FULL HOUSE

OTHER BOOKS BY REX STOUT

NOVELS

HOW LIKE A GOD
GOLDEN REMEDY
SEED ON THE WIND

O CARELESS LOVE!
MR. CINDERELLA
FOREST FIRE

THE PRESIDENT VANISHES

NERO WOLFE MYSTERIES

FER-DE-LANCE
THE RUBBER BAND
THE RED BOX
SOME BURIED CAESAR
OVER MY DEAD BODY
BLACK ORCHIDS
WHERE THERE'S A WILL
NOT QUITE DEAD ENOUGH
TOO MANY COOKS
THE SILENT SPEAKER

TOO MANY WOMEN
TROUBLE IN TRIPLICATE
THE SECOND CONFESSION
THREE DOORS TO DEATH
IN THE BEST FAMILIES
MURDER BY THE BOOK
TRIPLE JEOPARDY
PRISONER'S BASE
THE GOLDEN SPIDERS
THREE MEN OUT

THE BLACK MOUNTAIN

TECUMSEH FOX MYSTERIES

DOUBLE FOR DEATH

THE BROKEN VASE

BAD FOR BUSINESS

MYSTERIES

THE HAND IN THE GLOVE
MOUNTAIN CAT

ALPHABET HICKS
RED THREADS

FULL HOUSE

a Nero Wolfe Omnibus

REX STOUT

*Barry College Library
Miami, Florida*

NEW YORK • 1955

THE VIKING PRESS

COPYRIGHT 1935, 1948, 1949, 1950 BY REX STOUT ©

PUBLISHED BY THE VIKING PRESS IN JUNE 1955

PUBLISHED ON THE SAME DAY IN THE DOMINION OF CANADA
BY THE MACMILLAN COMPANY OF CANADA LIMITED

LIBRARY OF CONGRESS CATALOG CARD NUMBER: 55–7629

PRINTED IN U.S.A.

CONTENTS

THE LEAGUE OF FRIGHTENED MEN   3

AND BE A VILLAIN   215

CURTAINS FOR THREE

    THE GUN WITH WINGS   373

    BULLET FOR ONE   426

    DISGUISE FOR MURDER   476

THE LEAGUE
OF FRIGHTENED MEN

1

WOLFE and I sat in the office Friday afternoon. As it turned out, the name of Paul Chapin, and his slick and thrifty notions about getting vengeance at wholesale without paying for it, would have come to our notice pretty soon in any event; but that Friday afternoon the combination of an early November rain and a lack of profitable business that had lasted so long it was beginning to be painful, brought us an opening scene—a prologue, not a part of the main action—of the show that was about ready to begin.

Wolfe was drinking beer and looking at pictures of snowflakes in a book someone had sent him from Czechoslovakia. I was reading the morning paper, off and on. I had read it at breakfast, and glanced through it again for half an hour after checking accounts with Horstmann at eleven o'clock, and here I was with it once more in the middle of the rainy afternoon, thinking halfheartedly to find an item or two that would tickle the brain, which seemed about ready to dry up on me. I do read books, but I never yet got any real satisfaction out of one; I always have a feeling there's nothing alive about it, it's all dead and gone, what's the use, you might as well try to enjoy yourself on a picnic in a graveyard. Wolfe asked me once why the devil I ever pretended to read a book, and I told him for cultural reasons, and he said I might as well forgo the pains, that culture was like money, it comes easiest to those who need it least. Anyway, since it was a morning paper and this was the middle of the afternoon, and I had already gone through it twice, it wasn't much better than a book and I was only hanging onto it as an excuse to keep my eyes open.

Wolfe seemed absorbed in the pictures. Looking at him, I said to myself, He's in a battle with the elements. He's fighting his way through a raging blizzard, just sitting there comfortably looking at pictures of snowflakes. That's the advantage of being an artist, of having imagination. I said aloud, "You mustn't go to sleep, sir, it's fatal. You freeze to death."

Wolfe turned a page, paying no attention to me. I said, "The shipment from Caracas, from Richardt, was twelve bulbs short. I never knew him to make good a shortage."

Still no result. I said, "Fritz tells me that the turkey they sent is too old to broil and will be tough unless it is roasted two hours, which according to you will attenuate the flavor. So the turkey at forty-one cents a pound will be a mess."

Wolfe turned another page. I stared at him a while and then said, "Did you see the piece in the paper about the woman who has a pet monkey which sleeps at the head of her bed and wraps its tail around her wrist? And keeps it there all night? Did you see the one about the man who found a necklace on the street and returned it to its owner and she claimed he stole two pearls from it and had him arrested? Did you see the one about the man on the witness-stand in a case about an obscene book, and the lawyer asked him what was his purpose in writing the book, and he said because he had committed a murder and all murderers had to talk about their crimes and that was his way of talking about it? Not that I get the idea, about the author's purpose. If a book's dirty it's dirty, and what's the difference how it got that way? The lawyer says if the author's purpose was a worthy literary purpose the obscenity don't matter. You might as well say that if my purpose is to throw a rock at a tin can it don't matter if I hit you in the eye with it. You might as well say that if my purpose is to buy my poor old grandmother a silk dress it don't matter if I grabbed the jack from a Salvation Army kettle. You might as well say—"

I stopped. I had him. He did not lift his eyes from the page, his head did not move, there was no stirring of his massive frame in the specially constructed enormous chair behind his desk; but I saw his right forefinger wiggle faintly—his minatory wand, as he once called it—and I knew I had him.

He said, "Archie. Shut up."

I grinned. "Not a chance, sir. Great God, am I just going to sit here until I die? Shall I phone Pinkerton's and ask if they want a hotel room watched or something? If you keep a keg of dynamite around the house you've got to expect some noise sooner or later. That's what I am, a keg of dynamite. Shall I go to a movie?"

Wolfe's huge head tipped forward a sixteenth of an inch, for him an emphatic nod. "By all means. At once."

I got up from my chair, tossed the newspaper halfway across the room to my desk, turned around, and sat down again. "What was wrong with my analogies?" I demanded.

Wolfe turned another page. "Let us say," he murmured patiently, "that as an analogist you are supreme. Let us say that."

"All right. Say we do. I'm not trying to pick a quarrel, sir. Hell no. I'm just breaking under the strain of trying to figure out a third way of crossing my legs. I've been at it over a week now." It flashed into my mind that Wolfe could never be annoyed by that problem, since his legs were so fat that there was no possibility of them ever getting crossed by any tactics whatever, but I decided not to mention that. I swerved. "I stick to it, if a book's dirty it's dirty, no matter if the author had a string of purposes as long as a rainy day. That guy on the witness-stand yesterday was a nut. Wasn't he? You tell me. Or else he wanted some big headlines no matter what it cost him. It cost him fifty berries for contempt of court. At that it was cheap advertising for his book; for half a century he could buy about four inches on the literary page of the *Times*, and that's not even a chirp. But I guess the guy was a nut. He said he had done a murder, and all murderers have to confess, so he wrote the book, changing the characters and circumstances, as a means of confessing without putting himself in jeopardy. The judge was witty and sarcastic. He said that even if the guy was an inventor of stories and was in a court, he needn't try for the job of court jester. I'll bet the lawyers had a good hearty laugh at that one. Huh? But the author said it was no joke, that was why he wrote the book and any obscenity in it was only incidental, he really had croaked a guy. So the judge soaked him fifty bucks for contempt of court and chased him off the stand. I guess he's a nut? You tell me."

Wolfe's great chest went up and out in a sigh; he put a marker in the book and closed it and laid it on the desk, and leaned himself back, gently ponderous, in his chair.

He blinked twice. "Well?"

I went across to my desk and got the paper and opened it out to the page. "Nothing maybe. I guess he's a nut. His name is Paul Chapin and he's written several books. The title of this one is *Devil Take the Hindmost*. He graduated from Harvard in nineteen-twelve. He's a lop; it mentions here about his getting up to the stand with his crippled leg but it doesn't say which one."

Wolfe compressed his lips. "Is it possible," he demanded, "that lop is an abbreviation of lopsided, and that you use it as a metaphor for cripple?"

"I wouldn't know about the metaphor, but lop means cripple in my circle."

Wolfe sighed again, and set about the process of rising from his chair. "Thank God," he said, "the hour saves me from further analogies and colloquialisms." The clock on the wall said one minute till four—time for him to go up to the plant rooms. He made it to his feet, pulled the points of his vest down but failed as usual to cover with it the fold of bright yellow shirt that had puffed out, and moved across to the door.

At the threshold he paused. "Archie."

"Yes, sir."

"Phone Murger's to send over at once a copy of *Devil Take the Hindmost*, by Paul Chapin."

"Maybe they won't. It's suppressed, pending the court decision."

"Nonsense. Speak to Murger or Ballard. What good is an obscenity trial except to popularize literature?"

He went on toward the elevator, and I sat down at my desk and reached for the telephone.

II

AFTER breakfast the next morning, Saturday, I fooled with the plant records a while and then went to the kitchen to annoy Fritz.

Wolfe, of course, wouldn't be down until eleven o'clock. The roof of the old brownstone house on West Thirty-fifth Street where he had lived for twenty years, and me with him for the last seven of them, was glassed in and partitioned into rooms where varying conditions of temperature and humidity were maintained—by the vigilance of Theodore Horstmann—for the ten thousand orchids that lined the benches and shelves. Wolfe had once remarked to me that the orchids were his concubines: insipid, expensive, parasitic, and temperamental. He brought them, in their diverse forms and colors, to the limits of their perfection, and then gave them away; he had never sold one. His patience and ingenuity, supported by Horstmann's fidelity, had produced remarkable results and gained for the roof a reputation in quite different circles from those whose interest centered in the downstairs office. In all weathers and under any circumstances whatever, his four hours a day on the roof with Horstmann—from nine to eleven in the morning and from four to six in the afternoon—were inviolable.

This Saturday morning I finally had to admit that Fritz's good humor was too much for me. By eleven o'clock I was back in the office, trying to pretend there might be something to do if I looked for it, but I'm not much good at pretending. I was thinking: Ladies and gentlemen, my friends and customers, I won't hold out for a real case with worry and action and profit in it, just give us any old kind of a break. I'll even tail a chorus girl for you, or hide in the bathroom for the guy that's stealing the toothpaste—anything this side of industrial espionage. Anything.

Wolfe came in and said good morning. The mail didn't take long. He signed a couple of checks I had made out for bills he had gone over the day before, and asked me with a sigh what the bank balance was, and gave me a few short letters. I tapped them off and went out with them to the mailbox. When I got back Wolfe was starting on a second bottle of beer, leaning back in his chair, and I thought I saw a look in his half-closed eyes. At least, I thought, he's not back on the pretty snowflakes again. I sat at my desk and let the typewriter down.

Wolfe said, "Archie. One would know everything in the world there is to know, if one waited long enough. The one fault in the passivity of Buddha as a technique for the acquisition of knowledge and wisdom is the miserably brief span of human life. He sat through the first stanza of the first canto of the preamble, and then left for an appointment with—let us say, with a certain chemist."

"Yes, sir. You mean, we just go on sitting here and we learn a lot."

"Not a lot. But more, a little more each century."

"You, maybe. Not me. If I sit here about two more days I'll be so damn goofy I won't know anything."

Wolfe's eyes flickered faintly. "I would not care to seem mystic, but might not that, in your case, mean an increase?"

"Sure." I grunted. "If you had not once instructed me never again to tell you to go to hell, I would tell you to go to hell."

"Good." Wolfe gulped beer and wiped his lips. "You are offended. So, probably, awake. My opening remark was in the nature of a comment on a recent fact. You will remember that last month you were away for ten days on a mission that proved to be highly unremunerative, and that during your absence two young men were here to perform your duties."

I nodded. I grinned. One of the men had been from the Metropolitan Agency as Wolfe's bodyguard, and the other had been a stenographer from Miller's. "Sure. Two could handle it on a sprint."

"Just so. On one of those days a man came here and asked me to intercept his destiny. He didn't put it that way, but that was the substance of it. It proved not feasible to accept his commission."

I had opened a drawer of my desk and taken out a loose-leaf binder, and I flipped through the sheets in it to the page I wanted. "Yes, sir. I've got it. I've read it twice. It's a bit spotty; the stenographer from Miller's wasn't so hot. He couldn't spell—"

"The name was Hibbard."

I nodded, glancing over the typewritten pages. "Andrew Hibbard. Instructor in psychology at Columbia. It was on October twentieth, a Saturday, that's two weeks ago today."

"Suppose you read it."

"*Viva voce?*"

"Archie." Wolfe looked at me. "Where did you pick that up, where did you learn to pronounce it, and what do you think it means?"

"Do you want me to read this stuff out loud, sir?"

"It doesn't mean out loud. Confound you." Wolfe emptied his glass, leaned back in his chair, got his fingers to meet in front of his belly, and laced them. "Proceed."

"Okay. First there's a description of Mr. Hibbard. 'Small gentleman, around fifty, pointed nose, dark eyes—'"

"Enough. For that I can plunder my memory."

"Yes, sir. Mr. Hibbard seems to have started out by saying, 'How do you do, sir, my name is—'"

"Pass the amenities."

I glanced down the page. "How will this do? Mr. Hibbard said, 'I was advised to come to you by a friend whose name need not be mentioned, but the motivating force was plain funk. I was driven here by fear.'"

Wolfe nodded. I read from the typewritten sheets:

"*Mr. Wolfe:* Yes. Tell me about it.

"*Mr. Hibbard:* My card has told you I am in the psychology department at Columbia. Since you are an expert, you probably observe on my face and in my bearing the stigmata of fright bordering on panic.

"*Mr. Wolfe:* I observe that you are upset. I have no means of knowing whether it is chronic or acute.

"*Mr. Hibbard:* It is chronic. At least it is becoming so. That is why I have resorted to—to you. I am under an intolerable strain. My life is in danger—no, not that, worse than that, my life has been forfeited. I admit it.

"*Mr. Wolfe:* Of course. Mine too, sir. All of us.

"*Mr. Hibbard:* Rubbish. Excuse me. I am not discussing original sin. Mr. Wolfe, I am going to be killed. A man is going to kill me.

"*Mr. Wolfe:* Indeed. When? How?"

Wolfe put in, "Archie. You may delete the 'Misters.' "

"Okay. This Miller boy was brought up right, he didn't miss one. Somebody told him, always regard your employer with respect forty-four hours a week, more or less, as the case may be. Well. Next we have:

"*Hibbard:* That I can't tell you, since I don't know. There are things about this I do know, also, which I must keep to myself. I can tell you—well, many years ago I inflicted an injury, a lasting injury, on a man. I was not alone, there were others in it, but chance made me chiefly responsible. At least I have so regarded it. It was a boyish prank—with a tragic outcome. I have never forgiven myself. Neither have the others who were concerned in it, at least most of them haven't. Not that I have ever been morbid about it—it was twenty-five years ago—I am a psychologist and therefore too involved in the morbidities of others to have room for any of my own. Well, we injured that boy. We ruined him—in effect. Certainly we felt the responsibility, and all through these twenty-five years some of us have had the idea of making up for it. We have acted on the idea—sometimes. You know how it is; we are busy men, most of us. But we have never denied the burden, and now and then some of us have tried to carry it. That was difficult, for pawn—that is, as the boy advanced into manhood he became increasingly peculiar. I learned that in the lower schools he had given evidence of talent, and certainly in college—that is to say, of my own knowledge, after the injury, he possessed brilliance. Later the brilliance perhaps remained, but became distorted. At a certain point—"

Wolfe interrupted me. "A moment. Go back a few sentences. Beginning 'That was difficult, for pawn'—did you say 'pawn'?"

I found it. "That's it. 'Pawn.' I don't get it."

"Neither did the stenographer. Proceed."

"At a certain point, some five years ago, I decided definitely he was psychopathic."

"*Wolfe:* You continued to know him, then?"

"*Hibbard:* Oh yes. Many of us did. Some of us saw him frequently; one or two associated with him closely. Around that time his latent brilliance seemed to find itself in maturity. He—well, he did things which aroused admiration and interest. Convinced as I was that he was psychopathic, I nevertheless felt less concern for him than I had for a long time, for he appeared to be genuinely involved in satisfactory—at least compensatory—achievement. The awakening came in a startling manner. There was a reunion—a gathering—of a group of us, and one of us was killed—died—obviously, we unanimously thought, by an accident. But he—that is, the man we had injured—was there; and a few days later each of us received through the mail a communication from him saying that he had killed one of us and that the rest would follow; that he had embarked on a ship of vengeance."

"*Wolfe:* Indeed. 'Psychopathic' must have begun to seem almost a euphemism."

"*Hibbard:* Yes. But there was nothing we could do."

"*Wolfe:* Since you were equipped with evidence, it might not have proved hazardous to inform the police."

"*Hibbard:* We had no evidence."

"*Wolfe:* The communications?"

"*Hibbard:* They were typewritten, unsigned, and were expressed in ambiguous terms which rendered them worthless for practical purposes such as evidence. He had even disguised his style, very cleverly; it was not his style at all. But it was plain enough to us. Each of us got one; not only those who had been present at the gathering, but all of us, all members of the league. Of course—"

"*Wolfe:* The league?"

"*Hibbard:* That was a slip. It doesn't matter. Many years ago, when a few of us were together discussing this, one—maudlin, of course—

suggested that we should call ourselves the League of Atonement. The phrase hung on, in a way. Latterly it was never heard except in jest. Now I fancy the jokes are ended. I was going to say, of course all of us do not live in New York, only about half. One got his warning, just the same, in San Francisco. In New York a few of us got together and discussed it. We made a sort of an investigation, and we saw— him, and had a talk with him. He denied sending the warnings. He seemed amused, in his dark soul, and unconcerned.

"*Wolfe:* 'Dark soul' is an odd phrase for a psychologist?

"*Hibbard:* I read poetry weekends.

"*Wolfe:* Just so. And?

"*Hibbard:* Nothing happened for some time—three months. Then another of us was killed—found dead. The police said suicide, and it seemed that all indications pointed in that direction. But two days later a second warning was mailed to each of us, with the same purport, and obviously from the same source. It was worded with great cleverness, with brilliance.

"*Wolfe:* This time, naturally, you went to the police.

"*Hibbard:* Why naturally? We were still without evidence.

"*Wolfe:* Only that you would. One or some of you would.

"*Hibbard:* They did. I was against it, but they did go—

"*Wolfe:* Why were you against it?

"*Hibbard:* I felt it was useless. Also—well, I could not bring myself to join in a demand for retribution—his life, perhaps—from the man we had injured. You understand . . .

"*Wolfe:* Quite. First, the police could find no proof. Second, they might.

"*Hibbard:* Very well. I was not engaged in an essay on logic. A man may debar nonsense from his library of reason, but not from the arena of his impulses.

"*Wolfe:* Good. Neat. And the police?

"*Hibbard:* They got nowhere. He made total asses of them. He described to me their questioning and his replies—

"*Wolfe:* You still saw him?

"*Hibbard:* Of course. We were friends. Oh yes. The police went into it, questioned him, questioned all of us, investigated all they could, and came out empty-handed. Some of them, some of the group, got private detectives. That was two weeks—twelve days—ago. The detectives are having the same success as the police. I'm sure of it.

"*Wolfe:* Indeed. What agency?

"*Hibbard:* That is irrelevant. The point is that something happened. I could speak of apprehensions and precautions and so forth; I know plenty of words of that nature; I could even frame the situation in technical psychological terms; but the plain fact is that I'm too scared to go on. I want you to save me from death. I want to hire you to protect my life.

"*Wolfe:* Yes. What happened?

"*Hibbard:* Nothing. Nothing of any significance except to me. He came to me and said something, that's all. It would be of no advantage to repeat it. My shameful admission is that I am at length completely frightened. I'm afraid to go to bed and I'm afraid to get up. I'm afraid to eat. I want whatever measure of security you can sell me. I am accustomed to the arrangement of words, and the necessity of talking intelligently to you has enforced a semblance of order and urbanity in a section of my brain, but around and beneath that order there is a veritable panic. After all my exploration, scientific and pseudoscientific, of that extraordinary phenomenon the human psyche, devil-possessed and heaven-soaring, I am all reduced to this single simple primitive concern: I am terribly afraid of being killed. The friend who suggested my coming here said that you possess a remarkable combination of talents and that you have only one weakness. She did not call it cupidity; I forget her phrasing. I am not a millionaire, but I have ample private means besides my salary, and I am in no state of mind for haggling.

"*Wolfe:* I always need money. That is of course my affair. I will undertake to disembark this gentleman from his ship of vengeance, in advance of any injury to you, for the sum of ten thousand dollars.

"*Hibbard:* Disembark him? You can't. You don't know him.

"*Wolfe:* Nor does he know me. A meeting can be arranged.

"*Hibbard:* I didn't mean—ha! It would take more than a meeting. It would take more, I think, than all your talents. But that is beside the point. I have failed to make myself clear. I would not pay ten thousand dollars, or any other sum, for you to bring this man to—justice? Ha! Call it justice—a word that reeks with maggots. Anyhow, I would not be a party to that, even in the face of death. I have not told you his name. I shall not. Already, perhaps, I have disclosed too much. I wish your services as a safeguard for myself, not as an agency for his destruction.

"*Wolfe:* If the one demands the other?"

"*Hibbard:* I hope not. I pray not—could I pray? No. Prayer has been washed from my strain of blood. Certainly I would not expect you to give me a warrant of security. But your experience and ingenuity—I am sure they would be worth whatever you might ask—"

"*Wolfe:* Nonsense. My ingenuity would be worth less than nothing, Mr. Hibbard. Do I understand that you wish to engage me to protect your life against the unfriendly designs of this man without taking any steps whatever to expose and restrain him?"

"*Hibbard*: Yes, sir. Precisely. And I have been told that once your talents are committed to an enterprise, any attempt to circumvent you will be futile."

"*Wolfe:* I have no talents. I have genius or nothing. In this case, nothing. No, Mr. Hibbard; and I do need money. What you need, should you persist in your quixotism, is first, if you have dependents, generous life insurance; and second, a patient acceptance of the fact that your death is only a matter of time. That of course is true of all of us; we all share that disease with you, only yours seems to have reached a rather acute stage. My advice would be, waste neither time nor money on efforts at precaution. If he has decided to kill you, and if he possesses ordinary intelligence—let alone the brilliance you grant him—you will die. There are so many methods available for killing a fellow being!—many more than there are for most of our usual activities, like pruning a tree or threshing wheat or making a bed or swimming. I have been often impressed, in my experience, by the ease and lack of bother with which the average murder is executed. Consider: with the quarry within reach, the purpose fixed, and the weapon in hand, it will often require up to eight or ten minutes to kill a fly, whereas the average murder, I would guess, consumes ten or fifteen seconds at the outside. In cases of slow poison and similar ingenuities, death of course is lingering, but the act of murder itself is commonly quite brief. Consider again: there are certainly not more than two or three methods of killing a pig, but there are hundreds of ways to kill a man. If your friend is half as brilliant as you think him, and doesn't get in a rut as the ordinary criminal does, he may be expected to evolve a varied and interesting repertory before your league is half disposed of. He may even invent something new. One more point: it seems to me there is a fair chance for you. You may not, after all, be the next, or even the next or the next; and it is quite possible that somewhere along the line he may miscalculate or run into bad luck; or one of your league members, less quixotic than you, may engage my services. That would save you."

I took my eyes from the sheet to look at Wolfe. "Pretty good, sir. Pretty nice. I'm surprised it didn't get him; he must have been tough. Maybe you didn't go far enough. You only mentioned poison really; you could have brought in strangling and bleeding and crushed skulls and convulsions—"

"Proceed."

"*Hibbard:* I will pay you five hundred dollars a week.

"*Wolfe:* I am sorry. To now my casuistry has managed a satisfactory persuasion that the money I have put in my bank has been earned. I dare not put this strain upon it.

"*Hibbard:* But—you wouldn't refuse. You can't refuse a thing like this. My God. You are my only hope. I didn't realize it, but you are.

"*Wolfe:* I do refuse. I can undertake to render this man harmless, to remove the threat—

"*Hibbard:* No. No!

"*Wolfe:* Very well. One little suggestion: if you take out substantial life insurance, which would be innocent of fraud from the legal standpoint, you should if possible manage so that when the event comes it cannot plausibly be given the appearance of suicide; and since you will not be aware of the event much beforehand you will have to keep your wit sharpened. That is merely a practical suggestion, that the insurance may not be voided, to the loss of your beneficiary.

"*Hibbard:* But— Mr. Wolfe— Look here, you can't do this. I came here— I tell you it isn't reasonable—"

Wolfe stopped me. "That will do, Archie."

I looked up. "There's only a little more."

"I know. I find it painful. I refused that five hundred dollars—thousands, perhaps—once; I maintained my position; your reading it causes me useless discomfort. Do not finish it. There is nothing further except Mr. Hibbard's confused protestations and my admirable steadfastness."

"Yes, sir. I've read it." I glanced over the remaining lines. "I'm surprised you let him go. After all—"

Wolfe reached to the desk to ring for Fritz, shifted a little in his chair, and settled back again. "To tell you the truth, Archie, I entertained a notion."

"Yeah. I thought so."

"But nothing came of it. As you know, it takes a fillip on the flank for my mare to dance, and the fillip was not forthcoming. You were away at the time, and since your return the incident has not been discussed. It is odd that you should have innocently been the cause, by mere chance, of its revival."

"I don't get you."

Fritz came with beer. Wolfe took the opener from the drawer, poured a glass, gulped, and leaned back again. He resumed, "By annoying me about the man on the witness-stand. I resigned myself to your tantrum because it was nearly four o'clock. As you know, the book came. I read it last night."

"Why did you read it?"

"Don't badger me. I read it because it was a book. I had finished *The Native's Return*, by Louis Adamic, and *Outline of Human Nature*, by Alfred Rossiter, and I read books."

"Yeah. And?"

"This will amuse you. Paul Chapin, the man on the witness-stand, the author of *Devil Take the Hindmost*, is the villain of Andrew Hibbard's tale. He is the psychopathic avenger of an old and tragic injury."

"The hell he is." I gave Wolfe a look; I had known him to invent for practice. "Why is he?"

Wolfe's eyelids went up a shade. "Do you expect me to explain the universe?"

"No, sir. Retake. How do you know he is?"

"By no flight. Pedestrian mental processes. Must you have them?"

"I'd greatly appreciate it."

"I suppose so. A few details will do. Mr. Hibbard employed the unusual phrase, 'embark on a ship of vengeance,' and that phrase occurs twice in *Devil Take the Hindmost*. Mr. Hibbard did not say, as the stenographer has it, 'That was difficult, for pawn,' which is of course meaningless; he said, 'That was difficult, for Paul,' and caught himself up pronouncing the name, which he did not intend to disclose. Mr. Hibbard said things indicating that the man was a writer—for instance, speaking of his disguising his style in the warnings. Mr. Hibbard said that five years ago the man began to be involved in compensatory achievement. I telephoned two or three people this morning. In nineteen-twenty-nine Paul Chapin's first successful book was published, and in nineteen-thirty his second. Also, Chapin is a cripple through an injury which he suffered twenty-five years ago in a hazing accident at Harvard. If more is needed—"

"No. Thank you very much. I see. All right. Now that you know who the guy is, everything is cozy. Why is it? Who are you going to send a bill to?"

Two of the folds in Wolfe's cheeks opened out a little, so I knew he thought he was smiling. I said, "But you may just be pleased because you know it's corn fritters with anchovy sauce for lunch, and it's only ten minutes to the bell."

"No, Archie." The folds were gently closing. "I mentioned that I entertained a notion. It may or may not be fertile. As usual, you have furnished the fillip. Luckily our stake will be negligible. There are several possible channels of approach, but I believe— Yes. Get Mr. Andrew Hibbard on the phone—at Columbia, or at his home."

"Yes, sir. Will you speak?"

"Yes. Keep your wire and take it down as usual."

I got the number from the book and called it. First the university. I didn't get Hibbard. I monkeyed around with two or three extensions and four or five people, and it finally leaked out that he wasn't anywhere around, but no one seemed to know where he was. I tried his home, an Academy number, up in the same neighborhood. There a dumb female nearly riled me. She insisted on knowing who I was and she sounded doubtful about everything. She finally seemed to decide Mr. Hibbard probably wasn't home. Through the last of it Wolfe was listening in on his wire.

I turned to him. "I can try again and maybe with luck get a human being."

He shook his head. "After lunch. It is two minutes to one."

I got up and stretched, thinking I would be able to do a lot of destructive criticism on a corn fritter myself, especially with Fritz's sauce. It was at that moment that Wolfe's notion decided to come to him instead of waiting longer for him to go to it. It was a coincidence, too, though that was of no importance; she must have been trying to get our number while I was talking.

The telephone rang. I sat down again and got it. It was a woman's voice, and she asked to speak to Nero Wolfe. I asked if I might have her name, and when she said "Evelyn Hibbard" I told her to hold the line and put my hand over the transmitter.

I grinned at Wolfe. "It's a Hibbard."

His brows lifted.

"A female Hibbard named Evelyn. Voice young, maybe a daughter. Take it."

He took his receiver off, and I put mine back to my ear and got my pad and pencil ready. As Wolfe asked her what she wanted I was deciding again that he was the only man I had ever met who used absolutely the same tone to a woman as to a man. He had plenty of changes in his voice, but they weren't based on sex. I scribbled on the pad my quick symbols, mostly private, for the sounds in the receiver.

"I have a note of introduction to you from a friend, Miss Sarah Barstow. You will remember her, Mr. Wolfe; you—you investigated the death of her father. Could I see you at once, if possible? I'm talking from the Bidwell, Fifty-second Street. I could be there in fifteen minutes."

"I'm sorry, Miss Hibbard, I am engaged. Could you come at a quarter past two?"

"Oh." A little gasp floated after that. "I had hopes— I just decided ten minutes ago. Mr. Wolfe, it is very urgent. If you could possibly—"

"If you would describe the urgency."

"I'd rather not, on the telephone—but that's silly. It's my uncle, Andrew Hibbard; he went to see you two weeks ago, you may remember. He has disappeared."

"Indeed. When?"

"Tuesday evening. Four days ago."

"You have had no word of him?"

"Nothing." The female Hibbard's voice caught. "Nothing at all."

"Indeed." I saw Wolfe's eyes shift to take in the clock—it was four minutes past one—and shift again toward the door to the hall, where Fritz stood on the threshold, straight for announcing. "Since ninety hours have passed, another one may be risked. At a quarter past two? Will that be convenient?"

"If you can't— All right. I'll be there."

Two receivers were returned simultaneously to their racks. Fritz spoke as usual.

"Luncheon, sir."

III

I'M FUNNY about women. I've seen dozens of them I wouldn't mind marrying, but I've never been pulled so hard I lost my balance. I don't know whether any of them would have married me or not, that's the truth, since I never gave one a chance to collect enough data to form an intelligent opinion. When I meet a new one there's no doubt that I'm interested and I'm fully alive to all the possibilities, and I've never dodged the issue as far as I can tell, but I never seem to get infatuated. For instance, take the women I meet in my line of business —that is, Nero Wolfe's business. I never run into one, provided she's not just an item for the cleaners, without letting my eyes do the best they can for my judgment, and, more than that, it puts a tickle in my blood. I can feel the nudge on the accelerator. But then of course the business gets started, whatever it may happen to be, and I guess the trouble is I'm too conscientious. I love to do a good job more than anything else I can think of, and I suppose that's what shorts the line.

This Evelyn Hibbard was little and dark and smart. Her nose was too pointed, and she took too much advantage of her eyelashes, but nobody that knew merchandise would have put her on a bargain counter. She had on a slick gray twill suit, with a fur piece, and a little red hat with a narrow brim on the side of her head. She sat straight without crossing her legs, and her ankles and halfway to her knees were well trimmed but without promise of any plumpness.

I was at my desk, of course, with my pad, and after the first couple of minutes got only glances at her in between. If worry about her uncle was eating her, and I suppose it was, she was following what Wolfe called the Anglo-Saxon theory of the treatment of emotions and desserts: freeze them and hide them in your belly. She sat straight in the chair I had shoved up for her, keeping her handsome dark eyes level on Wolfe but once in a while flapping her lashes in my direction. She had brought with her a package wrapped in brown paper and held it on her lap. Wolfe leaned back in his seat with his chin down and his forearms laid out on the arms of the chair; it was his custom to make no effort to join his fingers at the high point of his middle mound sooner than a full hour after a meal.

She said that she and her younger sister lived with their uncle in an apartment on 113th Street. Their mother had died when they were young. Their father was remarried and lived in California. Their uncle was single. He, Uncle Andrew, had gone out Tuesday evening around nine o'clock, and had not returned. There had been no word from him. He had gone out alone, remarking casually to Ruth, the younger sister, that he would get some air.

Wolfe asked, "This has no precedent?"

"Precedent?"

"He has never done this before? You have no idea where he may be?"

"No. But I have an idea. I think—he has been killed."

"I suppose so." Wolfe opened his eyes a little. "That would naturally occur to you. On the telephone you mentioned his visit to me. Do you know what its purpose was?"

"I know all about it. It was through my friend Sarah Barstow that I heard of you. I persuaded my uncle to come to see you. I know what he told you and what you said to him. I told my uncle he was a sentimental romantic. He was." She stopped and kept her lips closed a moment to get them firm again; I looked up to see it. "I'm not. I'm hard-boiled. I think my uncle has been murdered, and the man who killed him is Paul Chapin, the writer. I came here to tell you that."

So here was the notion Wolfe had entertained, coming right to his office and sitting on a chair. But too late? The five hundred a week had gone out to get some air.

Wolfe said, "Quite likely. Thank you for coming. But it might be possible, and more to the point, to engage the attention of the police and the District Attorney."

She nodded. "You are the way Sarah Barstow described you. The police have been engaged since Wednesday noon. They have been willing so far, at the request of the president of the university, to keep the matter quiet. There has been no publicity. But the police—you might as well match me at chess against Capablanca. Mr. Wolfe—" The fingers of her clasped hands, resting on the package on her lap, twisted in a closer knot, and her voice tightened. "You don't know. Paul Chapin has the cunning and subtlety of all the things he mentioned in his first warning, the one he sent after he killed Judge Harrison. He is genuinely evil—all evil, all dangerous. You know he is not a man—"

"There, Miss Hibbard. There now." Wolfe sighed. "Surely he is a man, by definition. Did he indeed kill a judge? In that instance the presumption is of course in his favor. But you mentioned the first warning. Do you by any chance have a copy of it?"

She nodded. "I have." She indicated the package. "I have all the warnings, including"—she swallowed—"the last one. Dr. Burton gave me his."

"The one after the apparent suicide."

"No—Mr. Dreyer's. No. The one—another one came this morning to them—I suppose to all of them; after Dr. Burton told me, I telephoned two or three. You see, my uncle has disappeared—you see—"

"I see. Indeed. Dangerous. For Mr. Chapin, I mean. Any kind of rut is dangerous in his sort of enterprise. So you have all the warnings. With you? In that package?"

"Yes. Also I have bundles of letters which Paul Chapin has at various times written to my uncle, and a sort of diary which my uncle kept, and a book of records showing sums advanced to Paul Chapin from nineteen-nineteen to nineteen-twenty-eight by my uncle and others, and a list of the names and addresses of the members—that is, of the men who were present in nineteen-nine when it happened. A few other things."

"Preposterous. You have all that? Why not the police?"

Evelyn Hibbard shook her head. "I decided not. These things were in a very private file of my uncle's. They were precious to him, and they are now precious to me—in a different way. The police would get no help from them, but you might. And you would not abuse them. Would you?"

At the pause I glanced up and saw Wolfe's lips pushing out a little, then in, then out again. That excited me. It always did, even when I had no idea what it was all about. I watched him. He said, "Miss Hibbard. You mean you removed this file from the notice of the police and kept it, and have now brought it to me? Containing the names and addresses of the members of the League of Atonement? Remarkable."

She stared at him. "Why not? It has no information that they cannot easily obtain elsewhere—from Mr. Farrell or Dr. Burton or Mr. Drummond—any of them."

"All the same, remarkable." Wolfe reached to his desk and pushed a button. "Will you have a glass of beer? I drink beer, but would not impose my preferences. There is available a fair port, Solera, Dublin stout, Madeira, and more especially a Hungarian *vin du pays* which comes to me from the cellar of the vineyard. Your choice?"

She shook her head. "Thank you."

"I may have beer?"

"Please do."

Wolfe did not lean back again. He said, "If the package could perhaps be opened? I am especially interested in that first warning."

She began to untie the string. I got up to help. She handed me the package and I put it on Wolfe's desk and got the paper off. It was a large cardboard letter-file, old and faded but intact. I passed it to Wolfe, and he opened it with the deliberate and friendly exactness which his hands displayed toward all inanimate things.

Evelyn Hibbard said, "Under 'I.' My uncle did not call them warnings. He called them intimations."

Wolfe nodded. "Of destiny, I suppose." He removed papers from the file. "Your uncle is indeed a romantic. Oh yes, I say 'is.' It is wise to reject all suppositions, even painful ones, until surmise can stand on the legs of fact. Here it is. Ah! 'Ye should have killed me, watched the last mean sigh.' Is Mr. Chapin in malevolence a poet? May I read it?"

She nodded. He read:

> "Ye should have killed me, watched the last mean sigh
> Sneak through my nostril like a fugitive slave
> Slinking from bondage.
> Ye should have killed me.
> Ye killed the man,
> Ye should have killed me!
>
> Ye killed the man, but not
> The snake, the fox, the mouse that nibbles his hole,
> The patient cat, the hawk, the ape that grins,
> The wolf, the crocodile, the worm that works his way
> Up through the slime and down again to hide.
> Ah! All these ye left in me,
> And killed the man.
> Ye should have killed me!
>
> Long ago I said, trust time.
> Banal I said, time will take its toll.

> I said to the snake, the ape, the cat, the worm:
> Trust time, for all your aptitudes together
> Are not as sure and deadly. But now they said:
> Time is too slow; let us, Master.
> Master, count for us!
> I said no.
> Master, let us. Master, count for us!
> I felt them in me. I saw the night, the sea,
> The rocks, the neutral stars, the ready cliff.
> I heard ye all about, and I heard them:
> Master, let us. Master, count for us!
> I saw one there, secure at the edge of death;
> I counted: One!
> I shall count two, I know, and three and four . . .
> Not waiting for time's toll.
> Ye should have killed me."

Wolfe sat with the paper in his hand, glancing from it to Miss Hibbard. "It would seem likely that Mr. Chapin pushed the judge over the edge of a cliff—presumably impromptu. I presume, also, totally unobserved, since no suspicions were aroused. There was a cliff around handy?"

"Yes. It was in Massachusetts, up near Marblehead—last June. A crowd was there at Fillmore Collard's place. Judge Harrison had come East from Indiana for commencement, for his son's graduation. They missed him that night, and the next morning they found his body at the foot of the cliff, beaten among the rocks by the surf."

"Mr. Chapin was among them?"

She nodded. "He was there."

"But don't tell me the gathering was for purposes of atonement. It was not a meeting of this incredible league?"

"Oh no. Anyway, Mr. Wolfe, no one ever quite seriously called it a league. Even Uncle Andrew was not—" she stopped short, shut her lips, stuck her chin up, and then went on—"as romantic as that. The crowd was just a crowd, mostly from the class of nineteen-twelve, that Fillmore Collard had taken up from Cambridge. Seven or eight of the —well, league—were there."

Wolfe nodded and regarded her for a moment, then got at the file again and began pulling things out of its compartments. He flipped through the sheets of a loose-leaf binder, glanced inside a record book, and shuffled through a lot of papers. Finally he looked at Miss Hibbard again.

"And this quasi-poetic warning came to each of them after they had returned to their homes, and astonished them?"

"Yes, a few days later."

"I see. You know, of course, that Mr. Chapin's little effort was sound traditionally. Many of the most effective warnings in history, particularly the ancient ones, were in verse. As for the merits of Mr. Chapin's execution, granted the soundness of the tradition, it seems to me verbose, bombastic, and decidedly spotty. I cannot qualify as an expert in prosody, but I am not without an ear."

It wasn't like Wolfe to babble when business was on hand, and I glanced up, wondering where he thought he was headed for. She was just looking at him. I had to cut my glance short, for he was going on.

"Further, I suspect him specifically, in his second stanza—I suppose he would call it stanza—of plagiarism. It has been many years since I have read Spenser, but in a crack of my memory not quite closed up there is a catalogue of beasts— Archie. If you wouldn't mind, bring me that Spenser? The third shelf, at the right of the door. No, farther over—more yet—dark blue, tooled. That's it."

I took the book over and handed it to him, and he opened it and began skimming.

"*The Shepheardes Calender*, I am certain, and I think 'September.' Not that it matters; even if I find it, a petty triumph, scarcely worth the minutes I waste. You will forgive me, Miss Hibbard? 'Bulls that bene bate . . . Cocke on his dunghill. . . . This wolvish sheepe would catchen his pray . . .' No, certainly not that. Beasts here and there, but not the catalogue in my memory. I shall forgo the triumph; it isn't here. Anyway, it was pleasant to meet Spenser again, even for so brief a nod." He slid forward in his chair to a perilous extreme, to hand the book to Miss Hibbard. "A fine example of bookmaking, worth a glance of friendship from you. Printed, of course, in London, but bound in this city by a Swedish boy who will probably starve to death during the coming winter."

She summoned enough politeness to look at it, turn it over in her hand, glance inside, and look at the backbone again. Wolfe was back at the papers he had taken from the file. She was obviously through with the book, so I got up and took it and returned it to the shelf.

Wolfe was saying, "Miss Hibbard. I know that what you want is action, and doubtless I have tried your patience. I am sorry. If I might ask you a few questions?"

"Certainly. It seems to me—"

"Of course. Pardon me. Only two questions, I think. First, do you know whether your uncle recently took out any life insurance?"

She nodded impatiently. "But Mr. Wolfe, that has nothing to do with—"

He broke in to finish for her, "With the totalitarian evil of Paul Chapin. I know. Possibly not. Was it a large amount of insurance?"

"I think so. Yes. Very large."

"Were you the beneficiary?"

"I don't know. I suppose so. He told me you spoke to him of insurance. Then, about a week ago, he told me he had rushed it through and they had distributed it among four companies. I didn't pay much attention because my mind was on something else. I was angry with him and was trying to persuade him— I suppose my sister Ruth and I were the beneficiaries."

"Not Paul Chapin?"

She looked at him and opened her mouth and closed it again. She said, "That hadn't occurred to me. Perhaps he would. I don't know."

Wolfe nodded. "Yes, a sentimental romantic might do that. Now, the second question. Why did you come to see me? What do you want me to do?"

She gave him her eyes straight. "I want you to find proof of Paul Chapin's guilt and see that he pays the penalty. I can pay you for it. You told my uncle ten thousand dollars. I can pay that."

"Do you have a personal hostility for Mr. Chapin?"

"Personal?" She frowned. "Is there any other kind of hostility except personal? I don't know. I hate Paul Chapin, and have hated him for years, because I loved my uncle, and my sister Ruth loved him, and he was a fine, sensitive, generous man, and Paul Chapin was ruining his life. Ruined his life—oh—now—"

"There, Miss Hibbard. Please. You did not intend to engage me to find your uncle? You had no hope of that?"

"I think not. Oh, if you do! If you do that— I think I have no hope, I think I dare not. But then—even if you find him, there will still be Paul Chapin."

"Just so." Wolfe sighed, and turned his eyes to me. "Archie. Please wrap up Miss Hibbard's file for her. If I have not placed the contents in their proper compartments, she will forgive me. The paper and string are intact? Good."

She was protesting, "But you will need that. I'll leave it—"

"No, Miss Hibbard. I'm sorry. I can't undertake your commission."

She stared at him. He said, "The affair is in the hands of the police and the District Attorney. I would be hopelessly handicapped. I shall have to bid you good day."

She found her tongue. "Nonsense. You don't mean it." She exploded, forward in her chair. "Mr. Wolfe, it's outrageous! I've told you all about it—you've asked me, and I've told you. The reason you give is no reason at all. Why—"

He stopped her, with his finger wiggling and the quality in his voice, without raising it, that always got me a little sore because I never understood how he did it. "Please, Miss Hibbard. I have said no, and I have given you my reason. That is sufficient. If you will just take the package from Mr. Goodwin. Of course I am being rude to you, and on such occasions I always regret that I do not know the art of being rude elegantly. I have all the simplicities, including that of brusqueness."

But he got up from his chair, which, though she didn't know it, was an extraordinary concession. She, on her feet too, had taken the package from me and was mad as hell. Before turning to go, though, she realized that she was more helpless than she was mad. She appealed to him. "But don't you see, this leaves me— What can I do?"

"I can make only one suggestion. If you have made no other arrangements and still wish my services, and the police have made no progress, come to see me next Wednesday."

"But that's four whole days—"

"I'm sorry. Good day, Miss Hibbard."

I went to open the door for her, and she certainly had completely forgotten about her eyelashes.

When I got back to the office Wolfe was seated again, with what I suppose Andrew Hibbard would have called the stigmata of pleasure. His chin was up, and he was making little circles with the tip of his finger on the arm of his chair.

I came to a stop by his desk, across from him, and said, "That girl's mad. I would say, on a guess, she's about one-fifth as mad as I am."

He murmured, "Archie. For a moment, don't disturb me."

"No, sir. I wouldn't for anything. A trick is okay, and a deep trick is the staff of life for some people, but where you've got us to at present is wallowing in the unplumbed depths of— Wait a minute, I'll look it up, I think it's in Spenser."

"Archie, I warn you, someday you are going to become dispensable." He stirred a little. "If you were a woman and I were married to you, which God forbid, no amount of space available on this globe, to separate us, would put me at ease. I regret the necessity for my rudeness to Miss Hibbard. It was desirable to get rid of her without delay, for there is a great deal to be done."

"Good. If I can help any—"

"You can. Your notebook, please. Take a telegram."

I sat down. I wasn't within a hundred miles of it, and that always irritated me.

Wolfe dictated: "Regarding recent developments and third Chapin warning you are requested to attend meeting this address nine o'clock Monday evening November fifth without fail. Sign it Nero Wolfe and address."

"Sure." I had it down. "Just send it to anybody I happen to think of?"

Wolfe had lifted up the edge of his desk blotter and taken a sheet of paper from underneath and was pushing it at me. He said, "Here are the names. Include those in Boston, Philadelphia, and Washington; those farther away can be informed later by letter. Also, make a copy of the list; two—one for the safe. Also—"

I had taken the paper from him and a glance showed me what it was. I stared at him, and I suppose something in my face stopped him. He interrupted himself. "Reserve your disapproval, Archie. Save your fake moralities for your solitude."

I said, "So that's why you had me get the Spenser, so she would have something to look at. Why did you steal it?"

"I borrowed it."

"You say. I've looked in the dictionary. That's what I mean, why didn't you borrow it? She would have let you have it."

"Probably not." Wolfe sighed. "I didn't care to risk it. In view of your familiarity with the finer ethical points, you must realize that I couldn't very well accept her as a client and then propose to others, especially to a group—"

"Sure, I see that all right. Now that the notion you entertained has drifted in on me, I'd have my hat off if I had one on. But she'd have let you have it. Or you could have got the dope—"

"That will do, Archie." He got a faint tone on. "We shall at any rate be acting in her interest. It appears likely that this will be a complicated and expensive business, and there is no reason why Miss Hibbard should bear the burden alone. In a few minutes I shall be going upstairs, and you will be fairly busy. First, send the telegrams and copy the list. Then—take this, a letter to Miss Hibbard, sign my name and mail it this evening by special delivery: 'I find that the enclosed paper did not get back into your file this afternoon, but remained on my desk. I trust that its absence has not caused you any inconvenience. If you are still of a mind to see me next Wednesday, do not hesitate to call upon me.'"

"Yes, sir. Send her the list."

"Naturally. Be sure your copies are correct. Make three copies. I believe you know the home address of Mr. Higgam of the Metropolitan Trust Company?"

I nodded. "Up at Sutton—"

"Find him tomorrow and give him a copy of the list. Ask him to procure first thing Monday morning a financial report on the men listed. No history is required; their present standing is the point. For those in other cities, telegraph. We want the information by six o'clock Monday."

"Hibbard's name is here—maybe the other dead ones."

"The bank's ingenuity may discover them, and not disturb their souls. Get in touch with Saul Panzer and tell him to report here Monday evening at eight-thirty. Durkin likewise. Find out if Gore and Cather and two others—your selection—will be available for Tuesday morning."

I grinned. "How about the Sixty-first Regiment?"

"They will be our reserve. As soon as you have sent the telegrams, phone Miss Hibbard at her home. Try until you get her. Employ your charm. Make an appointment to call on her this evening. If you get to see her, tell her that you regret that I refused her commission, and that you have my leave to offer her your assistance if she wishes it. It will save time. It will afford you an opportunity to amass a collection of facts from her, and possibly even to glance through the papers and effects of Mr. Hibbard—chiefly for any indication of an awareness on his part that he would not soon return. We are of course in agreement with some of the tendencies of the law—for instance, its reluctance to believe a man dead merely because he is not visible on the spot he is accustomed to occupy."

"Yes, sir. Take my own line with her?"

"Any that suggests itself."

"If I go up there I could take the list along."

"No, mail it." Wolfe was getting up from his chair. I watched him; it was always something to see.

Before he got started for the door, I asked, "Maybe I should know this; I didn't get it. What was the idea, asking her about the life insurance?"

"That? Merely the possibility that we were encountering a degree of vindictive finesse never before reached in our experience. Chapin's hatred, diluted of course, extended from the uncle to the niece. He learned of the large sum she would receive in insurance, and in planning Hibbard's murder planned also that the body would not be discovered, and the insurance money would not be paid her."

"It would someday."

"But even a delay in an enemy's good fortune is at least a minor pleasure. Worth such a finesse if you have it in you. That was the possibility. And another one: let us say Chapin himself was the beneficiary. Miss Hibbard was sure he would kill her uncle, would evade discovery, and would collect a huge fortune for his pains. The thought was intolerable. So she killed her uncle herself—he was about to die in any event—and disposed of the body so that it could not be found. You might go into that with her this evening."

I said, "You think I won't? I'll get her alibi."

IV

THERE was plenty doing Saturday evening and Sunday. I saw Evelyn Hibbard and had three hours with her, and got Saul and Fred and the other boys lined up, and had a lot of fun on the telephone, and finally got hold of Higgam, the bank guy, late Sunday evening after he returned from a Long Island weekend. The phone calls were from members of the league who had got the telegrams. There were five or six that phoned, various kinds—some scared, some sore, and one that was apparently just curious. I had made several copies of the list, and as the phone calls came I checked them off on one and made notes. The original, Hibbard's, had a date at the top, February 16, 1931, and was typewritten. Some of the addresses had been changed later with a pen, so evidently it had been kept up-to-date. Four of the names had no addresses at all. The list was like this, leaving out the addresses and putting in the businesses or professions as we got them Monday from the bank:

> Andrew Hibbard, psychologist
> Ferdinand Bowen, stockbroker
> Loring A. Burton, doctor
> Eugene Dreyer, art dealer
> Alexander Drummond, florist
> George R. Pratt, politician
> Nicholas Cabot, lawyer
> Augustus Farrell, architect
> Wm. R. Harrison, judge
> Fillmore Collard, textile-mill owner
> Edwin Robert Byron, magazine editor
> L. M. Irving, social worker
> Lewis Palmer, Federal Housing Administration
> Julius Adler, lawyer
> Theodore Gaines, banker
> Pitney Scott, taxi driver
> Michael Ayers, newspaperman
> Arthur Kommers, sales manager
> Wallace McKenna, congressman from Illinois
> Sidney Lang, real estate
> Roland Erskine, actor
> Leopold Elkus, surgeon
> F. L. Ingalls, travel bureau
> Archibald Mollison, professor
> Richard M. Tuttle, boys' school
> T. R. Donovan
> Phillip Leonard
> Allan W. Gardner
> Hans Weber

For the last four there were no addresses, and I couldn't find them in the New York or suburban phone books, so I couldn't ask the bank for a report. Offhand, I thought, reading the names and considering that they were all Harvard men, which meant starting better than scratch on the average—offhand it looked pretty juicy; but the bank reports would settle that. It was fun stalling them on the phone.

But the real fun Sunday came in the middle of the afternoon. Someone had leaked on Hibbard's disappearance, and the Sunday papers had it, though they didn't give it a heavy play. When the doorbell rang around three o'clock and I answered it because I happened to be handy and Fritz was busy out back, and I saw two huskies standing there shoulder to shoulder, I surmised at first glance it was a couple of Bureau dicks and someone had got curious about me up at Hibbard's the night before. Then I recognized one of them and threw the door wide with a grin.

"Hello, hello. You late from church?"

The one on the right spoke, the one with a scar on his cheek I had recognized. "Nero Wolfe in?"

I nodded. "You want to see him? Leap the doorsill, gentlemen."

While I was closing the door and putting the chain on they were taking off their hats and coats and hanging them on the rack. Then they were running their hands over their hair and pulling their vests down and clearing their throats. They were as nervous as greenhorns on their first tail. I was impressed. I was so used to Wolfe myself and so familiar with his prowess that I was apt to forget the dents some of his strokes had made on some tough professional skulls. I asked them to wait in the hall and went to the office and told Wolfe that Del Bascom of the Bascom Detective Agency was there with one of his men and wanted to see him.

"Did you ask them what they wanted?"

"No."

Wolfe nodded, and I went out and brought them in. Bascom went across to the desk to shake hands; the other gentleman got his big rumpus onto a chair I shoved up, but nearly missed it on the way down on account of staring at Wolfe. I suspected he wasn't overwhelmed by prestige as much as he was by avoirdupois, having never seen Wolfe before.

Bascom was saying, "It's been nearly two years since I've seen you, Mr. Wolfe. Remember? The hay-fever case. That's what I called it.

Remember the clerk that didn't see the guy lifting the emeralds because he was sneezing?"

"I do indeed, Mr. Bascom. That young man had invention, to employ so common an affliction for so unusual a purpose."

"Yeah. Lots of 'em are smart, but very few of them is quite smart enough. That was quite a case. I'd have been left scratching my ear for a bite if it hadn't been for you. I'll never forget that. Is business pretty good with you, Mr. Wolfe?"

"No. Abominable."

"I suppose so. We've got to expect it. Some of the agencies are doing pretty well on industrial work, but I never got into that. I used to be a working man myself. Hell, I still am." Bascom crossed his legs and cleared his throat. "You taken on anything new lately?"

"No."

"You haven't?"

"No."

I nearly jumped at the squeak, it was so unexpected. It came from the other dick, his chair between Bascom and me. He squeaked all of a sudden, "I heard different."

"Well, who opened your valve?" Bascom glared at him, disgusted. "Did I request you to clamp your trap when we came in here?" He turned to Wolfe. "Do you know what's eating him? You'll enjoy this, Mr. Wolfe. He's heard a lot of talk about the great Nero Wolfe, and he wanted to show you haven't got him buffaloed." He shifted and turned on the glare again. "You sap."

Wolfe nodded. "Yes, I enjoy that. I like bravado. You were saying, Mr. Bascom?"

"Yeah. I might as well come to the point. It's like this. I'm on a case. I've got five men on it. I'm pulling down close to a thousand dollars a week, four weeks now. When I wind it up I'll get a fee that will keep me off of relief all winter. I'm getting it sewed up. About all I need now is some wrapping paper and a piece of string."

"That's fine."

"All of that. And what I'm here for is to ask you to lay off."

Wolfe's brows went up a shade. "To ask me?"

"To lay off." Bascom slid forward in his chair and got earnest. "Look here, Mr. Wolfe. It's the Chapin case. I've been on it for four weeks. Pratt and Cabot and Dr. Burton are paying me—that's no secret, or, if it was, it wouldn't be for you after Monday. Pratt's a sort of a friend of mine; I've done him a good turn or two. He phoned me last night and said if I wanted to hang my own price tag on Paul Chapin I'd better get a move on because Nero Wolfe was about to begin. That was how I found out about the telegrams you sent. I dusted around and saw Burton and Cabot and one or two others. Burton had never heard of you before and asked me to get a report on you, but he phoned me this morning and told me not to bother. I suppose he had inquired and got an earful."

Wolfe murmured, "I am gratified at the interest they displayed."

"I don't doubt it." Bascom laid a fist on the desk for emphasis and got more earnest still. "Mr. Wolfe. I want to speak to you as one professional man to another. You would be the first to agree that ours is a dignified profession."

"Not explicitly. To assert dignity is to lose it."

"Huh? Maybe. Anyway, it's a profession, like the law. As you know, it is improper for a lawyer to solicit a client away from another lawyer. He would be disbarred. No lawyer with any decency would ever try it. And don't you think our profession is as dignified as the law? That's the only question. See?"

Bascom waited for an answer, his eyes on Wolfe's face, and probably supposed that the slow unfolding on Wolfe's cheeks was merely a natural phenomenon, like the ground swell on an ocean. Wolfe finally said, "Mr. Bascom. If you would abandon the subtleties of innuendo? If you have a request to make, state it plainly."

"Hell, didn't I? I asked you to lay off."

"You mean, keep out of what you call the Chapin case? I am sorry to have to refuse your request."

"You won't?"

"Certainly not."

"And you think it is absolutely okay to solicit another man's clients away from him?"

"I have no idea. I shall not enter into a defense of my conduct with you. What if it turned out to be indefensible? I merely say, I refuse your request."

"Yeah. I thought you would." Bascom took his fist off the desk and relaxed a little. "My brother claimed you regarded yourself as a gentleman and you'd fall for it. I said you might be a gentleman but you wasn't a sap."

"Neither, I fear."

"Well and good. Now that that's out of the way, maybe we can talk business. If you're going to take on the Chapin case, that lets us out."

"Probably. Not necessarily."

"Oh yes, it does. You'll soak them until they'll have to begin buying the cheaper cuts. I know when I'm done, I can take it. I couldn't hang onto it much longer anyhow. God help you. I'd love to drop in here once a week and ask you how's tricks. I'm telling you, this cripple Chapin is the deepest and slickest that's ever run around loose. I said I had it about sewed up. Listen. There's not the faintest chance. Not the faintest. I had really given that up, and had three men tailing him to catch him on the next one—and by God there goes Hibbard and we can't even find what's left of him, and do you know what? My three men don't know where Chapin was Tuesday night! Can you beat it? It sounds dumb, but they're not dumb; they're damn good men. So, as I say, I'd love to drop in here—"

Wolfe put in, "You spoke of talking business."

"So I did. I'm ready to offer you a bargain. Of course you've got your own methods, we all have, but in these four weeks we've dug up a lot of dope, and it's cost us a lot of money to get it. It's confidential, naturally, but if your clients are the same as mine that don't matter. It would save you a lot of time and expense and circling around. You can have all the dope, and I'll confer with you on it any time, as often as you want." Bascom hesitated a moment, wet his lips, and concluded, "For one thousand dollars."

Wolfe shook his head gently. "But Mr. Bascom, all of your reports will be available to me."

"Sure, but you know what reports are. You know, they're all right, but oh hell. You would really get some dope if I let you question any of my men you wanted to. I'd throw that in."

"I question its value."

"Oh, be reasonable."

"I often try. I will pay one hundred dollars for what you offer. Please! I will not haggle. And do not think me discourteous if I say that I am busy and need all the time the clock affords me. I thank you for your visit, but I am busy." Wolfe's finger moved to indicate the books before him on the desk, one of them with a marker in it. "There are the five novels written by Paul Chapin; I managed to procure the four earlier ones yesterday evening. I am reading them. I agree with you that this is a difficult case. It is possible, though extremely unlikely, that I shall have it solved by midnight."

I swallowed a grin. Wolfe liked bravado all right; for his reputation it was one of his best tricks.

Bascom stared at him. After a moment he pushed his chair back and got up, and the dick next to me lifted himself with a grunt. Bascom said, "Don't let me keep you. I believe I mentioned we all have our own methods, and all I've got to say is thank God for that."

"Yes. Do you wish the hundred dollars?"

Bascom, turning, nodded. "I'll take it. It looks to me like you're throwing the money away, since you've already bought the novels, but hell, I'll take it."

I went across to open the door, and they followed.

V

By DINNERTIME Monday we were all set, so we enjoyed the meal in leisure. Fritz was always happy and put on a little extra effort when he knew things were moving in the office. That night I passed him a wink when I saw how full the soup was of mushrooms, and when I tasted the tarragon in the salad dressing I threw him a kiss. He blushed. Wolfe frequently had compliments for his dishes and expressed them appropriately, and Fritz always blushed; and whenever I found occasion to toss him a tribute he blushed likewise, I'd swear to heaven, just to please me, not to let me down. I often wondered if Wolfe noticed it. His attention to food was so alert and comprehensive that I would have said offhand he didn't, but in making any kind of a guess about Wolfe, offhand wasn't good enough.

As soon as dinner was over Wolfe went up to his room, as he had explained he would do; he was staging it. I conferred with Fritz in the kitchen a few minutes and then went upstairs and changed my clothes. I put on the gray suit with pin checks, one of the best fits I ever had, and a light blue shirt and a dark blue tie. On my way back down I stopped in at Wolfe's room to ask him a question. He was in the tapestry chair by the reading lamp with one of Paul Chapin's novels, and I stood waiting while he marked a paragraph in it with a lead pencil.

I said, "What if one of them brings along some foreign object, like a lawyer for instance? Shall I let it in?"

Without looking up, he nodded. I went down to the office.

The first one was early. I hadn't looked for the line to start forming until around nine, but it lacked twenty minutes of that when I heard Fritz going down the hall and the front door opening. Then the knob of the office door turned, and Fritz ushered in the first victim. He almost needed a shave, his pants were baggy, and his hair wasn't combed. His pale blue eyes darted around and landed on me.

"Hell," he said, "you ain't Nero Wolfe."

I admitted it. I exposed my identity. He didn't offer to shake hands. He said, "I know I'm early for the party. I'm Mike Ayers, I'm in the city room at the *Tribune*. I told Oggie Reid I had to have the evening off to get my life saved. I stopped off somewhere to get a pair of drinks, and after a while it occurred to me I was a damn fool, there was no reason why there shouldn't be a drink here. I am not referring to beer."

I said, "Gin or gin?"

He grinned. "Good for you. Scotch. Don't bother to dilute it."

I went over to the table Fritz and I had fixed up in the alcove, and poured it. I was thinking, Hurrah for Harvard and bright college days and so on. I was also thinking, If he gets too loud he'll be a nuisance, but if I refuse to pander to his vile habit he'll beat it. And, having learned the bank reports practically by heart, I knew he had been on the *Post* four years and the *Tribune* three, and was pulling down ninety bucks a week. Newspapermen are one of my weak spots anyhow; I've never been able to get rid of a feeling that they know things I don't know.

I poured him another drink, and he sat down and held onto it and crossed his legs. "Tell me," he said, "is it true that Nero Wolfe was a eunuch in a Cairo harem and got his start in life by collecting testimonials from the girls for Pyramid Dental Cream?"

Like an ass, for half a second I was sore. "Listen," I said, "Nero Wolfe is exactly—" Then I stopped and laughed. "Sure," I said. "Except that he wasn't a eunuch, he was a camel."

Mike Ayers nodded. "That explains it. I mean it explains why it's hard for a camel to go through a needle's eye. I've never seen Nero Wolfe, but I've heard about him, and I've seen a needle. You got any other facts?"

I had to pour him another drink before the next customer arrived. This time it was a pair, Ferdinand Bowen, the stockbroker, and Dr. Loring A. Burton. I went to the hall for them to get away from Mike Ayers. Burton was a big fine-looking guy, straight but not stiff, well dressed and not needing any favors, with dark hair and black eyes and a tired mouth. Bowen was medium-sized, and he was tired all over. He was trim in black and white, and if I'd wanted to see him any evening, which I felt I wouldn't, I'd have gone to the theater where there was a first night and waited in the lobby. He had little feet in neat pumps, and neat little lady-hands in neat little gray gloves. When he was taking his coat off I had to stand back so as not to get socked in the eye with his arms swinging around, and I don't cotton to a guy with that sort of an attitude toward his fellow men in confined spaces. Particularly I think they ought to be kept out of elevators, but I'm not fond of them anywhere.

I took Burton and Bowen to the office and explained that Wolfe would be down soon and showed them Mike Ayers. He called Bowen "Ferdie" and offered him a drink, and he called Burton "Lorelei." Fritz brought in another one, Alexander Drummond the florist, a neat little duck with a thin mustache. He was the only one on the list who had ever been to Wolfe's house before, he having come a couple of years back with a bunch from an association meeting to look at the plants. I remembered him. After that they came more or less all together: Pratt, the Tammany assemblyman; Adler and Cabot, lawyers; Kommers, sales manager from Philadelphia; Edwin Robert Byron—all of that—magazine editor; Augustus Farrell, architect; and a bird named Lee Mitchell, from Boston, who said he represented both Collard and Gaines, the banker. He had a letter from Gaines.

That made twelve accounted for, figuring both Collard and Gaines in, at ten minutes past nine. Of course they all knew each other, but it couldn't be said they were getting much gaiety out of it, not even Mike Ayers, who was going around with an empty glass in his hand, scowling. The others were mostly sitting with their funeral manners on. I went to Wolfe's desk and gave Fritz's button three short pokes. In a couple of minutes I heard the faint hum of the elevator.

The door of the office opened, and they all turned their heads. Wolfe came in; Fritz pulled the door to behind him. He waddled halfway to his desk, stopped, turned, and said, "Good evening, gentlemen." He went to his chair, got the edge of the seat up against the backs of his knees and his grip on the arms, and lowered himself.

Mike Ayers demanded my attention by waving his glass at me and calling, "Hey! A eunuch *and* a camel!"

Wolfe raised his head a little and said in one of his best tones, "Are you suggesting those additions to Mr. Chapin's catalogue of his internal menagerie?"

"Huh? Oh. I'm suggesting—"

George Pratt said, "Shut up, Mike," and Farrell the architect grabbed him and pulled him into a chair.

I had handed Wolfe a list showing those who were present, and he had glanced over it. He looked up and spoke. "I am glad to see that Mr. Cabot and Mr. Adler are here—both, I believe, attorneys. Their knowledge and their trained minds will restrain us from vulgar errors. I note also the presence of Mr. Michael Ayers, a journalist. He is one of your number, so I merely remark that the risk of publicity, should you wish to avoid it—"

Mike Ayers growled, "I'm not a journalist, I'm a newshound. I interviewed Einstein—"

"How drunk are you?"

"Hell, how do I know?"

Wolfe's brow lifted. "Gentlemen?"

Farrell said, "Mike's all right. Forget him. He's all right."

Julius Adler the lawyer, about the build of a lead-pencil stub, looking like a necktie clerk except for his eyes and the way he was dressed, put in, "I would say yes. We realize that this is your house, Mr. Wolfe, and that Mr. Ayers is lit, but after all we don't suppose that you invited us here to censor our private habits. You have something to say to us?"

"Oh, yes—"

"My name is Adler."

"Yes, Mr. Adler. Your remark illustrates what I knew would be the chief hindrance in my conversation with you gentlemen. I was aware that you would be antagonistic at the outset. You are all badly frightened, and a frightened man is hostile almost by reflex, as a defense. He suspects everything and everyone. I knew that you would regard me with suspicion."

"Nonsense." It was Cabot, the other lawyer. "We are not frightened, and there is nothing to suspect you of. If you have anything to say to us, say it."

I said, "Mr. Nicholas Cabot."

Wolfe nodded. "If you aren't frightened, Mr. Cabot, there is nothing to discuss. I mean that. You might as well go home." Wolfe opened his eyes and let them move slowly across the eleven faces. "You see, gentlemen, I invited you here this evening only after making a number of assumptions. If any one of them is wrong, this meeting is a waste of time, yours and mine. The first assumption is that you are convinced that Mr. Paul Chapin has murdered two, possibly three, of your friends. The second, that you are apprehensive that unless something is done about it he will murder you. The third, that my abilities are equal to the task of removing your apprehension; and the fourth, that you will be willing to pay well for that service. Well?"

They glanced at one another. Mike Ayers started to get up from his chair, and Farrell pulled him back. Pratt muttered loud enough to reach Wolfe, "Good here."

Cabot said, "We are convinced that Paul Chapin is a dangerous enemy of society. That naturally concerns us. As to your abilities—"

Wolfe wiggled a finger at him. "Mr. Cabot. If it amuses you to maintain the fiction that you came here this evening to protect society, I would not dampen the diversion. The question is, how much is it worth to you?"

Mike Ayers startled all of us with a sudden shout, "Slick old Nick!" and followed it immediately with a falsetto whine, "Nicky darling." Farrell poked him in the ribs. Someone grumbled, "Gag him." But the glances of two or three others in the direction of Cabot showed that Wolfe was right; the only way to handle that bird was to rub it in.

A new voice broke in, smooth and easy. "What's the difference whether we're scared or not?" It was Edwin Robert Byron, the magazine editor. "I'd just as soon say I'm scared, what's the difference? It seems to me the point is, what does Mr. Wolfe propose to do about it? Grant him his premise—"

"Grant, hell!" Mike Ayers got up, flinging his arm free of Farrell's grasp, and started for the table in the alcove. Halfway there he turned and blurted at them, "You're damned tootin' we're scared. We jump at noises and we look behind us and we drop things, you know damn well we do. All of you that didn't lay awake last night wondering how he got Andy and what he did with him, raise your hands. You've heard of our little organization, Wolfe, you old faker? The League of Atonement? We're changing it to the Craven Club, or maybe the League of the White Feather." He filled his glass and lifted it; I didn't bother to call to him that he had got hold of the sherry decanter by mistake. "Fellow members! To the League of the White Feather!" He negotiated the drink with one heroic swallow. "You can make mine an ostrich plume." He scowled and made a terrific grimace of disgust and indignation. "Who the hell put horse manure in that whisky?"

Farrell let out a big handsome guffaw, and Pratt seconded him. Drummond the florist was giggling. Bowen the stockbroker, either bored or looking successfully like it, took out a cigar and cut off the end and lit it. I was over finding the right bottle for Mike Ayers, for I knew he'd have to wash the taste out of his mouth.

Lee Mitchell of Boston got to his feet. "If I may remark, gentlemen—" He coughed. "Of course I am not one of you, but I am authorized to say that both Mr. Collard and Mr. Gaines are in fact apprehensive, they have satisfied themselves of the standing of Mr. Wolfe, and they are ready to entertain his suggestions."

"Good." Wolfe's tone cut short the buzz of comment. He turned his eyes to me. "Archie. If you will just pass out those slips."

I had them in the top drawer of my desk—twenty copies, just in case —and I took them and handed them around. Wolfe had rung for beer and was filling his glass. After he had half emptied it he said, "That, as you see, is merely a list of your names with a sum of money noted after each. I can explain it most easily by reading to you a memorandum which I have here—or have I? Archie?"

"Here it is, sir."

"Thank you. I have dictated it thus; it may be put into formal legal phrasing or not, as you prefer. I would be content to have it an initialed memorandum. For the sake of brevity I have referred to you, those whose names are on the list you have—those absent as well as those present—as 'the league.' The memorandum provides:

"1. I undertake to remove from the league all apprehension and expectation of injury from
"(a) Paul Chapin.
"(b) The person or persons who sent the metrical typewritten warnings.
"(c) The person or persons responsible for the deaths of William R. Harrison and Eugene Dreyer, and for the disappearance of Andrew Hibbard.

"2. Decision as to the satisfactory performance of the undertaking shall be made by a majority vote of the members of the league.

"3. The expenses of the undertaking shall be borne by me, and in the event of my failure to perform it satisfactorily the league shall be under no obligation to pay them, nor any other obligation.

"4. Upon decision that the undertaking has been satisfactorily performed, the members of the league will pay me, each the amount set after his name on the attached list; provided that the members will be severally and jointly responsible for the payment of the total amount."

"I believe that covers it. Of course, should you wish to make it terminable after a stated period—"

Nicholas Cabot cut in. "It's preposterous. I won't even discuss it." Julius Adler said with a smile, "I think we should thank Mr. Wolfe's secretary for adding it up and saving us the shock. Fifty-six thousand, nine hundred and fifteen dollars. Well!" His brows went up and stayed up. Kommers, who had spent at least ten bucks coming from Philadelphia, made his maiden speech, "I don't know much about your abilities, Mr. Wolfe, but I've learned something new about nerve." Others began to join in the chorus; they were just going to crowd us right in the ditch.

Wolfe waited, and in about a minute put up his hand, palm out, which was a pretty violent gesture for him. "Please, gentlemen. There is really no ground for controversy. It is a simple matter: I offer to sell you something for a stated price on delivery. If you think the price exorbitant you are under no compulsion to buy. However, I may observe in that connection that on Saturday Miss Evelyn Hibbard offered to pay me ten thousand dollars for the service proposed. There is no single item on that list as high as ten thousand dollars; and Miss Hibbard is not herself in jeopardy."

George Pratt said, "Yeah, and you turned her down so you could soak us. You're just out to do all the good you can, huh?"

"Anyhow, the memorandum is preposterous throughout." Nicholas Cabot had gone to Wolfe's desk and reached for the memorandum, and was standing there looking at it. "What's all this hocus-pocus about person or persons responsible? What we want is Paul Chapin put where he belongs. This attempt at evasion—"

"I'm surprised at you, Mr. Cabot." Wolfe sighed. "I phrased it that way chiefly because I knew two shrewd lawyers would be here and I wished to forestall their objections. Circumstances have got the idea of Paul Chapin's guilt so firmly fixed in your mind that you are a little off balance. I could not undertake specifically to remove your apprehensions by getting Mr. Chapin convicted of murder, because if I did so and investigation proved him innocent two difficulties would present themselves. First, I would have to frame him in order to collect my money, which would be not only unfair to him but also a great bother to me, and second, the real perpetrator of these indiscretions would remain free to continue his career, and you gentlemen would still be scared—or dead. I wished to cover—"

"Rubbish." Cabot pushed the memorandum impatiently away. "We are convinced it is Chapin. We know it is."

"So am I." Wolfe nodded, down, and up, and at rest again. "Yes, I am convinced that it is Chapin you should fear. But in preparing this memorandum I thought it well to cover all contingencies, and you as a lawyer must agree with me. After all, what is really known? Very little. For instance, what if Andrew Hibbard, tormented by remorse, was driven to undertake vengeance on behalf of the man you all had injured? 'Ye should have killed me.' What if, after killing two of you, he found he couldn't stomach it, and went off somewhere and ended his own life? That would contradict nothing we now know. Or what if another of you, or even an outsider, proceeded to balance some personal accounts, and took advantage of the exudations of the Chapin stew to lay a false scent? That might be you, Mr. Cabot, or Dr. Burton, or Mr. Michael Ayers—anyone. You say rubbish, and really I do too, but why not cover the contingencies?"

Cabot pulled the memorandum back beneath his eyes. Julius Adler got up and went to the desk and joined in the inspection. There was some murmuring among the others. Mike Ayers was sprawled in his chair with his hands deep in his pockets and his eyes shut tight.

Julius Adler said, "This last provision is out of the question—this joint responsibility for the total amount. We wouldn't consider it."

Wolfe's cheeks unfolded a little. "I agree with you, Mr. Adler. I shall not insist upon it. As a matter of fact, I inserted it purposely, so there would be something for you to take out."

Adler grunted. Drummond the florist, who had gone to join them, as had Pratt and Arthur Kommers, giggled again. Cabot looked at

Wolfe with a frown and said, "You aren't at all nimble, are you?"

"Moderately. I'm really not much good at negotiation. I am too blunt. It is a shortcoming of temperament not to be overcome. For instance, my proposal to you: I can only present it and say, take it or leave it. I compensate for the handicap by making the proposal so attractive that it cannot very well be refused."

I was surprised, all of a sudden, to see the shadow of a smile on Cabot's face, and for a second I damn near liked him. He said, "Of course. I sympathize with your disability."

"Thank you." Wolfe moved his eyes to take in the others. "Well, gentlemen? I will mention two little points. First, I did not include in the memorandum a stipulation that you should cooperate with me, but I shall of course expect it. I can do little without your help. I would like to feel free to have Mr. Goodwin and another of my men call upon you at any reasonable time, and I would like to talk with a few of you myself. I may?"

Three or four heads nodded. George Pratt, with the group at the desk, said, "Good here." Cabot smiled openly and murmured, "Don't forget your disability."

"Good. The second point, about the money. In my opinion, the sums I have listed are adequate but not extortionate. If I fail to satisfy you I get nothing, so it comes to this: would Mr. Gaines be willing at this moment to pay me eight thousand dollars, and Dr. Burton seven thousand, and Mr. Michael Ayers one hundred and eighty, in return for a guarantee of freedom from the fear which has fastened itself upon them? I take it that you agree that it is proper to have the amounts graded in accordance with ability to pay."

Again heads nodded. He was easing them into it; he was sewing them up. I grinned to myself. Boss, you're cute, that's all, you're just cute.

Lee Mitchell from Boston spoke again. "Of course I can't speak definitely for Mr. Collard and Mr. Gaines. I think I may say—you can probably count them in. I'll go back to Boston tonight, and they'll wire you tomorrow."

Cabot said, "You can cross Elkus out. He wouldn't pay you a cent."

"No?"

"No. He's as sentimental as Andy Hibbard was. He'd sooner see us all killed than help catch Paul Chapin."

"Indeed. It is disastrous to permit the vagaries of the heart to infect the mind. We shall see. Gentlemen. I would like to satisfy myself now on one point. Frankly, I do not wish it to be possible for any of you to say, at any time in the future, that I have acted with a ruthlessness or vindictiveness which you did not contemplate or desire. My understanding is that you are all convinced that Paul Chapin is a murderer, that he has threatened you with murder, and that he should be caught, discovered, convicted, and executed. I am going to ask Mr. Goodwin to call off your names. If my understanding is correct, you will please respond with 'yes.'"

He nodded at me. I took up the list on which I had checked those present. Before I could call one, Lee Mitchell said, "On that I can answer for Mr. Collard and Mr. Gaines—unqualifiedly. Their response is *yes*."

There was a stir, but no one spoke. I said, "Ferdinand Bowen."

The broker said, husky but firm, "Yes."

"Dr. Loring A. Burton."

For a moment there was no reply; then Burton murmured in a tone so low it was barely heard, "No." Everyone looked at him. He looked around, swallowed, and said suddenly and explosively, "Nonsense! Yes, of course! Romantic nonsense. Yes!"

Farrell said to him, "I should hope so. The wonder is you weren't first."

I went on, "Augustus Farrell."

"Yes."

I called the others—Drummond, Cabot, Pratt, Byron, Adler, Kommers; they all said, "Yes." I called, "Michael Ayers." He was still sprawled in his chair. I said his name again. Farrell, next to him, dug him in the ribs. "Mike! Hey! Say yes." Mike Ayers stirred a little, opened his eyes into slits, bawled out, "Yes!" and shut his eyes again.

I turned to Wolfe, "That's all, sir."

I usually heard Fritz when he went down the front hall to answer the doorbell, but that time I didn't, I suppose because I was too interested in the roll I was calling. So I was surprised when I saw the door of the office opening. The others saw me look and they looked too. Fritz came in three steps and waited until Wolfe nodded at him.

"A gentleman to see you, sir. He had no card. He told me to say, Mr. Paul Chapin."

"Indeed." Wolfe didn't move. "Indeed. Show him in."

VI

Fritz went back to the hall to get the visitor. I missed a bet, but Wolfe probably didn't—I don't know. I should have been taking notice of the expressions on the faces of our guests, but I wasn't; my eyes were glued on the door. I imagine all the others were too, except Wolfe's. I heard the thud of Paul Chapin's walking-stick on the rubber tile of the hall.

He limped in and stopped a few paces from the door. From where he was he couldn't see Wolfe, on account of the group gathered at the desk. He looked at the group, and at those around on chairs, and tossed his head up twice, his chin out, like a nervous horse trying to shake the rein. He said, "Hello, fellows," and limped forward again, far enough into the room so he could see Wolfe, first sending a quick, sharp glance at me. He was standing less than eight feet from me. He was dressed for evening, a dinner coat. He wasn't a big guy at all, rather under medium size than over; you couldn't call him skinny, but you could see the bone structure of his face—flat cheeks, an ordinary nose, and light-colored eyes. When he turned his back to me so as to face Wolfe I saw that his coat didn't hang straight down over his right hip pocket, and I uncrossed my legs and brought my feet back to position, just in case.

There had been no audible replies to his salutation. He looked around again, back again at Wolfe, and smiled at him. "You are Mr. Wolfe?"

"Yes." Wolfe had his fingers intertwined on his belly. "You are Mr. Chapin."

Paul Chapin nodded. "I was at the theater. They've done a book of mine into a play. Then I thought I'd drop in here."

"Which book? I've read all of them."

"You have? Really. I wouldn't suppose— *The Iron Heel*."

"Oh yes. That one. Accept my congratulations."

"Thank you. I hope you don't mind my dropping in. I knew of this gathering, of course. I learned of it from three of my friends, Leo Elkus and Lorry Burton and Alex Drummond. You mustn't hold it against them, except possibly Leo. He meant well, I think, but the others were trying to frighten me. They were trying it with a bogy, but for a bogy to be effective its terrors must be known to the victim. Unfortunately you were unknown to me. You have terrors, I suppose?"

Since Chapin's first word he had kept his eyes on Wolfe, ignoring the others. They were regarding him with varying reactions on their faces: Mitchell of Boston with curiosity, Bowen with a sour poker face, Cabot with uncomfortable indignation, Mike Ayers with scowling disgust. I was looking them over.

Of a sudden Dr. Burton left his chair, strode to the desk, and grabbed Chapin by the arm. He said to him, "Paul, for God's sake! Get out of here! This is terrible. Get out!"

Drummond the florist put in, his cultured tenor transformed by intensity into a ferocious squeal, "This is the limit, Paul! After what we —after what I— You dirty, murdering rat!"

Others, breaking their tension, found their tongues. Wolfe stopped them. He said sharply, "Gentlemen! Mr. Chapin is my guest!" He looked at Chapin, leaning on his stick. "You should sit down. Take a chair. Archie."

"No, thanks. I'll be going in a moment." Chapin sent a smile around; it would have been merely a pleasant smile but for his light-colored eyes, where there was no smile at all. "I've been standing on one foot for twenty-five years. Of course all of you know that; I don't need to tell you. I'm sorry if I've annoyed you by coming here; really, I wouldn't disconcert you fellows for anything. You've all been too kind to me, you know very well you have. If I may get a little literary and sentimental about it—you have lightened life's burden for me. I'll never forget it, I've told you that a thousand times. Of course now that I seem to have found my métier, now that I am standing on my own feet—that is, my own foot"—he smiled around again—"I shall be able to find my way the rest of the journey without you. But I shall always be grateful." He turned to Wolfe. "That's how it is, you see. But I didn't come here to say that, I came to see you. I was thinking that possibly you are a reasonable and intelligent man. Are you?"

Wolfe was looking at him. I was saying to myself, Look out, Paul Chapin, look out for those half-closed eyes, and if you take my advice you'll shut up and beat it quick.

Wolfe said, "I reach that pinnacle occasionally, Mr. Chapin."

"I'll try to believe you. There are few who do. I just wanted to say this to you: my friends have wasted a lot of time and money pursuing a mirage which someone has cleverly projected for them. I tell you straight, Mr. Wolfe, it's been a shock to me—that they should suspect *me*, knowing as they do how grateful I am for all their kindness! Really incredible! I wanted to put this before you and save you from the loss of your time and money too. You would not be so fatuous as to chase a mirage?"

"I assure you, sir, I am far too immobile to chase anything whatever. But perhaps—since you are by your own admission definitely out of it—perhaps you have a theory regarding the incidents that have disturbed your friends? It might help us."

"I'm afraid not." Chapin shook his head regretfully. "Of course it appears more than likely that it's a practical joke, but I have no idea—"

"Murder isn't a joke, Mr. Chapin. Death is not a joke."

"Oh no? Really, no? Are you so sure? Take a good case. Take me, Paul Chapin. Would you dare to assert that my death would not be a joke?"

"Why, would it?"

"Of course. A howling anticlimax. Death's pretensions to horror, considering what in my case has preceded it, would be indescribably ludicrous. That is why I have so greatly appreciated my friends, their thoughtfulness, their solicitude—"

A cry from behind interrupted him; a cry, deeply anguished, in the voice of Dr. Burton. "Paul! Paul, for God's sake!"

Chapin wheeled about on his good leg. "Yes?" Without raising his voice a particle he got into it a concentrated scorn that would have withered the love of God. "Yes, Lorry?"

Burton looked at him, said nothing, shook his head, and turned his eyes away. Chapin turned back to Wolfe. Wolfe said, "So you adhere to the joke theory."

"Not adhere precisely. It seems likely. So far as I am concerned, Mr. Wolfe, the only point is this: I suffer from the delusion of my friends that I am a source of peril to them. Actually, they are afraid of me. Of *me!* I suffer considerably, I really do. The fact is that it would be difficult to conceive of a more harmless creature than I am. I am myself afraid—constitutionally afraid of all sorts of things! For instance, on account of my pathetic physical inadequacy, I go in constant fear of this or that sort of violent attack, and I habitually am armed. See?"

Paul Chapin had us going all right. As his right hand came around behind him and his fingers started under the edge of his dinner coat, there were two or three cries of warning from the group, and I took it on the jump. With my momentum and him balanced against his walking-stick, I damn near toppled him over, but I had my grip on his right wrist and saved him from a tumble. With my left hand I jerked the gat from his hip pocket.

"Archie!" Wolfe snapped at me. "Release Mr. Chapin."

I let go his wrist. Wolfe was still snapping. "Give him back his— article."

I looked at the gat. It was a thirty-two, an old veteran, and a glance showed me it wasn't loaded. Paul Chapin, his light-colored eyes having no look in them at all, held out his hand. I put the gun in it, and he let it sit there on his palm as if it was a dish of applesauce.

Wolfe said, "Confound you, Archie. You have deprived Mr. Chapin of the opportunity for a dramatic and effective gesture. I know, Mr. Chapin. I am sorry. May I see the gun?"

Chapin handed it to him, and he looked it over. He threw the cylinder out and back, cocked it, snapped the trigger, and looked it over again. He said, "An ugly weapon. It terrifies me. Guns always do. May I show it to Mr. Goodwin?"

Chapin shrugged his shoulders, and Wolfe handed the gat to me. I took it under my light and gave it a few warm glances, cocked it, saw what Wolfe had seen, and grinned. Then I looked up and saw Paul Chapin's eyes on me and stopped grinning. You could still have said there was no look in them, but behind them was something I wouldn't have cared to bring into plain sight. I handed him the gun, and he stuck it back into his hip pocket. He said, half to me and half to Wolfe, in an easy tone, "That's it, you see. The effect is psychological. I learned a good deal about psychology from my friend Andy Hibbard."

There were ejaculations. George Pratt stepped to Chapin and glared at him. Pratt's hands were working at his sides as he stammered, "You —you snake! If you weren't a goddam cripple I'd knock you so far I'll say you'd be harmless—"

Chapin showed no alarm. "Yes, George. And what made me a goddam cripple?"

Pratt didn't retreat. "I helped to, once. Sure I did. That was an accident; we all have 'em—maybe not as bad as yours. Christ, can't you ever forget it? Is there no man in you at all? Has your brain got twisted—"

"No. Man? No." Chapin cut him off and smiled at him with his mouth. He looked around at the others. "You fellows are all men, though. Aren't you? Every one. God bless you. That's an idea, depend on God's blessing. Try it. I tried it once. Now I must ask you to excuse me." He turned to Wolfe. "Good evening, sir. I'll go. Thank you for your courtesy. I trust I haven't put too great a strain on your intelligence."

He inclined his head to Wolfe and to me, turned, and made off. His stick had thumped three times on the rug when he was halted by Wolfe's voice.

"Mr. Chapin. I almost forgot. May I ask you for a very few minutes more? Just a small—"

Nicholas Cabot's voice broke in, "For God's sake, Wolfe, let him go—"

"Please, Mr. Cabot. May I, gentlemen? Just a small favor, Mr. Chapin. Since you are innocent of any ill intent, and as anxious as we are to see your friends' difficulties removed, I trust you will help me in a little test. I know it will seem nonsensical to you, quite meaningless, but I should like to try it. Would you help me out?"

Chapin had turned. I thought he looked careful. He said, "Perhaps. What is it?"

"Quite simple. You use a typewriter, I suppose?"

"Of course. I type all my manuscripts myself."

"We have a typewriter here. Would you be good enough to sit at Mr. Goodwin's desk and type something at my dictation?"

"Why should I?" He hesitated and was certainly being careful now. He looked around and saw twelve pairs of eyes at him; then he smiled and said easily, "But for that matter, why shouldn't I?" He limped back toward me.

I pulled the machine up into position, inserted a sheet of paper, got up, and held my chair for him. He shook his head, and I moved away, and he leaned his stick up against the desk and got himself into the chair, shoving his bum leg under with his hand. Nobody was saying a word. He looked around at Wolfe and said, "I'm not very fast. Shall I double-space it?"

"I would say, single-space. In that way it will most nearly resemble the original. Are you ready?" Wolfe suddenly and unexpectedly put volume and depth into his voice. " 'Ye should have killed me'—comma —'watched the last mean sigh—' "

There was complete silence. It lasted ten seconds. Then Chapin's fingers moved, and the typewriter clicked, firm and fast. I followed the words on it. It got through the first three, but at the fourth it faltered. It stopped at the second *l* in "killed," stopped completely. There was silence again. You could have heard a feather falling. The sounds that broke it came from Paul Chapin. He moved with no haste but with a good deal of finality. He pushed back, got himself onto his feet, took his stick, and thumped off. He brushed past me, and Arthur Kommers had to move out of his way. Before he got to the door he stopped and turned. He did not seem especially perturbed, and his light-colored eyes had nothing new in them as far as I could see from where I was.

He said, "I would have been glad to help in any authentic test, Mr. Wolfe, but I wouldn't care to be the victim of a trick. I was referring, by the way, to intelligence, not to a vulgar and obvious cunning."

He turned. Wolfe murmured, "Archie," and I went out to help Chapin on with his coat and open the door for him.

VII

WHEN I got back to the office everybody was talking. Mike Ayers had gone to the table to get a drink, and three or four others had joined him. Dr. Burton stood with his hands dug into his pockets, frowning, listening to Farrell and Pratt. Wolfe had untwined his fingers and was showing his inner tumult by rubbing his nose with one of them. When I got to his desk Cabot the lawyer was saying to him, "I have an idea you'll collect your fees, Mr. Wolfe. I begin to understand your repute."

"I shall make no discount for flummery, sir." Wolfe sighed. "For my part, I have an idea that if I collect my fees I shall have earned them. Your friend Mr. Chapin is a man of quality."

Cabot nodded. "Paul Chapin is a distorted genius."

"All genius is distorted. Including my own. But so, for that matter, is all life, a mad and futile ferment of substances meant originally to occupy space without disturbing it. But alas, here we are in the thick of the disturbance, and the only way that has occurred to us to make it tolerable is to join in and raise all the hell our ingenuity may suggest. How did Paul Chapin acquire his special distortion? I mean the famous accident. Tell me about it. I understand it was at college, a hazing affair."

"Yes. It was pretty terrible." Cabot sat on the edge of the desk. "No doubt of that, but good God, other men—the war, for instance— Oh well. I suppose Paul was distorted from the beginning. He was a freshman; the rest of us were sophomores and on up. Do you know the Yard?"

"The Yard?"

"At Harvard."

"I have never been there."

"Well. There were dormitories—Thayer Hall. This was at Thayer Middle Entry—Hell Bend. We were having a beer night downstairs, and there were some there from outside—that's how fellows like Gaines and Collard happened to be present. We were having a good time around ten o'clock when a fellow came in and said he couldn't get in his room; he had left his key inside, and the doors had snap locks. Of course we all began to clap."

"That was a masterpiece, to forget one's key?"

"Oh no. We were clapping the opportunity. By getting out a hall window, or another room, you could make your way along a narrow ledge to the window of any locked room and get in that way. It was quite a trick—I wouldn't try it now for my hope of the Supreme Court —but I had done it in my freshman year and so had many others. Whenever an upperclassman forgot his key it was the native custom to conscript a freshman for that service. There was nothing extraordinary about it, for the agility of youth. Well, when this fellow—it was Andy Hibbard—when he announced he had locked himself out, of course we welcomed the opportunity for a little discipline. We looked around for a victim. Somebody heard a noise in the hall and looked out and saw one going by, and called to him to come in. He came in. It was Chapin."

"He was a freshman."

Cabot nodded. "Paul had a personality, a force in him, already at that age. Maybe he was already distorted. I'm not a psychiatrist. Andy Hibbard has told me—but that wouldn't help you any. Anyhow, we had been inclined to let him alone. Now here he was, delivered to us by chance. Somebody told him what was expected of him. He was quite cool about it. He asked what floor Andy's room was on, and we told him the fourth, three flights up. He said he was sorry, in that case he couldn't do it. Ferd Bowen said to him, 'What's the matter, you're not a cripple, are you?' We remembered that on account of what happened. He said he was perfectly sound. Bill Harrison, who was serious-minded in his cradle, asked him if he had vertigo. He said no. We marched him upstairs. Ordinarily not more than a dozen or so would probably have gone up to see the fun, but on account of the way he was taking it thirty-five of us herded him up. We didn't touch him. He went because he knew what would happen if he didn't."

"What would happen?"

"Oh, things—whatever might occur to us. You know college kids."

"As few as possible."

"Yes. Well, he went. I'll never forget his face as he was getting out of the hall window, backwards. It was white as a sheet, but it was something else too, I don't know what. It got me. It got Andy Hibbard too, for he jumped forward and called to Chapin to come back in, he would do it himself. Others grabbed Andy and told him not to be a damn fool. All who could crowded up and looked out of the window. It was moonlight. Others ran to one of the rooms and looked out of the windows there. Chapin got onto the ledge all right, and got straightened up and moved along a little, his hand stretched out as far as he could, trying to reach the next window. I didn't see it—I wasn't looking—but they said that all of a sudden he began to tremble, and down he went."

Cabot stopped. He reached in his pocket for his case and lit a cigarette. He didn't hold the match to it as steady as he might have. He took a couple of puffs and said, "That's all. That's what happened."

Wolfe grunted. "You say there were thirty-five of you?"

"Yes. So it turned out." Cabot pulled at his cigarette. "We chipped in, of course, and did all we could. He was in the hospital two months and had three operations. I don't know where he got a list of our names; I suppose from Andy. Andy took it hard. Anyway, the day he left the hospital he sent all of us copies of a poem he had written—thanking us. It was clever. There was only one of us smart enough to see what kind of thanks it was. Pitney Scott."

"Pitney Scott is a taxi driver."

Cabot raised his brows. "You should write our class history, Mr. Wolfe. Pit took to drink in nineteen-thirty, one of the depression casualties—not, like Mike Ayers, for the annoyance of other people; for his own destruction. I see you have him down for five dollars. I'll pay it."

"Indeed. That would indicate that you are prepared to accept my proposal."

"Of course I am. We all are. But you know that. What else can we do? We are menaced with death, there's no question about it. I have no idea why, if Paul had this in him, he waited so long to get it out—possibly his recent success gave him a touch of confidence that he needed, or money to finance his plans—I don't know. Of course we accept your proposal. Did you know that a month ago Adler and Pratt and Bowen seriously discussed the notion of hiring a gangster to kill him? They invited me in, but I wouldn't—everyone's squeamishness begins somewhere, and I suppose that was the starting point for mine—and they abandoned the idea. What else can we do? The police are helpless, which is understandable and nothing against them; they are equipped to frustrate many kinds of men, but not Paul Chapin—I grant him his quality. Three of us hired detectives a month ago, and we might as well have engaged a troop of Boy Scouts. They spent days looking for the typewriter on which the warnings were written, and never even found it; and if they had found it they would not have been able to fasten it on Paul Chapin."

"Yes." Wolfe reached out and pressed the button for Fritz. "Your detectives called on me and offered to place their findings at my disposal—with your consent." Fritz appeared, and Wolfe nodded for beer. "Mr. Cabot. What does Mr. Chapin mean when he says that you killed the man in him?"

"Well—that's poetry, isn't it?"

"It might be called that. Is it merely poetry, or is it also technical information?"

"I don't know." Cabot's eyes fell. I watched him and thought to myself, He's actually embarrassed; so there's kinks in your love-life too, huh, smoothie? He went on, "I couldn't say; I doubt if any of us could. You'd have to ask his doctor."

A new voice cut in. Julius Adler and Alex Drummond had come over a few minutes before and stood listening—Adler, I suppose, because he was a lawyer and therefore didn't trust lawyers, and Drummond since he was a tenor. I never saw a tenor that wasn't inquisitive.

At this point Drummond horned in with a giggle. "Or his wife."

Wolfe snapped at him, "Whose wife?"

"Why, Paul's."

If I had seen Wolfe astonished only three times in seven years, which is what I would guess, this was the fourth. He even moved in his chair. He looked at Cabot, not at Drummond, and demanded, "What is this nonsense?"

Cabot nodded. "Sure, Paul has a wife."

Wolfe poured a glass of beer, gulped half of it, let it settle a second, and swallowed the rest. He looked around for his handkerchief, but it had dropped to the floor. I got him one out of the drawer where I kept them, and he wiped his lips.

He said, "Tell me about her."

"Well—" Cabot looked for words. "Paul Chapin is full of distortions, let us say, and his wife is one of them. Her name was Dora Ritter. He married her three years ago, and they live in an apartment on Perry Street."

"What is she like and who was she?"

Cabot hesitated again, differently. This time he didn't seem to be looking for words, he was looking for a way out. He finally said, "I don't see—I really don't see that this is going to help you any, but I suppose you'll want to know it. But I'd rather not—you'd better get it from Burton himself." He turned and called, "Lorry! Come over here a minute."

Dr. Burton was with the group at the table, talking and working on a highball. He looked around, made some remark to Farrell, the architect, and crossed to Wolfe's desk. Cabot said to him, "Mr. Wolfe has just asked me who Paul's wife was. Maybe I'm being more delicate than the circumstances require, but I'd rather you'd tell him."

Burton looked at Wolfe and frowned. He looked at Cabot, and his voice sounded irritated. "Why not you, or anybody? Everybody knows it."

Cabot smiled. "I said maybe I was overdelicate."

"I think you were." Burton turned to Wolfe. "Dora Ritter was a maid in my employ. She is around fifty, extremely homely, disconcertingly competent, and stubborn as a wet boot. Paul Chapin married her in nineteen-thirty-one."

"What did he marry her for?"

"I am as likely to tell you as he is. Chapin is a psychopath."

"So Mr. Hibbard informed me. What sort of maid was she?"

"What sort?"

"Was she in your office, for instance?"

Burton was frowning. "No. She was my wife's maid."

"How long have you known her and how long has Chapin known her? Wait." Wolfe wiggled a finger. "I must ask you to bear with me, Dr. Burton. I have just received a shock and am floundering in confusion. I have read all of Paul Chapin's novels, and so naturally supposed myself to be in possession of a fairly complete understanding of his character, his temperament, his processes of thought, and his modes of action. I thought him incapable of following any of the traditional channels leading to matrimony, either emotional or practical. Learning that he has a wife, I am greatly shocked; I am even desperate. I need to have disclosed everything about her that is discoverable."

"Oh. You do." Burton looked at him, sizing him up, with sour steadiness. "Then I might as well disclose it myself. It was common gossip." He glanced at the others. "I knew that, though naturally it didn't reach my ears. If I show reluctance, it is only because it was—unpleasant."

"Yes."

"Yes, it was. I presume you don't know that of all of us, this group, I was the only one who knew Paul Chapin before the college days. We came from the same town—I more or less grew up with him. He was in love with a girl. I knew her—one of the girls I knew, that was all. He was infatuated with her, and he finally, through persistence, reached an understanding with her before he went away to college. Then the accident occurred, and he was crippled, and it was all off. In my opinion it would have been off anyway, sooner or later, without the intervention of an accident. I didn't go home for my vacations; I spent my summers working. It wasn't until after I was through with medical school that I went back for a visit, and discovered that this girl had become—that is, I married her."

He glanced aside at Cabot's cigarette case thrust at him by the lawyer, shook his head, turned back to Wolfe, and went on, "We came to New York. I was lucky in my profession; I have a good bedside manner and a knack with people's insides, especially women. I made a lot of money. I think it was in nineteen-twenty-three that my wife engaged Dora Ritter—yes, she was with us eight years. Her competence was a jewel in a nigger's ear—"

"Ethiope."

"Well, that's a nigger. One day Paul came to me and said he was going to marry my wife's maid. That was what was unpleasant. He made a nasty scene out of it."

Wolfe inclined his head. "I can imagine him explaining that the action contemplated was by way of a paraphrase on the old institution of whipping-boy."

Dr. Burton jerked his head up, startled, and stared at him. "How the devil did you know that?"

"He said that?"

"Those words. He said 'paraphrase.'"

"I suspected he would have lit on that." Wolfe scratched his ear, and I knew he was pleased. "Having read his novels, I am not unacquainted with his style of thought and his taste in allusion. So he married her. She, of course, having but one jewel and the rest all slag, would not be finicky. Do they make a happy pair? Do you ever see her?"

"Not frequently." Burton hesitated, then went on, "I see her very seldom. She comes once or twice a week to dress my wife's hair, and occasionally to sew. I am usually not at home."

Wolfe murmured, "It is a temptation to cling to competence when we find it."

Burton nodded. "I suppose so. My wife finds it impossible to forgo the indulgence. Dora is an expert hag."

"Well." Wolfe took some beer. "Thank you, Doctor. It has often been said, you will find romance in the most unlikely spots. Mr. Chapin's no longer upsets me, since it fits my presumptions. By the way, this probably clears up another little point. Permit me. Archie, would you ask Mr. Farrell to join us?"

I went and got Farrell and brought him over. He was brisk; the scotch was putting some spring into him. He gave Wolfe an amiable look.

"Mr. Farrell. Earlier this evening you remarked to Dr. Burton that it was a wonder he was not the first. I supposed that you meant the first victim of Mr. Chapin's campaign. Did that remark mean anything in particular?"

Farrell looked uncomfortable. "Did I say that?"

"You did."

"I don't remember it. I suppose I thought I was cracking a joke—I don't know."

Wolfe said patiently, "Dr. Burton has just been telling me the exegesis of Chapin's marriage and the former occupation of his wife. I thought perhaps—"

"Oh, he has." Farrell shot a glance at Burton. "Then what are you asking me for?"

"Don't be testy, Mr. Farrell; let me save your life in amity. That was the basis of your remark?"

"Of course. But what the devil have Lorry Burton's private affairs got to do with it? Or mine or anybody's? I thought what we are going to pay you for is to stop—"

He broke off. He looked around at the others, and his face got red. He finished to Wolfe in a completely different tone. "Forgive me. I forgot for a moment."

"Forgot what?"

"Nothing of any importance. Only that I'm out of it. In your total of fifty-odd thousand, you've got me down for ten dollars. Your sources of information are up-to-date. Have you any idea what architects have been up against the past four years? Even good ones. I did the new city hall at Baltimore in nineteen-twenty-eight. Now I couldn't get— you're not thinking of doing any building, Mr. Wolfe? A telephone stand or a dog kennel or anything? I'd be glad to submit designs— Oh, the devil. Anyway, I forgot I'm just here ex-officio, I'm not paying my way. Come on, Lorry, come and finish your drink. You ought to be home in bed, you're sagging worse than I am." He took Burton's arm.

Moving off, they halted for Wolfe. "Mr. Farrell. I am under the same necessity of earning your ten dollars as Mr. Collard's nine thousand. If you have comments—"

"Hell no. I haven't even got a comment. Nor am I even contributing ten bucks to the pot of retribution, I'm taking it out in scotch."

George Pratt said to Cabot, "Come on, Nick, have a little refreshment," and they followed the other two.

Alex Drummond was left alone at the corner of Wolfe's desk; he jerked to join the procession, then jerked back. He looked at Wolfe with his bright little eyes, stepped closer to him, and made his voice low. "Uh—Mr. Wolfe. I imagine your sources of information are pretty good."

Wolfe said without looking at him, "They are superlative."

"I imagine so. Gus Farrell hasn't really been up against it for more than a couple of months, but I notice you are aware of it. Uh—I wonder if you would be willing to enlighten me regarding another item on your list—just curiosity."

"I haven't engaged to satisfy your curiosity."

"No. But I was wondering. Why have you got Gaines down for eight thousand and Burton for seven thousand and so on, and Ferd Bowen for only twelve hundred? He's something in Wall Street—I mean really something. Isn't he? The firm of Galbraith and Bowen." Drummond made his voice a little lower. "Frankly, it's more than curiosity. He handles a few little investments for me."

Wolfe looked at him and looked away again. I thought for a minute he wasn't going to reply at all, but he did, with his eyes shut. "Don't bother to disparage your investments. It can have no effect on the amount of your payment to me, for that has already been calculated and recorded. As for your question, my sources of information may be superlative, but they are not infallible. If Mr. Bowen ventures to object that I have belittled him, I shall consider his protest with an open mind."

"Of course," Drummond agreed. "But if you could just tell me in confidence—"

"If you will excuse me." Wolfe opened his eyes, got his chin up, and raised his voice a little. "Gentlemen. Gentlemen? Could I have a word with you?"

They approached his desk, three or four from the corner the bookshelves made, and the wet contingent from the alcove table. Two or three still in chairs stayed there. Drummond, his hide too thick to show any red from Wolfe's sandpapering, trotted around to the far side. Mike Ayers flopped into a chair again, stretching out his legs; his mouth gaped wide in a free-for-all yawn; then suddenly he clamped his lips tight with a look of indignant and wary surprise. I had a notion to go and move him off the rug, but decided he was going to hold it.

Wolfe was handing it to them in his handsome manner. "The hour is getting late, and I would not wish to detain you beyond necessity. I take it that we are in agreement—"

Arthur Kommers interrupted, "I ought to leave in a minute to catch the midnight back to Philadelphia. Do you want my initials on that thing?"

"Thank you, sir. Not at present. There is a phrase to be deleted. I shall ask Mr. Cabot to prepare copies in his office tomorrow morning and send them to me for distribution." He sent a glance at the lawyer, and Cabot nodded. "Thank you. In that connection, Mr. Farrell, I wish to make a proposal to you. You are broke, but you have a fairly intelligent face. To be broke is not a disgrace, it is only a catastrophe. You can help me. For instance, you can take, or send, copies of the memorandum to those members of the league not present this evening, and arrange for their cooperation. I will pay you twenty dollars a day. There will be other little jobs for you."

The architect was staring at him. "You're quite a guy, Mr. Wolfe. By God if you're not. But I'm not a detective."

"I shall keep my demands modest, and expect no intrepidity."

"All right." Farrell laughed. "I can use twenty dollars."

"Good. Report here tomorrow at eleven. Now, Dr. Burton. Your lifelong acquaintance with Paul Chapin places you in a special position, for my purpose. Could you dine with me tomorrow evening?"

Without hesitation Burton shook his head. "I'm sorry, I shall be engaged."

"Could you call on me after dinner? Forgive me for not asking permission to call on you instead. My disinclination to leave my home has a ponderable basis."

But Burton shook his head again. "I'm sorry, Mr. Wolfe, I can't come." He hesitated and went on, "More frankly, I won't. It's softness in me. I'm not as soft about it as Andy Hibbard and Leo Elkus. I answered yes to the question you put this evening, though you made it as raw as possible. Of course you did that purposely. I answered yes, and I'll pay my share, but that's as far as I'll go. I will not confer on ways and means of exposing Paul Chapin's guilt and getting him convicted and electrocuted. Oh, don't misunderstand me. I don't pretend to be standing on a principle; I'm perfectly aware it's only a temperamental prejudice. I wouldn't move a finger to protect Paul or save him from the consequences of his crimes. In fact, in so far as the thing may be considered a personal issue between him and myself, I am ready to defeat him by a violence equal to his own."

"You are ready?" Wolfe had opened his eyes on him. "You mean you are prepared?"

"Not specially." Burton looked irritated. "It is of no importance whatever. I always seem to talk too much when Paul Chapin is concerned; I wish to the Lord I'd never heard of him. As far as that goes, of course, we all do. I only meant—well, for years I've kept an automatic pistol in the drawer of my study table. One evening last week

Paul came to see me. For years, of course, he was welcome at my house, though he seldom came. On this occasion, on account of recent events, I told the butler to keep him in the reception hall; and before I went to the reception hall I took the pistol from the drawer and stuck it in my pocket. That was all I meant; I would be perfectly willing to use personal violence if the circumstances required it."

Wolfe sighed. "I regret your soft spot, Dr. Burton. But for that you might, for instance, tell us which evening Mr. Chapin went to see you and what it was he wanted."

"That wouldn't help you." Burton was brusque. "It was personal—that is, it was only neurotic nonsense."

"So, they say, was Napoleon's dream of empire. Very well, sir. By all means cling to the tattered shreds of humanity that are left you; there are enough of us in that respect quite unclothed. I must somehow manage my enterprise without stripping you. I would like to ask, gentlemen, which of you were most intimate with Mr. Hibbard?"

They looked at one another. George Pratt said, "We all saw Andy off and on." Julius Adler put in, "I would say that among us Roland Erskine was his closest friend. I would boast that I was next."

"Erskine the actor?" Wolfe glanced at the clock. "I was thinking he might join us after the theater, but scarcely at this hour. He is working, I believe."

Drummond said, "He's in *The Iron Heel*; he has the lead."

"Then he couldn't dine. Not at a civilized hour." Wolfe looked at Julius Adler. "Could you come here at two o'clock tomorrow afternoon and bring Mr. Erskine with you?"

"Perhaps." The lawyer looked annoyed. "I suppose I could manage it. Couldn't you come to my office?"

"I'm sorry, sir. Believe me, I am; but knowing my habits as I do, it seems extravagantly improbable. If you could arrange to bring Mr. Erskine—"

"All right. I'll see what I can do."

"Thank you. You had better run, Mr. Kommers, or you'll miss your train. Another reason, and one of the best, for staying at home. Gentlemen, so far as our business is concerned I need not further detain you. But in connection with my remark to Mr. Kommers it occurs to me that no publication either before or since the invention of printing, no theological treatise and no political or scientific creed, has ever been as narrowly dogmatic or as offensively arbitrary in its prejudices as a railway timetable. If any of you should care to remain half an hour or so to help me enlarge upon that . . ."

Byron, the magazine editor, who had stuck in his shell all evening, suddenly woke up. He got up from his chair and slipped his head in between a couple of shoulders to see Wolfe. "You know, that idea could be developed into a first-rate little article—six hundred to seven hundred words, about. The Tyranny of the Wheel, you could call it, with a colored margin of trains and airplanes and ocean liners at top speed—of course liners don't have wheels, but you could do something about that. If I could persuade you, Mr. Wolfe—"

"I'm afraid you could only bewilder me, Mr. Byron."

Cabot the lawyer smiled. "I never saw a man less likely to be bewildered, even by Eddie Byron. Good night, Mr. Wolfe." He picked up the memorandum and folded it and put it in his pocket. "I'll send you these in the morning."

They got moving. Pratt and Farrell went and got Mike Ayers to his feet and slapped him around a little. Byron started trying to persuade Wolfe again and was pulled off by Adler. Kommers had gone. The others drifted to the hall, and I went out and stood around while they got their hats and coats on. Bowen and Burton went off together, as they had come. I held the door for Pratt and Farrell to get Mike Ayers through; they were the last out.

After I had shut the door and bolted it I went to the kitchen for a pitcher of milk. Fritz was sitting there, reading that newspaper printed in French, with his butler shoes still on, in spite of how he loved to put on his slippers after dinner on account of things left on his toes and feet by the war to remember it by. We said what we always said under those circumstances. He said, "I could bring your milk, Archie, if you would just tell me," and I said, "If I can drink it I can carry it."

In the office, Wolfe sat back with his eyes closed. I took the milk to my desk and poured a glass and sat down and sipped at it. The room was full of smoke and the smell of different drinks, and chairs were scattered around, and cigar and cigarette ashes were all over the rugs. It annoyed me, and I got up and opened a window. Wolfe said, "Close it," and I got up and closed it again. I poured another glass of milk.

I said, "This bird Chapin is a lunatic, and it's long past midnight. I'm damn good and sleepy."

Wolfe kept his eyes shut and also ignored me in other ways. I said,

"Do you realize we could earn all that jack and save a lot of trouble just by having a simple little accident happen to Paul Chapin? Depression prices on accidents like that run from fifty bucks up. It's smart to be thrifty."

Wolfe murmured, "Thank you, Archie. When I exhaust my own expedients I shall know where to turn. A page in your notebook."

I opened a drawer and took out a book and pencil.

"Phone Mr. Cabot's office at nine o'clock and make sure that the memorandums will be here by eleven, ready for Mr. Farrell. Ask where the reports from the Bascom Agency are and arrange to get them. The men will be here at eight?"

"Yes, sir."

"Send one of them to get the reports. Put three of them on Paul Chapin, first thing. We want a complete record of his movements, and phone anything of significance."

"Durkin and Keems and Gore?"

"That is your affair. But Saul Panzer is to get his nose onto Andrew Hibbard's last discoverable footstep. Tell him to phone me at eleven-thirty."

"Yes, sir."

"Put Cather onto Chapin's past, outside the circle of our clients, especially the past two years. As complete as possible. He might succeed in striking a harmonious chord with Dora Chapin."

"Maybe I could do that myself. She's probably a lulu."

"I suspect that of being a vulgarization of the word 'allure.' If she is alluring, resist the temptation for the moment. Your special province will be the deaths of Harrison and Dreyer. First read the Bascom reports, then proceed. Wherever original investigation is indicated and seems still feasible after the lapse of time, undertake it. Use men as necessary, but avoid extravagance. Do not call upon any of our clients until Mr. Farrell has seen them. That's all. It's late."

Wolfe opened his eyes, blinked, and closed them again. But I noticed that the tip of his finger was doing a little circle on the arm of the chair. I grinned. "Maybe we've got this and that for tomorrow and next day, but maybe right now you're troubled by the same thing I am. Why is this Mr. Chapin giving hip room to a Civil War gat with the hammer nose filed off so that it's about as murderous as a bean-shooter?"

"I'm not troubled, Archie." But his finger didn't stop. "I'm wondering whether another bottle of beer before going to bed would be judicious."

"You've had six since dinner."

"Seven. One upstairs."

"Then for God's sake call it a day. Speaking of Chapin's cannon, do you remember the lady dope-fiend who carried a box of pellets made out of flour in her sock, the usual cache, and when they took that and thought she was frisked, she still had the real thing in the hem of her skirt? Of course I don't mean that Chapin had another gun necessarily, I just mean, psychologically—"

"Good heavens." Wolfe pushed back his chair, not, of course, with violence, but with determination. "Archie. Understand this. As a man of action you are tolerable, you are even competent. But I will not for one moment put up with you as a psychologist. I am going to bed."

VIII

I HAD heard Wolfe, at various times, make quite a few cracks about murder. He had said once that no man could commit so complicated a deed as a premeditated murder and leave no opening. He had also said that the only way to commit a murder and remain safe from detection, despite any ingenuity in pursuit and trusting to no luck, was to do it impromptu—await your opportunity, keep your wits about you, and strike when the instant offered; and he added that the luxury of the impromptu murder could be afforded only by those who happened to be in no great hurry about it.

By Tuesday evening I was convinced of one thing about the death of William R. Harrison, federal judge from Indianapolis: that if it had been murder at all it had been impromptu. I would like to say another thing right here, that I know when I'm out of my class. I've got my limitations, and I never yet have tried to give them the ritz. Paul Chapin hadn't been in Nero Wolfe's office more than three minutes Monday night when I saw he was all Greek to me; if it was left to me to take him apart he was sitting pretty. When people begin to get deep and complicated they mix me up. But pictures never do. With pictures, no matter how many pieces they've got that don't seem to fit at first, I'm there forty ways from Sunday. I spent six hours Tuesday with the picture of Judge Harrison's death—reading the Bascom reports, talking with six people, including thirty minutes on long-distance with Fillmore Collard, and chewing it along with two meals—and I decided three things about it: first, that if it was murder it was impromptu; second, that if anybody killed him it was Paul Chapin; and third, that there was as much chance of proving it as there was of proving that honesty was the best policy.

It had happened nearly five months back, but the things that had happened since, starting with the typewritten poems they had got in the mail, had kept their memories active. Paul Chapin had driven up to Harvard with Leopold Elkus, the surgeon, who had gone because he had a son graduating. Judge Harrison had come on from Indianapolis for the same reason. Drummond had been there, Elkus told me, because each year the doubt whether he had really graduated from a big university became overwhelming and he went back every June to make sure. Elkus was very fond of Drummond, the way a taxi driver is of a cop. Cabot and Sidney Lang had been in Boston on business, and Bowen had been a house guest at the home of Theodore Gaines; presumably they were hatching some sort of a financial deal. Anyway, Fillmore Collard had got in touch with his old classmates and invited them for the weekend to his place near Marblehead. There had been quite a party, more than a dozen altogether.

Saturday evening after dinner they had strolled through the grounds, as darkness fell, to the edge of a hundred-foot cliff at the base of which the surf roared among jagged rocks. Four, among them Cabot and Elkus, had stayed in the house, playing bridge. Paul Chapin had hobbled along with the strollers. They had separated, some going to the stables with Collard to see a sick horse, some back to the house, one or two staying behind. It was an hour or so later that they missed Harrison, and not until midnight did they become really concerned. Daylight came before the tide was out enough for them to find his cut and bruised body at the foot of the cliff, wedged among the rocks.

A tragic accident and a ruined party. It had had no significance beyond that until the Wednesday following, when the typewritten poem came to each of them. It said a good deal for Paul Chapin's character and quality, the fact that none of them for a moment doubted the poem's implications. Cabot said that what closed their minds to any doubt was the similarity in the manner of Harrison's death to the accident Chapin had suffered from many years before.

He had fallen from a height. They got together and considered and tried to remember. After the interval of four days there was a good deal of disagreement. A man named Meyer, who lived in Boston, had stated Saturday night that he had gone off leaving Harrison seated on the edge of the cliff and had jokingly warned him to be ready to pull his parachute cord, and that no one else had been around. Now they tried to remember about Chapin. Two were positive that he had limped along after the group strolling to the house, that he had come up to them on the veranda, and had entered with them. Bowen thought he remembered seeing him at the stables. Sidney Lang had seen him reading a book soon after the group returned, and was of the opinion that he had not stirred from his seat for an hour or more.

All the league was in on it now, for they had all got warnings. They got nowhere. Two or three were inclined to laugh it off. Leopold Elkus thought Chapin guiltless, even of the warnings, and advised looking elsewhere for the culprit. Some—quite a few, at first—were in favor of turning it over to the police, but they were talked down, chiefly by Hibbard and Burton and Elkus. Collard and Gaines came down from Boston, and they tried to reconstruct the evening and definitely outline Chapin's movements, but failed through disagreements. In the end they delegated Burton, Cabot, and Lang to call on Chapin.

Chapin had smiled at them. At their insistence he described his Saturday-evening movements, recollecting them clearly and in detail; he had caught up with them at the cliff and sat there on a bench, and had left with the group that returned to the house; he had not noticed Harrison sitting on the cliff's edge. At the house, not being a cardplayer, he had got into a chair with a book and had stayed there with it until aroused by the hubbub over Harrison's absence—approaching midnight. That was his smiling story. He had been not angry, but delicately hurt, that his best friends could think him capable of wishing injury to one of them, knowing as they did that the only struggle in his breast was between affection and gratitude, for the lead. Smiling, but hurt. As for the warnings they had received, that was another matter. Regarding that, he said, his sorrow that they should suspect him not only of violence, but threats of additional violence, was lost in his indignation that he should be accused of so miserable a piece of versifying. He criticized it in detail and with force. As a threat it might be thought effective, he couldn't say as to that, but as poetry it was rotten, and he had certainly never supposed that his best friends could accuse him of such an offense. But then, he had ended, he realized that he would have to forgive them and he did so, fully and without reservation, since it was obvious that they were having quite a scare and so should not be held to account.

Who had sent the warnings, if he hadn't? He had no idea. Of course it could have been done by anyone knowing of that ancient accident who had also learned of this recent one. One guess was as good as another, unless they could uncover something to point their suspicion. The postmark might furnish a hint, or the envelopes and paper, or the typewriting itself. Maybe they had better see if they couldn't find the typewriter.

The committee of three had called on him at his apartment in Perry Street, and were sitting with him in the little room that he used for a study. As he had offered his helpful suggestion he had got up and limped over to his typewriter, patted it, and smiled at them.

"I'm sure that discreditable stuff wasn't written on this, unless one of you fellows sneaked in here and used it when I wasn't looking."

Nicholas Cabot had been tough enough to go over and stick in a sheet of paper and type a few lines on it, and put the sheet in his pocket and take it away with him, but a later examination had shown that Chapin was quite correct. The committee had made its report, and subsequent discussions had taken place, but weeks had gone by and the thing had petered out. Most of them, becoming a little ashamed of themselves and convinced that someone had tried a practical joke, made a point of continuing their friendly relations with Chapin. So far as was known by the six men I talked to, it hadn't been mentioned to him again.

I reported all this in brief outline to Wolfe, Tuesday evening. His comment was, "Then the death of this Judge Harrison—this man who in his conceit permitted himself the awful pretensions of a reader of chaos—whether designed by providence or by Paul Chapin, his death was extempore. Let us forget it; it might clutter up our minds, but it cannot crowd oblivion. If Mr. Chapin had been content with that man's death and had restrained his impulse to rodomontade, he might have considered himself safely avenged—in that instance. But his vanity undid him; he wrote that threat and sent it broadcast. That was dangerous."

"How sure are you?"

"Sure—"

"That he sent the threat."

"Did I not say he did?"

"Yeah. Excuse me for living."

"I would not take that responsibility; I have all I can do to excuse myself. But so much for Judge Harrison; whatever chaos he inhabits now, let us hope he contemplates it with a wiser modesty. I would tell you about Mr. Hibbard. That is, I would tell you nothing, for there is nothing to tell. His niece, Miss Evelyn Hibbard, called on me this morning."

"Oh, she did. I thought she was coming Wednesday."

"She anticipated it, having received a report of last evening's gathering."

"Did she spill anything new?"

"She could add nothing to what she told you Saturday evening. She has made another thorough search of the apartment, helped by her sister, and can find nothing whatever missing. Either Mr. Hibbard's absence was unforeseen by him, or he was a remarkably intelligent and strong-willed man. He was devoted to two pipes, which he smoked alternately. One of them is there in its usual place. He made no uncommon withdrawal from his bank, but he always carried a good deal of cash."

"Didn't I tell you about the pipe?"

"You may have. Saul Panzer, after a full day, had to offer one little morsel. A news vendor at One Hundred Sixteenth Street and Broadway, who has known Mr. Hibbard by sight for several years, saw him enter the subway between nine and ten o'clock last Tuesday evening."

"That was the only bite Saul got?"

Wolfe nodded, on his way slanting forward to reach the button on his desk. "The police had got that too, and no more, though it has been a full week since Mr. Hibbard disappeared. I telephoned Inspector Cramer this morning, and Mr. Morley at the District Attorney's office. As you know, they lend information only at usurious rates, but I gathered that they have exhausted even conjecture."

"Morley would deal you an extra card any time."

"Perhaps, but not when he has none to deal. Saul Panzer is following a suggestion I offered him, but its promise is negligible. There is no point in his attempting a solitary fishing expedition; if Mr. Chapin went for a walk with Mr. Hibbard and pushed him off a bridge into the East River, we cannot expect Saul to dive for the corpse. The routine facilities of the police and Bascom's men have covered, and are covering, possibilities of that nature. As for Mr. Chapin, it would be useless to question him. He has told both Bascom and the police that he spent last Tuesday evening in his apartment, and his wife sustains him. No one in the neighborhood remembers seeing him venture forth."

"You suggested something to Saul?"

"Merely to occupy him." Wolfe poured a glass of beer. "But on the most critical front, at the moment, we have met success. Mr. Farrell has gained the adherence of twenty individuals to the memorandum —all but Dr. Elkus in the city, and all but one without, over the telephone. Mr. Pitney Scott, the taxi driver, is excluded from these statistics; there would be no profit in hounding him, but you might find occasion to give him a glance; he arouses my curiosity, faintly, in another direction. Copies of the memorandum have been distributed, for return. Mr. Farrell is also collecting the warnings, all copies except those in the possession of the police. It will be well to have—"

The telephone rang. I nearly knocked my glass of milk over getting it. I'm always like that when we're on a case, and I suppose I'll never get over it; if I had just landed ten famous murderers and had them salted down, and was at the moment engaged in trying to run down a guy who had put a slug in a subway turnstile, Fritz going to answer the doorbell would put a quiver in me.

I heard a few words, and nodded at Wolfe. "Here's Farrell now." Wolfe pulled his phone over, and I kept my receiver to my ear. They talked only a minute or two.

After we had hung up I said, "What, what? Farrell taking Mr. Somebody to lunch at the Harvard Club? You're spending money like a drunken sailor."

Wolfe rubbed his nose. "I am not spending it. Mr. Farrell is. Decency will of course require me to furnish it. I requested Mr. Farrell to arrange for an interview with Mr. Oglethorpe; I did not contemplate feeding him. It is now beyond remedy. Mr. Oglethorpe is a member of the firm which publishes Mr. Chapin's books, and Mr. Farrell is slightly acquainted with him."

I grinned. "Well, you're stuck. I suppose you want him to publish your essay on The Tyranny of the Wheel. How's it coming on?"

Wolfe ignored my wit. He said, "Upstairs this morning I spent twenty minutes considering where Paul Chapin might elect to type something which he would not wish to be traced to him. The suggestion in one of Bascom's reports, that Chapin has a duplicate set of type-bars for his machine which he substitutes on occasion, I regard as infantile. Not only would the changing of the bars be a difficult, laborious, and uninspired proceeding; there is also the fact that the duplicate set would have to be concealed in some available spot, and that would be hazardous. No. Not that. Then there is the old trick of going to a typewriter agency and using one of their machines exposed for sale. But a visit from Paul Chapin, with his infirmity, would be remembered; also, that is excluded by the fact that all three of the warnings were executed on the same typewriter. I considered other possibilities, including some of those explored by Bascom, and one seemed to offer at least a faint promise. Mr. Chapin might call at the office of his publisher and, wishing to alter a manuscript, or even merely to write a letter, request the use of a typewriter. I am counting on Mr. Farrell to discover that; having discovered it, he may be able to get Mr. Oglethorpe's permission to take a sample of the work of the machine that Chapin used—or if that is not known, of each machine in their office."

I nodded. "That's not very dumb. I'm surprised that Farrell can still pay his dues at the Harvard Club."

"When a man of a certain type is forced into drastic financial retrenchment, he first deserts his family, then goes naked, and then gives up his club. Which reminds me, I gave Mr. Farrell twenty dollars this afternoon. Please record it. You may also note on your list those who have initialed the memorandum, and file the various copies. Also, note that we have an additional contributor, Miss Evelyn Hibbard. I arranged it with her this morning. The amount is three thousand dollars." He sighed. "I made a large reduction from the ten thousand she offered Saturday on account of the altered circumstances."

I had been waiting for that, or something like it. I made the Farrell entry in the cashbook, but didn't get out the list. I felt like clearing my throat, but I knew that wouldn't do, so I swallowed instead. I put the cashbook back and turned to Wolfe. "You understand, sir, I wouldn't accuse you of trying to put anything over. I know you just forgot about it."

His eyes opened at me. "Archie. You are trying the cryptic approach again. To what this time?"

"No, sir. This is on the level. You just forgot that Miss Evelyn Hibbard is *my* client. I went to see her Saturday at your suggestion; you couldn't take her on because you had other plans in mind. Remember, sir? So of course any arrangement she might make in this connection could only be with my advice and consent."

Wolfe was keeping his eyes open. He murmured, "Preposterous. Puerile trickery. You would not attempt to maintain that position."

I sighed, as much like one of his sighs as I could make it. "I hate to, sir. I really do. But it's the only honest thing I can do, protect my client. Of course you understand the ethics of it. I don't have to explain—"

He cut me off. "No. I would suggest that you refrain from explaining. How much would you advise your client to pay?"

"One thousand bucks."

"Absurd. In view of her original offer—"

"All right. I won't haggle. I'll split the difference with you. Two thousand. I stick there. I'm glued."

Wolfe shut his eyes. "Done, confound you. Enter it. Now take your notebook. Tomorrow morning . . ."

IX

WEDNESDAY morning pretty early I was sitting in the kitchen with the *Times* propped up in front of me, but not really seeing it because I was busy in my mind mapping out the day, getting on toward the bottom of my second cup of coffee, when Fritz returned from a trip to the front door to say that Fred Durkin wanted to see me. One thing I hate to be disturbed at is my last two healthy swallows of morning coffee, so I nodded and took my time. When I got to the office Fred was sitting there scowling at his hat on the floor, where it had landed when he had tried to toss it so it would hook on the back of my chair. He always missed.

I picked it up and handed it to him and said, "A dollar even you can't do it once out of ten tries."

He shook his big Irish bean. "No time. I'm a working man. I was just waiting for you to pick your teeth. Can I see Wolfe?"

"You know damn well you can't. Up to eleven o'clock Mr. Nero Wolfe is a horticulturist."

"Uh-huh. This is special."

"Not special enough for that. Spill it to the chief of staff. Has the lop put dust in your eyes? Why aren't you on his tail?"

"I don't relieve Johnny until nine. I'll be there." Durkin grabbed his hat by the brim, squinted for an aim, tossed it at the back of my chair again, and missed it by a mile. He grunted with disgust. "Listen here, Archie. It's a washout."

"What's the matter with it?"

"Well, you put three of us on this to cover him twenty-four hours a day. When Wolfe spends money like that, that shows it's important. He really wants this bird's program. Also, you told us to use taxis all we needed to, and so on. Well, it's a washout. Chapin lives in an apartment house at Two-o-three Perry Street with six floors and an elevator. He's on the fifth. The house has a big court in the back, with a couple of trees and some shrubs, and in the spring it's full of tulips—the elevator boy told me three thousand tulips. But the idea is that there's another house on the court, facing on Eleventh Street, built by the same landlord, and so what? Anybody that wants to can go out of the Perry Street house the back way instead of the front. They can cross the court and go through a passage and come out on Eleventh Street. Of course they could get back in the same way if they felt like it. So parked in a cigar store the other side of Perry Street with my eye fastened on the house, I feel about as useful as if I was watching one of the tunnel exits at the Yankee Stadium for a woman in a dark hat. Not that I've got any kick coming; my only trouble is my honest streak. I just wanted to see Wolfe and tell him what he's paying me money for."

"You could have phoned him last night."

"I could not. I got lit last night. This is the first job I've had in a month."

"Got any expense money left?"

"Enough for a couple of days. I've learned self-control."

"Okay." I picked his hat up and put it on my desk. "That's a nice picture you've got down there. It's no good. It looks to me like there's no way out of it but three more men for Eleventh Street. That would be buying it, six tails for one cripple and—"

"Wait a minute." Fred waved a hand at me. "That's not all of it. The other trouble is that the traffic cop at the corner is going to run us in. For blocking the street. There's too many of us, all after that cripple. There's a city feller there—I guess from the Homicide Squad, I don't recognize him—and a little guy with a brown cap and a pink necktie that must be one of Bascom's men. I don't recognize him either. But get this, for example. Yesterday afternoon a taxi drives up and stops in front of Two-o-three, and in a minute Chapin hobbles out of the building on his stick, and gets in the taxi. You should have seen the hustle around there. It was like Fifth Avenue in front of St. Patrick's at one o'clock Sunday, only Perry Street is narrow. There was another taxi coming along and I beat the town dick to it by a jump, and he had to run half a block to find one. Bascom's pet got into one that apparently he had waiting. I had a notion to yell to Chapin to wait a minute till we got lined up, but it wasn't necessary. It was all right, his driver went slow and none of us lost him. He went to the Harvard Club and stayed there a couple of hours and then stopped off at Two-forty-eight Madison Avenue and then went back home, and we all followed him. Honest to God, Archie, three of us, but I was in front."

"Yeah. It sounds swell."

"Sure it was. I kept looking around to see if they was all right. My idea was this; it came to me while I was riding along. Why couldn't we pal up? You get one more man, and him and Bascom and the town dick could cover Eleventh Street and let us on Perry Street have a little peace. I suppose they're on twelve hours now; maybe they've got reliefs, I don't know. How's that for an idea?"

"Rotten." I got up and handed him his hat. "No good at all, Fred. Out. Wolfe's not using any secondhand tailing. I'll get three men from the Metropolitan, and we'll cover Eleventh Street. It's a damn shame, because, as I told you, Wolfe wants Chapin covered as tight as a drum. Get back on the job and don't lose him. It sounds sad, the way you describe that traffic jam, but do the best you can. I'll get in touch with Bascom, and maybe he'll call his dog off. I didn't know he had any more money to spend. Run along now; I've got some errands you wouldn't understand."

"I'm not due till nine o'clock."

"Run along anyway. Oh, all right. One shot, just one. A quarter to a dime."

He nodded, shifted in his seat to get good position, and let her go. It was a close call; the hat hung there on its edge for a tenth of a second, then toppled off. Durkin fished a dime out of his pocket and handed it to me, and beat it.

I thought at first I'd run up to Wolfe's room and get his okay on covering Eleventh Street, but it was only eight-twenty and it always made me half sick to see him in bed with that black silk cover, drinking chocolate, not to mention that he would be sure to raise hell, so I got the Metropolitan Agency on the telephone and gave them the dope. I only ordered six-dollar men because it was nothing but a check anyway; I couldn't see why Chapin should be trying to pull anything foxy like rear exits. Then I sat for a minute and wondered who was keeping Bascom on the job, and I thought I'd phone him on the chance of his spilling it, but nobody answered. All this had made me a little late on my own schedule, so I grabbed my hat and coat and went to the garage for the roadster.

I had collected a few facts about the Dreyer business in my wanderings the day before. Eugene Dreyer, art dealer, had been found dead on the morning of Thursday, September 20, in the office of his gallery on Madison Avenue near Fifty-sixth Street. His body had been found by three cops, one a lieutenant, who had broken in the door on orders. He had been dead about twelve hours, and the cause had been nitroglycerin poisoning. After an investigation the police had pronounced it suicide, and the inquest had verified it. But on the Monday following, the second warnings arrived; everybody got one. We had several copies in Wolfe's office, and they read like this:

> Two.
> Ye should have killed me.
> Two;
> And with no ready cliff, rocks waiting below
> To rub the soul out; no ready waves
> To lick it off and clean it of old crimes,
> I let the snake and fox collaborate.
> They found the deadly oil, sweet-burning, cunningly
> Devised in tablets easily dissolved.
> And I, their Master, I,
> I found the time, the safe way to his throat,
> And counted: two.

One, and two, and eighty long days between.
But wait in patience; I am unhurried but sure.
Three and four and five and six and seven. . . .
Ye should have killed me.

Wolfe said it was better than the first one, because it was shorter and there were two good lines in it. I took his word for it.

Hell had popped right off. They forgot all about practical jokes and yelled to the cops and the D. A.'s office to come on back and nab him; suicide was out. When I got a description of the run-around that little poem had started, I was inclined to agree with Mike Ayers and cross out League of Atonement and make it the League of the White Feather. The only ones that hadn't seemed to develop an acute case of knee-tremor were Dr. Burton and Leopold Elkus the surgeon. Hibbard had been as much scared as anyone—more, if anything—but had still been against the police. Apparently he had been ready to go to bed with the willies, but also ready for the sacrifice. Elkus, of course, had been in on it, but I'm coming to that.

My date with Elkus that Wednesday morning was for nine-thirty, but I made an early start because I wanted to stop off at Fifty-sixth Street for a look at the Dreyer gallery, where it had happened. I got there before nine. It wasn't a gallery any more, but a bookstore. A middle-aged woman with a wart in front of her ear was nice to me and said of course I could look around, but there wasn't much to be made of it because everything had been changed. The little room on the right, where the conference had taken place on a Wednesday evening and the body had been found the following morning, was still an office, with a desk and a typewriter and so on, but a lot of shelves had been put in that were obviously new. I called the woman over and she came into the office. I pointed at a door in the back wall and said, "I wonder if you could tell me, is that the closet where Mr. Eugene Dreyer kept the materials for mixing his drinks?"

She looked hazy. "Mr. Dreyer—oh, that's the man—"

"The man that committed suicide in this room, yes, ma'am. I suppose you wouldn't know."

"Well, really—" She seemed startled. "I hadn't realized it was right in this little room. Of course I've heard about it—"

I said, "Thank you, ma'am," and went back to the street and got in the roadster. People who quit living a year ago Christmas and haven't found out about it yet give me a pain, and all I've got for them is politeness and damn little of that.

Leopold Elkus hadn't quit living, I discovered when I got to him in his private room, but he was a sad guy. He was medium-sized, with a big head and big hands and strong black eyes that kept floating away from you, not sideways or up or down but back into his head. He invited me to sit down and said in a friendly, soft voice, "Understand, Mr. Goodwin, I am seeing you only as a courtesy to my friends, who have requested it. I have explained to Mr. Farrell that I will not support the enterprise of your employer. Nor will I lend any assistance."

"Okay." I grinned at him. "I didn't come to pick a scrap, Dr. Elkus. I just want to ask some questions about September nineteenth, when Eugene Dreyer died—questions of fact."

"I have already answered any question you could possibly put—to the police several times, and to that incredibly ignorant detective—"

"Right. So far we agree. Just as a matter of courtesy to your friends, there's no reason why you shouldn't answer them once more, is there? To converse with the cops and Del Bascom and then draw the line at Nero Wolfe and me—well, that would be like—"

He smiled a sad smile. "Swallow a camel and strain at a gnat?" God that guy was sad.

"Yeah, I guess so. Only if you saw Nero Wolfe you wouldn't call him a gnat. It's like this, Dr. Elkus. I know you won't lend a hand to get the goods on Paul Chapin. But in this Dreyer business you're my only source of firsthand information, and so I had to get at you. I understand the other man, the art expert, has gone back to Italy."

He nodded. "Mr. Santini sailed some time ago."

"Then there's only you. There's no sense in my trying to ask you a lot of trick questions. Why don't you just tell me about it?"

He smiled, sad again. "I presume you know that two or three of my friends suspect me of lying to shield Paul Chapin?"

"Yeah. Are you?"

"No. I would neither shield him nor injure him, beyond the truth. Here is the story, Mr. Goodwin. You know, of course, that Eugene Dreyer was an old friend of mine, a classmate in college. He was pretty successful with his art gallery before the depression. I bought things from him occasionally. I have never been under the necessity of pursuing success, since I inherited wealth. My reputation as a surgeon is a by-product of my conviction that there is something wrong with all human beings beneath the surface. By chance I have a sure and skillful hand."

I looked at his big hands folded on his lap, and nodded at his black eyes floating back into his head. He went on. "Six years ago I gave Eugene Dreyer a tentative order for three Mantegnas—two small ones and a larger one. The price was one hundred and sixty thousand dollars. The paintings were in France. Paul Chapin happened to be in Europe at that time, and I wrote to ask him to look at them. After I received his report I ordered them. You know, I suppose, that for ten years Paul Chapin tried to be a painter. His work showed great sensitiveness, but his line was erratic and he had no feeling for form. It was interesting, but not good. I am told that he is finding himself in literature—I do not read novels.

"The paintings arrived at a time when I was overworked and had no leisure for a proper examination. I accepted them and paid for them. I was never happy with them; the friendly overtures which I made to those pictures from time to time—and there were many— were always repelled by them with an indelicacy, a faint harshness, which embarrassed and irritated me. I did not at first suspect them of imposture; I simply could not get along with them. But a few remarks made by expert persons finally aroused my suspicion. In September, nearly two months ago now, Enrico Santini, who knows Mantegna as I know the human viscera, visited this country. I asked him to look at my Mantegnas, and he pronounced them frauds. He further said that he knew their source, a certain talented swindler in Paris, and that it was not possible that any reputable dealer had handled them in good faith.

"I imagine it was the uncomfortable five years those pictures had given me, more than anything else, that caused me to act as I did with Dreyer. Ordinarily I am far too weak in my convictions to display any sort of ruthlessness, but on this occasion there was no hesitation in me at all. I told Eugene that I wished to return the pictures and receive my money back without delay. He said he had not the money, and I knew he hadn't, since I had within a year lent him considerable sums to tide him over. Nevertheless, I insisted that he must find it or suffer the consequences. I suspect that in the end I would have weakened as usual, and agreed to any sort of compromise, but unfortunately it is a trick of my temperament now and then to show the greatest determination of purpose when the resolution is most likely to falter. Unfortunately also, Mr. Santini was about to return to Italy. Eugene demanded an interview with him; that, of course, was a bluff.

"It was arranged that I should call at five o'clock Wednesday afternoon with Mr. Santini and Paul Chapin. Paul was included on account of the inspection he had given the pictures in France. I surmised that Eugene had arranged for his support, but as it turned out that was probably incorrect. We arrived. Eugene's suavity—"

I interrupted, "Just a minute, Doctor. Did Paul Chapin get to the gallery before you did?"

"No. We arrived together. I was in my car and called for him at the Harvard Club."

"Had he been there earlier that afternoon?"

"My dear sir." Elkus looked sad at me.

"Okay. You wouldn't know that. Anyway, the girl there says he hadn't."

"So I understand. I was saying, Eugene's suavity was painful, because of the nervousness it failed to hide. He mixed highballs for us, jerkily, not himself. I was embarrassed and therefore brusque. I asked Mr. Santini to make a statement, and he did so; he had written it down. Eugene contradicted him. They argued; Eugene was somewhat excited, but Mr. Santini remained cool. Finally Eugene called on Paul for his views, in obvious expectation of support. Paul smiled around at us, the smile that comes from his Malpighian capsules, and made a calm, brief statement. He said that three months after his inspection of the pictures—a month after they had been shipped to New York —he had learned definitely that they had been painted by Vasseult, the greatest forger of the century, in nineteen-twenty-four. That was the man Mr. Santini had named. Paul also said that he had kept silent about it because his affection for both Eugene and myself was so great that he could take no step that would injure either of us.

"I feared Eugene would collapse. He was plainly as astonished as he was hurt. I was of course embarrassed into silence. I do not now know whether Eugene had in desperation swindled me, or whether he had himself been imposed upon. Mr. Santini rose. I did likewise, and we left. Paul Chapin came with us. It was noon the following day when I learned that Eugene had committed suicide by drinking nitroglycerin, apparently within a few minutes—at the most, an hour—after we left. I learned it when the police arrived at my office to question me."

I nodded and sat and looked at him awhile. Then all of a sudden I straightened up in my chair and shot at him, "What made *you* think it was suicide?"

"Now, Mr. Goodwin." He smiled at me, sadder than ever. "Are all detectives alike? You know perfectly well why I thought it was suicide. The police thought so, and the circumstances indicated it."

"My mistake." I grinned. "I said no trick questions, didn't I? If you're willing to grant that a detective can have an idea in his mind, you know what mine is. Did Paul Chapin have any opportunity to put the nitroglycerin tablets in Dreyer's highball? That ignorant detective and all the bright cops seem to have the impression that you think he didn't."

Dr. Elkus nodded. "I labored to produce that impression. You know, of course, that Mr. Santini agreed with me. We are perfectly certain that Paul had no such opportunity. He went to the gallery with us, and we all entered the office together. Paul sat at my left, near the door, at least six feet away from Eugene. He touched no glass but his own. Eugene prepared the drinks and handed them around; we had only one. Departing, Paul preceded me through the door. Mr. Santini was ahead."

"Yeah. That's on the record. But in a fracas like that, so much excitement, there must have been some moving around, getting up and sitting down, walking back and forth—"

"Not at all. We were not excited, except possibly Eugene. He was the only one who left his chair."

"Did he change his coat, or put it on, or anything, after you got there?"

"No. He wore a morning coat. He did not remove it."

"The bottle with what was left of the nitroglycerin was found in the pocket of his coat."

"So I understand."

I sat back and looked at him again. I would have given the roadster and a couple of extra tires to know if he was lying. He was as much out of my class as Paul Chapin was. There was no way for me to get at him that I could see. I said, "Will you have lunch with Mr. Nero Wolfe tomorrow at one o'clock?"

"I'm sorry. I shall be engaged."

"Friday?"

He shook his head. "No. Not any day. You are in error regarding me,

Mr. Goodwin. I am not a knot to be untangled or a nut to be cracked. Give up your hope that I am deceptive, as most men are; I am really as simple as I seem. Give up your hope, too, to demonstrate the guilt of Paul Chapin in the death of Eugene Dreyer. It is not feasible. I know it isn't; I was there."

"Could you make it Saturday?"

He shook his head and smiled, still sad. I got up from my chair and picked up my hat and thanked him. But before I started for the door I said, "By the way, you know that second warning Paul Chapin wrote —anyhow, somebody wrote it. Is nitroglycerin oily and sweet-burning?"

"I am a surgeon, not a pharmacologist."

"Well, try one guess."

He smiled. "Nitroglycerin is unquestionably oily. It is said to have a sweet, burning taste. I have never tried it."

I thanked him again and went out and down to the street, and got in the roadster and stepped on the starter. As I rolled off downtown I was thinking that Dr. Leopold Elkus was exactly the kind of man that so often makes life a damn nuisance. I never yet have had any serious trouble with an out-and-out liar, but a man that might be telling the truth is an unqualified pain in the rumpus. And what with the Harrison line-up, and now this, I suspected that I began to perceive dimly that the memorandum Wolfe had concocted was going to turn out to be just a sheet of paper to be used for any purpose that might occur to you, unless we managed somehow to bust Elkus's story wide open.

I had intended to stop off again at Fifty-sixth Street for another look at the Dreyer gallery, but after listening to Elkus I decided it would be a waste of time, considering how the place had been done over. I kept on downtown, headed for home. The best bet I could think of at the moment was a try at Santini. The police had only questioned him once, on account of his sailing for Italy that Thursday night, and of course the warnings hadn't been received yet and they had no particular suspicions. Wolfe had connections in several cities in Europe, and there was a smart guy in Rome who had turned in a good one on the Whittemore bonds. We could cable him and set him on Santini and maybe get a wedge started. I'd have to persuade Wolfe it was worth about ninety-nine dollars in transatlantic words.

It was a quarter to eleven when I got there. In the office the phone was ringing, so I went on in with my hat and coat on. I knew Wolfe would eventually answer it from upstairs, but I thought I might as well get it. It was Saul Panzer. I asked him what he wanted, and he said he wanted to report. I asked him report what, and he said, nothing, just report. I was sore at everything anyway, so I got sarcastic. I said if he couldn't find Hibbard alive or dead, maybe he could rig up a dummy that would do. I said I had just got a smack in the eye on another angle of the case, and if he was no better than I was he'd better come on down to the office with a pinochle deck, and I hung up on him, which alone is enough to aggravate a nun.

It took me five minutes to dig the address of the Roman snoop out of the file. Wolfe came down on time, right at eleven. He said good morning, sniffed at the air, and got seated at his desk. I was impatient, but I knew I'd have to wait until he had glanced through the mail, fixed the orchids in the vase, tried his pen to see if it was working, and rung for beer. After that was all over he murmured at me, "Had you thought of venturing forth?"

"I tiptoed out at eight-thirty and just got back. Saul just telephoned. Another nickel wasted. If you want to get puckered up, here's a nice pickle to chew on."

Fritz brought his beer, and he poured a glass. I told him all about Elkus, every word of it, even that nitroglycerin was oily and sweet-burning. I thought if I gave him all of Elkus I could, he might get a notion. Then I handed him my own notion about the Roman.

Right away, as I expected, he got restive. He blinked and drank some more beer. He said, "You can cable four thousand miles for a fact or an object, but not for a subtlety like this. As a last resort you or Saul Panzer might go to call on Mr. Santini in Florence; it might in the end be worth that chance."

I tried an argument on him, for I couldn't see any other move. I didn't seem to be making much impression, but I kept on anyway, getting stubborn, because my main point was that it was only a matter of a hundred bucks. I was forgetting that I still had to tell him about the three Metropolitan men I had ordered for Eleventh Street. I got good and stubborn.

I was stopped in the middle of my stride by the sound of Fritz going down the hall to answer the doorbell. I didn't try to pick it up again, but waited to see who it was.

Fritz stepped in and closed the door behind him. He said there was a lady there to see Wolfe. No card.

"Her name?"

Fritz shook his head; usually he was more correct. He looked uncertain.

"Show her in, Fritz."

I felt uncertain too, when I saw her. They don't come any uglier. She came in and stood looking straight at Wolfe, as if she was deciding how to do him over. At that, she wasn't really ugly; I mean she wasn't hideous. Wolfe said it right the next day: it was more subtle than plain ugliness; to look at her made you despair of ever seeing a pretty woman again. Her eyes were rather small, gray, and looked as if they'd never move again when they got fixed. She had on a dark gray woolen coat with a hat to match, and an enormous gray fur piece was fastened around her neck. She sat down on the chair I pulled up for her and said in a strong voice, "I had a hard time getting here. I think I'm going to faint."

Wolfe said, "I hope not. A little brandy."

"No." She gave a little gasp. "No, thank you." She put her hand up to the fur piece and seemed to be trying to reach under it, behind. "I've been wounded—back there. I think you'd better look at it."

Wolfe shot me a glance, and I went. She got the thing unfastened in front, and I pulled it around and lifted it off. I gave a gasp then myself. Not that I haven't seen a little blood here and there, but not often that much, and it was so unexpected. The back of the fur piece, inside, was soaked. The collar of her coat was soaked too. She was a sight. It was still oozing out, plenty, from gashes across the back of her neck; I couldn't tell how deep they were. She moved, and it came out in a little spurt. I dropped the fur piece on the floor and said to her, "For God's sake keep still. Don't move your head." I looked at Wolfe and said, "Somebody's tried to cut her head off. I can't tell how far they got."

She spoke to Wolfe. "My husband. He wanted to kill me."

Wolfe's eyes on her were half closed. "Then you're Dora Ritter."

She shook her head, and the blood started, and I told her to quit. She said, "I am Dora Chapin. I have been married three years."

X

Wolfe didn't say anything. I stood behind her and waited, ready to catch her if she started to faint and fall forward, because I didn't know how much it might open up. Wolfe hadn't moved. He sat looking at her with his eyes nearly shut and his lips pushing out and in, and out and in again.

She said, "He got into a fit—one of his cold fits."

Wolfe said politely, "I didn't know Mr. Chapin had fits. Feel her pulse."

I reached out and got her wrist and placed my fingers. While I was counting she began to talk. "He doesn't have fits exactly. It's a look that comes into his eyes. I am always afraid of him, but when I see that look I am terrified. He has never done anything to me before. This morning when I saw him look like that I said something I shouldn't have said— Look here."

She jerked her hand away from me to use it for getting into her handbag, a big leather one. Out of it she pulled something wrapped in newspaper. She unrolled the newspaper and held up a kitchen knife that had blood on it, still wet and red.

"He had this, and I didn't know it. He must have been getting ready for me when he was out in the kitchen."

I took the knife from her and laid it on the desk, on top of the newspaper, and said to Wolfe, "Her pulse is on a little sprint, but it's okay."

Wolfe put his hands on the arms of the chair, braced himself, and got to his feet. He said, "Please do not move, Mrs. Chapin," and walked around behind her and took a look at her neck. He bent down with his eyes close to her; I hadn't seen him so active for a month or more. Peering at the gashes, he said, "Please tilt your head forward, just a little, and back again." She did so, and the blood came out again; in one spot it nearly spurted at him.

Wolfe straightened up. "Indeed. Get a doctor, Archie."

She started to turn around at him, and I stopped her. She protested, "I don't need a doctor. I got here; I can get home again. I just wanted to show you, and ask you—"

"Yes, madam. For the moment my judgment must prevail. If you please . . ."

I was at the phone, giving a number. Someone answered, and I asked for Dr. Vollmer. She said he wasn't there, he was just leaving; if it was urgent she might be able to catch him out in front. I started to ask her to do that, then it occurred to me that I might be quicker at it myself, and I hung up and took it on the trot. Fritz was in the hall, dusting, and I told him to stick around. As I hopped down the stoop I noticed a taxi there at the curb: our visitor's, of course. A couple of hundred feet east Dr. Vollmer's blue coupé was standing, and he was just getting in. I sprinted for him and let out a yell. He heard me and by the time I got there he was out on the sidewalk again. I told him about the casualty that had dropped in on us, and he got his bag out of the coupé and came along.

In my business I've seen it proved a hundred times that one thing you never want to leave in the bureau drawer is your curiosity. As we turned in at our stoop I took another look at the taxi standing there, and I nearly lost my aplomb for a second when the driver looked straight at me and tipped me a wink.

I went on in with the doc. Fritz was in the hall and told me that Wolfe had gone to the kitchen and would return when the doctor had finished. I told Fritz for God's sake not to let him get started eating, and took Vollmer into the office. Dora Chapin was still in her chair. I introduced them, and he put his bag on the desk and went to take a look at her. He poked around a little and said she might have to be sewed up, and he could tell better if he could wash her off.

I showed him where the bathroom was and said there were bandages and iodine and so on, and then said, "I'll call Fritz in to help you. I've got an errand out front. If you need me I'll be there."

He said all right, and I went to the hall and explained Fritz's new duties to him. Then I went out to the sidewalk.

The taxi was still there. The driver wasn't winking any more; he just looked at me. I said, "Greetings."

He said, "I very seldom talk that much."

"How much?"

"Enough to say 'Greetings'—any form of salutation."

"I don't blame you. May I glance inside?"

I pulled the door open and stuck my head in far enough to get a good look at the framed card fastened to the panel, showing the driver's picture and name. That was only a wild guess, but I thought if it happened to hit, it would save time.

I backed out again and put a foot up on the runningboard and grinned at him. "I understand you're a good engineer."

He looked funny for a second; then he laughed. "That was when I was in burlesque. Now I'm just doing straight parts. Damn it, quit grinning at me. I've got a headache."

I rubbed the grin off. "Why did you wink at me as I went by?"

"Why shouldn't I?"

"I don't know. Hell, don't try to be quaint. I just asked you a friendly question. What was the idea of the wink?"

He shook his head. "I'm a character. Didn't I say I had a headache? Let's see if we can't think of some place for you to go to. Is your name Nero Wolfe?"

"No. But yours is Pitney Scott. I've got you down on a list I made up, for a contribution of five dollars."

"I heard about that list."

"Yes? Who from?"

"Oh—people. You can cross me off. Last week I made eighteen dollars and twenty cents."

"You know what it's for."

He nodded. "I know that too. You want to save my life. Listen, my dear fellow, to charge five dollars for saving my life would be outrageous—believe me, exorbitant. Rank profiteering." He laughed. "These things have a bottom, I suppose. There is no such thing as a minus quantity except in mathematics. You have no idea what a feeling of solidity and assurance that reflection can give a man. Have you got a drink in your house?"

"How about two dollars? Make it two."

"You're still way high."

"One even buck."

"Still you flatter me. Listen." Though it was cold for November, with a raw wind, he had no gloves, and his hands were red and rough. He got his stiff fingers into a pocket, came out with some chicken feed, picked a nickel, and pushed it at me. "I'll pay up now and get it off my mind. Now that I don't owe you anything, have you got a drink?"

"What flavor do you want?"

"I—if it were good rye—" He leaned toward me, and a look came into his eyes. Then he jerked back. His voice got harsh and not friendly at all. "Can't you take a joke? I don't drink when I'm driving. Is that woman hurt much?"

"I don't think so; her head's still on. The doctor'll fix her up. Do you take her places often? Or her husband?"

He was still harsh. "I take her when she calls me—her husband too. I'm a taxi driver. Mr. Paul Chapin. They give me their trade when they can, for old time's sake. Once or twice they've let me get drunk at their place. Paul likes to see me drunk, and he furnishes the liquor." He laughed, and the harshness went. "You know, you take this situation in all its aspects, and you couldn't ask for anything more hilarious. I'm going to have to stay sober so as not to miss any of it. I winked at you because you're in on it now, and you're going to be just as funny as all the rest."

"That won't worry me any; I always have been pretty ludicrous. Does Chapin get drunk with you?"

"He doesn't drink. He says it makes his leg hurt."

"Did you know that there's a reward of five thousand dollars for finding Andrew Hibbard?"

"No."

"Alive or dead."

It looked to me as if, just stabbing around, I had hit something. His face had changed; he looked surprised, as if confronted with an idea that hadn't occurred to him. He said, "Well, he's a valuable man, that's not too much to offer for him. At that, Andy's not a bad guy. Who offered the reward?"

"His niece. It'll be in the papers tomorrow."

"Good for her. God bless her." He laughed. "It is an incontrovertible fact that five thousand dollars is a hell of a lot more money than a nickel. How do you account for that? I want a cigarette."

I got a packet out and lit us both up. His fingers weren't steady at all, and I began to feel sorry for him. So I said, "Just figure it out. Hibbard's home is up at University Heights. If you drove downtown somewhere—say around the Perry Street neighborhood, I don't know just where—and from there to One Hundred Sixteenth Street, ordinarily what would you get for it? Let's see—two, eight miles—that'd be around a dollar and a half. But if going uptown you happened to have your old classmate Andrew Hibbard with you—or just his corpse, maybe even only a piece of it, say his head and a couple of arms—instead of a dollar-fifty you'd get five grand. As you see, it all depends on your cargo." So as not to take my eyes off him, I blew cigarette smoke out of the corner of my mouth. Of course, riding a guy who needed a drink bad and wouldn't take it was like knocking a cripple's crutch from under him, but I didn't need to remind myself that all's fair in love and business. Basic truths like that are either born right in a man or they're not.

At that he had enough grip on himself to keep his mouth shut. He looked at his fingers trembling, holding the cigarette, so long that I finally looked at them too. Finally he let his hand fall to his knee and looked at me and began to laugh. He demanded, "Didn't I say you were going to be funny?" His voice went harsh again. "Listen, you. Beat it. Come on, now, beat it. Go back in the house or you'll catch cold."

I said, "All right, how about that drink?"

But he was through. I prodded at him a little, but he had gone completely dumb and unfriendly. I thought of bringing out some rye and letting him smell it, but decided that would just screw him down tighter. I said to myself, Anon, and passed him up.

Before going in the house I went around back of the taxi and got the license number.

I went to the kitchen. Wolfe was still there, in the wooden chair with arms where he always sat to direct Fritz and to eat when he was on a relapse.

I said, "Pitney Scott's out front—the taxi driver. He brought her. He paid me a nickel for his share, and he says that's all it's worth. He knows something about Andrew Hibbard."

"What?"

"You mean what does he know? Search me. I told him about the reward Miss Hibbard, my client, is offering, and he looked like get thee behind me, Satan. He's shy, he wants to be coaxed. My surmise is that he may not exactly know where Hibbard or his remains has been cached, but he thinks he might guess. He's got about seven months to go to pink snakes and crocodiles. I tried to get him to come in for a drink, but he fought that off too. He won't come in. He may not be workable at the present moment, but I was thinking of suggesting that you go out and look at him."

"Out?" Wolfe raised his head at me. "Out and down the stoop?"

"Yeah, just on the sidewalk; you wouldn't have to step off the curb. He's right there."

Wolfe shut his eyes. "I don't know, Archie. I don't know why you persist in trying to badger me into frantic sorties. Dismiss the notion entirely. It is not feasible. You say he actually gave you a nickel?"

"Yes, and where's it going to get you to act eccentric with a dipsomaniac taxi driver even if he did go to Harvard? Honest to God, sir, sometimes you run it into the ground."

"That will do. Definitely. Go and see if Mrs. Chapin has been made presentable."

I went. I found that Dr. Vollmer had finished with his patient in the bathroom and had her back in a chair in the office, with her neck bandaged so that she had to hold it stiff whether she wanted to or not. He was giving her instructions how to conduct herself, and Fritz was taking away basins and rags and things. I waited till the doc was through, then took him to the kitchen. Wolfe opened his eyes at him.

Vollmer said, "Quite a novel method of attack, Mr. Wolfe. Quite original, hacking at her from behind like that. He got into one of the posterior externals; I had to shave off some of her hair."

"He?"

The doctor nodded. "She explained that her husband, to whom she has been married three years, did the carving. With a little caution, which I urged upon her, she should be all right in a few days. I took fourteen stitches. Her husband must be a remarkable and unconventional man. She is remarkable too, in her way: the Spartan type. She didn't even clench her hands while I was sewing her; the fingers were positively relaxed."

"Indeed. You will want her name and address for your record."

"I have it, thanks. She wrote it down for me."

"Thank you, Doctor."

Vollmer went. Wolfe got to his feet, pulled at his vest in one of his vain attempts to cover the strip of canary-yellow shirt which encircled his magnificent middle, and preceded me to the office. I stopped to ask Fritz to clean off the inside of the fur piece as well as he could.

By the time I joined them Wolfe was back in his chair and she was sitting facing him. He was saying to her, "I am glad it was no worse, Mrs. Chapin. The doctor has told you, you must be careful not to jerk the stitches loose for a few days. By the way, his fee—did you pay him?"

"Yes. Five dollars."

"Good. Reasonable, I should say. Mr. Goodwin tells me your cab is waiting. Tell the driver to go slowly; jolting is always abominable, in your present condition even dangerous. We need not detain you longer."

She had her eyes fixed on him again. Getting washed off and wrapped up hadn't made her any handsomer. She took a breath through her nose and let it out again so you could hear it.

She said finally, "Don't you want me to tell you about it? I want to tell you what he did."

Wolfe's head went left and right. "It isn't necessary, Mrs. Chapin. You should go home and rest. I undertake to notify the police of the affair; I can understand your reluctant delicacy; after all, one's own husband to whom one has been married three years— I'll attend to that for you."

"I don't want the police." That woman could certainly pin her eyes. "Do you think I want my husband arrested? With his standing and position—all the publicity—do you think I want that? That's why I came to you—to tell you about it."

"But, Mrs. Chapin." Wolfe wiggled a finger at her. "You see, you came to the wrong place. Unfortunately for you, you came to the one man in New York, the one man in the world, who would at once understand what really happened at your home this morning. It was unavoidable, I suppose, since it was precisely that man, myself, whom you wished to delude. The devil of it is, from your standpoint, that I have a deep aversion to being deluded. Let's just call it quits. You really do need rest and quiet, after your nervous tension and your loss of blood. Go on home."

Of course, as had happened a few times before, I had missed the boat; I was swimming along behind, trying to keep up. For a minute I thought she was going to get up and go. She started to. Then she was back again, looking at him. She said, "I'm an educated woman, Mr. Wolfe. I've been in service, and I'm not ashamed of that, but I'm educated. You're trying to talk so I won't understand you, but I do."

"Good. Then there is no need—"

She snapped at him suddenly and violently. "You're a fat fool!"

Wolfe shook his head. "Fat visibly, though I prefer 'Gargantuan.' A fool only in the broader sense, as a common characteristic of the race. It was not magnanimous of you, Mrs. Chapin, to blurt my corpulence at me, since I had spoken of your fatuity only in general terms and had refrained from demonstrating it. I'll do that now." He moved a finger to indicate the knife, which still lay on the newspaper on the desk. "Archie, will you please clean that homely weapon."

I didn't know, I thought maybe he was bluffing her. I picked up the knife and stood there with it, looking from her to him. "Wash off the evidence?"

"If you please."

I took the knife to the bathroom and turned on the faucet, rubbed the blood off with a piece of gauze, and wiped it. Through the open door I couldn't hear any talking. I went back.

"Now," Wolfe instructed me, "grip the handle firmly in your right hand. Come toward the desk so Mrs. Chapin can see you better; turn your back. So. Elevate your arm and pull the knife across your neck; kindly be sure to use the back of the blade, not to carry the demonstration too far. You noted the length and the position of the cuts on Mrs. Chapin? Duplicate them on yourself. Yes. Yes, quite good. A little higher for that one. Another, somewhat lower. Confound you, be careful. That will do. You see, Mrs. Chapin? He did it quite neatly, don't you think? I am not insulting your intelligence by hinting that you expected us to think the wounds could not have been self-inflicted in the position you chose for them. More likely you selected it purely as a matter of precaution, knowing that the front, the neighborhood of the anterior jugular—"

He stopped, because he had no one to talk to except me. When I turned around after my demonstration she was already getting up from her chair, holding her head stiff and a clamp on her mouth. Without a word, without bothering to make any passes at him with her little gray glass eyes, she just got up and went; and he paid no attention, he went on with his speech until she had opened the office door and was through it. I noticed she was leaving her knife, but thought we might as well have it in our collection of odds and ends. Then all of a sudden I jumped for the hall.

"Hey, lady, wait a minute! Your fur!"

I got it from Fritz and caught her at the front door and put it around her. Pitney Scott got out of his cab and came over to help her down the stoop, and I went back in.

Wolfe was glancing through a letter from Hoehn and Company that had come in the morning mail. When he had finished he put it under a paperweight—a piece of petrified wood that had once been used to bust a guy's skull—and said, "The things a woman will think of are beyond belief. I knew a woman once in Hungary whose husband had frequent headaches. It was her custom to relieve them by the devoted application of cold compresses. It occurred to her one day to stir into the water with which she wetted the compresses a large quantity of a penetrating poison which she had herself distilled from an herb. The result was gratifying to her. The man on whom she tried the experiment was myself. The woman—"

He was just trying to keep me from annoying him about business. I cut in. "Yeah, I know. The woman was a witch you had caught riding around in the curl of a pig's tail. In spite of all that, it's time for me to brush up a little on this case we've got. You can give me a shove by explaining in long words how you knew Dora Chapin did her own manicuring."

Wolfe shook his head. "That would not be a shove, Archie; it would be a laborious and sustained propulsion. I shall not undertake it. I remind you merely: I have read all of Paul Chapin's novels. In two of them Dora Chapin is a character. He, of course, appears in all. The woman who married Dr. Burton, Paul Chapin's unattainable, seems to be in four out of five; I cannot discover her in the latest one. Read the books, and I shall be more inclined to discuss the conclusions they have led me to. But even then, of course, I would not attempt to place plain to your eyes the sights my own have discerned. God made you and me, in certain respects, quite unequal, and it would be futile to try any interference with His arrangements."

Fritz came to the door and said lunch was ready.

XI

SOMETIMES I thought it was a wonder Wolfe and I got on together at all. The differences between us, some of them, showed up plainer at the table than anywhere else. He was a taster, and I was a swallower. Not that I didn't know good from bad; after seven years of education from Fritz's cooking I could even tell, usually, superlative from excellent. But the fact remained that what chiefly attracted Wolfe about food in his pharynx was the affair it was having with his taste buds, whereas with me the important point was that it was bound for my belly. To avoid any misunderstanding, I should add that Wolfe was never disconcerted by the problem of what to do with it when he was through tasting it. He could put it away. I have seen him, during a relapse, dispose completely of a ten-pound goose between eight o'clock and midnight, while I was in a corner with ham sandwiches and milk, hoping he would choke. At those times he always ate in the kitchen.

It was the same in business, when we were on a case. A thousand times I've wanted to kick him, watching him progress leisurely to the elevator on his way to monkey with the plants upstairs; or read a book, tasting each phrase; or discuss with Fritz the best storage place for dry herbs; when I was running around barking my head off and expecting him to tell me where the right hole was. I admit he was a great man. When he called himself a genius he had a right to mean it whether he did or not. I admit that he never lost us a bet by his piddling around. But since I'm only human, I couldn't keep myself from wanting to kick him just because he was a genius. I came awful close to it sometimes, when he said things like, "Patience, Archie; if you eat the apple before it's ripe your only reward is a bellyache."

Well, this Wednesday afternoon, after lunch, I was sore. He went indifferent on me; he even went contrary. He wouldn't cable the guy in Rome to get into converse with Santini; he said it was futile and expected me to take his word for it. He wouldn't help me concoct a loop we could use to drag Leopold Elkus into the office; according to him, that was futile too. He kept trying to read in a book while I was after him. He said there were only two men in the case whom he felt any inclination to talk to: Andrew Hibbard and Paul Chapin; and he wasn't ready yet for Chapin and he didn't know where Hibbard was, or whether he was alive or dead. I knew Saul Panzer was going to the morgue every morning and afternoon to look over the stiffs, but I didn't know what else he was doing. I also knew that Wolfe had talked with Inspector Cramer on the phone that morning, but that was nothing to get excited about; Cramer had shot his bolt a week ago at Paul Chapin, and all that was keeping him awake was the routine of breathing.

Saul had phoned around noon and Wolfe had talked to him from the kitchen while I was out with Pitney Scott. A little after two Fred Durkin phoned. He said that Paul Chapin had been to the barber and a drugstore, and that the town dick and the guy in the brown cap and pink necktie were still on deck, and he was thinking of forming a club. Wolfe went on reading. About a quarter to three Orrie Cather called up and said he had got hold of something he wanted to show us and could he come on up with it; he was at the Fourteenth Street subway station. I told him yes. Then, just before Orrie arrived, a call came that made Wolfe put down his book. It was from Farrell, the architect, and Wolfe talked to him. He said he had had a nice lunch with Mr. Oglethorpe, and he had had a tough argument but had finally persuaded him. He was phoning from the publisher's office. Paul Chapin had on several occasions found it convenient to make use of a typewriter there, but there was some disagreement as to which one or ones, so he was going to take samples from a dozen of them. Wolfe told him to be sure that the factory number of the machine appeared on each sample.

I said, after we hung up, "Okay, that one's turning brown. But even if you hang the warnings on him, you've just started. The Harrison demise is out; you'll never tie that up. And I'm telling you that the same goes for Dreyer, unless you get Leopold Elkus down here and perform an operation on him. You've got to find a hole in his story and open it up, or we're licked. What the hell are we waiting for? It's all right for you, you can keep occupied, you've got a book to read—what the devil is it, anyhow?"

I got up to take a squint at it, a dark gray cover stamped in gold: *The Chasm of the Mind*, by Andrew Hibbard. I grunted. "Huh, maybe that's where he is, maybe he fell in."

"Long ago." Wolfe sighed. "Poor Hibbard, he couldn't exclude his poetic tendencies even from his title. Any more than Chapin can exclude his savagery from his plots."

I dropped back into my chair. "Listen, boss." There was nothing he hated more than being called "boss." "I'm beginning to catch on. I suppose Dr. Burton has written books too, and Byron, and maybe Dreyer, and of course Mike Ayers. I'll take the roadster and drive out to Pike County for a little duck hunting, and when you get caught up with your reading just wire me care of Cleve Sturgis, and I'll mosey back and we'll tackle this murder case. And take it easy, take your time; if you eat the apple after it is too ripe you'll get ptomaine poisoning or erysipelas or something, at least I hope to God you will." I was glaring at him, with no result except to make me feel like a sap, because he merely shut his eyes so as not to see me. I got up from my chair and glared anyhow. "Damn it, all I'm asking for is just a little halfway cooperation! One little lousy cablegram to that Roman wop! I ask you, should I have to work myself into a turmoil— Now what the hell do *you* want?"

The last was for Fritz. He had appeared in the door. He was frowning, because he never liked to hear me yell at Wolfe, and I frowned back at him. Then I saw someone standing behind him and I let the frown go and said, "Come on in, Orrie. What's the loot?" I turned to Wolfe and smoothed my voice out and opened up the respect. "He phoned a while ago and said he had got hold of something he wanted to show us. I told you, but you were engrossed in your book."

Orrie Cather had a bundle about the size of a small suitcase, wrapped in brown paper and tied with heavy string.

I said, "I hope it's books."

He shook his head. "It's not heavy enough for books." He set it down on the desk and looked around, and I shoved up a chair for him.

"What is it?"

"Search me. I brought it here to open it. It may be just a lot of nothing at all, but I had a hunch."

I got out my pocket knife, but Wolfe shook his head. He said to Orrie, "Go on."

Orrie grinned. "Well, as I say, it may be a lot of nothing at all, but I'd got so fed up after a day and a half finding out nothing whatever about that cripple except where he buys his groceries and how often he gets his shoes shined, that when something came along that looked like it might be a little break I guess I got excited. I've just been following your instructions—"

"Yes. Let us arrive at the package."

"Right. This morning I dropped in at the Greenwich Bookshop. I got talking with the guy, and I said I supposed he had Paul Chapin's books in his circulating library, and he said sure, and I said I might like to get one, and he handed me one and I looked it over—"

I couldn't help it; I snorted and stopped him. Orrie looked surprised, and Wolfe moved his eyes at me. I sat down.

"Then I said Chapin must be an interesting guy and had he ever seen him, and he said sure, Chapin lived in that neighborhood and bought books there and came in pretty often. He showed me a photograph of Chapin, autographed, on the wall with some others. A woman with black hair was sitting at a desk in the back of the shop, and she called out to the guy that that reminded her, Mr. Chapin never had come for the package he had left there a couple of weeks ago, and with Christmas stuff coming in, the package was in the way, and hadn't he better phone Mr. Chapin to send for it. The guy said maybe he would a little later, it was too early for Chapin to be up. I deposited my dollar and got my book and went down the street to a lunch counter and sat down with a cup of coffee to think."

Wolfe nodded sympathetically. Orrie looked at him suspiciously and went on. "I figured it this way. Two weeks ago was about the time the cops were warming up on Chapin. What if he got hep they would pull a search on him, and he had something in his place he didn't want them to see? There were a lot of things he might do, and one of them was to wrap it up and take it to his friends at the bookshop and ask them to keep it for him. It would be about as safe there as anywhere. Anyhow, I decided I liked Chapin well enough to do him the favor of taking a look at his package for him. I got an envelope and a piece of paper from a stationery store and went to a real-estate office and bummed the use of a typewriter. I wrote a nice note to the bookshop. I had used my eyes on Chapin's signature on the autographed photograph and got it pretty good. But then I was afraid to send it, so soon after I'd been there and heard the package mentioned. I decided to wait until afternoon. So a while ago I got a boy and sent him to the bookshop with the note, and I'm telling you it worked and they gave it to him." Orrie nodded his head at the desk. "That's it."

I got up and got out my knife again. Wolfe said, "No. Untie it." I started to work at the knot, which was a lulu. Orrie wiped his hand across his forehead and said, "By God, if it's just fishing tackle or electric-light bulbs or something, you'll have to give me a drink. This is the only break I've had."

I said, "Among other things, there's just a chance we might find a set of typewriter type bars. Or love letters from Mrs. Loring A. Burton, huh? There's nothing doing on this knot. He didn't want me to untie it, or anybody else. Even if I do get it, I could never tie it back again the same." I picked up my knife again, and looked at Wolfe. He nodded, and I slashed the string.

I took off the paper, several thicknesses. It wasn't a suitcase, but it was leather, and not imitation. It was an oblong box made out of light tan calfskin, a special job, beautifully made, with fine lines of tooling around the edges. It was a swell number.

Orrie grunted. "Jesus, I may be in for grand larceny."

Wolfe said, "Go on," but he didn't get up so he could see.

"I can't. It's locked."

"Well."

I went to the safe and got a couple of my bunches of keys, and went back and started trying. The lock was nothing remarkable; in a few minutes I had it. I laid the keys down and lifted the lid. Orrie stood up and looked in with me. We didn't say anything for a second; then we looked at each other. I never saw him look so disgusted.

Wolfe said, "Empty?"

"No, sir. We'll have to give Orrie a drink. It's not his, it's hers—I mean Dora Chapin's. It's her hand-and-foot box. Gloves and stockings and maybe other dainties."

"Indeed." To my surprise Wolfe showed interest. His lips pushed out and in. He was even going to get up. He did so, and I shoved the box across.

"Indeed. I suspect—yes, it must be. Archie. Kindly remove them and spread them on the desk. Here, I'll help. No, Orrie, not unless you wash your hands first. Ha, more intimate still! But mostly stockings and gloves. Less roughly, Archie, out of respect for the dignity the race aspires to; what we are displaying on this desk-top is the soul of a man. Qualities may be deduced—for instance, do you notice that the gloves, varying as they do in color and material, are all of a size? Among twenty pairs or more, not one exception? Could you ask more of loyalty and fidelity? 'O, that I were a glove upon that hand . . .' But with Romeo it was only rhetoric; for Paul Chapin the glove is the true treasure, with no hope beyond, either of sweet or of bitter. Again, let us not be carried away; it is a distortion to regard this or that aspect of a phenomenon to the exclusion of others. In the present case, for example, we cannot afford to forget that these articles are of expensive materials and workmanship, that they must have cost Dr. Burton something around three hundred dollars, and that he therefore had a right to expect that they should get more wear. Some of them, indeed, are practically new. To strike a balance—"

Orrie was sitting down again, staring at him. It was I who cut him off. "Where does Burton come in? I'm asking that in English."

Wolfe fingered the gloves some more, and held up a stocking to look through it at the light. To see him handling female hosiery as if he understood it gave me a new insight into the extent of his pretensions. He held up another one, dropped it back gently to the table, and took a handkerchief from his pocket and wiped his hands carefully, fingers and palms. Then he sat down.

"Read your Anglo-Saxon poets, Archie. Romeo himself was English, in spite of geography. I am not trying to befuddle you, I am adhering to a tradition."

"All right. Where does Burton come in?"

"I have said, he paid the bills. He paid for these articles, his wife wore them, Dora Ritter, later Chapin, appropriated them, and Paul Chapin treasured them."

"How do you know all that?"

"How could I help but know it? Here are these worn things, kept by Paul Chapin in an elegant and locked receptacle, and in a time of crisis removed by him to a place of safety against unfriendly curiosity. You saw the size of Dora Chapin's hands, you see these gloves; they are not hers. You heard Monday evening the story of Chapin's infatuation with the woman who is now Dr. Burton's wife. You know that for years Dora Chapin, then Ritter, was Mrs. Burton's personal maid, and that she still attends her, to do something to her hair, at least once a week. Knowing these things, it would seem to me that only the most desperate stupidity—"

"Yes, sir. Okay on the stupidity. But why does it have to be that Dora took them? Maybe Chapin took them himself."

"He might. But most unlikely. Surely he did not strip the stockings from her legs, and I doubt if he was familiar with her dressing room. The faithful Dora—"

"Faithful to who? Mrs. Burton, swiping her duds?"

"But Archie. Having seen Dora, can you not grant her rarity? Anyone can be faithful to an employer; millions are, daily, constantly; it is one of the dullest and most vulgar of loyalties. We need not, even if we could, conjecture as to the first stirring of sympathy in Dora's breast on her perceiving the bitter torment in the romantic cripple's heart. I would like to believe it was a decent and honorable bargain, that Paul Chapin offered to pay her money, and did pay her, to get him a pair of gloves his unattainable beloved had worn, but I fear not. Having seen Dora, I suspect that it was the service of romance to which she dedicated herself; and that has been her faithfulness. It may even account for her continuing to visit Mrs. Burton when her marriage freed her from the practical necessity; doubtless fresh specimens are added from time to time. What a stroke of luck for Chapin! The beloved odor, the intimate textile from the skin of his adored, is delivered to him as it may be required; more, the fingers which an hour ago played in his lady's hair are now passing him his dinner coffee. He enjoys daily all the more delicate associations with the person of his passion, and escapes entirely the enforced and commonplace contacts which usually render the delights of dubious profit. So much for the advantage, the peculiar thirst, called emotional, of the individual; it is true that the race of man cannot be continued by keeping gloves and stockings in leather boxes. The biological problem is another matter."

Orrie Cather said, "I knew a guy in the Army that used to take out a girl's handkerchief and kiss it before he went to sleep. One day a couple of us sneaked it out of his shirt and put something on it, and you should have heard him when he stuck his snout against it that night. He burned it up. Later he laid and cried; he was like that."

I said, "It took brains to think up one as good as that."

Wolfe looked at Orrie, shut his eyes for a few seconds, and opened them again. He said, "There are no ubiquitous handkerchiefs in this collection. Mr. Chapin is an epicure. Archie. Repack the box with feeling, lock it, wrap it up, and find a place for it in the cabinet. Orrie, you may resume; you know your instructions. You have not brought us the solution of our case, but you have lifted the curtain to another room of the edifice we are exploring. Telephone at five after six as usual."

Orrie went down the hall, whistling.

XII

I HAD a nice piece of leather of my own, not as big as Paul Chapin's treasure box, but fancier. Sitting at my desk around five o'clock that Wednesday afternoon, killing time waiting for a visitor who had phoned, I took it out of my inside breast pocket and looked at it; I had only had it a couple of weeks. It was brown, ostrich-skin, and was tooled in gold all over the outside. On one side the tooling was fine lines about half an inch apart, with flowers stemming out from them;

the flowers were orchids; the workmanship was so good that you could tell Wolfe had given the guy a cattleya to work from. The other side was covered with Colt automatics, fifty-two perfect little gold pistols all aiming at the center. Inside was stamped in gold: A. G. *from* N. W. Wolfe had given it to me on October 23, at the dinner table, and I didn't even know he knew when my birthday was. I carried my police and fire cards in it, and my operator's license. I might have traded it for New York City if you had thrown in a couple of good suburbs.

When Fritz came and said Inspector Cramer was there I put it back in my pocket.

I let Cramer get eased into a chair and then I went upstairs to the plant rooms. Wolfe was at the potting bench with Horstmann, spreading out some osmundine and leaning over to smell it; a dozen or so pots of odontoglossums, overgrown, were at his elbow. I waited until he looked around, and I felt my throat drying up.

"Well?"

I swallowed. "Cramer's downstairs. The rugged inspector."

"What of it? You heard me speaking to him on the telephone."

"Look here," I said, "I want this distinctly understood. I came up here only for one reason, because I thought maybe you had changed your mind and would like to see him. Yes or no will do it. If you give me a bawling out it will be nothing but pure childishness. You know what I think."

Wolfe opened his eyes a little wider, winked the left one at me twice, and turned to face the potting bench again. All I could see was his broad back that might have been something in a Macy Thanksgiving Day parade. He said to Horstmann, "This will do. Get the charcoal. No sphagnum, I think."

I went back down to the office and told Cramer, "Mr. Wolfe can't come down. He's too infirm."

The inspector laughed. "I didn't expect him to. I've known Nero Wolfe longer than you have, sonny. You don't suppose I thought I was going to tear any secrets out of him? Anything he would tell me he has already told you. Can I light a pipe?"

"Shoot. Wolfe hates it. To hell with him."

"What's this, you staging on me?" Cramer packed his pipe, held a match to it, and puffed. "You don't—need to. Did Wolfe tell you what —I told him on the phone?"

"I heard it." I patted my notebook. "I've got it down."

"The hell you have. Okay. I don't want George Pratt riding me; I'm too old to enjoy it. What went on here night before last?"

I grinned. "Just what Wolfe told you. That's all. He closed a little contract."

"Is it true that he nicked Pratt for four thousand dollars?"

"He didn't nick anybody. He offered something for sale, and they gave him the order."

"Yeah." He puffed. "You know Pratt? Pratt thinks that it's funny that he has to shell out to a private dick when the city maintains such a magnificent force of brave and intelligent men to cope with such problems. He said 'cope.' I was there. He was talking to the Deputy Commissioner."

"Indeed." I bit my lip. I always felt like a sap when I caught myself imitating Wolfe. "Maybe he was referring to the Department of Health. That never occurred to me before, a cop coping."

Cramer grunted. He sat back and looked at the vase of orchids and pulled at his pipe. Pretty soon he said, "I had a funny experience this afternoon. A woman called up downtown and said she wanted Nero Wolfe arrested because he had tried to cut her throat. They put her onto me because they knew I had Wolfe in mind about this case. I said I'd send a man up to get the details, and she gave me her name and address. You could have flipped me cold with a rubber band when I heard it."

I said, "That's a hot one. I wonder who it could have been."

"Sure you do. I'll bet you're puzzled. Then a couple of hours later a guy came to see me—by invitation. He was a taxi driver. He said that no matter how much diversion it offered he didn't care to take the rap for perjury, and that he saw blood on her when she got in his cab on Perry Street. That was one of the things I was wanting to mention to Wolfe on the phone, but the picture in my mind's eye of him slicing a lady's gullet was so damn remarkable that I didn't get it out." He puffed at his pipe, lit a match, and got it going again. He went on, more forceful and rugged. "Look here, Goodwin. What the hell's the idea? I've tried that Chapin woman three times, and I couldn't get her to break down enough to tell me what her name was. She put on the clamp and left it. Wolfe gets in the case late Monday night, and here already, Wednesday morning, she's chasing up to his office to show him her operation. What the hell is it about him that gets them coming like that?"

I grinned. "It's his sympathetic nature, Inspector."

"Yeah. Who carved her neck?"

"Search me. She told you, Wolfe. Pull him in and give him the works."

"Was it Chapin?"

I shook my head. "If I know that secret, it's buried here." I tapped my chest.

"Much obliged. Now listen to me. I'm being serious. Am I on the level?"

"Absolutely."

"I am?"

"You know damn well you are."

"Okay. Then I'm telling you I didn't come here to lift the silver. I've been after Chapin more than six weeks, ever since Dreyer was croaked, and what I've got on him is exactly nothing. Maybe he killed Harrison, and I'm damn sure he killed Dreyer, and it looks like he got Hibbard, and he's got me feeling like a Staten Island flatfoot. He's as slick as a wet pavement. Right in a courtroom he confesses he committed murder, and the judge fines him fifty bucks for contempt of court! Later I find that he mentioned it beforehand to his publisher, as a publicity stunt! Covered everywhere. Is he slick?"

I nodded. "He's slick."

"Yes. Well, I've tried this and that. For one thing, I've got it figured that his wife hates him and she's afraid of him, and probably she knows enough about it to fill out a hand for us, if we could get her to spill it. So when I heard that she had dashed up here to see Wolfe, I naturally surmised that he had learned things. And I want to say this. You don't need to tell me a damn thing if you don't want to. I'm not trying to horn in. But whatever you got out of that Chapin woman, maybe you can make better use of it if you see whether it fits a few pieces I've got hold of, and you're welcome—"

"But Inspector, wait a minute. If you think she came here friendly, to dump the can, how do you account for her calling up to get Wolfe arrested?"

"Now, sonny." Cramer's sharp eyes twinkled at me. "Didn't I say I've known Nero Wolfe longer than you have? If he wanted me to think she hadn't got confidential with him, that would be about exactly what he would tell her to do."

I laughed. While I was laughing it occurred to me that it wouldn't do any particular harm if Cramer continued to nurse that notion, so I laughed some more. I said, "He might, he sure might, but he didn't. Why she phoned you to arrest him—wait till I get a chance to tell Wolfe about it—why she did that, she's psychopathic. So's her husband. They're both psychopathic. That's Park Avenue for batty."

Cramer nodded. "I've heard the word. We've got a department—oh, well."

"And you're damn sure he killed Dreyer."

He nodded again. "I think Dreyer was murdered by Paul Chapin and Leopold Elkus."

"You don't say!" I looked at him. "That might turn out to be bright. Elkus, huh?"

"Yeah. You and Wolfe won't talk. Do you want me to talk?"

"I'd love it."

He filled his pipe again. "You know about the Dreyer thing. Do you know who bought the nitroglycerin tablets? Dreyer did. Sure. A week before he died, the day after Elkus phoned him that the pictures were phony and he wanted his money back. Maybe he had ideas about suicide and maybe he didn't; I think he didn't; there's several things people take nitroglycerin for in small doses."

He took a drag at the pipe, pulled it in until I expected to see smoke squirt out at his belly button, and went on, leaving it to find its way out by instinct. "Now, how did Chapin get the tablets out of the bottle that day? Easy. He didn't. Dreyer had had them for a week, and Chapin was in and out of the gallery pretty often. He had been there a couple of hours Monday afternoon, probably for a talk about Elkus's pictures. He could have got them then and saved them for an opening. The opening came Wednesday afternoon. Wait a minute. I know what Elkus says. That Thursday morning a detective questioned Santini too, the Italian expert, and it checked, but of course at that time it looked like nothing but routine. Since then I've sent a request to Italy, and they found Santini in Florence and had a good long talk with him. He says it was like he told the detective in the first place, but he forgot to mention that after they all left the office Elkus went back for something and was in the office alone for maybe half a minute.

What if Dreyer's glass was there, maybe half full, and Elkus, having got the tablets from Chapin, fixed it up for him?"

"What for? Just for a prank?"

"I'm not saying what for. That's one thing we're working on now. For instance, what if the pictures Dreyer sold Elkus were the real thing —it was six years ago—and Elkus put them away and substituted phonies for them, and then demanded his money back? We're looking into that. The minute I get any evidence what for, I'll arrange for some free board and room for Elkus *and* Chapin."

"You haven't got any yet."

"No."

I grinned. "Anyway, you're working in a lot of nice complications. I'll have to tell Wolfe about it; I hope to God it don't bore him. Why don't you just decide to believe it was suicide after all, and let it go at that?"

"Nothing doing. Especially since Hibbard disappeared. And even if I wanted to, George Pratt and that bunch wouldn't let me. They got those warnings. I don't blame them. Those things sound like business to me, even if they are dolled up. I suppose you've read them."

I nodded. He stuck his paw in his breast pocket and pulled out some papers and began looking through them. He said, "I'm a damn fool. I carry copies of them around with me, because I can't get rid of a hunch that there's a clue in them somewhere, some kind of a clue, if I could find it. Listen to this one, the one he sent last Friday, three days after Hibbard disappeared:

> "One. Two. Three.
> Ye cannot see what I see:
> His bloody head, his misery, his eyes
> Dead but for terror and the wretched hope
> That this last blow, this finis, will not fall.

> "One. Two. Three.
> Ye cannot hear what I hear:
> His moan for pity, now his desperate breath
> To suck the air in through the bubbling blood.

> "And I hear, too, in me the happy rhythm,
> The happy boastful strutting of my soul.

Yes! Hear! It boasts:
One. Two. Three.
Ye should have killed me.

"I ask you, does that sound like business?" Cramer folded it up again. "Did you ever see a guy that had been beaten around the head enough so that things were busted inside? Did you ever notice one? All right, get this: 'To suck the air in through the bubbling blood.' Does that describe it? I'll say it does. The man that wrote that was looking at it, I'm telling you he was looking right at it. That's why, as far as Andrew Hibbard is concerned, all I'm interested in is stiffs. Chapin got Hibbard as sure as hell, and the only question is, where did he put the leavings? Also, he got Dreyer, only with that one Elkus helped him."

The inspector stopped for a couple of pulls at his pipe. When that had been attended to he screwed his nose up at me and demanded, "Why, do *you* think it was suicide?"

"Hell no. I think Chapin killed him. And maybe Harrison, and maybe Hibbard. I'm just waiting to see you and Nero Wolfe and the Epworth League prove it on him. Also I'm annoyed about Elkus. If you get Elkus wrong you may gum it."

"Uh-huh." Cramer screwed his nose again. "You don't like me after Elkus? I wonder if Nero Wolfe will like it. I hope not to gum it, I really do. I suppose you know Elkus has got a shadow on Paul Chapin? What's he suspicious about?"

I lifted my brows a little and hoped that was all I did. "No. I didn't know that."

"The hell you didn't."

"No. Of course you have one, and we have—" I remembered that I never had got hold of Del Bascom to ask him about the dick in the brown cap and pink necktie. "I thought that runt keeping the boys company down there was one of Bascom's experts."

"Sure you did. You didn't know Bascom's been off the case since yesterday morning. Try having a talk with the runt. I did, last night, for two hours. He says he's got a goddam legal right to keep his goddam mouth shut. That's the way he talks, he's genteel. Finally I just shooed him away, and I'm going to find out who he's reporting to."

"I thought you said Elkus."

"That's my idea. Who else could it be? Do you know?"

I shook my head. "Hope to die."

"All right, if you do, don't tell me, I want to guess. Of course you realize that I'm not exactly a boob. If you don't, Nero Wolfe does. I arrested a man once, and he turned out to be guilty; that's why I was made an inspector. I know Wolfe expects to open up this Mr. Chapin and get well paid for it, and therefore if I expected him to pass me any cards out of his hand I *would* be a boob. But I'll be frank with you, in the past six weeks I've made so many grabs at this cripple without getting anything that I don't like him at all and in fact I'd like to rip out his guts. Also they're giving me such a riding that I'm beginning to get saddle sores. I would like to know two things. First, how far has Wolfe got? Sure, I know he's a genius. Okay. But has he got enough of it to stop that cripple?"

I said, and I meant it, "He's got enough to stop any guy that ever started."

"When? I won't lose any sleep if he nicks Pratt for four grand. Can you say when, and can I help?"

I shook my head. "No twice. But he'll do it."

"All right. I'll go on poking around myself. The other thing, you might tell me this, and I swear to God you won't regret it. When Dora Chapin was here this morning did she tell Wolfe she saw nitroglycerin tablets in her husband's pocket any time between September eleventh and September nineteenth?"

I grinned at him. "There are two ways I could answer that, Inspector. One way would be if she had said it, in which case I would try to answer it so you couldn't tell whether she had or not. The other way is the one you're hearing: she wasn't asked about it, and she said nothing about it. She just came here to get her throat cut."

"Uh-huh." Cramer got up from his chair. "And Wolfe started working on her from behind. He would. He's the damnedest guy at getting in the back door—well. So long. I'll say much obliged some other day. Give Wolfe a Bronx cheer for me, and tell him that as far as I'm concerned he can have the money *and* the applause of the citizens in this Chapin case, and the sooner the better. I'd like to get my mind on something else."

"I'll tell him. Like to have a glass of beer?"

He said no and went. Since he was an inspector, I went to the hall and helped him on with his coat and opened the door for him. At the curb was a police car, one of the big Cadillacs, with a chauffeur. Now, I thought, that's what I call being a detective.

I went back to the office. It looked dismal and gloomy; it was nearly six o'clock, and the dark had come over half an hour ago and I had only turned on one light. Wolfe was still upstairs, monkeying with the plants; he wasn't due down for seven minutes. I didn't feel like sitting watching him drink beer, and had no reason to expect anything more pertinent out of him, and I decided to go out and find a stone somewhere and turn it up to see what was under it. I opened a couple of windows to let Cramer's pipe smoke out, got my Colt from the drawer and put it in my pocket from force of habit, went to the hall for my hat and coat, and beat it.

XIII

I DIDN'T know Perry Street much, and was surprised when I walked up in front of Number 203, across the street, having left the roadster half a block away. It was quite a joint, stucco to look like Spanish, with black iron entrance lamps and no fire escapes. On both sides were old brick houses. A few cars were parked along the block, and a couple of taxis. On my side of the street was a string of dingy stores: stationery, laundry, delicatessen, cigar store, and so on. I moved along and looked in. At the delicatessen I stopped and went inside. There were two or three customers, and Fred Durkin was leaning against the end of the counter with a cheese sandwich and a bottle of beer. I turned around and went out, and walked back down to where the roadster was and got inside. In a couple of minutes Fred came along and climbed in beside me. He was still chewing and working his tongue in the corners. He asked me what was up. I said, nothing, I had just come down to gossip. I asked him, "Where's the other club members?"

He grinned. "Oh, they're around. The city feller is probably in the laundry; I think he likes the smell. I suppose Pinkie is down at the next corner, in the coffeepot. He usually deserts his post around this time to put on the nosebag."

"You call him Pinkie?"

"Oh, I can call him anything. That's for his necktie. What do you want me to call him?"

I looked at him. "You've had one or ten drinks. What's the big idea?"

"I swear to God I haven't, Archie. I'm just glad to see you. It's lonesome as hell around here."

"You chinned any with this Pinkie?"

"No. He's reticent. He hides somewhere and thinks."

"Okay. Go on back to your pickle emporium. If you see any kids scratching their initials on my car, pat 'em on the head."

Fred climbed out and went. In a minute I got out too and walked down to the next corner, where if you were blind the smell would have told you: coffeepot. I went in. There were three little tables along the wall, and half a dozen customers at the counter. Pinkie was there all right, alone at one of the little tables, working on a bowl of soup, trying to get the spoon out of his mouth. He had his brown cap on, over one ear.

I went over alongside his table and said to him, keeping my voice low, "Oh, here you are."

He looked up. I said, "The boss wants to see you right away. I'll sit on the lid here a while. Make it snappy."

He stared at me a couple of seconds, and then squeaked so that I nearly jumped. "You're a goddam filthy liar."

The little runt! I could have reached down and jerked his gold teeth out. I slid the other chair back with my toe and sat down and put my elbows on the table and looked at him. "I said, the boss wants to see you."

"Oh yeah?" He sneered at me with his mouth open, showing his gilded incisors. "You wouldn't string a guy, would you, mister? By God, I'll tell the goddam world you wouldn't. Who was I talking to a while ago on the goddam telephone?"

I grinned. "That was me. Listen here a minute. I can see you're tough. Do you want a good job?"

"Yeah. That's why I've got one. If you'd just move your goddam carcass away from my table—"

"All right, I will. Go on and eat your soup, and don't try to scare me with your bad manners. I might decide to remove your right ear and put it where the left one is, and hang the left one on your belt for a spare. Go on and eat."

He dropped his spoon in the soup bowl and wiped his mouth with the back of his hand. "What the hell do you want, anyway?"

"Well," I said, "I was having tea with my friend Inspector Cramer this afternoon, and he was telling me how much he enjoyed his talk with you last night, and I thought I'd like to meet you. That's one story. Then another story might be that a certain guy whose name I needn't mention has got the idea that you're selling him out, and I'm supposed to find out, and I thought the quickest way was to ask you. How many people are you working for?"

"Of all the goddam curiosity!" He sucked something from between his teeth with his tongue. "Last night the goddam inspector, and now you. Hell, my soup's getting cold."

He got up from his chair and picked up the bowl and carried it ten feet to the table at the end. Then he came back for the bread and butter and glass of water and took them. I waited till he was through moving, then I got up and went to the end table and sat down across from him. I was sore because my nifty opening had gone wild. The counterman and the customers were watching us, but only to pass the time. I reached in my pocket and got out my roll and peeled off a pair of twenties.

"Look here," I said, "I could spot you in a day or two, but it would cost both money and time, and I'd just as soon you'd get it. Here's forty bucks—half now if you tell me who's paying you, and the other half as soon as I check it. I'll find out anyhow; this'll just save time."

I'll be damned if he didn't get up and pick up his soup again and start back for the first table. A couple of the customers began to laugh, and the counterman called out, "Hey, let the guy eat his soup, maybe he just don't like you." I felt myself getting sore enough to push in somebody's nose, but I knew there was no profit in that, so I swallowed it and put on a grin. I picked up the runt's bread and butter and water and took it down and set it in front of him. Then I went and tossed a dime on the counter and said, "Give him some hot soup and put poison in it." Then I left.

I walked the block back to the roadster, not in a hurry. Fred Durkin was in the cigar store as I passed by. I had a notion to see him and tell him to keep an eye on his friend Pinkie and maybe catch him on a phone call or something, but, knowing how his mind worked, I thought it would be better to let it stay on his main job. I got in the roadster and headed uptown.

I couldn't figure the runt at all. Was it possible that a dick that looked like that was as honest as that? Who was paying him enough to make him look at forty dollars like it was soap wrappers? Who was so particular about its not being known that he was having Paul Chapin tailed? The inspector's idea didn't seem to me to make sense, even if Leopold Elkus had helped out that day with Dreyer's highball. Why would he put a shadow on Chapin? Of course it was possible, but my practice was to let the brain off easy on an idea until it got a little better than possible. If it wasn't Elkus, who was it? It might have been any one of the bunch who was too scared for Wolfe's memorandum to quiet him down and thought he needed his own reports of the cripple's activities, but in that case why all the mystery? Driving uptown, I went over the list in my mind without any result.

I put the roadster in the garage and walked home. It was nearly dinnertime when I got there. Wolfe was in the office, at his desk. He was doing something. His beer tray had been pushed to one side, and he was leaning over a piece of paper, inspecting it with a magnifying glass, with the strong light turned on. He looked up to nod at me, and then resumed. There was a little pile of similar papers under a weight. The typewriting on the paper began: "Ye should have killed me, watched the last mean sigh." It was the first warning.

Pretty soon he looked up again and blinked. He put the magnifying glass on the table. I asked, "These are Farrell's samples?"

"Yes. Mr. Farrell brought them ten minutes ago. He decided to get a specimen from each machine in Mr. Oglethorpe's office. I have examined two and discarded them—those marked with red pencil." He sighed. "You know, Archie, it is remarkable how the shortening of the days at this time of year, the early darkness, seems to lengthen the period between luncheon and dinner. I suppose I have made that comment before."

"Not very often, sir. Not more than once or twice a day."

"Indeed. It deserves more. You haven't washed."

"No, sir."

"There are two pheasants which should not be kept waiting."

I went upstairs.

After dinner we worked together at Farrell's samples; there were sixteen of them. He wasn't so good at the typewriter; he had x-ed out a good deal, but for our purpose that didn't matter. I brought a glass down from the plant rooms, and Wolfe went on with his. It didn't matter which of the originals we used, so long as it wasn't one of the carbons, since it had been definitely determined that they had all been written on the same machine. We did a thorough job of it, not finally eliminating one until we had both examined it. Wolfe loved that kind of work, every minute of it; when he had gone through a sample and made sure that the *a* wasn't off the line and the *n* wasn't cockeyed, he grunted with satisfaction. I liked it only when it got results. As we neared the bottom of the pile with the red pencil unanimous, I wasn't getting any gayer.

Around ten o'clock I got up and handed the last one across to him, and then went to the kitchen and got a pitcher of milk. Fritz, sitting there reading the French paper, giggled at me. "You drink milk looking like that, you curdle it."

I stuck my tongue out at him and went back to the office. Wolfe had fastened the sheets together with a clip and was putting the originals back in the envelope.

I said, "Well. This has been a fine pregnant evening. Huh?" I drank some milk and licked my lips.

Wolfe leaned back and got his fingers twined. He kept his eyes nearly open. He finally remarked, "We have sacrificed it to Mr. Chapin's adroitness—a tribute to him—and established a fact: that he did not type the warnings in his publisher's office. But he did type them, and doubtless holds himself in readiness to type another; so the machine exists and can be found. I have already another suggestion ready for Mr. Farrell—a little complicated, but worth the experiment."

"Maybe I could offer one. Tell him to get samples from the machines in Leopold Elkus's office."

Wolfe's brows went up. "Why particularly Elkus?"

"Well, for one thing Inspector Cramer got the idea of having someone in Italy get in touch with Mr. Santini. Dumb idea, of course, but he got it. Santini says that he has remembered that after they all left the office that day Elkus went back for something and was in there alone for maybe half a minute—plenty of time to drop some tablets into a highball."

"But hardly enough to filch the bottle from Mr. Dreyer's pocket and return it again, not to mention the dexterity required."

"That's all right. Chapin did that himself some time previously, maybe the week before, and gave them to Elkus."

"Indeed. This was in the newsreels?"

"It's in Cramer's bean. But it may also be in his bag one of these days. We would have to get a mirror and see how we look in it, if it turns out to be the dope and he bags it first. Another item is that Elkus has got a shadow on Chapin."

"That likewise is in Mr. Cramer's bean?"

"Yeah, likewise. But one of those dicks—"

"Archie." Wolfe wiggled a finger at me. "I think it would be as well to correct your perspective. You must not let the oddities of this case perplex you to the point of idiocy. For instance, Inspector Cramer. He is an excellent man. In nine murder cases out of ten his services would be much more valuable than mine; to mention a few points only, I need to keep regular hours, I could not function even passably where properly chilled beer was not continually available, and I cannot run fast. If I am forced to engage in extreme physical effort, such as killing a snake, I am hungry for days. But it is utterly futile, in this case or any other case in which we are interested, to give consideration to the contents of Mr. Cramer's bean. I supposed that in seven years you had learned that."

"Sure. His bean's out." I waved it out with my hand. "But what about his facts? Such as Elkus going back alone to the office?"

Wolfe shook his head. "You see, Archie? The dizzy revolutions of Mr. Chapin's cunning wheel of vengeance have hurled you off on a tangent. Consider what we have engaged to do under our memorandum: free our clients from fear of Paul Chapin's designs. Even if it were possible to prove that Dr. Elkus poisoned Mr. Dreyer's drink—which I strongly doubt—to what purpose should we attempt it? No; let us stick to the circumference of our own necessities and desires. Inspector Cramer might someday have a fact for us, as anyone might; there is no denying that; but he is welcome to this one. It is beyond our circle of endeavor."

"Still I don't see it. Look here. Say Elkus put the stuff in Dreyer's glass. Of course Chapin was in on it—look at the second warning. How are you going to prove Chapin guilty of Dreyer's murder unless you also prove how Elkus did his part?"

Wolfe nodded. "Your logic is impeccable. Your premise is absurd. I haven't the slightest expectation of proving Chapin guilty of Dreyer's murder."

"Then what the devil—"

I got that much out before I realized exactly what he had said. I stared at him.

He went on. "It could not be expected that you should know Paul

Chapin as I know him, because you have not had the extended and intimate association that I have enjoyed—through his books. He is possessed of a demon—a fine old melodramatic phrase. The same thing can be said in modern scientific terms, but it would mean no more and its flavor would be much impaired. He is possessed of a demon, but he is also, within certain limits, an extraordinarily astute man. Emotionally he is infantile—he even prefers a vicar to a replacement, when the original object is unattainable, as witness his taking Dora Ritter to proxy for her mistress. But his intellectual competence is such that it is problematical whether factual proof could ever be obtained of any act of his which he intended to remain anonymous."

He stopped for some beer. I said, "If you mean you give up, you're wasting a lot of time and money. If you mean you're waiting for him to croak another one, and you're tailing him to watch him do it, and he's as smart as you say he is—"

I drank milk. Wolfe wiped his lips and went on. "Of course we have our usual advantage: we are on the offensive. And of course the place to attack the enemy is his weak spot; those are truisms. Since Mr. Chapin has an aversion to factual proof and has the intellectual equipment to preclude it, let us abandon the intellectual field, and attack him where he is weak—his emotions. I am acquainting you now with this decision, which was made last Sunday. We are gathering what ammunition we may. Certainly facts are not to be sneered at; I need two more of them, possibly three, before I can feel confident of persuading Mr. Chapin to confess his guilt."

Wolfe emptied his glass. I said, "Confess, huh? That cripple?"

He nodded. "It would be simple. I am sure it will be."

"What are the three facts?"

"First, to find Mr. Hibbard. His meat and bone; we can do without the vital spark if it has found another errand. That, however, is more for the satisfaction of our clients and the fulfillment of the terms of our memorandum than for the effect on Mr. Chapin. That sort of fact will not impress him. Second, to find the typewriter on which he wrote the menacing verses. That I must have, for him. Third—the possibility—to learn if he has ever kissed his wife. That may not be needed. Given the first two, I probably should not wait for it."

"And with that you can make him confess?"

"I should think so. I see no other way out for him."

"That's all you need?"

"It seems ample."

I looked at him. Sometimes I thought I could tell how much he was being fanciful; sometimes I knew I couldn't. I grunted. "Then I might as well phone Fred and Bill and Orrie and the others to come up and check out."

"By no means. Mr. Chapin himself might lead us to the typewriter or the Hibbard meat and bone."

"And I've been useful too, according to you. Why did you buy the gasoline I burned up yesterday and today if you decided Sunday night you couldn't get the goods on him? It seems as if I'm like a piece of antique furniture or a pedigreed dog—I'm in the luxury class. You keep me on for beauty. Do you know what I think? I think that all this is just your delicate way of telling me that on the Dreyer thing you've decided I'm a washout and you think I might try something else. Okay. What?"

Wolfe's cheeks unfolded a little. "Veritably, Archie, you are overwhelming. The turbulence of a Carpathian torrent. It would be gratifying if you should discover Mr. Hibbard."

"I thought so. Forget Dreyer?"

"Let him rest in peace. At least for tomorrow."

"A thousand dicks and fifteen thousand cops have been looking for Hibbard for eight days. Where shall I bring him when I find him?"

"If alive, here. If dead, he will care as little as I. But his niece will care, I presume—to her."

"Do you tell me where to look?"

"Our little globe."

"Okay."

I went upstairs. I was riled. We had never had a case, and I suppose never will have, without Wolfe getting cryptic about it sooner or later; I was used to it and expected it, but it always riled me. In the Fairmont-Avery thing he had deliberately waited for twenty-four hours to close in on Pete Avery after he had him completely sewed up, just for the pleasure of watching me and Dick Morley of the D. A.'s office play fox-and-goose with that old fool that couldn't find his ear trumpet. I suppose his awful conceit was one of the wheels that worked the machinery that got his results, but that didn't make it any more enjoyable when I was doing the worrying for both of us. That Wednesday night I nearly took the enamel off of my teeth with the brush, stabbing with it at Wolfe's conceit.

The next morning, Thursday, I had had my breakfast and was in the office by eight o'clock, taking another good look at the photograph of her uncle which Evelyn Hibbard had given to us. Saul Panzer had phoned, and I had told him to meet me in the McAlpin lobby at eight-thirty. After I had soaked in all I could of the photograph I made a couple of phone calls, one to Evelyn Hibbard and one to Inspector Cramer. Cramer was friendly. He said that on Hibbard he had spread the net pretty wide. If a body of a man was washed up on the sand at Montauk Point, or found in a coal mine at Scranton, or smelled in a trunk in a Village rooming house, or pulled out of a turnip pit in South Jersey, he would know about it in ten minutes, and would be asking for specifications. That satisfied me that there was no sense in my wasting time or shoe leather looking for a dead Hibbard; I'd better concentrate on the possibility of a live one.

I went to the McAlpin and talked it over with Saul Panzer. He, with his wrinkled little mug not causing any stranger to suspect how cute he was—and he could be pretty damn cute—he sat on the edge of a tapestry chair, smoking a big slick light brown cigar that smelled like something they scatter on lawns in the early spring, and told me about it to date. It was obvious from the instructions Saul had been following, either that Wolfe had reached the same conclusion that I had—that if Hibbard had been croaked the police routine was the best and quickest way of finding him—or that Wolfe thought Hibbard was still alive. Saul had been digging up every connection Hibbard had had in and around the city for the past five years, every degree of intimacy, man, woman, and child, and calling on them. Since Hibbard had been an instructor at a large university, and also a sociable man, Saul hadn't made much more than a start. I supposed that Wolfe's idea was that there was a possibility that Chapin's third warning was a fake, that Hibbard had just got too scared to breathe and had run off to hide, and that in that case he was practically certain to get in touch with someone he knew.

My heart wasn't really in it. For my part, I believed the cripple, third warning and all. In the first place, Wolfe hadn't said definitely that he didn't; and secondly, I had known Wolfe to be wrong, not often, but more than once. When the event proved that he had been wrong about something, it was a delight to see him handle it. He would wiggle his finger a little more rapidly and violently than usual, and mutter with his eyes nearly open at me, "Archie. I love to make a mistake; it is my only assurance that I cannot reasonably be expected to assume the burden of omniscience."

But although I believed the cripple and was perfectly comfortable with the notion that Hibbard wasn't using up any more air, I couldn't see that there was anything better to be done than to smell around places where he had once been alive. I left the general list—neighbors, friends, pupils, and miscellaneous—to Saul, and chose for myself the members of the League of the White Feather.

The *Tribune* office was only seven blocks away, so I called there first, but Mike Ayers wasn't in. Next I went up on Park Avenue, to Drummond's florist shop, and the little fat tenor was all ready for a talk. He wanted to know many things, and I hope he believed what I told him, but he had nothing to offer in exchange that helped me any. From there I went back down to Thirty-ninth Street to see Edwin Robert Byron, the editor, and that was also empty. For over half an hour about all he found time for was "Excuse me" as he was reaching for the telephone. I was thinking, With all that practice, if he should happen to get fired as an editor he could step right in anywhere as a telephone girl.

When I was out working I was supposed to phone in at eleven o'clock, at which time Wolfe got down from the plant rooms, to ask if there were any new instructions. Leaving Edwin Robert Byron's office a little before eleven, I decided I might as well roll over to the house in person, since it was only a couple of blocks out of my way to the next call.

Wolfe wasn't down yet. I went to the kitchen and asked Fritz if anyone had left a corpse on the stoop for us, and he said he didn't think so. I heard the elevator and went to the office.

Wolfe was in one of his sighing moods. He sighed as he said good morning, and he sighed as he got into his chair. It might have meant anything from one measly little orchid getting bugs on it up to a major relapse. I waited until he got his little routine chores done before trying to pass a couple of words.

Out of one of the envelopes in the morning mail he took some pieces of paper that looked familiar from where I stood. I approached. Wolfe looked up at me and back at the papers.

I asked, "What's that, Farrell's second edition?"

He handed me one of the sheets, a different size from the others. I read it:

> Dear Mr. Wolfe:
>
> Here are two more samples which I failed to deliver with the others. I found them in another pocket. I am called suddenly to Philadelphia on a chance at a commission, and am mailing them to you so you will have them first thing in the morning.
>
> Sincerely,
> Augustus Farrell

Wolfe had already got his magnifying glass and was inspecting one of the samples. I felt my blood coming up to my head, which meant a hunch. I told myself to hang onto the aplomb, that there was no more reason to expect it of these than of the others, and there were only two chances. I stood and watched Wolfe. After a little he pushed the sheet aside and shook his head, and reached for the other one.

One more, I thought. If it's that one he's got one of his facts. I looked for an expression on his face as he examined it, but of course I might as well have saved my eyes the strain. He moved the glass along, intent, but a little too rapidly for me not to suspect that he had had a hunch too. At length he looked up at me and sighed. "No."

I demanded, "You mean it's not it?"

"No, I believe, is negative. No."

"Let me see the damn things."

He pushed them across, and I got the glass and gave them a look. I didn't need to be very thorough, after the practice I had had the night before. I was really almost incredulous, and sore as the devil, because in the detective business nothing is more important than to find your hunches good as often as possible. If you once get off of your hunches you might as well give up and go and get a job on the Homicide Squad. Not to mention that Wolfe had said that that typewriter was one of the two things he needed.

He was saying, "It is a pity Mr. Farrell has deserted us. I am not sure that my next suggestion should await his return; and he does not, by the way, mention his return." He picked up the note from Farrell and looked at it. "I believe, Archie, that you had best abandon the Hibbard search temporarily—"

He stopped himself and said in a different tone, "Mr. Goodwin. Hand me the glass."

I gave it to him. His using my formal handle when we were alone meant that he was excited almost beyond control, but I had no idea what about. Then I saw what he wanted the glass for. He was looking through it at the note from Farrell! I stared at him. He kept on looking. I didn't say anything. A beautiful suspicion was getting into me that you shouldn't ever ignore a hunch.

Finally Wolfe said, "Indeed."

I held out my hand, and he gave me the note and the glass. I saw it at a glance, but I kept on looking, it was so satisfactory to see that *a* off the line and a little to the left, and the *n* cockeyed, and all the other signs. I laid it on the table and grinned at Wolfe.

"Old Eagle Eye. Damn me for missing it."

He said, "Take off your coat and hat, Archie. Whom can we telephone in Philadelphia to learn where an architect there in pursuit of a commission might possibly be found?"

XIV

I STARTED for the hall to put my coat and hat away, but before I got to the door I turned and went back.

"Listen," I said, "the roadster needs some exercise. We might fool around with the phone all afternoon and not get anywhere. Why don't we do this: you phone Farrell's friends here and see if you can get a line on him. I'll roll down to Philly and call you up as soon as I arrive. If you haven't found out anything, I'll be on the ground to look for him. I can get there by two-thirty."

"Excellent," Wolfe agreed. "But the noon train will reach Philadelphia at two o'clock."

"Yeah, I know, but—"

"Archie. Let us agree on the train."

"Okay. I thought I might get away with it."

There was plenty of time to discuss a few probabilities, since it was only a five-minute walk to the Pennsylvania Station. I caught the noon train, had lunch on the diner, and phoned Wolfe from the Broad Street Station at two minutes after two.

He had no dope, except the names of a few friends and acquaintances of Farrell's in Philadelphia. I telephoned all I could get hold of, and chased around all afternoon—the Fine Arts Club, and an architectural magazine, and the newspaper offices to see if they knew who intended to build something, and so on. I was beginning to wonder if an idea that had come to me on the train could possibly have anything in it. Was Farrell himself entangled somehow in the Chapin business, and had he written that note on that typewriter for some reason maybe to be discovered, and then beat it? Was there a chance that he hadn't come to Philadelphia at all but was somewhere else, even perhaps on a transatlantic liner?

But around six o'clock I got him. I had taken to phoning architects. After about three dozen I found one who told me that a Mr. Allenby who had got rich and sentimental was going to build a library for a Missouri town that had been lucky enough to give birth to him and then lose him. That was a building project I hadn't heard of before. I phoned Allenby, and was told that Mr. Farrell was expected at his home at seven o'clock for dinner.

I snatched a pair of sandwiches and went out there, and then had to wait until he had finished his meal.

He came to me in Mr. Allenby's library. Of course he couldn't understand how I got there. I allowed him ten seconds for surprise and so forth, and then I asked him, "Last night you wrote a note to Nero Wolfe. Where's the typewriter you wrote it on?"

He smiled like a gentleman being bewildered. He said, "I suppose it's where I left it. I didn't take it away."

"Well, where was it? Excuse me for taking you on the jump like this. I've been hunting you for over five hours and I'm out of breath. The machine you wrote that note on is the one Paul Chapin used for his poems. That's the little detail."

"No!" He stared at me and laughed. "By God, that's good. You're sure? After working so hard to get all those samples, and then to write that note—I'll be damned."

"Yeah. When you get around to it—"

"Certainly. I used a typewriter at the Harvard Club."

"Oh. You did."

"I did indeed. I'll be damned."

"Yeah. Where do they keep this typewriter?"

"Why, it's one—it's available to any of the members. I was there last evening when the telegram came from Mr. Allenby, and I used it to write two or three notes. It's in a little room off the smoking room, sort of an alcove. A great many of the fellows use it off and on."

"Oh. They do." I sat down. "Well, this is nice. It's sweet enough to make you sick. It's available to anybody, and thousands of them use it."

"Hardly thousands, but quite a few—"

"Dozens is enough. Have you ever seen Paul Chapin use it?"

"I couldn't say—I believe, though—yes, in that little chair with his game leg pushed under—I'm pretty sure I have."

"Any of your other friends, this bunch?"

"I really couldn't say."

"Do many of them belong to the club?"

"Oh yes, nearly all. Mike Ayers doesn't, and I believe Leo Elkus resigned a few years ago—"

"I see. Are there any other typewriters in the alcove?"

"There's one more, but it belongs to a public stenographer. I understand this one was donated by some club member. They used to keep it in the library, but some of the one-finger experts made too much noise with it."

"All right." I got up. "You can imagine how I feel, coming all the way to Philadelphia to get a kick in the pants. Can I tell Wolfe when you're coming back, in case he wants you?"

He said probably tomorrow, he had to prepare drawings to submit to Mr. Allenby, and I thanked him for nothing and went out to seek the air and a streetcar to North Philadelphia.

The train ride back to New York, in a smoker filled with the discard from a hundred pairs of assorted lungs, was not what I needed to cheer me up. I couldn't think up anything to keep me awake, and I couldn't go to sleep. We pulled in at the Pennsylvania Station at midnight, and I walked home.

The office was dark; Wolfe had gone to bed. There was no note for me on my desk, so nothing startling had happened. I got a pitcher of milk from the refrigerator and went upstairs. I thought possibly Wolfe was still awake and would like to hear the joyous news, so I went toward the back of the hall to see if there was light under his door—not going close, for when he went to bed there was a switch he turned on, and if anyone stepped within eight feet of his door or touched any of his windows a gong went off in my room that was enough to paralyze you. The slit under his door was dark, so I went on with my milk, and drank it while I was getting ready for bed.

Friday morning after breakfast I was still sitting in the office at eight-thirty. I sat there, first because I was sour on the Hibbard search anyway, and second because I was going to wait until nine o'clock and see Wolfe as soon as he got to the plant rooms. But at eight-thirty the inside phone buzzed and I got on. It was Wolfe from his bedroom. He asked me if I had had a pleasant journey. I told him that all it would have needed to make it perfect was Dora Chapin for company. He asked if Mr. Farrell had remembered what typewriter he had used.

I told him. "A thing at the Harvard Club, in a little room off the smoking room. It seems that the members all play tunes on it whenever the spirit moves them. The good thing about this is that it narrows it down, it rules out all Yale men and other roughnecks. You can see Chapin wanted to make it as simple as possible."

Wolfe's low murmur was in my ear. "Excellent."

"Yeah. One of the facts you wanted. Swell."

"No, Archie. I mean it. This will do nicely. I told you, proof will not be needed in this case; facts will do for us. But we must be sure beyond peradventure of the facts. Please find someone willing to favor us who is a member of the Harvard Club—not one of our present clients. Perhaps Albert Wright would do; if not him, find someone. Ask him to go to the club this morning and take you as a guest. On that typewriter make a copy—no. Not that. There must be no hole for Mr. Chapin to squirm through, should he prove more difficult than I anticipate. In spite of his infirmity, he is probably capable of carrying a typewriter. Do this: after making arrangements for a host, purchase a new typewriter—any good one, follow your fancy—and take it with you to the club. Bring away the one that is there and leave the new one; manage it as you please, by arrangement with the steward, by prestidigitation, whatever suggests itself—with, however, the knowledge of your host, for he must be qualified to furnish corroboration, at any future time, as to the identity of the machine you remove. Bring it here."

"A new typewriter costs one hundred dollars."

"I know that. It is not necessary to speak of it."

"Okay."

I hung up and reached for the telephone book.

That was how it happened that at ten o'clock that Friday morning I sat in the smoking room of the Harvard Club with Albert Wright a vice-president of Eastern Electric, drinking vermouth, with a typewriter under a shiny rubberized cover on the floor at my feet. Wright had been very nice, as he should have been, since about all he owed to Wolfe was his wife and family. That was one of the neatest blackmailing cases . . . but let it rest. It was true that he had paid Wolfe's bill, which hadn't been modest, but what I've seen of wives and families has convinced me that they can't be paid for in cash; either they're way above any money price that could be imagined or they're clear out of sight in the other direction. Anyway, Wright had been nice about it.

I was saying, "This is it. It's that typewriter in there that I showed you the number of and had you put a scratch under it. Mr. Wolfe wants it."

Wright raised his brows. I went on. "Of course you don't care why, but if you do maybe he'll tell you someday. The real reason is that he's fond of culture and he don't like to see the members of a swell organization like the Harvard Club using a piece of junk like that in there. I've got a brand-new Underwood." I touched it with my toe. "I just bought it; it's a new standard machine. I take it in there and leave it and bring away the junk, that's all. If anyone sees me I am unconcerned. It's just a playful lark; the club gets what it needs, and Mr. Wolfe gets what he wants."

Wright, smiling, sipped his vermouth. "I hesitate chiefly because you had me mark the junk for identification. I would do about anything for Nero Wolfe, but I would dislike getting in a mess and having the club dragged in too, perhaps. I suppose you couldn't offer any guarantees on that score?"

I shook my head. "No guarantees, but, knowing how Mr. Wolfe is arranging this charade, I'd take you on a thousand to one."

Wright sat a minute and looked at me, and then smiled again. "Well, I have to get back to the office. Go on with your lark. I'll wait here."

There was nothing to it. I picked up the Underwood and walked into the alcove with it and set it down on the desk. The public stenographer was there only ten feet away, brushing up his machine, but I merely got too nonchalant even to glance at him. I pulled the junk aside and transferred the shiny cover to it, put the new one in its place, and picked up the junk and walked out. Wright got up from his chair and walked beside me to the elevator.

On the sidewalk, at the street entrance, Wright shook hands with me. He wasn't smiling; I guessed from the look on his face that his mind had gone back four years to another time we shook hands. He said, "Give Nero Wolfe my warmest regards, and tell him they will still be warm even if I get kicked out of the Harvard Club for helping to steal a typewriter."

I grinned. "Steal, my eye. It nearly broke my heart to leave that new Underwood there."

I carried my loot to where I had parked the roadster on Forty-fifth Street, put it on the seat beside me, and headed downtown. Having it there made me feel like we were getting somewhere. Not that I knew where, but Wolfe either did or thought he did. I didn't very often get really squeamish about Wolfe's calculations; I worried, all right, and worked myself into a stew when it seemed to me that he was overlooking a point that was apt to trip us up, but down in my heart I nearly always knew that anything he was missing would turn out in the end to be something we didn't need. In this case I wasn't so sure, and what made me not so sure was that damn cripple. There was something in the way the others spoke about him, in the way he looked and acted that Monday night, in the way those warnings sounded, that gave me an uneasy idea that for once Wolfe might be underrating a guy. That wasn't like him, for he usually had a pretty high opinion of the people whose fate he was interfering with. I was thinking that maybe the mistake he had made in this case was in reading Chapin's books. He had definite opinions about literary merit, and possibly, having rated the books pretty low, he had done the same for the man who wrote them. If he was rating Chapin low, I was all ready to fall in on the other side. For instance, here beside me was the typewriter on which the warnings had been written, all three of them, no doubt about it, and it was a typewriter to which Paul Chapin had had easy and constant access, but there was no way in the world of proving that he had done it. Not only that, it was a typewriter to which most of the other persons connected with the business had had access too. No, I thought, as far as writing those warnings went, nearly anything you might say about Chapin would be underrating him.

When I got to the house it wasn't eleven o'clock yet. I carried the typewriter to the hall and put it down on the stand while I removed my hat and coat. There was another hat and coat there; I looked at them; they weren't Farrell's; I didn't recognize them. I went to the kitchen to ask Fritz who the visitor was, but he wasn't there—upstairs, probably—so I went back and got the typewriter and took it to the office. But I didn't get more than six feet inside the door before I stopped. Sitting there, turning over the pages of a book, with his stick leaning against the arm of his chair, was Paul Chapin.

Something I don't often do, I went tonguetied. I suppose it was because I had under my arm the typewriter he had written his poems on, though certainly he couldn't recognize it under the cover. But he could tell it was a typewriter. I stood and stared at him.

He glanced up and informed me politely, "I'm waiting for Mr. Wolfe."

He turned another page in the book, and I saw it was *Devil Take the Hindmost*, the one Wolfe had marked things in. I said, "Does he know you're here?"

"Oh yes. His man told him some time ago. I've been here"—he glanced at his wrist—"half an hour."

There hadn't been any sign of his noticing what I was carrying. I went over and put it down on my desk and shoved it to the back edge. I went to Wolfe's desk and glanced through the envelopes of the morning mail, the corner of my eye telling me that Chapin was enjoying his book. I brushed off Wolfe's blotter and twisted his fountain pen around. Then I got sore, because I realized that I wasn't inclined to go and sit at my desk, and the reason was that it would put me with my back to Paul Chapin. So I went there and got into my chair and got some plant records from the drawer and began looking at them. It was a damn funny experience; I don't know what it was about that cripple that got under my skin so. Maybe he was magnetic. I actually had to clamp my jaw to keep from turning around to look at him, and while I was trying to laugh it off ideas kept flashing through my mind such as whether he had a gun and if so was it the one with the hammer nose filed down. I had a good deal stronger feeling of Paul Chapin behind me than I've had of lots of people under my eyes, and sometimes under my hands too.

I flipped the pages of the record book, and I didn't turn around until Wolfe came in.

I had many times seen Wolfe enter the office when a visitor was there waiting for him, and I watched him to see if he would vary his common habit for the sake of any effect on the cripple. He didn't. He stopped inside the door and said, "Good morning, Archie." Then he turned to Chapin, and his trunk and head went forward an inch and a half from the perpendicular, in a sort of mammoth elegance. "Good morning, sir." He proceeded to his desk, fixed the orchids in the vase, sat down, and looked through the mail. He rang for Fritz, took out his pen and tried it on the scratchpad, and, when Fritz came, nodded for beer.

He looked at me. "You saw Mr. Wright? Your errand was successful?"

"Yes, sir. In the bag."

"Good. If you would please move a chair up for Mr. Chapin. If you would be so good, sir? For either amenities or hostilities, the distance is too great. Come closer." He opened a bottle of beer.

Chapin got up, grasped his stick, and hobbled over to the desk. He paid no attention to the chair I placed for him, nor to me, but stood there leaning on his stick, his flat cheeks pale, his lips showing a faint movement like a race horse not quite steady at the barrier, his light-colored eyes betraying neither life nor death—neither the quickness of the one nor the glassy stare of the other. I got at my desk and shuffled my pad in among a pile of papers, ready to take my notes while pretending to do something else, but Wolfe shook his head at me. "Thank you, Archie, it will not be necessary."

The cripple said, "There need be neither amenities nor hostilities. I've come for my box."

"Ah! Of course. I might have known." Wolfe had turned on his gracious tone. "If you wouldn't mind, Mr. Chapin, may I ask how you knew I had it?"

"You may ask." Chapin smiled. "Any man's vanity will stand a pat on the back, won't it, Mr. Wolfe? I inquired for my package where I had left it, and was told it was not there, and learned of the ruse by which it had been stolen. I reflected, and it was obvious that the likeliest thief was you. You must believe me; this is not flattery; I really did come to you first."

"Thank you. I do thank you." Wolfe, having emptied a glass, leaned back and got comfortable. "I am considering—this shouldn't bore you, since words are the tools of your trade—I am considering the comical and tragical scantiness of all vocabularies. Take, for example, the procedure by which you acquired the contents of that box, and I got box and all; both our actions were, by definition, stealing, and both of us are thieves—words implying condemnation and contempt, and yet neither of us would concede that he has earned them. So much for words—but of course you know that, since you are a professional."

"You said contents. You haven't opened the box."

"My dear sir! Could Pandora herself have resisted such a temptation?"

"You broke the lock."

"No. It is intact. It is simple, and surrendered easily."

"And—you opened it. You probably—" He stopped and stood silent. His voice had gone thin on him, but I couldn't see that his face displayed any feeling at all, not even resentment. He continued, "In that case—I don't want it. I don't want to see it. But that's preposterous. Of course I want it. I must have it."

Wolfe, looking at him with half-closed eyes, motionless, said nothing. That lasted for seconds.

All of a sudden Chapin demanded, suddenly hoarse, "Damn you, where is it?"

Wolfe wiggled a finger at him. "Mr. Chapin. Sit down."

"No."

"Very well. You can't have the box. I intend to keep it."

Still there was no change on the cripple's face. I didn't like him, but I was admiring him. His light-colored eyes had kept straight into Wolfe's, but now they moved; he glanced aside at the chair I had placed for him, firmed his hand on the crook of his stick, and limped three steps and sat down. He looked at Wolfe again and said, "For twenty years I lived on pity. I don't know if you are a sensitive man, I don't know if you can guess what a diet like that would do. I despised it, but I lived on it, because a hungry man takes what he can get. Then I found something else to sustain me. I got a measure of pride in achievement; I ate bread that I earned; I threw away the stick that I needed to walk with—one that had been given me—and bought one of my own. Mr. Wolfe, I was done with pity. I had swallowed it to the extreme of toleration. I was sure that, whatever gestures I might be brought, foolishly or desperately, to accept from my fellow creatures, it would never again be pity."

He stopped. Wolfe murmured, "Not sure. Not sure unless you carried death ready at hand."

"Right. I learn that today. I seem to have acquired a new and active antipathy to death."

"And as regards pity—"

"I need it. I ask for it. I discovered an hour ago that you had got my box, and I have been considering ways and means. I can see no other way to get it than to plead with you. Force"—he smiled the smile that his eyes ignored—"is not feasible. The force of law is, of course, under the circumstances, out of the question. Cunning—I have no cunning, except with words. There is no way but to call upon your pity. I do so; I plead with you. The box is mine by purchase. The contents are mine by—by sacrifice. By purchase, I can say, though not with money. I ask you to give it back to me."

"Well. What plea have you to offer?"

"The plea of my need, my very real need, and your indifference."

"You are wrong there, Mr. Chapin. I need it too."

"No. It is you who are wrong. It is valueless to you."

"But my dear sir"—Wolfe wiggled a finger—"if I permit you to be the judge of your own needs you must grant me the same privilege. What other plea?"

"None. I tell you I will take it in pity."

"Not from me. Mr. Chapin. Let us not keep from our tongues what is in our minds. There is one plea you could make that would be effective. Wait, hear me. I know that you are not prepared to make it, not yet, and I am not prepared to ask for it. Your box is being kept in a safe place, intact. I need it here in order to be sure that you will come to see me whenever I am ready for you. I am not yet ready. When the time comes, it will not be merely my possession of your box that will persuade you to give me what I want and intend to get. I am preparing for you. You said you have acquired a new and active antipathy to death. Then you should prepare for me; for the best I shall be able to offer you, the day you come for your box, will be your choice between two deaths. I shall leave that, for the moment, as cryptic as it sounds; you may understand me, but you certainly will not try to anticipate me. Archie. In order that Mr. Chapin may not suspect us of gullery, bring the box, please."

I went and unlocked the cabinet and got the box from the shelf and took it and put it down on Wolfe's desk. I hadn't looked at it since Wednesday and had forgotten how swell it was; it certainly was a pip. I put it down with care. The cripple's eyes were on me, I thought, rather than on the box, and I had a notion of how pleased he probably was to see me handling it. For nothing but pure damn meanness I rubbed my hand back and forth along the top of it. Wolfe told me to sit down.

Chapin's hands were grasping the arms of his chair, as if to lift himself up. He said, "May I open it?"

"No."

He got to his feet, disregarding his stick, leaning on a hand on the desk. "I'll just—lift it."

"No. I'm sorry, Mr. Chapin. You won't touch it."

The cripple leaned there, bending forward, looking Wolfe in the eyes. His chin was stuck out. All of a sudden he began to laugh. It was a hell of a laugh; I thought it was going to choke him. He went on with it. Then it petered out, and he turned around and got hold of his stick. He seemed to me about half hysterical, and I was ready to jump him if he tried any child's play like bouncing the stick on Wolfe's bean, but I had him wrong again. He got into his regular posture, leaning to the right side with his head a little to the left to even up, and from his light-colored eyes steady on Wolfe again you would never have guessed he had any sentiments at all.

Wolfe said, "The next time you come here, Mr. Chapin, you may take the box with you."

Chapin shook his head. His tone was new, sharper. "I think not. You're making a mistake. You're forgetting that I've had twenty years' practice at renunciation."

Wolfe shook his head. "Oh no. On the contrary, that's what I'm counting on. The only question will be, which of two sacrifices you will select. If I know you, and I think I do, I know where your choice will lie."

"I'll make it now." I stared at the cripple's incredible smile; I thought to myself that in order to break him Wolfe would have to wipe that smile off, and it didn't look practical by any means I'd ever heard of. With the smile still working, fixed, Chapin put his left hand on the desk to steady himself, and with his right hand he lifted his stick up, pointing it in front of him like a rapier, and gently let its tip come to rest on the surface of the desk. He slid the tip along until it was against the side of the box, and then pushed, not in a hurry, just a steady push. The box moved, approached the edge, kept going, and tumbled to the floor. It bounced a little and rolled toward my feet.

Chapin retrieved his stick and got his weight on it again. He didn't look at the box; he directed his smile at Wolfe. "I told you, sir, I had learned to live on pity. I am learning now to live without it."

He tossed his head up twice, like a horse on the rein, got himself turned around, and hobbled to the door and on out. I sat and watched him; I didn't go to the hall to help him. We heard him out there, shuffling to keep his balance as he got into his coat; then the outer door opening and closing.

Wolfe sighed. "Pick it up, Archie. Put it away. It is astonishing, the effect a little literary and financial success will produce on a spiritual ailment."

He rang for beer.

XV

I DIDN'T go out again that morning. Wolfe got loquacious. Leaning back with his fingers interlaced in front of his belly, with his eyes mostly shut, he favored me with one of his quiet endless orations, his subject this time being what he called bravado of the psyche. He said there were two distinct species of bravado: one having as its purpose to impress outside spectators, the other being calculated solely for an internal audience. The latter was bravado of the psyche. It was a show put on by this or that factor of the ego to make a hit with all the other factors. And so on. I did manage before one o'clock to make a copy of the first warning on the Harvard Club junk, and put it under the glass. It was it. Chapin had typed his poems of friendship on that machine.

After lunch I got in the roadster to hunt for Hibbard. The usual reports had come from the boys, including Saul Panzer: nothing. Fred Durkin had cackled over the phone at a quarter to one that he and his colleagues had made a swell procession following Paul Chapin to Nero Wolfe's house, and had retired around the corner to Tenth Avenue to await news of Wolfe's demise. Then they had trailed Chapin back home again.

I had about as much hope of finding Hibbard as of getting a mash note from Greta Garbo, but I went on poking around. Of course I was phoning his niece Evelyn twice a day, not in the expectation of getting any dope, since she would let us know if she got any kind of news, but because she was my client and you've got to keep reminding your clients you're on the job. She was beginning to sound pretty sick on the telephone, and I hardly had the heart to try to buck her up, but I made a few passes at it.

Among other weak stabs I made that Friday afternoon was a visit to the office of Ferdinand Bowen, the stockbroker. Hibbard had an account with Galbraith & Bowen that had been fairly active, fooling with bonds, not much margin stuff, and while I more or less took Bowen in my stride, calling on all the members of the league, there was a little more chance of a hint there than with the others. Entering the office on the twentieth floor of one of the Wall Street buildings, I told myself I'd better advise Wolfe to give a boost to Bowen's contribution to the pot, no matter what the bank report said. Surely they had the rent paid, and that alone must have been beyond the dreams of avarice. It was one of those layouts, a whole floor, that give you the feeling that a girl would have to be at least a duchess to get a job there as a stenographer.

I was taken into Bowen's own room. It was as big as a dance hall, and the rugs made you want to walk around them. Bowen sat behind a beautiful dark brown desk with nothing on it but the *Wall Street Journal* and an ashtray. One of his little hands held a long fat cigarette with smoke curling up from it that smelled like a Turkish harlot—at least it smelled like what I would expect if I ever got close to one. I didn't like that guy. If I'd had my choice of pinning a murder on him or Paul Chapin, I'd have been compelled to toss a coin.

He thought he was being decent when he grunted at me to sit down. I can stand a real tough baby, but a bird that fancies himself for a hot mixture of John D. Rockefeller and Lord Chesterfield, being all the time innocent of both ingredients, gives me a severe pain in the sitter. I told him what I was telling all of them, that I would like to know about the last time he had seen Andrew Hibbard, and all details. He had to think. Finally he decided the last time had been more than a week before Hibbard disappeared, around the twentieth of October, at the theater. It had been a party, Hibbard with his niece, and Bowen with his wife. Nothing of any significance had been said, Bowen declared, nothing with any bearing on the present situation. As he remembered it, there had been no mention of Paul Chapin, probably because Bowen had been one of the three who had hired the Bascom detectives, and Hibbard disapproved of it and didn't want to spoil the evening with an argument.

I asked him, "Hibbard had a trading account with your firm?"

He nodded. "For a long while, over ten years. It wasn't very active, mostly back and forth in bonds."

"Yeah. I gathered that from the statements among his papers. You see, one thing that might help would be any evidence that when Hibbard left his apartment that Tuesday evening he had an idea that he might not be back again. I can't find any. I'm still looking. For instance, during the few days preceding his disappearance, did he make any unusual arrangements or give any unusual orders regarding his account here?"

Bowen shook the round thing that he used to grow his hair on. "No. I would have been told—but I'll make sure." From a row on the wall behind him he pulled out a telephone and talked into it. He waited a while and talked some more. He pushed the phone back and turned to me. "No, as I thought. There has been no transaction on Andy's account for over two weeks, and there were no instructions from him."

I bade him farewell.

That was a good sample of the steady progress I made that day in the search for Andrew Hibbard. It was a triumph. I found out as much from the other six guys I saw as I did from Ferdinand Bowen, so I was all elated when I breezed in home around dinnertime, not to mention the fact that with the roadster parked on Ninetieth Street some dirty lout scraped the rear fender while I was in seeing Dr. Burton. I didn't feel like anything at all, not even like listening to the charming gusto of Wolfe's dinner conversation—during a meal he refused to remember that there was such a thing as a murder case in the world—so I was glad that he picked that evening to leave the radio turned on.

After dinner we went to the office. Out of spite and bitterness I started to tell him about all the runs I had scored that afternoon, but he asked me to bring him the atlas and began to look at maps. There were all sorts of toys he was apt to begin playing with when he should have had his mind on business, but the worst of all was the atlas. When he got that out I gave up. I fooled around a while with the plant records and the expense account; then I closed my affairs for the night and went over to his desk to look him over. He was doing China! The atlas was a Gouchard, the finest to be had, and did China more than justice. He had the folded map opened out, and, with his pencil in one hand and his magnifying glass in the other, there he was, buried in the Orient. Without bothering to say good night to him, for I knew he wouldn't answer, I picked up his copy of *Devil Take the Hindmost* and went upstairs to my room, stopping in the kitchen for a pitcher of milk.

After I had got into pajamas and slippers I deposited myself in my most comfortable chair, under the reading lamp, with the milk handy on the little tile-top table, and took a crack at Paul Chapin's book. I thought it was about time I caught up with Wolfe. I flipped through it and saw there were quite a few places he had marked—sometimes only a phrase, sometimes a whole sentence, occasionally a long passage of two or three paragraphs. I decided to concentrate on those, and I skipped around and took them at random:

> . . . not by the intensity of his desire, but merely by his inborn impulse to act; to do, disregarding all pale considerations . . .
>
> For Alan there was no choice in the matter, for he knew that the fury that spends itself in words is but the mumbling of an idiot, beyond the circumference of reality.

I read a dozen more, yawned, and drank some milk. I went on.

> She said, "That's why I admire you. . . . I don't like a man too squeamish to butcher his own meat."
>
> . . . and scornful of all the whining eloquence deploring the awful brutalities of war; for the true objection to war is not the blood it soaks into the grass and the thirsty soil, not the bones it crushes, not the flesh it mangles, not the warm nutritious viscera it exposes to the hunger of the innocent birds and beasts. These things have their beauty, to compensate for the fleeting agonies of this man and that man. The trouble with war is that its noble and quivering excitements transcend the capacities of our weakling nervous systems; we are not men enough for it; it properly requires for its sublime sacrifices the blood and bones and flesh of heroes, and what

have we to offer? This little coward, that fat sniveler, all these regiments of puny cravens . . .

There was a lot of that. I got through it, and went on to the next. Then some more. It got monotonous, and I skipped around. There were some places that looked interesting, some conversations, and a long scene with three girls in an apple orchard, but Wolfe hadn't done any marking there. Around the middle of the book he had marked nearly a whole chapter which told about a guy croaking two other guys by manicuring them with an ax, with an extended explanation of how psychology entered into it. I thought that was a pretty good job of writing. Later I came across things like this, for instance:

> . . . for what counted was not the worship of violence, but the practice of it. Not the turbulent and complex emotion, but the act. What had killed Art Billings and Curly Stephens? Hate? No. Anger? No. Jealousy, vengefulness, fear, enmity? No, none of these things. They had been killed by an ax, gripped by his fingers and wielded by the muscles of his arm . . .

At eleven o'clock I gave up. The milk was all gone, and it didn't seem likely that I would catch up with where Wolfe thought he was if I sat up all night. I thought I detected a hint here and there that the author of that book was reasonably bloodthirsty, but I had some faint suspicions on that score already. I dropped the book on the table, stretched for a good yawn, went and opened the window and stood there looking down on the street long enough to let the sharp cold air make me feel like blankets, and hopped for the hay.

Saturday morning I started out again. It was all stale bread to me, and I suppose I did a rotten job of it; if one of those guys had had some little fact tucked away that might have helped there wasn't much chance of my prying it loose, the way I was going about it. I kept moving, anyhow. I called on Elkus, Lang, Mike Ayers, Adler, Cabot, and Pratt. I phoned Wolfe at eleven o'clock, and he had nothing to say. I decided to tackle Pitney Scott, the taxi driver. Maybe my wild guess that day had been right; there was a chance that he did know something about Andrew Hibbard. But I couldn't find him. I called up the office of his cab company and was told that he wasn't expected to report in until four o'clock. They told me that his usual cruising radius was from Fourteenth to Fifty-ninth streets, but that he might be anywhere. I went down and looked around Perry Street, but he wasn't there. At a quarter to one I phoned Wolfe again, expecting to be invited home to lunch, and instead he handed me a hot one. He asked me to grab a bite somewhere and run out to Mineola for him. Ditson had phoned to say that he had a dozen bulbs of a new miltonia just arrived from England, and had offered to give Wolfe a couple if he would send for them.

The only times I ever really felt like turning Communist were the occasions when, in the middle of a case, Wolfe sent me chasing around after orchids. It made me feel too damn silly. But it wasn't as bad this time as usual, since the particular job I was on looked like a washout anyhow. It was cold and raw that Saturday afternoon, and kept trying to make out that it was going to snow, but I opened both windows of the roadster and enjoyed the air a lot and the Long Island traffic not at all.

I got back to Thirty-fifth Street around three-thirty and took the bulbs in the office to show them to Wolfe. He felt them and looked them over carefully and asked me to take them upstairs to Horstmann and tell him not to snip the roots. I went up, and came back down to the office, intending to stop only a minute to enter the bulbs in the record book and then beat it again to get Pitney Scott. But Wolfe, from his chair, said, "Archie."

I knew from the tone it was the start of a speech, so I settled back. He went on. "Now and then I receive the impression that you suspect me of neglecting this or that detail of our business. Ordinarily you are wrong, which is as it should be. In the labyrinth of any problem that confronts us, we must select the most promising paths; if we attempt to follow all at once we shall arrive nowhere. In any art—and I am an artist or nothing—one of the deepest secrets of excellence is a discerning elimination. Of course that is a truism."

"Yes, sir."

"Yes. Take the art of writing. I am, let us say, describing the actions of my hero rushing to greet his beloved, who has just entered the forest. 'He sprang up from the log on which he had been sitting, with his left foot forward; as he did so, one leg of his trousers fell properly into place but the other remained hitched up at the knee. He began running toward her, first his right foot, then his left, then his right again, then left, right, left, right, left, right . . .' As you see, some of that can surely be left out—indeed, must be, if he is to accomplish his welcoming embrace in the same chapter. So the artist must leave out vastly more than he puts in, and one of his chief cares is to leave out nothing vital to his work."

"Yes, sir."

"You follow me. I assure you that the necessity I have just described is my constant concern when we are engaged in an enterprise. When you suspect me of neglect you are in a sense justified, for I do ignore great quantities of facts and impingements which might seem to another intelligence—let it go without characterization—to be of importance to our undertaking. But I should consider myself an inferior workman if I ignored a fact which the event proved actually to have significance. That is why I wish to make this apology to myself, thus publicly, in your hearing."

I nodded. "I'm still hanging on. Apology for what?"

"For bad workmanship. It may prove not to have been disastrous; it may even turn out of no importance whatever. But sitting here this afternoon, contemplating my glories and sifting out the sins, it occurred to me, and I need to ask you about it. You may remember that on Wednesday evening, sixty-five hours ago, you were describing for me the contents of Inspector Cramer's bean."

I grinned. "Yeah."

"You told me that it was his belief that Dr. Elkus was having Mr. Chapin shadowed."

"Yep."

"And then you started a sentence; I think you said, 'But one of those dicks—' Something approximating that. I was impatient, and I stopped you. I should not have done so. My impulsive reaction to what I knew to be nonsense betrayed me into an error. I should have let you finish. Pray do so now."

I nodded. "Yeah, I remember. But since you've dumped the Dreyer thing into the ashcan, what does it matter whether Elkus—"

"Archie. Confound it, I care nothing about Elkus; what I want is your sentence about a dick. What dick? Where is he?"

"Didn't I say? Tailing Paul Chapin."

"One of Mr. Cramer's men."

I shook my head. "Cramer has a man there too. And we've got Durkin and Gore and Keems, eight-hour shifts. This bird's an extra. Cramer wondered who was paying him and had him in for a conference, but he's tough, he never says anything but cuss words. I thought maybe he was Bascom's, but no."

"Have you seen him?"

"Yeah, I went down there. He was eating soup, and he's like you about meals, business is out. I waited on him a little, carried his bread and butter and so on, and came on home."

"Describe him."

"Well—he hasn't much to offer to the eye. He weighs a hundred and thirty-five, five feet seven. Brown cap and pink necktie. A cat scratched him on the cheek, and he didn't clean it up very well. Brown eyes; pointed nose; wide, thin mouth, but not tight; pale, healthy skin."

"Hair?"

"He kept his cap on."

Wolfe sighed. I noticed that the tip of his finger was doing a little circle on the arm of his chair. He said, "Sixty-five hours. Get him and bring him here at once."

I got up. "Yeah. Alive or dead?"

"By persuasion if possible, certainly with a minimum of violence, but bring him."

"It's five minutes to four. You'll be in the plant rooms."

"Well? This house is comfortable. Keep him."

I got some things from a drawer of my desk and stuffed them in my pockets and beat it.

XVI

I WAS NOT ever, in the Chapin case or any other case, quite as dumb as the prosecution would try to make you believe if I was on trial for it. For instance, as I went out and got into the roadster, in spite of all the preconceptions that had set up housekeeping in my belfry, I wasn't doing any guessing as to the nature of the fancy notion Wolfe had plucked out of his contemplation of his sins. My guessing had been completed before I left the office. On account of various considerations it was my opinion that he was cuckoo—I had told him that Cramer had had the dick in for a talk—but it was going to be diverting, whether it turned out that he was or he wasn't.

I drove to Perry Street and parked fifty feet down from the coffeepot. I had already decided on my tactics. Considering what I had learned of Pinkie's reaction to the diplomatic approach, it didn't seem practical to waste any time on persuasion. I walked to the coffeepot and glanced in. Pinkie wasn't there; of course it was nearly two hours till his soup time. I strolled back down the street, looking in at all the chances, and I went the whole long block to the next corner without a sign of either Pinkie, Fred Durkin, or anything that looked like a city detective. I went back again, clear to the coffeepot, with the same result. Not so good, I thought, for of course all the desertion meant that the beasts of prey were out trailing their quarry, and the quarry might stay out for a dinner and a show and get home at midnight. That would be enjoyable, with me substituting for Fred on the delicatessen sandwiches and Wolfe waiting at home to see what his notion looked like.

I drove around the block to get the roadster into a better position for surveying the scene, and sat in it and waited. It was getting dark, and it got dark, and I waited.

A little before six a taxi came along and stopped in front of 203. I tried to get a glimpse of the driver, having Pitney Scott on my mind, and made out that it wasn't him. But it was the cripple that got out. He paid and hobbled inside the building, and the taxi moved off. I looked around, taking in the street and the sidewalk.

Pretty soon I saw Fred Durkin walking up from the corner. He was with another guy. I climbed out to the sidewalk and stood there near a street light as they went by. Then I got back in. In a couple of minutes Fred came along, and I moved over to make room for him.

I said, "If you and the town dick want to cop a little expense money by pairing up on a taxi, okay. As long as nothing happens; then it might be your funeral."

Durkin grinned. "Aw, forget it. This whole layout's a joke. If I didn't need the money—"

"Yeah. You take the money and let me do the laughing. Where's Pinkie?"

"Huh? Don't tell me you're after the runt again!"

"Where is he?"

"He's around. He was behind us on the ride just now. There he goes —look, the coffeepot. He must have gone down Eleventh. He takes chances. It's time for his chow."

I had seen him going in. I said, "All right. Now listen. I'm going to funny up your joke for you. You and the town dick are pals."

"Well, we speak."

"Find him. Do they sell beer at that joint on the corner? Okay. Take him there and quench his thirst—on expense. Keep him there until my car's gone from in front of the coffeepot. I'm going to take Pinkie for a ride."

"No! I'll be damned. Keep his necktie for me."

"All right. Let's go. Beat it."

He climbed out and went. I sat and waited. Pretty soon I saw him come out of the laundry with the snoop and start off in the other direction. I stepped on the starter and pushed the gear lever and rolled along. This time I stopped right in front of the coffeepot. I got out and went in. I saw no cop around.

Pinkie was there, at the same table as before, with what looked like the same bowl of soup. I glanced at the other customers, on the stools, and observed nothing terrifying. I walked over to Pinkie and stopped at his elbow.

He looked up and said, "Well, goddam it."

Looking at him again, I thought there was a chance Wolfe was right. I said, "Come on, Inspector Cramer wants to see you," and took bracelets out of one pocket and my automatic out of another.

There must have been something in my eyes that made him suspicious, and I'll say the little devil had nerve. He said, "I don't believe it. Show me your goddam badge."

I couldn't afford an argument. I grabbed his collar and lifted him up out of his chair and set him on his feet. Then I snapped the handcuffs on him. I kept the gat completely visible and told him, "Get going." I heard one or two mutters from the lunch counter but didn't bother to look. Pinkie said, "My overcoat." I grabbed it off the hook and hung it on my arm and marched him out. He went nice. Instead of trying to hide the bracelets, like most of them do, he held his hands stuck out in front.

The only danger was that a flatfoot might happen along outside and offer to help me, and the roadster wasn't a police car. But all I saw was curious citizens. I herded him to the car, opened the door and shoved him in, and climbed in after him. I had left the engine running, just in case of a hurry. I rolled off, got to Seventh Avenue, and turned north.

I said, "Now listen. I've got two pieces of information. First, to ease your mind, I'm taking you to Thirty-fifth Street to call on Mr. Nero Wolfe. Second, if you open your trap to advertise anything, you'll go there just the same, only faster and more unconscious."

"I have no desire to call—"

"Shut up." But I was grinning inside, for his voice was different; he was already jumping his character.

The evening traffic was out playing tag, and it took long enough to get to West Thirty-fifth Street. I pulled up in front of the house, told my passenger to sit still, got out and walked around and opened his door, and told him to come on. I went behind him up the steps, used my key on the portal, and nodded him in. While I was taking off my hat and coat he started reaching up for his cap, but I told him to leave it on and steered him for the office.

Wolfe was sitting there with an empty beer glass, looking at the design the dried foam had left. I shut the office door and stood there, but the runt kept going, clear to the desk.

Wolfe looked at him, nodded faintly, and then looked some more. He spoke suddenly to me. "Archie. Take Mr. Hibbard's cap, remove the handcuffs, and place a chair for him."

I did those things. This gentleman, it appeared, represented the second fact Wolfe had demanded, and I was glad to wait on him. He held his hands out for me to take the bracelets off, but it seemed to be an effort for him, and a glance at his eyes showed me that he wasn't feeling any too prime. I eased the chair up back of his knees, and all of a sudden he slumped into it, buried his face in his hands, and stayed that way. Wolfe and I regarded him with not as much commiseration as he might have thought he had a right to expect if he had been looking at us. To me he was the finest hunk of bacon I had lamped for several moons.

Wolfe tipped me a nod, and I went to the cabinet and poured a stiff one and brought it over. I said, "Here, try this."

Finally he looked up. "What is it?"

"It's a goddam drink of rye whisky."

He shook his head and reached for the drink simultaneously. I knew he had some soup in him so didn't look for any catastrophe. He downed half of it, spluttered a little, and swallowed the rest.

I said to Wolfe, "I brought him in with his cap on so you could see him that way. Anyhow, all I ever saw was a photograph. And he was supposed to be dead. And I'm here to tell you, it would have been a pleasure to plug him, and no kinds of comments will be needed now or any other time."

Wolfe, disregarding me, spoke to the runt. "Mr. Hibbard. You know of the ancient New England custom of throwing a suspected witch into the river, and if she drowned she was innocent. My personal opinion of a large drink of straight whisky is that it provides a converse test: if you survive it you can risk anything. Mr. Goodwin did not in fact plug you?"

Hibbard looked at me and blinked, and at Wolfe and blinked again. He cleared his throat twice and said conversationally, "The truth of the matter is, I am not an adventurous man. I have been under a terrible strain for eleven days. And shall be—for many more."

"I hope not."

Hibbard shook his head. "And shall. God help me. And shall."

"You call on God now?"

"Rhetorically. I am farther than ever from Him, as a reliance." He looked at me. "Could I have a little more whisky?"

I got it for him. This time he started sipping it and smacked his lips. He said, "This is a relief. The whisky is too, of course, but I was referring particularly to this opportunity to become articulate again. No; I am farther than ever from a Deity in the stratosphere, but much closer to my fellow man. I have a confession to make, Mr. Wolfe, and it might as well be to you as anyone. I have learned more in these eleven days masquerading as a roughneck than in all the previous forty-three years of my existence."

"Harun al-Rashid—"

"No. Excuse me. He was seeking entertainment; I was seeking life—first, I thought, merely my own life, but I found much more. For instance, if you were to say to me now what you said three weeks ago, that you would undertake to remove my fear of Paul Chapin by destroying him, I would say: 'Certainly, by all means, how much do I owe you?' For I understand now that the reason for my former attitude was nothing but a greater fear than the fear of death, the fear of accepting responsibility for my own preservation. You don't mind if I talk? God, how I want to talk!"

Wolfe murmured, "This room is hardened to it." He rang for beer.

"Thank you. In these eleven days I have learned that psychology, as a formal science, is pure hocus-pocus. All written and printed words, aside from their function of relieving boredom, are meaningless drivel. I have fed a half-starved child with my own hands. I have seen two men batter each other with their fists until the blood ran. I have watched boys picking up girls. I have heard a woman tell a man, in public and with a personal application, facts which I had dimly supposed were known, academically, only to those who have read Havelock Ellis. I have observed hungry working men eating in a coffeepot. I have seen a tough boy of the street pick up a wilted daffodil from the gutter. It is utterly amazing, I tell you, how people do things they happen to feel like doing. And I have been an instructor in psychology for seventeen years! *Merde!* Could I have a little more whisky?"

I didn't know whether Wolfe needed him sober, but I saw no warning gesture from him, so I went and filled the glass again. This time I brought some White Rock for a chaser, and he started on that first.

Wolfe said, "Mr. Hibbard. I am fascinated at the prospect of your education, and I shall insist on hearing it entire, but I wonder if I could interpose a question or two. First I shall need to contradict you by observing that before your eleven days' education began you had learned enough to assume a disguise simple and effective enough to preserve your incognito, though the entire police force—and one or two other people—were looking for you. Really an achievement."

The fizz had ascended into the psychologist's nose, and he pinched it. "Oh no. That sort of thing is rule of thumb. The first rule, of course, is, nothing that looks like disguise. My best items were the necktie and the scratch on my cheek. My profanity, I fear, was not well done; I should not have undertaken it. But my great mistake was the teeth; it was the very devil to get the gold leaf cemented on, and I was forced to confine my diet almost exclusively to milk and soup. Of course, having once made my appearance, I could not abandon them. The clothing I am proud of."

"Yes, the clothing." Wolfe looked him over. "Excellent. Where did you get it?"

"A secondhand store on Grand Street. I changed in a subway toilet, and so was properly dressed when I went to rent a room on the lower West Side."

"And you left your second pipe at home. You have estimable qualities, Mr. Hibbard."

"I was desperate."

"A desperate fool is still a fool. What, in your desperation, did you hope to accomplish? Did your venture pretend to any intelligent purpose?"

Hibbard had to consider. He swallowed some whisky, washed it off with fizz, and coated that with another sip of whisky. He finally said, "So help me, I don't know. I mean I don't know now. When I left home, when I started this, all that I felt moving me was fear. The whole long story of what that unlucky episode, twenty-five years ago—of what it did to me—would sound fantastic if I tried to tell it. I was too highly sensitized in spots; I suppose I still am; doubtless it will show again in the proper surroundings. I am inclining now to the environmental school—you hear that? Atavism! Anyhow, fear had me, and all I was aware of was a desire to get near Paul Chapin and keep him under my eye. I had no plans further than that. I wanted to watch him. I knew if I told anyone, even Evelyn, my niece, there would be danger of his getting onto me, so I made a thorough job of it. But the last few days I have begun to suspect that in some gully of my mind, far below consciousness, was a desire to kill him. Of course there is no such thing as a desire without an intention, no matter how nebulous it may be. I believe I meant to kill him. I believe I have been working up to it, and I still am. I have no idea what this talk with you will do to me. I see no reason why it should have any effect one way or another."

"You will see, I think." Wolfe emptied his glass. "Naturally you do not know that Mr. Chapin has mailed verses to your friends stating explicitly that he killed you by clubbing you over the head."

"Oh yes. I know that."

"The devil you do. Who told you?"

"Pit. Pitney Scott."

I gritted my teeth and wanted to bite myself. Another chance underplayed, and all because I had believed the cripple's warning.

Wolfe was saying, "Then you did keep a bridge open."

"No. He opened it himself. The third day I was around there I met him face to face by bad luck, and of course he recognized me." Hibbard suddenly stopped, and turned a little pale. "By heaven—ha, there goes another illusion—I thought Pit—"

"Quite properly, Mr. Hibbard. Keep your illusion; Mr. Scott has told us nothing; it was Mr. Goodwin's acuteness of observation, and my feeling for phenomena, that uncovered you. But to resume: if you knew that Mr. Chapin had sent those verses, falsely boasting of murdering you, it is hard to see how you could keep your respect for him as an assassin. If you knew one of his murders, the latest one, to be nothing but rodomontade—"

Hibbard nodded. "You make a logical point, certainly. But logic has nothing to do with it. I am not engaged in developing a scientific thesis. There are twenty-five years behind this—and Bill Harrison, Gene Dreyer, and Paul that day in the courtroom. I was there, to testify to the psychological value of his book. It was on the day that Pit Scott showed me those verses about me sucking air in through my blood that I discovered that I wanted to kill Paul, and if I wanted it I intended it, or what the devil was I doing there?"

Wolfe sighed. "It is a pity. The back-seat driving of the less charitable emotions often makes me wonder that the brain does not desert the wheel entirely, in righteous exasperation. Not to mention their violent and senseless oscillations. Mr. Hibbard. Three weeks ago you were filled with horrified aversion at the thought of engaging me to arrange that Mr. Chapin should account legally for his crimes; today you are determined to kill him yourself. You do intend to kill him?"

"I think so." The psychological runt put his whisky glass on the desk. "That doesn't mean that I will. I don't know. I intend to."

"You are armed? You have a weapon?"

"No. I—no."

"You what?"

"Nothing. I should have said 'he.' He is physically a weakling."

"Indeed." The shadows on Wolfe's face altered; his cheeks were unfolding. "You will rip him apart with your bare hands. Into quivering bloody fragments—"

"I might," Hibbard snapped. "I don't know whether you taunt me through ignorance or through design. You should know that despair is still despair, even when there is an intellect to perceive it and control its hysteria. I can kill Paul Chapin and still know what I am doing. My physical build is negligible, next to contemptible, and my mental equipment has reached the decadence which sneers at the blood that feeds it, but in spite of those incongruities I can kill Paul Chapin. I think I understand now why it was such a relief to be able to talk again in my proper person, and I thank you for it. I think I needed to put this determination into words. It does me good to hear it. Now I would like you to let me go. I can go on, of course, only by your sufferance. You have interfered with me, and frankly I'm grateful for it, but there is no reason—"

"Mr. Hibbard." Wolfe wiggled a finger at him. "Permit me. The least offensive way of refusing a request is not to let it be made. Don't make it. Wait, please. There are several things you either do not know or fail to consider. For instance, do you know of an arrangement I have entered into with your friends?"

"Yes. Pit Scott told me. I'm not interested—"

"But I am. In fact I know of nothing else, at the moment, that interests me in the slightest degree; certainly not your recently acquired ferocity. Further, do you know that there, on Mr. Goodwin's desk, is the typewriter on which Mr. Chapin wrote his sanguinary verses? Yes, it was at the Harvard Club; we negotiated a trade. Do you know that I am ready for a complete penetration of Mr. Chapin's defenses, in spite of his pathetic bravado? Do you know that within twenty-four hours I shall be prepared to submit to you and your friends a confession from Mr. Chapin of his guilt, and to remove satisfactorily all your apprehensions?"

Hibbard was staring at him. He emptied his whisky glass, which he had been holding, half full, and put it on the desk and stared at Wolfe again. "I don't believe it."

"Of course you do. You merely don't want to. I'm sorry, Mr. Hibbard, you'll have to readjust yourself to a world of words and compromises and niceties of conduct. I would be glad— Well?"

He stopped to look at Fritz, who had appeared on the threshold. Wolfe glanced at the clock; it was seven-twenty-five. He said, "I'm sorry, Fritz. Three of us will dine, at eight o'clock. Will that be possible?"

"Yes, sir."

"Good. As I was saying, Mr. Hibbard, I would like to help make the readjustment as pleasant as possible for you, and at the same time serve my own convenience. The things I have just told you are the truth, but to help me in realizing the last one I shall need your cooperation. I mentioned twenty-four hours. I would like to have you remain here as my guest for that period. Will you?"

Hibbard shook his head with emphasis. "I don't believe you. You may have the typewriter, but you don't know Paul Chapin as I do. I don't believe you'll get him to confess, ever in God's world."

"I assure you I will. But that can be left to the event. Will you stay here until tomorrow evening and communicate with no one? My dear sir, I will bargain with you. You were about to make a request of me. I counter with one of my own. Though I am sure twenty-four hours will do, let us allow for contingencies; make it forty-eight. If you will agree to stay under this roof incommunicado until Monday evening, I engage that at that time, if I have not done as I said and closed the Chapin account forever, you will be free to resume your whimsical adventure without fear of any betrayal from us. Do I need to add a recommendation of our discretion and intelligence?"

As Wolfe finished speaking Hibbard unaccountably burst into laughter. For a runt he had a good laugh, deeper than his voice, which was baritone but a little thin. When he had laughed it out he said, "I was thinking that you probably have an adequate bathtub."

"We have."

"But tell me this. I am still learning. If I refused, if I got up now to walk out, what would you do?"

"Well—you see, Mr. Hibbard, it is important to my plans that your discovery should remain unknown until the proper moment. Certain shocks must be administered to Mr. Chapin, and they must be well timed. There are various ways of keeping a desired guest. The most amiable is to persuade him to accept an invitation; another would be to lock him up."

Hibbard nodded. "You see? What did I tell you? You see how people go ahead and do things they feel like doing? Miraculous!"

"It is indeed. And now the bathtub, if we are to dine at eight. Archie, if you would show Mr. Hibbard the south room, the one above mine."

I got up. "It'll be clammy as the devil. It hasn't been used— He can have mine."

"No. Fritz has aired it, and the heat is on; it has been properly prepared, even to brassocattlaelias truffautianas in the bowl."

"Oh." I grinned. "You had it prepared."

"Certainly. Mr. Hibbard. Come down when you are ready. I warn you, I am prepared to demonstrate that the eighth and ninth chapters of *The Chasm of the Mind* are mystic nonsense. If you wish to repel my attack, bring your wits to the table."

I started out with Hibbard, but Wolfe's voice came again and we turned. "You understand the arrangement, sir; you are to communicate with no one whatever. Away from your masquerade, the desire to reassure your niece will be next to irresistible."

"I'll resist it."

Since it was two flights up, I took him to Wolfe's elevator. The door of the south room stood open, and the room was nice and warm. I looked around: the bed had been made, comb and brush and nail file were on the dresser, orchids were in the bowl on the table, fresh towels were in the bathroom. Not bad for a strictly male household. I went out, but at the door was stopped by Hibbard.

"Say. Do you happen to have a dark brown necktie?"

I grinned and went to my room and picked out a genteel solid-color and took it up to him.

Down in the office Wolfe sat with his eyes shut. I went to my desk. I was sore as hell. I was still hearing the tone of Wolfe's voice when he said, "Sixty-five hours," and though I knew the reproach had been for himself and not for me, I didn't need a whack on the shins to inform me that I had made a bad fumble. I sat and considered the general and particular shortcomings of my conduct.

Finally I said aloud, as if to myself, not looking at him, "The one thing I won't ever do again is believe a cripple. It was all because I believed that damn warning. If it hadn't been imbedded in my nut that Andrew Hibbard was dead I would have been receptive to a decent suspicion no matter where it showed up. I suppose that goes for Inspector Cramer too, and I suppose that means that I'm of the same general order as he is. In that case—"

"Archie." I glanced at Wolfe enough to see that he had opened his eyes. He went on. "If that is meant as a defense offered to me, none is needed. If you are merely rubbing your vanity to relieve a soreness, please defer it. There are still eighteen minutes before dinner, and we might as well make use of them. I am suffering from my habitual impatience when nothing remains but the finishing touches. Take your notebook."

I got it out, and a pencil.

"Make three copies of this, the original on the good bond. Date it tomorrow, November eleventh—ha, Armistice Day! Most appropriate. It will have a heading in caps, as follows: CONFESSION OF PAUL CHAPIN REGARDING THE DEATHS OF WILLIAM R. HARRISON AND EUGENE DREYER AND THE WRITING AND DISPATCHING OF CERTAIN INFORMATIVE AND THREATENING VERSES. It is a concession to him to call them verses, but we should be magnanimous somewhere, let us select that for it. There will then be divisions, properly spaced and subheaded. The subheadings will also be in caps. The first one is DEATH OF WILLIAM R. HARRISON. Then begin, thus—"

I interrupted. "Listen, wouldn't it be fitting to type this on the machine from the Harvard Club? Of course it's crummy, but it would be a poetic gesture."

"Poetic? Oh. Sometimes, Archie, the association of your ideas reminds me of a hummingbird. Very well, you may do that. Let us proceed." When he was giving me a document Wolfe usually began slow and speeded up as he went along. He began, "I, Paul Chapin, of Two-o-three Perry Street, New York City, hereby confess that—"

The telephone rang.

I put my notebook down and reached for it. My practice was to answer calls by saying, crisp but friendly, "Hello, this is the office of Nero Wolfe." But this time I didn't get to finish it. I got about three words out, but the rest of it was stopped by an excited voice in my ear, excited but low, nearly a whisper, fast but trying to make it plain.

"Archie, listen. Quick, get it; I may be pulled off. Get up here as fast as you can—Doc Burton's, Ninetieth Street. Burton's croaked. The lop got him with a gat, pumped him full. They got him clean, I followed him—"

There were noises, but no more words. That was enough to last a while, anyway. I hung up and turned to Wolfe. I suppose my face wasn't very placid, but the expression on his didn't change any as he looked at me. I said, "That was Fred Durkin. Paul Chapin has just shot Dr. Burton and killed him—at his apartment on Ninetieth Street. They caught him red-handed. Fred invites me up to see the show."

Wolfe sighed. He murmured, "Nonsense."

"Nonsense, hell. Fred's not a genius, but I never saw him mistake a pinochle game for a murder. He's got good eyes. It looks like tailing Chapin wasn't such a bad idea after all, since it got Fred there on the spot. We've got him—"

"Archie. Shut up." Wolfe's lips were pushing out and in as fast as I had ever seen them. After ten seconds he said, "Consider this, please. Durkin's conversation was interrupted?"

"Yeah, he was pulled off."

"By the police, of course. The police take Chapin for murdering Burton; he is convicted and executed; and where are we? What of our engagements? We are lost."

I stared at him. "Good God. Damn that cripple—"

"Don't damn him. Save him. Save him for us. The roadster is in front? Good. Go there at once, fast. You know what to do; get it, the whole thing. I need the scene, the minutes and seconds, the participants—I need the facts. I need enough of them to save Paul Chapin. Go and get them."

I jumped.

XVII

I KEPT on the West Side as far as Eighty-sixth Street and then shot crosstown and through the park. I stepped on it only up to the limit, because I didn't want to get stopped. I felt pretty good and pretty rotten, both. She had cracked wide open, and I was on my way, and that was all sweetness and light; but on the other hand Fred's story of the event, decorated by Wolfe's comments, looked like nothing but bad weather. I swung left into Fifth Avenue, with only five blocks to go.

I pulled up short of the Burton number on Ninetieth Street, locked the ignition, and jumped to the sidewalk. There were canopies and entrances to big apartment houses all around. I walked east. I was nearly to the entrance I was headed for when I saw Fred Durkin. From somewhere he came trotting toward me. I stopped, and he jerked his head back and started west, and I went along behind him. I followed him to the corner of Fifth, and around it a few feet.

I said, "Am I poison? Spill it."

He said, "I didn't want that doorman to see you with me. He saw me getting the bum's rush. They caught me phoning you and kicked me out."

"That's too bad. I'll complain at headquarters. Well?"

"Well, they've got him, that's all. We followed him up here, the town dick and me, got here at seven-thirty. It was nice and private, without Pinkie. Of course we knew who lived here, and we talked it over whether we ought to phone and decided not to. We decided to go inside the lobby, and when the hall flunkey got unfriendly Murphy—that's the town dick—flashed his badge and shut him up. People were going and coming; there's two elevators. All of a sudden one of the elevator doors bangs open and a woman comes running out, popeyed, and yells, 'Where's Dr. Foster, catch Dr. Foster,' and the hall flunkey says he just saw him go out, and the woman runs for the street, yelling, 'Dr. Foster,' and Murphy nabs her by the arm and asks why not try Dr. Burton, and she looks at him funny and says Dr. Burton's been shot. He turns her loose and jumps for the elevator, and on the way up to the fifth floor discovers that I'm in it with him. He says—"

"Come on, for Christ's sake."

"Okay. The door of Burton's apartment is open. The party's in the first room we go into. Two women is there, one of them whining like a sick dog and jiggling a telephone, and the other one kneeling by a guy laying on the floor. The lop is sitting in a chair, looking like he's waiting his turn in a barber shop. We got busy. The guy was dead. Murphy got on the phone, and I looked around. A gat, a Colt automatic, was on the floor by the leg of a chair next to a table in the middle of the room. I went over and gave Chapin a rub to see if he had any more tools. The woman that was kneeling by the meat began to heave, and I went and got her up and led her away. Two men came in, a doctor and a house guy. Murphy got through on the phone and came over and slipped some irons on Chapin. I stayed with the woman, and when a couple of precinct cops came loping in I took the woman out of the room. The woman that had gone for Dr. Foster came back; she came running through the place and took the other woman away from me and took her off somewhere. I went into another room and saw books and a desk and a telephone, and called you up. One of the precinct men came snooping around and heard me, and that's when I left. He brought me downstairs and gave me the air."

"Who else has come?"

"Only a couple of radios and some more precinct guys."

"Cramer or the D. A.'s office?"

"Not yet. Hell, they don't need to bother. A package like that, they could just have it sent parcel post."

"Yeah. You go to Thirty-fifth Street and tell Fritz to feed you. As soon as Wolfe has finished his dinner, tell him about it. He may want you to get Saul and Orrie—he'll tell you."

"I'll have to phone my wife—"

"Well, you got a nickel? Beat it."

He went downtown, toward Eighty-ninth, and I went around the corner and east again. I approached the entrance; I didn't see any reason why I couldn't crash it, though I didn't know anyone up there. Just as I was under the canopy a big car came along and stopped quick, and two men got out. I took a look, then I got in the way of one of them. I grinned at him.

"Inspector Cramer! This is luck." I started to walk along in with him.

He stopped. "Oh! You. Nothing doing. Beat it."

I started to hand him a line, but he got sharp. "Beat it, Goodwin. If there's anything up there that belongs to you I'll save it for you. Nothing doing."

I fell back. People were gathering, there was already quite a crowd, and a cop was there herding them. In the confusion I was pretty sure he hadn't heard the little passage between Cramer and me. I faded away and went to where I had parked the roadster. I opened up the back and got out a black bag I kept a few things in for emergencies; it didn't look just right, but good enough. I went back to the entrance and pushed through the line while the cop was busy on the other side, and got through the door. Inside were the doorman and another cop. I stepped up to them and said, "Medical Examiner. What apartment is it?" The cop looked me over and took me to the elevator and said to the boy, "Take this gent to the fifth floor." Inside, going up, I gave the black bag a pat.

I breezed into the apartment. As Durkin had said, the party was right there, the first room you entered, a big reception hall. There was a mob there, mostly flatfeet and dicks standing around looking bored. Inspector Cramer was by the table, listening to one of the latter. I walked over to him and said his name.

He looked around and seemed surprised. "Well, in the name of—"

"Now listen, Inspector. Just a second. Forget it. I'm not going to steal the prisoner or the evidence or anything else. You know damn well I've got a right to curiosity, and that's all I expect to satisfy. Have a heart. My God, we've all got mothers."

"What have you got in that bag?"

"Shirts and socks. I used it to bring me up. I'd just as soon have one of your men take it down to my car for me."

He grunted. "Leave it here on the table, and if you get in the way—"

"I won't. Much obliged."

Being careful not to bump anyone, I got back against the wall. I took a look. It was a room seventeen by twenty, on a guess, nearly square. One end was mostly windows, curtained. At the other end was the entrance door. One long wall, the one I was standing against, had pictures and a couple of stands with vases of flowers. In the other wall, nearly to the corner, was a double door, closed, leading of course to the apartment proper. The rest of that wall, about ten feet of it, had curtains to match those at the end, but there couldn't have been windows. I figured it was closets for wraps. The light was from the ceiling, indirect, with switches at the double door and the entrance door. There was one large rug, and a good-sized table in the middle. Near where I stood was a stand with a telephone and a chair.

There were only four chairs altogether. In one of them, at the end of the table, Paul Chapin was sitting. I couldn't see his face; he was turned wrong. At the other end of the table Doc Burton was on the floor. He just looked dead and fairly comfortable; either he had landed straight when he fell, or someone had stretched him out, and his arms were neatly along his sides. His head was at a funny angle, but they always are until they're propped up. Looking at him, I thought to myself that Wolfe had had him down for seven thousand bucks, and now he'd never have that to worry about again, along with a lot of other things. From where I was I couldn't see much blood.

A few details had happened since I arrived. There had been phone calls. One of the dicks had gone out and come back in a couple of minutes with an Assistant Medical Examiner; apparently there had been difficulty downstairs. I hoped he wouldn't take my bag by mistake when he went. They buzzed around. Inspector Cramer had left the room by the double door—to see the women, I supposed. A young woman came in from outside and made a scene, but all in all she did pretty well with it, since it appeared that it was her father that had been croaked. She had been out somewhere, and she took it hard. I've often observed that the only thing that makes it a real hardship to have dealings with stiffs is the people that are still living. This girl was the kind that makes your throat clog up because you see how she's straining to fight it back in and you know she's licked. I was glad when a dick took her away, in to her mother.

I moseyed around to get a slant at the cripple. I went around the table and got in front of him. He looked at me, but there wasn't any sign of his being aware he had ever seen me before. His stick was on the table beside him, and his hat. He had on a brown overcoat, unbuttoned, and tan gloves. He was slouched over; his hands were resting on his good knee, fastened with the bracelets. There was nothing in his face, just nothing; he looked more like a passenger in the subway than anything else. His light-colored eyes looked straight at me. I thought to myself that this was the first piece of real hundred-percent bad luck I had ever known Nero Wolfe to have. He had had his share of bad breaks all right, but this wasn't a break, it was an avalanche.

Then I remembered what I was there for, and I said to myself that I had gone around for two days pretending to hunt Andrew Hibbard, knowing all the time it was hopeless, and Hibbard was at that moment eating scallops and arguing psychology with Wolfe. And until Wolfe himself said finish for that case one way or the other, hopeless was out. It was up to me to dig up a little hope.

I got against the wall again and surveyed the field. The medical guy was done. There was no telling how long Cramer would be with the women, but unless their tale was more complicated than it seemed likely to be there was no reason why it should be very long. When he returned there would probably be no delay in removing the stiff and the cripple, and then there would be nothing to keep anybody else. Cramer wouldn't be apt to go off and leave me behind; he'd want me for company. Nor could I see any reason why he would leave anyone behind, except a dick out in the hall maybe, and possibly one downstairs, to keep annoyance away from the family.

That was the way it looked. I couldn't go back to Wolfe with nothing but a sob story about a poor cripple and a dead man and a grief-stricken daughter. I wandered around again to the other side of the table, to the other wall where the curtains were. I stood with my back to the curtains. Then I saw my bag on the table. That wouldn't do, so I went over and got it, casually, and went back against the curtains again. I figured the chances were about fifty to one against me, but the worst I could get was an escort to the elevator. Keeping my eyes carelessly on the array of dicks and flatfeet scattered around, I felt behind me with my foot and found that back of the curtains the floor continued flush, with no sill. If it was a closet it was built into the wall, and I had no idea how deep it was or what was in there. I kept my eyes busy; I had to pick an instant when every guy there had his face turned, at least not right on me. I was waiting for something, and luck came that time; it happened. The phone rang, on the stand by the other wall. Having nothing to occupy them, they all turned involuntarily. I had my hand behind me, ready to pull the curtain aside, and back I went, and let the curtain fall again, with me behind.

I had ducked going in, in case there happened to be a hat shelf at the usual height, but the shelf was farther back; the closet was all of three feet deep and I had plenty of room. I held my breath for a few seconds, but heard none of the bloodhounds baying. I eased the black bag onto the floor in a corner and got behind what felt like a woman's fur coat. One thing there had been no help for: the cripple had seen me. His light-colored eyes had been right at me as I backed in. If he should decide to open his trap I hoped he would find something else to talk about.

I stood there in the dark, and after a while wished I had remembered to bring an oxygen tank. To amuse me I had the voices of the dicks outside, but they were low and I couldn't pick out many words. Somebody came in, some woman, and a little later a man. It was all of half an hour before Cramer returned. I heard the double door opening, close to my curtain, and then Cramer handing out orders. He sounded snappy and satisfied. A dick with a hoarse voice told another one, right in front of me, to carry Chapin's stick and he'd help him walk; they were taking him away. There were noises, and directions from Cramer about removing the corpse, and in a couple of minutes heavy feet as they carried it out. I was hoping to God that Cramer or someone else hadn't happened to hang his coat in my closet, but that wasn't likely; there had been three or four piled on the table. I heard a voice telling someone to go ask for a rug to put over the soiled place where Burton had been, and Cramer and others shoving off. It sounded like there were only two left, after the guy came back with the rug; they were kidding each other about some kind of a girl. I began to be afraid Cramer had spotted them to stay for some reason or other, but pretty soon I heard them going to the door, and it opened and closed.

I'd been in the closet long enough as far as my lungs were concerned, but I thought it was just possible one was still inside the main apartment, and I waited five minutes, counting. Then I pulled the edge of the curtain a little and took a slant. I opened it up and stepped out. Empty. All gone. The double doors were closed. I went over and turned the knob and pushed, and walked through. I was in a room about five times the size of the reception hall, dimly lighted, furnished up to the hilt. There was a door at the far end and a wide-open arch halfway down one side. I heard voices from somewhere.

I went on in a ways and called, "Hello! Mrs. Burton!"

The voices stopped, and there were footsteps coming. A guy appeared in the arch, trying to look important. I grinned inside. He was just a kid, around twenty-two, nice and handsome and dressed up. He said, "We thought you had all gone."

"Yeah. All but me. I have to see Mrs. Burton."

"But he said—the inspector said she wouldn't be bothered."

"I'm sorry, I have to see her."

"She's lying down."

"Tell her just a few questions."

He opened his mouth and shut it, looked as if he thought he ought to do something, and turned and beat it. In a minute he came back and nodded me along. I followed.

We went through a room and a sort of a hall and into another room. This was not so big, but was better lit and not so dolled up. A maid in uniform was going out another door with a tray. A woman was sitting on a couch, another woman in a chair, and the daughter I had seen in the reception hall was standing behind the couch. I walked over there.

I suppose Mrs. Loring A. Burton wasn't at her best that evening, but she could have slipped a few more notches and still have been in the money. A glance was enough to show you she was quite a person. She had a straight, thin nose, a warm mouth, fine dark eyes. Her hair was piled in braids at the back, pulled back just right for you to see her temples and brow, which maybe made most of the effect—that and the way she held her head. Her neck knew some artist's trick that I've seen many a movie star try to copy without quite getting it. It had been born in her spine.

With her head up like that I could see it would take more than a murdered husband to overwhelm her into leaving decisions to daughters and so on, so I disregarded the others. I told her I had a few confidential questions to ask and I'd like to see her alone. The woman in the chair muttered something about cruel and unnecessary. The daughter stared at me with red eyes.

Mrs. Burton asked, "Confidential to whom?"

"To Paul Chapin. I'd rather not—" I looked around.

She looked around too. I saw that the kid wasn't the son and heir after all, it was the daughter he was interested in, probably had it signed up. Mrs. Burton said, "What does it matter? Go to my room— you don't mind, Alice?"

The woman in the chair said she didn't, and got up. The kid took hold of the daughter's arm to steer her; by golly, he wasn't going to let her fall and hurt herself. They went on out.

Mrs. Burton said, "Well?"

I said, "The confidential part is really about me. Do you know who Nero Wolfe is?"

"Nero Wolfe? Yes."

"Dr. Burton and his friends entered into an agreement—"

She interrupted me. "I know all about it. My husband—" She stopped. The way she suddenly clasped her fingers tight and tried to keep her lips from moving showed that a bust-up was nearer to coming through than I had supposed. But she soon got it shoved under again. "My husband told me all about it."

I nodded. "That saves time. I'm not a city detective, I'm private. I work for Nero Wolfe; my name's Goodwin. If you ask me what I'm here for there's lots of ways to answer you, but you'd have to help me pick the right one. It depends on how you feel." I had the innocence turned on, the candid eye. I was talking fast. "Of course you feel terrible, certainly, but no matter how bad it is inside of you right now, you'll go on living. I've got some questions to ask for Nero Wolfe, and I can't be polite and wait for a week until your nerves have had a chance to grow some new skin, I've got to ask them now or never. I'm here now; just tell me this and get rid of me. Did you see Paul Chapin shoot your husband?"

"No. But I've already—"

"Sure. Let's get it done. Did anybody see him?"

"No."

I took a breath. At least, then, we weren't floating with our bellies up. I said, "All right. Then it's a question of how you feel. How you feel about this, for instance—that Paul Chapin didn't shoot your husband at all."

She stared at me. "What do you mean? I saw him—"

"You didn't see him shoot. Here's what I'm getting at, Mrs. Burton. I know your husband didn't hate Paul Chapin. I know he felt sorry for him and was willing to go with the crowd because he saw no help for it. How about you, did you hate him? Disregard what happened tonight. How much did you hate him?"

For a second I thought I had carried her along; then I saw a change coming in her eyes and her lips beginning to tighten up. She was going to ritz me out.

I rushed in ahead of it. "Listen, Mrs. Burton, I'm not just a smart pup nosing around somebody's back yard, seeing what I can smell. I really know all about this, maybe even some things you don't know. Right now, in a cabinet down in Nero Wolfe's office, there is a leather box. I put it there—this big. It's beautiful tan leather, with fine gold tooling on it, and it's locked, and it's full nearly to the top with your gloves and stockings—some you've worn. Now wait a minute, give me a chance. It belongs to Paul Chapin. Dora Ritter hooked them and gave them to him. It's his treasure. Nero Wolfe says his soul is in that box. I wouldn't know about that, I'm no expert on souls. I'm just telling you. The reason I want to know whether you hate Paul Chapin, regardless of his killing your husband, is this: what if he didn't kill him? Would you like to see them hang it on him anyway?"

She was looking at me, with the idea of ritzing me out put aside for the moment. She said, "I don't know what you're driving at. I saw him dead. I don't know what you mean."

"Neither do I. That's what I'm here to find out. I'm trying to make you understand that I'm not annoying you just for curiosity, I'm here on business, and it may turn out to be your business as well as mine. I'm interested in seeing that Paul Chapin gets no more than is coming to him. Right now I don't suppose you're interested in anything. You've had a shock that would lay most women flat. Well, you're not flat, and you might as well talk to me as sit and try not to think about it. I'd like to sit here and ask you a few things. If you look like you are going to faint I'll call the family and get up and go."

She unclasped her hands. She said, "I don't faint. You may sit down."

"Okay." I used the chair Alice had left. "Now tell me how it happened—the shooting. Who was here?"

"My husband and I, and the cook and the maid. One of the maids was out."

"No one else? What about the woman you called Alice?"

"That is my oldest friend. She came to—just a little while ago. There was no one else here."

"And?"

"I was in my room, dressing. We were dining out; my daughter was out somewhere. My husband came to my room for a cigarette; he always—he never remembered to have any, and the door between our rooms is always open. The maid came and said Paul Chapin was there. My husband left to go to the foyer to see him, but he didn't go direct; he went back through his room and his study. I mention that because I stood and listened. The last time Paul had come my husband had told the maid to keep him in the foyer, and before he went there he had gone to his study and got a revolver out of the drawer. I had thought it was childish. This time I listened to see if he did it again, and he did; I heard the drawer opening. Then he called to me, called my name, and I answered, 'What is it?' and he called back, nothing, never mind, he would tell me after he had speeded his guest. That was the last—those were his last words I heard. I heard him walking through the apartment—I listened, I suppose, because I was wondering what Paul could want. Then I heard noises—not loud, the foyer is so far away from my room—and then shots. I ran. The maid came out of the dining room and followed me. We ran to the foyer. It was dark, and the light in the drawing room was dim and we couldn't see anything. I heard a noise, someone falling, and Paul's voice saying my name. I turned on the light switch, and Paul was there on his knee, trying to get up. He said my name again, and said he was trying to hop to the switch. Then I saw Lorry, on the floor at the end of the table. I ran to him, and when I saw him I called to the maid to go for Dr. Foster, who lives a floor below us. I don't know what Paul did then; I didn't pay any attention to him; the first I knew some men came—"

"All right, hold it."

She stopped. I looked at her a minute, getting it. She had clasped her hands again and was doing some extra breathing, but not obtrusively. I quit worrying about her. I took out a pad and pencil and said, "This thing, the way you tell it, needs a lot of fixing. The worst item, of course, is the light being out. That's plain silly. Now wait a minute, I'm just talking about what Nero Wolfe calls a feeling for phenomena; I'm trying to enjoy one. Let's go back to the beginning. On his way to see Paul Chapin, your husband called to you from the study, and then said never mind. Have you any idea what he was going to say?"

"No, how could I—"

"Okay. The way you told it, he called to you after he opened the drawer. Was that the way it was?"

She nodded. "I'm sure it was after I heard the drawer open. I was listening."

"Yeah. Then you heard him walking to the foyer, and then you heard noises. What kind of noises?"

"I don't know. Just noises, movements. It is far away, and doors were closed. The noises were faint."

"Voices?"

"No. I didn't hear any."

"Did you hear your husband closing the foyer door after he got there?"

"No. I wouldn't hear that unless it banged."

"Then we'll try this. Since you were listening to his footsteps, even if you couldn't hear them any more after he got into the drawing room, there was a moment when you figured that he had reached the foyer. You know what I mean—the feeling that he was there. When I say 'Now,' that will mean that he has just reached the foyer, and you begin feeling the time, the passing of time. Feel it as near the same as you can, and when it's time for the first shot to go off, you say, 'Now.' Get it? *Now.*"

I looked at the second hand of my watch; it went crawling up from the 30. She said, "*Now.*"

I stared at her. "My God, that was only six seconds."

She nodded. "It was as short as that; I'm sure it was."

"In that case—all right. Then you ran to the foyer, and there was no light there. Of course you couldn't be wrong about that."

"No. The light was off."

"And you switched it on and saw Chapin kneeling, getting up. Did he have a gun in his hand?"

"No. He had his coat and gloves on. I didn't see a gun—anywhere."

"Did Inspector Cramer tell you about the gun?"

She nodded. "It was my husband's. He shot—it had been fired four times. They found it on the floor."

"Cramer showed it to you."

"Yes."

"And it's gone from the drawer in the study."

"Of course."

"When you turned on the light Chapin was saying something."

"He was saying my name. After the light was on he said—I can tell you exactly what he said. 'Anne, a cripple in the dark, my dear Anne; I was trying to hop to the switch.' He had fallen."

"Yeah. Naturally." I finished scratching on the pad and looked up at her. She was sitting tight. I said, "Now to go back again. Were you at home all afternoon?"

"No. I was at a gallery, looking at prints, and then at a tea. I got home around six."

"Was your husband here when you got here?"

"Yes, he comes early—on Saturday. He was in his study with Ferdinand Bowen. I went in to say hello. We always—said hello, no matter who was here."

"So Mr. Bowen was here. Do you know what for?"

"No. That is— No."

"Now come, Mrs. Burton. You've decided to put up with this, and it's pretty swell of you, so come ahead. What was Bowen here for?"

"He was asking a favor. That's all I know."

"A financial favor?"

"I suppose so, yes."

"Did he get it?"

"No. But this has no connection—no more of this."

"Okay. When did Bowen leave?"

"Soon after I arrived; I should say a quarter past six—perhaps twenty after; it was about ten minutes before Dora came, and she was punctual at six-thirty."

"You don't say so." I looked at her. "You mean Dora Chapin."

"Yes."

"She came to do your hair."

"Yes."

"I'll be damned. Excuse me. Nero Wolfe doesn't permit me to swear in front of ladies. And Dora Chapin got here at six-thirty. Well. When did she leave?"

"It always takes her three-quarters of an hour, so she left at a quarter past seven." She paused to calculate. "Yes, that would be right. A few minutes later, perhaps. I figured that I had fifteen minutes to finish dressing."

"So Dora Chapin left here at seven-twenty, and Paul Chapin arrived at half-past. That's interesting; they almost collided. Who else was here after six o'clock?"

"No one. That's all. My daughter left around half-past six, a little before Dora came. Of course I don't understand— What is it, Alice?"

A door had opened behind me, and I turned to see. It was the woman, the old friend. She said, "Nick Cabot is on the phone—they notified him. He wants to know if you want to talk to him."

Mrs. Burton's dark eyes flashed aside for an instant, at me. I let my head go sideways enough for her to see it. She spoke to her friend, "No, there is nothing to say. I won't talk to anyone. Are you folks finding something to eat?"

"We'll make out. Really, Anne, I think—"

"Please, Alice. Please—"

After a pause the door closed again. I had a grin inside, a little cocky. I said, "You started to say, something you don't understand . . ."

She didn't go on. She sat looking at me with a frown in her eyes but her brow smooth and white. She got up and went to a table, took a cigarette from a box and lit it, and picked up an ashtray. She came back to the couch and sat down and took a couple of whiffs. Then she looked at the cigarette as if wondering where it had come from, and crushed it dead on the tray and set the tray down. She straightened up and seemed to remember I was looking at her. She spoke suddenly. "What did you say your name is?"

"Archie Goodwin."

"Thank you. I should know your name. Strange things can happen, can't they? Why did you tell me not to talk to Mr. Cabot?"

"No special reason. Right now I don't want you to be talking to anybody but me."

She nodded. "And I'm doing it. Mr. Goodwin, you're not much over half my age, and I never saw you before. You seem to be clever.

You realized, I suppose, what the shock of seeing my husband dead, shot dead, has done to me. It has shaken things loose. I am doing something very remarkable, for me. I don't usually talk below the surface. I never have, since childhood, except with two people—my husband, my dear husband, and Paul Chapin. But we aren't talking about my husband; there's nothing to say about him. He's dead. He is dead—I shall have to tell myself many times—he is dead. He wants to go on living in me, or I want him to. I think—this is what I am really saying—I think I would want Paul to. Oh, it's impossible!" She jerked herself up, and her hands got clasped again. "It's absurd to try to talk about this—even to a stranger—and with Lorry dead—absurd."

I said, "Maybe it's absurd not to. Let it crack open once; spill it out."

She shook her head. "There's nothing to crack open. There's no reason why I should want to talk about it, but I do. Otherwise why should I let you question me? I saw farther inside myself this evening than I have ever seen before. It wasn't when I saw my husband dead; it wasn't when I stood alone in my room, looking at a picture of him, trying to realize he was dead. It was sitting here with that police inspector, with him telling me that a plea of guilty is not accepted in first-degree murder, and that I would have to talk with a representative of the District Attorney, and would have to testify in court so that Paul Chapin can be convicted and punished. I don't want him punished. My husband is dead, isn't that enough? And if I don't want him punished, what is it I want to hold on to? Is it pity? I have never pitied him. I have been pretty insolent with life, but not insolent enough to pity Paul Chapin. You told me that he has a box filled with my gloves and stockings which Dora stole from me, and that Nero Wolfe said it holds his soul. Perhaps my soul has been put away in a box too, and I didn't even know it."

She got up, abruptly. The ashtray slid off the couch to the floor. She stooped over and, with deliberate fingers that showed no sign of trembling, picked up the burned matchstick and the cigarette and put them on the tray. I didn't move to help her. She went to the table with the tray and then came back to the couch and sat down again.

She said, "I have always disliked Paul Chapin. Once, when I was eighteen years old, I promised to marry him. When I learned of his accident, that he was crippled for life, I was delighted because I wouldn't have to keep my promise. I didn't know that then, but I realized it later. At no time have I pitied him. I claim no originality in that; I think no woman has ever pitied him, only men. Women do not like him—even those who have been briefly fascinated by him. I dislike him intensely. I have thought about this; I have had occasion to analyze it; it is his deformity that is intolerable—not his physical deformity, the deformity of his nervous system, of his brain. You have heard of feminine cunning, but you don't understand it as Paul does, for he has it himself. It is a hateful quality in a man. Women have been fascinated by it, but the two or three who surrendered to it—I not among them, not even at eighteen—got only contempt for a reward."

"He married Dora Ritter. She's a woman?"

"Oh yes, Dora's a woman. But she is consecrated to a denial of her womanhood. I am fond of her, I understand her. She knows what beauty is, and she sees herself. That forced her, long ago, to the denial, and her strength of will has maintained it. Paul understood her too. He married her to show his contempt for me; he told me so. He could risk it with Dora because she might be relied upon never to embarrass him with the only demand that he would find humiliating. And as for Dora—she hates him, but she would die for him. Fiercely and secretly, against her denial, she longed for the dignity of marriage, and it was a miracle of luck that Paul offered it under the only circumstances that could make it acceptable to her. Oh, they understand each other!"

I said, "She hates him, and she married him."

"Yes. Dora could do that."

"I'm surprised she was here today. I understood she had a bad accident Wednesday morning. I saw her. She seems to have some character."

"It could be called that. Dora is insane. Legally, I suppose not, but nevertheless she is insane. Paul has told her so many times. She tells me about it, in the same tone she uses for the weather. There are two things she can't bear the thought of: that any woman should suspect her of being capable of tenderness, or that any man should regard her as a woman at all. Her character comes from her indifference to everything else, except Paul Chapin."

"She bragged to Nero Wolfe that she was married."

"Of course. It removes her from the field. Oh, it is impossible to laugh at her, and you can't pity her any more than you can Paul. A monkey might as well pity me because I haven't got a tail."

I said, "You were talking about your soul."

"Was I? Yes. To you, Mr. Goodwin. I could not speak about it to my friend Alice—I tried but nothing came. Wasn't I saying that I don't want Paul Chapin punished? Perhaps that's wrong, perhaps I do want him punished, but not crudely by killing him. What have I in my mind? What is in my heart? God knows. But I started to answer your questions when you said something—something about his punishment."

I nodded. "I said he shouldn't get more than is coming to him. Of course to you it looks open and shut, and apparently it looks the same way to the cops. You heard shots and ran to the foyer, and there it was, a live man and a dead man and a gun. And of course Inspector Cramer has already got the other fixings—for instance, the motive, all dressed up and its shoes shined, not to mention a willingness to even up with Chapin for certain inconveniences he has been put to. But, as Nero Wolfe says, a nurse that pushes the perambulator in the park without putting the baby in it has missed the point. Maybe if I look around I'll find the baby. For example, Dora Chapin left here at seven-twenty. Chapin arrived at seven-thirty, ten minutes later. What if she waited in the hall outside and came back in with him? Or if she couldn't do that because the maid let him in, he could have opened the door for her while the maid was gone to tell Dr. Burton. She could have snatched the gun from Burton's pocket and done the shooting and beat it before you could get there. That might explain the light being out; she might have flipped the switch before she opened the outer door so if anyone happened to be passing in the outside hall they couldn't see in. You say she hates Chapin. Maybe to him it was entirely unexpected; he had no idea what she was up to—"

She was shaking her head. "I don't believe that. It's possible, but I don't believe it."

"You say she's crazy."

"No. As far as Dora could like any man, she liked Lorry. She wouldn't do that."

"Not to make a reservation for Chapin in the electric chair?"

Mrs. Burton looked at me, and a little shudder ran over her. She said, "That's no better—than the other. That's horrible."

"Of course it's horrible. Whatever we pull out of this bag, it won't be a pleasant surprise for anyone concerned, except maybe Chapin.

I ought to mention another possibility: Dr. Burton shot himself. He turned the light out so Chapin couldn't see what he was doing in time to let out a yell that might have given it away. That's horrible too, but it's quite possible."

That didn't seem to discompose her as much as my first guess. She merely said calmly, "No, Mr. Goodwin. It might be barely conceivable that Lorry wanted—had some reason to kill himself without my knowing it, but that he would try to put the guilt on Paul—on anyone—no, that isn't even possible."

"Okay. You said it yourself a while ago, Mrs. Burton; strange things can happen. But as far as that's concerned, anyone at all might have done it—anyone who could get into that foyer and who knew Chapin was there and that Dr. Burton would come. By the way, what about the maid that's out this evening? Does she have a key? What's she like?"

"Yes, she has a key. She is fifty-six years old, has been with us nine years, and calls herself the housekeeper. You would waste time asking about her."

"I could still be curious about her key."

"She will have it when she comes in the morning. You may see her then if you wish."

"Thanks. Now the other maid. Could I see her now?"

She got up and went to the table and pushed a button and took another cigarette and lit it. I noticed that with her back turned you could have taken her for twenty, except for the coil of hair. But she was slumping a little; as she stood her shoulders sagged. She pulled them up again and turned and came back to the couch, as the inner door opened and the whole outfit appeared: cook, maid, friend Alice, daughter, and boy friend. The cook was carrying a tray.

Mrs. Burton said, "Thank you, Henny, not now. Don't try it again, please don't. I really couldn't swallow. And the rest of you—if you don't mind—we wish to see Rose a few minutes. Just Rose."

"But Mother, really—"

"No, dear. Please, just a few minutes. Johnny, this is very nice of you. I appreciate it very much. Come here, Rose."

The kid blushed. "Aw, don't mention it, Mrs. Burton."

They faded back through the door. The maid came and stood in front of us and tried some swallowing which didn't seem to work. Her face looked quite peculiar because it intended to be sympathetic but she was too shocked and scared, and it would have been fairly peculiar at any time with its broad flat nose and plucked eyebrows. Mrs. Burton told her I wanted to ask her some questions, and she looked at me as if she had been informed that I was going to sell her down the river. Then she stared at the pad on my knee and looked even worse.

I said, "Rose, I know exactly what's in your mind. You're thinking that the other man wrote down your answers to his questions and now I'm going to do the same, and then we'll compare them and if they're not alike we'll take you to the top of the Empire State Building and throw you off. Forget that silly stuff. Come on, forget it. By the way"—I turned to Mrs. Burton—"does Dora Chapin have a key to the apartment?"

"No."

"Okay. Rose, did you go to the door when Dora Chapin came this evening?"

"Yes, sir."

"You let her in, and she was alone."

"Yes, sir."

"When she left did you let her out?"

"No, sir. I never do. Mrs. Kurtz don't either. She just went."

"Where were you when she went?"

"I was in the dining room. I was there a long while. We weren't serving dinner, and I was dusting the glasses in there."

"Then I suppose you didn't let Mr. Bowen out either. That was the man—"

"Yes, sir, I know Mr. Bowen. No, I didn't let him out, but that was a long time before."

"I know. All right, you let nobody out. Let's go back to in. You answered the door when Mr. Chapin came."

"Yes, sir."

"Was he alone?"

"Yes, sir."

"You opened the door, and he came in, and you shut the door again."

"Yes, sir."

"Now see if you can remember this. It doesn't matter much if you can't, but maybe you can. What did Mr. Chapin say to you?"

She looked at me, and aside at Mrs. Burton, and down at the floor.

At first I thought maybe she was trying to fix up a fake for an answer; then I saw that she was just bewildered at the terrible complexity of the problem I had confronted her with by asking her a question that couldn't be answered "yes" or "no." I said, "Come on, Rose. You know, Mr. Chapin came in, and you took his hat and coat, and he said—"

She looked up. "I didn't take his hat and coat. He kept his coat on, and his gloves. He said to tell Dr. Burton he was there."

"Did he stand there by the door or did he walk to a chair to sit down?"

"I don't know. I think he would sit down. I think he came along behind me, but he came slow, and I came back in to tell Dr. Burton."

"Was the light turned on in the foyer when you left there?"

"Yes, sir. Of course."

"After you told Dr. Burton, where did you go?"

"I went back to the dining room."

"Where was the cook?"

"In the kitchen. She was there all the time."

"Where was Mrs. Burton?"

"She was in her room, dressing—wasn't you, madam?"

I grinned. "Sure she was. I'm just getting all of you placed. Did Dr. Burton go to the foyer right away?"

She nodded. "Well—maybe not right away. He went pretty soon. I was in the dining room and heard him go by the door."

"Okay." I got up from my chair. "Now I'm going to ask you to do something. I suppose I shouldn't tell you it's important, but it is. You go to the dining room and start taking down the glasses, or whatever you were doing after you told Dr. Burton. I'll walk past the dining-room door and on to the foyer. Was Dr. Burton going fast or slow?"

She shook her head and her lip began to quiver. "He was just going."

"All right, I'll just go. You hear me go by, and you decide when enough time has passed for the first shot to go off. When the time has come for the first shot, you yell, 'Now,' loud enough for me to hear you in the foyer. Do you understand? First you'd better tell—"

I stopped on account of her lip. It was getting into high. I snapped at her, "Come on out of that. Take a look at Mrs. Burton and learn how to behave yourself. You're doing this for her. Come on now."

She clamped her lips together and held them that way while she swallowed twice. Then she opened them to say, "The shots all came together."

"All right, say they did. You yell, 'Now,' when the time comes. First you'd better go and tell the people inside that you're going to yell or they'll be running out here—"

Mrs. Burton interposed, "I'll tell them. Rose, take Mr. Goodwin to the study and show him how to go."

She was quite a person, that Mrs. Burton. I was getting so I liked her. Maybe her soul was put away in a box somewhere, but other items of her insides, meaning guts, were all where they ought to be. If I was the kind that collected things I wouldn't have minded having one of her gloves myself.

Rose and I went out. Apparently she avoided the bedrooms by taking me around by a side hall, for we entered the study direct from that. She showed me how to go, by another door, and left me there. I looked around: books, leather chairs, radio, smoke stands, and a flat-top desk by a window. There was the drawer, of course, where the gat had been kept. I went over to it and pulled it open and shut it again. Then I went out by the other door and followed directions. I struck a medium pace, past the dining-room door, across the central hall, through a big room, and from that through the drawing room; got my eye on my watch, opened the door into the foyer, went in and closed it.

It was a good thing the folks had been warned, for Rose yelling, "Now," so I could hear it sounded even to me, away off in the foyer, like the last scream of doom. I went back in faster than I had come, for fear she might try it again. She had beat it back to the room where Mrs. Burton was. When I entered she was standing by the couch with her face white as a sheet, looking seasick. Mrs. Burton was reaching up to pat her arm. I went over and sat down.

I said, "I almost didn't get there. Two seconds at the most. Of course she rushed it, but it shows it must have been quick. Okay, Rose. I won't ask you to do any more yelling. You're a good, brave girl. Just a couple more questions. When you heard the shots you ran to the foyer with Mrs. Burton. Is that right?"

"Yes, sir."

"What did you see when you got there?"

"I didn't see anything. It was dark."

"What did you hear?"

"I heard something on the floor, and then I heard Mr. Chapin saying Mrs. Burton's name, and then the light went on and I saw him."

"What was he doing?"

"He was trying to get up."

"Did he have a gun in his hand?"

"No, sir. I'm sure he didn't because he had his hands on the floor, getting up."

"And then you saw Dr. Burton."

"Yes, sir." She swallowed. "I saw him after Mrs. Burton went to him."

"What did you do then?"

"Well—I stood there, I guess. Then Mrs. Burton told me to go for Dr. Foster, and I ran out and ran downstairs, and they told me Dr. Foster had just left, and I went to the elevator—"

"Okay, hold it."

I looked back over my notes. Mrs. Burton was patting Rose's arm again, and Rose was looking at her with her lip ready to sag. My watch said five minutes till eleven; I had been in that room nearly two hours. There was one thing I hadn't gone into at all, but it might not be needed, and in any event it could wait. I had got enough to sleep on. But as I flipped the pages of my pad there was another point that occurred to me which I thought ought to be attended to.

I put the pad and pencil in my pocket and looked at Mrs. Burton. "That's all for Rose. It's all for me too, except if you would just tell Rose—"

She looked up at the maid and nodded at her. "You'd better go to bed, Rose. Good night."

"Oh, Mrs. Burton—"

"All right now. You heard Mr. Goodwin say you're a brave girl. Go and get some sleep."

The maid gave me a look, not any too friendly, looked again at her mistress, and turned and went. As soon as the door had closed behind her I got up from my chair.

I said, "I'm going, but there's one more thing. I've got to ask a favor of you. You'll have to take my word for it that Nero Wolfe's interest in this business is the same as yours. I'm telling you that straight. You don't want Paul Chapin to burn in the electric chair for killing your husband, and neither does he. I don't know what his next move will be, that's up to him, but it's likely he'll need some kind of standing. For instance, if he wants to ask Inspector Cramer to let him see the gun he'll have to give a better reason than idle curiosity. I can't quite see Paul Chapin engaging him, but how about you? If we could say we were acting on a commission from you it would make things simple. Of course there wouldn't be any fee, even if we did something you wanted done. If you want me to I'll put that in writing."

I looked at her. Her head was still up, but the signs of a flop were in her eyes and at the corners of her mouth. I said to her, "I'm going. I won't stay and bark at you about this, just say yes or no. If you don't lie down somewhere and relax, let it go ahead and bust, you'll be doing another kind of relaxing. What about it?"

She shook her head. I thought she was saying no to me, but then she spoke—though this didn't sound as if it was directed at me any more than the headshake. "I loved my husband, Mr. Goodwin. Oh yes, I loved him. I sometimes disapproved of things he did. He disapproved of things I did, more often—though he seldom said so. He would disapprove of what I am doing now—I think he would. He would say, let fate do her job. He would say that as he so often said it—gallantly—and about Paul Chapin too. He is dead. Oh yes, he is dead—but let him live enough to say that now, and let me live enough to say what I always said: I will not keep my hand from any job if I think it's mine. He would not want me to make any new concessions to him, dead." She rose to her feet abruptly, and abruptly added, "And even if he wanted me to I doubt if I could. Good night, Mr. Goodwin." She held out her hand.

I took it. I said, "Maybe I get you, but I like plain words. Nero Wolfe can say he is acting in your behalf, is that it?"

She nodded. I turned and left the room.

In the foyer I took a glance around as I got my hat and coat from the table and put them on. I took the black bag from the closet. When I opened the door I gave the lock an inspection and saw it was the usual variety in houses of that class, the kind where you can press a button countersunk in the edge of the door to free the cylinder. I tried it and it worked. I heard a noise in the hall and stepped out and shut the door behind me. There, sitting in a chair, twisting the hide on his neck to see who had been monkeying with the door but not bothering to get up, was the snoop Cramer had left to protect the family from annoyance, as I had suspected he would.

I started pulling on my gloves. I said to him, friendly and brisk, "Thank you, my man, I assure you we appreciate this," and went on to the elevator.

XVIII

AT TWO O'CLOCK that night—Sunday morning—I sat at my desk in the office and yawned. Wolfe, behind his own desk, was looking at a schedule I had typed out for him, keeping a carbon for myself, during one of the intervals in my report when he had called time out to do a little arranging in his mind. The schedule looked like this:

> 6:05 Mrs. Burton arrives home. Present in apartment: Burton, daughter, Bowen, maid, cook.
> 6:20 Bowen leaves.
> 6:25 Daughter leaves.
> 6:30 Dora Chapin arrives.
> 7:20 Dora leaves.
> 7:30 Paul Chapin arrives.
> 7:33 Burton is shot.
> 7:50 Fred Durkin phones.

I looked at my carbon and yawned. Fritz had kept some squirrel stew hot for me, and it had long since been put away, with a couple of rye highballs because the black sauce Fritz used for squirrel made milk taste like stale olive juice. After I had imparted a few of the prominent details without saying how I had got hold of them, Wolfe had explained to Hibbard that it is the same with detectives as with magicians, their primary and constant concern is to preserve the air of mystery which is attached to their profession, and Hibbard had gone up to bed. The development that had arrived over the telephone while he was taking his bath had changed his world. He had eaten no dinner to speak of, though the need to chaperon the gold leaf on his teeth had departed. He had insisted on phoning fifty or sixty people, beginning with his niece, and had been restrained only by some tall talk about his word of honor. In fact, that question seemed not entirely closed, for Wolfe had had Fritz cut the wire of the telephone which was in Hibbard's room. Now he was up there, maybe asleep, maybe doping out a psychological detour around words of honor. I had gone on and given Wolfe the story, every crumb I had, and there had been discussions.

I threw the carbon onto the desk and did some more yawning. Finally Wolfe said, "You understand, Archie. I think it would be possible for us to go ahead without assuming the drudgery of discovering the murderer of Dr. Burton. I would indeed regard that as obvious, if only men could be depended upon to base their decisions on reason. Alas, there are only three or four of us in the world, and even we will bear watching. And our weak spot is that we are committed not to refer our success to a fact, we must refer it to the vote of our group of clients. We must not only make things happen, we must make our clients vote that they have happened. That arrangement was unavoidable. It makes it necessary for us to learn who killed Dr. Burton, so that if the vote cannot be sufficiently swayed by reason it can be bullied by melodrama. You see that."

I said, "I'm sleepy. When I have to wait until nearly midnight for my dinner and then it's squirrel stew—"

Wolfe nodded. "Yes, I know. Under those circumstances I would be no better than a maniac. Another thing. The worst aspect of this Burton development, from our standpoint, is what it does to the person of Mr. Chapin. He cannot come here to get his box—or for anything else. It will be necessary to make arrangements through Mr. Morley, and go to see him. What jail will they keep him in?"

"I suppose Centre Street. There are three or four places they could stick him, but the Tombs is the most likely."

Wolfe sighed. "That abominable clatter. It's more than two miles —nearer three, I suppose. The last time I left this house was early in September, for the privilege of dining at the same table with Albert Einstein, and, coming home, it rained. You remember that."

"Yeah. Will I ever forget it. There was such a downpour the pavements were damp."

"You deride me. Confound it— Ah well. I will not make a virtue of necessity, but neither will I whimper under its lash. Since there is no such thing as bail for a man charged with murder, and since I must have a conversation with Mr. Chapin, there is no escaping an expedition to Centre Street. Not, however, until we know who killed Dr. Burton."

"And not forgetting that before the night's out the cripple may empty the bag for Cramer by confessing that he did it."

"Archie." Wolfe wiggled a finger at me. "If you persist—but no. King Canute tried that. I only say again, nonsense. Have I not made it clear to you? It is the fashion to say anything is possible. The truth is, very few things are possible, pitiably few. That Mr. Chapin killed Dr. Burton is not among them. We are engaged on a project. It is futile to ask you to exclude from your brain all the fallacies which creep, familiar worms, through its chambers, but I do expect you not to let them interfere with our necessary operations. It is late, past two o'clock, time for bed. I have outlined your activities for tomorrow— today. I have explained what may be done, and what may not. Good night. Sleep well."

I stood up and yawned. I was too sleepy to be sore, so it was automatic that I said, "Okay, boss." I went upstairs to bed.

Sunday morning I slept late. I had been given three chores for that day, and the first on the list probably wouldn't be practical at any early hour, so twice when I woke up to glance at the clock I burrowed in again. I finally tumbled out around nine-thirty and got the body rinsed off and the face scraped. When I found myself whistling as I buttoned my shirt I stopped to seek the source of all the gaiety, and discovered I probably felt satisfied because Paul Chapin was behind bars and couldn't see the sunshine which I was seeing on the front of the houses across the street. I stopped whistling. That was no way to feel about a guy when I was supposed to be fighting for his freedom.

It was Sunday morning in November, and I knew what had happened when I had called down to Fritz that I was out of the bathtub: he had lined a casserole with butter, put in it six tablespoons of cream, three fresh eggs, four Lambert sausages, salt, pepper, paprika, and chives, and conveyed it to the oven. But before I went to the kitchen I stopped in the office. Andrew Hibbard was there with the morning paper. He said that he hadn't been able to sleep much, that he had had breakfast, and that he wished to God he had some of his own clothes. I told him that Wolfe was up on the top floor with the orchids and that he would be welcome up there if he cared to see them. He decided to go. I went to the phone and called up Centre Street and was told that Inspector Cramer hadn't shown up yet and they weren't sure when he would. So I went to the kitchen and took my time with the casserole and accessories. Of course the murder of Dr. Burton was front page in both papers. I read the pieces through and enjoyed them very much.

Then I went to the garage and got the roadster and moseyed downtown.

Cramer was in his office when I got there, and didn't keep me waiting. He was smoking a big cigar and looked contented. I sat down and listened to him discussing with a couple of dicks the best way to persuade some Harlem citizen to quit his anatomy experiments on the skulls of drugstore cashiers, and when they went I looked at him and grinned. He didn't grin back. He whirled his chair around to face me and asked me what I wanted. I told him I didn't want anything, I just wanted to thank him for letting me squat on the sidelines up at Doc Burton's last night.

He said, "Yeah. You were gone when I came out. Did it bore you?"

"It did. I couldn't find any clue."

"No." But still he didn't grin. "This case is one of those mean babies where nothing seems to fit. All we've got is the murderer and the gun and two witnesses. Now what do you want?"

I told him, "I want lots of things. You've got it, Inspector. Okay. You can afford to be generous, and George Pratt ought to hand you two grand, half of what you saved him. I'd like to know if you found any fingerprints on the gun. I'd like to know if Chapin has explained why he planned it so amateur, with him a professional. But what I'd really like is to have a little talk with Chapin. If you could arrange that for me—"

Cramer was grinning. He said, "I wouldn't mind having a talk with Chapin myself."

"Well, I'd be glad to put in a word for you."

He pulled on his cigar, and then took it out and got brisk. "I'll tell you, Goodwin. I'd just as soon sit and chin with you, but the fact is it's Sunday and I'm busy. So take this down. First, even if I passed you in to Chapin you wouldn't get anywhere. That cripple is part mule. I spent four hours on him last night, and I swear to God he wouldn't even tell me how old he is. He is not talking, and he won't talk to anyone except his wife. He says he don't want a lawyer, or rather he don't say anything when we ask him who he wants. His wife has seen him twice, and they won't say anything that anyone can hear. You know I've had a little experience greasing tongues, but he stops them all."

"Yeah. Did you try pinching him, just between you and me?"

He shook his head. "Haven't touched him. But to go on. After what Nero Wolfe said on the phone last night—I suppose you heard that talk—I had an idea you'd be wanting to see him. And I've decided nothing doing. Even if he was talking a blue streak—not a chance. Considering how we got him, I don't see why you're interested anyhow. Hell, can't Wolfe take the short end once in his life? Now wait a minute. You don't need to remind me Wolfe has always been better than square with me and there's one or two things I owe him. I'll hand him a favor when I've got one the right size. But no matter how tight I've got this cripple sewed up, I'm going to play safe with him."

"Okay. It just means extra trouble. Wolfe will have to arrange it at the D. A.'s office."

"Let him. If he does, I won't butt in. As far as I'm concerned, the only two people that get to see Chapin are his wife and his lawyer, and he's got no lawyer, and, if you ask me, not much wife. Listen, now that you've asked me a favor and I've turned you down, how about doing one for me? Tell me what you want to see him for? Huh?"

I grinned. "You'd be surprised. I have to ask him what he wants us to do with what is left of Andrew Hibbard until he gets a chance to tend to it."

Cramer stared at me. He snorted. "You wouldn't kid me."

"I wouldn't dream of it. Of course if he's not talking he probably wouldn't tell me, but I might find a way to turn him on. Look here, Inspector, there must be some human quality in you somewhere. Today's my birthday. Let me see him."

"Not a chance."

I got up. "How straight is it that he's not talking?"

"That's on the level. We can't get a peep."

I told him much obliged for all his many kindnesses, and left.

I got in the roadster and headed north. I wasn't downcast. I hadn't made any history, but I hadn't expected to. Remembering the mask that Paul Chapin had been using for a face as I saw him sitting in the Burton foyer the night before, I wasn't surprised that Cramer hadn't found him much of a conversationalist, and I wouldn't have expected to hear anything even if I had got to see him.

At Fourteenth Street I parked and went to a cigar store and phoned Wolfe. I told him, "Right again. They have to ask his wife whether he prefers white or dark meat, because he won't even tell them that. He's not interested in a lawyer. Cramer wouldn't let me see him."

Wolfe said, "Excellent. Proceed to Mrs. Burton."

I went back to the roadster and rolled on uptown.

When they telephoned from the lobby to the Burton apartment to say that Mr. Goodwin was there, I was hoping she hadn't got a new slant on this and that during the night. As Wolfe had said once, you can depend on a woman for anything except constancy. But she had stayed put; I was nodded to the elevator. Upstairs I was taken into the same room as the night before by a maid I hadn't seen—the housekeeper, Mrs. Kurtz, I surmised. She looked hostile and determined enough to make me contented that I didn't need to question her about a key or anything else.

Mrs. Burton sat in a chair by a window. She looked pale. If people had been with her she had sent them away. I told her I wouldn't sit down, I only had a few questions Nero Wolfe had given me.

I read the first one from my pad. "Did Paul Chapin say anything whatever to you last night besides what you have already told me, and if so, what?"

She said, "No. Nothing."

"Inspector Cramer showed you the gun that your husband was shot with. How sure are you that it was your husband's, the one he kept in the drawer of his desk?"

She said, "Quite sure. His initials were on it; it was a gift from a friend."

"During the fifty minutes that Dora Chapin was in the apartment last evening, was there any time when she went, or could have gone, to the study, and if so was there anyone else in the study at that time?"

She said, "No." Then the frown came into her eyes. "But wait—yes, there was. Soon after she came I sent her to the study for a book. I suppose there was no one there. My husband was in his room, dressing."

"This next one is the last. Do you know if Mr. Bowen was at any time alone in the study?"

She said, "Yes, he was. My husband came to my room to ask me a question."

I put the pad in my pocket and said to her, "You might tell me what the question was."

"No, Mr. Goodwin. I think not."

"It might be important. This isn't for publication."

Her eyes frowned again, but the hesitation was brief. "Very well. He asked me if I cared enough for Estelle Bowen—Mr. Bowen's wife —to make a considerable sacrifice for her. I said no."

"Did he tell you what he meant?"

"No."

"All right. That's all. You haven't slept any."

"No."

Ordinarily I've got as much to say as there's time for, but on that occasion no more observations suggested themselves. I told her thank you, and she nodded without moving her head, which sounds unlikely but I swear that's what she did, and I beat it. As I went out through the foyer I paused for another glance at one or two details, such as the location of the light switch by the double door.

On my way downtown I phoned Wolfe again. I told him what I had gathered from Mrs. Burton, and he told me that he and Andrew Hibbard were playing cribbage.

It was twenty minutes past noon when I got to Perry Street. It was deserted for Sunday—sidewalks empty, only a couple of cars parked in the whole block, and a taxi in front of the entrance at 203. I let the roadster slide to the curb opposite and got out. I had noted the number on the taxi's license plate and had seen the driver on his seat. I stepped across to the sidewalk and went alongside; his head was tilted over against the frame and his eyes were closed.

I put a foot on the runningboard and leaned in and said, "Good morning, Mr. Scott."

He came to with a start and looked at me. He blinked. "Oh," he said, "it's little Nero Wolfe."

I nodded. "Names don't bother me, but mine happens to be Archie Goodwin. How's tips?"

"My dear fellow." He made noises and spat out to the left, to the pavement. "Tips is copious. When was it I saw you, Wednesday? Only four days ago. You keeping busy?"

"I'm managing." I leaned in a little farther. "Look here, Pitney Scott. I wasn't looking for you, but I'm glad I found you. When Nero Wolfe heard how you recognized Andrew Hibbard over a week ago, but didn't claim the five grand reward when it was offered, he said you have an admirable sense of humor. Knowing how easy it is to find excuses for a friendly feeling for five grand, I'd say something different, but Wolfe meant well, he's just eccentric. Seeing you here, it just occurred to me that you ought to know that your friend Hibbard is at present a guest up at our house. I took him there yesterday in time for dinner. If it's all the same to you, he'd like to stay under cover for another couple of days, till we get this whole thing straightened out. If you should happen to turn mercenary, you won't lose anything by keeping your sense of humor."

He grunted. "So. You got Andy. And you only need a couple of days to straighten it all out. I thought *all* detectives were dumb."

"Sure, we are. I'm so dumb I don't even know whether it was you that took Dora Chapin up to Ninetieth Street last evening and brought her back again. I was just going to ask you."

"All right, ask me. Then I'll say it wasn't." He made noises and spat again—another futile attack on the imaginary obstruction in the throat of a man with a constant craving for a drink. He looked at me and went on, "You know, brother—if you will pardon the argot—I'm sore at you for spotting Andy, but I admire you for it too because it was halfway smart. And anyway, Lorry Burton was a pretty good guy. With him dead, and Mr. Paul Chapin in jail, the fun's gone. It's not funny any more, even to me, and Nero Wolfe's right about my sense of humor. It is admirable. I'm a character. I'm sardonic." He spat again. "But to hell with it. I didn't drive Mrs. Chapin to Burton's last night because she went in her own coupé."

"Oh. She drives herself."

"Sure. In the summertime she and her husband go to the country on picnics. Now that was funny, for instance, and I don't suppose they'll ever do that again. I don't know why she's using me today, unless it's because she doesn't want to park it in front of the Tombs— There she comes now."

I got off the runningboard and back a step. Dora Chapin had come out of the 203 entrance and was headed for the taxi. She had on another coat and another fur piece, but the face was the same, and so were the little gray eyes. She was carrying an oblong package about the size of a shoebox, and I supposed that was dainties for her husband's Sunday dinner. She didn't seem to have noticed me, let alone recognize me; then she stopped with one foot on the runningboard and turned the eyes straight at me, and for the first time I saw an expression in them that I could give a name to, and it wasn't fondness. You could call it an inviting expression if you went on to describe what she was inviting me to.

I stepped into it anyway. I said, "Mrs. Chapin. Could I ride with you? I'd like to tell you—"

She climbed inside and slammed the door to. Pitney Scott stepped on the starter, put the gear in, and started to roll. I stood and watched the taxi go, not very jubilant, because it was her I had come down there to see.

I walked to the corner and phoned Wolfe I wouldn't be home to lunch—which I didn't mind much because the eggs and cream and sausages I had shipped on at ten o'clock were still undecided what to do about it—bought a *Times,* and went to the roadster and made myself comfortable. Unless she had some kind of pull that Inspector Cramer didn't know about, they wouldn't let her stay very long at the Tombs.

At that I had to wait close to an hour and a half. It was nearly two o'clock, and I was thinking of hitting up the delicatessen where Fred Durkin had been a tenant for most of the week, when I looked up for the eightieth time at the sound of a car and saw the taxi slowing down. I had decided what to do. With all that animosity in Dora's eyes I calculated it wouldn't pay to try to join her downstairs and go up with her; I would wait till she was inside and then persuade Pitney Scott to take me up. With him along she might let me in. But again I didn't get the break. Instead of stopping at the entrance Scott rolled down a few yards, and then they both got out and both went in. I stared at them and did a little cussing, and decided not to do any more waiting. I got out and entered 203 for the first and last time, and went to the elevator and said, "Fifth floor." The man looked at me with the usual mild and weary suspicion but didn't bother with questions. I got out at the fifth and rang the bell at 5C.

I can't very well pretend to be proud of what happened that afternoon at Paul Chapin's apartment. I pulled a boner, no doubt of that, and it wasn't my fault that it didn't have a result that ended a good deal more than the Chapin case, but the opinion you have of it depends entirely on how you see it. I can't honestly agree that it was quite as dumb as one or two subsequent remarks of Wolfe's might seem to indicate. Anyway, this is how it happened.

Dora Chapin came to the door and opened it, and I got my foot inside the sill. She asked me what I wanted, and I said I had something to ask Pitney Scott. She said he would be down in half an hour and I could wait downstairs, and started to shut the door and got it as far as my foot.

I said, "Listen, Mrs. Chapin. I want to ask you something too. You think I'm against your husband, but I'm not; I'm for him. That's on the level. He hasn't got many friends left, and anyway it won't hurt you to listen to me. I've got something to say. I could say it to the police instead of you, but take it from me you wouldn't like that nearly as well. Let me in. Pitney Scott's here."

She threw the door wide open and said, "Come in."

Maybe that shift in her welcome should have made me suspicious, but it didn't. It merely made me think I had scared her, and also made me add a few chips to the stack I was betting that if her husband hadn't croaked Dr. Burton, she had. I went in and shut the door behind me and followed her across the hall and through a sitting room and dining room and into the kitchen. The rooms were big and well furnished and looked prosperous; and sitting in the kitchen at an enamel-top table was Pitney Scott, consuming a hunk of brown fried chicken. There was a platter of it with four or five pieces left.

I said to Dora Chapin, "Maybe we can go in front and leave Mr. Scott to enjoy himself."

She nodded at a chair and pointed to the chicken. "There's plenty." She turned to Scott. "I'll fix you a drink."

He shook his head and chewed and swallowed. "I've been off for ten days now, Mrs. Chapin. It wouldn't be funny, take my word for it. When the coffee's ready I'd appreciate that. Come on—you said Goodwin, didn't you?—come on and help me. Mrs. Chapin says she has dined."

I was hungry, and the chicken looked good, I admit that, but the psychology of it was that it looked like I ought to join in. Not to mention the salad, which had green peppers in it. I got into the chair, and Scott passed the platter. Dora Chapin had gone to the stove to turn the fire down under the percolator. There was still a lot of bandage at the back of her neck, and it looked unattractive where her hair had been shaved off. She was bigger than I had realized in the office that day, fairly hefty. She went into the dining room for something, and I got more intimate with the chicken after the first couple of bites and started a conversation with Scott. After a while Dora Chapin came back, with coffee cups and a bowl of sugar.

Of course it was in the coffee; she probably put it right in the pot, since she didn't drink any; but I didn't notice a taste. It was strong but it tasted all right. However, she must have put in all the sleeping tablets and a few other things she could get hold of, for God knows it was potent. I began to feel it when I was reaching to hand Scott a cigarette, and at the same time I saw the look on his face. He was a few seconds ahead of me. Dora Chapin was out of the room again. Scott looked at the door she had gone through, and tried to get up out of his chair, but couldn't make it. That was the last I really remember, him trying to get out of his chair, but I must have done one or two things after that, because when I came out of it I was in the dining room, halfway across to the door which led to the sitting room and the hall.

When I came out of it, it was dark. That was the first thing I knew, and for a while it was all I knew, because I couldn't move and I was fighting to get my eyes really open. I could see, off to my right—at a great distance, it seemed—two large oblongs of dim light, and I concentrated on deciding what they were. It came with a burst that they were windows, and it was dark in the room where I was, and the street was lit. Then I concentrated on what room I was in.

Things came back, but all in a jumble. I still didn't know where I was, though I was splitting my head fighting for it. I rolled over on the floor, and my hand landed on something metal, sharp, and I shrank from it. I pulled myself to my knees and began to crawl. I bumped into a table and a chair or two, and finally into the wall. I crawled around the wall with my shoulder against it, detouring for furniture, stopping every couple of feet to feel it, and at last I felt a door. I tried to stand up, but couldn't make it, and compromised by feeling above me. I found the switch and pushed on it, and the light went on. I crawled over to where there was some stuff on the floor, stretching the muscles in my brow and temples to keep my eyes open, and saw that the metal thing that had startled me was my ring of keys. My wallet was there too, and my pad and pencil, pocketknife, fountain pen, handkerchief—things from my pockets.

I got hold of a chair and pulled myself to my feet, but I couldn't navigate. I tried and fell down. I looked around for a telephone, but there wasn't any, so I crawled to the sitting room and found the light switch by the door and turned it on. The phone was on a stand by the farther wall. It looked so far away that the desire to lie down and give it up made me want to yell to show I wouldn't do that, but I couldn't yell. I finally got to the stand and sat down on the floor against it and reached up for the phone and got the receiver off and shoved it against my ear, and heard a man's voice, very faint. I said the number of Wolfe's phone and heard him say he couldn't hear me, so then I yelled it and that way got enough steam behind it.

After a while I heard another voice, and I yelled, "I want Nero Wolfe!"

The other voice mumbled, and I said to talk louder and asked who it was, and got it into my bean that it was Fritz. I told him to get Wolfe on, and he said Wolfe wasn't there, and I said he was crazy, and he mumbled a lot of stuff, and I told him to say it again, louder and slower.

"I said, Archie, Mr. Wolfe is not here. He went to look for you. Somebody came to get him, and he told me he was going for you. Archie, where are you? Mr. Wolfe said—"

I was having a hard time holding the phone, and it dropped to the floor, the whole works, and my head fell into my hands with my eyes closed, and I suppose what I was doing you would call crying.

XIX

I HAVEN'T the slightest idea how long I sat there on the floor with my head laying in my hands, trying to force myself out of it enough to pick up the telephone again. It may have been a minute and it may have been an hour. The trouble was that I should have been concentrating on the phone, and it kept sweeping over me that Wolfe was gone. I couldn't get my head out of my hands. Finally I heard a noise. It kept on and got louder, and at last it seeped into me that someone seemed to be trying to knock the door down. I grabbed the top of the telephone stand and pulled myself up, and decided I could keep my feet if I didn't let go of the wall, so I followed it around to the door to the hall, and around the hall to the entrance door where the noise was. I got my hands on it and turned the lock and the knob, and it flew open, and down I went again. The two guys that came in walked on me and then stood and looked at me, and I heard remarks about full to the gills and leaving the receiver off the hook.

By that time I could talk better. I said I don't know what, enough so that one of them beat it for a doctor, and the other one helped me get up and steered me to the kitchen. He turned the light on. Scott had slewed off of his chair and was curled up on the floor. My chair was turned over on its side. I felt cold air, and the guy said something about the window, and I looked at it and saw the glass was shattered with a big hole in it. I never did learn what it was I had thrown through the window, maybe the plate of chicken; anyway it hadn't aroused enough curiosity down below to do any good. The guy stooped over Scott and shook him, but he was dead to the world. By working the wall again, and furniture, I got back to the dining room and sat on the floor and began collecting my things and putting them in my pockets. I got worried because I thought something was missing and I couldn't figure out what it was, and then I realized it was the leather case Wolfe had given me, with pistols on one side and orchids on the other, that I carried my police and fire cards in. And by God I started to cry again. I was doing that when the other guy came back with the doctor. I was crying, and trying to push my knuckles into my temples hard enough to get my brain working on why Dora Chapin had fed me a knockout so she could frisk me and then took nothing but that leather case.

I had a fight with the doctor. He insisted that before he could give me anything he'd have to know just what it was I had inside of me, and he went to the bathroom to investigate bottles and boxes, and I went after him with the idea of plugging him. I was beginning to have thoughts, and they were starting to bust in my head. I got nearly to the bathroom when I forgot all about the doctor because I suddenly remembered that there had been something peculiar about Scott curled up on the floor, and I turned around and started for the kitchen. I was getting overconfident and fell down again, but I picked myself up and went on. I looked at Scott and saw what it was: he was in his shirtsleeves. His gray taxi driver's jacket was gone. I was trying to decide why that was important when the doctor came in with a glass of brown stuff in his hand. He said something and handed me the glass and watched me drink it, and then went over and knelt down by Scott.

The stuff tasted bitter. I put the empty glass on the table and got hold of the guy who had gone for the doctor—by this time I recognized him as the elevator man—and told him to go downstairs and switch the Chapin phone in, and then go outside and see if Scott's taxi was at the curb. Then I made it through the dining room again into the sitting room and got into a chair by the telephone stand. I got the operator and gave her the number.

Fritz answered. I said, "This is Archie. What was it you told me a while ago about Mr. Wolfe?"

"Why—Mr. Wolfe is gone." I could hear him better, and I could tell he was trying not to let his voice shake. "He told me he was going to get you, and that he suspected you of trying to coerce him into raising your pay. He went—"

"Wait a minute, Fritz. Talk slow. What time is it? My watch says a quarter to seven."

"Yes. That's right. Mr. Wolfe has been gone nearly four hours. Archie, where are you?"

"To hell with where I am. What happened? Someone came for him?"

"Yes. I went to the door, and a man handed me an envelope."

"Was it a taxi driver?"

"Yes, I think so. I took the envelope to Mr. Wolfe, and pretty soon he came to the kitchen and told me he was going. Mr. Hibbard helped him into his coat, the brown one with the big collar, and I got his hat and stick and gloves—"

"Did you see the taxi?"

"Yes, I went out with Mr. Wolfe and opened the door of the cab for him. Archie, for God's sake, tell me what I can do—"

"You can't do anything. Let me talk to Mr. Hibbard."

"But Archie—I am so disturbed—"

"So am I. Hold the fort, Fritz, and sit tight. Put Hibbard on."

I waited, and before long heard Hibbard's hello. I said to him, "This is Archie Goodwin, Mr. Hibbard. Now listen, I can't talk much. When Nero Wolfe gets home again we want to be able to tell him that you've kept your word. You promised him to stay dead until Monday evening. Understand?"

Hibbard sounded irritated. "Of course I understand, Mr. Goodwin, but it seems to me—"

"For God's sake forget how it seems to you. Either you keep your word or you don't."

"Well—I do."

"That's fine. Tell Fritz I'll call again as soon as I have anything to say."

I hung up. The brown stuff the doctor had given me seemed to be working, but not to much advantage; my head was pounding like the hammers of hell. The elevator man had come back and was standing there. I looked at him, and he said Scott's taxi was gone. I got hold of the phone again and called Spring 7-3100.

Cramer wasn't in his office, and they couldn't find him around. I got my wallet out of my pocket and with some care managed to find my lists of telephone numbers, and called Cramer's home. At first they said he wasn't there, but I persuaded them to change their minds, and finally he came to the phone. I didn't know a cop's voice could ever sound so welcome to me. I told him where I was and what had happened to me, and said I was trying to remember what it was he had said that morning about doing a favor for Nero Wolfe. He said, whatever it was, he had meant it.

I told him, "Okay, now's your chance. That crazy Chapin bitch has stolen a taxi, and she's got Nero Wolfe in it, taking him somewhere. I don't know where and I wouldn't know even if my head was working. She got him four hours ago and she's had time to get to Albany or anywhere else. No matter how she got him; I'll settle for that some other day. Listen, Inspector, for God's sake. Send out a general for a brown taxi, a Stuyvesant, MO two-nine-six-three-four-two. Got it down? Say it back. Will you put the radios on it? Will you send it to Westchester and Long Island and Jersey? Listen, the dope I was cooking up was that it was her that croaked Doc Burton. By God, if I ever get my hands on her— What? I'm not excited. Okay. Okay, Inspector, thanks."

I hung up. Someone had come in and was standing there, and I looked up and saw it was a flatfoot wearing a silly grin, directed at me. He asked me something, and I told him to take his shoes off to rest his brains. He made me some kind of a reply that was intended to be smart, and I laid my head down on the top of the telephone stand to get the range, and banged it up and down a few times on the wood, but it didn't seem to do any good. The elevator man said something to the cop, and he went toward the kitchen.

I got up and went to open a window and damn near fell out. The cold air was like ice. The way I felt I was sure of two things: first, that if my head went on like that much longer it would blow up, and second, that Wolfe was dead. It seemed obvious that after that woman once got him into that taxi there was nothing for her to do with him but kill him. I stood looking out onto Perry Street, trying to hold my head together, and I had a feeling that all of New York was there in front of me, between me and the house fronts I could see across the street—the Battery, the river fronts, Central Park, Flatbush, Harlem, Park Avenue, all of it—and Wolfe was there somewhere, and I didn't know where. Something occurred to me, and I held on to the window jamb and leaned out enough so I could see below. There was the roadster, where I had parked it, its fender shining with the reflection from a street light. I had an idea that if I could get down there and get it started I could drive it all right.

I decided to do that, but before I moved away from the window I thought I ought to decide where to go. One man in one roadster, even if he had a head on him that would work, wouldn't get far looking for that taxi. It was absolutely hopeless. But I had a notion that there was something important I could do, somewhere important I could go, if only I could figure out where it was. All of a sudden it came to me that where I wanted to go was home. I wanted to see Fritz and the office, and go over the house and see for myself that Wolfe wasn't there, look at things . . .

I didn't hesitate. I let go of the window jamb and started across the room, and just as I got to the hall the telephone rang. I could walk a little better. I went back to the telephone stand and picked up the receiver and said hello.

A voice said, "Chelsea two-three-nine-two-four? Please give me Mr. Chapin's apartment."

I nearly dropped the receiver, and I went stiff. I said, "Who is this?"

The voice said, "This is someone who wishes to be connected with Mr. Chapin's apartment. Didn't I make that clear?"

I let the phone down and pressed it against one of my ribs for a moment, not wanting to make a fool of myself. Then I put it up to my mouth again. "Excuse me for asking who it is. It sounded like Nero Wolfe. Where are you?"

"Ah! Archie. After what Mrs. Chapin has told me, I scarcely expected to find you operating an apartment-house switchboard. I am much relieved. How are you feeling?"

"Swell. Wonderful. How are you?"

"Fairly comfortable. Mrs. Chapin drives staccato, and the jolting of that infernal taxicab— Ah well. Archie. I am standing, and I dislike to talk on the telephone while standing. Also I would dislike very much to enter that taxicab again. If it is practical, get the sedan and come for me. I am at the Bronx River Inn, near the Woodlawn railroad station. You know where that is?"

"I know. I'll be there."

"No great hurry. I am fairly comfortable."

"Okay."

The click of his ringing off was in my ear. I hung up and sat down.

I was damn good and sore. Certainly not at Wolfe, not even at myself, just sore. Sore because I had phoned Cramer an SOS, sore because Wolfe was to hell and gone up beyond the end of the Grand Concourse and I didn't really know what shape he was in, sore because it was up to me to get there and there was no doubt at all about the shape I was in. I felt my eyes closing and jerked my head up. I decided that the next time I saw Dora Chapin, no matter when or where, I would take my pocketknife and cut her head off, completely loose from the rest of her. I thought of going to the kitchen and asking the doctor for another shot of the brown stuff, but didn't see how it could do me any good.

I picked up the phone and called the garage on Tenth Avenue and told them to fill the sedan with gas and put it at the curb. Then I got up and proceeded to make myself scarce. I would rather have done almost anything than try walking again, except go back to crawling. I made it to the hall and opened the door, and on out to the elevator. There I was faced by two new troubles: the elevator was right there, the door standing wide open, and I didn't have my hat and coat. I didn't want to go back to the kitchen for the elevator man because in the first place it was too far, and secondly if the flatfoot found out I was leaving he would probably want to detain me for information, and there was no telling how I would act if he tried it. I did go back to the hall, having left the door open. I got my hat and coat and returned to the elevator, inside, and somehow got the door closed and pulled the lever, hitting down by luck. It started down, and I leaned against the wall.

I thought I was releasing the lever about the right time, but the first thing I knew the elevator hit bottom like a ton of brick and shook me loose from the wall. I picked myself up and opened the door and saw there was a dark hall about two feet above my level. I climbed out and got myself stood up. It was the basement. I turned right, which seemed to be correct, and for a change it was. I came to a door and went through, and through a gate, and there I was outdoors with nothing between me and the sidewalk but a flight of concrete steps. I negotiated them and crossed the street and found the roadster and got in.

I don't believe yet that I drove that car from Perry Street to Thirty-sixth, to the garage. I might possibly have done it by caroms, bouncing back from the buildings first on one side of the street and then on the other, but the trouble with that theory is that next day the roadster didn't have a scratch on it. If anyone is keeping a miracle score, chalk one up for me. I got there, but I stopped out in front, deciding not to try for the door. I blew my horn, and Steve came out. I described my condition in round figures and told him I hoped there was someone there he could leave in charge of the joint, because he had to get in the sedan and drive me to the Bronx. He asked if I wanted a drink, and I snarled at him. He grinned and went inside, and I transferred to the sedan standing at the curb. Pretty soon he came back with an overcoat on and got in and shoved off. I told him where to go and let my head fall back in the corner against the cushion, but I didn't dare to let my eyes shut. I stretched them open and kept on stretching them every time I blinked. My window was down, and the cold air slapped me, and it seemed we were going a million miles a minute in a swift sweeping circle, and it was hard to keep up with my breathing.

Steve said, "Here we are, mister."

I grunted and lifted my head up and stretched my eyes again. We had stopped. There it was, Bronx River Inn, just across the sidewalk. I had a feeling it had come to us instead of us to it. Steve asked, "Can you navigate?"

"Sure." I set my jaw again and opened the door and climbed out. Then, after crossing the sidewalk, I tried to walk through a lattice, and set my jaw some more and detoured. I crossed the porch, with cold bare tables around and no one there, and opened the door and went inside to the main room. There some of the tables had cloths on them and a few customers were scattered here and there. The customer I was looking for was at a table in the far corner, and I approached it. There sat Nero Wolfe, all of him, on a chair which would have been economical for either half. His brown greatcoat covered another chair, beside him, and across the table from him I saw the bandages on the back of Dora Chapin's neck. She was facing him, with her rear to me. I walked over there.

Wolfe nodded at me. "Good evening, Archie. I am relieved again. It occurred to me after I phoned you that you were probably in no condition to pilot a car through this confounded labyrinth. I am greatly relieved. You have met Mrs. Chapin. Sit down. You don't look as if standing was very enjoyable."

He lifted his glass of beer and took a couple of swallows. I saw the remains of some kind of a mess on his plate, but Dora Chapin had cleaned hers up. I moved his hat and stick off of a chair and sat down on it. He asked me if I wanted a glass of milk, and I shook my head.

He said, "I confess it is a trifle mortifying, to set out to rescue you and end by requesting you to succor me, but if that is Mr. Scott's taxicab he should get new springs for it. If you get me home intact—and no doubt you will—that will not be your only triumph for this day. By putting me in touch with Mrs. Chapin in unconventional circumstances—though, it seems, inadvertently—you have brought us to the solution of our problem. I tell you that at once because I know it will be welcome news. Mrs. Chapin has been kind enough to accept my assurances—"

That was the last word I heard. The only other thing I remembered was that a tight wire which had been stretched between my temples, holding them together, suddenly parted with a twang. Wolfe told me afterward that when I folded up, my head hit the edge of the table with a loud thud before he could catch me.

XX

Monday morning when I woke up I was still in bed. That sounds as if I meant something else, but I don't. When I got enough awake to realize where I was I had a feeling that I had gone to bed sometime during Lent and here it was Christmas. Then I saw Doc Vollmer standing there beside me.

I grinned at him. "Hello, Doc. You got a job here as house physician?"

He grinned back. "I just stopped in to see how it went with what I pumped into you last night. Apparently—"

"What? Oh. Yeah. Good God." It struck me that the room seemed full of light. "What time is it?"

"Quarter to twelve."

"No!" I twisted to see the clock. "Holy murder!" I jerked myself upright, and someone jabbed a thousand icepicks into my skull. "Whoa,

Bill." I put my hands up to it and tried moving it slowly. I said to Vollmer, "What's this I've got here, my head?"

He laughed. "It'll be all right."

"Yeah. You're not saying when. Wowie! Is Mr. Wolfe down in the office?"

He nodded. "I spoke to him on the way up."

"And it's noon." I slid to my feet. "Look out, I might run into you." I started for the bathroom.

I began soaping up, and he came to the bathroom door and said he had left instructions with Fritz for my breakfast. I told him I didn't want instructions, I wanted ham and eggs. He laughed again and beat it. I was glad to hear him laugh, because it seemed likely that if there really were icepicks sticking in my head he, being a doctor, would be taking them out instead of laughing at me.

I made it as snappy as I could with my dizziness, cleansing the form and assuming the day's draperies, and went downstairs in pretty good style but hanging onto the banister.

Wolfe, in his chair, looked up and said good morning and asked me how I felt. I told him I felt like twin colts and went to my desk.

He said, "But Archie. Seriously. Should you be up?"

"Yeah. Not only should I be up, I should have been up. You know how it is, I'm a man of action."

His cheeks unfolded. "And I, of course, am supersedentary. A comical interchange of roles, that you rode home last evening from the Bronx River Inn, a matter of ten miles or more, with your head on my lap all the way."

I nodded. "Very comical. I told you a long while ago, Mr. Wolfe, that you pay me half for the chores I do and half for listening to you brag."

"So you did. And if I did not then remark, I do so now—but no. We can pursue these amenities another time; now there is business. Could you take some notes and break your fast with our lunch? Good. I spoke on the telephone this morning with Mr. Morley, and with the District Attorney himself. It has been arranged that I shall see Mr. Chapin at the Tombs at two-thirty this afternoon. You will remember that on Saturday evening I was beginning to dictate to you the confession of Paul Chapin when we were interrupted by news from Fred Durkin which caused a postponement. If you will turn to that page we can go on. I'll have to have it by two o'clock."

So as it turned out I not only didn't get to tie into the ham and eggs I had yearned for, I didn't even eat lunch with Wolfe and Hibbard. The dictating wasn't done until nearly one, and I had the typing to do. But by that time the emptiness inside had got to be a vacuum, or whatever it may be that is emptier than emptiness, and I had Fritz bring some hot egg sandwiches and milk and coffee to my desk. I wanted this typed just right, this document that Paul Chapin was to sign, and, with my head not inclined to see the importance of things like spelling and punctuation, I had to take my time and concentrate. Also, I wasted three minutes phoning the garage to tell them to bring the sedan around, for I supposed of course I would take Wolfe in it; but they said they already had instructions from Wolfe, and that the instructions included a driver. I thought maybe I ought to be sore about that, but decided not to.

Wolfe ate a quick lunch, for him. When he came into the office at a quarter to two I barely had the thing finished and was getting the three copies clipped into brown folders. He took them and put them in his pocket and told me to take my notebook and started on the instructions for my afternoon. He explained that he had asked for a driver from the garage because I would be busy with other things. He also explained that on account of the possibility of visitors he had procured from Hibbard a promise that he would spend the entire afternoon in his room, until dinnertime. Hibbard had gone there from the lunch table.

Fritz came to the door and said the car was there, and Wolfe told him he would be ready in a few minutes.

What gave me a new idea of the dimensions of Wolfe's nerve was the disclosure that a good part of the arrangements had been completed for a meeting of the League of the White Feather, in the office that evening at nine o'clock. Before he had seen Chapin at all! Of course I didn't know what Dora might have told him, except a couple of details that had been included in the confession, but it wasn't Dora that was supposed to sign on the dotted line, it was her little crippled husband with the light-colored eyes; and that was a job I was glad Wolfe hadn't bestowed on me, even if it did mean his sashaying out of the house twice in two days, which was an all-time record. But he had gone ahead and telephoned Boston and Philadelphia and Washington, and six or eight of them in New York, after we got home Sunday evening and from his room early that morning, and the meeting was on.

My immediate job was to get in touch with the others, by phone if possible, and ensure as full an attendance as we could get.

He gave me another one, more immediate, just before he left. He told me to go and see Mrs. Burton at once, and dictated two questions to ask her. I suggested the phone, and he said no, it would be better if I saw the daughter and the maids also. Fritz was standing there holding his coat.

Wolfe said, "And I was almost forgetting that our guests will be thirsty. Fritz, put the coat down and come here, and we shall see what we need. Archie, if you don't mind you had better start; you should be back by three. Let us see, Fritz. I noticed last week that Mr. Cabot prefers Aylmer's soda—"

I beat it. I walked to the garage for the roadster, and the sharp air glistened in my lungs. After I got the roadster out into the light I looked it over and couldn't find a scratch on it, and it was then I reflected on miracles. I got back in and headed uptown.

I was worried about Wolfe. It looked to me like he was rushing things beyond reason. It was true that Andrew Hibbard's parole was up that evening, but probably he could have been persuaded to extend it, and besides, it certainly wasn't vital to produce him at the meeting as a stunt. But it was like Wolfe not to wait until the confession was actually in the bag. That sort of gesture, thumbing his nose at luck, was a part of him, and maybe an important part; there were lots of things about Wolfe I didn't pretend to know. Anyhow, there was no law against worrying, and it didn't make my head feel any better to reflect on the outcome of the meeting that evening if Paul Chapin stayed mule. So that was what I reflected on, all the way to Ninetieth Street.

Wolfe had said that both of the questions I was to ask Mrs. Burton were quite important. The first was simple: Did Dr. Burton telephone Paul Chapin between six-fifty and seven o'clock Saturday evening and ask him to come to see him?

The second was more complicated: At six-thirty Saturday evening a pair of gray gloves was lying on the table in the Burton foyer, near the end toward the double doors. Were the gloves removed between then and seven-twenty by anyone in the apartment?

I got a break. Everybody was home. The housekeeper had me wait in the drawing room, and Mrs. Burton came to me there. She looked sick, I thought, and had on a gray dress that made her look sicker, but the spine was still doing its stuff. The first question took about nine seconds; the answer was no, definitely. Dr. Burton had done no telephoning after six-thirty Saturday evening. The second question required more time. Mrs. Kurtz was out of it, since she hadn't been there. The daughter, having left before six-thirty, seemed out of it too, but I asked Mrs. Burton to call her in anyhow, to make sure. She came and said she had left no gloves on the foyer table and had seen none there. Mrs. Burton herself had not been in the foyer between the time she returned home around six, and 7:33, when the sound of the shots had taken her there on the run. She said she had left no gloves on that table and certainly had removed none. She sent for Rose. Rose came, and I asked her if she had removed a pair of gloves from the foyer table between six-thirty and seven-twenty Saturday evening.

Rose looked at Mrs. Burton instead of me. She hesitated, and then she spoke. "No, ma'am, I didn't take the gloves. But Mrs. Chapin—"

She stopped. I said, "You saw some gloves there."

"Yes, sir."

"When?"

"When I went to let Mrs. Chapin in."

"Did Mrs. Chapin take them?"

"No, sir. That's when I noticed them, when she picked them up. She picked them up and then put them down again."

"You didn't go back later and get them?"

"No, sir, I didn't."

That settled that. I thanked Mrs. Burton and left. I wanted to tell her that before tomorrow noon we would have definite news for her that might help a little, but I thought Wolfe had already done enough discounting for the firm and I'd better let it ride.

It was after three when I got back to the office, and I got busy on the phone. There were eight names left for me, that Wolfe hadn't been able to get. He had told me the line to take, that we were prepared to mail our bills to our clients, the signers of the memorandum, but that before doing so we would like to explain to them in a body and receive their approval. Which again spoke fairly well for Wolfe's nerve, inasmuch as our clients knew damn well that it was the cops who had grabbed Chapin for Burton's murder and that we had had about as much to do with it as the lions in front of the library. But I agreed that it was a good line, since the object was to get them to the office.

I was doing pretty well with my eight, having hooked five of them in a little over half an hour, when, at a quarter to four, while I was looking in the book for the number of the Players' Club, on the trail of Roland Erskine, the phone rang. I answered, and it was Wolfe. As soon as I heard his voice I thought to myself, Uh-huh, here we go, the party's up the flue. But it didn't appear that that was the idea. He said to me, "Archie? What luck at Mrs. Burton's?"

"All negatives. Burton didn't phone, and nobody took any gloves."

"But perhaps the maid saw them?"

"Oh. You knew that too. She did. She saw Mrs. Chapin pick them up and put them down again."

"Excellent. I am telephoning because I have just made a promise and I wish to redeem it without delay. Take Mr. Chapin's box from the cabinet, wrap it carefully, and convey it to his apartment and deliver it to Mrs. Chapin. I shall probably be at home by your return."

"Okay. You got any news?"

"Nothing startling."

"I wouldn't expect anything startling. Let's try a plain straightforward question. Did you get the confession signed or didn't you?"

"I did."

"It's really signed?"

"It is. But I forgot to say, before you wrap Mr. Chapin's box take out a pair of gloves, gray leather, and keep them. Please get the box to Mrs. Chapin at once."

"Okay."

I hung up. The fat devil had put it over. I had no idea what items of ammunition he had procured from Dora Chapin, and of course he had the advantage that Chapin was already in the Tombs with a first-degree murder charge glued on him, but even so I handed it to him. I would say that that cripple was the hardest guy to deal with I had ever run across, except the perfume salesman up in New Rochelle who used to drown kittens in the bathtub and one day got hold of his wife by mistake. I would have loved to see Wolfe inserting the needle in him.

Wolfe had said without delay, so I let the last three victims wait. I wrapped the box up and drove down to Perry Street with it, removing a pair of gloves first, in accordance with instructions, and putting them in a drawer of my desk. I parked across the street from 203 and got out.

I had decided on the proper technique for that delivery. I went across to where the elevator man was standing inside the entrance and said to him, "Take this package up to Mrs. Chapin on the fifth floor. Then come back here and I'll give you a quarter."

He took the package and said, "The cop was sore as a boil yesterday when he found you'd gone. How're you feeling?"

"Magnificent. Run ahead, mister."

He went and came back, and I gave him a quarter. I asked him, "Did I break anything on your vertical buggy? The lever wouldn't work."

He grinned about a sixteenth of an inch. "I'll bet it wouldn't. Naw, you didn't break it."

So I kept Wolfe's promise for him and got the package delivered without running any unnecessary risk of being invited in for tea, and all it cost me was two bits, which was cheap enough.

Wolfe returned before I got back home. I knew that in the hall, seeing his hat and coat there. Since it was after four o'clock he would of course be upstairs with the plants, but all of his traipsing around had me nervous, and before going to the office I went up the three flights. I had hardly seen the orchids for more than brief glances for nearly a week. Wolfe was in the tropical room, going down the line, looking for aphids, and from the expression on his face I knew he had found some. I stood there, and pretty soon he turned and looked at me as if I was either an aphid myself or had them all over me. There was no use attempting any conversation. I beat it downstairs to resume at the telephone.

I only got two of the remaining three, couldn't find Roland Erskine anywhere. As it was, we had done pretty good. A telegram had come from Boston saying that Collard and Gaines would be there, and Mollison was coming down from New Haven. I suspected that Wolfe would have handled the long-distance babies himself even if I hadn't been in bed.

Wolfe didn't come to the office directly from the plant rooms at six o'clock as usual. Apparently he had stopped in his room, for when he appeared around six-thirty he was lugging a stack of books, and I saw they were Paul Chapin's novels. He put them on his desk and sat down and rang for beer.

I told him Mrs. Chapin had the box, and read him the notes of my afternoon call on Mrs. Burton. He gave me some instructions for the evening, which I made notes of, because he liked to have everything down, and then he got playful. He made a lot of random remarks, and

I took them like a gentleman, and then, because it was getting on toward dinner, I observed that it was about time I got acquainted with the mystery of the pair of gloves on the foyer table. To my surprise he agreed with me.

He said, "That was the contribution of Mrs. Chapin. She furnished other information too, but nothing as interesting as that. She arrived at the Burton apartment, as you know, at six-thirty. The maid called Rose let her in. As she passed through the foyer she saw a pair of gloves on the table, and she stopped to pick them up. She says she intended to take them in to Mrs. Burton, but it would not be uncharitable to surmise that she had in mind starting a new treasure box for her husband; and that is supported by the reasons she gives for returning the gloves to the table. She gives two reasons: that the maid had turned and was looking at her, and that the gloves seemed a little heavier than any she had known Mrs. Burton to wear. At any rate, she left them there. But when she went through the foyer alone on the way out, she thought to look at them again to satisfy herself whether they were Mrs. Burton's or not. The gloves were gone. She even looked around for them. They were gone."

"I see. And that proves she didn't croak Burton."

"It does. And it identifies the murderer. If it should turn out that factual corroboration is needed of Mrs. Chapin's innocence, which seems unlikely, it can be established that at half-past seven she was receiving a summons from a policeman at Park Avenue and Fiftieth Street for passing a red light. Not to mention the probability that the hallman and doorman saw her leaving the building before the event occurred. But none of that should be needed."

"Uh-huh. I suppose you got her confidence by giving her some orchids."

"No. But as a matter of fact I promised her some. Make a note of that for tomorrow. I got her confidence by telling her the truth, that the conviction of her husband for murder would cost me many thousands of dollars. You see, what happened— What time is it? Good. She was convinced, as was Chapin himself, that I was responsible for his predicament. Not knowing the nature of my agreement with his friends, he thought I had framed him. Having seen me, he could not of course suppose that I myself had performed the acrobatics in the foyer. Do you know who did that? You. Yes indeed, you did the killing, I merely devised it. Mrs. Chapin, believing that, seized an opportunity. With you and Pitney Scott fast asleep, she went through your pockets, took his cap and jacket, sat down and wrote a note, and drove the taxicab here. She handed the envelope to Fritz at the door and returned to the cab. The note was brief and quite clear; I can quote it verbatim: 'Archie Goodwin will be dead in two hours unless you get in my taxi and go where I drive you.' And it was signed with her name, Dora Chapin. Admirably forthright. What persuaded me that some sort of action was called for was the presence in the envelope of the leather case you had seemed to like."

He paused for a glass of beer. I grunted and thought I ought to say something, but all I could think of was, "Yeah, I liked it. And you've still got it."

He nodded, and resumed. "The only aspect of the episode that was really distressing came from Mrs. Chapin's romantic idea of what constitutes a remote and secluded spot. Since I was committed to follow her, a bush in a corner of Central Park would have done her just as well, but that infernal female ass bounced that cab far beyond the limits of the city. I learned subsequently that she had in mind an isolated wood somewhere on the edge of Long Island Sound where she and her husband had gone last summer to have a picnic. It became unendurable. I lowered the glass between us and shouted at the back of her ear that if she did not stop within three minutes I would call for help at every passing car and every visible human being. I convinced her. She turned into a byroad and soon stopped under a clump of trees.

"This will amuse you. She had a weapon. A kitchen knife! By the way, that carving she exhibited to us last Wednesday was done on her own initiative; her husband disapproved. At that time the game was still one of establishing Mr. Chapin in the minds of his friends as a dangerous and murderous fellow, without involving him in any demonstrable guilt. He already suspected that I might uncover him, and his wife's bloody neck was a red herring, though her own idea. Well. She could not very well have expected to kill me with a knife, since none could be long enough to reach a vital spot; I suppose no gun was available, or perhaps she mistrusts them as I do. Perhaps she meant merely to hack me into acquiescence; and of course she had in reserve my anxiety as to the peril of your situation. At all events, her purpose was to force me to reveal the skulduggery by which her husband had been entrapped. I was to write it. She had pen and paper with her. That attention to detail endeared her to me."

"Yeah. And?"

He drank beer. "Nothing much. You know my fondness for talking. It was an excellent opportunity. She was calm from the outset. She and I have much in common—for instance, our dislike of perturbation. It would have been instructive to see her using the knife on the back of her neck that day; I would wager she did it much as one trims a chop. After I had explained the situation to her, we discussed it. The moment arrived when it seemed pointless to continue our conference in that cold, dark, forbidding spot, and besides, I had learned what had happened to you. She seemed so uncertain as to what she had used to flavor your coffee that I thought it best to reach a telephone with as little delay as possible. Ah! Mr. Hibbard, I trust the long afternoon has been fairly tolerable."

Hibbard walked in, looking a little groggy, still wearing my brown necktie. Behind him came Fritz to announce dinner.

XXI

THEY piled in early. By nine o'clock ten of them had already arrived, checked off on my list, and I was doing the honors. Four of them I hadn't seen before: Collard and Gaines from Boston, Irving from Philadelphia, and Professor Mollison of Yale. Mike Ayers, stony sober on arrival, helped me get drinks around. At nine sharp Leopold Elkus joined the throng. I had no idea what Wolfe had told him to get him there; anyway, there he was, and what he wanted to drink was a glass of port, and I restrained an impulse to tell him there was no nitroglycerin in it. He recognized me and acted gracious. Some more came, among them Augustus Farrell, who had phoned on Saturday that he was back from Philadelphia and had landed the commission for Mr. Allenby's library. Wolfe, surmising that what he was really phoning about was the twenty bucks due him for Wednesday's work, had had me mail him a check.

They didn't seem as subdued as they had a week before. They took to the drinks with more gusto and gathered in groups and talked, and two or three of them even came up to me and got impatient. Collard, the Boston textile man who owned the cliff that Judge Harrison had fallen off of, told me he hoped to see the last act of the opera, and I said I was sorry but I myself had had to give up that hope long ago.

I overheard Elkus telling Ferdinand Bowen that it appeared likely that Nero Wolfe was in an advanced stage of megalomania, and tried to get Bowen's reply but missed it.

There were fifteen of them present at a quarter past nine, which was the time Wolfe had told me he would make his entrance.

It was a good entrance, all right. He did it in perfect style. I was watching for him, not to miss it. He came in, three paces in, and stood there until they had all turned to look at him and the talking had stopped. He inclined his head and used his resonance. "Good evening, gentlemen." Then he faced the door and nodded at Fritz, who was standing on the threshold. Fritz moved aside, and Andrew Hibbard walked in.

That started the first uproar. Pratt and Mike Ayers were the quickest to react. They both yelled "Andy!" and jumped for him. Others followed. They encircled him, shouted at him, grabbed his hands, and pounded him on the back. They had him hemmed in so that I couldn't see any of him, to observe what kind of psychology he was taking it with. It was easy to imagine, hearing them and looking at them, that they really liked Andy Hibbard. Maybe even Drummond and Bowen liked him; you've got to take the bitter along with the sweet.

Wolfe had eluded the stampede. He had got to his desk and lowered himself into his chair, and Fritz had brought him beer. I looked at him and was glad I did, for it wasn't often he felt like winking at me and I wouldn't have wanted to miss it. He returned my look and gave me the wink, and I grinned at him. Then he drank some beer.

The commotion went on a while longer. Mike Ayers came over to Wolfe's desk and said something which I couldn't hear on account of the noise, and Wolfe nodded and replied something. Mike Ayers went back and began shooing them into chairs, and Cabot and Farrell helped him. They subsided. Pratt took Hibbard by the arm and steered him to one of the big armchairs, and then sat down next to him and took out his handkerchief and wiped his eyes.

Wolfe started the ball rolling. He sat pretty straight, his forearms on the arms of his chair, his chin down, his eyes open on them.

"Gentlemen. Thank you for coming here this evening. Even if we should later come to disagreement, I am sure we are in accord as to the felicitous nature of our preamble. We are all glad that Mr. Hibbard is with us. Mr. Goodwin and I are gratified that we were able to play the Stanley to his Livingstone. As to the particular dark continent that Mr. Hibbard chose to explore, and the method of our finding him, those details must wait for another occasion, since we have more pressing business. I believe it is enough at present to say that Mr. Hibbard's disappearance was a venture on his own account, a sally in search of education. That is correct, Mr. Hibbard?"

They all looked at Hibbard. He nodded. "That's correct."

Wolfe took some papers from his drawer, spread them out, and picked one up. "I have here, gentlemen, a copy of the memorandum of our agreement. One of my undertakings herein was to remove from you all apprehension and expectation of injury from the person or persons responsible for the disappearance of Andrew Hibbard. I take it that that has been accomplished? You have no fear of Mr. Hibbard himself? Good. Then that much is done." He paused to look them over, face by face, and went on. "For the rest, it will be necessary to read you a document." He put the memorandum down and picked up another paper, sheets clipped to a brown paper jacket. "This, gentlemen, is dated November twelfth, which is today. It is signed with the name of Paul Chapin. At the top it is headed: CONFESSION OF PAUL CHAPIN REGARDING THE DEATHS OF WILLIAM R. HARRISON AND EUGENE DREYER AND THE WRITING AND DISPATCHING OF CERTAIN INFORMATIVE AND THREATENING VERSES. It reads as follows—"

Cabot the lawyer butted in. He would. He interrupted. "Mr. Wolfe. Of course this is interesting, but in view of what has happened do you think it's necessary?"

"Quite." Wolfe didn't look up. "If you will permit me."

"I, Paul Chapin, of Two-o-three Perry Street, New York City, hereby confess that I was in no way concerned in the death of Judge William R. Harrison. To the best of my knowledge and belief his death was accidental.

"I further confess that I was in no way concerned in the death of Eugene Dreyer. To the best of my knowledge and belief he committed suicide.

"I further confess—"

There was an explosive snort from Mike Ayers, and mutterings from some of the others. Julius Adler's mild sarcastic voice took the air. "This is drivel. Chapin has maintained throughout—"

Wolfe stopped him, and all of them. "Gentlemen! Please. I ask your indulgence. If you will withhold comments until the end."

Drummond squeaked, "Let him finish," and I made a mental note to give him an extra drink.

Wolfe continued:

"I further confess that the verses received by certain persons on three separate occasions were composed, typed, and mailed by me. They were intended to convey by implication the information that I had killed Harrison, Dreyer, and Hibbard, and that it was my purpose to kill others. They were typed on the typewriter in the alcove of the smoking room at the Harvard Club, a fact which was discovered by Nero Wolfe. That ends my confession. The rest is explanation, which I offer at Nero Wolfe's request.

"The idea of the verses, which came to me after Harrison's death, was at first only one of the fantasies which occupy a mind accustomed to invention. I composed them. They were good, at least for one purpose, and I decided to send them. I devised details as to paper, envelopes, and typing, which would leave no possibility of proving that they had been sent by me. They worked admirably, beyond my expectations.

"Three months later the death of Dreyer, and the circumstances under which it occurred, offered another opportunity which of course was irresistible. This was more risky than the first, since I had been present at the gallery that afternoon, but careful consideration convinced me that there was no real danger. I typed the second verses and sent them. They were even more successful than the first ones. I need not try to describe the satisfaction it gave me to fill with trepidation and terror the insolent breasts which for so many years had bulged their pity at me. They had called themselves the League of Atonement—oh yes, I knew that. Now at last atonement had in fact begun.

"I supplemented the effect of the verses verbally, with certain of my friends, whenever a safe opportunity offered, and this was more fertile with Andrew Hibbard than with anyone else. It ended by his becoming so terrified that he ran away. I do not know where he is; it is quite possible that he killed himself. As soon as I learned of his disappearance I decided to take advantage of it. Of course if he reappeared the game was up, but I had not supposed that I could continue the business indefinitely, and this was too good a chance to be missed. I sent the third verses. The result was nothing short of magnificent; indeed it proved to be too magnificent. I had never heard of Nero Wolfe. I went to his office that evening for the pleasure of seeing my friends, and to look at Wolfe. I saw that he was acute and intuitive, and that my diversion was probably at an end. An attempt was made by my wife to impress Wolfe, but it failed.

"There are other points that might be touched upon, but I believe none of them require explanation. I would like to mention, though, that my testimony on the witness-stand regarding my reason for writing my novel *Devil Take the Hindmost* was in my opinion a superlative bit of finesse, and Nero Wolfe agrees with me.

"I will add that I am not responsible for the literary quality of this document. It was written by Nero Wolfe.

"Paul Chapin."

Wolfe finished, dropped the confession to the table, and leaned back. "Now, gentlemen. If you wish to comment."

There were mumblings. Ferdinand Bowen, the stockbroker, spoke up. "It seems to me Adler has commented for all of us. Drivel."

Wolfe nodded. "I can understand that viewpoint. In fact, I suppose that under the circumstances it is inevitable. But let me expound my own viewpoint. My position is that I have met my obligations under the memorandum and that the payments are due."

"My dear sir!" It was Nicholas Cabot. "Preposterous."

"I think not. What I undertook to do was to remove your fear of Paul Chapin. That's what it amounts to, with the facts we now have. Well, as for Andrew Hibbard, here he is. As for the deaths of Harrison and Dreyer, it should have been obvious to all of you, from the beginning, that Chapin had nothing to do with them. You had known him all his mature life. I had merely read his books, but I was aware last Monday evening, when you gentlemen were here, that Chapin could not possibly commit a premeditated murder, and not even an impromptu one unless suddenly demented. And you, Mr. Hibbard, a psychologist! Have you read Chapin's books? Why are they so concerned with murder and the delight of it? Why does every page have its hymn to violence and the brute beauty of vehement action? Or, to change heroes, why did Nietzsche say, 'Thou goest to woman, forget not thy whip'? Because he had not the temerity to touch a woman with the tip of a goose feather. The truth is that Paul Chapin did murder Harrison and Dreyer, and all of you. He has murdered you, and will doubtless do so again, in his books. Let him, gentlemen, and go on breathing.

"No. Harrison and Dreyer and Hibbard are out of it. Consult the memorandum. There remains only the matter of the warnings. Chapin admits he sent them, and tells you how and why and where. The trilogy is done. There will be no sequels, and even if there were I should not suppose they would alarm you. If he should desire to use the same typewriter again he would have to come to this office for it, for it rests there on Mr. Goodwin's desk."

They all looked, and I moved out of the way so they could see it.

Wolfe drank beer, and wiped his lips. He resumed. "I know, of course, where the trouble lies. Paul Chapin is in the Tombs, charged with the murder of Dr. Burton. If that had not happened, if Dr. Burton were here with us this evening alive and well, I have no doubt that all of you would acquiesce in my position. I have done the work I was engaged for. But as it is, you are confused; and what confuses you is this, that whereas you formerly had no security at all against Paul Chapin's injurious designs, you now have more than you need. I offer you the security I undertook to get for you, but you are no longer interested in it because you already have something just as good: namely, that Chapin is going to be electrocuted and can no longer murder you even in books. Mr. Cabot, I ask you, as a lawyer, is that exposition of the situation correct? What do you think of it?"

"I think—" Cabot pursed his lips, and after a moment went on, "I think it is remarkably ingenious rubbish."

Wolfe nodded. "I would expect you to. I take it, gentlemen, that Mr. Cabot's opinion is approximately unanimous. Yes? So it becomes necessary for me to introduce a new consideration. This: that Chapin did not kill Dr. Burton, that I can establish his innocence, and that if tried he will be acquitted."

That started the second uproar. It began as a muttering of incredulity and astonishment; it was Leopold Elkus that put the noise in it. He jumped out of his chair and ran around Wolfe's desk to get at him and grabbed his hand and began pumping it. He seemed to be excited; he was yelling at Wolfe something about justice and gratitude and how great and grand Wolfe was; I didn't hear anything about megalomania. The others, busy with their own remarks, didn't pay any attention to him. Mike Ayers, roaring with laughter, got up and went to the table for a drink. I got up too, thinking I might have to go and haul Elkus off of Wolfe, but he finally trotted back to the others, gesticulating and still talking.

Wolfe lifted his hand at them. "Gentlemen! If you please. I seem to have startled you. Similarly, I suppose, the police and the District Attorney will be startled, though they should not be. You of course expect me to support my statement with evidence, but if I do that I must ask you for more impartiality than I observe at the moment on most of your faces. You cannot be at the same time juridical and partisan, at least not with any pretense at competence.

"I offer these items. First, at a few minutes before seven on Saturday evening Paul Chapin answered the telephone in his apartment. It was Dr. Burton, who asked Chapin to come to see him immediately. A little later Chapin left to go to Ninetieth Street, arriving there at seven-thirty. But there was something wrong with that telephone call, namely, that Dr. Burton never made it. For that we have the word of his wife, who says that her husband telephoned no one around that time Saturday. It seems likely, therefore, that there was somewhere a third person who was taking upon himself the functions of fate. I know, Mr. Adler. And I think I perceive, Mr. Bowen, that your face carries a similar expression. You would ask if I am gullible enough to believe Mr. Chapin. I am not gullible, but I believe him. He told his wife of the telephone call, and she told me; and there is the switchboard operator at the Chapin apartment house.

"Item two. Consider the details of what is supposed to have happened in the Burton foyer. Dr. Burton took the pistol from his desk and went to the foyer. Chapin, there waiting for him, took the pistol from him, shot him four times, turned out the light, threw the pistol on the floor and then got down on his hands and knees to look for it in the dark. What a picture! According to the story of Mrs. Burton and of the maid, Dr. Burton had been in the foyer not more than six seconds, possibly less, when the shots were fired. Burton was a good-sized man, and powerful. Chapin is small and is handicapped by a major deformity; he cannot even walk without support. Well, I am now going to count six seconds for you. One . . . two . . . three . . . four . . . five . . . six. That was six seconds. In that space of time, or less, the crippled Chapin is supposed to have got the gun from Burton's pocket, God knows how, shot him, dropped the gun, hobbled to the switch to turn off the light, and hobbled back to the table to fall to the floor. In your juridical capacity, gentlemen, what do you think of that?"

Leopold Elkus stood up. His black eyes were not floating back into his head now; he was using them for glaring. He let the bunch have the glare, right and left, saying loudly and clearly, "Anyone who ever believed that is no better than a cretin." He looked at Wolfe. "I shall have apologies for you, sir, when this kindergarten is over." He sat down.

"Thank you, Dr. Elkus. Item three, for what conceivable reason did Chapin turn out the light? I shall not take your time by listing conjectures only to have you reject them as I have done. Make your own when you have leisure for it, if it amuses you. I only say the actions even of a murderer should be in some degree explicable, and to believe that Chapin shot Burton and then hobbled to the wall to turn out the light is to believe nonsense. I doubt if any of you believe that. Do you?"

They looked at one another as if, having no opinions of their own, they would like to borrow one. Two or three shook their heads. George Pratt spoke up. "I'll tell you what I believe, Wolfe. I believe we hired you to get Paul Chapin into trouble, not out of it." Drummond giggled, and Mike Ayers laughed.

Nicholas Cabot demanded, "What does Chapin have to say? Did he shoot or didn't he? Did he turn out the light or didn't he? What does he say happened during those six seconds?"

Wolfe shook his head, and his cheeks unfolded a little. "Oh no, Mr. Cabot. It is possible that Mr. Chapin will have to tell his story on the witness-stand in his own defense. You can hardly expect me to disclose it in advance to those who may consider themselves his enemies."

"What the hell, no one would believe him anyway." It was Ferdinand Bowen relieving himself. "He'd cook up a tale, of course."

Wolfe turned his eyes on Bowen, and I had mine there too. I was curious to see if he would take it. I didn't think he would, but he did; he kept his gaze steady back at Wolfe.

Wolfe sighed. "Well, gentlemen, I have presented my case. I could offer further points for your consideration—for instance, the likelihood that if Chapin intended to kill Dr. Burton as soon as he set eyes on him he would have gone provided with a weapon. Also, Chapin's constitutional incapacity for any form of violent action, which I discovered through his novels, and which all of you must be acquainted with as a fact. And in addition there are items of evidence which I cannot divulge to you now, out of fairness to him, but which will certainly be used should he come to trial. Surely, surely I have offered enough to show you that if your minds have been cleared of any fear of injury from Paul Chapin, it is not because a policeman found him sitting in Dr. Burton's foyer, stunned by an event he could not have foreseen; it is because I have laid bare the purely literary nature of his attempt at vengeance. The question is this, have I satisfactorily performed my undertaking? I think I have. But it is you who are to decide it, by vote. I ask you to vote yes. Archie. If you will please call the names."

They began to talk. Bowen muttered to his neighbor, Gaines of Boston, "Pretty slick, but he's a damn fool if he thinks we'll fall for it." Elkus glared at him. I caught a few other observations. Cabot said to Wolfe, "I shall vote no. In case Chapin does get an acquittal, and evidence is presented—"

Wolfe nodded at him. "I am aware, Mr. Cabot, that this vote is not the last dingdong of doom. As you shall see, if I lose." He nodded at me, and I started the roll call. On the list I was using they were alphabetical.

"Julius Adler."

"No. I would like to say—"

Wolfe cut him off. "The no is sufficient. Proceed, Archie."

"Michael Ayers."

"Yes!" He made it emphatic. I thought, Good for him, with two weeks' wages up.

"Ferdinand Bowen."

"No."

"Edwin Robert Byron."

"Yes." That evened it up.

"Nicholas Cabot."

"No."

"Fillmore Collard."

"Yes." Wowie. Nine thousand berries. I paused because I had to look at him.

"Alexander Drummond."

"No." Sure, the damn canary.

"Leopold Elkus."

"Yes!" And it was even again, four and four.

"Augustus Farrell."

"Yes."

"Theodore Gaines."
"No."
"L. M. Irving."
"No."
"Arthur Kommers."
"No." Three out-of-town babies, three noes in a row, and I hoped Wolfe was proud of his long-distance phoning.
"Sidney Lang."
"Yes."
"Archibald Mollison."
"Yes."

It was even again, seven and seven, and just one more to go, but I knew what it would be before I called it. It was George Pratt, the Tammany bird who had tried to get Inspector Cramer worried about his four grand.

I said it. "George R. Pratt."
"No."

I counted them over to make sure, and turned to Wolfe. "Seven yeses and eight noes."

He didn't look at me. They all began talking. Wolfe had rung for another bottle of beer, and now he opened it, poured a glass, watched the foam go down, and drank. I put the list with the vote on it down in front of him, but he didn't look at it. He drank some more beer and wiped his lips with his usual care. Then he leaned back and shut his eyes. They were all talking, and two or three of them directed questions or remarks at him, but he kept his eyes closed and paid no attention. Leopold Elkus walked to the desk and stood and looked at him a minute, and then went back again. They were getting louder, and the arguments were warming up.

Finally Wolfe came to. He opened his eyes and saw that a fresh bottle of beer had arrived, which I had attended to, and opened it and drank some. Then he picked up a paperweight and rapped on the desk. They looked around, but went on talking. He rapped again, and they began to quiet down.

He spoke. "Gentlemen. I must again ask your indulgence—"

But Cabot was feeling his oats. He broke in, snappy. "We have voted. According to the memorandum, that settles it."

Wolfe got snappy too. "It settles that vote, sir. It does not settle the destiny of the human race. If you wish to leave us, of course you may, but we would still have a quorum without you. Good. I have two appeals to make. First, to those eight who voted no. Please heed me. I appeal to each and all of you—you understand, to each one of you—to change your vote to yes. I have a specific reason to hope that one of you will decide to change. Well, gentlemen? I shall give you one minute."

They shook their heads. One or two spoke, but mostly they were silent, gazing at Wolfe. There had been a new tone in his voice. He had taken out his watch and kept his eyes on it. At the end of the minute he returned it to his pocket and looked up.

He sighed. "Then I must proceed to my second appeal. This time, Mr. Bowen, it is to you alone. I ask you to vote yes. You of course know why. Will you vote yes?"

They all looked at the stockbroker. Including me. He was still taking it, but not so good. He damn near stuttered, shooting it back at Wolfe. I would say he did just fair with it. "Certainly not. Why should I?" His mouth stayed open; he thought he would talk some more, and then he thought he wouldn't.

Wolfe sighed again. "Mr. Bowen, you are a simpleton. Gentlemen, I would like to explain briefly why I have not done sooner what I am going to do now. There were two reasons: because I am not fond of interfering in affairs that are not my concern, and because it would be expensive for me. To be exact, it will cost me twelve hundred dollars, the amount of Mr. Bowen's payment under the memorandum. Besides that, as I have said, it was none of my business. If any person is suspected of having committed a crime, and if I am offered a sufficient sum of money to catch him up, I will do it. That is my business. I understand that there are individuals who will undertake to apprehend wrongdoers, especially murderers, without being paid for it. They do it, I presume, for amusement, which is not astonishing when you consider what odd diversions have been sought by various members of our race. I myself have other means of escaping boredom, but this is the only one I have developed of avoiding penury. I will hunt anyone down if you pay me enough. But no one has offered to pay me for discovering the murderer of Dr. Burton. By exposing him and delivering him to justice I shall lose twelve hundred dollars, but I shall ensure the collection of a larger sum. Now. Mr. Farrell, would you mind moving to another chair? If you please. And you, Archie, take the seat Mr. Farrell is vacating, next to Mr. Bowen."

I moved. My eyes hadn't left Bowen since Wolfe had asked him to vote yes, and now all eyes were on him. Nobody was saying a word. The stockbroker was up against it. By skating all around him with inference and insinuation but not directly accusing him, and prolonging it, Wolfe had him plenty perplexed. The others staring at him didn't help him any. I suppose he was trying to decide whether it was time for him to jump up and begin resenting things. He didn't glance at me as I sat down by him; he was looking at Wolfe.

Wolfe was on the phone. He kept his usual tempo, taking his time, though he had to try three numbers before he reached the man he wanted. He finally got him. Nobody on the chairs moved by a hair while he was talking.

"Inspector Cramer? This is Nero Wolfe. That's right. Good evening, sir. Inspector, I would like you to do me a favor. I have guests in my office, and no leisure at present for long explanations. I believe you know how much reliance may be placed in any positive statement I may make. Well. Will you send a man to my office—perhaps two would be better—for the murderer of Dr. Loring A. Burton? I have him here. No. No, indeed. I beg you. Explanations can come later. Of course, proof; what good is certainty without proof? By all means, if you wish to come yourself. Certainly."

He pushed the phone back, and Bowen jumped up. His knees were trembling, and so were his little lady-hands, which I was watching to see that he didn't make a pass. I took advantage of his being up to feel his rear for a gun, and my hands on him startled him. He forgot what he was going to say to Wolfe and turned on me, and by God he hauled off and kicked me on the shin. I got up and grabbed him and pushed him back into his chair and observed to him, "You try another friendly gesture like that and I'll paste you one."

Drummond, who had been sitting next to Bowen on the other side, moved away. Several others got up.

Wolfe said, "Sit down, gentlemen. I beg you, there is no occasion for turmoil. Archie, if you will kindly bring Mr. Bowen closer; I would like to see him better while talking to him. If it is necessary to prod him, you may do so."

I stood up and told the stockbroker to find his feet. He didn't move and he didn't look up; his hands were in his lap, twisting in a knot, and there were various colors distributed over his face and neck, and I was surprised not to see any yellow. I said, "Get a move on or I'll move you."

From behind me I heard George Pratt's voice, "You don't have to prove you're tough. Look at the poor devil."

"Yeah?" I didn't turn because I didn't care to take my eyes off of Bowen. "Was it your shin he kicked? Speak when you're spoken to."

I grabbed Bowen's collar and jerked him up, and he came. I admit he was pitiful. He stood for a second, trying to look around at them, and he tried to keep the quaver out of his voice. "Fellows. You understand why—if I don't say anything now to—to this ridiculous—"

He couldn't finish it anyhow, so I hauled him away. I put a chair up and sat him in it, then I perched on the edge of Wolfe's desk so as to face him. Two or three of the bunch got to their feet and approached us.

Wolfe turned to face the stockbroker. "Mr. Bowen. It gives me no pleasure to prolong your discomfiture in the presence of your friends, but in any event we must wait until the police arrive to take you away. Just now you used the word 'ridiculous'; may I borrow it from you? You are the most ridiculous murderer I have ever met. I do not know you well enough to be able to say whether it was through vast stupidity or extraordinary insouciance; however that may be, you planned the most hazardous of all crimes as if you were devising a harmless parlor game.

"I am not merely taunting you; I am depriving you of your last tatters of hope and courage in order to break you down. You stole a large sum from Dr. Burton through his account with your firm. I know nothing of the mechanism of your theft; that will be uncovered when the District Attorney examines your books. You found that Dr. Burton had discovered the theft, or suspected it, and on Saturday you went to his apartment to appeal to him, but already you had arranged an alternative in case the appeal failed. You were with Burton in his study. He went to his wife's room to ask her if she cared enough for Estelle Bowen to make a big sacrifice for her, and his wife said no. Burton returned to the study, and you got your answer; but during his absence you had got his automatic pistol from the drawer of his desk and put it in your pocket. Since you were his close friend you had probably known for a long time that he kept a gun there; if not, you heard him in this room a week ago tonight telling all of us that on the occasion of Paul Chapin's last visit to him he had got the gun from the drawer before he went to see Chapin in the foyer. Would you like a drink?"

Bowen made no reply or movement. Mike Ayers went to the table and got a shot of rye and came over with it and offered it to him, but Bowen paid no attention. Mike Ayers shrugged his shoulders and drank it himself.

Wolfe was going on. "Soon you left, at twenty minutes past six. No one went to the foyer with you; or if Burton did go, you pushed the button on the edge of the door as you went out, so it would not lock, and in a moment re-entered. At all events, you were alone in the foyer and the Burtons thought you had gone. You listened. Hearing no one, you went to the telephone. You had your gloves in your hand, and, not to be encumbered with them while phoning, you laid them on the table. But before your call had gone through you were interrupted by the sound of someone approaching in the drawing room. Alarmed, you ran for the concealment which you had already decided on: the curtained closet next to the light switch and the double doors. You got behind the curtain in time, before Miss Burton, the daughter of the house, came through, leaving the apartment.

"You realized that you had left your gloves lying on the table, and that concerned you, for you would need them to keep fingerprints from the gun—and, by the way, did it not occur to you that the phone would show prints? Or did you wipe them off? No matter. But you did not at once dash out for the gloves, for you needed a little time to collect yourself after the alarm the daughter had given you. You waited, and probably congratulated yourself that you did, for almost at once you heard the double door opening again, and footsteps, and the opening of the entrance door. It was Dora Chapin, arriving to do Mrs. Burton's hair.

"Mr. Paul Chapin was out Saturday afternoon and did not return until rather late. This morning on the telephone the switchboard operator at his apartment house told me that there was a phone call for Mr. Chapin some fifteen or twenty minutes before he arrived home. So it seems likely that about six-forty you emerged from your hiding place, got the gloves, and tried the phone again, but there was no answer from the Chapin apartment. You returned to the closet and, fifteen minutes later, tried again. Of course you did not know that that last phone call of yours, at about five minutes to seven, happened to coincide with Mr. Chapin's entrance into the hall of the Perry Street house; the switchboard operator called to him, and he answered that call at the switchboard itself, so the operator heard it. Apparently you imitated Dr. Burton's voice with some success, for Mr. Chapin was deceived. He went upstairs to his apartment for a few minutes, and then came down to take a cab to Ninetieth Street.

"After phoning Chapin you returned again to the closet and waited there, with an accelerated pulse, I presume, and an emergency demand on your supply of adrenalin. Indeed, you seem practically to have exhausted the latter. I imagine that it seemed quite a while before Chapin arrived, and you were surprised later to find that it had been only thirty-five minutes since your phone call. At all events, he came, was admitted by the maid, and sat down. In your closet you kept your ears keen to learn if he took a chair that would turn his back to you; you had your gloves on, and the gun in your right hand ready for action. Still you strained your ears to hear the approach of Dr. Burton. You heard his steps crossing the drawing room, and the instant the sound came of his hand on the doorknob, you moved. Here, I confess, you showed efficiency and accuracy. Your left arm shot out past the edge of the curtain, your fingers found the light switch and pushed it, and the foyer was in darkness except for the dim light that wandered through the door from the drawing room after Dr. Burton had opened it. With the light off, you jumped from the closet, found Chapin in his chair, and shoved him off onto the floor—not difficult with a cripple, was it, Mr. Bowen? By that time Dr. Burton had approached the commotion and was quite close when you shot him, and there was enough light from the drawing-room door for you to tell where his middle was. You pulled the trigger and held it for four shots, then threw the gun to the floor—and made your exit, after closing the double door. In the hall you ran to the stairs and ran down them. There were only four flights, and one more to the basement, and a short stretch of hall to the service entrance. You calculated that even if you encountered someone there would be no great danger in it, for the guilt of Paul Chapin would be so obvious that no questions would be asked of anyone outside of the apartment.

"Now, Mr. Bowen, you made many mistakes, but none so idiotic as your sole reliance on Chapin's obvious guilt, for that one was the father of all the others. Why in the name of heaven didn't you turn on the light again as you went out? And why didn't you wait until Chapin and Burton had talked a minute or two before you acted? You could have done just as well. Another inexcusable thing was your carelessness in leaving the gloves on the table. I know; you were so sure that they would be sure of Chapin that you thought nothing else mattered.

You were worse than a tyro, you were a donkey. I tell you this, sir, your exposure is a credit to no one, least of all to me. Pfui!"

Wolfe stopped abruptly and turned to ring for Fritz, for beer. Bowen's fingers had been twisting in and out, but now they had stopped that and were locked together. He was shaking all over, just sitting in his chair, shaking, with no nerve left, no savvy, no nothing; he was nothing but a gob of scared meat.

Leopold Elkus came up and stood three feet from Bowen and stood staring at him; I had a feeling that he had a notion to cut him open and see what was inside. Mike Ayers appeared with another drink, but this time it wasn't for Bowen; he held it out to me, and I took it and drank it. Andrew Hibbard went to my desk and got the telephone and gave the operator the number of his home. Drummond was squeaking something to George Pratt.

Nicholas Cabot passed around Bowen's chair, went up to Wolfe, and said to him in a tone not low enough for me not to hear, "I'm going, Mr. Wolfe. I have an appointment. I want to say there's no reason why you shouldn't get that twelve hundred dollars from Bowen. It's a legal obligation. If you'd like me to handle the collection I'd be glad to do it and expect no fee. Let me know."

That lawyer was tough.

XXII

THREE days later, Thursday around noon, we had a caller. I had just got back from taking a vast and voluminous deposit to the bank, and was sitting at my desk, bending my thoughts toward a little relaxation in the shape of an afternoon movie. Wolfe was in his chair, leaning back with his eyes shut, still and silent as a mountain, probably considering the adequacy of the plans for lunch.

Fritz came to the door and said, "A man to see you, sir. Mr. Paul Chapin."

Wolfe opened his eyes to a slit and nodded. I whirled my chair around and stood up.

The cripple hobbled in. It was a bright day outside, and the strong light from the windows gave me a better look at him than I had ever had. I saw that his eyes weren't quite as light-colored as I had thought, they were about the shade of dull aluminum; and his skin wasn't dead pale, it was more like bleached leather; it looked tough. He gave me only half a glance as he thumped across to Wolfe's desk. I moved a chair around for him.

"Good morning, Mr. Chapin." Wolfe nearly opened his eyes. "You won't be seated? I beg you—thanks. It gives me genuine discomfort to see people stand. Allow me to congratulate you on your appearance. If I had spent three days in the Tombs prison, as you did, I would be nothing but a wraith, a tattered remnant. How were the meals? I presume, unspeakable?"

The cripple lifted his shoulders and dropped them. He didn't appear to be settling down for a chat; he had lowered himself onto the edge of the chair I had placed for him, and perched there with his stick upright in front and both his hands resting on the crook. His aluminum eyes had the same amount of expression in them that aluminum usually has.

He said, "I sit for courtesy, to relieve you of discomfort—for a moment only. I came for the pair of gloves which you removed from my box."

"Ah!" Wolfe's eyes opened the rest of the way. "So your blessings are numbered. Indeed!"

Chapin nodded. "Luckily. May I have them?"

"Another disappointment." Wolfe sighed. "I was thinking you had taken the trouble to call to convey your gratitude for my saving you from the electric chair. You are, of course, grateful?"

Chapin's lips twisted. "I am as grateful as you would expect me to be. So we needn't waste time on that. May I have the gloves?"

"You may. Archie, if you please. To me."

I got the gloves from a drawer of my desk and handed them across to Wolfe. He came forward in his chair to place them in front of him on his own desk, one neatly on top of the other, and to smooth them out. Chapin's gaze was fastened on the gloves.

Wolfe leaned back and sighed again. "You know, Mr. Chapin, I never got to use them. I retained them, from your box, to demonstrate a point Monday evening by showing how nearly they fitted Mr. Bowen, thus explaining how Dora Chapin—your wife—could mistake Mr. Bowen's gloves for a pair of Mrs. Burton's; but since he wilted like a dendrobium with root-rot there was no occasion for it. Now"— Wolfe wiggled a finger—"I don't expect you to believe this, but it is nevertheless true that I halfway suspected that your knowledge of the contents of your box was intimate enough to make you aware of the absence of any fraction of the inventory, so I did not return these. I kept them. I wanted to see you."

Paul Chapin, saying nothing, took a hand from his walking-stick and reached out for the gloves. Wolfe shook his head and pulled them back a little. The cripple tossed his head up.

"Just a morsel of patience, Mr. Chapin. I wanted to see you because I had an apology to make. I am hoping that you will accept it."

"I came for my gloves. You may keep the apology."

"But, my dear sir!" Wolfe wiggled a finger again. "Permit me at least to describe my offense. I wish to apologize for forging your name."

Chapin lifted his brows.

Wolfe turned to me. "A copy of the confession, Archie."

I went to the safe and got it and gave it to him. He unfolded it and handed it across to the cripple. I sat down and grinned at Wolfe, but he pretended not to notice; he leaned back with his eyes half closed, laced his fingers at his belly, and sighed.

Chapin read the confession twice. He first glanced at it indifferently and ran through it rapidly, then took a squint at Wolfe, twisted his lips a little, and read the confession all over again, not nearly so fast.

He tossed it over to the desk. "Fantastic," he declared. "Set down that way, prosaically, baldly, it sounds fantastic. Doesn't it?"

Wolfe nodded. "It struck me, Mr. Chapin, that you went to a great deal of trouble for a pitifully meager result. Of course you understand that I required this document for the impression it would make on your friends, and, knowing the impossibility of persuading you to sign it for me, I was compelled to write your name myself. That is what I wish to apologize for. Here are your gloves, sir. I take it that my apology is accepted."

The cripple took the gloves, felt them, put them in his inside breast pocket, grabbed the arms of his chair, and raised himself. He stood leaning on his stick.

"You knew I wouldn't sign such a document? How did you know that?"

"Because I had read your books. I had seen you. I was acquainted with your—let us say, your indomitable spirit."

"You have another name for it?"

"Many. Your appalling infantile contumacy. It got you a crippled leg. It got you a wife. It very nearly got you two thousand volts of electricity."

Chapin smiled. "So you read my books. Read the next one. I'm putting you in it—a leading character."

"Naturally." Wolfe opened his eyes. "And of course I die violently. I warn you, Mr. Chapin, I resent that. I actively resent it. I have a deep repugnance for violence in all its forms. I would go to any length in an effort to persuade you—"

He was talking to no one—or at least, merely to the back of a cripple who was hobbling to the door.

At the threshold Chapin turned for a moment, long enough for us to see him smile and hear him say, "You will die, sir, in the most abhorrent manner conceivable to an appalling infantile imagination. I promise you."

He went.

Wolfe leaned back and shut his eyes. I sat down. Later I could permit myself a grin at the thought of the awful fate in store for Nero Wolfe, but for the moment I had my mind back on Monday afternoon, examining details of various events. I remembered that, when I had left to call on Mrs. Burton, Wolfe had been there discussing soda water with Fritz, and when I returned he had gone, and so had the sedan. But not to the Tombs to see Paul Chapin. He had never left the house. The sedan had gone to the garage, and Wolfe to his room, with his coat and hat and stick and gloves, to drink beer in his easy chair. And at a quarter to four it was from his room that he had telephoned me to take the box to Mrs. Chapin, to give him a chance to fake a return. Of course Fritz had been in on it, so he had fooled me too. And Hibbard shooed off to the third floor for the afternoon . . .

They had made a monkey of *me* all right.

I said to Wolfe, "I had intended to go to a movie after lunch, but now I can't. I've got work ahead. I've got to figure out certain suggestions to make to Paul Chapin for his next book. My head is full of ideas."

"Indeed." Wolfe's bulk came forward to permit him to ring for beer. "Archie." He nodded at me gravely. "Your head full of ideas? Even my death by violence is not too high a price for so rare and happy a phenomenon as that."

AND BE A VILLAIN

> Meet it is I set it down,
> That one may smile, and smile, and be a villain. . . .
> —HAMLET, *Act I*

I

For the third time I went over the final additions and subtractions on the first page of Form 1040, to make good and sure. Then I swiveled my chair to face Nero Wolfe, who was seated behind his desk to the right of mine, reading a book of poems by a guy named Van Doren, Mark Van Doren. So I thought I might as well use a poetry word.

"It's bleak," I said.

There was no sign that he heard.

"Bleak," I repeated. "If it means what I think it does. Bleak!"

His eyes didn't lift from the page, but he murmured, "What's bleak?"

"Figures." I leaned to slide the Form 1040 across the waxed grain of his desk. "This is March thirteenth. Four thousand three hundred and twelve dollars and sixty-eight cents, in addition to the four quarterly installments already paid. Then we have to send in 1040-ES for 1948, and a check for ten thousand bucks goes with it." I clasped my fingers at the back of my head and asked grimly, "Bleak or not?"

He asked what the bank balance was and I told him. "Of course," I conceded, "that will take care of the two wallops from our rich uncle just mentioned, also a loaf of bread and a sliver of shad roe, but weeks pass and bills arrive, not to be so crude as to speak of paying Fritz and Theodore and me."

Wolfe had put down the poetry and was scowling at the Form 1040, pretending he could add.

I raised my voice. "But you own this house and furniture, except the chair and other items in my room which I bought myself, and you're the boss and you know best. Sure. That electric-company bird would have been good for at least a grand over and above expenses on his forgery problem, but you couldn't be bothered. Mrs. What's-her-name would have paid twice that, plenty, for the lowdown on that so-called musician, but you were too busy reading. That lawyer by the name of Clifford was in a bad hole and had to buy help, but he had dandruff. That actress and her gentleman protector—"

"Archie. Shut up."

"Yes, sir. Also what do you do? You come down from your beautiful orchids day before yesterday and breeze in here and tell me merrily to draw another man-size check for that World Government outfit. When I meekly mention that the science of bookkeeping has two main branches, first addition and second subtraction—"

"Leave the room!"

I snarled in his direction, swiveled back to my desk position, got the typewriter in place, inserted paper with carbon, and started to tap out, from my work sheet, Schedule G for line 6 of Schedule C. Time passed and I went on with the job, now and then darting a glance to the right to see if he had had the brass to resume on the book. He hadn't. He was leaning back in his chair, which was big enough for two but not two of him, motionless, with his eyes closed. The tempest was raging. I had a private grin and went on with my work. Somewhat later, when I was finishing Schedule F for line 16 of Schedule C, a growl came from him.

"Archie."

"Yes, sir." I swiveled.

"A man condemning the income tax because of the annoyance it gives him or the expense it puts him to is merely a dog baring its teeth, and he forfeits the privileges of civilized discourse. But it is permissible to criticize it on other and impersonal grounds. A government, like an individual, spends money for any or all of three reasons: because it needs to, because it wants to, or simply because it has it to spend. The last is much the shabbiest. It is arguable, if not manifest, that a substantial proportion of this great spring flood of billions pouring into the Treasury will in effect get spent for that last shabby reason."

"Yeah. So we deduct something? How do I word it?"

Wolfe half opened his eyes. "You are sure of your figures?"

"Only too sure."

"Did you cheat much?"

"Average. Nothing indecent."

"I have to pay the amounts you named?"

"Either that or forfeit some privileges."

"Very well." Wolfe sighed clear down, sat a minute, and straightened in his chair. "Confound it. There was a time when a thousand dinars a year was ample for me. Get Mr. Richards of the Federal Broadcasting Company."

I frowned at him, trying to guess; then, because I knew he was using up a lot of energy sitting up straight, I gave up, found the number in the book, dialed, and, by using Wolfe's name, got through to Richards three minutes under par for a vice-president.

Wolfe took his phone, exchanged greetings, and went on. "In my office two years ago, Mr. Richards, when you handed me a check, you said that you felt you were still in my debt—in spite of the size of the check. So I'm presuming to ask a favor of you. I want some confidential information. What amount of money is involved, weekly let us say, in the radio program of Miss Madeline Fraser?"

"Oh." There was a pause. Richards's voice had been friendly and even warm. Now it backed off a little. "How did you get connected with that?"

"I'm not connected with it, not in any way. But I would appreciate the information—confidentially. Is it too much for me?"

"It's an extremely unfortunate situation, for Miss Fraser, for the network, for the sponsors—everyone concerned. You wouldn't care to tell me why you're interested?"

"I'd rather not." Wolfe was brusque. "I'm sorry I bothered you—"

"You're not bothering me, or if you are you're welcome. The information you want isn't published, but everyone in radio knows it. Everyone in radio knows everything. Exactly what do you want?"

"The total sum involved."

"Well—let's see—counting air time, it's on nearly two hundred stations—production, talent, scripts, everything—roughly, thirty thousand dollars a week."

"Nonsense," Wolfe said curtly.

"Why nonsense?"

"It's monstrous. That's over a million and a half a year."

"No, around a million and a quarter, on account of the summer vacation."

"Even so. I suppose Miss Fraser gets a material segment of it?"

"Quite material. Everyone knows that too. Her take is around five thousand a week, but the way she splits it with her manager, Miss Koppel, is one thing everyone doesn't know—at least I don't." Richards's voice had warmed up again. "You know, Mr. Wolfe, if you felt like doing me a little favor right back you could tell me confidentially what you want with this."

But all he got from Wolfe was thanks, and he was gentleman enough to take them without insisting on the return favor. After Wolfe had pushed the phone away he remarked to me, "Good heavens. Twelve hundred thousand dollars!"

I, feeling better because it was obvious what he was up to, grinned at him. "Yes, sir. You would go over big on the air. You could read poetry. By the way, if you want to hear her earn her segment, she's on every Tuesday and Friday morning from eleven to twelve. You'd get pointers. Was that your idea?"

"No." He was gruff. "My idea is to land a job I know how to do. Take your notebook. These instructions will be a little complicated on account of the contingencies to be provided for."

I got my notebook from a drawer.

II

AFTER three tries that Saturday at the listed Manhattan number of Madeline Fraser, with "don't answer" as the only result, I finally resorted to Lon Cohen of the *Gazette* and he dug it out for me that both Miss Fraser and her manager, Miss Deborah Koppel, were weekending up in Connecticut.

As a citizen in good standing—anyway, pretty good—my tendency was to wish the New York Police Department good luck in its contacts with crime, but I frankly hoped that Inspector Cramer and his Homicide scientists wouldn't get Scotch tape on the Orchard case before we had a chance to inspect the contents. Judging from the newspaper accounts I had read, it didn't seem likely that Cramer was getting set to toot a trumpet, but you can never tell how much is being held back, so I was all for driving to Connecticut and horning in on the weekend, but Wolfe vetoed it and told me to wait until Monday.

By noon Sunday he had finished the book of poems and was drawing pictures of horses on sheets from his memo pad, testing a theory he had run across somewhere that you can analyze a man's character from the way he draws a horse. I had completed Forms 1040 and 1040-ES and, with checks enclosed, they had been mailed. After lunch

I hung around the kitchen a while, listening to Wolfe and Fritz Brenner, the chef and household jewel, arguing whether horse mackerel is as good as Mediterranean tunny fish for *vitello tonnato*—which, as prepared by Fritz, is the finest thing on earth to do with tender young veal. When the argument began to bore me because there was no Mediterranean tunny fish to be had anyhow, I went up to the top floor, to the plant rooms that had been built on the roof, and spent a couple of hours with Theodore Horstmann on the germination records. Then, remembering that on account of a date with a lady I wouldn't have the evening for it, I went down three flights to the office, took the newspapers for five days to my desk, and read everything they had on the Orchard case.

When I had finished I wasn't a bit worried that Monday morning's paper would confront me with a headline that the cops had wrapped it up.

III

THE BEST I was able to get on the phone was an appointment for three P.M., so at that hour Monday afternoon I entered the lobby of an apartment house in the upper Seventies between Madison and Park. It was the palace type, with rugs bought by the acre, but with the effect somewhat spoiled, as it so often is, by a rubber runner on the main traffic lane merely because the sidewalk was wet with rain. That's no way to run a palace. If a rug gets a damp dirty footprint, what the hell, toss it out and roll out another one, that's the palace spirit.

I told the distinguished-looking hallman that my name was Archie Goodwin and I was bound for Miss Fraser's apartment. He got a slip of paper from his pocket, consulted it, nodded, and inquired, "And? Anything else?"

I stretched my neck to bring my mouth within a foot of his ear, and whispered to him, "Oatmeal."

He nodded again, signaled with his hand to the elevator man, who was standing outside the door of his car fifteen paces away, and said in a cultivated voice, "Ten B."

"Tell me," I requested, "about this password gag, is it just since the murder trouble or has it always been so?"

He gave me an icy look and turned his back. I told the back, "That costs you a nickel. I fully intended to give you a nickel."

With the elevator man I decided not to speak at all. He agreed. Out at the tenth floor, I found myself in a box no bigger than the elevator, another palace trick, with a door to the left marked 10A and one to the right marked 10B. The elevator man stayed there until I had pushed the button on the latter, and the door had opened and I had entered.

The woman who had let me in, who might easily have been a female wrestling champion twenty years back, said, "Excuse me, I'm in a hurry," and beat it on a trot. I called after her, "My name's Goodwin!" but got no reaction.

I advanced four steps, took off my hat and coat and dropped them on a chair, and made a survey. I was in a big square sort of a hall, with doors off to the left and in the wall ahead. To the right, instead of a wall and doors, it just spread out into an enormous living room which contained at least twenty different kinds of furniture. My eye was professionally trained to take in anything from a complicated street scene to a speck on a man's collar, and really get it, but for the job of accurately describing that room I would have charged double. Two of the outstanding items were a chrome-and-red-leather bar with stools to match and a massive old black walnut table with carved legs and edges. That should convey the tone of the place.

There was nobody in sight, but I could hear voices. I advanced to pick out a chair to sit on, saw none that I thought much of, and settled on a divan ten feet long and four feet wide, covered with green burlap. A nearby chair had pink embroidered silk. I was trying to decide what kind of a horse the person who furnished that room would draw, when company entered the square hall sector from one of the doors in the far wall—two men, one young and handsome, the other middle-aged and bald, both loaded down with photographic equipment, including a tripod.

"She's showing her age," the young man said.

"Age, hell," the bald man retorted, "She's had a murder, hasn't she? Have you ever had a murder?" He caught sight of me and asked his companion, "Who's that?"

"I don't know, never saw him before." The young man was trying to open the entrance door without dropping anything. He succeeded, and they passed through, and the door closed behind them.

In a minute another of the doors in the square hall opened and the female wrestler appeared. She came in my direction, but, reaching me, trotted on by, made for a door near a corner off to the left, opened it, and was gone.

I was beginning to feel neglected.

Ten minutes more and I decided to take the offensive. I was on my feet and had taken a couple of steps when there was another entrance, again from an inside door at the far side of the square hall, and I halted. The newcomer headed for me, not at a jerky trot but with a smooth easy flow, saying as she approached, "Mr. Goodwin?"

I admitted it.

"I'm Deborah Koppel." She offered her hand. "We never really catch up with ourselves around here."

She had already given me two surprises. At first glance I had thought her eyes were small and insignificant, but when she faced me and talked I saw they were quite large, very dark, and certainly shrewd. Also, because she was short and fat, I had expected the hand I took to be pudgy and moist, but it was firm and strong though small. Her complexion was dark and her dress was black. Everything about her was either black or dark, except the gray, almost white by comparison, showing in her night-black hair.

"You told Miss Fraser on the phone," she was saying in her high, thin voice, "that you have a suggestion for her from Mr. Nero Wolfe."

"That's right."

"She's very busy. Of course she always is. I'm her manager. Would you care to tell me about it?"

"I'd tell you anything," I declared. "But I work for Mr. Wolfe. His instructions are to tell Miss Fraser, but now, having met you, I'd like to tell her *and* you."

She smiled. The smile was friendly, but it made her eyes look even shrewder. "Very good ad libbing," she said approvingly. "I wouldn't want you to disobey your instructions. Will it take long?"

"That depends. Somewhere between five minutes and five hours."

"By no means five hours. Please be as brief as you can. Come this way."

She turned and started for the square hall and I followed. We went through a door, crossed a room that had a piano, a bed, and an electric refrigerator in it, which left it anybody's guess how to name it, and on through another door into a corner room big enough to have six windows, three on one side and three on another. Every object in it, and it was anything but empty, was either pale yellow or pale blue. The wood, both the trim and the furniture, was painted blue, but other things—rugs, upholstery, curtains, bed coverlet—were divided indiscriminately between the two colors. Among the few exceptions were the bindings of the books on the shelves and the clothes of the blond young man who was seated on a chair. The woman lying on the bed kept to the scheme, with her lemon-colored house gown and her light blue slippers.

The blond young man rose and came to meet us, changing expression on the way. My first glimpse of his face had shown me a gloomy frown, but now his eyes beamed with welcome and his mouth was arranged into a smile that would have done a brush salesman proud. I suppose he did it from force of habit, but it was uncalled for because I was the one who was going to sell something.

"Mr. Goodwin," Deborah Koppel said. "Mr. Meadows."

"Bill Meadows. Just make it Bill, everyone does." His handshake was out of stock but he had the muscle for it. "So you're Archie Goodwin? This is a real pleasure! The next best thing to meeting the great Nero Wolfe himself!"

A rich contralto voice broke in. "This is my rest period, Mr. Goodwin, and they won't let me get up. I'm not even supposed to talk, but when the time comes that I don't talk—!"

I stepped across to the bed, and as I took the hand Madeline Fraser offered she smiled. It wasn't a shrewd smile like Deborah Koppel's or a synthetic one like Bill Meadows's, but just a smile from her to me. Her gray-green eyes didn't give the impression that she was measuring me, though she probably was, and I sure was measuring her. She was slender but not skinny and she looked quite long, stretched out on the bed. With no makeup on it at all it was quite possible to look at her face without having to resist an impulse to look somewhere else, which was darned good for a woman certainly close to forty and probably a little past it, especially since I personally can see no point in spending eyesight on females over thirty.

"You know," she said, "I have often been tempted—bring chairs up, Bill—to ask Nero Wolfe to be a guest on my program."

She said it like a trained broadcaster, breaking it up so it would sound natural but arranging the inflections so that listeners of any mental age whatever would get it.

"I'm afraid," I told her with a grin, "that he wouldn't accept unless you ran wires to his office and broadcast from there. He never leaves home on business, and rarely for anything at all." I lowered myself onto one of the chairs Bill had brought up, and he and Deborah Koppel took the other two.

Madeline Fraser nodded. "Yes, I know." She had turned on her side to see me without twisting her neck, and the hip curving up under the thin yellow gown made her seem not quite so slender. "Is that just a publicity trick or does he really like it?"

"I guess both. He's very lazy, and he's scared to death of moving objects, especially things on wheels."

"Wonderful! Tell me all about him."

"Some other time, Lina," Deborah Koppel put in. "Mr. Goodwin has a suggestion for you, and you have a broadcast tomorrow and haven't even looked at the script."

"My God, is it Monday already?"

"Monday and half-past three," Deborah said patiently.

The radio prima donna's torso propped up to perpendicular as if someone had given her a violent jerk. "What's the suggestion?" she demanded, and flopped back again.

"What made him think of it," I said, "was something that happened to him Saturday. This great nation took him for a ride. Two rides. The Rides of March."

"Income tax? Me too. But what—"

"That's good!" Bill Meadows exclaimed. "Where did you get it? Has it been on the air?"

"Not that I know of. I created it yesterday morning while I was brushing my teeth."

"We'll give you ten bucks for it—no, wait a minute." He turned to Deborah. "What percentage of our audience ever heard of the Ides of March?"

"One-half of one," she said as if she were quoting a published statistic. "Cut."

"You can have it for a dollar," I offered generously. "Mr. Wolfe's suggestion will cost you a lot more. Like everyone in the upper brackets, he's broke." My eyes were meeting the gray-green gaze of Madeline Fraser. "He suggests that you hire him to investigate the murder of Cyril Orchard."

"Oh, Lord," Bill Meadows protested, and brought his hands up to press the heels of his palms against his eyes. Deborah Koppel looked at him, then at Madeline Fraser, and took in air for a deep sigh. Miss Fraser shook her head, and suddenly looked older and more in need of makeup.

"We have decided," she said, "that the only thing we can do about that is forget it as soon as possible. We have ruled it out of conversation."

"That would be fine and sensible," I conceded, "if you could make everyone, including the cops and the papers, obey the rule. But aside from the difficulty of shutting people up about any old kind of a murder, even a dull one, it was simply too good a show. Maybe you don't realize how good. Your program has an eight million audience, twice a week. Your guests were a horse-race tipster and a professor of mathematics from a big university. And smack in the middle of the program one of them makes terrible noises right into the microphone, and keels over, and pretty soon he's dead, and he got the poison right there on the broadcast, in the product of one of your sponsors."

I darted glances at the other two and then back to the woman on the bed. "I knew I might meet any one of a dozen attitudes here, but I sure didn't expect this one. If you don't know, you ought to, that one like that doesn't get ruled out of conversation, not only not in a week, but not in twenty years—not when the question is still open who provided the poison. Twenty years from now people would still be arguing about who was it, Madeline Fraser or Deborah Koppel or Bill Meadows or Nathan Traub or F. O. Savarese or Elinor Vance or Nancylee Shepherd or Tully Strong—"

The door came open and the female wrestler entered and announced in a hasty breath, "Mr. Strong is here."

"Send him in, Cora," Miss Fraser told her.

I suppose I would have been struck by the contrast between Tully Strong and his name if I hadn't known what to expect from his pictures in the papers. He looked like them in the obvious points—the rimless spectacles, the thin lips, the long neck, the hair brushed flat—but somehow in the flesh he didn't look as dumb and vacant as the pictures. I got that much noted while he was being greeted, by the time he turned to me for the introduction.

"Mr. Strong," Deborah Koppel told me, "is the secretary of our Sponsors' Council."

"Yes, I know."

"Mr. Goodwin," she told him, "has called with a suggestion from Nero Wolfe. Mr. Wolfe is a private detective."

"Yes, I know." Tully Strong smiled at me. With lips as thin as his it is often difficult to tell whether it's a smile or a grimace, but I would have called it a smile, especially when he added, "We are both famous, aren't we? Of course you are accustomed to the glare of the spotlight, but it is quite new to me." He sat down. "What does Mr. Wolfe suggest?"

"He thinks Miss Fraser ought to hire him to look into the murder of Cyril Orchard."

"Damn Cyril Orchard." Yes, it had been a smile, for now it was a grimace, and it was quite different. "Damn him to hell!"

"That's pretty tough," Bill Meadows objected, "since he may be there right now."

Strong ignored him to ask me, "Aren't the police giving us enough trouble without deliberately hiring someone to give us more?"

"Sure they are," I agreed, "but that's a shortsighted view of it. The person who is really giving you trouble is the one who put the poison in the Starlite. As I was explaining when you came, the trouble will go on for years unless and until he gets tapped on the shoulder. Of course the police may get him, but they've had it for six days now and you know how far they've got. The one that stops the trouble will be the one that puts it where it belongs. Do you know that Mr. Wolfe is smart or shall I go into that?"

"I had hoped," Deborah Koppel put in, "that Mr. Wolfe's suggestion would be something concrete. That he had a—an idea."

"Nope." I made it definite. "His only idea is to get paid twenty thousand dollars for ending the trouble."

Bill Meadows let out a whistle. Deborah Koppel smiled at me.

Tully Strong protested indignantly. "Twenty thousand!"

"Not from me," said Madeline Fraser, fully as definite as I had been. "I really must get to work on my broadcast, Mr. Goodwin."

"Now wait a minute." I concentrated on her. "That's only one of my points, getting the trouble over, and not the best one. Look at it this way. You and your program have had a lot of publicity out of this, haven't you?"

She groaned. "Publicity, my God! The man calls it publicity!"

"So it is," I maintained, "but out of the wrong barrel. And it's going to keep coming, still out of the wrong barrel, whether you like it or not. Again tomorrow every paper in town will have your name in a front-page headline. You can't help that, but you can decide what the headline will say. As it stands now you know darned well what it will say. What if, instead of that, it announces that you have engaged Nero Wolfe to investigate the murder of the guest on your program because of your passionate desire to see justice done? The piece would explain the terms of the arrangement; you are to pay the expenses of the investigation—unpadded, we don't pad expenses—and that's all you are to pay unless Mr. Wolfe gets the murderer with evidence to convict. If he comes through you pay him a fee of twenty thousand dollars. Would that get the headline or not? What kind of publicity would it be, still out of the wrong barrel? What percentage of your audience and the general public would it persuade, not only that you and yours are innocent, but that you are a hero to sacrifice a fortune for the sake of justice? Ninety-nine and one-half per cent. Very few of them would stop to consider that both the expenses and the fee will be deductible on your income tax and, in your bracket, the actual cost to you would be around four thousand dollars, no more. In the public mind you would no longer be one of the suspects in a sensational murder case, being hunted—you would be a champion of the people, *hunting* a murderer."

I spread out my hands. "And you would get all that, Miss Fraser, even if Mr. Wolfe had the worst flop of his career and all it cost you was expenses. Nobody could say you hadn't tried. It's a big bargain for you. Mr. Wolfe almost never takes a case on a contingent basis, but when he needs money he breaks rules, especially his own."

Madeline Fraser had closed her eyes. Now she opened them again, and again her smile was just from her to me. "The way you tell it," she said, "it certainly is a bargain. What do you think, Debby?"

"I think I like it," Miss Koppel said cautiously. "It would have to be discussed with the network and agencies and sponsors."

"Mr. Goodwin."

I turned my head. "Yes, Mr. Strong?"

Tully Strong had removed his spectacles and was blinking at me. "You understand that I am only the secretary of the Council of the sponsors of Miss Fraser's program, and I have no real authority. But I know how they feel about this, two of them in particular, and of course it is my duty to report this conversation to them without delay, and I can tell you off the record that it is extremely probable they would prefer to accept Mr. Wolfe's offer on their own account. For the impression on the public I think they would consider it desirable that Mr. Wolfe should be paid by them—on the terms stated by you. Still off the record, I believe this would apply especially to the makers of Starlite. That's the bottled drink the poison was put into."

"Yeah, I know it is." I looked around at the four faces. "I'm sort of in a hole. I hoped to close a deal with Miss Fraser before I left here, but Miss Koppel says it has to be discussed with others, and now Mr. Strong thinks the sponsors may want to take it over. The trouble is the delay. It's already six days old, and Mr. Wolfe should get to work at once. Tonight if possible, tomorrow at the latest."

"Not to mention," Bill Meadows said, smiling at me, "that he has to get ahead of the cops and keep ahead if he wants to collect. It seems to me— Hello, Elinor!" He left his chair in a hurry. "How about it?"

The girl who had entered without announcement tossed him a nod and a word and came toward the bed with rapid steps. I say girl because, although according to the newspapers Elinor Vance already had under her belt a Smith diploma, a play written and nearly produced, and two years as script writer for the Madeline Fraser program, she looked as if she had at least eight years to go to reach my deadline. As she crossed to us the thought struck me how few there are who still look attractive even when they're obviously way behind on sleep and played out to the point where they're about ready to drop.

"I'm sorry to be so late, Lina," she said all in a breath, "but they kept me down there all day, at the District Attorney's office—I couldn't make them understand. They're terrible, those men are—"

She stopped, and her body started to shake all over.

"Goddam it," Bill Meadows said savagely. "I'll get you a drink."

"I'm already getting it, Bill," Tully Strong called from a side of the room.

"Flop here on the bed," Miss Fraser said, getting her feet out of the way.

"It's nearly five o'clock." It was Miss Koppel's quiet, determined voice. "We're going to start to work right now or I'll phone and cancel tomorrow's broadcast."

I stood up, facing Madeline Fraser, looking down at her. "What about it? Can this be settled tonight?"

"I don't see how." She was stroking Elinor Vance's shoulder. "With a broadcast to get up, and people to consult—"

"Then tomorrow morning?"

Tully Strong, approaching with the drink for Elinor Vance, handed it to her and then spoke to me. "I'll phone you tomorrow, before noon if possible."

"Good for you," I told him, and beat it.

IV

WITHOUT at all intending to, I certainly had turned it into a seller's market.

The only development that Monday evening came not from the prospective customers, but from Inspector Cramer of Homicide, in the form of a phone call just before Fritz summoned Wolfe and me to dinner. It was nothing shattering. Cramer merely asked to speak to Wolfe, and asked him, "Who's paying you on the Orchard case?"

"No one," Wolfe said curtly.

"No? Then Goodwin drives your car up to Seventy-eighth Street just to test the tires?"

"It's my car, Mr. Cramer, and I help to pay for the streets."

It ended in a stalemate, and Wolfe and I moved across the hall to the dining room, to eat fried shrimps and Cape Cod clam cakes. With those items Fritz serves a sour sauce thick with mushrooms which is habit-forming.

Tuesday morning the fun began, with the first phone call arriving before Wolfe got down to the office. Of course that didn't mean sunup, since his morning hours upstairs with Theodore and the orchids are always and forever from nine to eleven. First was Richards of the Federal Broadcasting Company. It is left to my discretion whether to buzz the plant rooms or not, and this seemed to call for it, since Richards had done us a favor the day before. When I got him through to Wolfe it appeared that what he wanted was to introduce another FBC vice-president, a Mr. Beech. What Mr. Beech wanted was to ask why the hell Wolfe hadn't gone straight to the FBC with his suggestion about murder, though he didn't put it that way. He was very affable. The impression I got, listening in as instructed, was that the network had had its tongue hanging out for years, waiting and hoping for an excuse to hand Wolfe a hunk of dough. Wolfe was polite to him but didn't actually apologize.

Second was Tully Strong, the secretary of the Sponsors' Council, and I conversed with him myself. He strongly hoped that we had made no commitment with Miss Fraser or the network or anyone else because, as he had surmised, some of the sponsors were interested and one of them was excited. That one, he told me off the record, was the Starlite Company, which, since the poison had been served to the victim in a bottle of Starlite, The Drink You Dream Of, would fight for its exclusive right to take Wolfe up. I told him I would refer it to Wolfe without prejudice when he came down at eleven o'clock.

Third was Lon Cohen of the *Gazette*, who said talk was going around and would I kindly remember that on Saturday he had moved heaven and earth for me to find out where Madeline Fraser was, and how did it stand right now? I bandied words with him.

Fourth was a man with a smooth, low-pitched voice who gave his name as Nathan Traub, which was one of the names that had been made familiar to the public by the newspaper stories. I knew, naturally, that he was an executive of the advertising agency which handled the accounts of three of the Fraser sponsors, since I had read the papers. He seemed to be a little confused as to just what he wanted, but I gathered that the agency felt that it would be immoral for Wolfe to close any deal with anyone concerned without getting an okay from the agency. Having met a few agency men in my travels, I thought it was nice of them not to extend it to cover any deal with anyone about anything. I told him he might hear from us later.

Fifth was Deborah Koppel. She said that Miss Fraser was going on the air in twenty minutes and had been too busy to talk with the people who must be consulted, but that she was favorably inclined toward Wolfe's suggestion and would give us something definite before the day ended.

So by eleven o'clock, when two things happened simultaneously —Wolfe's entering the office and my turning on the radio and tuning it to the FBC station, WPIT—it was unquestionably a seller's market.

Throughout Madeline Fraser's broadcast Wolfe leaned back in his chair behind his desk with his eyes shut. I sat until I got restless and then moved around, with the only interruptions a couple of phone calls. Bill Meadows was of course on with her, as her stooge and feeder, since that was his job, and the guests for the day were an eminent fashion designer and one of the Ten Best-Dressed Women. The guests were eminently lousy and Bill was nothing to write home about, but there was no getting away from it that Fraser was good. Her voice was good, her timing was good, and even when she was talking about White Birch Soap you would almost as soon leave it on as turn it off. I had listened in on her the preceding Friday for the first time, no doubt along with several million others, and again I had to hand it to her for sitting on a very hot spot without a twitch or a wriggle.

It must have been sizzling hot when she got to that place in the program where bottles of Starlite were opened and poured into glasses —drinks for the two guests and Bill Meadows and herself. I don't know who had made the decision the preceding Friday, her first broadcast after Orchard's death, to leave that in, but if she did she had her nerve. Whoever had made the decision, it had been up to her to carry the ball, and she had sailed right through as if no bottle of Starlite had ever been known even to make anyone belch, let alone utter a shrill cry, claw at the air, have convulsions, and die. Today she delivered again. There was no false note, no quiver, no slack or speedup, nothing; and I must admit that Bill handled it well too. The guests were terrible, but that was the style to which they had accustomed us.

When it was over and I had turned the radio off Wolfe muttered, "That's an extremely dangerous woman."

I would have been more impressed if I hadn't known so well his conviction that all women alive are either extremely dangerous or extremely dumb. So I merely said, "If you mean she's damn clever I agree. She's awful good."

He shook his head. "I mean the purpose she allows her cleverness to serve. That unspeakable prepared biscuit flour! Fritz and I have tried it. Those things she calls Sweeties! Pfui! And that salad dressing abomination—we have tried that too, in an emergency. What they do to stomachs heaven knows, but that woman is ingeniously and deliberately conspiring in the corruption of millions of palates. She should be stopped!"

"Okay, stop her. Pin a murder on her. Though I must admit, having seen—"

The phone rang. It was Mr. Beech of FBC, wanting to know if we had made any promises to Tully Strong or to anyone else connected with any of the sponsors, and if so whom and what?

When he had been attended to I remarked to Wolfe, "I think it would be a good plan to line up Saul and Orrie and Fred—"

The phone rang. It was a man who gave his name as Owen, saying he was in charge of public relations for the Starlite Company, asking if he could come down to West Thirty-fifth Street on the run for a talk with Nero Wolfe. I stalled him with some difficulty and hung up.

Wolfe observed, removing the cap from a bottle of beer which Fritz had brought, "I must first find out what's going on. If it appears that the police are as stumped as—"

The phone rang. It was Nathan Traub, the agency man, wanting to know everything.

Up till lunch, and during lunch, and after lunch, the phone rang. They were having one hell of a time trying to get it decided how they would split the honor. Wolfe began to get really irritated and so did I. His afternoon hours upstairs with the plants are from four to six, and it was just as he was leaving the office, headed for his elevator in the hall, that word came that a big conference was on in Beech's office in the FBC building on Forty-sixth Street.

At that, when they once got together apparently they dealt the cards and played the hands without any more horsing around, for it was still short of five o'clock when the phone rang once more. I answered it and heard a voice I had heard before that day.

"Mr. Goodwin? This is Deborah Koppel. It's all arranged."

"Good. How?"

"I'm talking on behalf of Miss Fraser. They thought you should be told by her, through me, since you first made the suggestion to her and therefore you would want to know that the arrangement is satisfactory to her. An FBC lawyer is drafting an agreement to be signed by Mr. Wolfe and the other parties."

"Mr. Wolfe hates to sign anything written by a lawyer. Ten to one he won't sign it. He'll insist on dictating it to me, so you might as well give me the details."

She objected. "Then someone else may refuse to sign it."

"Not a chance," I assured her. "The people who have been phoning here all day would sign anything. What's the arrangement?"

"Well, just as you suggested. As you proposed it to Miss Fraser. No one objected to that. What they've been discussing was how to divide it up, and this is what they've agreed on . . ."

As she told it to me I scribbled it in my notebook, and this is how it looked:

	Per cent of expenses	Share of fee
Starlite	50	$10,000
FBC	28	5,500
M. Fraser	15	3,000
White Birch Soap	5	1,000
Sweeties	2	500
	100	$20,000

I called it back to check and then stated, "It suits us if it suits Miss Fraser. Is she satisfied?"

"She agrees to it," Deborah said. "She would have preferred to do it alone, all herself, but under the circumstances that wasn't possible. Yes, she's satisfied."

"Okay. Mr. Wolfe will dictate it, probably in the form of a letter, with copies for all. But that's just a formality and he wants to get started. All we know is what we've read in the papers. According to them there are eight people that the police regard as—uh, possibilities. Their names—"

"I know their names. Including mine."

"Sure you do. Can you have them all here at this office at half-past eight this evening?"

"All of them?"

"Yes, ma'am."

"But is that necessary?"

"Mr. Wolfe thinks so. This is him talking through me, to Miss Fraser through you. I ought to warn you, he can be an awful nuisance when a good fee depends on it. Usually when you hire a man to do something he thinks you're the boss. When you hire Wolfe he thinks he's the boss. He's a genius and that's merely one of the ways it shows. You can either take it or fight it. What do you want, just the publicity, or do you want the job done?"

"Don't bully me, Mr. Goodwin. We want the job done. I don't know if I can get Professor Savarese. And that Shepherd girl—she's a bigger nuisance than Mr. Wolfe could ever possibly be."

"Will you get all you can? Half-past eight. And keep me informed?"

She said she would. After I had hung up I buzzed Wolfe on the house phone to tell him we had made a sale.

It soon became apparent that we had also bought something. It was only twenty-five to six, less than three-quarters of an hour since I had finished with Deborah Koppel, when the doorbell rang. Sometimes Fritz answers it and sometimes me—usually me, when I'm home and not engaged on something that shouldn't be interrupted. So I marched to the hall and to the front door and pulled it open.

On the stoop was a surprise party. In front was a man-about-town in a topcoat the Duke of Windsor would have worn any day. To his left and rear was a red-faced plump gentleman. Back of them were three more, miscellaneous, carrying an assortment of cases and bags. When I saw what I had to contend with I brought the door with me and held it, leaving only enough of an opening for room for my shoulders.

"We'd like to see Mr. Nero Wolfe," the topcoat said like an old friend.

"He's engaged. I'm Archie Goodwin. Can I help?"

"You certainly can! I'm Fred Owen, in charge of public relations for the Starlite Company." He was pushing a hand at me and I took it. "And this is Mr. Walter B. Anderson, the president of the Starlite Company. May we come in?"

I reached to take the president's hand and still keep my door block intact. "If you don't mind," I said, "it would be a help if you'd give me a rough idea."

"Certainly, glad to! I would have phoned, only this has to be rushed if we're going to make the morning papers. So I just persuaded Mr. Anderson, and collected the photographers, and came. It shouldn't take ten minutes—say a shot of Mr. Anderson looking at Mr. Wolfe as he signs the agreement, or vice versa, and one of them shaking hands, and one of them side by side, bending over in a huddle inspecting some object that can be captioned as a clue—how about that one?"

"Wonderful!" I grinned at him. "But damn it, not today. Mr. Wolfe cut himself shaving, and he's wearing a patch, and vain as he is it would be very risky to aim a camera at him."

That goes to show how a man will degrade himself on account of money. Meaning me. The proper and natural thing to do would have been to kick them off the stoop down the seven steps to the sidewalk, especially the topcoat, and why didn't I do it? Ten grand. Maybe even twenty, for if Starlite had been insulted they might have soured the whole deal.

The effort, including sacrifice of principle, that it took to get them on their way without making them too sore put me in a frame of mind that accounted for my reaction somewhat later, after Wolfe had come down to the office, when I had explained the agreement our clients had come to, and he said, "No. I will not." He was emphatic. "I will not draft or sign an agreement one of the parties to which is that Sweeties."

I knew perfectly well that was reasonable and even noble. But what pinched me was that I had sacrificed principle without hesitation, and here he was refusing to. I glared at him. "Very well." I stood up. "I resign as of now. You are simply too conceited, too eccentric, and too fat to work for."

"Archie. Sit down."

"No."

"Yes. I am no fatter than I was five years ago. I am considerably more conceited, but so are you, and why the devil shouldn't we be? Someday there will be a crisis. Either you'll get insufferable and I'll fire you, or I'll get insufferable and you'll quit. But this isn't the day and you know it. You also know I would rather become a policeman and take orders from Mr. Cramer than work for anything or anyone called Sweeties. Your performance yesterday and today has been highly satisfactory."

"Don't try to butter me."

"Bosh. I repeat that I am no fatter than I was five years ago. Sit down and get your notebook. We'll put it in the form of a letter, to all of them jointly, and they can initial our copy. We shall ignore Sweeties"—he made a face—"and add that two per cent and that five hundred dollars to the share of the Federal Broadcasting Company."

That was what we did.

By the time Fritz called us to dinner there had been phone calls from Deborah Koppel and others, and the party for the evening was set.

V

THERE are four rooms on the ground floor of Wolfe's old brownstone house on West Thirty-fifth Street not far from the Hudson River. As you enter from the stoop, on your right are an enormous old oak clothes rack with a mirror, the elevator, the stairs, and the door to the dining room. On your left are the doors to the front room, which doesn't get used much, and to the office. The door to the kitchen is at the rear, the far end of the hall.

The office is twice as big as any of the other rooms. It is actually our living room too, and since Wolfe spends most of his time there you have to allow him his rule regarding furniture and accessories: nothing enters it or stays in it that he doesn't enjoy looking at. He enjoys the contrast between the cherry of his desk and the cardato of his chair, made by Meyer. The bright yellow couch has to be cleaned every two months, but he likes bright yellow. The three-foot globe over by the bookshelves is too big for a room that size, but he likes to look at it. He loves a comfortable chair so much that he won't have any other kind in the place, though he never sits on any but his own.

So that evening at least our guests' fannies were at ease, however the rest of them may have felt. There were nine of them present, six invited and three gate-crashers. Of the eight I had wanted Deborah Koppel to get, Nancylee Shepherd hadn't been asked, and Professor F. O. Savarese couldn't make it. The three gate-crashers were Starlite's president and public-relations man, Anderson and Owen, who had previously only got as far as the stoop, and Beech, the FBC vice-president.

At nine o'clock they were all there, all sitting, and all looking at Wolfe. There had been no friction at all except a little brush I had with Anderson. The best chair in the room, not counting Wolfe's, is one of red leather which is kept not far from one end of Wolfe's desk. Soon after entering Anderson had spotted it and squat-claimed it. When I asked him courteously to move to the other side of the room he went rude on me. He said he liked it there.

"But," I said, "this chair, and those, are reserved for the candidates."

"Candidates for what?"

"For top billing in a murder trial. Mr. Wolfe would like them sort of together, so they'll all be under his eye."

"Then arrange them that way."

He wasn't moving. "I can't ask you to show me your stub," I said pointedly, "because this is merely a private house, and you weren't invited, and my only argument is the convenience and pleasure of your host."

He gave me a dirty look but no more words, got up, and went across to the couch. I moved Madeline Fraser to the red leather chair, which gave the other five candidates more elbow room in their semicircle fronting Wolfe's desk. Beech, who had been standing talking to Wolfe, went and took a chair near the end of the couch. Owen had joined his boss, so I had the three gate-crashers off to themselves, which was as it should be.

Wolfe's eyes swept the semicircle, starting at Miss Fraser's end. "You are going to find this tiresome," he said conversationally, "because I'm just starting on this and so shall have to cover details that you're sick of hearing and talking about. All the information I have has come from newspapers, and therefore much of it is doubtless inaccurate and some of it false. How much you'll have to correct me on I don't know."

"It depends a lot," said Nathan Traub with a smile, "on which paper you read."

Traub, the agency man, was the only one of the six I hadn't seen before, having only heard his smooth low-pitched voice on the phone, when he had practically told me that everything had to be cleared through him. He was much younger than I had expected, around my age, but otherwise he was no great surprise. The chief difference between any two advertising executives is that one goes to buy a suit at Brooks Brothers in the morning and the other one goes in the afternoon. It depends on the conference schedule. The suit this Traub had bought was a double-breasted gray which went very well with his dark hair and the healthy color of his cheeks.

"I have read them all." Wolfe's eyes went from left to right again. "I did so when I decided I wanted a job on this case. By the way, I assume you all know who has hired me, and for what?"

There were nods. "We know all about it," Bill Meadows said.

"Good. Then you know why the presence of Mr. Anderson, Mr. Owen, and Mr. Beech is being tolerated. With them here, and of course

Miss Fraser, ninety-five per cent of the clients' interest is represented. The only one absent is White Birch Soap."

"They're not absent." Nathan Traub was politely indignant. "I can speak for them."

"I'd rather you'd speak for yourself," Wolfe retorted. "The clients are here to listen, not to speak." He rested his elbows on the arms of his chair and put the tips of his thumbs together. With the gate-crashers put in their places, he went on, "As for you, ladies and gentlemen, this would be much more interesting and stimulating for you if I could begin by saying that my job is to learn which one of you is guilty of murder—and to prove it. Unfortunately we can't have that fillip, since two of the eight—Miss Shepherd and Mr. Savarese—didn't come. I am told that Mr. Savarese had an engagement, and there is a certain reluctance about Miss Shepherd that I would like to know more about."

"She's a nosy little chatterbox." From Tully Strong, who had removed his spectacles and was gazing at Wolfe with an intent frown.

"She's a pain in the neck." From Bill Meadows.

Everybody smiled, some nervously, some apparently meaning it.

"I didn't try to get her," Deborah Koppel said. "She wouldn't have come unless Miss Fraser herself had asked her, and I didn't think that was necessary. She hates all the rest of us."

"Why?"

"Because she thinks we keep her away from Miss Fraser."

"Do you?"

"Yes. We try to."

"Not from me too, I hope." Wolfe sighed down to where a strip of his yellow shirt divided his vest from his trousers, and curled his palms and fingers over the ends of his chair arms. "Now. Let's get at this. Usually when I talk I dislike interruptions, but this is an exception. If you disagree with anything I say, or think me in error, say so at once.

"With that understood: Frequently, twice a week or oftener, you consider the problem of guests for Miss Fraser's program. It is in fact a problem, because you want interesting people, famous ones if possible, but they must be willing to submit to the indignity of lending their presence, and their assent by silence, if nothing more, to the preposterous statements made by Miss Fraser and Mr. Meadows regarding the products they advertise. Recently—"

"What's undignified about it?"

"There are no preposterous statements!"

"What's this got to do with what we're paying you for?"

"You disagree." Wolfe was unruffled. "I asked for it. Archie, include it in your notes that Mr. Traub and Mr. Strong disagree. You may ignore Mr. Owen's protest, since my invitation to interrupt did not extend to him."

He took in the semicircle again. "Recently a suggestion was made that you corral, as a guest, a man who sells tips on horse races. I understand that your memories differ as to when that suggestion was first made."

Madeline Fraser said, "It's been discussed off and on for over a year."

"I've always been dead against it," Tully Strong asserted.

Deborah Koppel smiled. "Mr. Strong thought it would be improper. He thinks the program should never offend anybody, which is impossible. Anything and everything offends somebody."

"What changed your mind, Mr. Strong?"

"Two things," said the secretary of the Sponsors' Council. "First, we got the idea of having the audience vote on it—the air audience—and out of over fourteen thousand letters ninety-two point six per cent were in favor. Second, one of the letters was from an assistant professor of mathematics at Columbia University, suggesting that the second guest on the program should be him, or some other professor, who could speak as an expert on the law of averages. That gave it a different slant entirely, and I was for it. Nat Traub, for the agency, was still against it."

"And I still am," Traub declared. "Can you blame me?"

"So," Wolfe asked Strong, "Mr. Traub was a minority of one?"

"That's right. We went ahead. Miss Vance, who does research for the program in addition to writing scripts, got up a list of prospects. I was surprised to find, and the others were too, that more than thirty tip sheets of various kinds are published in New York alone. We boiled it down to five and they were contacted."

I should have warned them that the use of "contact" as a verb was not permitted in that office. Now Wolfe would have it in for him.

Wolfe frowned. "All five were invited?"

"Oh no. Appointments were made for them to see Miss Fraser—the publishers of them. She had to find out which one was most likely to go over on the air and not pull something that would hurt the program. The final choice was left to her."

"How were the five selected?"

"Scientifically. The length of time they had been in business, the quality of paper and printing of the sheets, the opinions of sports writers, things like that."

"Who was the scientist? You?"

"No—I don't know—"

"I was," a firm, quiet voice stated. It was Elinor Vance. I had put her in the chair nearest mine because Wolfe isn't the only one who likes to have things around that he enjoys looking at. Obviously she hadn't caught up on sleep yet, and every so often she had to clamp her teeth to keep her chin from quivering, but she was the only one there who could conceivably have made me remember that I was not primarily a detective, but a man. I was curious how her brown eyes would look if and when they got fun in them again someday.

She was going on. "First I took out those that were plainly impossible, more than half of them, and then I talked it over with Miss Koppel and Mr. Meadows, and I think one or two others—I guess Mr. Strong—yes, I'm sure I did—but it was me more than them. I picked the five names."

"And they all came to see Miss Fraser?"

"Four of them did. One of them was out of town—in Florida."

Wolfe's gaze went to the left. "And you, Miss Fraser, chose Mr. Cyril Orchard from those four?"

She nodded. "Yes."

"How did you do that? Scientifically?"

"No." She smiled. "There's nothing scientific about me. He seemed fairly intelligent, and he had much the best voice of the four and was the best talker, and I liked the name of his sheet, *Track Almanac*—and then I guess I was a little snobbish about it too. His sheet was the most expensive—ten dollars a week."

"Those were the considerations that led you to select him?"

"Yes."

"You had never seen or heard of him before he came to see you as one of the four?"

"I hadn't seen him, but I had heard of him, and I had seen his sheet."

"Oh?" Wolfe's eyes went half shut. "You had?"

"Yes, about a month before that, maybe longer, when the question of having a tipster on the program had come up again, I had subscribed to some of the sheets—three or four of them—to see what they were like. Not in my name, of course. Things like that are done in my manager's name—Miss Koppel. One of them was this *Track Almanac*."

"How did you happen to choose that one?"

"My God, I don't know!" Madeline Fraser's eyes flashed momentarily with irritation. "Do you remember, Debby?"

Deborah shook her head. "I think we phoned somebody."

"The New York State Racing Commission," Bill Meadows offered sarcastically.

"Well." Wolfe leaned forward to push a button on his desk. "I'm going to have some beer. Aren't some of you thirsty?"

That called for an intermission. No one had accepted a previous offer of liquids I had made, but now they made it unanimous in the affirmative, and I got busy at the table at the far wall, already equipped. Two of them joined Wolfe with the beer, brought by Fritz from the kitchen, and the others suited their fancy. I had suggested to Wolfe that it would be fitting to have a case of Starlite in a prominent place on the table, but he had merely snorted. On such occasions he always insisted that a red wine and a chilled white wine must be among those present. Usually they had no takers, but this time there were two, Miss Koppel and Traub, who went for the Montrachet; and, being strongly in favor of the way its taste insists on sneaking all over the inside of your head, I helped out with it. There is only one trouble about serving assorted drinks to a bunch of people in the office on business. I maintain that it is a legitimate item for the expense account for the clients, and Wolfe says no, that what anyone eats or drinks in his house is on him. Another eccentricity. Also he insists that they must all have stands or tables at their elbows for their drinks.

So they did.

VI

WOLFE, for whom the first bottle of beer is merely a preamble, filled his glass from the second bottle, put the bottle down, and leaned back.

"What I've been after," he said in his conversational tone again, "is how that particular individual, Mr. Cyril Orchard, became a guest on that program. The conclusion from the newspaper accounts is that none of you, including Miss Shepherd and Mr. Savarese, knew him from Adam. But he was murdered. Later I'll discuss this with you severally, but for now I'll just put it to all of you: had you had any dealings with, or connection with, or knowledge of, Cyril Orchard prior to his appearance on that program? Other than what I have just been told?"

Starting with Madeline Fraser, he got either a no or a shake of the head from each of the six.

He grunted. "I assume," he said, "that the police have unearthed no contradiction to any of your negatives, since if they had you would hardly be foolish enough to try to hold to them with me. My whole approach to this matter is quite different from what it would be if I didn't know that the police have spent seven days and nights working on it. They have been after you, and they have their training and talents; also they have authority and a thousand men—twenty thousand. The question is whether their methods and abilities are up to this job; all I can do is use my own."

Wolfe came forward to drink beer, used his handkerchief on his lips, and leaned back again.

"But I need to know what happened—from you, not the newspapers. We now have you in the broadcasting studio Tuesday morning, a week ago today. The two guests—Mr. Cyril Orchard and Professor Savarese—have arrived. It is a quarter to eleven. The rest of you are there, at or near the table which holds the microphones. Seated at one side of the narrow table are Miss Fraser and Professor Savarese; across from them, facing them, are Mr. Orchard and Mr. Meadows. Voice levels are being taken. About twenty feet from the table is the first row of chairs provided for the studio audience. That audience consists of some two hundred people, nearly all women, many of whom, devoted followers of Miss Fraser, frequently attend the broadcasts. Is that picture correct—not approximately correct, but correct?"

They nodded. "Nothing wrong with it," Bill Meadows said.

"Many of them," Miss Fraser stated, "would come much oftener if they could get tickets. There are always twice as many applications for tickets as we can supply."

"No doubt," Wolfe growled. He had shown great restraint, not telling her how dangerous she was. "But the applicants who didn't get tickets, not being there, do not concern us. An essential element of the picture which I haven't mentioned is not yet visible. Behind the closed door of an electric refrigerator over against the wall are eight bottles of Starlite. How did they get there?"

An answer came from the couch, from Fred Owen. "We always have three or four cases in the studio, in a locked cab—"

"If you please, Mr. Owen." Wolfe wiggled a finger at him. "I want to hear as much as I can of the voices of these six people."

"They were there in the studio," Tully Strong said. "In a cabinet. It's kept locked because if it wasn't they wouldn't be there long."

"Who had taken the eight bottles from the cabinet and put them in the refrigerator?"

"I had." It was Elinor Vance, and I looked up from my notebook for another glance at her. "That's one of my chores every broadcast."

One trouble with her, I thought, is overwork. Script writer, researcher, bartender—what else?

"You can't carry eight bottles," Wolfe remarked, "at one time."

"I know I can't, so I took four and then went back for four more."

"Leaving the cabinet unlocked— No." Wolfe stopped himself. "Those refinements will have to wait." His eyes passed along the line again. "So there they are, in the refrigerator. By the way, I understand that the presence at the broadcast of all but one of you was routine and customary. The exception was you, Mr. Traub. You very rarely attend. What were you there for?"

"Because I was jittery, Mr. Wolfe." Traub's advertising smile and smooth low-pitched voice showed no resentment at being singled out. "I still thought having a race tout on the program was a mistake, and I wanted to be on hand."

"You thought there was no telling what Mr. Orchard might say?"

"I knew nothing about Orchard. I thought the whole idea was a stinker."

"If you mean the whole idea of the program, I agree—but that's not what we're trying to decide. We'll go on with the broadcast. First, one more piece of the picture. Where are the glasses they're going to drink from?"

"On a tray at the end of the table," Deborah Koppel said.

"The broadcasting table? Where they're seated at the microphones?"

"Yes."

"Who put them there?"

"That girl, Nancylee Shepherd. The only way to keep her back of the line would be to tie her up. Or of course not let her in, and Miss Fraser will not permit that. She organized the biggest Fraser Girls' Club in the country. So we—"

The phone rang. I reached for it and muttered into it.

"Mr. Bluff," I told Wolfe, using one of my fifteen aliases for the caller. Wolfe got his receiver to his ear, giving me a signal to stay on.

"Yes, Mr. Cramer?"

Cramer's sarcastic voice sounded as if he had a cigar stuck in his mouth, as he probably had. "How are you coming up there?"

"Slowly. Not really started yet."

"That's too bad, since no one's paying you on the Orchard case. So you told me yesterday."

"This is today. Tomorrow's paper will tell you all about it. I'm sorry, Mr. Cramer, but I'm busy."

"You certainly are, from the reports I've got here. Which one is your client?"

"You'll see it in the paper."

"Then there's no reason—"

"Yes. There is. That I'm extremely busy and exactly a week behind you. Good-by, sir."

Wolfe's tone and his manner of hanging up got a reaction from the gate-crashers. Mr. Walter B. Anderson, the Starlite president, demanded to know if the caller had been Police Inspector Cramer, and, told that it was, got critical. His position was that Wolfe should not have been rude to the inspector. It was bad tactics and bad manners. Wolfe, not bothering to draw his sword, brushed him aside with a couple of words, but Anderson leaped for his throat. He had not yet, he said, signed any agreement, and if that was going to be Wolfe's attitude maybe he wouldn't.

"Indeed." Wolfe's brows went up a sixteenth of an inch. "Then you'd better notify the press immediately. Do you want to use the phone?"

"By God, I wish I could. I have a right to—"

"You have no right whatever, Mr. Anderson, except to pay your share of my fee if I earn it. You are here in my office on sufferance.

Confound it, I am undertaking to solve a problem that has Mr. Cramer so nonplused that he desperately wants a hint from me before I've even begun. He doesn't mind my rudeness; he's so accustomed to it that if I were affable he'd haul me in as a material witness. Are you going to use the phone?"

"You know damn well I'm not."

"I wish you were. The better I see this picture the less I like it." Wolfe went back to the line of candidates. "You say, Miss Koppel, that this adolescent busybody, Miss Shepherd, put the tray of glasses on the table?"

"Yes, she—"

"She took them from me," Elinor Vance put in, "when I got them from the cabinet. She was right there with her hand out and I let her take them."

"The locked cabinet that the Starlite is kept in?"

"Yes."

"And the glasses are heavy and dark blue, quite opaque so that anything in them is invisible?"

"Yes."

"You didn't look into them from the top?"

"No."

"If one of them had something inside you wouldn't have seen it?"

"No." Elinor went on, "If you think my answers are short and quick, that's because I've already answered these questions, and many others, hundreds of times. I could answer them in my sleep."

Wolfe nodded. "Of course. So now we have the bottles in the refrigerator and the glasses on the table, and the program is on the air. For forty minutes it went smoothly. The two guests did well. None of Mr. Traub's fears were realized."

"It was one of the best broadcasts of the year," Miss Fraser said.

"Exceptional," Tully Strong declared. "There were thirty-two studio laughs in the first half-hour."

"How did you like the second half?" Traub asked pointedly.

"We're coming to it." Wolfe sighed. "Well, here we are. The moment arrives when Starlite is to be poured, drunk, and eulogized. Who brought it from the refrigerator? You again, Miss Vance?"

"No, me," Bill Meadows said. "It's part of the show for the mikes, me pushing back my chair, walking, opening the refrigerator door and closing it, and coming back with the bottles. Then someone—"

"There were eight bottles in the refrigerator. How many did you get?"

"Four."

"How did you decide which ones?"

"I didn't decide. I always just take the four in front. You realize that all Starlite bottles are exactly alike. There wouldn't be any way to tell them apart, so how would I decide?"

"I couldn't say. Anyway, you didn't?"

"No. As I said, I simply took the four bottles that were nearest to me. That's natural."

"So it is. And carried them to the table and removed the caps?"

"I took them to the table, but about removing the caps, that's something we don't quite agree on. We agree that I didn't do it, because I put them on the table as usual and then got back into my chair, quick, to get on the mike. Someone else always takes the caps from the bottles, not always the same one, and that day Debby—Miss Koppel was right there, and Miss Vance, and Strong, and Traub. I was on the mike and didn't see who removed the caps. The action there is a little tight and needs help, with taking off the caps, pouring into the glasses, and getting the glasses passed around—and the bottles have to be passed around too."

"Who does the passing?"

"Oh, someone—or, rather, more than one. You know, they just get passed—the glasses and bottles both. After pouring into the glasses the bottles are still about half full, so the bottles are passed too."

"Who did the pouring and passing that day?"

Bill Meadows hesitated. "That's what we don't agree about." He was not at ease. "As I said, they were all right there—Miss Koppel and Miss Vance, and Strong and Traub. That's why it was confusing."

"Confusing or not," Wolfe said testily, "it should be possible to remember what happened, so simple a thing as that. This is the detail where, above all others, clarity is essential. We know that Mr. Orchard got the bottle and glass which contained the cyanide, because he drank enough of it to kill him. But we do not know, at least I don't, whether he got it by a whim of circumstance or by the deliberate maneuver of one or more of those present. Obviously that's a vital point. That glass and bottle were placed in front of Mr. Orchard by somebody—not this one, or this one, but that one. Who put them there?"

Wolfe's gaze went along the line. They all met it. No one had anything to say, but neither was anyone impelled to look somewhere else. Finally Tully Strong, who had his spectacles back on, spoke. "We simply don't remember, Mr. Wolfe."

"Pfui." Wolfe was disgusted. "Certainly you remember. No wonder Mr. Cramer has got nowhere. You're lying, every one of you."

"No," Miss Fraser objected. "They're not lying really."

"The wrong pronoun," Wolfe snapped at her. "My comment included you, Miss Fraser."

She smiled at him. "You may include me if you like, but I don't. It's like this. These people are not only associated with one another in connection with my program, they are friends. Of course they have arguments—there's always bound to be some friction when two people are often together, let alone five or six—but they are friends and they like one another." Her timing and inflections were as good as if she had been on the air. "This is a terrible thing, a horrible thing, and we all knew it was the minute the doctor came and looked at him, and then looked up and said nothing should be touched and no one should leave. So could you really expect one of them to say—or, since you include me, could you expect one of us to say—'Yes, I gave him the glass with poison in it'?"

"What was left in the bottle was also poisoned."

"All right, the bottle too. Or could you expect one of us to say, 'Yes, I saw my friend give him the glass and bottle'? And name the friend?"

"Then you're agreeing with me. That you're all lying."

"Not at all." Miss Fraser was too earnest to smile now. "The pouring and passing the glasses and bottles was commonplace routine, and there was no reason for us to notice details enough to keep them in our minds at all. Then came that overwhelming shock, and the confusion, and later came the police, and the strain and tension of it, and we just didn't remember. That isn't the least bit surprising. What would surprise me would be if someone did remember, for instance if Mr. Traub said positively that Mr. Strong put that glass and bottle in front of Mr. Orchard, it would merely prove that Mr. Traub hates Mr. Strong, and that would surprise me because I don't believe that any one of us hates another one."

"Nor," Wolfe murmured dryly, "that any of you hated Mr. Orchard—or wanted to kill him."

"Who on earth could have wanted to kill that man?"

"I don't know. That's what I've been hired to find out—provided the poison reached its intended destination. You say you're not surprised, but I am. I'm surprised the police haven't locked you all up."

"They damn near did," Traub said grimly.

"I certainly thought they would arrest me," Madeline Fraser declared. "That was what was in my mind—it was all that was in my mind—as soon as I heard the doctor say cyanide. Not who had given him that glass and bottle, not even what the effect would be on my program, but the death of my husband. He died of cyanide poisoning six years ago."

Wolfe nodded. "The papers haven't neglected that. It was what leaped first to your mind?"

"Yes, when I heard the doctor say cyanide. I suppose you wouldn't understand—or perhaps you would—anyway it did."

"It did to mine too," Deborah Koppel interposed, in a tone that implied that someone had been accused of something. "Miss Fraser's husband was my brother. I saw him just after he died. Then that day I saw Cyril Orchard, and—" She stopped. Having her in profile, I couldn't see her eyes, but I saw her clasped hands. In a moment she went on, "Yes, it came to my mind."

Wolfe stirred impatiently. "Well. I won't pretend that I'm exasperated that you're such good friends that you haven't been able to remember what happened. If you had, and had told the police, I might not have this job." He glanced at the clock on the wall. "It's after eleven. I had thought it barely possible that I might get a wedge into a crack by getting you here together, but it seems hopeless. You're much too fond of one another. Our time has been completely wasted. I haven't got a thing, not a microscopic morsel, that I hadn't already got from the papers. I may never get anything, but I intend to try. Which of you will spend the night here with me? Not all the night; probably four or five hours. I shall need that long, more or less, with each of you, and I would like to start now. Which of you will stay?"

There were no eager volunteers.

"My Lord!" Elinor Vance protested. "Over and over and over again."

"My clients," Wolfe said, "are your employer, your network, and your sponsors. Mr. Meadows?"

"I've got to take Miss Fraser home," Bill objected. "I could come back."

"I'll take her," Tully Strong offered.

"That's foolish." Deborah Koppel was annoyed. "I live only a block away and we'll take a taxi together."

"I'll go with you," Elinor Vance suggested. "I'll drop you and keep the taxi on uptown."

"I'll ride with you," Tully Strong insisted.

"But you live in the Village!"

"Count me in," Bill Meadows said stubbornly. "I can be back here in twenty minutes. Thank God tomorrow's Wednesday."

"This is all unnecessary," the president of Starlite broke in with authority. He had left the couch and was among the candidates, who were also on their feet. "My car is outside and I can take all of you who are going uptown. You can stay here with Wolfe, Meadows." He turned and stepped to the desk. "Mr. Wolfe, I haven't been greatly impressed this evening. Hardly at all impressed."

"Neither have I," Wolfe agreed. "It's a dreary outlook. I would prefer to abandon it, but you and I are both committed by that press release." Seeing that some of them were heading for the hall, he raised his voice. "If you please? A moment. I would like to make appointments. One of you tomorrow from eleven to one, another from two to four, another in the evening from eight-thirty to twelve, and another from midnight on. Will you decide on that before you go?"

They did so, with me helping them and making notes of the decisions. It took a little discussion, but they were such good friends that there was no argument. The only thing that soured the leave-taking at all was when Owen made an opportunity to pass me a crack about no patch or cut being visible on Wolfe's face. He might at least have had the decency to let it lay.

"I said nothing about his face," I told him coldly. "I said he cut himself shaving. He shaves his legs. I understood you wanted him in kilts for the pictures."

Owen was too offended to speak. Utterly devoid of a sense of humor.

When the others had gone Bill Meadows was honored with the red leather chair. On a low table at his elbow I put a replenished glass, and Fritz put a tray holding three sandwiches made with his own bread, one of minced rabbit meat, one of corned beef, and one of Georgia country ham. I arranged myself at my desk with my notebook, a plate of sandwiches to match Bill's, a pitcher of milk, and a glass. Wolfe had only beer. He never eats between dinner and breakfast. If he did he never would be able to say he is no fatter than he was five years ago, which isn't true anyhow.

In a way it's a pleasure to watch Wolfe doing a complete overhaul on a man, or a woman either, and in another way it's enough to make you grit your teeth. When you know exactly what he's after and he's sneaking up on it without the slightest sound to alarm the victim, it's a joy to be there. But when he's after nothing in particular, or if he is you don't know what, and he pokes in this hole a while and then tries another one, and then goes back to the first one, and as far as you can see is getting absolutely nowhere, and the hours go by, and your sandwiches and milk are all gone long ago, sooner or later the time comes when you don't even bother to get a hand in front of your yawns, let alone swallow them.

If, at four o'clock that Wednesday morning, Wolfe had once more started in on Bill Meadows about his connections with people who bet on horse races, or about the favorite topics of conversation among the people we were interested in when they weren't talking shop, or about how he got into broadcasting and did he like it much, I would either have thrown my notebook at him or gone to the kitchen for more milk. But he didn't. He pushed back his chair and manipulated himself to his feet. If anyone wants to know what I had in the notebook he can come to the office any time I'm not busy and I'll read it to him for a dollar a page, but he would be throwing his money away at any price.

I ushered Bill out. When I returned to the office Fritz was there tidying up. He never goes to bed until after Wolfe does. He asked me, "Was the corned beef juicy, Archie?"

"Good God," I demanded, "do you expect me to remember that far back? That was days ago." I went to spin the knob on the safe and jiggle the handle, remarking to Wolfe, "It seems we're still in the paddock, not even at the starting post. Who do you want in the morning? Saul and Orrie and Fred and Johnny? For what? Why not have them tail Mr. Anderson?"

"I do not intend," Wolfe said glumly, "to start spending money until I know what I want to buy—not even our clients' money. If this poisoner is going to be exposed by such activities as investigation of sales of potassium cyanide or of sources of it available to these people, it is up to Mr. Cramer and his twenty thousand men. Doubtless they have already done about all they can in those directions, and many others, or he wouldn't have phoned me, squealing for help. The only person I want to see in the morning is—who is it? Who's coming at eleven?"

"Debby. Miss Koppel."

"You might have taken the men first, on the off chance that we'd have it before we got to the women." He was at the door to the hall. "Good night."

VII

If, THIRTY-THREE hours later, at lunch time on Thursday, anyone had wanted to know how things were shaping up, he could have satisfied his curiosity by looking in the dining room and observing Wolfe's behavior at the midday meal, which consisted of corn fritters with autumn honey, sausages, and a bowl of salad. At meals he is always expansive, talkative, and good-humored, but throughout that one he was grim, sullen, and peevish. Fritz was worried stiff.

Wednesday we had entertained Miss Koppel from eleven to one, Miss Fraser from two to four, Miss Vance from eight-thirty in the evening until after eleven, and Nathan Traub from midnight on; and Tully Strong Thursday morning from eleven until lunch time.

We had got hundreds of notebook pages of nothing.

Gaps had of course been filled in, but with what? We even had confessions, but of what? Bill Meadows and Nat Traub both confessed that they frequently bet on horse races. Elinor Vance confessed that her brother was an electroplater, and that she was aware that he constantly used materials which contained cyanide. Madeline Fraser confessed that it was hard to believe that anyone would have put poison into one of the bottles without caring a damn which one of the four broadcasters it got served to. Tully Strong confessed that the police had found his fingerprints on all four of the bottles, and accounted for them by explaining that while the doctor had been kneeling to examine Cyril Orchard, he, Strong, had been horrified by the possibility that there had been something wrong with a bottle of Starlite, the product of the most important sponsor on the Council. In a panic he had seized the four bottles, with the idiotic notion of caching them somewhere, and Miss Fraser and Traub had taken them from him and replaced them on the table. That was a particularly neat confession, since it explained why the cops had got nowhere from prints on the bottles.

Deborah Koppel confessed that she knew a good deal about cyanides, their uses, effects, symptoms, doses, and accessibility, because she had read up on them after the death of her brother six years ago. In all the sessions those were the only two times Wolfe got really disagreeable, when he was asking about the death of Lawrence Koppel— first with Deborah, the sister, and then with Madeline Fraser, the widow. The details had of course been pie for the newspapers during the past week, on account of the coincidence of the cyanide, and one of the tabloids had even gone so far as to run a piece by an expert, discussing whether it had really been suicide, though there hadn't been the slightest question about it at the time or at any time since.

But that wasn't the aspect that Wolfe was disagreeable about. Lawrence Koppel's death had occurred at his home in a little town in Michigan called Fleetville, and what Wolfe wanted to know was whether there had been anyone in or near Fleetville who was named Orchard, or who had relatives named Orchard, or who had later changed his name to Orchard. I don't know how it had entered his head that that was a hot idea, but he certainly wrung it dry and kept going back to it for another squeeze. He spent so much time on it with Madeline Fraser that four o'clock, the hour of his afternoon date with the orchids, came before he had asked her anything at all about horse races.

The interviews with those five were not all that happened that day and night and morning. Wolfe and I had discussions, of the numerous ways in which a determined and intelligent person can get his hands on a supply of cyanide, of the easy access to the bottles in the refrigerator in the broadcasting studio, of the advisability of trying to get Inspector Cramer or Sergeant Purley Stebbins to cough up some data on things like fingerprints. That got us exactly as far as the interviews did. Then there were two more phone calls from Cramer, and some from Lon Cohen and various others; and there was the little detail of arranging for Professor F. O. Savarese to pay us a visit.

Also the matter of arranging for Nancylee Shepherd to come and be processed, but on that we were temporarily stymied. We knew all about her: she was sixteen, she lived with her parents at 829 Wixley Avenue in the Bronx, she had light yellow hair and gray eyes, and her father worked in a storage warehouse. They had no phone, so at four Wednesday, when Miss Fraser had left and Wolfe had gone up to the plants, I got the car from the garage and drove to the Bronx.

Eight-twenty-nine Wixley Avenue was the kind of apartment house where people live not because they want to, but because they have to. It should have been ashamed of itself and probably was. There was no click when I pushed the button marked Shepherd, so I went to the basement and dug up the janitor. He harmonized well with the building. He said I was way behind time if I expected to get any effective results—that's what he said—pushing the Shepherd button. They had been gone three days now. No, not the whole family, Mrs. Shepherd and the girl. He didn't know where they had gone, and neither did anyone else around there. Some thought they had skipped, and some thought the cops had 'em. He personally thought they might be dead. No, not Mr. Shepherd too. He came home from work every afternoon a little after five, and left every morning at half-past six.

A glance at my wrist showing me ten to five, I offered the animal a buck to stick around the front and give me a sign when Shepherd showed up, and the look in his eye told me that I had wasted at least four bits of the clients' money.

It wasn't a long wait. When Shepherd appeared I saw that it wouldn't have been necessary to keep the janitor away from his work, for from the line of the eyebrows it was about as far up to the beginning of his hair as it was down to the point of his chin, and a sketchy description would have been enough. Whoever designs the faces had lost all sense of proportion. As he was about to enter the vestibule I got in front of him and asked without the faintest touch of condescension, "Mr. Shepherd?"

"Get out," he snarled.

"My name's Goodwin and I'm working for Miss Madeline Fraser. I understand your wife and daughter—"

"Get out!"

"But I only want—"

"Get out!"

He didn't put a hand on me or shoulder me, and I can't understand yet how he got past me to the vestibule without friction, but he did, and got his key in the door. There were of course a dozen possible courses for me, anything from grabbing his coat and holding on, to plugging him in the jaw, but while that would have given me emotional release it wouldn't have got what I wanted. It was plain that as long as he was conscious he wasn't going to tell me where Nancylee was, and unconscious he couldn't. I passed.

I drove back down to Thirty-fifth Street, left the car at the curb, went in to the office, and dialed Madeline Fraser's number. Deborah Koppel answered, and I asked her, "Did you folks know that Nancylee has left home? With her mother?"

Yes, she said, they knew that.

"You didn't mention it when you were here this morning. Neither did Miss Fraser this afternoon."

"There was no reason to mention it, was there? We weren't asked."

"You were asked about Nancylee, both of you."

"But not if she had left home or where she is."

"Then may I ask you now? Where is she?"

"I don't know."

"Does Miss Fraser?"

"No. None of us knows."

"How did you know she was gone?"

"She phoned Miss Fraser and told her she was going."

"When was that?"

"That was . . . that was Sunday."

"She didn't say where she was going?"

"No."

That was the best I could get. When I was through trying and had hung up, I sat and considered. There was a chance that Purley Stebbins of Homicide would be in the mood for tossing me a bone, since Cramer had been spending nickels on us, but if I asked him for it he would want to make it a trade, and I had nothing to offer. So when I reached for the phone again it wasn't that number, but the *Gazette*'s, that I dialed.

Lon Cohen immediately got personal. Where, he wanted to know, had I got the idea that an open press release made an entry in my credit column?

I poohed him. "Someday, chum, you'll get a lulu. Say in about six months, the way we're going. A newspaper is supposed to render public service, and I want some. Did you know that Nancylee Shepherd and her mother have blown?"

"Certainly. The father got sore because she was mixed up in a murder case. He damn near killed two photographers. Father has character."

"Yeah, I've met Father. What did he do with his wife and daughter, bury them?"

"Shipped 'em out of town. With Cramer's permission, as we got it here, and of course Cramer knew where but wasn't giving out. Naturally we thought it an outrage. Is the great public, are the American people, to be deceived and kept in ignorance? No. You must have had a hunch, because we just got it here—it came in less than an hour ago. Nancylee and her mother are at the Ambassador in Atlantic City, sitting room, bedroom, and bath."

"You don't say. Paid for by?"

He didn't know. He agreed that it was intolerable that the American people, of whom I was one, should be uninformed on so vital a point, and before he hung up he said he would certainly do something about it.

When Wolfe came down to the office I reported developments. At that time we still had three more to overhaul, but it was already apparent that we were going to need all we could get, so Wolfe told me to get Saul Panzer on the phone. Saul wasn't in, but an hour later he called back.

Saul Panzer free-lances. He has no office and doesn't need one. He is so good that he demands, and gets, double the market, and any day of the week he gets so many offers that he can pick as he pleases. I have never known him to turn Wolfe down except when he was so tied up he couldn't shake loose.

He took this on. He would take a train to Atlantic City that evening, sleep there, and in the morning persuade Mrs. Shepherd to let Nancylee come to New York for a talk with Wolfe. He would bring her, with Mother if necessary.

As Wolfe was finishing with Saul, Fritz entered with a tray. I looked at him with surprise, since Wolfe seldom takes on beer during the hour preceding dinner, but then, as he put the tray on the desk, I saw it wasn't beer. It was a bottle of Starlite, with three glasses. Instead of turning to leave, Fritz stood by.

"It may be too cold," Fritz suggested.

With a glance of supercilious distaste at the bottle, Wolfe got the opener from his top drawer, removed the cap, and started pouring.

"It seems to me," I remarked, "like a useless sacrifice. Why suffer? If Orchard had never drunk Starlite before he wouldn't know whether it tasted right or not, and even if he didn't like it they were on the air and just for politeness he would have gulped some down." I took the glass that Fritz handed me, a third full. "Anyway he drank enough to kill him, so what does it matter what we think?"

"He may have drunk it before." Wolfe held the glass to his nose, sniffed, and made a face. "At any rate, the murderer had to assume that he might have. Would the difference in taste be too great a hazard?"

"I see." I sipped. "Not so bad." I sipped again. "The only way we can really tell is to drink this and then drink some cyanide. Have you got some?"

"Don't bubble, Archie." Wolfe put his glass down after two little tastes. "Good heavens. What the devil is in it, Fritz?"

Fritz shook his head. "Ipecac?" he guessed. "Horehound? Would you like some sherry?"

"No. Water. I'll get it." Wolfe got up, marched to the hall, and turned toward the kitchen. He believes in some good healthy exercise before dinner.

That evening, Wednesday, our victims were first Elinor Vance and then Nathan Traub. It was more than three hours after midnight when Wolfe finally let Traub go, which made two nights in a row.

Thursday morning at eleven we started on Tully Strong. In the middle of it, right at noon, there was a phone call from Saul Panzer. Wolfe took it, giving me the sign to stay on. I knew from the tone of Saul's voice, just pronouncing my name, that he had no bacon.

"I'm at the Atlantic City railroad station," Saul said, "and I can either catch a train to New York in twenty minutes or go jump in the ocean, whichever you advise. I couldn't get to Mrs. Shepherd just by asking, so I tried a trick but it didn't work. Finally she and the daughter came down to the hotel lobby, but I thought it would be better to wait until they came outside, if they came, and they did. My approach was one that has worked a thousand times, but it didn't with her. She called a cop and wanted him to arrest me for annoying her. I made another try later, on the phone again, but four words was as far as I got. Now it's no use. This is the third time I've flopped on you in ten years, and that's too often. I don't want you to pay me, not even expenses."

"Nonsense." Wolfe never gets riled with Saul. "You can give me the details later, if there are any I should have. Will you reach New York in time to come to the office at six o'clock?"

"Yes."

"Good. Do that."

Wolfe resumed with Traub. As I have already mentioned, the climax of that two hours' hard work was when Traub confessed that he frequently bet on horse races. As soon as he had gone Wolfe and I went to the dining room for the lunch previously described, corn fritters with autumn honey, sausages, and a bowl of salad. Of course what added to his misery was the fact that Savarese was expected at two o'clock, because he likes to have the duration of a meal determined solely by the inclination of him and the meal, not by some extraneous phenomenon like the sound of a doorbell.

But the bell rang right on the dot.

VIII

You HAVE heard of the exception that proves the rule. Professor F. O. Savarese was it.

The accepted rule is that an Italian is dark and, if not actually a runt, at least not tall; that a professor is dry and pedantic, with eye trouble; and that a mathematician really lives in the stratosphere and is here just visiting relatives. Well, Savarese was an Italian-American professor of mathematics, but he was big and blond and buoyant, two inches taller than me, and he came breezing in like a March morning wind.

He spent the first twenty minutes telling Wolfe and me how fascinating and practical it would be to work out a set of mathematical formulas that could be used in the detective business. His favorite branch of mathematics, he said, was the one that dealt with the objective numerical measurement of probability. Very well. What was any detective work, any kind at all, but the objective measurement of probability? All he proposed to do was to add the word "numerical," not as a substitute or replacement, but as an ally and reinforcement.

"I'll show you what I mean," he offered. "May I have paper and pencil?"

He had bounded over to me before I could even uncross my legs, took the pad and pencil I handed him, and bounded back to the red leather chair. When the pencil had jitterbugged on the pad for half a minute he tore off the top sheet and slid it across the desk to Wolfe, then went to work on the next sheet and in a moment tore that off and leaped to me with it.

"You should each have one," he said, "so you can follow me."

I wouldn't try to pretend I could put it down from memory, but I still have both of those sheets, in the folder marked ORCHARD, and this is what is on them:

$$u = \frac{1}{V_{2\pi} \cdot D} \left\{ 1 - \frac{1}{2} k \left(\frac{X}{D} - \frac{1}{3} \frac{X^3}{D^3} \right) \right\} e^{-\frac{1}{2} X^2/D^2}$$

"That," Savarese said, his whole face smiling with eager interest and friendliness and desire to help, "is the second approximation of the normal law of error, sometimes called the generalized law of error. Let's apply it to the simplest kind of detective problem, say the question which one of three servants in a house stole a diamond ring from a locked drawer. I should explain that X is the deviation from the mean, D is the standard deviation, k is—"

"Please!" Wolfe had to make it next door to a bellow, and did. "What are you trying to do, change the subject?"

"No." Savarese looked surprised and a little hurt. "Am I? What was the subject?"

"The death of Mr. Cyril Orchard and your connection with it."

"Oh. Of course." He smiled apologetically and spread his hands, palms up. "Perhaps later? It is one of my favorite ideas, the application of the mathematical laws of probability and error to detective problems, and a chance to discuss it with you is a golden opportunity."

"Another time. Meanwhile"—Wolfe tapped the generalized law of error with a fingertip—"I'll keep this. Which one of the people at that broadcast placed that glass and bottle in front of Mr. Orchard?"

"I don't know. I'm going to find it very interesting to compare your handling of me with the way the police did it. What you're trying to do, of course, is to proceed from probability toward certainty, as close as you can get. Say you start, as you see it, with one chance in five that I poisoned Orchard. Assuming that you have no subjective bias, your purpose is to move as rapidly as possible from that position, and you don't care which direction. Anything I say or do will move you one way or the other. If one way, the one-in-five will become one-in-four, one-in-three, and so on until it becomes one-in-one and a minute fraction, which will be close enough to affirmative certainty so that you will say you know that I killed Orchard. If it goes the other way, your one-in-five will become one-in-ten, one-in-one-hundred, one-in-one-thousand; and when it gets to one-in-ten-billion you will be close enough to negative certainty so that you will say you know that I did not kill Orchard. There is a formula—"

"No doubt." Wolfe was controlling himself very well. "If you want to compare me with the police you'll have to let me get a word in now and then. Had you ever seen Mr. Orchard before the day of the broadcast?"

"Oh, yes, six times. The first time was thirteen months earlier, in February nineteen-forty-seven. You're going to find me remarkably exact, since the police have had me over all this, back and forth. I might as well give you everything I can that will move you toward affirmative certainty, since subjectively you would prefer that direction. Shall I do that?"

"By all means."

"I thought that would appeal to you. As a mathematician I have always been interested in the application of the calculation of probabilities to the various forms of gambling. The genesis of normal distributions—"

"Not now," Wolfe said sharply.

"Oh—of course not. There are reasons why it is exceptionally difficult to calculate probabilities in the case of horse races, and yet people bet hundreds of millions of dollars on them. A little over a year ago, studying the possibilities of some formulas, I decided to look at some tip sheets, and subscribed to three. One of them was the *Track Almanac*, published by Cyril Orchard. Asked by the police why I chose that one, I could only say that I didn't know. I forget. That is suspicious, for them and you; for me, it is simply a fact that I don't remember. One day in February last year a daily double featured by Orchard came through, and I went to see him. He had some intelligence, and if he had been interested in the mathematical problems involved I could have made good use of him, but he wasn't. In spite of that I saw him occasionally, and he once spent a weekend with me at the home of a friend in New Jersey. Altogether, previous to that broadcast, I had seen him, been with him, six times. That's suspicious, isn't it?"

"Moderately," Wolfe conceded.

Savarese nodded. "I'm glad to see you keep as objective as possible. But what about this? When I learned that a popular radio program on a national network had asked for opinions on the advisability of having a horse-race tipster as a guest, I wrote a letter strongly urging it, asked for the privilege of being myself the second guest on the program, and suggested that Cyril Orchard should be the tipster invited." Savarese smiled all over, beaming. "What about your one-in-five now?"

Wolfe grunted. "I didn't take that position. You assumed it for me. I suppose the police have that letter you wrote?"

"No, they haven't. No one has it. It seems that Miss Fraser's staff doesn't keep correspondence more than two or three weeks, and my letter has presumably been destroyed. If I had known that in time I might have been less candid in describing the letter's contents to the police, but on the other hand I might not have been. Obviously my treatment of that problem had an effect on my calculations of the probability of my being arrested for murder. But for a free decision I would have had to know, first, that the letter had been destroyed, and, second, that the memories of Miss Fraser's staff were vague about its contents. I learned both of those facts too late."

Wolfe stirred in his chair. "What else on the road to affirmative certainty?"

"Let's see." Savarese considered. "I think that's all, unless we go into observation of distributions, and that should be left for a secondary formula. For instance, my character, a study of which, *a posteriori*, would show it to be probable that I would commit murder for the sake of a sound but revolutionary formula. One detail of that would be my personal finances. My salary as an assistant professor is barely enough to live on endurably, but I paid ten dollars a week for that *Track Almanac*."

"Do you gamble? Do you bet on horse races?"

"No. I never have. I know too much—or rather, I know too little. More than ninety-nine per cent of the bets placed on horse races are outbursts of emotion, not exercises of reason. I restrict my emotions to the activities for which they are qualified." Savarese waved a hand. "That starts us in the other direction, toward a negative certainty, with its conclusion that I did not kill Orchard, and we might as well go on with it. Items: I could not have managed that Orchard got the poison. I was seated diagonally across from him, and I did not help pass the bottles. It cannot be shown that I have ever purchased, stolen, borrowed, or possessed any cyanide. It cannot be established that I would, did, or shall profit in any way from Orchard's death. When I arrived at the broadcasting studio, at twenty minutes to eleven, everyone else was already there and I would certainly have been observed if I had gone to the refrigerator and opened its door. There is no evidence that my association with Orchard was other than as I have described it, with no element of animus or of any subjective attitude."

Savarese beamed. "How far have we gone? One-in-one-thousand?"

"I'm not with you," Wolfe said with no element of animus. "I'm not on that road at all, nor on any road. I'm wandering around poking at things. Have you ever been in Michigan?"

For the hour that was left before orchid time Wolfe fired questions at him, and Savarese answered him briefly and to the point. Evidently the professor really did want to compare Wolfe's technique with that of the police, for, as he gave close attention to each question as it was asked, he had more the air of a judge or referee sizing something up than of a murder suspect, guilty or innocent, going through an ordeal. The objective attitude.

He maintained it right up to four o'clock, when the session ended, and I escorted the objective attitude to the front door, and Wolfe went to his elevator.

A little after five Saul Panzer arrived. Coming only up to the middle of my ear, and of slight build, Saul doesn't even begin to fill the red leather chair, but he likes to sit in it, and did so. He is pretty objective too, and I have rarely seen him either elated or upset about anything that had happened to him, or that he had caused to happen to someone else, but that day he was really riled.

"It was bad judgment," he told me, frowning and glum. "Rotten judgment. I'm ashamed to face Mr. Wolfe. I had a good story ready, one that I fully expected to work, and all I needed was ten minutes with the mother to put it over. But I misjudged her. I had discussed her with a couple of the bellhops, and had talked with her on the phone, and had a good chance to size her up in the hotel lobby and when she came outside, and I utterly misjudged her. I can't tell you anything about her brains or character, I didn't get that far, but she certainly knows how to keep the dogs off. I came mighty close to spending the day in the pound."

He told me all about it, and I had to admit it was a gloomy tale. No operative likes to come away empty from as simple a job as that, and Saul Panzer sure doesn't. To get his mind off of it, I mixed him a highball and got out a deck of cards for a little congenial gin. When six o'clock came and brought Wolfe down from the plant rooms, ending the game, I had won something better than three bucks.

Saul made his report. Wolfe sat behind his desk and listened, without interruption or comment. At the end he told Saul he had nothing to apologize for, asked him to phone after dinner for instructions, and let him go. Left alone with me, Wolfe leaned back and shut his eyes and was not visibly even breathing. I got at my typewriter and tapped out a summary of Saul's report, and was on my way to the cabinet to file it when Wolfe's voice came. "Archie."

"Yes, sir."

"I am stripped. This is no better than a treadmill."

"Yes, sir."

"I have to talk with that girl. Get Miss Fraser."

I did so, but we might as well have saved the nickel. Listening in on my phone, I swallowed it along with Wolfe. Miss Fraser was sorry that we had made little or no progress. She would do anything she could to help, but she was afraid, in fact she was certain, that it would be useless for her to call Mrs. Shepherd at Atlantic City and ask her to bring her daughter to New York to see Wolfe. There was no doubt that Mrs. Shepherd would flatly refuse. Miss Fraser admitted that she had influence with the child, Nancylee, but asserted that she had none at all with the mother. As for phoning Nancylee and persuading her to scoot and come on her own, she wouldn't consider it. She couldn't very well, since she had supplied the money for the mother and daughter to go away.

"You did?" Wolfe allowed himself to sound surprised. "Miss Koppel told Mr. Goodwin that none of you knew where they had gone."

"We didn't, until we saw it in the paper today. Nancylee's father was provoked, and that's putting it mildly, by all the photographers and reporters and everything else, and he blamed it on me, and I offered to pay the expense of a trip for them, but I didn't know where they decided to go."

We hung up, and discussed the outlook. I ventured to suggest two or three other possible lines of action, but Wolfe had his heart set on Nancylee, and I must admit I couldn't blame him for not wanting to start another round of conferences with the individuals he had been working on.

Finally he said, in a tone that announced he was no longer discussing but telling me, "I have to talk with that girl. Go and bring her."

I had known it was coming. "Conscious?" I asked casually.

"I said with her, not to her. She must be able to talk. You could revive her after you get her here. I should have sent you in the first place, knowing how you are with young women."

"Thank you very much. She's not a young woman, she's a minor. She wears socks."

"Archie."

"Yes, sir."

"Get her."

IX

I HAD A bad break. An idea that came to me at the dinner table, while I was pretending to listen to Wolfe telling how men with mustaches a foot long used to teach mathematics in schools in Montenegro, required, if it was to bear fruit, some information from the janitor at 829 Wixley Avenue. But when, immediately after dinner, I drove up there, he had gone to the movies and I had to wait over an hour for him. I got what I hoped would be all I needed, generously ladled out another buck of Starlite money, drove back downtown and put the car in the garage, and went home and up to my room. Wolfe, of course, was in the office, and the door was standing open, but I didn't even stop to nod as I went by.

In my room I gave my teeth an extra good brush, being uncertain how long they would have to wait for the next one, and then did my packing for the trip by putting a comb and hairbrush in my topcoat pocket. I didn't want to have a bag to take care of. Also I made a phone call. I made it there instead of in the office because Wolfe had put it off on me without a trace of a hint regarding ways and means, and if he wanted it like that, okay. In that case there was no reason why he should listen to me giving careful and explicit instructions to Saul Panzer. Downstairs again, I did pause at the office door to tell him good night, but that was all I had for him.

Tuesday night I had had a little over three hours' sleep, and Wednesday night about the same. That night, Thursday, I had less than three, and only in snatches. At six-thirty Friday morning, when I emerged to the cab platform at the Atlantic City railroad station, it was still half dark, murky, chilly, and generally unattractive. I had me a good yawn, shivered from head to foot, told a taxi driver I was his customer but he would please wait for me a minute, and then stepped to the taxi just behind him and spoke to the driver of it.

"This time of day one taxi isn't enough for me, I always need two. I'll take the one in front and you follow, and when we stop we'll have a conference."

"Where you going?"

"Not far." I pushed a dollar bill at him. "You won't get lost."

He nodded without enthusiasm and kicked his starter. I climbed into the front cab and told the driver to pull up somewhere in the vicinity of the Ambassador Hotel. It wasn't much of a haul, and a few minutes later he rolled to the curb, which at that time of day had space to spare. When the other driver stopped right behind us I signaled to him, and he came and joined us.

"I have enemies," I told them.

They exchanged a glance and one of them said, "Work it out yourself, bud, we're just hackies. My meter says sixty cents."

"I don't mean that kind of enemies. It's wife and daughter. They're ruining my life. How many ways are there for people to leave the Ambassador Hotel? I don't mean dodges like fire escapes and coal chutes, just normal ways."

"Two," one said.

"Three," the other said.

"Make up your minds."

They agreed on three, and gave me the layout.

"Then there's enough of us," I decided. "Here." I shelled out two finifs, with an extra single for the one who had carried me to even them up. "The final payment will depend on how long it takes, but you won't have to sue me. Now listen."

They did so.

Ten minutes later, a little before seven, I was standing by some kind of a bush with no leaves on it, keeping an eye on the ocean-front entrance of the Ambassador. Gobs of dirty gray mist being batted around by icy gusts made it seem more like a last resort than a resort. Also I was realizing that I had made a serious mistake when I had postponed breakfast until there would be time to do it right. My stomach had decided that since it wasn't going to be needed any more it might as well try shriveling into a ball and see how I liked that. I tried to kid it along by swallowing, but because I hadn't brushed my teeth it didn't taste like me at all, so I tried spitting instead, but that only made my stomach shrivel faster. After less than half an hour of it, when my watch said a quarter past seven, I was wishing to God I had done my planning better when one of my taxis came dashing around a corner to a stop, and the driver called to me and opened the door.

"They're off, bud."

"The station?"

"I guess so. That way." He made a U turn and stepped on the gas. "They came out the cab entrance and took one there. Tony's on their tail."

I didn't have to spur him on because he was already taking it hop, skip, and jump. My wrist watch told me nineteen past—eleven minutes before the seven-thirty for New York would leave. Only four of them had been used up when we did a fancy swerve and jerked to a stop in front of the railroad station. I hopped out. Just ahead of us a woman was paying her driver while a girl stood at her elbow.

"Duck, you damn fool," my driver growled at me. "They ain't blind, are they?"

"That's all right," I assured him. "They know I'm after them. It's a war of nerves."

Tony appeared from somewhere, and I separated myself from another pair of fives and then entered the station. There was only one ticket window working, and mother and child were at it, buying. I moseyed on to the train shed, still with three minutes to go, and was about to glance over my shoulder to see what was keeping them when they passed me on the run, holding hands, daughter in front and pulling Mom along. From the rear I saw them climb on board the train, but I stayed on the platform until the signal had been given and the wheels had started to turn, and then got on.

The diner wasn't crowded. I had a double orange juice, griddle cakes with broiled ham, coffee, French toast with sausage cakes, grape jelly, and more coffee. My stomach and I made up, and we agreed to forget it ever happened.

I decided to go have a look at the family, and here is something I'm not proud of. I had been so damn hungry that no thought of other stomachs had entered my head. But when, three cars back, I saw them and the look on their faces, the thought did come. Of course they were under other strains too, one in particular, but part of that pale, tight, anguished expression unquestionably came from hunger. They had had no time to grab anything on the way, and their manner of life was such that the idea of buying a meal on a train might not even occur to them.

I went back to the end of the car, stood facing the occupants, and called out, "Get your breakfast in the dining car, three cars ahead! Moderate prices!"

Then I passed down the aisle, repeating it at suitable intervals, once right at their seat. It worked. They exchanged some words and then got up and staggered forward. Not only that, I had made other sales too: a woman, a man, and a couple.

By the time the family returned we were less than an hour from New York. I looked them over as they came down the aisle. Mother was small and round-shouldered and her hair was going gray. Her nose still looked thin and sharp-pointed, but not as much so as it had when she was starving. Nancylee was better-looking, and much more intelligent-looking, than I would have expected from her pictures in the papers or from Saul's description. She had lots of medium-brown hair coming below her shoulders, and blue eyes, so dark that you had to be fairly close to see the blue, that were always on the go. She showed no trace either of Mom's pointed nose or of Pop's acreage of brow. If I had been in high school I would gladly have bought her a Coke or even a sundae.

Danger would begin, I well knew, the minute they stepped off the train at Pennsylvania Station and mounted the stairs. I had decided what to do if they headed for a taxi or bus or the subway, or if Mom started to enter a phone booth. So I was right on their heels when the moment for action came, but the only action called for was a pleasant walk. They took the escalator to the street level, left the station by the north exit, and turned left. I trailed. At Ninth Avenue they turned uptown, and at Thirty-fifth Street left again. That cinched it that they were aiming straight for Wolfe's house, non-stop, and naturally I was anything but crestfallen, but what really did my heart good was the timing. It was exactly eleven o'clock, and Wolfe would get down from the plant rooms and settled in his chair just in time to welcome them.

So it was. West of Tenth Avenue they began looking at the numbers, and I began to close up. At our stoop they halted, took another look, and mounted the steps. By the time they were pushing the button I was at the bottom of the stoop, but they had taken no notice of me. It would have been more triumphant if I could have done it another way, but the trouble was that Fritz wouldn't let them in until he had checked with Wolfe. So I took the steps two at a time, used my key and flung the door open, and invited them.

"Mrs. Shepherd? Go right in."

She crossed the threshold. But Nancylee snapped at me, "You were on the train. There's something funny about this."

"Mr. Wolfe's expecting you," I said, "if you want to call that funny. Anyway, come inside to laugh, so I can shut the door."

She entered, not taking her eyes off of me. I asked them if they wanted to leave their things in the hall, and they didn't, so I escorted them to the office. Wolfe, in his chair behind his desk, looked undecided for an instant and then got to his feet. I really appreciated that. He never rises when men enter, and his customary routine when a woman enters is to explain, if he feels like taking the trouble, that he keeps his chair because getting out of it and back in again is a more serious undertaking for him than for most men. I knew why he was breaking his rule. It was a salute to me, not just for producing them, but for getting them there exactly at the first minute of the day that he would be ready for them.

"Mrs. Shepherd," I said, "this is Mr. Nero Wolfe. Miss Nancylee Shepherd."

Wolfe bowed. "How do you do, ladies."

"My husband," Mom said in a scared but determined voice. "Where's my husband?"

"He'll be here soon," Wolfe assured her. "He was detained. Sit down, madam."

I grinned at him and shook my head. "Much obliged for trying to help, but that's not the line." I shifted the grin to the family. "I'll have to explain not only to you but to Mr. Wolfe too. Have you got the telegram with you? Let me have it a minute?"

Mom would have opened her handbag, but Nancylee stopped her. "Don't give it to him!" She snapped at me, "You let us out of here right now!"

"No," I said, "not right now, but I will in about five minutes if you still want to go. What are you afraid of? Didn't I see to it that you got some breakfast? First I would like to explain to Mr. Wolfe, and then I'll explain to you." I turned to Wolfe. "The telegram Mrs. Shepherd has in her bag reads as follows: 'Take first train to New York and go to office of Nero Wolfe at Nine-eighteen West Thirty-fifth Street. He is paying for this telegram. Bring Nan with you. Meet me there. Leave your things in your hotel room. Shake a leg. Al.' Saul sent it from a telegraph office in the Bronx at six-thirty this morning. You will understand why I had to go up there again to see the janitor. The 'shake a leg' made it absolutely authentic, along with other things."

"Then Father didn't send it!" Nancylee was glaring at me. "I thought there was something funny about it!" She took her mother's arm. "Come on, we're going!"

"Where, Nan?"

"We're leaving here!"

"But where are we going?" Near panic was in Mom's eyes and voice. "Home?"

"That's the point," I said emphatically. "That's just it. Where? You have three choices. First, you can go home and when the head of the family comes from work you can tell him how you were taken in by a fake telegram. Your faces show how much that appeals to you. Second, you can take the next train back to Atlantic City, but in that case I phone immediately, before you leave, to Mr. Shepherd at the warehouse where he works, and tell him that you're here with a wild tale about a telegram, and of course he'll want to speak to you. So again you would have to tell him about being fooled by a fake telegram."

Mom looked as if she needed some support, so I moved a chair up behind her and she sat.

"You're utterly awful," Nancylee said. "Just utterly!"

I ignored her and continued to her mother. "Or, third, you can stay here and Mr. Wolfe will discuss some matters with Nancylee, and ask her some questions. It may take two hours, or three, or four, so the sooner he gets started the better. You'll get an extra good lunch. As soon as Mr. Wolfe is through I'll take you to the station and put you on a train for Atlantic City. We'll pay your fare both ways and all expenses, such as taxi fare, and your breakfast, and dinner on the train going back. Mr. Shepherd, whom I have met, will never know anything about it." I screwed my lips. "Those are the only choices I can think of, those three."

Nancylee sat down and—another indication of her intelligence—in the red leather chair.

"This is terrible," Mom said hopelessly. "This is the worst thing—you don't look like a man that would do a thing like this. Are you absolutely sure my husband didn't send that telegram? Honestly?"

"Positively not," I assured her. "He doesn't know a thing about it and never will. There's nothing terrible about it. Long before bedtime you'll be back in that wonderful hotel room."

She shook her head as if all was lost.

"It's not so wonderful," Nancylee asserted. "The shower squirts sideways and they won't fix it." Suddenly she clapped a hand to her mouth, went pop-eyed, and sprang from the chair.

"Jumping cats!" she squealed. "Where's your radio? It's Friday! She's broadcasting!"

"No radio," I said firmly. "It's out of order. Here, let me take your coat and hat."

X

DURING the entire performance, except when we knocked off for lunch, Mrs. Shepherd sat with sagging shoulders on one of the yellow chairs. Wolfe didn't like her there and at various points gave her suggestions, such as going up to the south room for a nap or up to the top to look at the orchids, but she wasn't moving. She was of course protecting her young, but I swear I think her main concern was that if she let us out of her sight we might pull another telegram on her, signed Al.

I intend to be fair and just to Nancylee. It is quite true that this is on record, on a page of my notebook:

W: You have a high regard for Miss Fraser, haven't you, Miss Shepherd?

N: Oh, yes! She's simply utterly!

On another page:

W: Why did you leave high school without graduating if you were doing so well?

N: I was offered a modeling job. Just small time, two dollars an hour not very often and mostly legs, but the cash was simply sweet!

W: You're looking forward to a life of that—modeling?

N: Oh no! I'm really very serious-minded. *Am* I! I'm going into radio. I'm going to have a program like Miss Fraser—you know, human and get the laughs, but worth while and *good*. How often have you been on the air, Mr. Wolfe?

On still another page:

W: How have you been passing your time at Atlantic City?

N: Rotting away. That place is as dead as last week's date. Simply stagnating. Utterly!

Those are verbatim, and there are plenty more where they came from, but there are other pages to balance them. She could talk to the point when she felt like it, as for instance when she explained that she would have been suspicious of the telegram, and would have insisted that her mother call her father at the warehouse by long distance, if she hadn't learned from the papers that Miss Fraser had engaged Nero Wolfe to work on the case. And when he got her going on the subject of Miss Fraser's staff, she not only showed that she had done a neat little job of sizing them up, but also conveyed it to us without including anything that she might be called upon either to prove or to eat.

It was easy to see how desperate Wolfe was from the way he confined himself, up to lunch time, to skating around the edges, getting her used to his voice and manner and to hearing him ask any and every kind of question. By the time Fritz summoned us to the dining room I couldn't see that he had got the faintest flicker of light from any direction.

When we were back in the office and settled again, with Mom in her same chair and Nancylee dragging on a cigarette as if she had been at it for years, Wolfe resumed as before, but soon I noticed that he was circling in toward the scene of the crime. After getting himself up to date on the East Bronx Fraser Girls' Club and how Nancylee had organized it and put it at the top, he went right on into the studio and began on the Fraser broadcasts. He learned that Nancylee was always there on Tuesday, and sometimes on Friday too. Miss Fraser had promised her that she could get on a live mike someday, at least for a line or two. On the network! Most of the time she sat with the audience, front row, but she was always ready to help with anything, and frequently she was allowed to, but only on account of Miss Fraser. The others thought she was a nuisance.

"Are you?" Wolfe asked.

"You bet I am! But Miss Fraser doesn't think so because she knows

I think she's the very hottest thing on the air, simply super, and then there's my club, so you see how that is. The old ego mego."

You can see why I'd like to be fair and just to her.

Wolfe nodded as man to man. "What sort of things do you help with?"

"Oh." She waved a hand. "Somebody drops a page of script, I pick it up. One of the chairs squeaks, I hear it first and bring another one. The day it happened, I got the tray of glasses from the cabinet and took them to the table."

"You did? The day Mr. Orchard was a guest?"

"Sure, I often did that."

"Do you have a key to the cabinet?"

"No, Miss Vance has. She opened it and got the tray of glasses out." Nancylee smiled. "I broke one once, and did Miss Fraser throw a fit? No definitely. She just told me to bring a paper cup, that's how super she is."

"Marvelous. When did that happen?"

"Oh, a long while ago, when they were using the plain glasses, before they changed to the dark blue ones."

"How long ago was it?"

"Nearly a year, it must be." Nancylee nodded. "Yes, because it was when they first started to drink Starlite on the program, and the first few times they used plain clear glasses and then they had to change—" She stopped short.

"Why did they have to change?"

"I don't know."

I expected Wolfe to pounce, or at least to push. There was no doubt about it. Nancylee had stopped herself because she was saying, or starting to say, something that she didn't intend to let out, and when she said she didn't know she was lying. But Wolfe whirled and skated off.

"I suspect to get them so heavy they wouldn't break." He chuckled as if that were utterly amusing. "Have you ever drunk Starlite, Miss Shepherd?"

"Me? Are you kidding? When my club got to the top they sent me ten cases. Truckloads!"

"I don't like it much. Do you?"

"Oh—I guess so. I guess I adore it, but not too much at a time. When I get my program and have Shepherd Clubs I'm going to work it a different way." She frowned. "Do you think Nancylee Shepherd is a good radio name, or is Nan Shepherd better, or should I make one up? Miss Fraser's name was Oxhall, and she married a man named Koppel but he died, and when she got into radio she didn't want to use either of them and made one up."

"Either of yours," Wolfe said judiciously, "would be excellent. You must tell me sometime how you're going to handle your clubs. Do you think Starlite has pepper in it?"

"I don't know, I never thought. It's a lot of junk mixed together. Not at all frizoo."

"No," Wolfe agreed, "not frizoo. What other things do you do to help out at the broadcasts?"

"Oh, just like I said."

"Do you ever help pass the glasses and bottles around—to Miss Fraser and Mr. Meadows and the guests?"

"No, I tried to once, but they wouldn't let me."

"Where were you—the day we're talking about—while that was being done?"

"Sitting on the piano bench. They want me to stay in the audience while they're on the air, but sometimes I don't."

"Did you see who did the passing—to Mr. Orchard, for instance?"

Nancylee smiled in good-fellowship. "Now you'd like to know that, wouldn't you? But I didn't. The police asked me that about twenty million times."

"No doubt. I ask you once. Do you ever take the bottles from the cabinet and put them in the refrigerator?"

"Sure, I often do that—or I should say I help. That's Miss Vance's job, and she can't carry them all at once, so she has to make two trips, so quite often she takes four bottles and I take three."

"I see. I shouldn't think she would consider you a nuisance. Did you help with the bottles that Tuesday?"

"No, because I was looking at the new hat Miss Fraser had on, and I didn't see Miss Vance starting to get the bottles."

"Then Miss Vance had to make two trips, first four bottles and then three?"

"Yes, because Miss Fraser's hat was really something for the preview. Utterly first run! It had—"

"I believe you." Wolfe's voice sharpened a little, though perhaps only to my experienced ear. "That's right, isn't it, first four bottles and then three?"

"Yes, that's right."

"Making a total of seven?"

"Oh, you can add!" Nancylee exclaimed delightedly. She raised her right hand with four fingers extended, then her left hand with three, and looked from one to the other. "Correct. Seven!"

"Seven," Wolfe agreed. "I can add, and you can, but Miss Vance and Mr. Meadows can't. I understand that only four bottles are required for the program, but that they like to have extra ones in the refrigerator to provide for possible contingencies. But Miss Vance and Mr. Meadows say that the total is eight bottles. You say seven. Miss Vance says that they are taken from the cabinet to the refrigerator in two lots, four and four. You say four and three."

Wolfe leaned forward. "Miss Shepherd." His voice cut. "You will explain to me immediately, and satisfactorily, why they say eight and you say seven. Why?"

She didn't look delighted at all. She said nothing.

"Why?" It was the crack of a whip.

"I don't know!" she blurted.

I had both eyes on her, and even from a corner of one, with the other one shut, it would have been as plain as daylight that she did know, and furthermore that she had clammed and intended to stay clammed.

"Pfui." Wolfe wiggled a finger at her. "Apparently, Miss Shepherd, you have the crackbrained notion that whenever the fancy strikes you you can say you don't know, and I'll let it pass. You tried it about the glasses, and now this. I'll give you one minute to start telling me why the others said the customary number of bottles taken to the refrigerator is eight, and you say seven—Archie, time it."

I looked at my wrist, and then back at Nancylee. But she merely stayed a clam. Her face showed no sign that she was trying to make one up, or even figuring what would happen if she didn't. She was simply utterly not saying anything. I let her have an extra ten seconds, and then announced, "It's up."

Wolfe sighed. "I'm afraid, Miss Shepherd, that you and your mother will not return to Atlantic City. Not today. It is—"

A sound of pain came from Mom—not a word, just a sound. Nancy cried, "But you promised—"

"No. I did not. Mr. Goodwin did. You can have that out with him, but not until after I have given him some instructions." Wolfe turned to me. "Archie, you will escort Miss Shepherd to the office of Inspector Cramer. Her mother may accompany you or go home, as she prefers. But first take this down, type it, and take it with you. Two carbons. A letter to Inspector Cramer."

Wolfe leaned back, closed his eyes, pursed his lips, and in a moment began. "Regarding the murder of Cyril Orchard, I send you this information by Mr. Goodwin, who is taking Miss Nancylee Shepherd to you. He will explain how Miss Shepherd was brought to New York from Atlantic City. Paragraph.

"I suggest that Miss Madeline Fraser should be arrested without delay, charged with the murder of Cyril Orchard. It is obvious that the members of her staff are joined in a conspiracy. At first I assumed that their purpose was to protect her, but I am now convinced that I was wrong. At my office Tuesday evening it was ludicrously transparent that they were all deeply concerned about Miss Fraser's getting home safely, or so I then thought. I now believe that their concern was of a very different kind. Paragraph.

"That evening, here, Mr. Meadows was unnecessarily explicit and explanatory when I asked him how he decided which bottles to take from the refrigerator. There were various other matters which aroused my suspicion, plainly pointing to Miss Fraser, among them their pretense that they cannot remember who placed the glass and bottle in front of Mr. Orchard, which is of course ridiculous. Certainly they remember; and it is not conceivable that they would conspire unanimously to defend one of their number from exposure, unless that one were Miss Fraser. They are moved, doubtless, by varying considerations—loyalty, affection, or merely the desire to keep their jobs, which they will no longer have after Miss Fraser is arrested and disgraced—and, I hope, punished as the law provides. Paragraph.

"All this was already in my mind, but not with enough conviction to put it to you thus strongly, so I waited until I could have a talk with Miss Shepherd. I have now done that. It is plain that she too is in the conspiracy, and that leaves no doubt that it is Miss Fraser who is being shielded from exposure, since Miss Shepherd would do anything for her but nothing for any of the others. Miss Shepherd has lied to me twice that I am sure of, once when she said that she didn't know why the glasses that they drank from were changed, and once when she would give no explanation of her contradiction of the others regarding the number of bottles put in the refrigerator. Mr. Goodwin will give you the details of that. Paragraph.

"When you have got Miss Fraser safely locked in a cell, I would suggest that in questioning her you concentrate on the changing of the glasses. That happened nearly a year ago, and therefore it seems likely that the murder of Mr. Orchard was planned far in advance. This should make it easier for you, not harder, especially if you are able to persuade Miss Shepherd, by methods available to you, to tell all she knows about it. I do not— Archie!"

If Nancylee had had a split personality and it had been the gungirl half of her that suddenly sprang into action, I certainly would have been caught with my fountain pen down. But she didn't pull a gat. All she did was come out of her chair like a hurricane, get to me before I could even point the pen at her, snatch the notebook and hurl it across the room, and turn to blaze away at Wolfe, "That's a lie! It's all a lie!"

"Now, Nan," came from Mrs. Shepherd, in a kind of shaky, hopeless moan.

I was on my feet at the hurricane's elbow, feeling silly. Wolfe snapped at me, "Get the notebook and we'll finish. She's hysterical. If she does it again put her in the bathroom."

Nancylee was gripping my coat sleeve. "No!" she cried. "You're a stinker, you know you are! Changing the glasses had nothing to do with it! And I don't know why they changed them either—you're just a stinker—"

"Stop it!" Wolfe commanded her. "Stop screaming. If you have anything to say, sit down and say it. Why did they change the glasses?"

"I don't know!"

In crossing the room for it I had to detour around Mom, and, doing so, I gave her a pat on the shoulder, but I doubt if she was aware of it. From her standpoint there was nothing left. When I got turned around again Nancylee was still standing there, and from the stiffness of her back she looked put for the day. But as I reached my desk, suddenly she spoke, no screaming.

"I honestly don't know why they changed the glasses, because I was just guessing, but if I tell you what I was guessing I'll have to tell you something I promised Miss Fraser I would never tell anybody."

Wolfe nodded. "As I said. Shielding Miss Fraser."

"I'm not shielding her! She doesn't have to be shielded!"

"Don't get hysterical again. What was it you guessed?"

"I want to phone her."

"Of course you do. To warn her. So she can get away."

Nancylee slapped a palm on his desk.

"Don't do that!" he thundered.

"You're such a stinker!"

"Very well. Archie, lock her in the bathroom and phone Mr. Cramer to send for her."

I stood up, but she paid no attention to me. "All right," she said, "then I'll tell her how you made me tell, and my mother can tell her, too. When they got the new glasses I didn't know why, but I noticed right away, the broadcast that day, about the bottles too. That day Miss Vance didn't take eight bottles, she only took seven. If it hadn't been for that I might not have noticed, but I did, and when they were broadcasting I saw that the bottle they gave Miss Fraser had a piece of tape on it. And every time after that it has always been seven bottles, and they always give Miss Fraser the one with tape on it. So I thought there was some connection, the new glasses and the tape on the bottle, but I was just guessing."

"I wish you'd sit down, Miss Shepherd. I don't like tipping my head back."

"I wouldn't care if you broke your old neck!"

"Now, Nan," her mother moaned.

Nancylee went to the red leather chair and lowered herself onto the edge of it.

"You said," Wolfe murmured, "that you promised Miss Fraser not to tell about this. When did you promise, recently?"

"No, a long time ago. Months ago. I was curious about the tape on the bottle, and one day I asked Miss Vance about it, and afterward Miss Fraser told me it was something very personal to her and she made me promise never to tell. Twice since then she has asked me if I was keeping the promise and I told her I was and I always would. And now here I am! But you saying she should be arrested for murder—just because I said I didn't know—"

"I gave other reasons."

"But she won't be arrested now, will she? The way I've explained?"

"We'll see. Probably not." Wolfe sounded comforting. "No one has ever told you what the tape is on the bottle for?"

"No."

"Haven't you guessed?"

"No, I haven't, and I'm not going to guess now. I don't know what it's for or who puts it on or when they put it on, or anything about it except what I've said, that the bottle they give Miss Fraser has a piece of tape on it. And that's been going on a long time, nearly a year, so it couldn't have anything to do with that man getting murdered just last week. So I hope you're satisfied."

"Fairly well," Wolfe conceded.

"Then may I phone her now?"

"I'd rather you didn't. You see she has hired me to investigate this murder, and I'd prefer to tell her about this myself—and apologize for suspecting her. By the way, the day Mr. Orchard was poisoned—did Miss Fraser's bottle have tape on it that day as usual?"

"I didn't notice it that day, but I suppose so, it always did."

"You're sure you didn't notice it?"

"What do you think? Am I lying again?"

Wolfe shook his head. "I doubt it. You don't sound like it. But one thing you can tell me, about the tape. What was it like and where was it on the bottle?"

"Just a piece of Scotch tape, that's all, around the neck of the bottle, down nearly to where the bottle starts to get bigger."

"Always in the same place?"

"Yes."

"How wide is it?"

"You know, Scotch tape, about that wide." She held a thumb and fingertip about half an inch apart.

"What color?"

"Brown—or maybe it looks brown because the bottle is."

"Always the same color?"

"Yes."

"Then it couldn't have been very conspicuous."

"I didn't say it was conspicuous. It wasn't."

"You have good eyesight, of course, at your age." Wolfe glanced at the clock and turned to me. "When is the next train for Atlantic City?"

"Four-thirty," I told him.

"Then you have plenty of time. Give Mrs. Shepherd enough to cover all expenses. You will take her and her daughter to the station.

Since they do not wish it to be known that they have made this trip, it would be unwise for them to do any telephoning, and of course you will make sure that they board the right train, and that the train actually starts. As you know, I do not trust trains either to start or, once started, to stop."

"We're going back," Mom said, unbelieving but daring to hope.

XI

THERE was one little incident I shouldn't skip, on the train when I had found their seats for them and was turning to go. I had made no effort to be sociable, since their manner, especially Nancylee's, had made it plain that if I had stepped into a manhole they wouldn't even have halted to glance down in. But as I turned to go Mom suddenly reached up to pat me on the shoulder. Apparently the pat I had given her at one of her darkest moments had been noticed after all, or maybe it was because I had got them Pullman seats. I grinned at her, but didn't risk offering to shake hands in farewell. I ride my luck only so far.

Naturally another party was indicated, but I didn't realize how urgent it was until I got back to the office and found a note, on a sheet from Wolfe's memo pad, waiting for me under a paperweight on my desk—he being, as per schedule, up in the plant rooms. The note said:

AG—
Have all seven of them here at six o'clock.
NW

Just like snapping your fingers. I scowled at the note. Why couldn't it be after dinner, allowing more time both to get them and to work on them? Not to mention that I already had a fairly good production record for the day, with the eleven A.M. delivery I had made. My watch said ten to five. I swallowed an impulse to mount to the plant rooms and give him an argument, and reached for the phone.

I ran into various difficulties, including resistance to a summons on such short notice, with which I was in complete sympathy. Bill Meadows balked good, saying that he had already told Wolfe everything he knew, including the time he had thrown a baseball through a windowpane, and I had to put pressure on him with menacing hints. Madeline Fraser and Deborah Koppel were reluctant but had to admit that Wolfe should either be fired or given all possible help. They agreed to bring Elinor Vance. Nathan Traub, whom I got first, at his office, was the only one who offered no objection, though he commented that he would have to call off an important appointment. The only two I fell down on were Savarese and Strong. The professor had left town for the weekend, I supposed to hunt formulas, and Tully Strong just couldn't be found, though I tried everywhere, including all the sponsors.

Shortly before six I phoned up to Wolfe to report. The best he had for me was a grunt. I remarked that five out of seven, at that hour on a Friday, was nothing to be sneezed at. He replied that seven would have been better.

"Yeah," I agreed. "I've sent Savarese and Strong telegrams signed Al, but what if they don't get them on time?"

So there were five. Wolfe doesn't like to be seen, by anyone but Fritz or me, sitting around waiting for people, I imagine on the theory that it's bad for his prestige, and therefore he didn't come down to the office until I passed him the word that all five were there. Then he favored us by appearing. He entered, bowed to them, crossed to his chair, and got himself comfortable. It was cozier and more intimate than it had been three days earlier, with the gate-crashers absent.

There was a little conversation. Traub offered some pointed remarks about Wolfe's refusal to admit reporters for an interview. Ordinarily, with an opening like that, Wolfe counters with a nasty crusher, but now he couldn't be bothered. He merely waved it away.

"I got you people down here," he said, perfectly friendly, "for a single purpose, and if you're not to be late for your dinners we'd better get at it. Tuesday evening I told you that you were all lying to me, but I didn't know then how barefaced you were about it. Why the devil didn't you tell me about the piece of tape on Miss Fraser's bottle?"

They all muffed it badly, even Miss Fraser, with the sole exception of Traub. He alone looked just bewildered.

"Tape?" he asked. "What tape?"

It took the other four an average of three seconds even to begin deciding what to do about their faces.

"Who is going to tell me about it?" Wolfe inquired. "Not all of you at once. Which one?"

"But," Bill Meadows stammered, "we don't know what you're talking about."

"Nonsense." Wolfe was less friendly. "Don't waste time on that. Miss Shepherd spent most of the day here and I know all about it." His eyes stopped on Miss Fraser. "She couldn't help it, madam. She did quite well for a child, and she surrendered only under the threat of imminent peril to you."

"What's this all about?" Traub demanded.

"It's nothing, Nat," Miss Fraser assured him. "Nothing of any importance. Just a little—a sort of joke among us, that you don't know about."

"Nothing to it!" Bill Meadows said, a little too loud. "There's a perfectly simple—"

"Wait, Bill." Deborah Koppel's voice held quiet authority. Her gaze was at Wolfe. "Will you tell us exactly what Nancylee said?"

"Certainly," Wolfe assented. "The bottle served to Miss Fraser on the broadcast is always identified with a strip of Scotch tape. That has been going on for months, nearly a year. The tape is either brown, the color of the bottle, or transparent, is half an inch wide, and encircles the neck of the bottle near the shoulder."

"Is that all she told you?"

"That's the main thing. Let's get that explained. What's the tape for?"

"Didn't Nancylee tell you?"

"She said she didn't know."

Deborah was frowning. "Why she must know! It's quite simple. As we told you, when we get to the studio the day of a broadcast Miss Vance takes the bottles from the cabinet and puts them in the refrigerator. But that gives them only half an hour or a little longer to get cold, and Miss Fraser likes hers as cold as possible, so a bottle for her is put in earlier and the tape put on to tell it from the others."

"Who puts it there and when?"

"Well—that depends. Sometimes one of us puts it there the day before. Sometimes it's one left over from the preceding broadcast."

"Good heavens," Wolfe murmured. "I didn't know you were an imbecile, Miss Koppel."

"I am not an imbecile, Mr. Wolfe."

"I'll have to have more than your word for it. I presume the explanation you have given me was concocted to satisfy the casual curiosity of anyone who might notice the tape on the bottle—and, incidentally, I wouldn't be surprised if it was offered to Miss Shepherd and after further observation she rejected it. That's one thing she didn't tell me. For that purpose the explanation would be adequate—except with Miss Shepherd—but to try it on me! I'll withdraw the 'imbecile,' since I blurted it at you without warning, but I do think you might have managed something a little less flimsy."

"It may be flimsy," Bill Meadows put in aggressively, "but it happens to be true."

"My dear sir." Wolfe was disgusted. "You too? Then why didn't it satisfy Miss Shepherd, if it was tried on her, and why was she sworn to secrecy? Why weren't all the bottles put in the refrigerator in advance, to get them all cold, instead of just the one for Miss Fraser? There are—"

"Because someone—" Bill stopped short.

"Precisely," Wolfe agreed with what he had cut off. "Because hundreds of people use that studio between Miss Fraser's broadcasts, and someone would have taken them from the refrigerator, which isn't locked. That's what you were about to say, but didn't, because you realized there would be the same hazard for one bottle as for eight." Wolfe shook his head. "No, it's no good. I'm tired of your lies; I want the truth; and I'll get it because nothing else can meet the tests I am now equipped to apply. Why is the tape put on the bottle?"

They looked at one another.

"No," Deborah Koppel said to anybody and everybody.

"What *is* all this?" Traub demanded peevishly.

No one paid any attention to him.

"Why not," Wolfe inquired, "try me with the same answer you have given the police?"

No reply.

Elinor Vance spoke, not to Wolfe. "It's up to you, Lina. I think we have to tell him."

"No," Miss Koppel insisted.

"I don't see any other way out of it, Debby," Madeline Fraser declared. "You shouldn't have told him that silly lie. It wasn't good enough for him and you know it." Her gray-green eyes went to Wolfe. "It would be fatal for me, for all of us, if this became known. I don't suppose you would give me your word to keep it secret?"

"How could I, madam?" Wolfe turned a palm up. "Under the circumstances? But I'll share it as reluctantly, and as narrowly, as the circumstances will permit."

"All right. Damn that Cyril Orchard, for making this necessary. The tape on the bottle shows that it is for me. My bottle doesn't contain Starlite. I can't drink Starlite."

"Why not?"

"It gives me indigestion."

"Good God!" Nathan Traub cried, his smooth low-pitched voice transformed into a squeak.

"I can't help it, Nat," Miss Fraser told him firmly, "but it does."

"And that," Wolfe demanded, "is your desperate and fatal secret?"

She nodded. "My Lord, could anything be worse? If that got around? If Leonard Lyons got it, for instance? I stuck to it the first few times, but it was no use. I wanted to cut that from the program, serving it, but by that time the Starlite people were crazy about it, especially Anderson and Owen, and of course I couldn't tell them the truth. I tried faking it, not drinking much, but even a few sips made me sick. It must be an allergy."

"I congratulate you," Wolfe said emphatically.

"Good God," Traub muttered. He pointed a finger at Wolfe. "It is absolutely essential that this get to no one. No one whatever!"

"It's out now," Miss Koppel said quietly but tensely. "It's gone now."

"So," Wolfe asked, "you used a substitute?"

"Yes." Miss Fraser went on. "It was the only way out. We used black coffee. I drink gallons of it anyhow, and I like it either hot or cold. With sugar in it. It looks enough like Starlite, which is dark brown, and of course in the bottle it can't be seen anyway, and we changed to dark blue glasses so it couldn't be seen that it didn't fizz."

"Who makes the coffee?"

"My cook, in my apartment."

"Who bottles it?"

"She does—my cook—she puts it in a Starlite bottle, and puts the cap on."

"When, the day of the broadcast?"

"No, because it would still be hot, or at least warm, so she does it the day before and puts it in the refrigerator."

"Not at the broadcasting studio?"

"Oh, no, in my kitchen."

"Does she put the tape on it?"

"No, Miss Vance does that. In the morning she gets it—she always comes to my apartment to go downtown with me—and she puts the tape on it, and takes it to the studio in her bag, and puts it in the refrigerator there. She has to be careful not to let anyone see her do that."

"I feel better," Bill Meadows announced abruptly. He had his handkerchief out and was wiping his forehead.

"Why?" Wolfe asked him.

"Because I knew this had to come sooner or later, and I'm glad it was you that got it instead of the cops. It's been a cockeyed farce, all this digging to find out who had it in for this guy Orchard. Nobody wanted to poison Orchard. The poison was in the coffee and Orchard got it by mistake."

That finished Traub. A groan came from him, his chin went down, and he sat shaking his head in despair.

Wolfe was frowning. "Are you trying to tell me that the police don't know that the poisoned bottle held coffee?"

"Oh, sure, they know that." Bill wanted to help now. "But they've kept it under their hats. You notice it hasn't been in the papers. And none of us has spilled it, you can see why we wouldn't. They know it was coffee all right, but they think it was meant for Orchard, and it wasn't, it was meant for Miss Fraser."

Bill leaned forward and was very earnest. "Damn it, don't you see what we're up against? If we tell it and it gets known, God help the program! We'd get hooted off the air. But as long as we don't tell it, everybody thinks the poison was meant for Orchard, and that's why I said it was a farce. Well, we didn't tell, and as far as I'm concerned we never would."

"How have you explained the coffee to the police?"

"We haven't explained it. We didn't know how the poison got in the bottle, did we? Well, we didn't know how the coffee got there either. What else could we say?"

"Nothing, I suppose, since you blackballed the truth. How have you explained the tape?"

"We haven't explained it."

"Why not?"

"We haven't been asked to."

"Nonsense. Certainly you have."

"I haven't."

"Thanks, Bill." It was Madeline Fraser, smiling at him. "But there's no use trying to save any pieces." She turned to Wolfe. "He's trying to protect me from—don't they call it tampering with evidence? You remember that after the doctor came Mr. Strong took the four bottles from the table and started off with them, just a foolish impulse he had, and Mr. Traub and I took them from him and put them back on the table."

Wolfe nodded.

"Well, that was when I removed the tape from the bottle."

"I see. Good heavens! It's a wonder all of you didn't collectively gather them up, and the glasses, and march to the nearest sink to wash up." Wolfe went back to Bill. "You said Mr. Orchard got the poisoned coffee by mistake. How did that happen?"

"Traub gave it to him. Traub didn't—"

Protests came at him from both directions, all of them joining in. Traub even left his chair to make it emphatic.

Bill got a little flushed, but he was stubborn and heedless. "Since we're telling it," he insisted, "we'd better tell it all."

"You're not sure it was Nat," Miss Koppel said firmly.

"Certainly I'm sure! You know damn well it was! You know damn well we all saw—all except Lina—that Orchard had her bottle, and of course it was Traub that gave it to him, because Traub was the only one that didn't know about the tape. Anyhow I saw him! That's the way it was, Mr. Wolfe. But when the cops started on us apparently we all had the same idea—I forget who started it—that it would be best not to remember who put the bottle in front of Orchard. So we didn't. Now that you know about the tape, I do remember, and if the others don't they ought to."

"Quit trying to protect me, Bill," Miss Fraser scolded him. "It was my idea, about not remembering. I started it."

Again several of them spoke at once. Wolfe showed them a palm.

"Please! Mr. Traub. Manifestly it doesn't matter whether you give me a yes or a no, since you alone were not aware that one of the bottles had a distinction; but I ask you pro forma, did you place that bottle before Mr. Orchard?"

"I don't know," Traub said belligerently, "and I don't care. Meadows doesn't know either."

"But you did help pass the glasses and bottles around?"

"I've told you I did. I thought it was fun." He threw up both hands. "Fun!"

"There's one thing," Madeline Fraser put in, for Wolfe. "Mr. Meadows said that they all saw that Mr. Orchard had my bottle, except me. That's only partly true. I didn't notice it at first, but when I lifted the glass to drink and smelled the Starlite I knew someone else had my glass. I went ahead and faked the drinking, and as I went on with the script I saw that the bottle with the tape on it was a little nearer to him than to me—as you know, he sat across from me. I had to decide quick what to do—not me with the Starlite, but him with the coffee. I was afraid he would blurt out that it tasted like coffee, especially since he had taken two big gulps. I was feeling relieved that apparently he wasn't going to, when he sprang up with that terrible cry. So what Mr. Meadows said was only partly true. I suppose he was protecting me some more, but I'm tired of being protected by everybody."

"He isn't listening, Lina," Miss Koppel remarked.

It was a permissible conclusion, but not necessarily sound. Wolfe had leaned back in his chair and closed his eyes, and even to me it might have seemed that he was settling for a snooze but for two details: first, dinnertime was getting close, and second, the tip of his right forefinger was doing a little circle on the arm of his chair, around and around. The silence held for seconds, made a minute, and started on another one.

Someone said something.

Wolfe's eyes came half open and he straightened up.

"I could," he said, either to himself or to them, "ask you to stay to dinner. Or to return after dinner. But if Miss Fraser is tired of being protected, I am tired of being humbugged. There are things I need to know, but I don't intend to try to pry them out of you without a lever. If you are ready to let me have them, I'm ready to take them. You know what they are as well as I do. It now seems obvious that this was an attempt to kill Miss Fraser. What further evidence is there to support that assumption, and what evidence is there, if any, to contradict it? Who wants Miss Fraser to die, and why? Particularly, who of those who had access to the bottle of coffee, at any time from the moment it was bottled at her apartment to the moment when it was served at the broadcast? And so on. I won't put all the questions; you know what I want. Will any of you give it to me—any of it?"

His gaze passed along the line. No one said a word.

"One or more of you," he said, "might prefer not to speak in the presence of the others. If so, do you want to come back later? This evening?"

"If I had anything to tell you," Bill Meadows asserted, "I'd tell you now."

"You sure would," Traub agreed.

"I thought not," Wolfe said grimly. "To get anything out of you another Miss Shepherd would be necessary. One other chance: if you prefer not even to make an appointment in the presence of the others, we are always here to answer the phone. But I would advise you not to delay." He pushed his chair back and got erect. "That's all I have for you now, and you have nothing for me."

They didn't like that much. They wanted to know what he was going to do. Especially and unanimously, they wanted to know what about their secret. Was the world going to hear of what a sip of Starlite did to Madeline Fraser? On that Wolfe refused to commit himself. The stubbornest of the bunch was Traub. When the others finally left he stayed behind, refusing to give up the fight, even trying to follow Wolfe into the kitchen. I had to get rude to get rid of him.

When Wolfe emerged from the kitchen, instead of bearing left toward the dining room he returned to the office, although dinner was ready.

I followed. "What's the idea? Not hungry?"

"Get Mr. Cramer."

I went to my desk and obeyed.

Wolfe got on.

"How do you do, sir." He was polite but far from servile. "Yes. No. No, indeed. If you will come to my office after dinner, say at nine o'clock, I'll tell you why you haven't got anywhere on that Orchard case. No, not only that, I think you'll find it helpful. No, nine o'clock would be better."

He hung up, scowled at me, and headed for the dining room. By the time he had seated himself, tucked his napkin in the V of his vest, and removed the lid from the onion soup, letting the beautiful strong steam sail out, his face had completely cleared and he was ready to purr.

XII

INSPECTOR CRAMER, adjusted to ease in the red leather chair, with beer on the little table at his elbow, manipulated his jaw so that the unlighted cigar made a cocky upward angle from the left side of his mouth.

"Yes," he admitted. "You can have it all for a nickel. That's where I am. Either I'm getting older or murderers are getting smarter."

He was in fact getting fairly gray, and his middle, though it would never get into Wolfe's class, was beginning to make pretensions, but his eyes were as sharp as ever and his heavy broad shoulders showed no inclination to sink under the load.

"But," he went on, sounding more truculent than he actually was because keeping the cigar where he wanted it made him talk through his teeth, "I'm not expecting any nickel from you. You don't look as if you needed anything. You look as pleased as if someone had just given you a geranium."

"I don't like geraniums."

"Then what's all the happiness about? Have you got to the point where you're ready to tell Archie to mail out the bills?"

He not only wasn't truculent; he was positively mushy. Usually he called me Goodwin. He called me Archie only when he wanted to peddle the impression that he regarded himself as one of the family, which he wasn't.

Wolfe shook his head. "No, I'm far short of that. But I am indeed pleased. I like the position I'm in. It seems likely that you and your trained men—up to a thousand of them, I assume, on a case as blazoned as this one—are about to work like the devil to help me earn a fee. Isn't that enough to give me a smirk?"

"The hell you say." Cramer wasn't so sugary. "According to the papers your fee is contingent."

"So it is."

"On what you do. Not on what we do."

"Of course," Wolfe agreed. He leaned back and sighed comfortably. "You're much too clearsighted not to appraise the situation, which is a little peculiar, as I do. Would you like me to describe it?"

"I'd love it. You're a good describer."

"Yes, I think I am. You have made no progress, and after ten days you are sunk in a morass, because there is a cardinal fact which you have not discovered. I have. I have discovered it by talking with the very persons who have been questioned by you and your men many times, and it was not given to me willingly. Only by intense and sustained effort did I dig it out. Then why should I pass it on to you? Why don't I use it myself, and go on to triumph?"

Cramer put his beer glass down. "You're telling me."

"That was rhetoric. The trouble is that, while without this fact you can't even get started, with it there is still a job to be done; that job will require further extended dealing with these same people, their histories and relationships; and I have gone as far as I can with them unless I hire an army. You already have an army. The job will probably need an enormous amount of the sort of work for which your men are passably equipped, some of them even adequately, so why shouldn't they do it? Isn't it the responsibility of the police to catch a murderer?"

Cramer was now wary and watchful. "From you," he said, "that's one hell of a question. More rhetoric?"

"Oh no. That one deserves an answer. Yours, I feel sure, is yes, and the newspapers agree. So I submit a proposal: I'll give you the fact, and you'll proceed to catch the murderer. When that has been done, you and I will discuss whether the fact was essential to your success; whether you could possibly have got the truth and the evidence without it. If we agree that you couldn't, you will so inform my clients, and I shall collect my fee. No document will be required; an oral statement will do; and of course only to my clients. I don't care what you say to journalists or to your superior officers."

Cramer grunted. He removed the cigar from his mouth, gazed at the mangled end suspiciously as if he expected to see a bug crawling, and put it back where it belonged. Then he squinted at Wolfe. "Would you repeat that?"

Wolfe did so, as if he were reading it off, without changing a word.

Cramer grunted again. "You say if we agree. You mean if you agree with me, or if I agree with you?"

"Bah. It couldn't be plainer."

"Yeah. When you're plainest you need looking at closest. What if I've already got this wonderful fact?"

"You didn't have it two hours ago. If you have it now, I have nothing to give and shall get nothing. If when I divulge it you claim to have had it, you'll tell me when and from whom you got it." Wolfe stirred impatiently. "It is, of course, connected with facts in your possession—for instance, that the bottle contained sugared coffee instead of Starlite."

"Sure, they've told you that."

"Or that your laboratory has found traces of a certain substance, in a band half an inch wide, encircling the neck of the bottle."

"They haven't told you *that*." Cramer's eyes got narrower. "There are only six or seven people who could have told you that, and they all get paid by the City of New York, and by God you can name him before we go any farther."

"Pfui." Wolfe was disgusted. "I have better use for my clients' money than buying information from policemen. Why don't you like my proposal? What's wrong with it? Frankly, I hope to heaven you accept it, and immediately. If you don't I'll have to hire two dozen men and begin all over again on those people, and I'd rather eat baker's bread—almost."

"All right." Cramer did not relax. "Hell, I'd do anything to save you from that. I'm on. Your proposal, as you have twice stated it, provided I get the fact, and all of it, here and now."

"You do. Here it is, and Mr. Goodwin will have a typed copy for you. But first—a little detail—I owe it to one of my clients to request that one item of it be kept confidential, if it can possibly be managed."

"I can't keep murder evidence confidential."

"I know you can't. I said if it can possibly be managed."

"I'll see, but I'm not promising, and if I did promise I probably wouldn't keep it. What's the item? Give it to me first."

"Certainly. Miss Fraser can't drink Starlite because it gives her indigestion."

"What the hell." Cramer goggled at him. "Orchard didn't drink Starlite, he drank coffee, and it didn't give him indigestion, it killed him."

Wolfe nodded. "I know. But that's the item, and on behalf of my clients I ask that it be kept undisclosed if possible. This is going to take some time, perhaps an hour, and your glass and bottle are empty. Archie?"

I got up and bartended without any boyish enthusiasm because I wasn't very crazy about the shape things were taking. I was keeping my fingers crossed. If Wolfe was starting some tricky maneuver and only fed him a couple of crumbs, with the idea of getting a full-sized loaf, not baker's bread, in exchange, that would be one thing, and I was ready to applaud if he got away with it. If he really opened the bag and dumped it out, letting Cramer help himself, that would be something quite different. In that case he was playing it straight, and that could only mean that he had got fed up with them, and really intended to sit and read poetry or draw horses and let the cops earn his fee for him. That did not appeal to me. Money may be everything, but it makes a difference how you get it.

He opened the bag and dumped it. He gave Cramer all we had. He even quoted, from memory, the telegram that had been sent to Mom Shepherd, and as he did so I had to clamp my jaw to keep from making one of four or five remarks that would have fitted the occasion. I had composed that telegram, not him. But I kept my trap shut. I do sometimes ride him in the presence of outsiders, but rarely for Cramer to hear, and not when my feelings are as strong as they were then.

Also Cramer had a lot of questions to ask, and Wolfe answered them like a lamb. And I had to leave my chair so Cramer could rest his broad bottom on it while he phoned his office.

"Rowcliff? Take this down, but don't broadcast it." He was very crisp and executive, every inch an inspector. "I'm at Wolfe's office, and he did have something, and for once I think he's dealing off the top of the deck. We've got to start all over. It's one of those goddam babies where the wrong person got killed. It was intended for the Fraser woman. I'll tell you when I get there, in half an hour, maybe a little more. Call in everybody that's on the case. Find out where the commissioner is, and the D.A. Get that Elinor Vance and that Nathan Traub, and get the cook at the Fraser apartment. Have those three there by the time I come. We'll take the others in the morning. Who was it went to Michigan—oh, I remember, Darst. Be sure you don't miss him, I want to see him. . . ."

And so forth. After another dozen or so executive orders Cramer hung up and returned to the red leather chair.

"What else?" he demanded.

"That's all," Wolfe declared. "I wish you luck."

Having dropped his chewed-up cigar in my wastebasket when he usurped my chair, Cramer got out another one and stuck it in his mouth without looking at it. "I'll tell you," he said. "You gave me a fact, no doubt about that, but this is the first time I ever saw you turn out all your pockets, so I sit down again. Before I leave I'd like to sit here a couple of minutes and ask myself, What for?"

Wolfe chuckled. "Didn't I just hear you telling your men to start to work for me?"

"Yeah, I guess so." The cigar slanted up. "It seems plausible, but I've known you to seem plausible before. And I swear to God if there's a gag in this it's buried too deep for me. You don't even make any suggestions."

"I have none."

And he didn't. I saw that. And there wasn't any gag. I didn't wonder that Cramer suspected him, considering what his experiences with him had been in the past years, but to me it was only too evident that Wolfe had really done a strip act, to avoid overworking his brain. I have sat in that office with him too many hours, and watched him put on his acts for too many audiences, not to know when he is getting up a charade. I certainly don't always know what he is up to, but I do know when he is up to nothing at all. He was simply utterly going to let the city employees do it.

"Would you suggest, for instance," Cramer inquired, "hauling Miss Fraser in on a charge of tampering with evidence? Or the others for obstructing justice?"

Wolfe shook his head. "My dear sir, you are after a murderer, not tamperers or obstructers. Anyway, you can't get convictions on charges like that, except in very special cases, and you know it. You are hinting that it isn't like me to expose a client to such a charge, but will you arrest her? No. What you will do, I hope, is find out who it is that wants to kill her. How could I have suggestions for you? You know vastly more about it than I do. There are a thousand lines of investigation, in a case like this, on which I haven't moved a finger; and doubtless you have explored all of them. I won't insult you by offering a list of them. I'll be here, though, I'm always here, should you want a word with me."

Cramer got up and went.

XIII

I can't deny that from a purely practical point of view the deal that Wolfe made with Cramer that Friday evening was slick, even fancy, and well designed to save wear and tear on Wolfe's energy and the contents of his skull. No matter how it added up at the end it didn't need one of Professor Savarese's formulas to show how probable it was that the fact Wolfe had furnished Cramer would turn out to be an essential item. That was a good bet at almost any odds.

But.

There was one fatal flaw in the deal. The city scientists, in order to earn Wolfe's fee for him while he played around with his toys, had to crack the case. That was the joker. I have never seen a more completely uncracked case than that one was, a full week after Wolfe had made his cute little arrangement to have his detective work done by proxy. I kept up to date on it both by reading the newspapers and by making jaunts down to Homicide headquarters on Twentieth Street, for chats with Sergeant Purley Stebbins or other acquaintances, and twice with Cramer himself. That was humiliating, but I did want to keep myself informed somehow about the case Wolfe and I were working on. For the first time in history I was perfectly welcome at Homicide, especially after three or four days had passed. It got to be pathetic, the way they would greet me like a treasured pal, no doubt thinking it was just possible I had come to contribute another fact. God knows they needed one. For of course they were reading the papers too, and the press was living up to one of its oldest traditions by bawling hell out of the cops for bungling a case which, by prompt and competent— You know how it goes.

So far the public had not been informed that Starlite gave Miss Fraser indigestion. If the papers had known that!

Wolfe wasn't lifting a finger. It was not, properly speaking, a relapse. Relapse is my word for it when he gets so offended or disgusted by something about a case, or so appalled by the kind or amount of work it is going to take to solve it, that he decides to pretend he has never heard of it, and rejects it as a topic of conversation. This wasn't like that. He just didn't intend to work unless he had to. He was perfectly willing to read the pieces in the papers, or to put down his book and listen when I returned from one of my visits to Homicide. But if I tried to badger him into some mild exertion like hiring Saul and Fred and Orrie to look under some stones, or even thinking up a little errand for me, he merely picked up his book again.

If any of the developments, such as they were, meant anything to him, he gave no sign of it. Elinor Vance was arrested, held as a material witness, and after two days released on bail. The word I brought from Homicide was that there was nothing to it except that she had by far the best opportunity to put something in the coffee, with the exception of the cook. Not that there weren't plenty of others; the list had been considerably lengthened by the discovery that the coffee had been made, bottled, and kept overnight in Miss Fraser's apartment, with all the coming and going there.

Then there was the motive-collecting operation. In a murder case you can always get some motives together, but the trouble is you can never be sure which ones are sunfast for the people concerned. It all depends. There was the guy in Brooklyn a few years ago who stabbed a dentist in and around the heart eleven times because he had pulled the wrong tooth. In this case the motive assortment was about average, nothing outstanding but fairly good specimens. Six months ago Miss Fraser and Bill Meadows had had a first-class row, and she had fired him and he had been off the program for three weeks. They both claimed that they now dearly loved each other.

Not long ago Nat Traub had tried to persuade a soup manufacturer, one of the Fraser sponsors, to leave her and sign up for an evening comedy show, and Miss Fraser had retaliated by talking the sponsor into switching to another agency. Not only that, there were vague hints that Miss Fraser had started a campaign for a similar switch by other sponsors, including Starlite, but they couldn't be nailed down. Again, she and Traub insisted that they were awful good friends.

The Radio Writers Guild should have been delighted to poison Miss Fraser on account of her tough attitude toward demands of the Guild for changes in contracts, and Elinor Vance was a member of the Guild in good standing. As for Tully Strong, Miss Fraser had opposed the formation of a Sponsors' Council, and still didn't like it, and of course if there were no Council there would be no secretary.

And so on. As motives go, worth tacking up but not spectacular. The one that would probably have got the popular vote was Deborah

Koppel's. Somebody in the D.A.'s office had induced Miss Fraser to reveal the contents of her will. It left ten grand each to a niece and nephew, children of her sister who lived in Michigan, and all the rest to Deborah. It would be a very decent chunk, somewhere in six figures, with the first figure either a two or a three, certainly worth a little investment in poison for anyone whose mind ran in that direction. There was, however, not the slightest indication that Deborah's mind did. She and Miss Fraser, then Miss Oxhall, had been girlhood friends in Michigan, had taught at the same school, and had become sisters-in-law when Madeline had married Deborah's brother Lawrence.

Speaking of Lawrence, his death had of course been looked into again, chiefly on account of the coincidence of the cyanide. He had been a photographer, and therefore, when needing cyanide, all he had to do was reach to a shelf for it. What if he hadn't killed himself after all? Or what if, even if he had, someone thought he hadn't, believed it was his wife who had needed the cyanide in order to collect five thousand dollars in insurance money, and had now arranged, after six years, to even up by giving Miss Fraser a dose of it herself?

Naturally the best candidate for that was Deborah Koppel. But they couldn't find one measly scrap to start a foundation with. There wasn't the slightest evidence, ancient or recent, that Deborah and Madeline had ever been anything but devoted friends, bound together by mutual interest, respect, and affection. Not only that, the Michigan people refused to bat an eye at the suggestion that Lawrence Koppel's death had not been suicide. He had been a neurotic hypochondriac, and the letter he had sent to his best friend, a local lawyer, had cinched it. Michigan had been perfectly willing to answer New York's questions, but for themselves they weren't interested.

Another of the thousand lines that petered out into nothing was the effort to link up one of the staff, especially Elinor Vance, with Michigan. They had tried it before with Cyril Orchard, and now they tried it with the others. No soap. None of them had ever been there.

Wolfe, as I say, read some of this in the papers, and courteously listened to the rest of it, and much more, from me. He was not, however, permitted to limit himself strictly to the role of spectator. Cramer came to our office twice during that week, and Anderson, the Starlite president, once; and there were others.

There was Tully Strong, who arrived Saturday afternoon, after a six-hour session with Cramer and an assortment of his trained men.

He had probably been pecked at a good deal, as all of them had, since they had told the cops a string of barefaced lies, and he was not in good humor. He was so sore that when he put his hands on Wolfe's desk and leaned over at him to make some remarks about treachery, and his spectacles slipped forward nearly to the tip of his nose, he didn't bother to push them back in place.

His theory was that the agreement with Wolfe was null and void because Wolfe had violated it. Whatever happened, Wolfe not only would not collect his fee, he would not even be reimbursed for expenses. Moreover, he would be sued for damages. His disclosure of a fact which, if made public, would inflict great injury on Miss Fraser and her program, the network, and Starlite, was irresponsible and inexcusable, and certainly actionable.

Wolfe told him bosh, he had not violated the agreement.

"No?" Strong straightened up. His necktie was to one side and his hair needed a comb and brush. His hand went up to his spectacles, which were barely hanging on, but instead of pushing them back he removed them. "You think not? You'll see. And, besides, you have put Miss Fraser's life in danger! I was trying to protect her! We all were!"

"All?" Wolfe objected. "Not all. All but one."

"Yes, all!" Strong had come there to be mad and would have no interference. "No one knew, no one but us, that it was meant for her! Now everybody knows it! Who can protect her now? I'll try, we all will, but what chance have we got?"

It seemed to me he was getting illogical. The only threat to Miss Fraser, as far as we knew, came from the guy who had performed on the coffee, and surely we hadn't told him anything he didn't already know.

I had to usher Tully Strong to the door and out. If he had been capable of calming down enough to be seated for a talk I would have been all for it, but he was really upset. When Wolfe told me to put him out I couldn't conscientiously object. At that he had spunk. Anybody could have told from one glance at us that if I was forced to deal with him physically I would have had to decide what to do with my other hand, in case I wanted to be fully occupied, but when I took hold of his arm he jerked loose and then turned on me as if stretching me out would be pie. He had his specs in one hand, too. I succeeded in herding him out without either of us getting hurt.

As was to be expected, Tully Strong wasn't the only one who had the notion that Wolfe had committed treason by giving their fatal secret to the cops. They all let us know it, too, either by phone or in person. Nat Traub's attitude was specially bitter, probably because of the item that had been volunteered by Bill Meadows, that Traub had served the bottle and glass to Orchard. Cramer's crew must have really liked that one, and I could imagine the different keys they used playing it for Traub to hear. One thing I preferred not to imagine was what we would have got from Mr. Walter B. Anderson, the Starlite president, and Fred Owen, the director of public relations, if anyone had told them the full extent of Wolfe's treachery. Apparently they were still ignorant about the true and horrible reason why one of the bottles had contained coffee instead of The Drink You Dream Of.

Another caller, this one Monday afternoon, was the formula hound, Professor Savarese. He too came to the office straight from a long conference with the cops, and he too was good and mad, but for a different reason. The cops had no longer been interested in his association with Cyril Orchard, or in anything about Orchard at all, and he wanted to know why. They had refused to tell him. They had reviewed his whole life, from birth to date, all over again, but with an entirely different approach. It was plain that what they were after now was a link between him and Miss Fraser. Why? What new factor had entered? The intrusion of a hitherto unknown and unsuspected factor would raise hell with his calculation of probabilities, but if there was one he had to have it, and quick. This was the first good chance he had ever had to test his formulas on the most dramatic of all problems, a murder case, from the inside, and he wasn't going to tolerate any blank spaces without a fight.

What was the new factor? Why was it now a vital question whether he had had any previous association, direct or indirect, with Miss Fraser?

Up to a point Wolfe listened to him without coming to a boil, but he finally got annoyed enough to call on me again to do some more ushering. I obeyed in a halfhearted way. For one thing, Wolfe was passing up another chance to do a dime's worth of work himself, with Savarese right there and more than ready to talk, and for another, I was resisting a temptation. The question had popped into my head, How would this figure wizard go about getting Miss Fraser's indigestion into a mathematical equation? It might not be instructive to get him to answer it, but at least it would pass the time, and it would help as much in solving the case as anything Wolfe was doing. But, not wanting to get us any more deeply involved in treachery than we already were, I skipped it.

I ushered him out.

Anyhow, that was only Monday. By the time four more days had passed and another Friday arrived, finishing a full week since we had supplied Cramer with a fact, I was a promising prospect for a strait jacket. That evening, as I returned to the office with Wolfe after an unusually good dinner which I had not enjoyed, the outlook for the next three or four hours revolted me. As he got himself adjusted comfortably in his chair and reached for his book, I announced, "I'm going to my club."

He nodded, and got his book open.

"You do not even," I said cuttingly, "ask me which club, though you know damn well I don't belong to any. I am thoroughly fed up with sitting here day after day and night after night, waiting for the moment when the idea will somehow seep into you that a detective is supposed to detect. You are simply too goddam lazy to live. You think you're a genius. Say you are. If in order to be a genius myself I had to be as self-satisfied, as overweight, and as inert as you are, I like me better this way."

Apparently he was reading.

"This," I said, "is the climax I've been leading up to for a week—or rather, that you've been leading me up to. Sure, I know your alibi, and I'm good and sick of it—that there is nothing we can do that the cops aren't already doing. Of all the sausage." I kept my voice dry, factual, and cultured. "If this case is too much for you why don't you try another one? The papers are full of them. How about the gang that stole a truckload of cheese yesterday right here on Eleventh Avenue? How about the fifth-grade boy that hit his teacher in the eye with a jelly bean? Page fifty-eight in the *Times*. Or, if everything but murder is beneath you, what's wrong with the political and economic fortune-teller, a lady named Beula Poole, who got shot in the back of her head last evening? Page one of any paper. You could probably sew that one up before bedtime."

He turned over a page.

"Tomorrow," I said, "is Saturday. I shall draw my pay as usual. I'm going to a fight at the Garden. Talk about contrasts—you in that chair and a couple of good middleweights in a ring."

I blew.

But I didn't go to the Garden. My first stop was the corner drugstore, where I went to a phone booth and called Lon Cohen of the *Gazette*. He was in, and about through, and saw no reason why I shouldn't buy him eight or ten drinks, provided he could have a two-inch steak for a chaser.

So an hour later Lon and I were at a corner table at Pietro's. He had done well with the drinks and had made a good start on the steak. I was having highballs, to be sociable, and was on my third, along with my second pound of peanuts. I hadn't realized how much I had short-changed myself on dinner, sitting opposite Wolfe, until I got into the spirit of it with the peanuts.

We had discussed the state of things from politics to prize-fights, by no means excluding murder. Lon had had his glass filled often enough, and had enough of the steak in him, to have reached a state of mind where he might reasonably be expected to be open to suggestion. So I made an approach by telling him, deadpan, that in my opinion the papers were riding the cops too hard on the Orchard case.

He leered at me. "For God's sake, has Cramer threatened to take your license or something?"

"No, honest," I insisted, reaching for peanuts, "this one is really tough and you know it. They're doing as well as they can with what they've got. Besides that, it's so damn commonplace. Every paper always does it—after a week start crabbing and after two weeks start screaming. It's got so everybody always expects it and nobody ever reads it. You know what I'd do if I ran a newspaper? I'd start running stuff that people would read."

"Jesus!" Lon gawked at me. "What an idea! Give me a column on it. Who would teach 'em to read?"

"A column," I said, "would only get me started. I need at least a page. But in this particular case, where it's at now, it's a question of an editorial. This is Friday night. For Sunday you ought to have an editorial on the Orchard case. It's still hot and the public still loves it. But—"

"I'm no editor, I'm a newsman."

"I know, I'm just talking. Five will get you ten that your sheet will have an editorial on the Orchard case Sunday, and what will it say? It will be called OUR PUBLIC GUARDIANS, and it will be the same old crap, and not one in a thousand will read beyond the first line. Phooey. If it was me I would call it TOO OLD OR TOO FAT, and I wouldn't mention the cops once. Nor would I mention Nero Wolfe, not by name. I would refer to the blaze of publicity with which a certain celebrated private investigator entered the Orchard case, and to the expectations it aroused. That his record seemed to justify it. That we see now how goofy it was, because in ten days he hasn't taken a trick. That the reason may be that he is getting too old, or too fat, or merely that he hasn't got what it takes when a case is really tough, but no matter what the reason is, this shows us that for our protection from vicious criminals we must rely on our efficient and well-trained police force, and not on any so-called brilliant geniuses. I said I wouldn't mention the cops, but I think I'd better, right at the last. I could add a sentence that while they may have got stuck in the mud on the Orchard case, they are the brave men who keep the structure of our society from you know."

Lon, having swallowed a hunk of steak, would have spoken, but I stopped him. "They would read that, don't think they wouldn't. I know you're not an editor, but you're the best man they've got and you're allowed to talk to editors, aren't you? I would love to see an editorial like that tried, just as an experiment. So much so that if a paper ran it I would want to show my appreciation the first opportunity I get, by stretching a point a hell of a ways to give it first crack at some interesting little item."

Lon had his eyebrows up. "If you don't want to bore me, turn it the other side up so the interesting little item will be on top."

"Nuts. Do you want to talk about it or not?"

"Sure, I'll talk about anything."

I signaled the waiter for refills.

XIV

I WOULD give anything in the world, anyway up to four bits, to know whether Wolfe saw or read that editorial before I showed it to him late Sunday afternoon. I think he did. He always glances over the editorials in three papers, of which the *Gazette* is one, and if his eye caught it at all he must have read it. It was entitled THE FALSE ALARM, and it carried out the idea I had given Lon to a T.

I knew of course that Wolfe wouldn't do any spluttering, and I should have realized that he probably wouldn't make any sign or offer any comment. But I didn't, and therefore by late afternoon I was in a hole. If he hadn't read it I had to see that he did, and that was risky. It had to be done right or he would smell an elephant. So I thought it over. What would be the natural thing? How would I naturally do it if I suddenly ran across it?

What I did do was turn in my chair to grin at him and ask casually, "Did you see this editorial in the *Gazette* called THE FALSE ALARM?"

He grunted. "What's it about?"

"You'd better read it." I got up, crossed over, and put it on his desk. "A funny thing, it gave me the feeling I had written it myself. It's the only editorial I've seen in weeks that I completely agree with."

He picked it up. I sat down facing him, but he held the paper so that it cut off my view. He isn't a fast reader, and he held the pose long enough to read it through twice, but that's exactly what he would have done if he already knew it by heart and wanted me to think otherwise.

"Bah!" The paper was lowered. "Some little scrivener who doubtless has ulcers and is on a diet."

"Yeah, I guess so. The rat. The contemptible louse. If only he knew how you've been sweating and stewing, going without sleep—"

"Archie. Shut up."

"Yes, sir."

I hoped to God I was being natural.

That was all for then, but I was not licked. I had never supposed that he would tear his hair or pace up and down. A little later an old friend of his, Marko Vukcic dropped in for a Sunday-evening snack—five kinds of cheese, guava jelly, freshly roasted chestnuts, and almond tarts. I was anxious to see if he would show the editorial to Marko, which would have been a bad sign. He didn't. After Marko had left, to return to Rusterman's Restaurant, which was the best in New York because he managed it, Wolfe settled down with his book again, but hadn't turned more than ten pages before he dogeared and closed it and tossed it to a far corner of his desk. He then got up, crossed the room to the big globe, and stood and studied geography. That didn't seem to satisfy him any better than the book, so he went and turned on the radio. After dialing to eight different stations, he muttered to himself, stalked back to his chair behind his desk, and sat and scowled. I took all this in only from a corner of one eye, since I was buried so deep in a magazine that I didn't even know he was in the room.

He spoke. "Archie."

"Yes, sir?"

"It has been nine days."

"Yes, sir."

"Since that tour de force of yours. Getting that Miss Shepherd here."

"Yes, sir."

He was being tactful. What he meant was that it had been nine days since he had passed a miracle by uncovering the tape on the bottle and Miss Fraser's indigestion, but he figured that if he tossed me a bone I would be less likely either to snarl or to gloat. He went on. "It was not then flighty to assume that a good routine job was all that was needed. But the events of those nine days have not supported that assumption."

"No, sir."

"Get Mr. Cramer."

"As soon as I finish this paragraph."

I allowed a reasonable number of seconds to go by, but I admit I wasn't seeing a word. Then, getting on the phone, I was prepared to settle for less than the inspector himself, since it was Sunday evening, and hoped that Wolfe was too, but it wasn't necessary. Cramer was there, and Wolfe got on and invited him to pay us a call.

"I'm busy." Cramer sounded harrassed. "Why, have you got something?"

"Yes."

"What?"

"I don't know. I won't know until I've talked with you. After we've talked your busyness may be more productive than it has been."

"The hell you say. I'll be there in half an hour."

That didn't elate me at all. I hadn't cooked up a neat little scheme, and devoted a whole evening to it, and bought Lon Cohen twenty bucks' worth of liquids and solids, just to prod Wolfe into getting Cramer in to talk things over. As for his saying he had something, that was a plain lie. All he had was a muleheaded determination not to let his ease and comfort be interfered with.

So when Cramer arrived I didn't bubble over. Neither did he, for that matter. He marched into the office, nodded a greeting, dropped into the red leather chair, and growled, "I wish to God you'd forget you're eccentric and start moving around more. Busy as I am, here I am. What is it?"

"My remark on the phone," Wolfe said placidly, "may have been blunt, but it was justified."

"What remark?"

"That your busyness could be more productive. Have you made any progress?"

"No."

"You're no further along than you were a week ago?"

"Further along to the day I retire, yes. Otherwise no."

"Then I'd like to ask some questions about that woman, Beula Poole, who was found dead in her office Friday morning. The papers say that you say it was murder. Was it?"

I gawked at him. This was clear away from me. When he jumped completely off the track like that I never knew whether he was stalling, being subtle, or trying to show me how much of a clod I was. Then I saw a gleam in Cramer's eye which indicated that even he had left me far behind, and all I could do was gawk some more.

Cramer nodded. "Yeah, it was murder. Why, looking for another client so I can earn another fee for you?"

"Do you know who did it?"

"No."

"No glimmer? No good start?"

"No start at all, good or bad."

"Tell me about it."

Cramer grunted. "Most of it has been in the papers, all but a detail or two we've saved up." He moved farther back in the chair, as if he might stay longer than he had thought. "First you might tell me what got you interested, don't you think?"

"Certainly. Mr. Cyril Orchard, who got killed, was the publisher of a horse-race tip sheet for which subscribers paid ten dollars a week, an unheard-of price. Miss Beula Poole, who also got killed, was the publisher of a sheet which purported to give inside advance information on political and economic affairs, for which subscribers paid the same unheard-of price of ten dollars a week."

"Is that all?"

"I think it's enough to warrant a question or two. It is true that Mr. Orchard was poisoned and Miss Poole was shot, a big variation in method. Also that it is now assumed that Mr. Orchard was killed by misadventure, the poison having been intended for another, whereas the bullet that killed Miss Poole must have been intended for her.

But even so, it's a remarkable coincidence—sufficiently so to justify some curiosity, at least. For example, it might be worth the trouble to compare the lists of subscribers of the two publications."

"Yeah, I thought so too."

"You did?" Wolfe was a little annoyed, as he always was at any implication that someone else could be as smart as him. "Then you've compared them. And?"

Cramer shook his head. "I didn't say I'd compared them, I said I'd thought of it. What made me think of it was the fact that it couldn't be done, because there weren't any lists to compare."

"Nonsense. There must have been. Did you look for them?"

"Sure we did, but too late. In Orchard's case there was a little bad management. His office, a little one-room hole in a building on Forty-second Street, was locked, and there was some fiddling around looking for an employee or a relative to let us in. When we finally entered by having the superintendent admit us, the next day, the place had been cleaned out—not a piece of paper or an address plate or anything else. It was different with the woman, Poole, because it was in her office that she was shot—another one-room hole, on the third floor of an old building on Nineteenth Street, only four blocks from my place. But her body wasn't found until nearly noon the next day, and by the time we got there that had been cleaned out too. The same way. Nothing."

Wolfe was no longer annoyed. Cramer had had two coincidences and he had had only one. "Well." He was purring. "That settles it. In spite of variations, it is now more than curiosity. Of course you have inquired?"

"Plenty. The sheets were printed at different shops, and neither of them had a list of subscribers or anything else that helps. Neither Orchard nor the woman employed any help. Orchard left a widow and two children, but they don't seem to know a damn thing about his business, let alone who his subscribers were. Beula Poole's nearest relatives live out West, in Colorado, and they don't know anything, apparently not even how she was earning a living. And so on. As for the routine, all covered and all useless. No one seen entering or leaving—it's only two flights up—no weapon, no fingerprints that help any, nobody heard the shot—"

Wolfe nodded impatiently. "You said you hadn't made any start, and naturally routine has been followed. Any discoverable association of Miss Poole with Mr. Orchard?"

"If there was we can't discover it."

"Where were Miss Fraser and the others at the time Miss Poole was shot?"

Cramer squinted at him. "You think it might even develop that way?"

"I would like to put the question. Wouldn't you?"

"Yeah. I have. You see, the two offices being cleaned out is a detail we've saved up." Cramer looked at me. "And you'll kindly not peddle it to your pal Cohen of the *Gazette*." He went on to Wolfe. "It's not so easy because there's a leeway of four or five hours on when she was shot. We've asked all that bunch about it, and no one can be checked off."

"Mr. Savarese? Miss Shepherd? Mr. Shepherd?"

"What?" Cramer's eyes widened. "Where the hell does Shepherd come in?"

"I don't know. Archie doesn't like him, and I have learned that it is always quite possible that anyone he doesn't like may be a murderer."

"Oh, comic relief. The Shepherd girl was in Atlantic City with her mother, and still is. On Savarese I'd have to look at the reports, but I know he's not checked off because nobody is. By the way, we've dug up two subscribers to Orchard's tip sheet, besides Savarese and the Fraser woman. With no result. They bet on the races and they subscribed, that's all, according to them."

"I'd like to talk with them," Wolfe declared.

"You can. At my office any time."

"Pfui. As you know, I never leave this house on business. If you'll give Archie their names and addresses he'll attend to it."

Cramer said he'd have Stebbins phone and give them to me. I never saw him more cooperative, which meant that he had never been more frustrated.

They kept at it a while longer, but Cramer had nothing more of any importance to give Wolfe, and Wolfe hadn't had anything to give Cramer to begin with. I listened with part of my brain, and with the other part tried to do a little offhand sorting and arranging. I had to admit that it would take quite a formula to have room for the two coincidences as such, and therefore they would probably have to be joined together somehow, but it was no part-brain job for me. Whenever dough passes without visible value received the first thing you think of is blackmail, so I thought of it, but that didn't get me anywhere because there were too many other things in the way. It was obvious that the various aspects were not yet in a condition that called for the application of my particular kind of talent.

After Cramer had gone Wolfe sat and gazed at a distant corner of the ceiling with his eyes open about a thirty-second of an inch. I sat and waited, not wanting to disturb him, for when I saw his lips pushing out, and in again, and out and in, I knew he was exerting himself to the limit, and I was perfectly satisfied. There had been a good chance that he would figure that he had helped all he could for a while, and go back to his reading until Cramer made a progress report or somebody else got killed. But the editorial had stung him good. Finally he transferred the gaze to me and pronounced my name.

"Yes, sir," I said brightly.

"Your notebook. Take this."

I got ready.

"Former subscribers to the publication of Cyril Orchard, or to that of Beula Poole, should communicate with me immediately. Put it in three papers, the *Gazette*, the *News*, and the *Herald Tribune*. A modest display, say two inches. Reply to a box number. A good page if possible."

"And I'll call for the replies? It saves time."

"Then do so."

I put paper in the typewriter. The phone rang. It was Sergeant Purley Stebbins, to give me the names and addresses of the two Orchard subscribers they had dug up.

XV

So BEGINNING Monday morning we were again a going concern, instead of a sitting-and-waiting one, but I was not in my element. I like a case you can make a diagram of. I don't object to complications, that's all right, but if you're out for bear it seems silly to concentrate on hunting for moose tracks. Our fee depended on our finding out how and why Orchard got cyanided by drinking Madeline Fraser's sugared coffee, and here we were spending our time and energy on the shooting of a female named Beula Poole. Even granting it was one and the same guy who pinched the lead pencils and spilled ink on the rug, if you've been hired to nail him for pencil-stealing that's what you should work at.

I admit that isn't exactly fair, because most of our Monday activities had to do with Orchard. Wolfe seemed to think it was important for him to have a talk with those two subscribers, so instead of using the phone I went out after them. I had one of them in the office waiting for him at eleven A.M.—an assistant office manager for a big tile company. Wolfe spent less than a quarter of an hour on him, knowing, of course, that the cops had spent more and had checked him. He had bet on the races for years. In February a year ago he had learned that a Hialeah daily double featured in a sheet called *Track Almanac* had come through for a killing, and he had subscribed, though the ten bucks a week was a sixth of his salary. He had stayed with it for nine weeks and then quit. So much for him.

The other one was a little different. Her name was Marie Leconne, and she owned a snooty beauty parlor on Madison Avenue. She wouldn't have accepted my invitation if she hadn't been under the illusion that Wolfe was connected with the police, though I didn't precisely tell her so. That Monday evening she was with us a good two hours, but left nothing of any value behind. She had subscribed to *Track Almanac* in August, seven months ago, and had remained a subscriber up to the time of Orchard's death. Prior to subscribing she had done little or no betting on the races; she was hazy about whether it was little, or no. Since subscribing she had bet frequently, but she firmly refused to tell where, through whom, or in what amounts. Wolfe, knowing that I occasionally risk a finif, passed me a hint to have some conversation with her about pertinent matters like horses and jockeys, but she declined to cooperate. All in all, she kept herself nicely under control, and flew off the handle only once, when Wolfe pressed her hard for a plausible reason why she had subscribed to a tip sheet at such a price. That aggravated her terribly, and since the one thing that scares Wolfe out of his senses is a woman in a tantrum, he backed away fast.

He did keep on trying, from other angles, but when she finally left all we knew for sure was that she had not subscribed to *Track Almanac* in order to get guesses on the ponies. She was slippery, and nobody's fool, and Wolfe had got no further than the cops in opening her up.

I suggested to Wolfe, "We might start Saul asking around in her circle."

He snorted. "Mr. Cramer is presumably attending to that, and, anyway, it would have to be dragged out of her inch by inch. The advertisement should be quicker."

It was quicker, all right, in getting results, but not the results we were after. There had not been time to make the Monday papers, so the ad's first appearance was Tuesday morning. Appraising it, I thought it caught the eye effectively for so small a space. After breakfast, which I always eat in the kitchen with Fritz while Wolfe has his in his room on a tray, and after dealing with the morning mail and other chores in the office, I went out to stretch my legs and thought I might as well head in the direction of the *Herald Tribune* Building. Expecting nothing so soon but thinking it wouldn't hurt to drop in, I did so. There was a telegram. I tore it open and read:

> CALL MIDLAND FIVE THREE SEVEN EIGHT FOUR
> LEAVE MESSAGE FOR DUNCAN GIVING APPOINTMENT

I went to a phone booth and put a nickel in the slot, with the idea of calling Cramer's office to ask who Midland 5-3784 belonged to, but changed my mind. If it happened that this led to a hot trail we didn't want to be hampered by city interference, at least I didn't. However, I thought I might as well get something for my nickel and dialed another number. Fritz answered, and I asked him to switch it to the plant rooms.

"Yes, Archie?" Wolfe's voice came, peevish. He was at the bench, repotting, as I knew from his schedule, and he hates to be interrupted at that job. I told him about the telegram.

"Very well, call the number. Make an appointment for eleven o'clock or later."

I walked back home, went to my desk, dialed the Midland number, and asked for Mr. Duncan. Of course it could have been Mrs. or Miss, but I preferred to deal with a man after our experience with Marie Leconne. A gruff voice with an accent said that Mr. Duncan wasn't there and was there a message.

"Will he be back soon?"

"I don't know. All I know is that I can take a message."

I thereupon delivered one, that Mr. Duncan would be expected at Nero Wolfe's office at eleven o'clock, or as soon thereafter as possible.

He didn't come. Wolfe descended in his elevator sharp at eleven as usual, got himself enthroned, rang for beer, and began sorting plant cards he had brought down with him. I had him sign a couple of checks and then started to help with the cards. At half-past eleven I asked if I should ring the Midland number to see if Duncan had got the message, and he said no, we would wait until noon.

The phone rang. I went to my desk and told it, "Nero Wolfe's office, Goodwin speaking."

"I got your message for Duncan. Let me speak to Mr. Wolfe, please."

I covered the transmitter and told Wolfe, "He says Duncan, but it's a voice I've heard. It's not a familiar voice, but by God I've heard it. See if you have."

Wolfe lifted his instrument. "Yes, Mr. Duncan? This is Nero Wolfe."

"How are you?" the voice asked.

"I'm well, thank you. Do I know you, sir?"

"I really don't know. I mean I don't know if you would recognize me, seeing me, because I don't know how foolishly inquisitive you may have been. But we have talked before, on the phone."

"We have?"

"Yes. Twice. On June ninth, nineteen-forty-three, I called to give you some advice regarding a job you were doing for General Carpenter. On January sixteenth, nineteen-forty-six, I called to speak about the advisability of limiting your efforts in behalf of a Mrs. Tremont."

"Yes. I remember."

I remembered too. I chalked it against me that I hadn't recognized the voice with the first six words, though it had been over two years since I had heard it—hard, slow, precise, and cold as last week's corpse. It was continuing. "I was pleased to see that you did limit your efforts as I suggested. That showed—"

"I limited them because no extension of them was required to finish the job I was hired for. I did not limit them because you suggested it, Mr. Zeck." Wolfe was being fairly icy himself.

"So you know my name." The voice never changed.

"Certainly. I went to some trouble and expense to ascertain it. I don't pay much attention to threats, I get too many of them, but at least I like to know who the threatener is. Yes, I know your name, sir. Is that temerarious? Many people know Mr. Arnold Zeck."

"You have had no occasion to. This, Mr. Wolfe, does *not* please me."

"I didn't expect it to."

"No. But I am much easier to get along with when I am pleased. That's why I sent you that telegram and am talking with you now. I have strong admiration for you, as I've said before. I wouldn't want to lose it. It would please me better to keep it. Your advertisement in the papers has given me some concern. I realize that you didn't know that, you couldn't have known it, so I'm telling you. The advertisement disturbs me. It can't be recalled; it has appeared. But it is extremely important that you should not permit it to lead you into difficulties that will be too much for you. The wisest course for you will be to drop the matter. You understand me, don't you, Mr. Wolfe?"

"Oh yes, I understand you. You put things quite clearly, Mr. Zeck, and so do I. I have engaged to do something, and I intend to do it. I haven't the slightest desire either to please you or to displease you, and unless one or the other is inherent in my job you have no reason to be concerned. You understand me, don't you?"

"Yes. I do. But now you know."

The line went dead.

Wolfe cradled the phone and leaned back in his chair, with his eyes closed to a slit. I pushed my phone away, swiveled, and gazed at him through a minute's silence.

"So," I said. "That sonofabitch. Shall I find out about the Midland number?"

Wolfe shook his head. "Useless. It would be some little store that merely took a message. Anyway, he has a number of his own."

"Yeah. He didn't know you knew his name. Neither did I. How did that happen?"

"Two years ago I engaged some of Mr. Bascom's men without telling you. He had sounded as if he were a man of resource and resolution, and I didn't want to get you involved."

"It's the Zeck with the place in Westchester, of course?"

"Yes. I should have signaled you off as soon as I recognized his voice. I tell you nothing because it is better for you to know nothing. You are to forget that you know his name."

"Like that." I snapped my fingers, and grinned at him. "What the hell? Does he eat human flesh, preferably handsome young men?"

"No. He does worse." Wolfe's eyes came half open. "I'll tell you this. If ever, in the course of my business, I find that I am committed against him and must destroy him, I shall leave this house, find a place where I can work—and sleep and eat if there is time for it—and stay there until I have finished. I don't want to do that, and therefore I hope I'll never have to."

"I see. I'd like to meet this bozo. I think I'll make his acquaintance."

"You will not. You'll stay away from him." He made a face. "If this job leads me to that extremity—well, it will or it won't." He glanced at the clock. "It's nearly noon. You'd better go and see if any more answers have arrived. Can't you telephone?"

XVI

THERE were no more answers. That goes not only for Tuesday noon, but for the rest of the day and evening, and Wednesday morning, and Wednesday after lunch. Nothing doing.

It didn't surprise me. The nature of the phone call from the man whose name I had been ordered to forget made it seem likely that there was something peculiar about the subscribers to *Track Almanac* and *What to Expect,* which was the name of the political and economic dope sheet published by the late Beula Poole. But even granting that there wasn't, that as far as they were concerned it was all clean and straight, the two publishers had just been murdered, and who would be goop enough to answer such an ad just to get asked a lot of impertinent questions? In the office after lunch Wednesday I made a remark to that effect to Wolfe, and got only a growl for reply.

"We might at least," I insisted, "have hinted that they would get their money back or something."

No reply.

"We could insert it again and add that. Or we could offer a reward for anyone who would give us the name of an Orchard or Poole subscriber."

No reply.

"Or I could go up to the Fraser apartment and get into conversation with the bunch, and who knows?"

"Yes. Do so."

I looked at him suspiciously. He meant it.

"Now?"

"Yes."

"You sure are hard up when you start taking suggestions from me."

I pulled the phone to me and dialed the number. It was Bill Meadows who answered, and he sounded anything but gay, even when he learned it was me. After a brief talk, however, I was willing to forgive him. I hung up and informed Wolfe, "I guess I'll have to postpone it. Miss Fraser and Miss Koppel are both out. Bill was a little vague, but I gather that the latter has been tagged by the city authorities for some reason or other, and the former is engaged in trying to remove the tag. Maybe she needs help. Why don't I find out?"

"I don't know. You might try."

I turned and dialed Watkins 9-8241. Inspector Cramer wasn't available, but I got someone just as good, or sometimes I think even better, Sergeant Stebbins.

"I need some information," I told him, "in connection with this fee you folks are earning for Mr. Wolfe."

"So do we," he said frankly. "Got any?"

"Not right now. Mr. Wolfe and I are in conference. How did Miss Koppel hurt your feelings, and where is she, and if you see Miss Fraser give her my love."

He let out a roar of delight. Purley doesn't laugh often, at least when he's on duty, and I resented it. I waited until I thought he might hear me and then demanded, "What the hell is so funny?"

"I never expected the day to come," he declared. "You calling me to ask where your client is. What's the matter, is Wolfe off his feed?"

"I know another one even better. Call me back when you're through laughing."

"I'm through. Haven't you heard what the Koppel dame did?"

"No. I only know what you tell me."

"Well, this isn't loose yet. We may want to keep it a while if we can, I don't know."

"I'll help you keep it. So will Mr. Wolfe."

"That's understood?"

"Yes."

"Okay. Of course they've all been told not to leave the jurisdiction. This morning Miss Koppel took a cab to La Guardia. She was nabbed as she was boarding the nine-o'clock plane for Detroit. She says she wanted to visit her sick mother in Fleetville, which is eighty miles from Detroit. But she didn't ask permission to go, and the word we get is that her mother is no sicker than she has been for a year. So we charged her as a material witness. Does that strike you as highhanded? Do you think it calls for a shakeup?"

"Get set for another laugh. Where's Miss Fraser?"

"With her lawyer at the D. A.'s office discussing bail."

"What kind of reasons have you got for Miss Koppel taking a trip that are any better than hers?"

"I wouldn't know. Now you're out of my class. If you want to go into details like that, Wolfe had better ask the inspector."

I tried another approach or two, but either Purley had given me all there was or the rest was in another drawer which he didn't feel like opening. I hung up and relayed the news to Wolfe.

He nodded as if it were no concern of his. I glared at him. "It wouldn't interest you to have one or both of them stop in for a chat on their way home? To ask why Miss Koppel simply had to go to Michigan would be vulgar curiosity?"

"Bah. The police are asking, aren't they?" Wolfe was bitter. "I've spent countless hours with those people, and got something for it only when I had a whip to snap. Why compound futility? I need another whip. Call those newspapers again."

"Am I still to go up there? After the ladies get home?"

"You might as well."

"Yeah." I was savage. "At least I can compound some futility."

I phoned all three papers. Nothing. Being in no mood to sit and concentrate on germination records, I announced that I was going out for a walk, and Wolfe nodded absently. When I got back it was after four o'clock and he had gone up to the plant rooms. I fiddled around, finally decided that I might as well concentrate on something and the germination records were all I had, and got Theodore's reports from the drawer, but then I thought why not throw away three more nickels? So I started dialing again.

Herald Tribune, nothing. *News,* nothing. But the *Gazette* girl said yes, they had one. The way I went for my hat and headed for Tenth Avenue to grab a taxi, you might have thought I was on my way to a murder.

The driver was a philosopher. "You don't see many eager happy faces like yours nowadays," he told me.

"I'm on my way to my wedding."

He opened his mouth to speak again, then clamped it shut. He shook his head resolutely. "No. Why should I spoil it?"

I paid him off outside the *Gazette* building and went in and got my prize. It was a square pale blue envelope, and the printed return on the flap said:

> Mrs. W. T. Michaels
> 890 East End Avenue
> New York City 28

Inside was a single sheet matching the envelope, with small neat handwriting on it:

> Box P304:
>   Regarding your advertisement, I am not a former subscriber to either of the publications, but I may be able to tell you something. You may write me, or call Lincoln 3-4808, but do not phone before ten in the morning or after five-thirty in the afternoon. That is important.
>   Hilda Michaels

It was still forty minutes this side of her deadline, so I went straight to a booth and dialed the number. A female voice answered. I asked to speak to Mrs. Michaels.

"This is Mrs. Michaels."

"This is the *Gazette* advertiser you wrote to, Box P304. I've just read—"

"What's your name?" She had a tendency to snap.

"My name is Goodwin, Archie Goodwin. I can be up there in fifteen minutes or less—"

"No, you can't. Anyway, you'd better not. Are you connected with the Police Department?"

"No. I work for Nero Wolfe. You may have heard of Nero Wolfe, the detective?"

"Of course. This isn't a convent. Was that his advertisement?"

"Yes. He—"

"Then why didn't he phone me?"

"Because I just got your note. I'm phoning from a booth in the *Gazette* building. You said not—"

"Well, Mr. Goodman, I doubt if I can tell Mr. Wolfe anything he would be interested in. I really doubt it."

"Maybe not," I conceded. "But he would be the best judge of that. If you don't want me to come up there, how would it be if you called on Mr. Wolfe at his office? West Thirty-fifth Street—it's in the phone book. Or I could run up now in a taxi and—"

"Oh, not now. Not today. I might be able to make it tomorrow—or Friday—"

I was annoyed. For one thing, I would just as soon be permitted to finish a sentence once in a while, and for another, apparently she had read the piece about Wolfe being hired to work on the Orchard case, and my name had been in it, and it had been spelled correctly. So I took on weight. "You don't seem to realize what you've done, Mrs. Michaels. You—"

"Why, what have I done?"

"You have landed smack in the middle of a murder case. Mr. Wolfe and the police are more or less collaborating on it. He would like to see you about the matter mentioned in his advertisement, not tomorrow or next week, but quick. I think you ought to see him. If you try to put it off because you've begun to regret sending this note he'll be compelled to consult the police, and then what? Then you'll—"

"I didn't say I regret sending the note."

"No, but the way you—"

"I'll be at Mr. Wolfe's office by six o'clock."

"Good! Shall I come—"

I might have known better than to give her another chance to chop me off. She said that she was quite capable of getting herself transported, and I could well believe it.

XVII

THERE was nothing snappy about her appearance. The mink coat, and the dark red woolen dress made visible when the coat had been spread over the back of the red leather chair, unquestionably meant well, but she was not built to cooperate with clothes. There was too much of her and the distribution was all wrong. Her face was so well padded that there was no telling whether there were any bones underneath, and the creases were considerably more than skin deep. I didn't like her. From Wolfe's expression it was plain, to me, that he didn't like her. As for her, it was a safe bet that she didn't like anybody.

Wolfe rustled the sheet of pale blue paper, glanced at it again, and looked at her. "You say here, madam, that you may be able to tell me something. Your caution is understandable and even commendable. You wanted to find out who had placed the advertisement before committing yourself. Now you know. There is no need—"

"That man threatened me," she snapped. "That's not the way to get me to tell something—if I have something to tell."

"I agree. Mr. Goodwin is headstrong. Archie, withdraw the threat."

I did my best to grin at her as man to woman. "I take it back, Mrs. Michaels. I was so anxious—"

"If I tell you anything," she said to Wolfe, ignoring me, "it will be because I want to, and it will be completely confidential. Whatever you do about it, of course I have nothing to say about that, but you will give me your solemn word of honor that my name will not be mentioned to anyone. No one is to know I wrote you or came to see you or had anything to do with it."

Wolfe shook his head. "Impossible. Manifestly impossible. You are not a fool, madam, and I won't try to treat you as if you were. It is even conceivable that you might have to take the witness-stand in a murder trial. I know nothing about it, because I don't know what you have to tell. Then how could I—"

"All right," she said, surrendering. "I see I made a mistake. I must be home by seven o'clock. Here's what I have to tell you: somebody I know was a subscriber to that *What to Expect* that was published by that woman, Beula Poole. I distinctly remember, one day two or three months ago, I saw a little stack of them somewhere—in some house or apartment or office. I've been trying to remember where it was, and I simply can't. I wrote you because I thought you might tell me something that would make me remember, and I'm quite willing to try, but I doubt if it will do any good."

"Indeed." Wolfe's expression was fully as sour as hers. "I said you're not a fool. I suppose you're prepared to stick to that under any circum—"

"Yes, I am."

"Even if Mr. Goodwin gets headstrong again and renews his threat?"

"That!" She was contemptuous.

"It's very thin, Mrs. Michaels. Even ridiculous. That you would go to the bother of answering that advertisement, and coming down here—"

"I don't mind being ridiculous."

"Then I have no alternative." Wolfe's lips tightened. He released them. "I accept your conditions. I agree, for myself and for Mr. Goodwin, who is my agent, that we will not disclose the source of our information, and that we will do our utmost to keep anyone from learning it. Should anyone ascertain it, it will be against our will and in spite of our precautions in good faith. We cannot guarantee; we can only promise; and we do so."

Her eyes had narrowed. "On your solemn word of honor."

"Good heavens. That ragged old patch? Very well. My solemn word of honor. Archie?"

"My solemn word of honor," I said gravely.

Her head made an odd ducking movement, reminding me of a fat-cheeked owl I had seen at the zoo, getting ready to swoop on a mouse.

"My husband," she said, "has been a subscriber to that publication, *What to Expect*, for eight months."

But the owl had swooped because it was hungry, whereas she was swooping just to hurt. It was in her voice, which was still hers but quite different when she said the word "husband."

"And that's ridiculous," she went on, "if you want something ridiculous. He hasn't the slightest interest in politics or industry or the stock market or anything like that. He is a successful doctor and all he ever thinks about is his work and his patients, especially his women patients. What would he want with a thing like that *What to Expect*? Why should he pay that Beula Poole money every week, month after month? I have my own money, and for the first few years after we married we lived on my income, but then he began to be successful, and now he doesn't need my money any more. And he doesn't—"

Abruptly she stood up. Apparently the habit had got so strong that sometimes she even interrupted herself. She was turning to pick up her coat.

"If you please," Wolfe said brusquely. "You have my word of honor and I want some details. What has your husband—"

"That's all," she snapped. "I don't intend to answer any silly questions. If I did you'd be sure to give me away, you wouldn't be smart enough not to, and the details don't matter. I've told you the one thing you need to know, and I only hope—"

She was proceeding with the coat, and I had gone to her to help.

"Yes, madam, what do you hope?"

She looked straight at him. "I hope you've got some brains. You don't look it."

She turned and made for the hall, and I followed. Over the years I have opened that front door to let many people out of that house, among them thieves, swindlers, murderers, and assorted crooks, but it has never been a greater pleasure than on that occasion. Added to everything else, I had noticed when helping her with her coat that her neck needed washing.

It had not been news to us that her husband was a successful doctor. Between my return to the office and her arrival there had been time for a look at the phone book, which had him as an M.D. with an office address in the Sixties just off Park Avenue, and for a call to Doc Vollmer. Vollmer had never met him, but knew his standing and reputation, which were up around the top. He had a good high-bracket practice, with the emphasis on gynecology.

Back in the office I remarked to Wolfe, "There goes my pendulum again. Lately I've been swinging toward the notion of getting myself a little woman, but good Godalmighty. Brother!"

He nodded, and shivered a little. "Yes. However, we can't reject it merely because it's soiled. Unquestionably her fact is a fact; otherwise she would have contrived an elaborate support for it." He glanced at the clock. "She said she had to be home by seven, so he may still be in his office. Try it."

I found the number and dialed it. The woman who answered firmly intended to protect her employer from harassment by a stranger, but I finally sold her.

Wolfe took it. "Dr. Michaels? This is Nero Wolfe, a detective. Yes, sir, so far as I know there is only one of that name. I'm in a little difficulty and would appreciate some help from you."

"I'm just leaving for the day, Mr. Wolfe. I'm afraid I couldn't undertake to give you medical advice on the phone." His voice was low, pleasant, and tired.

"It isn't medical advice I need, Doctor. I want to have a talk with you about a publication called *What to Expect*, to which you subscribed. The difficulty is that I find it impractical to leave my house. I could send my assistant or a policeman to see you, or both, but I would prefer to discuss it with you myself, confidentially. I wonder if you could call on me this evening after dinner?"

Evidently the interrupting mania in the Michaels family was confined to the wife. Not only did he not interrupt, he didn't even take a cue. Wolfe tried again. "Would that be convenient, sir?"

"If I could have another moment, Mr. Wolfe. I've had a hard day and am trying to think."

"By all means."

He took ten seconds. His voice came, even tireder. "I suppose it would be useless to tell you to go to hell. I would prefer not to discuss it on the phone. I'll be at your office around nine o'clock."

"Good. Have you a dinner engagement, Doctor?"

"An engagement? No. I'm dining at home. Why?"

"It just occurred to me—could I prevail on you to dine with me? You said you were just leaving for the day. I have a good cook. We are having fresh pork tenderloin, with all fiber removed, done in a casserole, with a sharp brown sauce moderately spiced. There will not be time to chambrer a claret properly, but we can have the chill off. We shall of course not approach our little matter until afterward, with the coffee—or even after that. Do you happen to know the brandy labeled Remisier? It is not common. I hope this won't shock you, but the way to do it is to sip it with bites of Fritz's apple pie. Fritz is my cook."

"I'll be damned. I'll be there—what's the address?"

Wolfe gave it to him, and hung up.

"I'll be damned too," I declared. "A perfect stranger? He may put horseradish on oysters."

Wolfe grunted. "If he had gone home to eat with that creature things might have been said. Even to the point of repudiation by her and defiance by him. I thought it prudent to avoid that risk."

"Nuts. There's no such risk and you know it. What you're trying to avoid is to give anyone an excuse to think you're human. You were being kind to your fellow man and you'd rather be caught dead. The idea of the poor devil going home to dine with that female hyena was simply too much for your great big warm heart, and you were so damn impetuous you even committed yourself to letting him have some of that brandy of which there are only nineteen bottles in the United States and they're all in your cellar."

"Bosh." He arose. "You would sentimentalize the multiplication table." He started for the kitchen, to tell Fritz about the guest, and to smell around.

XVIII

AFTER dinner Fritz brought us a second pot of coffee in the office, and also the brandy bottle and big-bellied glasses. Most of the two hours had been spent, not on West Thirty-fifth Street in New York, but in Egypt. Wolfe and the guest had both spent some time there in days gone by, and they had settled on that for discussion and a few arguments.

Dr. Michaels, informally comfortable in the red leather chair, put down his coffee cup, ditched a cigarette, and gently patted his midriff. He looked exactly like a successful Park Avenue doctor, middle-aged, well-built and well-dressed, worried but self-assured. After the first hour at the table the tired and worried look had gone, but now, as he cocked an eye at Wolfe after disposing of the cigarette, his forehead was wrinkled again.

"This has been a delightful recess," he declared. "It has done me a world of good. I have dozens of patients for whom I would like to prescribe a dinner with you, but I'm afraid I'd have to advise you not to fill the prescription." He belched, and was well-mannered enough not to try to cheat on it. "Well. Now I'll stop masquerading as a guest and take my proper role. The human sacrifice."

Wolfe disallowed it. "I have no desire or intention to gut you, sir."

Michaels smiled. "A surgeon might say that too, as he slits the skin. No, let's get it done. Did my wife phone you, or write you, or come to see you?"

"Your wife?" Wolfe's eyes opened innocently. "Has there been any mention of your wife?"

"Only by me, this moment. Let it pass. I suppose your solemn word of honor has been invoked—a fine old phrase, really, solemn word of honor—" He shrugged. "I wasn't actually surprised when you asked me about that blackmail business on the phone, merely momentarily confused. I had been expecting something of the sort, because it didn't seem likely that such an opportunity to cause me embarrassment—or perhaps worse—would be missed. Only I would have guessed it would be the police. This is much better, much."

Wolfe's head dipped forward, visibly, to acknowledge the compliment. "It may eventually reach the police, Doctor. There may be no help for it."

"Of course, I realize that. I can only hope not. Did she give you the anonymous letters, or just show them to you?"

"Neither. But that 'she' is your pronoun, not mine. With that understood—I have no documentary evidence, and have seen none. If there is some, no doubt I could get it." Wolfe sighed, leaned back, and half closed his eyes. "Wouldn't it be simpler if you assume that I know nothing at all, and tell me about it?"

"I suppose so, damn it." Michaels sipped some brandy, used his tongue to give all the membranes a chance at it, swallowed, and put the glass down. "From the beginning?"

"If you please."

"Well—it was last summer, nine months ago, that I first learned about the anonymous letters. One of my colleagues showed me one that he had received by mail. It strongly hinted that I was chronically guilty of—uh, unethical conduct—with women patients. Not long after that I became aware of a decided change in the attitude of one of my oldest and most valued patients. I appealed to her to tell me frankly what had caused it. She had received two similar letters. It was the next day—naturally my memory is quite vivid on this—that my wife showed me two letters, again similar, that had come to her."

The wrinkles on his forehead had taken command again. "I don't have to explain what that sort of thing could do to a doctor if it kept up. Of course I thought of the police, but the risk of possible publicity, or even spreading of rumor, through a police inquiry, was too great. There was the same objection, or at least I thought there was, to hiring a private investigator. Then, the day after my wife showed me the letters—no, two days after—I had a phone call at my home in the evening. I presume my wife listened to it on the extension in her room— But you're not interested in that. I wish to God you were—" Michaels abruptly jerked his head up as if he had heard a noise somewhere. "Now what did I mean by that?"

"I have no idea," Wolfe murmured. "The phone call?"

"It was a woman's voice. She didn't waste any words. She said she understood that people had been getting letters about me, and if it annoyed me and I wanted to stop it I could easily do so. If I would subscribe for one year to a publication called *What to Expect*—she gave me the address—there would be no more letters. The cost would be ten dollars a week, and I could pay as I pleased, weekly, monthly, or the year in advance. She assured me emphatically that there would be no request for renewal, that nothing beyond the one year's subscription would be required, that the letters would stop as soon as I subscribed, and that there would be no more."

Michaels turned a hand to show a palm. "That's all. I subscribed. I sent ten dollars a week for a while—eight weeks—and then I sent a check for four hundred and forty dollars. So far as I know there have been no more letters—and I think I would know."

"Interesting," Wolfe murmured. "Extremely."

"Yes," Michaels agreed. "I can understand your saying that. It's what a doctor says when he runs across something rare like a lung grown to a rib. But if he's tactful he doesn't say it in the hearing of the patient."

"You're quite right, sir. I apologize. But this is indeed a rarity—truly remarkable! If the execution graded as high as the conception— What were the letters like, typed?"

"Yes. Plain envelopes and plain cheap paper, but the typing was perfect."

"You said you sent a check. That was acceptable?"

Michaels nodded. "She made that clear. Either check or money order. Cash would be accepted, but was thought inadvisable on account of the risk in the mails."

"You see? Admirable. What about her voice?"

"It was medium in pitch, clear and precise, educated—I mean good diction and grammar—and matter-of-fact. One day I called the number of the publication—as you probably know, it's listed—and asked for Miss Poole. It was Miss Poole talking, she said. I discussed a paragraph in the latest issue, and she was intelligent and informed about it. But her voice was soprano, jerky and nervous, nothing like the voice that had told me how to get the letters stopped."

"It wouldn't be. That was what you phoned for?"

"Yes. I thought I'd have that much satisfaction at least, since there was no risk in it."

"You might have saved your nickel." Wolfe grimaced. "Dr. Michaels, I'm going to ask you a question."

"Go ahead."

"I don't want to, but though the question is intrusive it is also important. And it will do no good to ask it unless I can be assured of a completely candid reply or a refusal to answer at all. You would be capable of a fairly good job of evasion if you were moved to try, and I don't want that. Will you give me either candor or silence?"

Michaels smiled. "Silence is so awkward. I'll give you a straight answer or I'll say 'no comment.'"

"Good. How much substance was there in the hints in those letters about your conduct?"

The doctor looked at him, considered, and finally nodded his head. "It's intrusive, all right, but I'll take your word for it that it's important. You want a full answer?"

"As full as possible."

"Then it must be confidential."

"It will be."

"I accept that. I don't ask for your solemn word of honor. There was not even a shadow of substance. I have never, with any patient, even approached the boundaries of professional decorum. But I'm not like you; I have a deep and intense need for the companionship of a woman. I suppose that's why I married so early—and so disastrously. Possibly her money attracted me too, though I would vigorously deny it; there are bad streaks in me. Anyway, I do have the companionship of a woman, but not the one I married. She has never been my patient. When she needs medical advice she goes to some other doctor. No doctor should assume responsibility for the health of one he loves or one he hates."

"This companionship you enjoy—it could not have been the stimulus for the hints in the letters?"

"I don't see how. All the letters spoke of women patients—in the plural, and patients."

"Giving their names?"

"No, no names."

Wolfe nodded with satisfaction. "That would have taken too much research for a wholesale operation, and it wasn't necessary." He came forward in his chair to reach for the pushbutton. "I am greatly obliged to you, Dr. Michaels. This has been highly distasteful for you, and you have been most indulgent. I don't need to prolong it, and I won't. I foresee no necessity to give the police your name, and I'll even engage not to do so, though heaven only knows what my informant will do. Now we'll have some beer. We didn't get it settled about the pointed arches in the Tulun mosque."

"If you don't mind," the guest said, "I've been wondering if it would be seemly to tip this brandy bottle again."

So he stayed with the brandy while Wolfe had beer. I excused myself and went out for a breath of air, for while they were perfectly welcome to do some more settling about the pointed arches in the Tulun mosque, as far as I was concerned it had been attended to long ago.

It was past eleven when I returned, and soon afterward Michaels arose to go. He was far from being pickled, but he was much more relaxed and rosy than he had been when I let him in. Wolfe was so mellow that he even stood up to say good-by, and I didn't see his usual flicker of hesitation when Michaels extended a hand. He doesn't care about shaking hands indiscriminately.

Michaels said impulsively, "I want to ask you something."

"Then do so."

"I want to consult you professionally—your profession. I need help. I want to pay for it."

"You will, sir, if it's worth anything."

"It will be, I'm sure. I want to know, if you are being shadowed, if a man is following you, how many ways are there of eluding him, and what are they, and how are they executed?"

"Good heavens." Wolfe shuddered. "How long has this been going on?"

"For months."

"Well. Archie?"

"Sure," I said. "Glad to."

"I don't want to impose on you," Michaels lied. He did. "It's late."

"That's okay. Sit down."

I really didn't mind, having met his wife.

XIX

THAT, I thought to myself as I was brushing my hair Thursday morning, covered some ground. That was a real step forward.

Then, as I dropped the brush into the drawer, I asked aloud, "Yeah? Toward what?"

In a murder case you expect to spend at least half your time barking up wrong trees. Sometimes that gets you irritated, but what the hell, if you belong in the detective business at all you just skip it and take another look. That wasn't the trouble with this one. We hadn't gone dashing around investigating a funny sound only to learn it was just a cat on a fence. Far from it. We had left all that to the cops. Every move we had made had been strictly pertinent. Our two chief discoveries—the tape on the bottle of coffee and the way the circulation department of *What to Expect* operated—were unquestionably essential parts of the picture of the death of Cyril Orchard, which was what we were working on.

So it was a step forward. Fine. When you have taken a step forward, the next thing on the program is another step in the same direction. And that was the pebble in the griddle cake I broke a tooth on that morning. Bathing and dressing and eating breakfast, I went over the situation from every angle and viewpoint, and I had to admit this: if Wolfe had called me up to his room and asked for a suggestion on how I should spend the day, I would have been tonguetied.

What I'm doing, if you're following me, is to justify what I did do. When he did call me up to his room, and wished me a good morning, and asked how I had slept, and told me to phone Inspector Cramer and invite him to pay us a visit at eleven o'clock, all I said was, "Yes, sir."

There was another phone call which I had decided to make on my own. Since it involved a violation of a law Wolfe had passed I didn't want to make it from the office, so when I went out for a stroll to the bank to deposit a check from a former client who was paying in installments, I patronized a booth. When I got Lon Cohen I told him I wanted to ask him something that had no connection with the detective business, but was strictly private. I said I had been offered a job at a figure ten times what he was worth, and fully half what I was, and, while I had no intention of leaving Wolfe, I was curious. Had he ever heard of a guy named Arnold Zeck, and what about him?

"Nothing for you," Lon said.

"What do you mean, nothing for me?"

"I mean you don't want a Sunday feature, you want the lowdown, and I haven't got it. Zeck is a question mark. I've heard that he owns twenty assemblymen and six district leaders, and I've also heard that he is merely a dried fish. There's a rumor that if you print something about him that he resents, your body is washed ashore at Montauk Point, mangled by sharks, but you know how the boys talk. One little detail—this is between us?"

"Forever."

"There's not a word on him in our morgue. I had occasion to look once, several years ago—when he gave his yacht to the Navy. Not a thing, which is peculiar for a guy that gives away yachts and owns the highest hill in Westchester. What's the job?"

"Skip it. I wouldn't consider it. I thought he still had his yacht."

I decided to let it lay. If the time should come when Wolfe had to sneak outdoors and look for a place to hide, I didn't want it blamed on me.

Cramer arrived shortly after eleven. He wasn't jovial, and neither was I. When he came, as I had known him to, to tear Wolfe to pieces, or at least to threaten to haul him downtown or send a squad with a paper signed by a judge, he had fire in his eye and springs in his calves. This time he was so forlorn he even let me hang up his hat and coat for him. But as he entered the office I saw him squaring his shoulders. He was so used to going into that room to be belligerent that it was automatic. He growled a greeting, sat, and demanded, "What have you got this time?"

Wolfe, lips compressed, regarded him a moment and then pointed a finger at him. "You know, Mr. Cramer, I begin to suspect I'm a jackass. Three weeks ago yesterday, when I read in the paper of Mr. Orchard's death, I should have guessed immediately why people paid him ten dollars a week. I don't mean merely the general idea of blackmail; that was an obvious possibility; I mean the whole operation, the way it was done."

"Why, have you guessed it now?"

"No. I've had it described to me."

"By whom?"

"It doesn't matter. An innocent victim. Would you like to have me describe it to you?"

"Sure. Or the other way around."

Wolfe frowned. "What? You know about it?"

"Yeah, I know about it. I do now." Cramer wasn't doing any bragging. He stayed glum. "Understand I'm saying nothing against the New York Police Department. It's the best on earth. But it's a large organization, and you can't expect everyone to know what everybody else did or is doing. My part of it is Homicide. Well. In September nineteen-forty-six, nineteen months ago, a citizen lodged a complaint with a precinct detective sergeant. People had received anonymous letters about him, and he had got a phone call from a man that if he subscribed to a thing called *Track Almanac* for one year there would be no more letters. He said the stuff in the letters was lies, and he wasn't going to be swindled, and he wanted justice. Because it looked as if it might be a real job the sergeant consulted his captain. They went together to the *Track Almanac* office, found Orchard there, and jumped him. He denied it, said it must have been someone trying to queer him. The citizen listened to Orchard's voice, both direct and on the phone, and said it hadn't been his voice on the phone, it must have been a confederate. But no lead to a confederate could be found. Nothing could be found. Orchard stood pat. He refused to let them see his subscription list, on the ground that he didn't want his customers pestered, which was within his rights in the absence of a charge. The citizen's lawyer wouldn't let him swear a warrant. There were no more anonymous letters."

"Beautiful," Wolfe murmured.

"What the hell is so beautiful?"

"Excuse me. And?"

"And nothing. The captain is now retired, living on a farm in Rhode Island. The sergeant is still a sergeant, as he should be, since apparently he doesn't read the papers. He's up in a Bronx precinct, specializing in kids that throw stones at trains. Just day before yesterday the name Orchard reminded him of something! So I've got that. I've put men onto the other Orchard subscribers that we know about, except the one that was just a sucker—plenty of men to cover anybody at all close to them, to ask about anonymous letters. There have been no results on Savarese or Madeline Fraser, but we've uncovered it on the Leconne woman, the one that runs a beauty parlor. It was the same routine—the letters and the phone call, and she fell for it. She says the letters were lies, and it looks like they were, but she paid up to get them stopped, and she pushed us off, and you too, because she didn't want a stink."

Cramer made a gesture. "Does that describe it?"

"Perfectly," Wolfe granted.

"Okay. You called me, and I came because I swear to God I don't see what it gets me. It was you who got brilliant and made it that the poison was for the Fraser woman, not Orchard. Now that looks crazy, but what don't? If it was for Orchard after all, who and why in that bunch? And what about Beula Poole? Were she and Orchard teaming it? Or was she horning in on his list? By God, I never saw anything like it! Have you been giving me a runaround? I want to know!"

Cramer pulled a cigar from his pocket and got his teeth closed on it.

Wolfe shook his head. "Not I," he declared. "I'm a little dizzy myself. Your description was sketchy, and it might help to fill it in. Are you in a hurry?"

"Hell no."

"Then look at this. It is important, if we are to see clearly the connection of the two events, to know exactly what the roles of Mr. Orchard and Miss Poole were. Let us say that I am an ingenious and ruthless man, and I decide to make some money by blackmailing wholesale, with little or no risk to myself."

"Orchard got poisoned," Cramer growled, "and she got shot."

"Yes," Wolfe agreed, "but I didn't. I either know people I can use or I know how to find them. I am a patient and resourceful man. I supply Orchard with funds to begin publication of *Track Almanac*. I have lists prepared, with the greatest care, of persons with ample incomes from a business or profession or job that would make them sensitive to my attack. Then I start operating. The phone calls are made neither by Orchard nor by me. Of course Orchard, who is in an exposed position, has never met me, doesn't know who I am, and probably isn't even aware that I exist. Indeed, of those engaged in the operation, very few know that I exist, possibly only one."

Wolfe rubbed his palms together. "All this is passably clever. I am taking from my victims only a small fraction of their incomes, and I am not threatening them with exposure of a fearful secret. Even if I knew their secrets, which I don't, I would prefer not to use them in the anonymous letters; that would not merely harass them, it would fill them with terror, and I don't want terror, I only want money. Therefore, while my lists are carefully compiled, no great amount of research is required, just enough to get only the kind of people who would be least likely to put up a fight, either by going to the police or by any other method. Even should one resort to the police, what will happen? You have already answered that, Mr. Cramer, by telling what did happen."

"That sergeant was dumb as hell," Cramer grumbled.

"Oh no. There was the captain too. Take an hour sometime to consider what you would have done and see where you come out. What if one or two more citizens had made the same complaint? Mr. Orchard would have insisted that he was being persecuted by an enemy. In the extreme case of an avalanche of complaints, most improbable, or of an exposure by an exceptionally capable policeman, what then? Mr. Orchard would be done for, but I wouldn't. Even if he wanted to squeal, he couldn't, not on me, for he doesn't know me."

"He has been getting money to you," Cramer objected.

"Not to me. He never gets within ten miles of me. The handling of the money is an important detail and you may be sure it has been well organized. Only one man ever gets close enough to me to bring me money. It shouldn't take me long to build up a fine list of subscribers to *Track Almanac*—certainly a hundred, possibly five hundred. Let us be moderate and say two hundred. That's two thousand dollars a week. If Mr. Orchard keeps half, he can pay all expenses and have well over thirty thousand a year for his net. If he has any sense, and he has been carefully chosen and is under surveillance, that will satisfy him. For me, it's a question of my total volume. How many units do I have? New York is big enough for four or five, Chicago for two or three, Detroit, Philadelphia, and Los Angeles for two each, at least a dozen cities for one. If I wanted to stretch it I could easily get twenty units working. But we'll be moderate again and stop at twelve. That would bring me in six hundred thousand dollars a year for my share. My operating costs shouldn't be more than half that; and when you consider that my net is really net, with no income tax to pay, I am doing very well indeed."

Cramer started to say something, but Wolfe put up a hand. "Please. As I said, all that is fairly clever, especially the avoidance of real threats about real secrets, but what makes it a masterpiece is the limitation of the tribute. All blackmailers will promise that this time is the last, but I not only make the promise, I keep it. I have an inviolable rule never to ask for a subscription renewal."

"You can't prove it."

"No, I can't. But I confidently assume it, because it is the essence, the great beauty, of the plan. A man can put up with a pain—and this was not really a pain, merely a discomfort, for people with good incomes—if he thinks he knows when it will stop, and if it stops when the time comes. But if I make them pay year after year, with no end in sight, I invite sure disaster. I'm too good a businessman for that. It is much cheaper and safer to get four new subscribers a week for each unit; that's all that is needed to keep it at a constant two hundred subscribers."

Wolfe nodded emphatically. "By all means, then, if I am to stay in business indefinitely, and I intend to, I must make that rule and rigidly adhere to it; and I do so. There will of course be many little difficulties, as there are in any enterprise, and I must also be prepared for an unforeseen contingency. For example, Mr. Orchard may get killed. If so I must know of it at once, and I must have a man in readiness to remove all papers from his office, even though there is nothing there that could possibly lead to me. I would prefer to have no inkling of the nature and extent of my operations reach unfriendly parties. But I am not panicky; why should I be? Within two weeks one of my associates—the one who makes the phone calls for my units that are managed by females—begins phoning the *Track Almanac* subscribers to tell them that their remaining payments should be made to another publication called *What to Expect*. It would have been better to discard my *Track Almanac* list and take my loss, but I don't know that. I only find it out when Miss Poole also gets killed. Luckily my surveillance is excellent. Again an office must be cleaned out, and this time under hazardous conditions and with dispatch. Quite likely my man has seen the murderer, and can even name him; but I'm not interested in catching a murderer; what I want is to save my business from these confounded interruptions. I discard both those cursed lists, destroy them, burn them, and start plans for two entirely new units. How about a weekly sheet giving the latest shopping information? Or a course in languages, any language? There are numberless possibilities."

Wolfe leaned back. "There's your connection, Mr. Cramer."

"The hell it is," Cramer mumbled. He was rubbing the side of his nose with his forefinger. He was sorting things out. After a moment he went on, "I thought maybe you were going to end up by killing both of them yourself. That would be a connection too, wouldn't it?"

"Not a very plausible one. Why would I choose that time and place and method for killing Mr. Orchard? Or even Miss Poole—why there in her office? It wouldn't be like me. If they had to be disposed of surely I would have made better arrangements than that."

"Then you're saying it was a subscriber."

"I make the suggestion. Not necessarily a subscriber, but one who looked at things from the subscriber's viewpoint."

"Then the poison was intended for Orchard after all."

"I suppose so, confound it. I admit that's hard to swallow. It's sticking in my throat."

"Mine too." Cramer was skeptical. "One thing you overlooked. You were so interested in pretending it was you, you didn't mention who it really is. This patient, ruthless bird that's pulling down over half a million a year. Could I have his name and address?"

"Not from me," Wolfe said positively. "I strongly doubt if you could finish him, and if you tried he would know who had named him. Then I would have to undertake it, and I don't want to tackle him. I work for money, to make a living, not just to keep myself alive. I don't want to be reduced to that primitive extremity."

"Nuts. You've been telling me a dream you had. You can't stand it for anyone to think you don't know everything, so you even have the brass to tell me to my face that you know his name. You don't even know he exists, any more than Orchard did."

"Oh yes, I do. I'm much more intelligent than Mr. Orchard."

"Have it your way," Cramer conceded generously. "You trade orchids with him. So what? He's not in my department. If he wasn't behind these murders I don't want him. My job is homicide. Say you didn't dream it, say it's just as you said, what comes next? How have I gained an inch—or you either? Is that what you got me here for, to tell me about your goddam units in twelve different cities?"

"Partly. I didn't know your precinct sergeant had been reminded of something. But that wasn't all. Do you feel like telling me why Miss Koppel tried to get on an airplane?"

"Sure I feel like it, but I can't because I don't know. She says to see her sick mother. We've tried to find another reason that we like better, but no luck. She's under bond not to leave the state."

Wolfe nodded. "Nothing seems to fructify, does it? What I really wanted was to offer a suggestion. Would you like one?"

"Let me hear it."

"I hope it will appeal to you. You said that you have had men working in the circles of the Orchard subscribers you know about, and that there have been no results on Professor Savarese or Miss Fraser. You might have expected that, and probably did, since those two have given credible reasons for having subscribed. Why not shift your aim to another target? How many men are available for that sort of work?"

"As many as I want."

"Then put a dozen or more onto Miss Vance—or, rather, onto her associates. Make it thorough. Tell the men that the object is not to learn whether anonymous letters regarding Miss Vance have been received. Tell them that that much has been confidently assumed, and that their job is to find out what the letters said, and who got them and when. It will require pertinacity to the farthest limit of permissible police conduct. The man good enough actually to secure one of the letters will be immediately promoted."

Cramer sat scowling. Probably he was doing the same as me, straining for a quick but comprehensive flashback of all the things that Elinor Vance had seen or done, either in our presence or to our knowledge. Finally he inquired, "Why her?"

Wolfe shook his head. "If I explained you would say I was telling you another dream. I assure you that in my opinion the reason is good."

"How many letters to how many people?"

Wolfe's brows went up. "My dear sir! If I knew that would I let you get a finger in it? I would have her here ready for delivery, with evidence. What the deuce is wrong with it? I am merely suggesting a specific line of inquiry on a specific person whom you have already been tormenting for over three weeks."

"You're letting my finger in now. If it's any good why don't you hire men with your clients' money and sail on through?"

Wolfe snorted. He was disgusted. "Very well," he said. "I'll do that. Don't bother about it. Doubtless your own contrivances are far superior. Another sergeant may be reminded of something that happened at the turn of the century."

Cramer stood up. I thought he was going to leave without a word, but he spoke. "That's pretty damn cheap, Wolfe. You would never have heard of that sergeant if I hadn't told you about him. Freely."

He turned and marched out. I made allowances for both of them because their nerves were on edge. After three weeks for Cramer, and more than two for Wolfe, they were no closer to the killer of Cyril Orchard than when they started.

XX

I HAVE to admit that for me the toss to Elinor Vance was a passed ball. It went by me away out of reach. I halfway expected that now at last we would get some hired help, but when I asked Wolfe if I should line up Saul and Fred and Orrie he merely grunted. I wasn't much surprised, since it was in accordance with our new policy of letting the cops do it. It was a cinch that Cramer's first move on returning to his headquarters would be to start a pack sniffing for anonymous letters about Elinor Vance.

After lunch I disposed of a minor personal problem by getting Wolfe's permission to pay a debt, though that wasn't the way I put it. I told him that I would like to call Lon Cohen and give him the dope on how subscriptions to *Track Almanac* and *What to Expect* had been procured, of course without any hint of a patient, ruthless mastermind who didn't exist, and naming no names. My arguments were (a) that Wolfe had fished it up himself and therefore Cramer had no copyright, (b) that it was desirable to have a newspaper under an obligation, (c) that it would serve them right for the vicious editorial they had run, and (d) that it might possibly start a fire somewhere that would give us a smoke signal. Wolfe nodded, but I waited until he had gone up to the plant rooms to phone Lon to pay up. If I had done it in his hearing he's so damn suspicious that some word, or a shade of a tone, might have started him asking questions.

Another proposal I made later on didn't do so well. He turned it down flat. Since it was to be assumed that I had forgotten the name Arnold Zeck, I used Duncan instead. I reminded Wolfe that he had told Cramer that it was likely that an employee of Duncan's had seen the killer of Beula Poole, and could even name him. What I proposed was to call the Midland number and leave a message for Duncan to phone Wolfe. If and when he did so Wolfe would make an offer: if Duncan would come through on the killer, not for quotation of course, Wolfe would agree to forget that he had ever heard tell of anyone whose name began with Z—pardon me, D.

All I got was my head snapped off. First, Wolfe would make no such bargain with a criminal, especially a dysgenic one; and second, there would be no further communication between him and that nameless buzzard unless the buzzard started it. That seemed shortsighted to me. If he didn't intend to square off with the bird unless he had to, why not take what he could get? After dinner that evening I tried to bring it up again, but he wouldn't discuss it.

The following morning, Friday, we had a pair of visitors that we hadn't seen for quite a while: Walter B. Anderson, the Starlite president, and Fred Owen, the director of public relations. When the doorbell rang a little before noon and I went to the front and saw them on the stoop, my attitude was quite different from what it had been the first time. They had no photographers along, and they were clients in good standing entitled to one hell of a beef if they only knew it, and there was a faint chance that they had a concealed weapon, maybe a hatpin, to stick into Wolfe. So without going to the office to check I welcomed them across the threshold.

Wolfe greeted them without any visible signs of rapture, but at least he didn't grump. He even asked them how they did. While they were getting seated he shifted in his chair so he could give his eyes to either one without excessive exertion for his neck muscles. He actually apologized. "It isn't astonishing if you gentlemen are getting a little impatient. But if you are exasperated, so am I. I had no idea it would drag on like this. No murderer likes to be caught, naturally; but this one seems to have an extraordinary aversion to it. Would you like me to describe what has been accomplished?"

"We know pretty well," Owen stated. He was wearing a dark brown double-breasted pin-stripe that must have taken at least five fittings to get it the way it looked.

"We know too well," the president corrected him. Usually I am tolerant of the red-faced plump type, but every time that geezer opened his mouth I wanted to shut it, and not by talking.

Wolfe frowned. "I've admitted your right to exasperation. You needn't insist on it."

"We're not exasperated with you, Mr. Wolfe," Owen declared.

"I am," the president corrected him again. "With the whole damn thing and everything and everyone connected with it. For a while I've been willing to string along with the idea that there can't be any argument against a Hooper in the high twenties, but I've thought I might be wrong and now I know I was. My God, blackmail! Were you responsible for that piece in the *Gazette* this morning?"

"Well—" Wolfe was being judicious. "I would say that the responsibility rests with the man who conceived the scheme. I discovered and disclosed it—"

"It doesn't matter." Anderson waved it aside. "What does matter is that my company and my product cannot and will not be connected in the public mind with blackmail. That's dirty. That makes people gag."

"I absolutely agree," Owen asserted.

"Murder is moderately dirty too," Wolfe objected.

"No," Anderson said flatly. "Murder is sensational and exciting, but it's not like blackmail and anonymous letters. I'm through. I've had enough of it."

He got a hand in his breast pocket and pulled out an envelope, from which he extracted an oblong strip of blue paper. "Here's a check for your fee, the total amount. I can collect from the others—or not. I'll see. Send me a bill for expenses to date. You understand, I'm calling it off."

Owen had got up to take the check and hand it to Wolfe. Wolfe took a squint at it and let it drop to the desk.

"Indeed." Wolfe picked up the check, gave it another look, and dropped it again. "Have you consulted the other parties to our arrangement?"

"No, and I don't intend to. What do you care? That's the full amount, isn't it?"

"Yes, the amount's all right. But why this headlong retreat? What has suddenly scared you so?"

"Nothing has scared me." Anderson came forward in his chair. "Look, Wolfe. I came down here myself to make sure there's no slip-up on this. The deal is off, beginning right now. If you listened to the Fraser program this morning you didn't hear my product mentioned. I'm paying that off too, and clearing out. If you think I'm scared you don't know me. I don't scare. But I know how to take action when the circumstances require it, and that's what I'm doing."

He left his chair, leaned over Wolfe's desk, stretched a short fat arm, and tapped the check with a short stubby forefinger. "I'm no welsher! I'll pay your expenses just like I'm paying this! I'm not blaming you, to hell with that, but from this minute—you—are—not—working—for —me!"

With the last six words the finger jabbed the desk, at the rate of about three jabs to a word.

"Come on, Fred," the president commanded, and the pair tramped out to the hall.

I moseyed over as far as the office door to see that they didn't make off with my new twenty-dollar gray spring hat, and, when they were definitely gone, returned to my desk, sat, and commented to Wolfe, "He seems to be upset."

"Take a letter to him."

I got my notebook and pen. Wolfe cleared his throat. "Not dear Mr. Anderson, dear sir. Regarding our conversation at my office this morning, I am engaged with others as well as you, and, since my fee is contingent upon a performance, I am obliged to continue until the performance is completed. The check you gave me will be held in my safe until that time."

I looked up. "Sincerely?"

"I suppose so. There's nothing insincere about it. When you go out to mail it go first to the bank and have the check certified."

"That shifts the contingency," I remarked, opening the drawer where I kept letterheads, "to whether the bank stays solvent or not."

It was at that moment, the moment when I was putting the paper in the typewriter, that Wolfe really settled down to work on the Orchard case. He leaned back, shut his eyes, and began exercising his lips. He was like that when I left on my errand, and still like that when I got back. At such times I don't have to tiptoe or keep from rustling papers; I can bang the typewriter or make phone calls or use the vacuum cleaner and he doesn't hear it.

All the rest of that day and evening, up till bedtime, except for intermissions for meals and the afternoon conclave in the plant rooms, he kept at it, with no word or sign to give me a hint what kind of trail he had found, if any. In a way it was perfectly jake with me, for at least it showed that he had decided we would do our own cooking, but in another way it wasn't so hot. When it goes on hour after hour, as it did that Friday, the chances are that he's finding himself just about cornered, and there's no telling how desperate he'll be when he picks a hole to bust out through. A couple of years ago, after spending most of a day figuring one out, he ended up with a charade that damn near got nine human beings asphyxiated with ciphogene, including him and me, not to mention Inspector Cramer.

When both the clock and my wristwatch said it was close to midnight, and there he still was, I inquired politely, "Shall we have some coffee to keep awake?"

His mutter barely reached me. "Go to bed."

I did so.

XXI

I NEEDN'T have worried. He did give birth, but not to one of his fantastic freaks. The next morning, Saturday, when Fritz returned to the kitchen after taking up the breakfast tray he told me I was wanted.

Since Wolfe likes plenty of air at night but a good warm room at breakfast time it had been necessary, long ago, to install a contraption that would automatically close his window at six A.M. As a result the eight-o'clock temperature permits him to have his tray on a table near the window without bothering to put on a dressing gown. Seated there, his hair not yet combed, his feet bare, and all the yardage of his yellow pajamas dazzling in the morning sun, he is something to blink at, and it's too bad that Fritz and I are the only ones who ever have the privilege.

I told him it was a nice morning, and he grunted. He will not admit that a morning is bearable, let alone nice, until, having had his second cup of coffee, he has got himself fully dressed.

"Instructions," he growled.

I sat down, opened my notebook, and uncapped my pen. He instructed. "Get some ordinary plain white paper of a cheap grade; I doubt if any of ours will do. Say five by eight. Type this on it, single-spaced, no date or salutation."

He shut his eyes. "Since you are a friend of Elinor Vance, this is something you should know. During her last year at college the death of a certain person was ascribed to natural causes and was never properly investigated. Another incident that was never investigated was the disappearance of a jar of cyanide from the electroplating shop of Miss Vance's brother. It would be interesting to know if there was any connection between those two incidents. Possibly an inquiry into both of them would suggest such a connection."

"That all?"

"Yes. No signature. No envelope. Fold the paper and soil it a little;

give it the appearance of having been handled. This is Saturday, but an item in the morning paper tells of the withdrawal of Starlite from sponsorship of Miss Fraser's program, so I doubt if those people will have gone off for weekends. You may even find that they are together, conferring; that would suit our purpose best. But either together or singly, see them; show them the anonymous letter, ask if they have ever seen it or one similar to it; be insistent and as pestiferous as possible."

"Including Miss Vance herself?"

"Let circumstances decide. If they are together and she is with them, yes. Presumably she has already been alerted by Mr. Cramer's men."

"The professor? Savarese?"

"No, don't bother with him." Wolfe drank coffee. "That's all."

I stood up. "I might get more or better results if I knew what we're after. Are we expecting Elinor Vance to break down and confess? Or am I nagging one of them into pulling a gun on me, or what?"

I should have known better, with him still in his pajamas and his hair tousled.

"You're following instructions," he said peevishly. "If I knew what you're going to get I wouldn't have had to resort to this shabby stratagem."

"Shabby is right," I agreed, and left him.

I would of course obey orders, for the same reason that a good soldier does, namely he'd better, but I was not filled with enough zeal to make me hurry my breakfast. My attitude as I set about the preliminaries of the operation was that if this was the best he could do he might as well have stayed dormant. I did not believe that he had anything on Elinor Vance. He does sometimes hire Saul or Orrie or Fred without letting me know what they're up to or, more rarely, even that they're working for him, but I can always tell by seeing if money has been taken from the safe. The money was all present or accounted for. You can judge my frame of mind when I state that I halfway suspected that he had picked on Elinor merely because I had gone to a little trouble to have her seated nearest to me the night of the party.

He was, however, right about the weekends. I didn't start on the phone calls until nine-thirty, not wanting to get them out of bed for something which I regarded as about as useful as throwing rocks at the moon. The first one I tried, Bill Meadows, said he hadn't had breakfast yet and he didn't know when he would have some free time, because he was due at Miss Fraser's apartment at eleven for a conference and there was no telling how long it would last. That indicated that I would have a chance to throw at two or more moons with one stone, and another couple of phone calls verified it. There was a meeting on. I did the morning chores, buzzed the plant rooms to inform Wolfe, and left a little before eleven and headed uptown.

To show you what a murder case will do to people's lives, the password routine had been abandoned. But it by no means followed that it was easier than it had been to get up to apartment 10B. Quite the contrary. Evidently journalists and others had been trying all kinds of dodges to get a ride in the elevator, for the distinguished-looking hallman wasn't a particle interested in what I said my name was, and he steeled himself to betray no sign of recognition. He simply used the phone, and in a few minutes Bill Meadows emerged from the elevator and walked over to us. We said hello.

"Strong said you'd probably show up," he said. Neither his tone nor his expression indicated that they had been pacing up and down waiting for me. "Miss Fraser wants to know if it's something urgent."

"Mr. Wolfe thinks it is."

"All right, come on."

He was so preoccupied that he went into the elevator first.

I decided that if he tried leaving me alone in the enormous living room with the assorted furniture, to wait until I was summoned, I would just stick to his heels, but that proved to be unnecessary. He couldn't have left me alone there because that was where they were.

Madeline Fraser was on the green burlap divan, propped against a dozen cushions. Deborah Koppel was seated on the piano bench. Elinor Vance perched on a corner of the massive old black walnut table. Tully Strong had the edge of his sitter on the edge of the pink silk chair, and Nat Traub was standing. That was all as billed, but there was an added attraction. Also standing, at the far end of the long divan, was Nancylee Shepherd.

"It was Goodwin," Bill Meadows told them, but they would probably have deduced it anyhow, since I had dropped my hat and coat in the hall and was practically at his elbow. He spoke to Miss Fraser, "He says it's something urgent."

Miss Fraser asked me briskly, "Will it take long, Mr. Goodwin?" She looked clean and competent, as if she had had a good night's sleep, a shower, a healthy vigorous rub, and a thorough breakfast.

I told her I was afraid it might.

"Then I'll have to ask you to wait." She was asking a favor. She certainly had the knack of being personal without making you want to back off. "Mr. Traub has to leave soon for an appointment, and we have to make an important decision. You know, of course, that we have lost a sponsor. I suppose I ought to feel low about it, but I really don't. Do you know how many firms we have had offers from, to take the Starlite place? Sixteen!"

"Wonderful!" I admired. "Sure, I'll wait." I crossed to occupy a chair outside the conference zone.

They forgot, immediately and completely, that I was there. All but one: Nancylee. She changed position so she could keep her eyes on me, and her expression showed plainly that she considered me tricky, ratty, and unworthy of trust.

"We've got to start eliminating," Tully Strong declared. He had his spectacles off, holding them in his hand. "As I understand it there are just five serious contenders."

"Four," Elinor Vance said, glancing at a paper she held. "I've crossed off Fluff, the biscuit dough. You said to, didn't you, Lina?"

"It's a good company," Traub said regretfully. "One of the best. Their radio budget is over three million."

"You're just making it harder, Nat," Deborah Koppel told him. "We can't take all of them. I thought your favorite was Meltettes."

"It is," Traub agreed, "but these are all very fine accounts. What do you think of Meltettes, Miss Fraser?" He was the only one of the bunch who didn't call her Lina.

"I haven't tried them." She glanced around. "Where are they?"

Nancylee, apparently not so concentrated on me as to miss any word or gesture of her idol, spoke up. "There on the piano, Miss Fraser. Do you want them?"

"We have got to eliminate," Strong insisted, stabbing the air with his spectacles for emphasis. "I must repeat, as representative of the other sponsors, that they are firmly and unanimously opposed to Sparkle, if it is to be served on the program as Starlite was. They never liked the idea and they don't want it resumed."

"It's already crossed off," Elinor Vance stated. "With Fluff and Sparkle out, that leaves four."

"Not on account of the sponsors," Miss Fraser put in. "We just happen to agree with them. They aren't going to decide this. We are."

"You mean you are, Lina." Bill Meadows sounded a little irritated. "What the hell, we all know that. You don't want Fluff because Cora made some biscuits and you didn't like 'em. You don't want Sparkle because they want it served on the program, and God knows I don't blame you."

Elinor Vance repeated, "That leaves four."

"All right, eliminate!" Strong persisted.

"We're right where we were before," Deborah Koppel told them. "The trouble is, there's no real objection to any of the four, and I think Bill's right, I think we have to put it up to Lina."

"I am prepared," Nat Traub announced, in the tone of a man burning bridges, "to say that I will vote for Meltettes."

For my part, I was prepared to say that I would vote for nobody. Sitting there taking them in, as far as I could tell the only strain they were under was the pressure of picking the right sponsor. If, combined with that, one of them was contending with the nervous wear and tear of a couple of murders, he was too good for me. As the argument got warmer it began to appear that, though they were agreed that the final word was up to Miss Fraser, each of them had a favorite among the four entries left. That was what complicated the elimination.

Naturally, on account of the slip of paper I had in my pocket, I was especially interested in Elinor Vance, but the sponsor problem seemed to be monopolizing her attention as completely as that of the others. I would of course have to follow instructions and proceed with my errand as soon as they gave me a chance, but I was beginning to feel silly. While Wolfe had left it pretty vague, one thing was plain, that I was supposed to give them a severe jolt, and I doubted if I had what it would take. When they got worked up to the point of naming the winner—settling on the lucky product that would be cast for the role sixteen had applied for—bringing up the subject of an anonymous letter, even one implying that one of them was a chronic murderer, would be an anticlimax. With a serious problem like that just triumphantly solved, what would they care about a little thing like murder?

But I was dead wrong. I found that out incidentally, as a by-product of their argument. It appeared that two of the contenders were deadly rivals, both clawing for children's dimes: a candy bar called Happy Andy and a little box of tasty delights called Meltettes. It was the latter that Traub had decided to back unequivocally, and he, when the question came to a head which of those two to eliminate, again asked Miss Fraser if she had tried Meltettes. She told him no. He asked if she had tried Happy Andy. She said yes. Then, he insisted, it was only fair for her to try Meltettes.

"All right," she agreed. "There on the piano, Debby, that little red box. Toss it over."

"No!" a shrill voice cried. It was Nancylee. Everyone looked at her.

Deborah Koppel, who had picked up the little red cardboard box, asked her, "What's the matter?"

"It's dangerous!" Nancylee was there, a hand outstretched. "Give it to me. I'll eat one first!"

It was only a romantic kid being dramatic, and all she rated from that bunch, if I had read their pulses right, was a laugh and a brush-off, but that was what showed me I had been dead wrong. There wasn't even a snicker. No one said a word. They all froze, staring at Nancylee, with only one exception. That was Deborah Koppel. She held the box away from Nancylee's reaching hand and told her contemptuously, "Don't be silly."

"I mean it!" the girl cried. "Let me—"

"Nonsense." Deborah pushed her back, opened the flap of the box, took out an object, popped it into her mouth, chewed once or twice, swallowed, and then spat explosively, ejecting a spray of little particles.

I was the first, by maybe a tenth of a second, to realize that there was something doing. It wasn't so much the spitting, for that could conceivably have been merely her way of voting against Meltettes, as it was the swift terrible contortion of her features. As I bounded across to her she left the piano bench with a spasmodic jerk, got erect with her hands flung high, and screamed, "Lina! Don't! Don't let—"

I was at her, with a hand on her arm, and Bill Meadows was there too, but her muscles all in convulsion took us along as she fought toward the divan, and Madeline Fraser was there to meet her and get supporting arms around her. But somehow the three of us together failed to hold her up or get her onto the divan. She went down until her knees were on the floor, with one arm stretched rigid across the burlap of the divan, and would have gone the rest of the way but for Miss Fraser, also on her knees.

I straightened, wheeled, and told Nat Traub, "Get a doctor quick!" I saw Nancylee reaching to pick up the little red cardboard box and snapped at her, "Let that alone and behave yourself." Then to the rest of them: "Let everything alone, hear me?"

XXII

AROUND four o'clock I could have got permission to go home if I had insisted, but it seemed better to stay as long as there was a chance of picking up another item for my report. I had already phoned Wolfe to explain why I wasn't following his instructions.

All of those who had been present at the conference were still there, very much so, except Deborah Koppel, who had been removed in a basket when several gangs of city scientists had finished their part of it. She had been dead when the doctor arrived. The others were still alive but not in a mood to brag about it.

At four o'clock Lieutenant Rowcliff and an assistant D. A. were sitting on the green burlap divan, arguing whether the taste of cyanide should warn people in time to refrain from swallowing. That seemed pointless, since whether it should or not it usually doesn't, and anyway the only ones who could qualify as experts are those who have tried it, and none of them is available. I moved on. At the big oak table another lieutenant was conversing with Bill Meadows, meanwhile referring to notes on loose sheets of paper. I went on by. In the dining room a sergeant and a private were pecking away at Elinor Vance. I passed through. In the kitchen a dick with a pug nose was holding a sheet of paper, one of a series, flat on the table while Cora, the female wrestler, put her initials on it.

Turning and going back the way I had come, I continued on to the square hall, opened a door at its far end, and went through. This, the room without a name, was more densely populated than the others. Tully Strong and Nat Traub were on chairs against opposite walls. Nancylee was standing by a window. A dick was seated in the center of the room, another was leaning against a wall, and Sergeant Purley Stebbins was sort of strolling around.

That called the roll, for I knew that Madeline Fraser was in the room beyond, her bedroom, where I had first met the bunch of them, having a talk with Inspector Cramer. The way I knew that, I had just been ordered out by Deputy Commissioner O'Hara, who was in there with them.

The first series of quickies, taking them one at a time on a gallop, had been staged in the dining room by Cramer himself. Cramer and an assistant D.A. had sat at one side of the table, with the subject across from them, and me seated a little to the rear of the subject's elbow. The theory of that arrangement was that if the subject's memory showed a tendency to conflict with mine, I could tip Cramer off by sticking out my tongue or some other signal without being seen by the subject. The dick-stenographer had been at one end of the table, and other units of the personnel had hung around.

Since they were by no means strangers to Cramer and he was already intimately acquainted with their biographies, he could keep it brief and concentrate chiefly on two points: their positions and movements during the conference, and the box of Meltettes. On the former there were some contradictions on minor details, but only what you might expect under the circumstances; and I, who had been there, saw no indication that anyone was trying to fancy it up.

On the latter, the box of Meltettes, there was no contradiction at all. By noon Friday, the preceding day, the news had begun to spread that Starlite was bowing out, though it had not yet been published. For some time Meltettes had been on the Fraser waiting list, to grab a vacancy if one occurred. Friday morning Nat Traub, whose agency had the Meltettes account, had phoned his client the news, and the client had rushed him a carton of its product by messenger. A carton held forty-eight of the little red cardboard boxes. Traub, wishing to lose no time on a matter of such urgency and importance, and not wanting to lug the whole carton, had taken one little box from it and dropped it in his pocket and hotfooted it to the FBC building, arriving at the studio just before the conclusion of the Fraser broadcast. He had spoken to Miss Fraser and Miss Koppel on behalf of Meltettes and handed the box to Miss Koppel.

Miss Koppel had passed the box on to Elinor Vance, who had put it in her bag—the same bag that had been used to transport sugared coffee in a Starlite bottle. The three women had lunched in a nearby restaurant and then gone to Miss Fraser's apartment, where they had been joined later by Bill Meadows and Tully Strong for an exploratory discussion of the sponsor problem. Soon after their arrival at the apartment Elinor had taken the box of Meltettes from her bag and given it to Miss Fraser, who had put it on the big oak table in the living room.

That had been between two-thirty and three o'clock Friday afternoon, and that was as far as it went. No one knew how or when the box had been moved from the oak table to the piano. There was a blank space, completely blank, of about eighteen hours, ending around nine o'clock Saturday morning, when Cora, on a dusting mission, had seen it on the piano. She had picked it up for a swipe of the dustcloth on the piano top and put it down again. Its next appearance was two hours later, when Nancylee, soon after her arrival at the apartment, had spotted it and been tempted to help herself, even going so far as to get her clutches on it, but had been scared off when she saw that Miss Koppel's eye was on her. That, Nancylee explained, was how she had known where the box was when Miss Fraser had asked.

As you can see, it left plenty of room for inch-by-inch digging and sifting, which was lucky for everybody from privates to inspectors who are supposed to earn their pay, for there was no other place to dig at all. Relationships and motives and suspicions had already had all the juice squeezed out of them. So by four o'clock Saturday afternoon a hundred grown men, if not more, were scattered around the city, doing their damnedest to uncover another little splinter of a fact, any old fact, about that box of Meltettes. Some of them, of course, were getting results. For instance, word had come from the laboratory that the box, as it came to them, had held eleven Meltettes; that one of them, which had obviously been operated on rather skillfully, had about twelve grains of cyanide mixed into its insides; and that the other ten were quite harmless, with no sign of having been tampered with. Meltettes, they said, fitted snugly into the box in pairs, and the cyanided one had been on top, at the end of the box which opened.

And other reports, including of course fingerprints. Most of them had been relayed to Cramer in my presence. Whatever he may have thought they added up to, it looked to me very much like a repeat performance by the artist who had painted the sugared-coffee picture: so many crossing lines and overlapping colors that no resemblance to any known animal or other object was discernible.

Returning to the densely populated room with no name after my tour of inspection, I made some witty remark to Purley Stebbins and lowered myself into a chair. As I said, I could probably have bulled my way out and gone home, but I didn't want to. What prospect did it offer? I would have fiddled around until Wolfe came down to the office, made my report, and then what? He would either have grunted in disgust, found something to criticize, and lowered his iron curtain again, or he would have gone into another trance and popped out around midnight with some bright idea like typing an anonymous letter about Bill Meadows flunking in algebra his last year in high school. I preferred to stick around in the faint hope that something would turn up.

And something did. I had abandoned the idea of making some sense out of the crossing lines and overlapping colors, given up trying to get a rise out of Purley, and was exchanging hostile glares with Nancylee, when the door from the square hall opened and a lady entered. She darted a glance around and told Purley that Inspector Cramer had sent for her. He crossed to the far door, which led to Miss Fraser's bedroom, opened it, and closed it after she had passed through.

I knew her by sight but not her name, and even had an opinion of her, namely that she was the most presentable of all the female dicks I had seen. With nothing else to do, I figured out what Cramer wanted with her, and had just come to the correct conclusion when the door opened again and I got it verified. Cramer appeared first, then Deputy Commissioner O'Hara.

Cramer spoke to Purley. "Get 'em all in here."

Purley flew to obey. Nat Traub asked wistfully, "Have you made any progress, Inspector?"

Cramer didn't even have the decency to growl at him, let alone reply. That seemed unnecessarily rude, so I told Traub, "Yeah, they've reached an important decision. You're all going to be frisked."

It was ill-advised, especially with O'Hara there, since he has never forgiven me for being clever once, but I was frustrated and edgy. O'Hara gave me an evil look and Cramer told me to close my trap.

The others came straggling in with their escorts. I surveyed the lot and would have felt genuinely sorry for them if I had known which one to leave out. There was no question now about the kind of strain they were under, and it had nothing to do with picking a sponsor.

Cramer addressed them. "I want to say to you people that as long as you cooperate with us we have no desire to make it any harder for you than we have to. You can't blame us for feeling we have to bear down on you, in view of the fact that all of you lied, and kept on lying, about the bottle that the stuff came out of that killed Orchard. I called you in here to tell you that we're going to search your persons. The position is this, we would be justified in taking you all down and booking you as material witnesses, and that's what we'll do if any of you object to the search. Miss Fraser made no objection. A policewoman is in there with her now. The women will be taken in there one at a time. The men will be taken by Lieutenant Rowcliff and Sergeant Stebbins, also one at a time, to another room. Does anyone object?"

It was pitiful. They were in no condition to object, even if he had announced his intention of having clusters of Meltettes tatooed on their chests. Nobody made a sound except Nancylee, who merely shrilled, "Oh, I never!"

I crossed my legs and prepared to sit it out. And so I did, up to a point. Purley and Rowcliff took Tully Strong first. Soon the female dick appeared and got Elinor Vance. Evidently they were being thorough, for it was a good eight minutes before Purley came back with Strong and took Bill Meadows, and the lady took just as long with Elinor Vance. The last two on the list were Nancylee in one direction and Nat Traub in the other.

That is, they were the last two as I had it. But when Rowcliff and Purley returned with Traub and handed Cramer some slips of paper, O'Hara barked at them, "What about Goodwin?"

"Oh, him?" Rowcliff asked.

"Certainly him! He was here, wasn't he?"

Rowcliff looked at Cramer. Cramer looked at me.

I grinned at O'Hara. "What if I object, Commissioner?"

"Try it! That won't help you any!"

"The hell it won't. It will either preserve my dignity or start a string of firecrackers. What do you want to bet my big brother can't lick your big brother?"

He took a step toward me. "You resist, do you?"

"You're damn right I do." My hand did a half-circle. "Before twenty witnesses."

He wheeled. "Send him down, Inspector. To my office. Charge him. Then have him searched."

"Yes, sir." Cramer was frowning. "First, would you mind stepping into another room with me? Perhaps I haven't fully explained the situation—"

"I understand it perfectly! Wolfe has cooperated, so you say—to what purpose? What has happened? Another murder! Wolfe has got you all buffaloed, and I'm sick and tired of it! Take him to my office!"

"No one has got me buffaloed," Cramer rasped. "Take him, Purley. I'll phone about a charge."

XXIII

THERE were two things I liked about Deputy Commissioner O'Hara's office. First, it was there that I had been clever on a previous occasion, and therefore it aroused agreeable memories, and second, I like nice surroundings and it was the most attractive room at Centre Street, being on a corner with six large windows, and furnished with chairs and rugs and other items which had been paid for by O'Hara's rich wife.

I sat at ease in one of the comfortable chairs. The contents of my pockets were stacked in a neat pile on a corner of O'Hara's big shiny mahogany desk, except for one item, which Purley Stebbins had in his paw. Purley was so mad his face was a red sunset, and he was stuttering.

"Don't be a g-goddam fool," he exhorted me. "If you clam it with O'Hara when he gets here he'll jug you sure as hell, and it's after six o'clock so where'll you spend the night?" He shook his paw at me, the one holding the item taken from my pocket. "Tell me about this!"

I shook my head firmly. "You know, Purley," I said without rancor, "this is pretty damn ironic. You frisked that bunch of suspects and got nothing at all—I could tell that from the way you and Rowcliff looked. But on me, absolutely innocent of wrongdoing, you find what you think is an incriminating document. So here I am, sunk, facing God knows what kind of doom. I try to catch a glimpse of the future, and what do I see?"

"Oh, shut up!"

"No, I've got to talk to someone." I glanced at my wrist. "As you say, it's after six o'clock. Mr. Wolfe has come down from the plant rooms, expecting to find me awaiting him in the office, ready for my report of the day's events. He'll be disappointed. You know how he'll feel. Better still, you know what he'll do. He'll be so frantic he'll start looking up numbers and dialing them himself. I am offering ten to one that he has already called the Fraser apartment and spoken to Cramer. How much of it do you want? A dime? A buck?"

"Can it, you goddam ape." Purley was resigning. "Save it for O'Hara; he'll be here pretty soon. I hope they give you a cell with bedbugs."

"I would prefer," I said courteously, "to chat."

"Then chat about this."

"No. For the hundredth time, no. I detest anonymous letters and I don't like to talk about them."

He went to a chair and sat facing me. I got up, crossed to bookshelves, selected *Crime and Criminals*, by Mercier, and returned to my seat with it.

Purley had been wrong. O'Hara was not there pretty soon. When I glanced at my wrist every ten minutes or so I did it on the sly because I didn't want Purley to think I was getting impatient. It was a little past seven when I looked up from my book at the sound of a buzzer. Purley went to a phone on the desk and had a talk with it. He hung up, returned to his chair, sat, and after a moment spoke.

"That was the Deputy Commissioner. He is going to have his dinner. I'm to keep you here till he comes."

"Good," I said approvingly. "This is a fascinating book."

"He thinks you're boiling. You bastard."

I shrugged.

I kept my temper perfectly for another hour or more, and then, still there with my book, I became aware that I was starting to lose control. The trouble was that I had begun to feel hungry, and that was making me sore. Then there was another factor: what the hell was Wolfe doing? That, I admit, was unreasonable. Any phoning he did would be to Cramer or O'Hara, or possibly someone at the D. A.'s office, and with me cooped up as I was I wouldn't hear even an echo. If he had learned where I was and tried to get me, they wouldn't have put him through, since Purley had orders from O'Hara that I was to make no calls. But what with feeling hungry and getting no word from the outside world, I became aware that I was beginning to be offended, and that would not do. I forced my mind away from food and other aggravating aspects, including the number of revolutions the minute hand of my watch had made, and turned another page.

It was ten minutes to nine when the door opened and O'Hara and Cramer walked in. Purley stood up. I was in the middle of a paragraph and so merely flicked one eye enough to see who it was. O'Hara hung his hat and coat on a rack, and Cramer dropped his on a chair. O'Hara strode to his desk, crossing my bow so close that I could easily have tripped him by stretching a leg.

Cramer looked tired. Without spending a glance on me he nodded at Purley. "Has he opened up?"

"No, sir. Here it is." Purley handed him the item.

They had both had it read to them on the phone, but they wanted to see it. Cramer read it through twice and then handed it to O'Hara. While that was going on I went to the shelves and replaced the book, had a good stretch and yawn, and returned to my chair.

Cramer glared down at me. "What have you got to say?"

"More of the same," I told him. "I've explained to the sergeant, who has had nothing to eat by the way, that that thing has no connection whatever with any murder or any other crime, and therefore questions about it are out of order."

"You've been charged as a material witness."

"Yeah, I know, Purley showed it to me. Why don't you ask Mr. Wolfe? He might be feeling generous."

"The hell he might. We have. Look, Goodwin—"

"I'll handle him, Inspector." O'Hara speaking. He was an energetic cuss. He had gone clear around his desk to sit down, but now he arose and came clear around it again to confront me. I looked up at him inquiringly, not a bit angry.

He was trying to control himself. "You can't possibly get away with it," he stated. "It's incredible that you have the gall to try it, both you and Wolfe. Anonymous letters are a central factor in this case, a vital factor. You went up to that apartment today to see those people, and you had in your pocket an anonymous letter about one of them, practically accusing her of murder. Do you mean to tell me that you take the position that that letter has no connection with the crimes under investigation?"

"I sure do. Evidently Mr. Wolfe does too." I made a gesture. "Corroboration."

"You take and maintain that position while aware of the penalty that may be imposed upon conviction for an obstruction of justice?"

"I do."

O'Hara turned and blurted at Cramer, "Get Wolfe down here! Damn it, we should have hauled him in hours ago!"

This, I thought to myself, is something like. Now we ought to see some fur fly.

But we didn't, at least not as O'Hara had it programed. What interfered was a phone call. The buzzer sounded, and Purley, seeing that his superiors were too worked up to hear it, went to the desk and answered. After a word he told Cramer, "For you, Inspector," and Cramer crossed and got it. O'Hara stood glaring down at me, but, having his attention called by a certain tone taken by Cramer's voice, turned to look that way. Finally Cramer hung up. The expression on his face was that of a man trying to decide what it was he just swallowed.

"Well?" O'Hara demanded.

"The desk just had a call," Cramer said, "from the WPIT newsroom. WPIT is doing the script for the ten-o'clock newscast, and they're including an announcement received a few minutes ago from Nero Wolfe. Wolfe announces that he has solved the murder cases, all three of them, with no assistance from the police, and that very soon, probably sometime tomorrow, he will be ready to tell the District Attorney the name of the murderer and to furnish all necessary information. WPIT wants to know if we have any comment."

Of course it was vulgar, but I couldn't help it. I threw back my head and let out a roar. It wasn't so much the news itself as it was the look on O'Hara's face as the full beauty of it seeped through to him.

"The fat bum!" Purley whimpered.

I told O'Hara distinctly, "The next time Cramer asks you to step into another room with him I'd advise you to step."

He didn't hear me.

"It wasn't a question," Cramer said, "of Wolfe having me buffaloed. With him the only question is what has he got and how and when will he use it. If that goes on the air I would just as soon quit."

"What—" O'Hara stopped to wet his lips. "What would you suggest?"

Cramer didn't answer. He pulled a cigar from his pocket, slow motion, got it between his teeth, took it out again and hurled it for the wastebasket, missing by two feet, walked to a chair, sat down, and breathed.

"There are only two things," he said. "Just let it land is one. The other is to ask Goodwin to call him and request him to recall the announcement—and tell him he'll be home right away to report." Cramer breathed again. "I won't ask Goodwin that. Do you want to?"

"No! It's blackmail!" O'Hara yelled in pain.

"Yeah," Cramer agreed. "Only when Wolfe does it there's nothing anonymous about it. The newscast will be on in thirty-five minutes."

O'Hara would rather have eaten soap. "It may be a bluff," he pleaded. "Pure bluff!"

"Certainly it may. And it may not. It's easy enough to call it—just sit down and wait. If you're not going to call on Goodwin I guess I'll have to see if I can get hold of the commissioner." Cramer stood up.

O'Hara turned to me. I have to hand it to him, he looked me in the eye as he asked, "Will you do it?"

I grinned at him. "That warrant Purley showed me is around somewhere. It will be vacated?"

"Yes."

"Okay, I've got witnesses." I crossed to the desk and began returning my belongings to the proper pockets. The anonymous letter was there where O'Hara had left it when he had advanced to overwhelm me, and I picked it up and displayed it. "I'm taking this," I said, "but I'll let you look at it again if you want to. May I use the phone?"

I circled the desk, dropped into O'Hara's personal chair, pulled the instrument to me, and asked the male switchboard voice to get Mr. Nero Wolfe. The voice asked who I was and I told it. Then we had some comedy. After I had waited a good two minutes there was a knock on the door and O'Hara called, "Come in." The door swung wide open and two individuals entered with guns in their hands, stern and alert. When they saw the arrangements they stopped dead and looked foolish.

"What do you want?" O'Hara barked.

"The phone," one said. "Goodwin. We didn't know—"

"For Christ's sake!" Purley exploded. "Ain't I here?" It was a breach of discipline, with his superiors present.

They bumped at the threshold, getting out, pulling the door after them. I couldn't possibly have been blamed for helping myself to another hearty laugh, but there's a limit to what even a Deputy Commissioner will take, so I choked it off and sat tight until there was a voice in my ear that I knew better than any other voice on earth.

"Archie," I said.

"Where are you?" The voice was icy with rage, but not at me.

"I'm in O'Hara's office, at his desk, using his phone. I am half starved. O'Hara, Cramer, and Sergeant Stebbins are present. To be perfectly fair, Cramer and Purley are innocent. This boneheaded play was a solo by O'Hara. He fully realizes his mistake and sincerely apologizes. The warrant for my arrest is a thing of the past. The letter about Miss Vance is in my pocket. I have conceded nothing. I'm free to go where I please, including home. O'Hara requests, as a personal favor, that you kill the announcement you gave WPIT. Can that be done?"

"It can if I choose. It was arranged through Mr. Richards."

"So I suspected. You should have seen O'Hara's face when the tidings reached him. If you choose, and all of us here hope you do, go ahead and kill it and I'll be there in twenty minutes or less. Tell Fritz I'm hungry."

"Mr. O'Hara is a nincompoop. Tell him I said so. I'll have the announcement suspended temporarily, but there will be conditions. Stay there. I'll phone you shortly."

I cradled the phone, leaned back, and grinned at the three inquiring faces. "He'll call back. He thinks he can head it off temporarily, but he's got some idea about conditions." I focused on O'Hara. "He said to tell you that he says you're a nincompoop, but I think it would be more tactful not to mention it, so I won't."

"Someday," O'Hara said through his teeth, "he'll land on his nose."

They all sat down and began exchanging comments. I didn't listen because my mind was occupied. I was willing to chalk up for Wolfe a neat and well-timed swagger, and to admit that it got the desired results, but now what? Did he really have anything at all, and if so how much? It had better be fairly good. Cramer and Stebbins were not exactly ready to clasp our hands across the corpses, and as for O'Hara, I only hoped to God that when Wolfe called back he wouldn't tell me to slap the Deputy Commissioner on the back and tell him it had been just a prank and wasn't it fun? All in all, it was such a gloomy outlook that when the buzzer sounded and I reached for the phone I would just as soon have been somewhere else.

Wolfe's voice asked if they were still there and I said yes. He said to tell them that the announcement had been postponed and would not be broadcast at ten o'clock, and I did so. Then he asked for my report of the day's events.

"Now?" I demanded. "On the phone?"

"Yes," he said. "Concisely, but including all essentials. If there is a contradiction to demolish I must know it."

Even with the suspicion gnawing at me that I had got roped in for a supporting role in an enormous bluff, I did enjoy it. It was a situation anyone would appreciate. There I was, in O'Hara's chair at his desk in his office, giving a detailed report to Wolfe of a murder I had witnessed and a police operation I had helped with, and for over half an hour those three bozos simply utterly had to sit and listen. Whatever position they might be in all too soon, all they could do now was to take it and like it. I did enjoy it. Now and then Wolfe interrupted with a question, and when I had finished he took me back to fill in a few gaps. Then he proceeded to give me instructions, and as I listened it became apparent that if it was a bluff at least he wasn't going to leave me behind the enemy lines to fight my way out. I asked him to repeat it to make sure I had it straight. He did so.

"Okay," I said. "Tell Fritz I'm hungry." I hung up and faced the three on chairs. "I'm sorry it took so long, but he pays my salary and what could I do? As I told you, the announcement has been postponed. He is willing to kill it, but that sort of depends. He thinks it would be appropriate for Inspector Cramer and Sergeant Stebbins to help with the windup. He would appreciate it if you will start by delivering eight people at his office as soon as possible. He wants the five who were at the Fraser apartment today, not including the girl, Nancylee, or Cora the cook. Also Savarese. Also Anderson, president of the Starlite Company, and Owen, the public-relations man. All he wants you to do is to get them there, and to be present yourselves, but with the understanding that he will run the show. With that provision, he states that when you leave you will be prepared to make an arrest and take the murderer with you, and the announcement he gave WPIT will not be made. You can do the announcing."

I arose and moved, crossing to a chair over by the wall near the door to reclaim my hat and coat. Then I turned. "It's after ten o'clock, and if this thing is on I'm not going to start it on an empty stomach. In my opinion, even if all he has in mind is a game of blind man's bluff, which I doubt, it's well worth it. Orchard died twenty-five days ago. Beula Poole nine days. Miss Koppel ten hours. You could put your inventory on a postage stamp." I had my hand on the doorknob. "How about it? Feel like helping?"

Cramer growled at me, "Why Anderson and Owen? What does he want them for?"

"Search me. Of course he likes a good audience."

"Maybe we can't get them."

"You can try. You're an inspector and murder is a very bad crime."

"It may take hours."

"Yeah, it looks like an all-night party. If I can stand it you can, not to mention Mr. Wolfe. All right, then we'll be seeing you." I opened the door and took a step, but turned.

"Oh, I forgot, he told me to tell you, this anonymous letter about

Elinor Vance is just some homemade bait that didn't get used. I typed it myself this morning. If you get a chance tonight you can do a sample on my machine and compare."

O'Hara barked ferociously, "Why the hell didn't you say so?"

"I didn't like the way I was asked, Commissioner. The only man I know of more sensitive than me is Nero Wolfe."

XXIV

IT WAS not surprising that Cramer delivered the whole order. Certainly none of those people could have been compelled to go out into the night, and let themselves be conveyed to Nero Wolfe's office, or any place else, without slapping a charge on them, but it doesn't take much compelling when you're in that kind of a fix. They were all there well before midnight.

Wolfe stayed up in his room until they all arrived. I had supposed that while I ate my warmed-over cutlets he would have some questions or instructions for me, and probably both, but no. If he had anything he already had it and needed no contributions from me. He saw to it that my food was hot and my salad crisp and then beat it upstairs.

The atmosphere, as they gathered, was naturally not very genial, but it wasn't so much tense as it was glum. They were simply sunk. As soon as Elinor Vance got onto a chair she rested her elbows on her knees and buried her face in her hands, and stayed that way. Tully Strong folded his arms, let his head sag until his chin met his chest, and shut his eyes. Madeline Fraser sat in the red leather chair, which I got her into before President Anderson arrived, looking first at one of her fellow beings and then at another, but she gave the impression that she merely felt she ought to be conscious of something and they would do as well as anything else.

Bill Meadows, seated near Elinor Vance, was leaning back with his hands clasped behind his head, glaring at the ceiling. Nat Traub was a sight, with his necktie off center, his hair mussed, and his eyes bloodshot. His facial growth was the kind that needs shaving twice a day, and it hadn't had it. He was so restless he couldn't stay in his chair, but when he left it there was no place he wanted to go, so all he could do was sit down again. I did not, on that account, tag him for it, since he had a right to be haggard. A Meltette taken from a box delivered by him had poisoned and killed someone, and it wasn't hard to imagine how his client had reacted to that.

Two conversations were going on. Professor Savarese was telling Purley Stebbins something at length, presumably the latest in formulas, and Purley was making himself an accessory by nodding now and then. Anderson and Owen, the Starlite delegates, were standing by the couch talking with Cramer, and, judging from the snatches I caught, they might finally decide to sit down and they might not. They had been the last to arrive. I, having passed the word to Wolfe that the delivery had been completed, was wondering what was keeping him when I heard the sound of his elevator.

They were so busy with their internal affairs that Traub and I were the only ones who were aware that our host had joined us until he reached the corner of his desk and turned to make a survey. The conversations stopped. Savarese bounded across to shake hands. Elinor Vance lifted her head, showing such a woebegone face that I had to restrain an impulse to take the anonymous letter from my pocket and tear it up then and there. Traub sat down for the twentieth time. Bill Meadows unclasped his hands and pressed his fingertips against his eyes.

President Anderson sputtered, "Since when have you been running the Police Department?"

That's what a big executive is supposed to do, go straight to the point.

Wolfe, getting loose from Savarese, moved to his chair and got himself arranged in it. I guess it's partly his size, unquestionably impressive, which holds people's attention when he is in motion, but his manner and style have a lot to do with it. You get both suspense and surprise. You know he's going to be clumsy and wait to see it, but by gum you never do. First thing you know there he is, in his chair or wherever he was bound for, and there was nothing clumsy about it at all. It was smooth and balanced and efficient.

He looked up at the clock, which said twenty to twelve, and remarked to the audience, "It's late, isn't it?" He regarded the Starlite president. "Let's not start bickering, Mr. Anderson. You weren't dragged here by force, were you? You were impelled either by concern or curiosity. In either case you won't leave until you hear what I have to say, so why not sit down and listen? If you want to be contentious wait until you learn what you have to contend with. It works better that way."

He took in the others. "Perhaps, though, I should answer Mr. Anderson's question, though it was obviously rhetorical. I am not running the Police Department, far from it. I don't know what you were told when you were asked to come here, but I assume you know that nothing I say is backed by any official authority, for I have none. Mr. Cramer and Mr. Stebbins are present as observers. That is correct, Mr. Cramer?"

The inspector, seated on the corner of the couch, nodded. "They understand that."

"Good. Then Mr. Anderson's question was not only rhetorical, it was gibberish. I shall—"

"I have a question!" a voice said, harsh and strained.

"Yes, Mr. Meadows, what is it?"

"If this isn't official, what happens to the notes Goodwin is making?"

"That depends on what we accomplish. They may never leave this house, and end up by being added to the stack in the cellar. Or a transcription of them may be accepted as evidence in a courtroom. I wish you'd sit down, Mr. Savarese. It's more tranquil if everyone is seated."

Wolfe shifted his center of gravity. During his first ten minutes in a chair minor adjustments were always required.

"I should begin," he said with just a trace of peevishness, "by admitting that I am in a highly vulnerable position. I have told Mr. Cramer that when he leaves here he will take a murderer with him; but though I know who the murderer is, I haven't a morsel of evidence against him, and neither has anyone else. Still—"

"Wait a minute," Cramer growled.

Wolfe shook his head. "It's important, Mr. Cramer, to keep this unofficial—until I reach a certain point, if I ever do—so it would be best for you to say nothing whatever." His eyes moved. "I think the best approach is to explain how I learned the identity of the murderer—and by the way, here's an interesting point: though I was already close to certitude, it was clinched for me only two hours ago, when Mr. Goodwin told me that there were sixteen eager candidates for the sponsorship just abandoned by Starlite. That removed my shred of doubt."

"For God's sake," Nat Traub blurted, "let the fine points go! Let's have it!"

"You'll have to be patient, sir," Wolfe reproved him. "I'm not merely reporting, I'm doing a job. Whether a murderer gets arrested, and tried, and convicted, depends entirely on how I handle this. There is no evidence, and if I don't squeeze it out of you people now, tonight, there may never be any. The trouble all along, both for the police and for me, has been that no finger pointed without wavering. In going for a murderer as well concealed as this one it is always necessary to trample down improbabilities to get a path started, but it is foolhardy to do so until a direction is plainly indicated. This time there was no such plain indication, and, frankly, I had begun to doubt if there would be one—until yesterday morning, when Mr. Anderson and Mr. Owen visited this office. They gave it to me."

"You're a liar!" Anderson stated.

"You see?" Wolfe upturned a palm. "Someday, sir, you're going to get on the wrong train by trying to board yours before it arrives. How do you know whether I'm a liar or not until you know what I'm saying? You did come here. You gave me a check for the full amount of my fee, told me that I was no longer in your hire, and said that you had withdrawn as a sponsor of Miss Fraser's program. You gave as your reason for withdrawal that the practice of blackmail had been injected into the case, and you didn't want your product connected in the public mind with blackmail because it is dirty and makes people gag. Isn't that so?"

"Yes. But—"

"I'll do the butting. After you left I sat in this chair twelve straight hours, with intermissions only for meals, using my brain on you. If I had known then that before the day was out sixteen other products were scrambling to take your Starlite's place, I would have reached my conclusion in much less than twelve hours, but I didn't. What I was exploring was the question, what had happened to you? You had been so greedy for publicity that you had even made a trip down here to get into a photograph with me. Now, suddenly, you were fleeing like a comely maiden from a smallpox scare. Why?"

"I told you—"

"I know. But that wasn't good enough. Examined with care, it was actually flimsy. I don't propose to recite all my twistings and windings for those twelve hours, but first of all I rejected the reason you gave.

What, then? I considered every possible circumstance and all conceivable combinations. That you were yourself the murderer and feared I might sniff you out; that you were not the murderer, but the blackmailer; that, yourself innocent, you knew the identity of one of the culprits, or both, and did not wish to be associated with the disclosure; and a thousand others. Upon each and all of my conjectures I brought to bear what I knew of you—your position, your record, your temperament, and your character. At the end only one supposition wholly satisfied me. I concluded that you had somehow become convinced that someone closely connected with that program, which you were sponsoring, had committed the murders, and that there was a possibility that that fact would be discovered. More: I concluded that it was not Miss Koppel or Miss Vance or Mr. Meadows or Mr. Strong, and certainly not Mr. Savarese. It is the public mind that you are anxious about, and in the public mind those people are quite insignificant. Miss Fraser is that program, and that program is Miss Fraser. It could only be her. You knew, or thought you knew, that Miss Fraser herself had killed Mr. Orchard, and possibly Miss Poole too, and you were getting as far away from her as you could as quickly as you could. Your face tells me you don't like that."

"No," Anderson said coldly, "and you won't either before you hear the last of it. You through?"

"Good heavens, no. I've barely started. As I say, I reached that conclusion, but it was nothing to crow about. What was I to do with it? I had a screw I could put on you, but it seemed unwise to be hasty about it, and I considered a trial of other expedients. I confess that the one I chose to begin with was feeble and even sleazy, but it was at breakfast this morning, before I had finished my coffee and got dressed, and Mr. Goodwin was fidgety and I wanted to give him something to do. Also, I had already made a suggestion to Mr. Cramer which was designed to give everyone the impression that there was evidence that Miss Vance had been blackmailed, that she was under acute suspicion, and that she might be charged with murder at any moment. There was a chance, I thought, that an imminent threat to Miss Vance, who is a personable young woman, might impel somebody to talk."

"So you started that," Elinor Vance said dully.

Wolfe nodded. "I'm not boasting about it. I've confessed it was worse than second-rate, but I thought Mr. Cramer might as well try it; and this morning, before I was dressed, I could devise nothing better than for Mr. Goodwin to type an anonymous letter about you and take it up there—a letter which implied that you had committed murder at least twice."

"Goddam pretty," Bill Meadows said.

"He didn't do it," Elinor said.

"Yes, he did," Wolfe disillusioned her. "He had it with him, but didn't get to use it. The death of Miss Koppel was responsible not only for that, but for other things as well—for instance, for this gathering. If I had acted swiftly and energetically on the conclusion I reached twenty-four hours ago, Miss Koppel might be alive now. I owe her an apology but I can't get it to her. What I can do is what I'm doing."

Wolfe's eyes darted to Anderson and fastened there. "I'm going to put that screw on you, sir. I won't waste time appealing to you, in the name of justice or anything else, to tell me why you abruptly turned tail and scuttled. That would be futile. Instead, I'll tell you a homely little fact: Miss Fraser drank Starlite only the first few times it was served on her program, and then had to quit and substitute coffee. She had to quit because your product upset her stomach. It gave her a violent indigestion."

"That's a lie," Anderson said. "Another lie."

"If it is it won't last long. Miss Vance. Some things aren't as important as they once were. You heard what I said. Is it true?"

"Yes."

"Mr. Strong?"

"I don't think this—"

"Confound it, you're in the same room and the same chair! Is it true or not?"

"Yes."

"Mr. Meadows?"

"Yes."

"That should be enough. So, Mr. Anderson—"

"A put-up job," the president sneered. "I left their damn program."

Wolfe shook his head. "They're not missing you. They had their choice of sixteen offers. No, Mr. Anderson, you're in a pickle. Blackmail revolts you, and you're being blackmailed. It is true that newspapers are reluctant to offend advertisers, but some of them couldn't possibly resist so picturesque an item as this, that the product Miss Fraser puffed so effectively to ten million people made her so ill that she didn't dare swallow a spoonful of it. Indeed yes, the papers will print it; and they'll get it in time for Monday morning."

"You sonofabitch." Anderson was holding. "They won't touch it. Will they, Fred?"

But the director of public relations was frozen, speechless with horror.

"I think they will," Wolfe persisted. "One will, I know. And open publication might be better than the sort of talk that would get around when once it's started. You know how rumors get distorted; fools would even say that it wasn't necessary to add anything to Starlite to poison Mr. Orchard. Really, the blackmail potential of this is very high. And what do you have to do to stop it? Something hideous and insupportable? Not at all. Merely tell me why you suddenly decided to scoot."

Anderson looked at Owen, but Owen was gazing fixedly at Wolfe as at the embodiment of evil.

"It will be useless," Wolfe said, "to try any dodge. I'm ready for you. I spent all day yesterday on this, and I doubt very much if I'll accept anything except what I have already specified: that someone or something had persuaded you that Miss Fraser herself was in danger of being exposed as a murderer or a blackmailer. However, you can try."

"I don't have to try." He was a stubborn devil. "I told you yesterday. That was my reason then, and it's my reason now."

"Oh, for God's sake!" Fred Owen wailed. "Oh, my God!"

"Goddam it," Anderson blurted at him. "I gave my word! I'm sewed up! I promised!"

"To whom?" Wolfe snapped.

"All right," Owen said bitterly, "keep your word and lose your shirt. This is ruin! This is dynamite!"

"To whom?" Wolfe persisted.

"I can't tell you, and I won't. That was part of the promise."

"Indeed. Then that makes it simple." Wolfe's eyes darted left. "Mr. Meadows, a hypothetical question. If it was you to whom Mr. Anderson gave the pledge that keeps him from speaking, do you now release him from it?"

"It wasn't me," Bill said.

"I didn't ask you that. You know what a hypothetical question is. Please answer to the if. If it was you, do you release him?"

"Yes. I do."

"Mr. Traub, the same question. With that if, do you release him?"

"Yes."

"Miss Vance? Do you?"

"Yes."

"Mr. Strong. Do you?"

Of course Tully Strong had had time, a full minute, to make up his mind what to say. He said it.

"No!"

XXV

ELEVEN pairs of eyes fastened on Tully Strong.

"Aha," Wolfe muttered. He leaned back, sighed deep, and looked pleased.

"Remarkable!" a voice boomed. It was Professor Savarese. "So simple!"

If he expected to pull some of the eyes his way, he got cheated. They stayed on Strong.

"That was a piece of luck," Wolfe said, "and I'm grateful for it. If I had started with you, Mr. Strong, and got your no, the others might have made it not so simple."

"I answered a hypothetical question," Tully asserted, "and that's all. It doesn't mean anything."

"Correct," Wolfe agreed. "In logic, it doesn't. But I saw your face when you realized what was coming, the dilemma you would be confronted with in a matter of seconds, and that was enough. Do you now hope to retreat into logic?"

Tully just wasn't up to it. Not only had his face been enough when he saw it coming; it was still enough. The muscles around his thin, tight lips quivered as he issued the command to let words through.

"I merely answered a hypothetical question," was the best he could do. It was pathetic.

Wolfe sighed again. "Well. I suppose I'll have to light it for you. I don't blame you, sir, for being obstinate about it, since it may be assumed that you have behaved badly. I don't mean your withholding information from the police; most people do that, and often for reasons much shoddier than yours. I mean your behavior to your employers. Since you are paid by the eight sponsors jointly your loyalty to them is indivisible; but you did not warn all of them that Miss Fraser was, or might be, headed for disgrace and disaster, and that therefore they had better clear out; apparently you confined it to Mr. Anderson. For value received or to be received, I presume—a good job?"

Wolfe shrugged. "But now it's all up." His eyes moved. "By the way, Archie, since Mr. Strong will soon be telling us how he knew it was Miss Fraser, you'd better take a look. She's capable of anything, and she's as deft as a bear's tongue. Look in her bag."

Cramer was on his feet. "I'm not going—"

"I didn't ask you," Wolfe snapped. "Confound it, don't you see how ticklish this is? I'm quite aware I've got no evidence yet, but I'm not going to have that woman displaying her extraordinary dexterity in my office. Archie?"

I had left my chair and stepped to the other end of Wolfe's desk, but I was in a rather embarrassing position. I am not incapable of using force on a woman, since after all men have never found anything else to use on them with any great success when it comes right down to it, but Wolfe had by no means worked up to a point where the audience was with me. And when I extended a hand toward the handsome leather bag in Madeline Fraser's lap, she gave me the full force of her gray-green eyes and told me distinctly, "Don't touch me."

I brought the hand back. Her eyes went to Wolfe.

"Don't you think it's about time I said something? Wouldn't it look better?"

"No." Wolfe met her gaze. "I'd advise you to wait, madam. All you can give us now is a denial, and of course we'll stipulate that. What else can you say?"

"I wouldn't bother with a denial," she said scornfully. "But it seems stupid for me to sit here and let this go on indefinitely."

"Not at all." Wolfe leaned toward her. "Let me assure you of one thing, Miss Fraser, most earnestly. It is highly unlikely, whatever you say or do from now on, that I shall ever think you stupid. I am too well convinced of the contrary. Not even if Mr. Goodwin opens your bag and finds in it the gun with which Miss Poole was shot."

"He isn't going to open it."

She seemed to know what she was talking about. I glanced at Inspector Cramer, but the big stiff wasn't ready yet to move a finger. I picked up the little table that was always there by the arm of the red leather chair, moved it over to the wall, went and brought one of the small yellow chairs, and sat, so close to Madeline Fraser that if we had spread elbows they would have touched. That meant no more notes, but Wolfe couldn't have everything. As I sat down by her, putting in motion the air that had been there undisturbed, I got a faint whiff of a spicy perfume, and my imagination must have been pretty active because I was reminded of the odor that had reached me that day in her apartment, from the breath of Deborah Koppel as I tried to get her onto the divan before she collapsed. It wasn't the same at all except in my fancy. I asked Wolfe, "This will do, won't it?"

He nodded and went back to Tully Strong. "So you have not one reason for reluctance, but several. Even so, you can't possibly stick it. It has been clearly demonstrated to Mr. Cramer that you are withholding important information directly pertinent to the crimes he is investigating, and you and others have already pushed his patience pretty far. He'll get his teeth in you now and he won't let go. Then there's Mr. Anderson. The promise he gave you is half gone, now that we know it was you he gave it to, and with the threat I'm holding over him he can't reasonably be expected to keep the other half."

Wolfe gestured. "And all I really need is a detail. I am satisfied that I know pretty well what you told Mr. Anderson. What happened yesterday, just before he took alarm and leaped to action? The morning papers had the story of the anonymous letters—the blackmailing device by which people were constrained to make payments to Mr. Orchard and Miss Poole. Then that story had supplied a missing link for someone. Who and how? Say it was Mr. Anderson. Say that he received, some weeks ago, an anonymous letter or letters blackguarding Miss Fraser. He showed them to her. He received no more letters. That's all he knew about it. A little later Mr. Orchard was a guest on the Fraser program and got poisoned, but there was no reason for Mr. Anderson to connect that event with the anonymous letters he had received. That was what the story in yesterday's papers did for him; they made that connection. It was now perfectly plain: anonymous letters about Miss Fraser; Miss Fraser's subscription to *Track Almanac*; the method by which those subscriptions were obtained; and Mr. Orchard's death by drinking poisoned coffee ostensibly intended for Miss Fraser. That did not convict Miss Fraser of murder, but at a minimum it made it extremely inadvisable to continue in the role of her sponsor. So Mr. Anderson skedaddled."

"I got no anonymous letters," Anderson declared.

"I believe you." Wolfe didn't look away from Tully Strong. "I rejected, tentatively, the assumption that Mr. Anderson had himself received the anonymous letters, on various grounds, but chiefly because it would be out of character for him to show an anonymous letter to the subject of it. He would be much more likely to have the letter's allegations investigated, and there was good reason to assume that that had not been done. So I postulated that it was not Mr. Anderson, but some other person, who had once received an anonymous letter or letters about Miss Fraser and who was yesterday provided with a missing link. It was a permissible guess that that person was one of those now present, and so I tried the experiment of having the police insinuate an imminent threat to Miss Vance, in the hope that it would loosen a tongue. I was too cautious. It failed lamentably; and Miss Koppel died."

Wolfe was talking only to Strong. "Of course, having no evidence, I have no certainty that the information you gave Mr. Anderson concerned anonymous letters. It is possible that your conviction, or suspicion, about Miss Fraser, had some other basis. But I like my assumption because it is neat and comprehensive; and I shall abandon it only under compulsion. It explains everything, and nothing contradicts it. It will even explain, I confidently expect, why Mr. Orchard and Miss Poole were killed. Two of the finer points of their operation were these, that they demanded only a small fraction of the victim's income, limited to one year, and that the letters did not expose, or threaten to expose, an actual secret in the victim's past. Even if they had known such secrets they would not have used them. But sooner or later—this is a point on which Mr. Savarese could speak with the authority of an expert, but not now, some other time—sooner or later, by the law of averages, they would use such a secret by inadvertence. Sooner or later the bugaboo they invented would be, for the victim, not a mischievous libel, but a real and most dreadful terror."

Wolfe nodded. "Yes. So it happened. The victim was shown the letter or letters by some friend—by you, Mr. Strong—and found herself confronted not merely by the necessity of paying an inconsequential tribute, but by the awful danger of some disclosure that was not to be borne; for she could not know, of course, that the content of the letter had been fabricated and that its agreement with reality was sheer accident. So she acted. Indeed, she acted! She killed Mr. Orchard. Then she learned, from a strange female voice on the phone, that Mr. Orchard had not been the sole possessor of the knowledge she thought he had, and again she acted. She killed Miss Poole."

"My God," Anderson cut in, "you're certainly playing it strong, with no cards."

"I am, sir," Wolfe agreed. "It's time I got dealt to, don't you think? Surely I've earned at least one card. You can give it to me, or Mr. Strong can. What more do you want, for heaven's sake? Rabbits from a hat?"

Anderson got up, moved, and was confronting the secretary of the Sponsors' Council. "Don't be a damn fool, Tully," he said with harsh authority. "He knows it all, you heard him. Go ahead and get rid of it!"

"This is swell for me," Tully said bitterly.

"It would have been swell for Miss Koppel," Wolfe said curtly, "if you had spoken twenty hours ago. How many letters did you get?"

"Two."

"When?"

"February. Around the middle of February."

"Did you show them to anyone besides Miss Fraser?"

"No, just her, but Miss Koppel was there so she saw them too."

"Where are they now?"

"I don't know. I gave them to Miss Fraser."

"What did they say?"

Tully's lips parted, stayed open a moment, and closed again.

"Don't be an ass," Wolfe snapped. "Mr. Anderson is here. What did they say?"

"They said that it was lucky for Miss Fraser that when her husband died no one had been suspicious enough to have the farewell letters he wrote examined by a handwriting expert."

"What else?"

"That was all. The second one said the same thing, only in a different way."

Wolfe's eyes darted to Anderson. "Is that what he told you, sir?"

The president, who had returned to the couch, nodded. "Yes, that's it. Isn't it enough?"

"Plenty, in the context." Wolfe's head jerked around to face the lady at my elbow. "Miss Fraser. I've heard of only one farewell letter your husband wrote, to a friend, a local attorney. Was there another? To you, perhaps?"

"I don't think," she said, "that it would be very sensible for me to try to help you." I couldn't detect the slightest difference in her voice. Wolfe had understated it when he said she was an extremely dangerous woman. "Especially," she went on, "since you are apparently accepting those lies. If Mr. Strong ever got any anonymous letters he never showed them to me—nor to Miss Koppel, I'm sure of that."

"I'll be damned!" Tully Strong cried, and his specs fell off as he gawked at her.

It was marvelous, and it certainly showed how Madeline Fraser got people. Tully had been capable of assuming that she had killed a couple of guys, but when he heard her come out with what he knew to be a downright lie he was flabbergasted.

Wolfe nodded at her. "I suppose," he admitted, "it would be hopeless to expect you to be anything but sensible. You are aware that there is still no evidence, except Mr. Strong's word against yours. Obviously the best chance is the letter your husband wrote to his friend, since the threat that aroused your ferocity concerned it." His face left us, to the right. "Do you happen to know, Mr. Cramer, whether that letter still exists?"

Cramer was right up with him. He had gone to the phone on my desk and was dialing. In a moment he spoke. "Dixon there? Put him on. Dixon? I'm at Wolfe's office. Yeah, he's got it, but by the end of the tail. Two things quick. Get Darst and have him phone Fleetville, Michigan. He was out there and knows 'em. Before Lawrence Koppel died he wrote a letter to a friend. We want to know if that letter still exists and where it is, and they're to get it if they can and keep it, but for God's sake don't scare the friend into burning it or eating it. Tell Darst it's so important it's the whole case. Then get set with a warrant for an all-day job on the Fraser woman's apartment. What we're looking for is cyanide, and it can be anywhere—the heel of a shoe, for instance. You know the men to get—only the best. Wolfe got it by the tail with one of his crazy dives into a two-foot tank, and now we've got to hang onto it. What? Yes, damn it, of course it's her! Step on it!"

He hung up, crossed to me, thumbed me away, moved the chair aside, and stood by Miss Fraser's chair, gazing down at her. Keeping his gaze where it was, he rumbled, "You might talk a little more, Wolfe."

"I could talk all night," Wolfe declared. "Miss Fraser is worth it. She had good luck, but most of the bad luck goes to the fumblers, and she is no fumbler. Her husband's death must have been managed with great skill, not so much because she gulled the authorities, which may have been no great feat, but because she completely deceived her husband's sister, Miss Koppel. The whole operation with Mr. Orchard was well conceived and executed, with the finest subtlety in even the lesser details—for instance, having the subscription in Miss Koppel's name. It was simple to phone Mr. Orchard that that money came from her, Miss Fraser. But best of all was the climax—getting the poisoned coffee served to the intended victim. That was one of her pieces of luck, since apparently Mr. Traub, who didn't know about the taped bottle, innocently put it in front of Mr. Orchard, but she would have managed without it. At that narrow table, with Mr. Orchard just across from her, and with the broadcast going on, she could have manipulated it with no difficulty, and probably without anyone becoming aware of any manipulation. Certainly without arousing any suspicion of intent, before or after."

"Okay," Cramer conceded. "That doesn't worry me. And the Poole thing doesn't either, since there's nothing against it. But the Koppel woman?"

Wolfe nodded. "That was the masterpiece. Miss Fraser had in her favor, certainly, years of intimacy during which she had gained Miss Koppel's unquestioning loyalty, affection, and trust. They held steadfast even when Miss Koppel saw the anonymous letters Mr. Strong had received. It is quite possible that she received similar letters herself. We don't know, and never will, I suppose, what finally gave birth to the worm of suspicion in Miss Koppel. It wasn't the newspaper story of the anonymous letters and blackmailing, since that appeared yesterday, Friday, and it was on Wednesday that Miss Koppel tried to take an airplane to Michigan. We may now assume, since we know that she had seen the anonymous letters, that something had made her suspicious enough to want to inspect the farewell letter her brother had sent to his friend, and we may certainly assume that Miss Fraser, when she learned what her dearest and closest friend had tried to do, knew why."

"That's plain enough," Cramer said impatiently. "What I mean—"

"I know. You mean what I meant when I said it was a masterpiece. It took resourcefulness, first-rate improvisation, and ingenuity to make use of the opportunity offered by Mr. Traub's delivery of the box of Meltettes; and only a maniacal stoicism could have left those deadly tidbits there on the piano where anybody might casually have eaten one. Probably inquiry would show that it was not as haphazard as it seems; that it was generally known that the box was there to be sampled by Miss Fraser and therefore no one would loot it. But the actual performance, as Mr. Goodwin described it to me, was faultless. There was then no danger to a bystander, for if anyone but Miss Koppel had started to eat one of the things Miss Fraser could easily have prevented it. If the box had been handed to Miss Fraser, she could either have postponed the sampling or have taken one from the second layer instead of the top. What chance was there that Miss Koppel would eat one of the things? One in five, one in a thousand? Anyway, she played for that chance, and again she had luck; but it was not all luck, and she performed superbly."

"This is incredible," Madeline Fraser said. "I knew I was strong, but I didn't know I could do this. Only a few hours ago my dearest friend Debby died in my arms. I should be with her, sitting with her through the night, but here I am, sitting here, listening to this—this nightmare—"

"Cut," Bill Meadows said harshly. "Night and nightmare. Cut one."

The gray-green eyes darted at him. "So you're ratting, are you, Bill?"

"Yes, I'm ratting. I saw Debby die. And I think he's got it. I think you killed her."

"Bill!" It was Elinor Vance, breaking. "Bill, I can't stand it!" She was on her feet, shaking all over. "I can't!"

Bill put his arms around her, tight. "All right, kid. I hope to God she gets it. You were there too. What if you had decided to eat one?"

The phone rang and I got it. It was for Cramer. Purley went and replaced him beside Miss Fraser, and he came to the phone. When he hung up he told Wolfe, "Koppel's friend still has that letter, and it's safe."

"Good," Wolfe said approvingly. "Will you please get her out of here? I've been wanting beer for an hour, and I'm not foolhardy enough to eat or drink anything with her in the house." He looked around. "The rest of you are invited to stay if you care to. You must be thirsty."

But they didn't like it there. They went.

XXVI

THE EXPERTS were enthusiastic about the letter Lawrence Koppel had written to his friend. They called it one of the cleverest forgeries they had ever seen. But what pleased Wolfe most was the finding of the cyanide. It was in the hollowed-out heel of a house slipper, and was evidently the leavings of the supply Mrs. Lawrence Koppel had snitched six years ago from her husband's shelf.

It was May eighteenth that she was sentenced on her conviction for the first-degree murder of Deborah Koppel. They had decided that was the best one to try her for. The next day, a Wednesday, a little before noon, Wolfe and I were in the office, checking over catalogues, when the phone rang. I went to my desk for it.

"Nero Wolfe's office, Archie Goodwin speaking."

"May I speak to Mr. Wolfe, please?"

"Who is it?"

"Tell him a personal matter."

I covered the transmitter. "Personal matter," I told Wolfe. "A man whose name I have forgotten."

"What the devil! Ask him."

"A man," I said distinctly, "whose name I have forgotten."

"Oh." He frowned. He finished checking an item and then picked up the phone on his desk, while I stayed with mine. "This is Nero Wolfe."

"I would know the voice anywhere. How are you?"

"Well, thank you. Do I know you?"

"Yes. I am calling to express my appreciation of your handling of the Fraser case, now that it's over. I am pleased and thought you should know it. I have been, and still am, a little annoyed, but I am satisfied that you are not responsible. I have good sources of information. I congratulate you on keeping your investigation within the limits I prescribed. That has increased my admiration of you."

"I like to be admired," Wolfe said curtly. "But when I undertake an investigation I permit prescription of limits only by the requirements of the job. If that job had taken me across your path you would have found me there."

"Then that is either my good fortune—or yours."

The connection went.

I grinned at Wolfe. "He's an abrupt bastard."

Wolfe grunted. I returned to my post at the end of his desk and picked up my pencil.

"One little idea," I suggested. "Why not give Dr. Michaels a ring and ask if anyone has phoned to switch his subscription? No, that won't do, he's paid up. Marie Leconne?"

"No. I invite trouble only when I'm paid for it. And to grapple with him the pay would have to be high."

"Okay." I checked an item. "You'd be a problem in a foxhole, but the day may come."

"It may. I hope not. Have you any Zygopetalum crinitum on that page?"

"Good God no. It begins with a Z!"

CURTAINS FOR THREE

THE GUN WITH WINGS

I

THE YOUNG woman took a pink piece of paper from her handbag, got up from the red leather chair, put the paper on Nero Wolfe's desk, and sat down again. Feeling it my duty to keep myself informed and also to save Wolfe the exertion of leaning forward and reaching so far, I arose and crossed to hand the paper to him after a glance at it. It was a check for five thousand dollars, dated that day, August fourteenth, made out to him, and signed Margaret Mion. He gave a look and dropped it back on the desk.

"I thought," she said, "perhaps that would be the best way to start the conversation."

In my chair at my desk, taking her in, I was readjusting my attitude. When, early that Sunday afternoon, she had phoned for an appointment, I had dug up a vague recollection of a picture of her in the paper some months back, and had decided it would be no treat to meet her, but now I was hedging. Her appeal wasn't what she had, which was only so-so, but what she did with it. I don't mean tricks. Her mouth wasn't attractive even when she smiled, but the smile was. Her eyes were just a pair of brown eyes, nothing at all sensational, but it was a pleasure to watch them move around, from Wolfe to me to the man who had come with her, seated off to her left. I guessed she had maybe three years to go to reach thirty.

"Don't you think," the man asked her, "we should get some questions answered first?"

His tone was strained and a little harsh, and his face matched it. He was worried and didn't care who knew it. With his deep-set gray eyes and well-fitted jaw he might on a happier day have passed for a leader of men, but not as he now sat. Something was eating him. When Mrs. Mion had introduced him as Mr. Frederick Weppler I had recognized the name of the music critic of the *Gazette*, but I couldn't remember whether he had been mentioned in the newspaper accounts of the event that had caused the publication of Mrs. Mion's picture.

She shook her head at him, not arbitrarily. "It wouldn't help, Fred, really. We'll just have to tell it and see what he says." She smiled at Wolfe—or maybe it wasn't actually a smile, but just her way of handling her lips. "Mr. Weppler wasn't quite sure we should come to see you, and I had to persuade him. Men are more cautious than women, aren't they?"

"Yes," Wolfe agreed, and added, "Thank heaven."

She nodded. "I suppose so." She gestured. "I brought that check with me to show that we really mean it. We're in trouble and we want you to get us out. We want to get married and we can't. That is—if I should just speak for myself—I want to marry him." She looked at Weppler, and this time it was unquestionably a smile. "Do you want to marry me, Fred?"

"Yes," he muttered. Then he suddenly jerked his chin up and looked defiantly at Wolfe. "You understand this is embarrassing, don't you? It's none of your business, but we've come to get your help. I'm thirty-four years old, and this is the first time I've ever been—" He stopped. In a moment he said stiffly, "I am in love with Mrs. Mion and I want to marry her more than I have ever wanted anything in my life." His eyes went to his love and he murmured a plea. "Peggy!"

Wolfe grunted. "I accept that as proven. You both want to get married. Why don't you?"

"Because we can't," Peggy said. "We simply can't. It's on account —you may remember reading about my husband's death in April, four months ago? Alberto Mion, the opera singer?"

"Vaguely. You'd better refresh my memory."

"Well, he died—he killed himself." There was no sign of a smile now. "Fred—Mr. Weppler and I found him. It was seven o'clock, a Tuesday evening in April, at our apartment on East End Avenue. Just that afternoon Fred and I had found out that we loved each other, and—"

"Peggy!" Weppler called sharply.

Her eyes darted to him and back to Wolfe. "Perhaps I should ask you, Mr. Wolfe. He thinks we should tell you just enough so you understand the problem, and I think you can't understand it unless we tell you everything. What do you think?"

"I can't say until I hear it. Go ahead. If I have questions, we'll see."

She nodded. "I imagine you'll have plenty of questions. Have you ever been in love but would have died rather than let anyone see it?"

"Never," Wolfe said emphatically. I kept my face straight.

"Well, I was, and I admit it. But no one knew it, not even him. Did you, Fred?"

"I did not." Weppler was emphatic too.

"Until that afternoon," Peggy told Wolfe. "He was at the apartment for lunch, and it happened right after lunch. The others had left, and all of a sudden we were looking at each other, and then he spoke or I did, I don't know which." She looked at Weppler imploringly. "I know you think this is embarrassing, Fred, but if he doesn't know what it was like he won't understand why you went upstairs to see Alberto."

"Does he have to?" Weppler demanded.

"Of course he does." She returned to Wolfe. "I suppose I can't make you see what it was like. We were completely—well, we were in love, that's all, and I guess we had been for quite a while without saying it, and that made it all the more—more overwhelming. Fred wanted to see my husband right away, to tell him about it and decide what we could do, and I said all right, so he went upstairs—"

"Upstairs?"

"Yes, it's a duplex, and upstairs was my husband's soundproofed studio, where he practiced. So he went—"

"Please, Peggy," Weppler interrupted her. His eyes went to Wolfe. "You should have it firsthand. I went up to tell Mion that I loved his wife, and she loved me and not him, and to ask him to be civilized about it. Getting a divorce has come to be regarded as fairly civilized, but he didn't see it that way. He was anything but civilized. He wasn't violent, but he was damned mean. After some of that I got afraid I might do to him what Gif James had done, and I left. I didn't want to go back to Mrs. Mion while I was in that state of mind, so I left the studio by the door to the upper hall and took the elevator there."

He stopped.

"And?" Wolfe prodded him.

"I walked it off. I walked across to the park, and after a while I had calmed down and I phoned Mrs. Mion, and she met me in the park. I told her what Mion's attitude was, and I asked her to leave him and come with me. She wouldn't do that." Weppler paused, and then went on, "There are two complications you ought to have if you're to have everything."

"If they're relevant, yes."

"They're relevant all right. First, Mrs. Mion had and has money of her own. That was an added attraction for Mion. It wasn't for me. I'm just telling you."

"Thank you. And the second?"

"The second was Mrs. Mion's reason for not leaving Mion immediately. I suppose you know he had been the top tenor at the Met for five or six years, and his voice was gone—temporarily. Gifford James, the baritone, had hit him on the neck with his fist and hurt his larynx—that was early in March—and Mion couldn't finish the season. It had been operated, but his voice hadn't come back, and naturally he was glum, and Mrs. Mion wouldn't leave him under those circumstances. I tried to persuade her to, but she wouldn't. I wasn't anything like normal that day, on account of what had happened to me for the first time in my life, and on account of what Mion had said to me, so I wasn't reasonable and I left her in the park and went downtown to a bar and started drinking. A lot of time went by and I had quite a few, but I wasn't pickled. Along toward seven o'clock I decided I had to see her again and carry her off so she wouldn't spend another night there. That mood took me back to East End Avenue and up to the twelfth floor, and then I stood there in the hall a while, perhaps ten minutes, before my finger went to the pushbutton. Finally I rang, and the maid let me in and went for Mrs. Mion, but I had lost my nerve or something. All I did was suggest that we should have a talk with Mion together. She agreed, and we went upstairs and—"

"Using the elevator?"

"No, the stairs inside the apartment. We entered the studio. Mion was on the floor. We went over to him. There was a big hole through the top of his head. He was dead. I led Mrs. Mion out, made her come, and on the stairs—they're too narrow to go two abreast—she fell and rolled halfway down. I carried her to her room and put her on her bed, and I started for the living room, for the phone there, when I thought of something to do first. I went out and took the elevator to the ground floor, got the doorman and elevator man together, and asked them who had been taken up to the Mion apartment, either the twelfth floor or the thirteenth, that afternoon. I said they must be damn sure not to skip anybody. They gave me the names and I wrote them down. Then I went back up to the apartment and phoned the police. After I did that it struck me that a layman isn't supposed to decide if a man is dead, so I phoned Dr. Lloyd, who has an apartment there in the building. He came at once, and I took him up to the studio. We hadn't been there more than three or four minutes when the first policeman came, and of course—"

"If you please," Wolfe put in crossly. "Everything is sometimes too much. You haven't even hinted at the trouble you're in."

"I'll get to it—"

"But faster, I hope, if I help. My memory has been jogged. The doctor and the police pronounced him dead. The muzzle of the revolver had been thrust into his mouth, and the emerging bullet had torn out a piece of his skull. The revolver, found lying on the floor beside him, belonged to him and was kept there in the studio. There was no sign of any struggle and no mark of any other injury on him. The loss of his voice was an excellent motive for suicide. Therefore, after a routine investigation, giving due weight to the difficulty of sticking the barrel of a loaded revolver into a man's mouth without arousing him to protest, it was recorded as suicide. Isn't that correct?"

They both said yes.

"Have the police reopened it? Or is gossip at work?"

They both said no.

"Then let's get on. Where's the trouble?"

"It's us," Peggy said.

"Why? What's wrong with you?"

"Everything." She gestured. "No, I don't mean that—not everything, just one thing. After my husband's death and the—the routine investigation, I went away for a while. When I came back—for the past two months Fred and I have been together some, but it wasn't right—I mean we didn't feel right. Day before yesterday, Friday, I went to friends in Connecticut for the weekend, and he was there. Neither of us knew the other was coming. We talked it out yesterday and last night and this morning, and we decided to come and ask you to help us—anyway, I did, and he wouldn't let me come alone."

Peggy leaned forward and was in deadly earnest. "You *must* help us, Mr. Wolfe. I love him so much—so much!—and he says he loves me, and I know he does! Yesterday afternoon we decided we would get married in October, and then last night we got started talking—but it isn't what we say, it's what is in our eyes when we look at each other. We just can't get married with that back of our eyes and trying to hide it—"

A little shiver went over her. "For years—forever? We can't! We know we can't—it would be horrible! What it is, it's a question: who killed Alberto? Did he? Did I? I don't really think he did, and he doesn't really think I did—I hope he doesn't—but it's there back of our eyes, and we know it is!"

She extended both hands. "We want you to find out!"

Wolfe snorted. "Nonsense. You need a spanking or a psychiatrist. The police may have shortcomings, but they're not nincompoops. If they're satisfied—"

"But that's it! They wouldn't be satisfied if we had told the truth!"

"Oh." Wolfe's brows went up. "You lied to them?"

"Yes. Or if we didn't lie, anyhow we didn't tell them the truth. We didn't tell them that when we first went in together and saw him, there was no gun lying there. There was no gun in sight."

"Indeed. How sure are you?"

"Absolutely positive. I never saw anything clearer than I saw that— that sight—all of it. There was no gun."

Wolfe snapped at Weppler, "You agree, sir?"

"Yes. She's right."

Wolfe sighed. "Well," he conceded, "I can see that you're really in trouble. Spanking wouldn't help."

I shifted in my chair on account of a tingle at the lower part of my spine. Nero Wolfe's old brownstone house on West Thirty-fifth Street was an interesting place to live and work—for Fritz Brenner, the chef and housekeeper, for Theodore Horstmann, who fed and nursed the ten thousand orchids in the plant rooms up on the roof, and for me, Archie Goodwin, whose main field of operations was the big office on the ground floor. Naturally I thought my job the most interesting, since a confidential assistant to a famous private detective is constantly getting an earful of all kinds of troubles and problems—everything from a missing necklace to a new blackmail gimmick. Very few clients actually bored me. But only one kind of case gave me that tingle in the spine: murder. And if this pair of lovebirds were talking straight, this was it.

II

I HAD filled two notebooks when they left, more than two hours later.

If they had thought it through before they phoned for an appointment with Wolfe, they wouldn't have phoned. All they wanted, as Wolfe pointed out, was the moon. They wanted him, first, to investigate a four-month-old murder without letting on there had been one; second, to prove that neither of them had killed Alberto Mion, which could be done only by finding out who had; and third, in case he concluded that one of them had done it, to file it away and forget it. Not that they put it that way, since their story was that they were both absolutely innocent, but that was what it amounted to.

Wolfe made it good and plain. "If I take the job," he told them, "and find evidence to convict someone of murder, no matter who, the use I make of it will be solely in my discretion. I am neither an Astraea nor a sadist, but I like my door open. But if you want to drop it now, here's your check, and Mr. Goodwin's notebooks will be destroyed. We can forget you have been here, and shall."

That was one of the moments when they were within an ace of getting up and going, especially Fred Weppler, but they didn't. They looked at each other, and it was all in their eyes. By that time I had about decided I liked them both pretty well and was even beginning to admire them, they were so damn determined to get loose from the trap they were in. When they looked at each other like that their eyes said, "Let's go and be together, my darling love, and forget this—come on, come on." Then they said, "It will be so wonderful!" Then they said, "Yes, oh yes, but— But we don't want it wonderful for a day or a week; it must be always wonderful—and we know . . ."

It took strong muscles to hold onto it like that, not to mention horse sense, and several times I caught myself feeling sentimental about it. Then of course there was the check for five grand on Wolfe's desk.

The notebooks were full of assorted matters. There were a thousand details which might or might not turn out to be pertinent, such as the mutual dislike between Peggy Mion and Rupert Grove, her husband's manager, or the occasion of Gifford James socking Alberto Mion in front of witnesses, or the attitudes of various persons toward

Mion's demand for damages; but you couldn't use it all, and Wolfe himself never needed more than a fraction of it, so I'll pick and choose. Of course the gun was Exhibit A. It was a new one, having been bought by Mion the day after Gifford James had plugged him and hurt his larynx—not, he had announced, for vengeance on James but for future protection. He had carried it in a pocket whenever he went out, and at home had kept it in the studio, lying on the base of a bust of Caruso. So far as known, it had never fired but one bullet, the one that killed Mion.

When Dr. Lloyd had arrived and Weppler had taken him to the studio the gun was lying on the floor not far from Mion's knee. Dr. Lloyd's hand had started for it but had been withdrawn without touching it, so it had been there when the law came. Peggy was positive it had not been there when she and Fred had entered, and he agreed. The cops had made no announcement about fingerprints, which wasn't surprising since none are hardly ever found on a gun that are any good. Throughout the two hours and a half, Wolfe kept darting back to the gun, but it simply didn't have wings.

The picture of the day and the day's people was all filled in. The morning seemed irrelevant, so it started at lunch time with five of them there: Mion, Peggy, Fred, one Adele Bosley, and Dr. Lloyd. It was more professional than social. Fred had been invited because Mion wanted to sell him the idea of writing a piece for the *Gazette* saying that the rumors that Mion would never be able to sing again were malicious hooey. Adele Bosley, who was in charge of public relations for the Metropolitan Opera, had come to help work on Fred. Dr. Lloyd had been asked so he could assure Weppler that the operation he had performed on Mion's larynx had been successful and it was a good bet that by the time the opera season opened in November the great tenor would be as good as ever. Nothing special had happened except that Fred had agreed to do the piece. Adele Bosley and Lloyd had left, and Mion had gone up to the soundproofed studio, and Fred and Peggy had looked at each other and suddenly discovered the most important fact of life since the Garden of Eden.

An hour or so later there had been another gathering, this time up in the studio, around half-past three, but neither Fred nor Peggy had been present. By then Fred had walked himself calm and phoned Peggy, and she had gone to meet him in the park, so their information on the meeting in the studio was hearsay. Besides Mion and Dr. Lloyd there had been four people: Adele Bosley for operatic public relations; Mr. Rupert Grove, Mion's manager; Mr. Gifford James, the baritone who had socked Mion in the neck six weeks previously; and Judge Henry Arnold, James' lawyer. This affair had been even less social than the lunch, having been arranged to discuss a formal request that Mion had made of Gifford James for the payment of a quarter of a million bucks for the damage to Mion's larynx.

Fred's and Peggy's hearsay had it that the conference had been fairly hot at points, with the temperature boosted right at the beginning by Mion's getting the gun from Caruso's bust and placing it on a table at his elbow. On the details of its course they were pretty sketchy, since they hadn't been there, but anyhow the gun hadn't been fired. Also there was plenty of evidence that Mion was alive and well—except for his larynx—when the party broke up. He had made two phone calls after the conference had ended, one to his barber and one to a wealthy female opera patron; his manager, Rupert Grove, had phoned him a little later; and around five-thirty he had phoned downstairs to the maid to bring him a bottle of vermouth and some ice, which she had done. She had taken the tray into the studio, and he had been upright and intact.

I was careful to get all the names spelled right in my notebook, since it seemed likely the job would be to get one of them tagged for murder, and I was especially careful with the last one that got in: Clara James, Gifford's daughter. There were three spotlights on her. First, the reason for James' assault on Mion had been his knowledge or suspicion—Fred and Peggy weren't sure which—that Mion had stepped over the line with James' daughter. Second, her name had ended the list, got by Fred from the doorman and elevator man, of people who had called that afternoon. They said she had come about a quarter past six and had got off at the floor the studio was on, the thirteenth, and had summoned the elevator to the twelfth floor a little later, maybe ten minutes, and had left. The third spotlight was directed by Peggy, who had stayed in the park a while after Fred had marched off, and had then returned home, arriving around five o'clock. She had not gone up to the studio and had not seen her husband. Sometime after six, she thought around half-past, she had answered the doorbell herself because the maid had been in the kitchen with the cook. It was Clara James. She was pale and tense, but she was always pale and tense. She had asked for Alberto, and Peggy had said she thought he was up in the studio, and Clara had said no, he wasn't there, and never mind. When Clara went for the elevator button, Peggy had shut the door, not wanting company anyway, and particularly not Clara James.

Some half an hour later Fred showed up, and they ascended to the studio together and found that Alberto was there all right, but no longer upright or intact.

That picture left room for a whole night of questions, but Wolfe concentrated on what he regarded as the essentials. Even so, we went into the third hour and the third notebook. He completely ignored some spots that I thought needed filling in: for instance, had Alberto had a habit of stepping over the line with other men's daughters and/or wives, and if so, names please. From things they said I gathered that Alberto had been broad-minded about other men's women, but apparently Wolfe wasn't interested. Along toward the end he was back on the gun again, and when they had nothing new to offer he scowled and got caustic. When they stayed glued he finally snapped at them, "Which one of you is lying?"

They looked hurt. "That won't get you anywhere," Fred Weppler said bitterly, "or us either."

"It would be silly," Peggy Mion protested, "to come here and give you that check and then lie to you. Wouldn't it?"

"Then you're silly," Wolfe said coldly. He pointed a finger at her. "Look here. All of this might be worked out, none of it is preposterous, except one thing. Who put the gun on the floor beside the body? When you two entered the studio it wasn't there; you both swear to that, and I accept it. You left and started downstairs; you fell, and he carried you to your room. You weren't unconscious. Were you?"

"No." Peggy was meeting his gaze. "I could have walked, but he—he wanted to carry me."

"No doubt. He did so. You stayed in your room. He went to the ground floor to compile a list of those who had made themselves available as murder suspects—showing admirable foresight, by the way—came back up and phoned the police and then the doctor, who arrived without delay since he lived in the building. Not more than fifteen minutes intervened between the moment you and Mr. Weppler left the studio and the moment he and the doctor entered. The door from the studio to the public hall on the thirteenth floor has a lock that is automatic with the closing of the door, and the door was closed and locked. No one could possibly have entered during that fifteen minutes. You say that you had left your bed and gone to the living room, and that no one could have used that route without being seen by you. The maid and cook were in the kitchen, unaware of what was going on. So no one entered the studio and placed the gun on the floor."

"Someone did," Fred said doggedly.

Peggy insisted, "We don't know who had a key."

"You said that before." Wolfe was at them now. "Even if everyone had keys, I don't believe it and neither would anyone else." His eyes came to me. "Archie. Would you?"

"I'd have to see a movie of it," I admitted.

"You see?" he demanded of them. "Mr. Goodwin isn't prejudiced against you—on the contrary. He's ready to fight fire for you; see how he gets behind on his notes for the pleasure of watching you look at each other. But he agrees with me that you're lying. Since no one else could have put the gun on the floor, one of you did. I have to know about it. The circumstances may have made it imperative for you, or you thought they did."

He looked at Fred. "Suppose you opened a drawer of Mrs. Mion's dresser to get smelling salts, and the gun was there, with an odor showing it had been recently fired—put there, you would instantly conjecture, by someone to direct suspicion at her. What would you naturally do? Exactly what you did do: take it upstairs and put it beside the body, without letting her know about it. Or—"

"Rot," Fred said harshly. "Absolute rot."

Wolfe looked at Peggy. "Or suppose it was you who found it there in your bedroom, after he had gone downstairs. Naturally you would have—"

"This is absurd," Peggy said with spirit. "How could it have been in my bedroom unless I put it there? My husband was alive at five-thirty, and I got home before that, and was right there, in the living room and my room, until Fred came at seven o'clock. So unless you assume—"

"Very well," Wolfe conceded, "Not the bedroom. But somewhere. I can't proceed until I get this from one of you. Confound it, the gun didn't fly. I expect plenty of lies from the others, at least one of them, but I want the truth from you."

"You've got it," Fred declared.

"No. I haven't."

"Then it's a stalemate." Fred stood up. "Well, Peggy?"

They looked at each other, and their eyes went through the performance again. When they got to the place in the script where it said, "It must be wonderful always," Fred sat down.

But Wolfe, having no part in the script, horned in. "A stalemate," he said dryly, "ends the game, I believe."

Plainly it was up to me. If Wolfe openly committed himself to no dice nothing would budge him. I arose, got the pretty pink check from his desk, put it on mine, placed a paperweight on it, sat down, and grinned at him.

"Granted that you're dead right," I observed, "which is not what you call apodictical, someday we ought to make up a list of the clients that have sat here and lied to us. There was Mike Walsh, and Calida Frost, and that cafeteria guy, Pratt—oh, dozens. But their money was good, and I didn't get so far behind with my notes that I couldn't catch up. All that for nothing?"

"About those notes," Fred Weppler said firmly. "I want to make something clear."

Wolfe looked at him.

He looked back. "We came here," he said, "to tell you in confidence about a problem and get you to investigate. Your accusing us of lying makes me wonder if we ought to go on, but if Mrs. Mion wants to I'm willing. But I want to make it plain that if you divulge what we've told you, if you tell the police or anyone else that we said there was no gun there when we went in, we'll deny it in spite of your damn notes. We'll deny it and stick to it!" He looked at his girl. "We've got to, Peggy! All right?"

"He wouldn't tell the police," Peggy declared, with fair conviction.

"Maybe not. But if he does, you'll stick with me on the denial. Won't you?"

"Certainly I will," she promised, as if he had asked her to help kill a rattlesnake.

Wolfe was taking them in, with his lips tightened. Obviously, with the check on my desk on its way to the bank, he had decided to add them to the list of clients who told lies and go on from there. He forced his eyes wide open to rest them, let them half close again, and spoke.

"We'll settle that along with other things before we're through," he asserted. "You realize, of course, that I'm assuming your innocence, but I've made a thousand wrong assumptions before now so they're not worth much. Has either of you a notion of who killed Mr. Mion?"

They both said no.

He grunted. "I have."

They opened their eyes at him.

He nodded. "It's only another assumption, but I like it. It will take work to validate it. To begin with, I must see the people you have mentioned—all six of them—and I would prefer not to string it out. Since you don't want them told that I'm investigating a murder, we must devise a stratagem. Did your husband leave a will, Mrs. Mion?"

She nodded and said yes.

"Are you the heir?"

"Yes, I—" She gestured. "I don't need it and don't want it."

"But it's yours. That will do nicely. An asset of the estate is the expectation of damages to be paid by Mr. James for his assault on Mr. Mion. You may properly claim that asset. The six people I want to see were all concerned in that affair, one way or another. I'll write them immediately, mailing the letters tonight special delivery, telling them that I represent you in the matter and would like them to call at my office tomorrow evening."

"That's impossible!" Peggy cried, shocked. "I couldn't! I wouldn't dream of asking Gif to pay damages—"

Wolfe banged a fist on his desk. "Confound it!" he roared. "Get out of here! Go! Do you think murders are solved by cutting out paper dolls? First you lie to me, and now you refuse to annoy people, including the murderer! Archie, put them out!"

"Good for you," I muttered at him. I was getting fed up too. I glared at the would-be clients. "Try the Salvation Army," I suggested. "They're old hands at helping people in trouble. You can have the notebooks to take along—at cost, six bits. No charge for the contents."

They were looking at each other.

"I guess he has to see them somehow," Fred conceded. "He has to have a reason, and I must admit that's a good one. You don't owe them anything—not one of them."

Peggy gave in.

After a few details had been attended to, the most important of which was getting addresses, they left. The manner of their going, and of our speeding them, was so far from cordial that it might have been thought that instead of being the clients they were the prey. But the check was on my desk. When, after letting them out, I returned to the office, Wolfe was leaning back with his eyes shut, frowning in distaste.

I stretched and yawned. "This ought to be fun," I said encouragingly. "Making it just a grab for damages. If the murderer is among the guests, see how long you can keep it from him. I bet he catches on before the jury comes in with the verdict."

"Shut up," he growled. "Blockheads."

"Oh, have a heart," I protested. "People in love aren't supposed to think, that's why they have to hire trained thinkers. You should be happy and proud they picked you. What's a good big lie or two when you're in love? When I saw—"

"Shut up," he repeated. His eyes came open. "Your notebook. Those letters must go at once."

III

MONDAY evening's party lasted a full three hours, and murder wasn't mentioned once. Even so, it wasn't exactly jolly. The letters had put it straight that Wolfe, acting for Mrs. Mion, wanted to find out whether an appropriate sum could be collected from Gifford James without resort to lawyers and a court, and what sum would be thought appropriate. So each of them was naturally in a state of mind: Gifford James himself; his daughter Clara; his lawyer, Judge Henry Arnold; Adele Bosley for Public Relations; Dr. Nicholas Lloyd as the technical expert; and Rupert Grove, who had been Mion's manager. That made six, which was just comfortable for our big office. Fred and Peggy had not been invited.

The James trio arrived together and were so punctual, right on the dot at nine o'clock, that Wolfe and I hadn't yet finished our after-dinner coffee in the office. I was so curious to have a look that I went to answer the door instead of leaving it to Fritz, the chef and house overseer who helps to make Wolfe's days and years a joy forever almost as much as I do. The first thing that impressed me was that the baritone took the lead crossing the threshold, letting his daughter and his lawyer tag along behind. Since I have occasionally let Lily Rowan share her pair of opera seats with me, James' six feet and broad shoulders and cocky strut were nothing new, but I was surprised that he looked so young, since he must have been close to fifty. He handed me his hat as if taking care of his hat on Monday evening, August 15, was the one and only thing I had been born for. Unfortunately I let it drop.

Clara made up for it by looking at me. That alone showed she was unusually observant, since one never looks at the flunkey who lets one in, but she saw me drop her father's hat and gave me a glance, and then prolonged the glance until it practically said, "What are you, in disguise? See you later." That made me feel friendly, but with reserve. Not only was she pale and tense, as Peggy Mion had said, but her blue eyes glistened, and a girl her age shouldn't glisten like that. Nevertheless, I gave her a grin to show that I appreciated the prolonged glance.

Meanwhile the lawyer, Judge Henry Arnold, had hung up his own hat. During the day I had of course made inquiries on all of them, and had learned that he rated the "Judge" only because he had once been a city magistrate. Even so, that's what they called him, so the sight of him was a letdown. He was a little sawed-off squirt with a bald head so flat on top you could have kept an ashtray on it, and his nose was pushed in. He must have been better arranged inside than out, since he had quite a list of clients among the higher levels on Broadway.

Taking them to the office and introducing them to Wolfe, I undertook to assign them to some of the yellow chairs, but the baritone spied the red leather one and copped it. I was helping Fritz fill their orders for drinks when the buzzer sounded and I went back to the front.

It was Dr. Nicholas Lloyd. He had no hat, so that point wasn't raised, and I decided that the searching look he aimed at me was merely professional and automatic, to see if I was anemic or diabetic or what. With his lined handsome face and worried dark eyes he looked every inch a doctor and even surgeon, fully up to the classy reputation my inquiries had disclosed. When I ushered him to the office his eyes lighted up at sight of the refreshment table, and he was the best customer—bourbon and water with mint—all evening.

The last two came together—at least they were on the stoop together when I opened the door. I would probably have given Adele Bosley the red leather chair if James hadn't already copped it. She shook hands and said she had been wanting to meet Archie Goodwin for years, but that was just public relations and went out the other ear. The point is that from my desk I get most of a party profile or three-quarters, but the one in the red leather chair fullface, and I like a view. Not that Adele Bosley was a pin-up, and she must have been in the fifth or sixth grade when Clara James was born, but her smooth tanned skin and pretty mouth without too much lipstick and nice brown eyes were good scenery.

Rupert Grove didn't shake hands, which didn't upset me. He may have been a good manager for Alberto Mion's affairs, but not for his own physique. A man can be fat and still have integrity, as for instance Falstaff or Nero Wolfe, but that bird had lost all sense of proportion. His legs were short, and it was all in the middle third of him. If you wanted to be polite and look at his face you had to concentrate. I did so, since I needed to size them all up, and saw nothing worthy of recording but a pair of shrewd and shifty black eyes.

When these two were seated and provided with liquid, Wolfe fired the starting gun. He said he was sorry it had been necessary to ask them to exert themselves on a hot evening, but that the question at issue could be answered fairly and equitably only if all concerned had a voice in it. The responding murmurs went all the way from acquiescence to extreme irritation. Judge Arnold said belligerently that there was no question at legal issue because Alberto Mion was dead.

"Nonsense," Wolfe said curtly. "If that were true you, a lawyer, wouldn't have bothered to come. Anyway, the purpose of this meeting is to keep it from becoming a legal issue. Four of you telephoned Mrs. Mion today to ask if I am acting for her, and were told that I am. On her behalf I want to collect the facts. I may as well tell you, without prejudice to her, that she will accept my recommendation. Should I decide that a large sum is due her you may of course contest; but if I form the opinion that she has no claim she will bow to it. Under that responsibility I need all the facts. Therefore—"

"You're not a court," Arnold snapped.

"No, sir, I'm not. If you prefer it in a court you'll get it." Wolfe's eyes moved. "Miss Bosley, would your employers welcome that kind of publicity? Dr. Lloyd, would you rather appear as an expert on the witness-stand or talk it over here? Mr. Grove, how would your client feel about it if he were alive? Mr. James, what do you think? You wouldn't relish the publicity either, would you? Particularly since your daughter's name would appear?"

"Why would her name appear?" James demanded in his trained baritone.

Wolfe turned up a palm. "It would be evidence. It would be established that just before you struck Mr. Mion you said to him, 'You let my daughter alone, you bastard.'"

I put my hand in my pocket. I have a rule, justified by experience, that whenever a killer is among those present, or may be, a gun must be handy. Not regarding the back of the third drawer of my desk, where they are kept, as handy enough, the routine is to transfer one to my pocket before guests gather. That was the pocket I put my hand in, knowing how cocky James was. But he didn't leave his chair. He merely blurted, "That's a lie!"

Wolfe grunted. "Ten people heard you say it. That would indeed be publicity, if you denied it under oath and all ten of them, subpoenaed to testify, contradicted you. I honestly think it would be better to discuss it with me."

"What do you want to know?" Judge Arnold demanded.

"The facts. First, the one already moot. When I lie I like to know it. Mr. Grove, you were present when that famous blow was struck. Have I quoted Mr. James correctly?"

"Yes." Grove's voice was a high tenor, which pleased me.

"You heard him say that?"

"Yes."

"Miss Bosley. Did you?"

She looked uncomfortable. "Wouldn't it be better to—"

"Please. You're not under oath, but I'm merely collecting facts, and I was told I lied. Did you hear him say that?"

"Yes, I did." Adele's eyes went to James. "I'm sorry, Gif."

"But it's not true!" Clara James cried.

Wolfe rasped at her, "We're all lying?"

I could have warned her, when she gave me that glance in the hall, to look out for him. Not only was she a sophisticated young woman, and not only did she glisten, but her slimness was the kind that comes from not eating enough, and Wolfe absolutely cannot stand people who don't eat enough. I knew he would be down on her from the go.

But she came back at him. "I don't mean that," she said scornfully.

"Don't be so touchy! I mean I had lied to my father. What he thought about Alberto and me wasn't true. I was just bragging to him because —it doesn't matter why. Anyway, what I told him wasn't true, and I told him so that night!"

"Which night?"

"When we got home—from the stage party after *Rigoletto*. That was where my father knocked Alberto down, you know, right there on the stage. When we got home I told him that what I had said about Alberto and me wasn't true."

"When were you lying, the first time or the second?"

"Don't answer that, my dear," Judge Arnold broke in, lawyering. He looked sternly at Wolfe. "This is all irrelevant. You're welcome to facts, but relevant facts. What Miss James told her father is immaterial."

Wolfe shook his head. "Oh no." His eyes went from right to left and back again. "Apparently I haven't made it plain. Mrs. Mion wants me to decide for her whether she has a just claim, not so much legally as morally. If it appears that Mr. James' assault on Mr. Mion was morally justified that will be a factor in my decision." He focused on Clara. "Whether my question was relevant or not, Miss James, I admit it was embarrassing and therefore invited mendacity. I withdraw it. Try this instead. Had you, prior to that stage party, given your father to understand that Mr. Mion had seduced you?"

"Well—" Clara laughed. It was a tinkly soprano laugh, rather attractive. "What a nice old-fashioned way to say it! Yes, I had. But it wasn't true!"

"But you believed it, Mr. James?"

Gifford James was having trouble holding himself in, and I concede that such leading questions about his daughter's honor from a stranger must have been hard to take. But after all it wasn't new to the rest of the audience, and anyway it sure was relevant. He forced himself to speak with quiet dignity. "I believed what my daughter told me, yes."

Wolfe nodded. "So much for that," he said in a relieved tone. "I'm glad that part is over with." His eyes moved. "Now. Mr. Grove, tell me about the conference in Mr. Mion's studio, a few hours before he died."

Rupert the Fat had his head tilted to one side, with his shrewd black eyes meeting Wolfe's. "It was for the purpose," he said in his high tenor, "of discussing the demand Mion had made for payment of damages."

"You were there?"

"I was, naturally. I was Mion's adviser and manager. Also Miss Bosley, Dr. Lloyd, Mr. James, and Judge Arnold."

"Who arranged the conference, you?"

"In a way, yes. Arnold suggested it, and I told Mion and phoned Dr. Lloyd and Miss Bosley."

"What was decided?"

"Nothing. That is, nothing definite. There was the question of the extent of the damage—how soon Mion would be able to sing again."

"What was your position?"

Grove's eyes tightened. "Didn't I say I was Mion's manager?"

"Certainly. I mean, what position did you take regarding the payment of damages?"

"I thought a preliminary payment of fifty thousand dollars should be made at once. Even if Mion's voice was soon all right he had already lost that and more. His South American tour had been canceled, and he had been unable to make a lot of records on contract, and then radio offers—"

"Nothing like fifty thousand dollars," Judge Arnold asserted aggressively. There was nothing wrong with his larynx, small as he was. "I showed figures—"

"To hell with your figures! Anybody can—"

"Please!" Wolfe rapped on his desk with a knuckle. "What was Mr. Mion's position?"

"The same as mine, of course." Grove was scowling at Arnold as he spoke to Wolfe. "We had discussed it."

"Naturally." Wolfe's eyes went left. "How did you feel about it, Mr. James?"

"I think," Arnold broke in, "that I should speak for my client. You agree, Gif?"

"Go ahead," the baritone muttered.

Arnold did, and took most of one of the three hours. I was surprised that Wolfe didn't stop him, and finally decided that he let him ramble on just to get additional support for his long-standing opinion of lawyers. If so, he got it. Arnold covered everything. He had a lot to say about tort-feasors, going back a couple of centuries, with emphasis on the mental state of a tort-feasor. Another item he covered at length was proximate cause. He got really worked up about proximate cause, but it was so involved that I lost track and passed.

Here and there, though, he made sense. At one point he said, "The idea of a preliminary payment, as they called it, was clearly inadmissible. It is not reasonable to expect a man, even if he stipulates an obligation, to make a payment thereon until either the total amount of the obligation, or an exact method of computing it, has been agreed upon."

At another point he said, "The demand for so large a sum can in fact be properly characterized as blackmail. They knew that if the action went to trial, and if we showed that my client's deed sprang from his knowledge that his daughter had been wronged, a jury would not be likely to award damages. But they also knew that we would be averse to making that defense."

"Not his knowledge," Wolfe objected. "Merely his belief. His daughter says she had misinformed him."

"We could have showed knowledge," Arnold insisted.

I looked at Clara with my brows up. She was being contradicted flatly on the chronology of her lie and her truth, but either she and her father didn't get the implication of it or they didn't want to get started on that again.

At another point Arnold said, "Even if my client's deed was tortious and damages would be collectible, the amount could not be agreed upon until the extent of the injury was known. We offered, without prejudice, twenty thousand dollars in full settlement, for a general release. They refused. They wanted a payment forthwith on account. We refused that on principle. In the end there was agreement on only one thing: that an effort should be made to arrive at the total amount of damage. Of course that was what Dr. Lloyd was there for. He was asked for a prognosis, and he stated that—but you don't need to take hearsay. He's here, and you can get it direct."

Wolfe nodded. "If you please, Doctor?"

I thought, My God, here we go again with another expert.

But Lloyd had mercy on us. He kept it down to our level and didn't take anything like an hour. Before he spoke he took another swallow from his third helping of bourbon and water with mint, which had smoothed out some of the lines on his handsome face and taken some of the worry from his eyes.

"I'll try to remember," he said slowly, "exactly what I told them. First I described the damage the blow had done. The thyroid and arytenoid cartilages on the left side had been severely injured, and to a lesser extent the cricoid." He smiled—a superior smile, but not supercilious. "I waited two weeks, using indicated treatment, thinking an operation might not be required, but it was. When I got inside I confess I was relieved; it wasn't as bad as I had feared. It was a simple operation, and he healed admirably. I wouldn't have been risking much that day if I had given assurance that his voice would be as good as ever in two months, three at the most, but the larynx is an extremely delicate instrument, and a tenor like Mion's is a remarkable phenomenon, so I was cautious enough merely to say that I would be surprised and disappointed if he wasn't ready, fully ready, for the opening of the next opera season, seven months from then. I added that my hope and expectation were actually more optimistic than that."

Lloyd pursed his lips. "That was it, I think. Nevertheless, I welcomed the suggestion that my prognosis should be reinforced by Rentner's. Apparently it would be a major factor in the decision about the amount to be paid in damages, and I didn't want the sole responsibility."

"Rentner? Who was he?" Wolfe asked.

"Dr. Abraham Rentner of Mount Sinai," Lloyd replied, in the tone I would use if someone asked me who Jackie Robinson was. "I phoned him and made an appointment for the following morning."

"I insisted on it," Rupert the Fat said importantly. "Mion had a right to collect not sometime in the distant future, but then and there. They wouldn't pay unless a total was agreed on, and if we had to name a total I wanted to be damn sure it was enough. Don't forget that that day Mion couldn't sing a note."

"He wouldn't have been able even to let out a pianissimo for at least two months," Lloyd bore him out. "I gave that as the minimum."

"There seems," Judge Arnold interposed, "to be an implication that we opposed the suggestion that a second professional opinion be secured. I must protest—"

"You did!" Grove squeaked.

"We did not!" Gifford James barked. "We merely—"

The three of them went at it, snapping and snarling. It seemed to me that they might have saved their energy for the big issue, was anything coming to Mrs. Mion and if so how much, but not those babies.

Their main concern was to avoid the slightest risk of agreeing on anything at all. Wolfe patiently let them get where they were headed for—nowhere—and then invited a new voice in. He turned to Adele and spoke.

"Miss Bosley, we haven't heard from you. Which side were you on?"

IV

ADELE BOSLEY had been sitting taking it in, sipping occasionally at her rum collins—now her second one—and looking, I thought, pretty damn intelligent. Though it was the middle of August, she was the only one of the six who had a really good tan. Her public relations with the sun were excellent.

She shook her head. "I wasn't on either side, Mr. Wolfe. My only interest was that of my employer, the Metropolitan Opera Association. Naturally we wanted it settled privately, without any scandal. I had no opinion whatever on whether—on the point at issue."

"And expressed none?"

"No. I merely urged them to get it settled if possible."

"Fair enough!" Clara James blurted. It was a sneer. "You might have helped my father a little, since he got your job for you. Or had you—"

"Be quiet, Clara!" James told her with authority.

But she ignored him and finished it. "Or had you already paid in full for that?"

I was shocked. Judge Arnold looked pained. Rupert the Fat giggled. Doc Lloyd took a gulp of bourbon and water.

In view of the mildly friendly attitude I was developing toward Adele I sort of hoped she would throw something at the slim and glistening Miss James, but all she did was appeal to the father. "Can't you handle the brat, Gif?"

Then, without waiting for an answer, she turned to Wolfe. "Miss James likes to use her imagination. What she implied is not on the record. Not anybody's record."

Wolfe nodded. "It wouldn't belong on this one anyhow." He made a face. "To go back to relevancies, what time did that conference break up?"

"Why—Mr. James and Judge Arnold left first, around four-thirty. Then Dr. Lloyd, soon after. I stayed a few minutes with Mion and Mr. Grove, and then went."

"Where did you go?"

"To my office, on Broadway."

"How long did you stay at your office?"

She looked surprised. "I don't know—yes, I do too, of course. Until a little after seven. I had things to do, and I typed a confidential report of the conference at Mion's."

"Did you see Mion again before he died? Or phone him?"

"See him?" She was more surprised. "How could I? Don't you know he was found dead at seven o'clock? That was before I left the office."

"Did you phone him? Between four-thirty and seven?"

"No." Adele was puzzled and slightly exasperated. It struck me that Wolfe was recklessly getting onto thin ice, mighty close to the forbidden subject of murder. Adele added, "I don't know what you're getting at."

"Neither do I," Judge Arnold put in with emphasis. He smiled sarcastically. "Unless it's force of habit with you, asking people where they were at the time a death by violence occurred. Why don't you go after all of us?"

"That's what I intend to do," Wolfe said imperturbably. "I would like to know why Mion decided to kill himself, because that has a bearing on the opinion I shall give his widow. I understand that two or three of you have said that he was wrought up when that conference ended, but not despondent or splenetic. I know he committed suicide; the police can't be flummoxed on a thing like that; but why?"

"I doubt," Adele Bosley offered, "if you know how a singer—especially a great artist like Mion—how he feels when he can't let a sound out, when he can't even talk except in an undertone or a whisper. It's horrible."

"Anyway, you never knew with him," Rupert Grove contributed. "In rehearsal I've heard him do an aria like an angel and then rush out weeping because he thought he had slurred a release. One minute he was up in the sky and the next he was under a rug."

Wolfe grunted. "Nevertheless, anything said to him by anyone during the two hours preceding his suicide is pertinent to this inquiry, to establish Mrs. Mion's moral position. I want to know where you people were that day, after the conference up to seven o'clock, and what you did."

"My God!" Judge Arnold threw up his hands. The hands came down again. "All right, it's getting late. As Miss Bosley told you, my client and I left Mion's studio together. We went to the Churchill bar and drank and talked. A little later Miss James joined us, stayed long enough for a drink, I suppose half an hour, and left. Mr. James and I remained together until after seven. During that time neither of us communicated with Mion, nor arranged for anyone else to. I believe that covers it?"

"Thank you," Wolfe said politely. "You corroborate, of course, Mr. James?"

"I do," the baritone said gruffly. "This is a lot of goddam nonsense."

"It does begin to sound like it," Wolfe conceded. "Dr. Lloyd? If you don't mind?"

He hadn't better, since he had been mellowed by four ample helpings of our best bourbon, and he didn't. "Not at all," he said cooperatively. "I made calls on five patients, two on upper Fifth Avenue, one in the East Sixties, and two at the hospital. I got home a little after six and had just finished dressing after taking a bath when Fred Weppler phoned me about Mion. Of course I went at once."

"You hadn't seen Mion or phoned him?"

"Not since I left after the conference. Perhaps I should have, but I had no idea—I'm not a psychiatrist, but I was his doctor."

"He was mercurial, was he?"

"Yes, he was." Lloyd pursed his lips. "Of course, that's not a medical term."

"Far from it," Wolfe agreed. He shifted his gaze. "Mr. Grove, I don't have to ask you if you phoned Mion, since it is on record that you did. Around five o'clock?"

Rupert the Fat had his head tilted again. Apparently that was his favorite pose for conversing. He corrected Wolfe. "It was after five. More like a quarter past."

"Where did you phone from?"

"The Harvard Club."

I thought, I'll be damned, it takes all kinds to make a Harvard Club.

"What was said?"

"Not much." Grove's lips twisted. "It's none of your damn business, you know, but the others have obliged, and I'll string along. I had forgotten to ask him if he would endorse a certain product for a thousand dollars, and the agency wanted an answer. We talked less than three minutes. First he said he wouldn't and then he said he would. That was all."

"Did he sound like a man getting ready to kill himself?"

"Not the slightest. He was glum, but naturally, since he still couldn't sing and couldn't expect to for at least two months."

"After you phoned Mion what did you do?"

"I stayed at the club. I ate dinner there and hadn't quite finished when the news came that Mion had killed himself. So I'm still behind that ice cream and coffee."

"That's too bad. When you phoned Mion, did you again try to persuade him not to press his claim against Mr. James?"

Grove's head straightened up. "Did I what?" he demanded.

"You heard me," Wolfe said rudely. "What's surprising about it? Naturally Mrs. Mion has informed me, since I'm working for her. You were opposed to Mion's asking for payment in the first place and tried to talk him out of it. You said the publicity would be so harmful that it wasn't worth it. He demanded that you support the claim and threatened to cancel your contract if you refused. Isn't that correct?"

"It is not." Grove's black eyes were blazing. "It wasn't like that at all! I merely gave him my opinion. When it was decided to make the claim I went along." His voice went up a notch higher, though I wouldn't have thought it possible. "I certainly did!"

"I see." Wolfe wasn't arguing. "What is your opinion now, about Mrs. Mion's claim?"

"I don't think she has one. I don't believe she can collect. If I were in James' place I certainly wouldn't pay her a cent."

Wolfe nodded. "You don't like her, do you?"

"Frankly, I don't. No. I never have. Do I have to like her?"

"No, indeed. Especially since she doesn't like you either." Wolfe shifted in his chair and leaned back. I could tell from the line of his lips, straightened out, that the next item on the agenda was one he didn't care for, and I understood why when I saw his eyes level at Clara James. I'll bet that if he had known that he would have to be dealing with that type he wouldn't have taken the job. He spoke to her testily. "Miss James, you've heard what has been said?"

"I was wondering," she complained, as if she had been holding in a grievance, "if you were going to go on ignoring me. I was around too, you know."

"I know. I haven't forgotten you." His tone implied that he only wished he could. "When you had a drink in the Churchill bar with your father and Judge Arnold, why did they send you up to Mion's studio to see him? What for?"

Arnold and James protested at once, loudly and simultaneously. Wolfe, paying no attention to them, waited to hear Clara, her voice having been drowned by theirs.

". . . nothing to do with it," she was finishing. "I sent myself."

"It was your own idea?"

"Entirely. I have one once in a while, all alone."

"What did you go for?"

"You don't need to answer, my dear," Arnold told her.

She ignored him. "They told me what had happened at the conference, and I was mad. I thought it was a holdup—but I wasn't going to tell Alberto that. I thought I could talk him out of it."

"You went to appeal to him for old times' sake?"

She looked pleased. "You have the nicest way of putting things! Imagine a girl my age having old times!"

"I'm glad you like my diction, Miss James." Wolfe was furious. "Anyhow, you went. Arriving at a quarter past six?"

"Just about, yes."

"Did you see Mion?"

"No."

"Why not?"

"He wasn't there. At least—" She stopped. Her eyes weren't glistening quite so much. She went on, "That's what I thought then. I went to the thirteenth floor and rang the bell at the door to the studio. It's a loud bell—he had it loud to be heard above his voice and the piano when he was practicing—but I couldn't hear it from the hall because the door is soundproofed too, and after I had pushed the button a few times I wasn't sure the bell was ringing so I knocked on the door. I like to finish anything I start, and I thought he must be there, so I rang the bell some more and took off my shoe and pounded on the door with the heel. Then I went down to the twelfth floor by the public stairs and rang the bell at the apartment door. That was really stupid, because I know how Mrs. Mion hates me, but anyway I did. She came to the door and said she thought Alberto was up in the studio, and I said he wasn't, and she shut the door in my face. I went home and mixed myself a drink—which reminds me, I must admit this is good scotch, though I never heard of it before."

She lifted her glass and jiggled it to swirl the ice. "Any questions?"

"No," Wolfe growled. He glanced at the clock on the wall and then along the line of faces. "I shall certainly report to Mrs. Mion," he told them, "that you were not grudging with the facts."

"And what else?" Arnold inquired.

"I don't know. We'll see."

That they didn't like. I wouldn't have supposed anyone could name a subject on which those six characters would have been in unanimous accord, but Wolfe turned the trick in five words. They wanted a verdict; failing that, an opinion; failing that, at least a hint. Adele Bosley was stubborn, Rupert the Fat was so indignant he squeaked, and Judge Arnold was next door to nasty. Wolfe was patient up to a point, but finally stood up and told them good night as if he meant it. The note it ended on was such that before going not one of them shelled out a word of appreciation for all the refreshment, not even Adele, the expert on public relations, or Doc Lloyd, who had practically emptied the bourbon bottle.

With the front door locked and bolted for the night, I returned to the office. To my astonishment Wolfe was still on his feet, standing over by the bookshelves, glaring at the backbones.

"Restless?" I asked courteously.

He turned and said aggressively, "I want another bottle of beer."

"Nuts. You've had five since dinner." I didn't bother to put much feeling into it, as the routine was familiar. He had himself set the quota of five bottles between dinner and bedtime, and usually stuck to it, but when anything sent his humor far enough down he liked to shift the responsibility so he could be sore at me too.

It was just part of my job. "Nothing doing," I said firmly. "I counted 'em. Five. What's the trouble, a whole evening gone and still no murderer?"

"Bah." He compressed his lips. "That's not it. If that were all we could close it up before going to bed. It's that confounded gun with wings." He gazed at me with his eyes narrowed, as if suspecting that

I had wings too. "I could, of course, just ignore it— No. No, in view of the state our clients are in, it would be foolhardy. We'll have to clear it up. There's no alternative."

"That's a nuisance. Can I help any?"

"Yes. Phone Mr. Cramer first thing in the morning. Ask him to be here at eleven o'clock."

My brows went up. "But he's interested only in homicides. Do I tell him we've got one to show him?"

"No. Tell him I guarantee that it's worth the trouble." Wolfe took a step toward me. "Archie."

"Yes, sir."

"I've had a bad evening and I'll have another bottle."

"You will not. Not a chance." Fritz had come in and we were starting to clear up. "It's after midnight and you're in the way. Go to bed."

"One wouldn't hurt him," Fritz muttered.

"You're a help," I said bitterly. "I warn both of you, I've got a gun in my pocket. What a household!"

V

FOR NINE months of the year Inspector Cramer of Homicide, big and broad and turning gray, looked the part well enough, but in the summertime the heat kept his face so red that he was a little gaudy. He knew it and didn't like it, and as a result he was some harder to deal with in August than in January. If an occasion arises for me to commit a murder in Manhattan I hope it will be winter.

Tuesday at noon he sat in the red leather chair and looked at Wolfe with no geniality. Detained by another appointment, he hadn't been able to make it at eleven, the hour when Wolfe adjourns the morning session with his orchids up in the plant rooms. Wolfe wasn't exactly beaming either, and I was looking forward to some vaudeville. Also I was curious to see how Wolfe would go about getting dope on a murder from Cramer without spilling it that there had been one, as Cramer was by no means a nitwit.

"I'm on my way uptown," Cramer grumbled, "and haven't got much time."

That was probably a barefaced lie. He merely didn't want to admit that an inspector of the NYPD would call on a private detective on request, even though it was Nero Wolfe and I had told him we had something hot.

"What is it," he grumbled on, "the Dickinson thing? Who brought you in?"

Wolfe shook his head. "No one, thank heaven. It's about the murder of Alberto Mion."

I goggled at him. This was away beyond me. Right off he had let the dog loose, when I had thought the whole point was that there was no dog on the place.

"Mion?" Cramer wasn't interested. "Not one of mine."

"It soon will be. Alberto Mion, the famous opera singer. Four months ago, on April nineteenth. In his studio on East End Avenue. Shot—"

"Oh." Cramer nodded. "Yeah, I remember. But you're stretching it a little. It was suicide."

"No. It was first-degree murder."

Cramer regarded him for three breaths. Then, in no hurry, he got a cigar from his pocket, inspected it, and stuck it in his mouth. In a moment he took it out again.

"I have never known it to fail," he remarked, "that you can be counted on for a headache. Who says it was murder?"

"I have reached that conclusion."

"Then that's settled." Cramer's sarcasm was usually a little heavy. "Have you bothered any about evidence?"

"I have none."

"Good. Evidence just clutters a murder up." Cramer stuck the cigar back in his mouth and exploded, "When did you start keeping your sentences so goddam short? Go ahead and talk!"

"Well—" Wolfe considered. "It's a little difficult. You're probably not familiar with the details, since it was so long ago and was recorded as suicide."

"I remember it fairly well. As you say, he was famous. Go right ahead."

Wolfe leaned back and closed his eyes. "Interrupt me if you need to. I had six people here for a talk last evening." He pronounced their names and identified them. "Five of them were present at a conference in Mion's studio which ended two hours before he was found dead. The sixth, Miss James, banged on the studio door at a quarter past six and got no reply, presumably because he was dead then. My conclusion that Mion was murdered is based on things I have heard said. I'm not going to repeat them to you—because it would take too long, because it's a question of emphasis and interpretation, and because you have already heard them."

"I wasn't here last evening," Cramer said dryly.

"So you weren't. Instead of 'you,' I should have said the Police Department. It must all be in the files. They were questioned at the time it happened, and told their stories as they have now told them to me. You can get it there. Have you ever known me to have to eat my words?"

"I've seen times when I would have liked to shove them down your throat."

"But you never have. Here are three more I shall not eat: Mion was murdered. I won't tell you, now, how I reached that conclusion; study your files."

Cramer was keeping himself under restraint. "I don't have to study them," he declared, "for one detail—how he was killed. Are you saying he fired the gun himself but was driven to it?"

"No. The murderer fired the gun."

"It must have been quite a murderer. It's quite a trick to pry a guy's mouth open and stick a gun in it without getting bit. Would you mind naming him?"

Wolfe shook his head. "I haven't got that far yet. But it isn't the objection you raise that's bothering me; that can be overcome; it's something else." He leaned forward and was earnest. "Look here, Mr. Cramer. It would not have been impossible for me to see this through alone, deliver the murderer and the evidence to you, and flap my wings and crow. But first, I have no ambition to expose you as a zany, since you're not; and second, I need your help. I am not now prepared to prove to you that Mion was murdered; I can only assure you that he was, and repeat that I won't have to eat it—and neither will you. Isn't that enough, at least to arouse your interest?"

Cramer stopped chewing the cigar. He never lit one. "Sure," he said grimly. "Hell, I'm interested. Another first-class headache. I'm flattered you want me to help. How?"

"I want you to arrest two people as material witnesses, question them, and let them out on bail."

"Which two? Why not all six?" I warned you his sarcasm was hefty.

"But"—Wolfe ignored it—"under clearly defined conditions. They must not know that I am responsible; they must not even know that I have spoken with you. The arrests should be made late this afternoon or early evening, so they'll be kept in custody all night and until they arrange for bail in the morning. The bail need not be high; that's not important. The questioning should be fairly prolonged and severe, not merely a gesture, and if they get little or no sleep so much the better. Of course this sort of thing is routine for you."

"Yeah, we do it constantly." Cramer's tone was unchanged. "But when we ask for a warrant we like to have a fairly good excuse. We wouldn't like to put down that it's to do Nero Wolfe a favor. I don't want to be contrary."

"There's ample excuse for these two. They *are* material witnesses. They are indeed."

"You haven't named them. Who are they?"

"The man and woman who found the body. Mr. Frederick Weppler, the music critic, and Mrs. Mion, the widow."

This time I didn't goggle, but I had to catch myself quick. It was a first if there ever was one. Time and again I have seen Wolfe go far, on a few occasions much too far, to keep a client from being pinched. He regards it as an unbearable personal insult. And here he was, practically begging the law to haul Fred and Peggy in, when I had deposited her check for five grand only the day before!

"Oh," Cramer said. "Them?"

"Yes, sir," Wolfe assured him cooperatively. "As you know or can learn from the files, there is plenty to ask them about. Mr. Weppler was there for lunch that day, with others, and when the others left he remained with Mrs. Mion. What was discussed? What did they do that afternoon; where were they? Why did Mr. Weppler return to the Mion apartment at seven o'clock? Why did he and Mrs. Mion ascend together to the studio? After finding the body, why did Mr. Weppler go downstairs before notifying the police, to get a list of names from the doorman and elevator man? An extraordinary performance. Was it Mion's habit to take an afternoon nap? Did he sleep with his mouth open?"

"Much obliged," Cramer said not gratefully. "You're a wonder at thinking of questions to ask. But even if Mion did take naps with his mouth open, I doubt if he did it standing up. And after the bullet left his head it went up to the ceiling, as I remember it. Now." Cramer put his palms on the arms of the chair, with the cigar in his mouth tilted up at about the angle the gun in Mion's mouth had probably been. "Who's your client?"

"No," Wolfe said regretfully. "I'm not ready to disclose that."

"I thought not. In fact, there isn't one single damn thing you have disclosed. You've got no evidence, or if you have any you're keeping it under your belt. You've got a conclusion you like, that will help a client you won't name, and you want me to test it for you by arresting two reputable citizens and giving them the works. I've seen samples of your nerve before, but this is tops. For God's sake!"

"I've told you I won't eat it, and neither will you. If—"

"You'd eat one of your own orchids if you had to earn a fee!"

That started the fireworks. I have sat many times and listened to that pair in a slugging match and enjoyed every minute of it, but this one got so hot that I wasn't exactly sure I was enjoying it. At 12:40 Cramer was on his feet, starting to leave. At 12:45 he was back in the red leather chair, shaking his fist and snarling. At 12:48 Wolfe was leaning back with his eyes shut, pretending he was deaf. At 12:52 he was pounding his desk and bellowing.

At ten past one it was all over. Cramer had taken it and was gone. He had made a condition, that there would first be a check of the record and a staff talk, but that didn't matter, since the arrests were to be postponed until after judges had gone home. He accepted the proviso that the victims were not to know that Wolfe had a hand in it, so it could have been said that he was knuckling under, but actually he was merely using horse sense. No matter how much he discounted Wolfe's three words that were not to be eaten—and he knew from experience how risky it was to discount Wolfe just for the hell of it—they made it fairly probable that it wouldn't hurt to give Mion's death another look; and in that case a session with the couple who had found the body was as good a way to start as any. As a matter of fact, the only detail that Cramer choked on was Wolfe's refusal to tell who his client was.

As I followed Wolfe into the dining room for lunch I remarked to his outspread back, "There are already eight hundred and nine people in the metropolitan area who would like to poison you. This will make it eight hundred and eleven. Don't think they won't find out sooner or later."

"Of course they will," he conceded, pulling his chair back. "But too late."

The rest of that day and evening nothing happened at all, as far as we knew.

VI

I WAS at my desk in the office at 10:40 the next morning when the phone rang. I got it and told the transmitter, "Nero Wolfe's office, Archie Goodwin speaking."

"I want to talk to Mr. Wolfe."

"He won't be available until eleven o'clock. Can I help?"

"This is urgent. This is Weppler, Frederick Weppler. I'm in a booth in a drugstore on Ninth Avenue near Twentieth Street. Mrs. Mion is with me. We've been arrested."

"Good God!" I was horrified. "What for?"

"To ask us about Mion's death. They had material-witness warrants. They kept us all night, and we just got out on bail. I had a lawyer arrange for the bail, but I don't want him to know about—that we consulted Wolfe, and he's not with us. We want to see Wolfe."

"You sure do," I agreed emphatically. "It's a damn outrage. Come on up here. He'll be down from the plant rooms by the time you arrive. Grab a taxi."

"We can't. That's why I'm phoning. We're being followed by two detectives and we don't want them to know we're seeing Wolfe. How can we shake them?"

It would have saved time and energy to tell him to come ahead, that a couple of official tails needn't worry him, but I thought I'd better play along.

"For God's sake," I said, disgusted. "Cops give me a pain in the neck. Listen. Are you listening?"

"Yes."

"Go to the Feder Paper Company, Five-thirty-five West Seventeenth Street. In the office ask for Mr. Sol Feder. Tell him your name is Montgomery. He'll conduct you along a passage that exits on Eighteenth Street. Right there, either at the curb or double-parked, will be a taxi with a handkerchief on the door handle. I'll be in it. Don't lose any time climbing in. Have you got it?"

"I think so. You'd better repeat the address."

I did so, and told him to wait ten minutes before starting, to give me time to get there. Then, after hanging up, I phoned Sol Feder to instruct him, got Wolfe on the house phone to inform him, and beat it.

I should have told him to wait fifteen or twenty minutes instead of ten, because I got to my post on Eighteenth Street barely in time. My taxi had just stopped, and I was reaching out to tie my handkerchief on the door handle, when here they came across the sidewalk like a bat out of hell. I swung the door wide, and Fred practically threw Peggy in and dived in after her.

"Okay, driver," I said sternly, "you know where," and we rolled.

As we swung into Tenth Avenue I asked if they had had breakfast and they said yes, not with any enthusiasm. The fact is, they looked as if they were entirely out of enthusiasm. Peggy's lightweight green jacket, which she had on over a tan cotton dress, was rumpled and not very clean, and her face looked neglected. Fred's hair might not have been combed for a month, and his brown tropical worsted was anything but natty. They sat holding hands, and about once a minute Fred twisted around to look through the rear window.

"We're loose all right," I assured him. "I've been saving Sol Feder just for an emergency like this."

It was only a five-minute ride. When I ushered them into the office Wolfe was there in his big custom-made chair behind his desk. He arose to greet them, invited them to sit, asked if they had breakfasted properly, and said that the news of their arrest had been an unpleasant shock.

"One thing," Fred blurted, still standing. "We came to see you and consult you in confidence, and forty-eight hours later we were arrested. Was that pure coincidence?"

Wolfe finished getting himself re-established in his chair. "That won't help us any, Mr. Weppler," he said without resentment. "If that's your frame of mind you'd better go somewhere and cool off. You and Mrs. Mion are my clients. An insinuation that I am capable of acting against the interest of a client is too childish for discussion. What did the police ask you about?"

But Fred wasn't satisfied. "You're not a double-crosser," he conceded, "I know that. But what about Goodwin here? He may not be a double-crosser either, but he might have got careless in conversation with someone."

Wolfe's eyes moved. "Archie. Did you?"

"No, sir. But he can postpone asking my pardon. They've had a hard night." I looked at Fred. "Sit down and relax. If I had a careless tongue I wouldn't last at this job a week."

"It's damn funny," Fred persisted. He sat. "Mrs. Mion agrees with me. Don't you, Peggy?"

Peggy, in the red leather chair, gave him a glance and then looked back at Wolfe. "I did, I guess," she confessed. "Yes, I did. But now that I'm here, seeing you—" She made a gesture. "Oh, forget it! There's no one else to go to. We know lawyers, of course, but we don't want to tell a lawyer what we know—about the gun. We've already told you. But now the police suspect something, and we're out on bail, and you've got to do something!"

"What did you find out Monday evening?" Fred demanded. "You stalled when I phoned yesterday. What did they say?"

"They recited facts," Wolfe replied. "As I told you on the phone, I made some progress. I have nothing to add to that—now. But I want to know, I *must* know, what line the police took with you. Did they know what you told me about the gun?"

They both said no.

Wolfe grunted. "Then I might reasonably ask that you withdraw your insinuation that I or Mr. Goodwin betrayed you. What did they ask about?"

The answers to that took a good half an hour. The cops hadn't missed a thing that was included in the picture as they knew it, and, with instructions from Cramer to make it thorough, they hadn't left a scrap. Far from limiting it to the day of Mion's death, they had been particularly curious about Peggy's and Fred's feelings and actions during the months both prior and subsequent thereto. Several times I had to take the tip of my tongue between my teeth to keep from asking the clients why they hadn't told the cops to go soak their heads, but I really knew why: they had been scared. A scared man is only half a man. By the time they finished reporting on their ordeal I was feeling sympathetic, and even a little guilty on behalf of Wolfe, when suddenly he snapped me out of it.

He sat a while tapping the arm of his chair with a fingertip, and then looked at me and said abruptly, "Archie. Draw a check to the order of Mrs. Mion for five thousand dollars."

They gawked at him. I got up and headed for the safe. They demanded to know what the idea was. I stood at the safe door to listen.

"I'm quitting," Wolfe said curtly. "I can't stand you. I told you Sunday that one or both of you were lying, and you stubbornly denied it. I undertook to work around your lie, and I did my best. But now that the police have got curious about Mion's death, and specifically about you, I refuse longer to risk it. I am willing to be a Quixote, but not a chump. In breaking with you, I should tell you that I shall immediately inform Inspector Cramer of all that you have told me, and also warn you that he knows me well and will believe me. If, when the police start the next round with you, you are fools enough to contradict me, heaven knows what will happen. Your best course will be to acknowledge the truth and let them pursue the investigation you hired me for; but I should also warn you that they are not simpletons and they too will know that you are lying—at least one of you. Archie, what are you standing there gaping for? Get the checkbook."

I opened the safe door.

Neither of them had uttered a peep. I suppose they were too tired to react normally. As I returned to my desk they just sat, looking at each other. As I started making the entry on the stub, Fred's voice came.

"You can't do this. This isn't ethical."

"Pfui." Wolfe snorted. "You hire me to get you out of a fix, and lie to me about it, and talk of ethics! Incidentally, I did make progress Monday evening. I cleared everything up but two details, but the devil of it is that one of them depends on you. I have got to know who put that gun on the floor beside the body. I am convinced that it was one of you, but you won't admit it. So I'm helpless, and that's a pity, because I am also convinced that neither of you was involved in Mion's death. If there were—"

"What's that?" Fred demanded. There was nothing wrong with his reaction now. "You're convinced that neither of us was involved?"

"I am."

Fred was out of his chair. He went to Wolfe's desk, put his palms on it, leaned forward, and said harshly, "Do you mean that? Look at me. Open your eyes and look at me! Do you mean that?"

"Yes," Wolfe told him. "Certainly I mean it."

Fred gazed at him another moment and then straightened up. "All right," he said, the harshness gone. "I put the gun on the floor."

A wail came from Peggy. She sailed out of her chair and to him and seized his arm with both hands. "Fred! No! Fred!" she pleaded. I wouldn't have thought her capable of wailing, but of course she was tired to begin with. He put a hand on top of hers and then decided that was inadequate and took her in his arms. For a minute he concentrated on her. Finally he turned his face to Wolfe and spoke.

"I may regret this, but if I do you will too. By God, you will." He was quite positive of it. "All right, I lied. I put the gun on the floor. Now it's up to you." He held the other client closer. "I did, Peggy. Don't say I should have told you—maybe I should—but I couldn't. It'll be all right, dearest, really it will—"

"Sit down," Wolfe said crossly. After a moment he made it an order. "Confound it, sit down!"

Peggy freed herself, Fred letting her go, and returned to her chair and dropped into it. Fred perched on its arm, with a hand on her far shoulder, and she put her hand up to his. Their eyes, suspicious, afraid, defiant, and hopeful all at once, were on Wolfe.

He stayed cross. "I assume," he said, "that you see how it is. You haven't impressed me. I already knew one of you had put the gun there. How could anyone else have entered the studio during those few minutes? The truth you have told me will be worse than useless, it will be extremely dangerous, unless you follow it with more truth. Try another lie and there's no telling what will happen; I might not be able to save you. Where did you find it?"

"Don't worry," Fred said quietly. "You've screwed it out of me and you'll get it straight. When we went in and found the body I saw the gun where Mion always kept it, on the base of Caruso's bust. Mrs. Mion didn't see it; she didn't look that way. When I left her in her bedroom I went back up. I picked the gun up by the trigger guard and smelled it; it had been fired. I put it on the floor by the body, returned to the apartment, went out, and took the elevator to the ground floor. The rest was just as I told you Sunday."

Wolfe grunted. "You may have been in love, but you didn't think much of her intelligence. You assumed that after killing him she hadn't had the wit to leave the gun where he might have dropped—"

"I did not, damn you!"

"Nonsense. Of course you did. Who else would you have wanted to shield? And afterward it got you in a pickle. When you had to agree with her that the gun hadn't been there when you and she entered, you were hobbled. You didn't dare tell her what you had done because of the implication that you suspected her, especially when she seemed to be suspecting you. You couldn't be sure whether she really did suspect you, or whether she was only—"

"I never did suspect him," Peggy said firmly. It was a job to make her voice firm, but she managed it. "And he never suspected me, not really. We just weren't sure—sure all the way down—and when you're in love and want it to last you've got to be sure."

"That was it," Fred agreed. They were looking at each other. "That was it exactly."

"All right, I'll take this," Wolfe said curtly. "I think you've told the truth, Mr. Weppler."

"I know damn well I have."

Wolfe nodded. "You sound like it. I have a good ear for the truth. Now take Mrs. Mion home. I've got to work, but first I must think it over. As I said, there were two details, and you've disposed of only one. You can't help with the other. Go home and eat something."

"Who wants to eat?" Fred demanded fiercely. "We want to know what you're going to do!"

"I've got to brush my teeth," Peggy stated. I shot her a glance of admiration and affection. Women's saying things like that at times like that is one of the reasons I enjoy their company. No man alive, under those circumstances, would have felt that he had to brush his teeth and said so.

Besides, it made it easier to get rid of them without being rude. Fred tried to insist that they had a right to know what the program was, and to help consider the prospects, but was finally compelled to accept Wolfe's mandate that when a man hired an expert the only authority he kept was the right to fire. That, combined with Peggy's longing for a toothbrush and Wolfe's assurance that he would keep them informed, got them on their way without a ruckus.

When, after letting them out, I returned to the office, Wolfe was drumming on his desk blotter with the paperknife, scowling at it, though I had told him a hundred times that it ruined the blotter. I went and got the checkbook and replaced it in the safe, having put nothing on the stub but the date, so no harm was done.

"Twenty minutes till lunch," I announced, swiveling my chair and sitting. "Will that be enough to hogtie the second detail?"

No reply.

I refused to be sensitive. "If you don't mind," I inquired pleasantly, "what is the second detail?"

Again no reply, but after a moment he dropped the paperknife, leaned back, and sighed clear down.

"That confounded gun," he growled. "How did it get from the floor to the bust? Who moved it?"

I stared at him. "My God," I complained, "you're hard to satisfy. You've just had two clients arrested and worked like a dog, getting the gun from the bust to the floor. Now you want to get it from the floor to the bust again? What the hell!"

"Not again. Prior to."

"Prior to what?"

"To the discovery of the body." His eyes slanted at me. "What do you think of this? A man—or a woman, no matter which—entered the studio and killed Mion in a manner that would convey a strong presumption of suicide. He deliberately planned it that way; it's not as difficult as the traditional police theory assumes. Then he placed the gun on the base of the bust, twenty feet away from the body, and departed. What do you think of it?"

"I don't think; I know. It didn't happen that way, unless he suddenly went batty after he pulled the trigger, which seems far-fetched."

"Precisely. Having planned it to look like suicide, he placed the gun on the floor near the body. That is not discussible. But Mr. Weppler found it on the bust. Who took it from the floor and put it there, and when and why?"

"Yeah." I scratched my nose. "That's annoying. I'll admit the question is relevant and material, but why the hell do you let it in? Why don't you let it lay? Get him or her pinched, indicted, and tried. The cops will testify that the gun was there on the floor, and that will suit the jury fine, since it was framed for suicide. Verdict, provided you've sewed up things like motive and opportunity, guilty." I waved a hand. "Simple. Why bring it up at all about the gun being so fidgety?"

Wolfe grunted. "The clients. I have to earn my fee. They want their minds cleared, and they know the gun wasn't on the floor when they discovered the body. For the jury, I can't leave it that the gun was on the bust, and for the clients I can't leave it that it stayed on the floor where the murderer put it. Having, through Mr. Weppler, got it from the bust to the floor, I must now go back and get it from the floor to the bust. You see that?"

"Only too plain." I whistled for help. "I'll be damned. How're you coming on?"

"I've just started." He sat up straight. "But I must clear my own mind, for lunch. Please hand me Mr. Shanks's orchid catalogue."

That was all for the moment, and during meals Wolfe excludes business not only from the conversation but also from the air. After lunch he returned to the office and got comfortable in his chair. For a while he just sat, and then began pushing his lips out and in, and I knew he was doing hard labor. Having no idea how he proposed to move the gun from the floor to the bust, I was wondering how long it might take, and whether he would have to get Cramer to arrest someone else, and if so who. I have seen him sit there like that, working, for hours on end, but this time twenty minutes did it. It wasn't three o'clock yet when he pronounced my name gruffly and opened his eyes.

"Archie."

"Yes, sir."

"I can't do this. You'll have to."

"You mean dope it? I'm sorry, I'm busy."

"I mean execute it." He made a face. "I will not undertake to handle that young woman. It would be an ordeal, and I might botch it. It's just the thing for you. Your notebook. I'll dictate a document and then we'll discuss it."

"Yes, sir. I wouldn't call Miss Bosley really young."

"Not Miss Bosley. Miss James."

"Oh." I got the notebook.

VII

AT A QUARTER past four, Wolfe having gone up to the plant rooms for his afternoon session with the orchids, I sat at my desk, glowering at the phone, feeling the way I imagine Jackie Robinson feels when he strikes out with the bases full. I had phoned Clara James to ask her to come for a ride with me in the convertible, and she had pushed my nose in.

If that sounds as if I like myself beyond reason, not so. I am quite aware that I bat close to a thousand on invitations to damsels only because I don't issue one unless the circumstances strongly indicate that it will be accepted. But that has got me accustomed to hearing yes, and therefore it was a rude shock to listen to her unqualified no. Besides, I had taken the trouble to go upstairs and change to a Pillater shirt and a tropical worsted made by Corley, and there I was, all dressed up.

I concocted three schemes and rejected them, concocted a fourth and bought it, reached for the phone, and dialed the number again. Clara's voice answered, as it had before. As soon as she learned who it was she got impatient.

"I told you I had a cocktail date! Please don't—"

"Hold it," I told her bluntly. "I made a mistake. I was being kind. I wanted to get you out into the nice open air before I told you the bad news. I—"

"What bad news?"

"A woman just told Mr. Wolfe and me that there are five people besides her, and maybe more, who know that you had a key to Alberto Mion's studio door."

Silence. Sometimes silences irritate me, but I didn't mind this one. Finally her voice came, totally different. "It's a silly lie. Who told you?"

"I forget. And I'm not discussing it on the phone. Two things and two only. First, if this gets around, what about your banging on the door for ten minutes, trying to get in, while he was in there dead? When you had a key? It would make even a cop skeptical. Second, meet me at the Churchill bar at five sharp and we'll talk it over. Yes or no."

"But this is so—you're so—"

"Hold it. No good. Yes or no."

Another silence, shorter, and then, "Yes," and she hung up.

I never keep a woman waiting and saw no reason to make an exception of this one, so I got to the Churchill bar eight minutes ahead of time. It was spacious, air-conditioned, well-fitted in all respects, and even in the middle of August well-fitted also in the matter of customers, male and female. I strolled through, glancing around but not expecting her yet, and was surprised when I heard my name and saw her in a booth. Of course she hadn't had far to come, but even so she had wasted no time. She already had a drink and it was nearly gone. I joined her and immediately a waiter was there.

"You're having?" I asked her.

"Scotch on the rocks."

I told the waiter to bring two and he went.

She leaned forward at me and began in a breath, "Listen, this is absolutely silly, you just tell me who told you that, why, it's absolutely crazy—"

"Wait a minute." I stopped her more with my eyes than my words. Hers were glistening at me. "That's not the way to start, because it won't get us anywhere." I got a paper from my pocket and unfolded it. It was a neatly typed copy of the document Wolfe had dictated. "The quickest and easiest way will be for you to read this first, then you'll know what it's about."

I handed her the paper. You might as well read it while she does. It was dated that day:

> I, Clara James, hereby declare that on Tuesday, April 19, I entered the apartment house at 620 East End Avenue, New York City, at or about 6:15 P.M., and took the elevator to the 13th floor. I rang the bell at the door of the studio of Alberto Mion. No one came to the door and there was no sound from within. The door was not quite closed. It was not open enough to show a crack, but was not latched or locked. After ringing again and getting no response, I opened the door and entered.
>
> Alberto Mion's body was lying on the floor over near the piano. He was dead. There was a hole in the top of his head. There was no question whether he was dead. I got dizzy and had to sit down on the floor and put my head down to keep from fainting. I didn't touch the body. There was a revolver there on the floor, not far from the body, and I picked it up. I think I sat on the floor about five minutes, but it might have been a little more or less. When I got back on my feet and started for the door I became aware that the revolver was still in my hand. I placed it on the base of the bust of Caruso. Later I realized I shouldn't have done that, but at the time I was too shocked and dazed to know what I was doing.
>
> I left the studio, pulling the door shut behind me, went

down the public stairs to the twelfth floor, and rang the bell at the door of the Mion apartment. I intended to tell Mrs. Mion about it, but when she appeared there in the doorway it was impossible to get it out. I couldn't tell her that her husband was up in the studio, dead. Later I regretted this, but I now see no reason to regret it or apologize for it, and I simply could not get the words out. I said I had wanted to see her husband, and had rung the bell at the studio and no one had answered. Then I rang for the elevator and went down to the street and went home.

Having been unable to tell Mrs. Mion, I told no one. I would have told my father, but he wasn't at home. I decided to wait until he returned and tell him, but before he came a friend telephoned me the news that Mion had killed himself, so I decided not to tell anyone, not even my father, that I had been in the studio, but to say that I had rung the bell and knocked on the door and got no reply. I thought that would make no difference, but it has now been explained to me that it does, and therefore I am stating it exactly as it happened.

As she got to the end the waiter came with the drinks, and she held the document against her chest as if it were a poker hand. Keeping it there with her left, she reached for the glass with her right and took a big swallow of scotch. I took a sip of mine to be sociable.

"It's a pack of lies," she said indignantly.

"It sure is," I agreed. "I have good ears, so keep your voice down. Mr. Wolfe is perfectly willing to give you a break, and anyhow it would be a job to get you to sign it if it told the truth. We are quite aware that the studio door was locked and you opened it with your key. Also that—no, listen to me a minute—also that you purposely picked up the gun and put it on the bust because you thought Mrs. Mion had killed him and left the gun there so it would look like suicide, and you wanted to mess it up for her. You couldn't—"

"Where were you?" she demanded scornfully. "Hiding behind the couch?"

"Nuts. If you didn't have a key why did you break a date to see me because of what I said on the phone? As for the gun, you couldn't have been dumber if you'd worked at it for a year. Who would believe anyone had shot him so it would look like suicide and then been fool enough to put the gun on the bust? Too dumb to believe, honest, but you did it."

She was too busy with her brain to resent being called dumb. Her frown creased her smooth pale forehead and took the glisten from her eyes. "Anyway," she protested, "what this says not only isn't true, it's impossible! They found the gun on the floor by his body, so this couldn't possibly be true!"

"Yeah." I grinned at her. "It must have been a shock when you read that in the paper. Since you had personally moved the gun to the bust, how come they found it on the floor? Obviously someone had moved it back. I suppose you decided that Mrs. Mion had done that too, and it must have been hard to keep your mouth shut, but you had to. Now it's a little different. Mr. Wolfe knows who put the gun back on the floor and he can prove it. What's more, he knows Mion was murdered and he can prove that too. All that stops him is the detail of explaining how the gun got from the floor to the bust." I got out my fountain pen. "Put your name to that, and I'll witness it, and we're all set."

"You mean sign this thing?" She was contemptuous. "I'm not *that* dumb."

I caught the waiter's eye and signaled for refills, and then, to keep her company, emptied my glass.

I met her gaze, matching her frown. "Lookit, Blue Eyes," I told her reasonably. "I'm not sticking needles under your nails. I'm not saying we can prove you entered the studio—whether with your key or because the door wasn't locked doesn't matter—and moved the gun. We know you did, since no one else could have and you were there at the right time, but I admit we can't prove it. However, I'm offering you a wonderful bargain."

I pointed the pen at her. "Just listen. All we want this statement for is to keep it in reserve, in case the person who put the gun back on the floor is fool enough to blab it, which is very unlikely. He would only be—"

"You say he?" she demanded.

"Make it he or she. As Mr. Wolfe says, the language could use another pronoun. He would only be making trouble for himself. If he doesn't spill it, and he won't, your statement won't be used at all, but we've got to have it in the safe in case he does. Another thing, if we have this statement we won't feel obliged to pass it along to the cops about your having had a key to the studio door. We wouldn't be interested in keys. Still another, you'll be saving your father a big chunk of dough. If you sign this statement we can clear up the matter of Mion's death, and if we do that I guarantee that Mrs. Mion will be in no frame of mind to push any claim against your father. She will be too busy with a certain matter."

I proffered the pen. "Go ahead and sign it."

She shook her head, but not with much energy because her brain was working again. Fully appreciating the fact that her thinking was not on the tournament level, I was patient. Then the refills came and there was a recess, since she couldn't be expected to think and drink all at once. But finally she fought her way through to the point I had aimed at.

"So you know," she declared with satisfaction.

"We know enough," I said darkly.

"You know she killed him. You know she put the gun back on the floor. I knew that too, I knew she must have. And now you can prove it? If I sign this you can prove it?"

Of course I could have covered it with doubletalk, but I thought, What the hell. "We certainly can," I assured her. "With this statement we're ready to go. It's the missing link. Here's the pen."

She lifted her glass, drained it, put it down, and damned if she didn't shake her head again, this time with energy. "No," she said flatly, "I won't." She extended a hand with the document in it. "I admit it's all true, and when you get her on trial if she says she put the gun back on the floor I'll come and swear to it that I put it on the bust, but I won't sign anything because once I signed something about an accident and my father made me promise that I would never sign anything again without showing it to him first. I could take it and show it to him and then sign it, and you could come for it tonight or tomorrow." She frowned. "Except that he knows I had a key, but I could explain that."

But she no longer had the document. I had reached and taken it. You are welcome to think I should have changed holds on her and gone on fighting, but you weren't there seeing and hearing her, and I was. I gave up. I got out my pocket notebook, tore out a page, and began writing on it.

"I could use another drink," she stated.

"In a minute," I mumbled, and went on writing, as follows:

> To Nero Wolfe:
> I hereby declare that Archie Goodwin has tried his best to persuade me to sign the statement you wrote, and explained its purpose to me, and I have told him why I must refuse to sign it.

"There," I said, handing it to her. "That won't be signing something; it's just stating that you refuse to sign something. The reason I've got to have it, Mr. Wolfe knows how beautiful girls appeal to me, especially sophisticated girls like you, and if I take that thing back to him unsigned he'll think I didn't even try. He might even fire me. Just write your name there at the bottom."

She read it over again and took the pen. She smiled at me, glistening. "You're not kidding me any," she said, not unfriendly. "I know when I appeal to a man. You think I'm cold and calculating."

"Yeah?" I made it a little bitter, but not too bitter. "Anyhow it's not the point whether you appeal to me, but what Mr. Wolfe will think. It'll help a lot to have that. Much obliged." I took the paper from her and blew on her signature to dry it.

"I know when I appeal to a man," she stated.

There wasn't another thing there I wanted, but I had practically promised to buy her another drink, so I did so.

It was after six when I got back to West Thirty-fifth Street, so Wolfe had finished in the plant rooms and was down in the office. I marched in and put the unsigned statement on his desk in front of him.

He grunted. "Well?"

I sat down and told him exactly how it had gone, up to the point where she had offered to take the document home and show it to her father.

"I'm sorry," I said, "but some of her outstanding qualities didn't show much in that crowd the other evening. I give this not as an excuse but merely a fact. Her mental operations could easily be carried on inside a hollowed-out pea. Knowing what you think of unsupported statements, and wanting to convince you of the truth of that one, I got evidence to back it up. Here's a paper she *did* sign."

I handed him the page I had torn from my notebook. He took a look at it and then cocked an eye at me.

"She signed this?"

"Yes, sir. In my presence."

"Indeed. Good. Satisfactory."

I acknowledged the tribute with a careless nod. It does not hurt my feelings when he says, "Satisfactory," like that.

"A bold, easy hand," he said. "She used your pen?"

"Yes, sir."

"May I have it, please?"

I arose and handed it to him, together with a couple of sheets of typewriter paper, and stood and watched with interested approval as he wrote "Clara James" over and over again, comparing each attempt with the sample I had secured. Meanwhile, at intervals, he spoke.

"It's highly unlikely that anyone will ever see it—except our clients. . . . That's better. . . . There's time to phone all of them before dinner—first Mrs. Mion and Mr. Weppler—then the others. . . . Tell them my opinion is ready on Mrs. Mion's claim against Mr. James. . . . If they can come at nine this evening— If that's impossible tomorrow morning at eleven will do. . . . Then get Mr. Cramer. . . . Tell him it might be well to bring one of his men along. . . ."

He flattened the typed statement on his desk blotter, forged Clara James' name at the bottom, and compared it with the true signature which I had provided.

"Faulty, to an expert," he muttered, "but no expert will ever see it. For our clients, even if they know her writing, it will do nicely."

VIII

It took a solid hour on the phone to get it fixed for that evening, but I finally managed it. I never did catch up with Gifford James, but his daughter agreed to find him and deliver him, and made good on it. The others I tracked down myself.

The only ones that gave me an argument were the clients, especially Peggy Mion. She balked hard at sitting in at a meeting for the ostensible purpose of collecting from Gifford James, and I had to appeal to Wolfe. Fred and Peggy were invited to come ahead of the others for a private briefing and then decide whether to stay or not. She bought that.

They got there in time to help out with the after-dinner coffee. Peggy had presumably brushed her teeth and had a nap and a bath, and manifestly she had changed her clothes, but even so she did not sparkle. She was wary, weary, removed, and skeptical. She didn't say in so many words that she wished she had never gone near Nero Wolfe, but she might as well have. I had a notion that Fred Weppler felt the same way about it but was being gallant and loyal. It was Peggy who had insisted on coming to Wolfe, and Fred didn't want her to feel that he thought she had made things worse instead of better.

They didn't perk up even when Wolfe showed them the statement with Clara James' name signed to it. They read it together, with her in the red leather chair and him perched on the arm.

They looked up together, at Wolfe.

"So what?" Fred demanded.

"My dear sir." Wolfe pushed his cup and saucer back. "My dear madam. Why did you come to me? Because the fact that the gun was not on the floor when you two entered the studio convinced you that Mion had not killed himself but had been murdered. If the circumstances had permitted you to believe that he had killed himself, you would be married by now and never have needed me. Very well. That is now precisely what the circumstances are. What more do you want? You wanted your minds cleared. I have cleared them."

Fred twisted his lips, tight.

"I don't believe it," Peggy said glumly.

"You don't believe this statement?" Wolfe reached for the document and put it in his desk drawer, which struck me as a wise precaution, since it was getting close to nine o'clock. "Do you think Miss James would sign a thing like that if it weren't true? Why would—"

"I don't mean that," Peggy said. "I mean I don't believe my husband killed himself, no matter where the gun was. I knew him too well. He would never have killed himself—*never*." She twisted her head to look up at her fellow client. "Would he, Fred?"

"It's hard to believe," Fred admitted grudgingly.

"I see." Wolfe was caustic. "Then the job you hired me for was not as you described it. At least you must concede that I have satisfied you about the gun; you can't wiggle out of that. So that job's done, but now you want more. You want a murder disclosed, which means, of necessity, a murderer caught. You want—"

"I only mean," Peggy insisted forlornly, "that I don't believe he killed himself, and nothing would make me believe it. I see now what I really—"

The doorbell sounded, and I went to answer it.

IX

So the clients stayed for the party.

There were ten guests altogether: the six who had been there Monday evening, the two clients, Inspector Cramer, and my old friend and enemy, Sergeant Purley Stebbins. What made it unusual was that the dumbest one of the lot, Clara James, was the only one who had a notion of what was up, unless she had told her father, which I doubted. She had the advantage of the lead I had given her at the Churchill bar. Adele Bosley, Dr. Lloyd, Rupert Grove, Judge Arnold, and Gifford James had had no reason to suppose there was anything on the agenda but the damage claim against James, until they got there and were made acquainted with Inspector Cramer and Sergeant Stebbins. God only knew what they thought then; one glance at their faces was enough to show *they* didn't know. As for Cramer and Stebbins, they had had enough experience of Nero Wolfe to be aware that almost certainly fur was going to fly, but whose and how and when? And as for Fred and Peggy, even after the arrival of the law, they probably thought that Wolfe was going to get Mion's suicide pegged down by producing Clara's statement and disclosing what Fred had told us about moving the gun from the bust to the floor, which accounted for the desperate and cornered look on their faces. But now they were stuck.

Wolfe focused on the inspector, who was seated in the rear over by the big globe, with Purley nearby. "If you don't mind, Mr. Cramer, first I'll clear up a little matter that is outside your interest."

Cramer nodded and shifted the cigar in his mouth to a new angle. He was keeping his watchful eyes on the move.

Wolfe changed his focus. "I'm sure you'll all be glad to hear this. Not that I formed my opinion so as to please you; I considered only the merits of the case. Without prejudice to her legal position, I feel that morally Mrs. Mion has no claim on Mr. James. As I said she would, she accepts my judgment. She makes no claim and will ask no payment for damages. You verify that before these witnesses, Mrs. Mion?"

"Certainly." Peggy was going to add something, but stopped it on the way out.

"This is wonderful!" Adele Bosley was out of her chair. "May I use a phone?"

"Later," Wolfe snapped at her. "Sit down, please."

"It seems to me," Judge Arnold observed, "that this could have been told us on the phone. I had to cancel an important engagement." Lawyers are never satisfied.

"Quite true," Wolfe agreed mildly, "if that were all. But there's the matter of Mion's death. When I—"

"What has that got to do with it?"

"I'm about to tell you. Surely it isn't extraneous, since his death resulted, though indirectly, from the assault by Mr. James. But my interest goes beyond that. Mrs. Mion hired me not only to decide about the claim of her husband's estate against Mr. James—that is now closed—but also to investigate her husband's death. She was convinced he had not killed himself. She could not believe it was in his character to commit suicide. I have investigated and I am prepared to report to her."

"You don't need us here for that," Rupert the Fat said in a high squeak.

"I need one of you. I need the murderer."

"You still don't need *us*," Arnold said harshly.

"Hang it," Wolfe snapped, "then go! All but one of you. Go!"

Nobody made a move.

Wolfe gave them five seconds. "Then I'll go on," he said dryly. "As I say, I'm prepared to report, but the investigation is not concluded. One vital detail will require official sanction, and that's why Inspector Cramer is present. It will also need Mrs. Mion's concurrence; and I think it well to consult Dr. Lloyd too, since he signed the death certificate." His eyes went to Peggy. "First you, madam. Will you give your consent to the exhumation of your husband's body?"

She gawked at him. "What for?"

"To get evidence that he was murdered, and by whom. It is a reasonable expectation."

She stopped gawking. "Yes. I don't care." She thought he was just talking to hear himself.

Wolfe's eyes went left. "You have no objection, Dr. Lloyd?"

Lloyd was nonplused. "I have no idea," he said slowly and distinctly, "what you're getting at, but in any case I have no voice in the matter. I merely issued the certificate."

"Then you won't oppose it. Mr. Cramer. The basis for the request for official sanction will appear in a moment, but you should know that what will be required is an examination and report by Dr. Abraham Rentner of Mount Sinai Hospital."

"You don't get an exhumation just because you're curious," Cramer growled.

"I know it. I'm more than curious." Wolfe's eyes traveled. "You all know, I suppose, that one of the chief reasons, probably the main one, for the police decision that Mion had committed suicide was the manner of his death. Of course other details had to fit—as for instance the presence of the gun there beside the body—and they did. But the determining factor was the assumption that a man cannot be murdered by sticking the barrel of a revolver in his mouth and pulling the trigger unless he is first made unconscious; and there was no evidence that Mion had been either struck or drugged, and besides, when the bullet left his head it went to the ceiling. However, though that assumption is ordinarily sound, surely this case was an exception. It came to my mind at once, when Mrs. Mion first consulted me. For there was present— But I'll show you with a simple demonstration. Archie. Get a gun."

I opened my third drawer and got one out.

"Is it loaded?"

I flipped it open to check. "No, sir."

Wolfe returned to the audience. "You, I think, Mr. James. As an opera singer you should be able to follow stage directions. Stand up, please. This is a serious matter, so do it right. You are a patient with a sore throat, and Mr. Goodwin is your doctor. He will ask you to open your mouth so he can look at your throat. You are to do exactly what you would naturally do under those circumstances. Will you do that?"

"But it's obvious." James, standing, was looking grim. "I don't need to."

"Nevertheless, please indulge me. There's a certain detail. Will you do it as naturally as possible?"

"Yes."

"Good. Will the rest of you all watch Mr. James' face? Closely. Go ahead, Archie."

With the gun in my pocket I moved in front of James and told him to open wide. He did so. For a moment his eyes came to mine as I peered into his throat, and then slanted upward. Not in a hurry,

I took the gun from my pocket and poked it into his mouth until it touched the roof. He jerked back and dropped into his chair.

"Did you see the gun?" Wolfe demanded.

"No. My eyes were up."

"Just so." Wolfe looked at the others. "You saw his eyes go up? They always do. Try it yourselves sometime. I tried it in my bedroom Sunday evening. So it is by no means impossible to kill a man that way, it isn't even difficult, if you're his doctor and he has something wrong with his throat. You agree, Dr. Lloyd?"

Lloyd had not joined the general movement to watch James' face during the demonstration. He hadn't stirred a muscle. Now his jaw was twitching a little, but that was all.

He did his best to smile. "To show that a thing could happen," he said in a pretty good voice, "isn't the same thing as proving it did happen."

"Indeed it isn't," Wolfe conceded. "Though we do have some facts. You have no effective alibi. Mion would have admitted you to his studio at any time without question. You could have managed easily to get the gun from the base of Caruso's bust, and slipped it into your pocket without being seen. For you, as for no one else, he would upon request have stood with his mouth wide open, inviting his doom. He was killed shortly after you had been compelled to make an appointment for Dr. Rentner to examine him. We do have those facts, don't we?"

"They prove nothing," Lloyd insisted. His voice was not quite as good. He came out of his chair to his feet. It did not look as if the movement had any purpose; apparently he simply couldn't stay put in his chair, and the muscles had acted on their own. And it had been a mistake because, standing upright, he began to tremble.

"They'll help," Wolfe told him, "if we can get one more—and I suspect we can, or what are you quivering about? What was it, Doctor? Some unfortunate blunder? Had you botched the operation and ruined his voice forever? I suppose that was it, since the threat to your reputation and career was grave enough to make you resort to murder. Anyhow we'll soon know, when Dr. Rentner makes his examination and reports. I don't expect you to furnish—"

"It wasn't a blunder!" Lloyd squawked. "It could have happened to anyone—"

Whereupon he did blunder. I think what made him lose his head completely was hearing his own voice and realizing it was a hysterical squawk and he couldn't help it. He made a dash for the door. I knocked Judge Arnold down in my rush across the room, which was unnecessary, for by the time I arrived Purley Stebbins had Lloyd by the collar, and Cramer was there too. Hearing a commotion behind me, I turned around. Clara James had made a dive for Peggy Mion, screeching something I didn't catch, but her father and Adele Bosley had stopped her and were getting her under control. Judge Arnold and Rupert the Fat were excitedly telling Wolfe how wonderful he was. Peggy was apparently weeping, from the way her shoulders were shaking, but I couldn't see her face because it was buried on Fred's shoulder, and his arms had her tight.

Nobody wanted me or needed me, so I went to the kitchen for a glass of milk.

BULLET FOR ONE

I

It was her complexion that made it hard to believe she was as scared as she said she was.

"Maybe I haven't made it clear," she persisted, twisting her fingers some more though I had asked her to stop. "I'm not making anything up, really I'm not. If they framed me once, isn't that a good enough reason to think they are doing it again?"

If her cheek color had been from a drugstore, with the patches showing because the fear in her heart was using extra blood for internal needs, I would probably have been affected more. But at first sight of her I had been reminded of a picture on a calendar hanging on the wall of Sam's Diner on Eleventh Avenue, a picture of a round-faced girl with one hand holding a pail and the other hand resting on the flank of a cow she had just milked or was just going to milk. It was her to a T, in skin tint, build, and innocence.

She quit the finger-twisting to make tight little fists and perch them on her thigh fronts. "Is he really such a puffed-up baboon?" she demanded. "They'll be here in twenty minutes, and I've got to see him first!" Suddenly she was out of the chair, on her feet. "Where is he, upstairs?"

Having suspected she was subject to impulses, I had, instead of crossing to my desk, held a position between her and the door to the hall.

"Give it up," I advised her. "When you stand up you tremble, I noticed that when you came in, so sit down. I've tried to explain, Miss Rooney, that while this room is Mr. Wolfe's office, the rest of this building is his home. From nine to eleven in the morning, and from four to six in the afternoon, he is absolutely at home, up in the plant rooms with his orchids, and bigger men than you have had to like it. But, what I've seen of you, I think possibly you're nice, and I'll do you a favor."

"What?"

"Sit down and quit trembling."

She sat down.

"I'll go up and tell him about you."

"What will you tell him?"

"I'll remind him that a man named Ferdinand Pohl phoned this morning and made a date for himself and four others, to come here to see Mr. Wolfe at six o'clock, which is sixteen minutes from now. I'll tell him your name is Audrey Rooney and you're one of the four others, and you're fairly good-looking and may be nice, and you're scared stiff because, as you tell it, they're pretending they think it was Talbott but actually they're getting set to frame you, and—"

"Not all of them."

"Anyhow some. I'll tell him that you came ahead of time to see him alone and inform him that you have not murdered anyone, specifically not Sigmund Keyes, and to warn him that he must watch these stinkers like a hawk."

"It sounds crazy—like that!"

"I'll put feeling in it."

She left her chair again, came to me in three swift steps, flattened her palms on my coat front, and tilted her head back to get my eyes.

"You may be nice too," she said hopefully.

"That would be too much to expect," I told her as I turned and made for the stairs in the hall.

II

Ferdinand Pohl was speaking.

Sitting there in the office with my chair swiveled so that my back was to my desk, with Wolfe himself behind his desk to my left, I took Pohl in. He was close to twice my age. Seated in the red leather chair beyond the end of Wolfe's desk, with his leg-crossing histing his pants so that five inches of bare shin showed above his garterless sock, there was nothing about him to command attention except an unusual assortment of facial creases, and nothing at all to love.

"What brought us together," he was saying in a thin peevish tone, "and what brought us here together, is our unanimous opinion that

Sigmund Keyes was murdered by Victor Talbott, and also our conviction—"

"Not unanimous," another voice objected.

The voice was soft and good for the ears, and its owner was good for the eyes. Her chin, especially, was the kind you can take from any angle. The only reason I hadn't seated her in the chair nearest mine was that on her arrival she had answered my welcoming smile with nothing but brow-lifting, and I had decided to hell with her until she learned her manners.

"Not unanimous, Ferdy," she objected.

"You said," Pohl told her, even more peevish, "that you were in sympathy with our purpose and wanted to join us and come here with us."

Seeing them and hearing them, I made a note that they hated each other. She had known him longer than I had, since she called him Ferdy, and evidently she agreed that there was nothing about him to love. I was about to start feeling that I had been too harsh with her when I saw she was lifting her brows at him.

"That," she declared, "is quite different from having the opinion that Vic murdered my father. I have no opinion, because I don't know."

"Then what are you in sympathy with?"

"I want to find out. So do you. And I certainly agree that the police are being extremely stupid."

"Who do you think killed him if Vic didn't?"

"I don't know." The brows went up again. "But since I have inherited my father's business, and since I am engaged to marry Vic, and since a few other things, I want very much to know. That's why I'm here with you."

"You don't belong here!"

"I'm here, Ferdy."

"I say you don't belong!" Pohl's creases were wriggling. "I said so and I still say so! We came, the four of us, for a definite purpose, to get Nero Wolfe to find proof that Vic killed your father!" Pohl suddenly uncrossed his legs, leaned forward to peer at Dorothy Keyes' face, and asked in a mean little voice, "And what if you helped him?"

Three other voices spoke at once. One said, "They're off again."
Another, "Let Mr. Broadyke tell it."
Another, "Get one of them out of here."

Wolfe said, "If the job is limited to those terms, Mr. Pohl, to prove that a man named by you committed murder, you've wasted your trip. What if he didn't?"

III

MANY things had happened in that office on the ground floor of the old brownstone house owned by Nero Wolfe during the years I had worked for him as his man Friday, Saturday, Sunday, Monday, Tuesday, Wednesday, and Thursday.

This gathering in the office, on this Tuesday evening in October, had its own special angle of interest. Sigmund Keyes, top-drawer industrial designer, had been murdered the preceding Tuesday, just a week ago. I had read about it in the papers and had also found an opportunity to hear it privately discussed by my friend and enemy Sergeant Purley Stebbins of Homicide, and from the professional-detective slant it struck me as a lulu.

It had been Keyes' custom, five days a week at six-thirty in the morning, to take a walk in the park, and to do it the hard and silly way by walking on four legs instead of two. He kept the four legs, which he owned and which were named Casanova, at the Stillwell Riding Academy on Ninety-eighth Street just west of the park. That morning he mounted Casanova as usual, promptly at six-thirty, and rode into the park. Forty minutes later, at seven-ten, he had been seen by a mounted cop, in the park on patrol, down around Sixty-sixth Street. His customary schedule would have had him about there at that time. Twenty-five minutes later, at seven-thirty-five, Casanova, with his saddle uninhabited, had emerged from the park uptown and strolled down the street to the academy. Curiosity had naturally been aroused, and in three-quarters of an hour had been satisfied, when a park cop had found Keyes' body behind a thicket some twenty yards from the bridle path in the park, in the latitude of Ninety-fifth Street. Later a .38-caliber revolver bullet had been dug out of his chest. The police had concluded, from marks on the path and beyond its edge, that he had been shot out of his saddle and had crawled, with difficulty, up a little slope toward a paved walk for pedestrians, and hadn't had enough life left to make it.

A horseman shot from his saddle within sight of the Empire State

Building was of course a natural for the tabloids, and the other papers thought well of it too. No weapon had been found, and no eyewitnesses. No citizen had even come forward to report seeing a masked man lurking behind a tree, probably because very few New Yorkers could possibly explain being up and dressed and strolling in the park at that hour of the morning.

So the city employees had had to start at the other end and look for motives and opportunities. During the week that had passed a lot of names had been mentioned and a lot of people had received official callers, and as a result the glare had pretty well concentrated on six spots. So the papers had it, and so I gathered from Purley Stebbins. What gave the scene in our office that Tuesday afternoon its special angle of interest was the fact that five of the six spots were there seated on chairs, and apparently what they wanted Wolfe to do was to take the glare out of their eyes and get it aimed exclusively at the sixth spot, not present.

IV

"Permit me to say," Frank Broadyke offered in a cultivated baritone, "that Mr. Pohl has put it badly. The situation is this, Mr. Wolfe, that Mr. Pohl got us together and we found that each of us feels that he is being harassed unreasonably. Not only that he is unjustly suspected of a crime he did not commit, but that in a full week the police have accomplished nothing and aren't likely to, and we will be left with this unjust suspicion permanently upon us."

Broadyke gestured with a hand. More than his baritone was cultivated; he was cultivated all over. He was somewhat younger than Pohl, and ten times as elegant. His manner gave the impression that he was finding it difficult just to be himself because (a) he was in the office of a private detective, which was vulgar, (b) he had come there with persons with whom one doesn't ordinarily associate, which was embarrassing, and (c) the subject for discussion was his connection with a murder, which was preposterous.

He was going on. "Mr. Pohl suggested that we consult you and engage your services. As one who will gladly pay my share of the bill, permit me to say that what I want is the removal of that unjust suspicion. If you can achieve that only by finding the criminal and evidence against him, very well. If the guilty man proves to be Victor Talbott, again very well."

"There's no if about it!" Pohl blurted. "Talbott did it, and the job is to pin it on him!"

"With me helping, Ferdy, don't forget," Dorothy Keyes told him softly.

"Aw, can it!"

Eyes turned to the speaker, whose only contribution up to that point had been the remark, "They're off again." Heads had to turn too because he was seated to the rear of the swing of the arc. The high pitch of his voice was a good match for his name, Wayne Safford, but not for his broad husky build and the strong big bones of his face. According to the papers he was twenty-eight, but he looked a little older, about my age.

Wolfe nodded at him. "I quite agree, Mr. Safford." Wolfe's eyes swept the arc. "Mr. Pohl wants too much for his money. You can hire me to catch a fish, ladies and gentlemen, but you can't tell me which fish. You can tell me what it is I'm after—a murderer—but you can't tell me who it is unless you have evidence, and in that case why pay me? Have you got evidence?"

No one said anything.

"Have you got evidence, Mr. Pohl?"

"No."

"How do you know it was Mr. Talbott?"

"I know it, that's all. We all know it! Even Miss Keyes here knows it, but she's too damn contrary to admit it."

Wolfe swept the arc again. "Is that true? Do you all know it?"

No word. No "yes" and no "no." No nods and no shakes.

"Then the identity of the fish is left to me. Is that understood? Mr. Broadyke?"

"Yes."

"Mr. Safford?"

"Yes."

"Miss Rooney?"

"Yes. Only I think it was Vic Talbott."

"Nothing can stop you. Miss Keyes?"

"Yes."

"Mr. Pohl?"

No answer.

"I must have a commitment on this, Mr. Pohl. If it proves to be Mr. Talbott you can pay extra. But in any case, I am hired to get facts?"

"Sure, the real facts."

"There is no other kind. I guarantee not to deliver any unreal facts." Wolfe leaned forward to press a button on his desk. "That is, indeed, the only guaranty I can give you. I should make it plain that you are responsible both collectively and individually for this engagement with me. Now if—"

The door to the hall had opened, and Fritz Brenner entered and approached.

"Fritz," Wolfe told him, "there will be five guests at dinner."

"Yes, sir," Fritz told him without a blink and turned to go. That's how good Fritz is, and he is not the kind to ring in omelets or canned soup. As he was opening the door a protest came from Frank Broadyke.

"Better make it four. I'll have to leave soon and I have a dinner engagement."

"Cancel it," Wolfe snapped.

"I'm afraid I can't, really."

"Then I can't take this job." Wolfe was curt. "What do you expect, with this thing already a week old?" He glanced at the clock on the wall. "I'll need you, all of you, certainly all evening, and probably most of the night. I must know all that you know about Mr. Keyes and Mr. Talbott. Also, if I am to remove this unjust suspicion of you from the minds of the police and the public, I must begin by removing it from my own mind. That will take many hours of hard work."

"Oh," Dorothy Keyes put in, her brows going up, "you suspect us, do you?"

Wolfe, ignoring her, asked Broadyke, "Well, sir?"

"I'll have to phone," Broadyke muttered.

"You may," Wolfe conceded, as if he were yielding a point. His eyes moved, left and right and left again, and settled on Audrey Rooney, whose chair was a little in the rear, to one side of Wayne Safford's. "Miss Rooney," he shot at her, "you seem to be the most vulnerable, since you were on the scene. When did Mr. Keyes dismiss you from his employ, and what for?"

Audrey had been sitting straight and still, with her lips tight. "Well, it was—" she began, but stopped to clear her throat and then didn't continue because of an interruption.

The doorbell had rung, and I had left it to Fritz to answer it, which was the custom when I was engaged with Wolfe and visitors, unless superseding orders had been given. Now the door to the hall opened, and Fritz entered, closed the door behind him, and announced, "A gentleman to see you, sir. Mr. Victor Talbott."

The name plopped in the middle of us like a paratrooper at a picnic.

"By God!" Wayne Safford exclaimed.

"How the devil—" Frank Broadyke started, and stopped.

"So you told him!" Pohl spat at Dorothy Keyes.

Dorothy merely raised her brows. I was getting fed up with that routine and wished she would try something else.

Audrey Rooney's mouth was hanging open.

"Show him in," Wolfe told Fritz.

V

LIKE millions of my fellow citizens, I had done some sizing up of Victor Talbott from pictures of him in the papers, and within ten seconds after he had joined us in the office I had decided the label I had tied on him could stay. He was the guy who, at a cocktail party or before dinner, grabs the tray of appetizers and passes it around, looking into eyes and making cracks.

Not counting me, he was easily the best-looking male in the room.

Entering, he shot a glance and a smile at Dorothy Keyes, ignored the others, came to a stop in front of Wolfe's desk, and said pleasantly, "You're Nero Wolfe, of course. I'm Vic Talbott. I suppose you'd rather not shake hands with me under the circumstances—that is, if you're accepting the job these people came to offer you. Are you?"

"How do you do, sir," Wolfe rumbled. "Good heavens, I've shaken hands with—how many murderers, Archie?"

"Oh—forty," I estimated.

"At least that. That's Mr. Goodwin, Mr. Talbott."

Evidently Vic figured I might be squeamish too, for he gave me a nod but extended no hand. Then he turned to face the guests. "What about it, folks? Have you hired the great detective?"

"Nuts," Wayne Safford squeaked at him. "You come prancing in, huh?"

Ferdinand Pohl had left his chair and was advancing on the gatecrasher. I was on my feet, ready to move. There was plenty of feeling loose in the room, and I didn't want any of our clients hurt. But all Pohl did was to tap Talbott on the chest with a thick forefinger and growl at him, "Listen, my boy. You're not going to sell anything here. You've made one sale too many as it is." Pohl whirled to Wolfe. "What did you let him in for?"

"Permit me to say," Broadyke put in, "that it does seem an excess of hospitality."

"By the way, Vic"—it was Dorothy's soft voice—"Ferdy says I was your accomplice."

The remarks from the others had made no visible impression on him, but it was different with Dorothy. He turned to her, and the look on his face was good for a whole chapter in his biography. He was absolutely all hers unless I needed an oculist. She could lift her lovely brows a thousand times a day without feeding him up. He let his eyes speak to her and then wheeled to use his tongue for Pohl. "Do you know what I think of you, Ferdy? I guess you do!"

"If you please," Wolfe said sharply. "You don't need my office for exchanging your opinions of one another; you can do that anywhere. We have work to do. Mr. Talbott, you asked if I've accepted a job that has been offered me. I have. I have engaged to investigate the murder of Sigmund Keyes. But I have received no confidences and can still decline it. Have you a better offer? What did you come here for?"

Talbott smiled at him. "That's the way to talk," he said admiringly. "No, I have nothing to offer in the way of a job, but I felt I ought to be in on this. I figured it this way: they were going to hire you to get me arrested for murder, so naturally you would like to have a look at me and ask me some questions—and here I am."

"Pleading not guilty, of course. Archie. A chair for Mr. Talbott."

"Of course," he agreed, thanking me with a smile for the chair I brought, and sitting down. "Otherwise you'd have no job. Shoot." Suddenly he flushed. "Under the circumstances, I guess I shouldn't have said 'shoot.'"

"You could have said 'Fire away,'" Wayne Safford piped up from the rear.

"Be quiet, Wayne," Audrey Rooney scolded him.

"Permit me—" Broadyke began, but Wolfe cut him off.

"No. Mr. Talbott has invited questions." He focused on the inviter.

"These other people think the police are handling this matter stupidly and ineffectively. Do you agree, Mr. Talbott?"

Vic considered a moment, then nodded. "On the whole, yes," he assented.

"Why?"

"Well—you see, they're up against it. They're used to working with clues, and while they found plenty of clues to show what happened, like the marks on the bridle path and leading to the thicket, there aren't any that help to identify the murderer. Absolutely none whatever. So they had to fall back on motive, and right away they found a man with the best motive in the world."

Talbott tapped himself on the necktie. "Me. But then they found that this man—me—that I couldn't possibly have done it because I was somewhere else. They found I had an alibi that was—"

"Phony!" From Wayne Safford.

"Made to order." From Broadyke.

"The dumbheads!" From Pohl. "If they had brains enough to give that switchboard girl—"

"Please!" Wolfe shut them up. "Go ahead, Mr. Talbott. Your alibi —but first the motive. What is the best motive in the world?"

Vic looked surprised. "It's been printed over and over again."

"I know. But I don't want journalistic conjectures when I've got you—unless you're sensitive about it."

Talbott's smile had some bitterness in it. "If I was," he declared, "I've sure been cured this past week. I guess ten million people have read that I'm deeply in love with Dorothy Keyes or some variation of that. All right, I am! Want a shot—want a picture of me saying it?" He turned to face his fiancée. "I love you, Dorothy, better than all the world, deeply, madly, with all my heart." He returned to Wolfe. "There's your motive."

"Vic, darling," Dorothy told his profile, "you're a perfect fool, and you're perfectly fascinating. I really am glad you've got a good alibi."

"You demonstrate love," Wolfe said dryly, "by killing your beloved's surviving parent. Is that it?"

"Yes," Talbott asserted. "Under certain conditions. Here was the situation. Sigmund Keyes was the most celebrated and successful industrial designer in America, and—"

"Nonsense!" Broadyke exploded, without asking permission to say.

Talbott smiled. "Sometimes," he said, as if offering it for consideration, "a jealous man is worse than any jealous woman. You know, of course, that Mr. Broadyke is himself an industrial designer—in fact, he practically invented the profession. Not many manufacturers would dream of tooling for a new model—steamship, railroad train, airplane, refrigerator, vacuum cleaner, alarm clock, no matter what—without consulting Broadyke, until I came along and took over the selling end for Sigmund Keyes. Incidentally, that's why I doubt if Broadyke killed Keyes. If he had got that desperate about it he wouldn't have killed Keyes, he would have killed me."

"You were speaking," Wolfe reminded him, "of love as a motive for murder under certain conditions."

"Yes, and Broadyke threw me off." Talbott cocked his head. "Let's see—oh, yes, and I was doing the selling for Keyes, and he couldn't stand the talk going around that I was mostly responsible for the big success we were having, but he was afraid to get rid of me. And I loved his daughter and wanted her to marry me, and will always love her. But he had great influence with her, which I did not and do not understand—anyway, if she loved me as I do her that wouldn't have mattered, but she doesn't—"

"My God, Vic," Dorothy protested, "haven't I said a dozen times I'd marry you like that"—she snapped her fingers—"if it weren't for Dad? Really, I'm crazy about you!"

"All right," Talbott told Wolfe, "there's your motive. It's certainly old-fashioned, no modern industrial design to it, but it's absolutely dependable. Naturally that's what the police thought until they ran up against the fact that I was somewhere else. That got them bewildered and made them sore, and they haven't recovered their wits, so I guess my good friends here are right that they're being stupid and ineffective. Not that they've crossed me off entirely. I understand they've got an army of detectives and stool pigeons hunting for the gunman I hired to do the job. They'll have to hunt hard. You heard Miss Keyes call me a fool, but I'm not quite fool enough to hire someone to commit a murder for me."

"I should hope not." Wolfe sighed. "There's nothing better than a good motive. What about the alibi? Have the police given up on that?"

"Yes, the damn idiots!" Pohl blurted. "That switchboard girl—"

"I asked Mr. Talbott," Wolfe snapped.

"I don't know," Talbott admitted, "but I suppose they had to. I'm still trembling at how lucky I was that I got to bed late that Monday night—I mean a week ago, the night before Keyes was killed. If I had been riding with him I'd be in jail now, and done for. It's a question of timing."

Talbott compressed his lips and loosened them. "Oh, boy! The mounted cop saw Keyes riding in the park near Sixty-sixth Street at ten minutes past seven. Keyes was killed near Ninety-sixth Street. Even if he had galloped all the way he couldn't have got there, the way that bridle path winds, before seven-twenty. And he didn't gallop, because if he had the horse would have shown it, and he didn't." Talbott twisted around. "You're the authority on that, Wayne. Casanova hadn't been in a sweat, had he?"

"You're telling it," was all he got from Wayne Safford.

"Well, he hadn't," Talbott told Wolfe. "Wayne is on record on that. So Keyes couldn't have reached the spot where he was killed before seven-twenty-five. There's the time for that, twenty-five minutes past seven."

"And you?" Wolfe inquired.

"Me, I was lucky. I sure was. I often rode in the park with Keyes at that ungodly hour—two or three times a week. He wanted me to make it every day, but I got out of it about half the time. There was nothing social or sociable about it. We would walk our horses side by side, talking business, except when he felt like trotting. I live at the Hotel Churchill. I got in late Monday night, but I left a call for six o'clock anyway, because I hadn't ridden with Keyes for several days and didn't want to get him sore. But when the girl rang my phone in the morning I was just too damn sleepy, and I told her to call the riding academy and say I wouldn't be there, and to call me again at seven-thirty. She did so, and I still didn't feel like turning out but I had to because I had a breakfast date with an out-of-town customer, so I told her to send up a double orange juice. A few minutes later a waiter brought it up. So was I lucky? Keyes was killed uptown at twenty-five past seven at the earliest, and probably a little later. I was in my room at the Churchill, nearly three miles away, at half-past seven. You can have three guesses how glad I was I left that seven-thirty call!"

Wolfe nodded. "You should give the out-of-town customer a discount. In that armor, why did you take the trouble to join this gathering?"

"A switchboard girl and a waiter, for God's sake!" Pohl snorted sarcastically.

"Nice honest people, Ferdy," Talbott told him, and answered Wolfe, "I didn't."

"No? You're not here?"

"Sure I'm here, but not to join any gathering. I came to join Miss Keyes. I don't regard it as trouble to join Miss Keyes. As for the rest of them, except maybe Broadyke—"

The doorbell rang again, and since additional gate-crashers might or might not be desirable, I upped myself in a hurry, stepped across and into the hall, intercepted Fritz just in time, and went to the front door to take a look through the panel of one-way glass.

Seeing who it was out on the stoop, I fastened the chain bolt, pulled the door open the two inches the chain would permit, and spoke through the crack. "I don't want to catch cold."

"Neither do I," a gruff voice told me. "Take that damn bolt off."

"Mr. Wolfe is engaged," I said politely. "Will I do?"

"You will not. You never have and you never will."

"Then hold it a minute. I'll see."

I shut the door, went to the office, and told Wolfe, "The man about the chair," which was my favorite alias for Inspector Cramer of Homicide.

Wolfe grunted and shook his head. "I'll be busy for hours and can't be interrupted."

I returned to the front, opened to the crack again, and said regretfully, "Sorry, but he's doing his homework."

"Yeah," Cramer said sarcastically, "he certainly is. Now that Talbott's here too you've got a full house. All six of 'em. Open the door."

"Bah. Who are you trying to impress? You have tails on one or more, possibly all, and I do hope you haven't abandoned Talbott because we like him. By the way, the phone girl and the waiter at the Churchill —what're their names?"

"I'm coming in, Goodwin."

"Come ahead. This chain has never had a real test, and I've wondered about it."

"In the name of the law, open this door!"

I was so astonished that I nearly did open it in order to get a good look at him. Through the crack I could use only one eye. "Well, listen to you," I said incredulously. "On me you try that? As you know, it's the law that keeps you out. If you're ready to make an arrest, tell me who, and I'll see that he or she doesn't pull a scoot. After all, you're not a monopoly. You've had them for a full week, day or night, and Wolfe has had them only an hour or so, and you can't bear it! Incidentally, they're not refusing to see you, they don't know you're here, so don't chalk that against them. It's Mr. Wolfe who can't be disturbed. I'll give you this much satisfaction: he hasn't solved it yet, and it may take till midnight. It will save time if you'll give me the names—"

"Shut up," Cramer rasped. "I came here perfectly friendly. There's no law against Wolfe having people in his office. And there's no law against my being there with them, either."

"There sure isn't," I agreed heartily, "once you're in, but what about this door? Here's a legal door, with a man on one side who can't open it, and a man on the other side who won't, and according to the statutes—"

"Archie!" It was a bellow from the office, Wolfe's loudest bellow, seldom heard, and there were other sounds. It came again. "Archie!"

I said hastily, "Excuse me," slammed the door shut, ran down the hall and turned the knob, and popped in.

It was nothing seriously alarming. Wolfe was still in his chair behind his desk. The chair Talbott had occupied was overturned. Dorothy was on her feet, her back to Wolfe's desk, with her brows elevated to a record high. Audrey Rooney was standing in the corner by the big globe, with her clenched fists pressed against her cheeks, staring. Pohl and Broadyke were also out of their chairs, also gazing at the center of the room. From the spectators' frozen attitudes you might have expected to see something really startling, but it was only a couple of guys slinging punches. As I entered Talbott landed a right hook on the side of Safford's neck, and as I closed the door to the hall behind me Safford countered with a solid stiff left to Talbott's kidney sector. The only noise besides their fists and feet was a tense mutter from Audrey Rooney in her corner. "Hit him, Wayne; hit him, Wayne."

"How much did I miss?" I demanded.

"Stop them!" Wolfe ordered me.

Talbott's right glanced off of Safford's cheek, and Safford got in another one over the kidney. They were operating properly and in an orderly manner, but Wolfe was the boss and he hated commotion in the office, so I stepped across, grabbed Talbott's coat collar and yanked him back so hard he fell over a chair, and faced Safford to block him. For a second I thought Safford was going to paste me with one he had waiting, but he let it drop.

"What started it so quick?" I wanted to know.

Audrey was there, clutching my sleeve, protesting fiercely, "You shouldn't have stopped him! Wayne would have knocked him down! He did before!" She sounded more bloodthirsty than milkthirsty.

"He made a remark about Miss Rooney," Broadyke permitted himself to say.

"Get him out of here!" Wolfe spluttered.

"Which one?" I asked, watching Safford with one eye and Talbott with the other.

"Mr. Talbott!"

"You did very well, Vic," Dorothy was saying. "You were fantastically handsome with the gleam of battle in your eye." She put her palms against Talbott's cheeks, pulled his head forward, and stretched her neck to kiss him on the lips—a quick one. "There!"

"Vic is going now," I told her. "Come on, Talbott, I'll let you out."

Before he came he enfolded Dorothy in his arms. I glanced at Safford, expecting him to counter by enfolding Audrey, but he was standing by with his fists still doubled up. So I herded Talbott out of the room ahead of me. In the hall, while he was getting his hat and coat, I took a look through the one-way panel, saw that the stoop was clear, and opened the door. As he crossed the sill I told him, "You go for the head too much. You'll break a hand that way someday."

Back in the office someone had righted the overturned chair, and they were all seated again. Apparently, though her knight had been given the boot, Dorothy was going to stick. As I crossed to resume my place at my desk Wolfe was saying, "We got interrupted, Miss Rooney. As I said, you seem to be the most vulnerable, since you were on the scene. Will you please move a little closer—that chair there? Archie, your notebook."

VI

AT 10:55 THE next morning I was sitting in the office—not still, but again—waiting for Wolfe to come down from the plant rooms on the roof, where he keeps ten thousand orchids and an assortment of other

specimens of vegetation. I was playing three-handed pinochle with
Saul Panzer and Orrie Cather, who had been phoned to come in for
a job. Saul always wore an old brown cap, was undersized and homely,
with a big nose, and was the best field man in the world for everything
that could be done without a dinner jacket. Orrie, who would be able
to get along without a hairbrush in a few years, was by no means up to
Saul but was a good all-round man.

At 10:55 I was three bucks down.

In a drawer of my desk were two notebookfuls. Wolfe hadn't kept
the clients all night, but there hadn't been much left of it when he
let them go, and we now knew a good deal more about all of them
than any of the papers had printed. In some respects they were all
alike, as they told it. For instance, none of them had killed Sigmund
Keyes; none was heartbroken over his death, not even his daughter;
none had ever owned a revolver or knew much about shooting one;
none could produce any evidence that would help to convict Talbott
or even get him arrested; none had an airtight alibi; and each had a
motive of his own which might not have been the best in the world,
like Talbott's, but was nothing to sneeze at.

So they said.

Ferdinand Pohl had been indignant. He couldn't see why time
should be wasted on them and theirs, since the proper and sole objective was to bust Talbott's alibi and nab him. But he came through with
his facts. Ten years previously he had furnished the hundred thousand
dollars that had been needed to get Sigmund Keyes started with the
style of setup suitable for a big-time industrial designer. In the past
couple of years the Keyes profits had been up above the clouds, and
Pohl had wanted an even split and hadn't got it. Keyes had ladled
out a measly annual five per cent on Pohl's ante, five thousand a year,
whereas half the profits would have been ten times that, and Pohl
couldn't confront him with the classic alternative, buy my share or
sell me yours, because Pohl had been making bad guesses on other
matters and was deep in debt. The law wouldn't have helped, since
the partnership agreement had guaranteed Pohl only the five per cent
and Keyes had given the profits an alias by taking the gravy as salary,
claiming it was his designing ability that made the money. It had been,
Pohl said, a case of misjudging a man's character. Now that Keyes was
dead it would be a different story, with the contracts on hand and
royalties to come for periods up to twenty years. If Pohl and Dorothy,

who inherited, couldn't come to an understanding, it would be up to a judge to make the divvy, and Pohl would get, he thought, at least two hundred thousand, and probably a lot more.

He denied that that was a good motive for murder—not for him, and anyway it was silly to discuss it, because that Tuesday morning at 7:28 he had taken a train to Larchmont to sail his boat. Had he boarded the train at Grand Central or One Hundred and Twenty-fifth Street? Grand Central, he said. Had he been alone? Yes. He had left his apartment on East Eighty-fourth Street at seven o'clock and taken the subway. Did he often ride the subway? Yes, fairly frequently, when it wasn't a rush hour. And so on, for fourteen pages of a notebook. I gave him a D minus, even granting that he could cinch it that he reached Larchmont on that train, since it would have stopped at One Hundred and Twenty-fifth Street at 7:38, ten minutes after it left Grand Central.

With Dorothy Keyes the big question was how much of the Keyes profits had been coming her way. Part of the time she seemed to have the idea that her father had been fairly liberal with the dough, and then she would toss in a comment which indicated that he had been as tight-fisted as a baby hanging onto another baby's toy. It was confusing because she had no head for figures. The conclusion I reached was that her take had averaged somewhere between five hundred and twenty thousand a year, which was a wide gap. The point was, which way was she sitting prettier, with her father alive and making plenty of dough and shelling it out, or with him dead and everything hers after Pohl had been attended to? She saw the point all right, and I must say it didn't seem to shock her much, since she didn't even bother to lift her brows.

If it was an act it was good. Instead of standing on the broad moral principle that daughters do not kill fathers, her fundamental position was that at the unspeakable hour in question, half-past seven in the morning, she couldn't even have been killing a fly, let alone her father. She was never out of bed before eleven, except in emergencies, as for instance the Tuesday morning under discussion, when word had come sometime between nine and ten that her father was dead. That had roused her. She had lived with her father in an apartment on Central Park South. Servants? Two maids. Wolfe put it to her: would it have been possible, before seven in the morning, for her to leave the apartment and the building, and later get back in again, without being seen? Not, she declared, unless someone had turned a hose on her to wake her up; that accomplished, possibly the rest could be managed, but she really couldn't say because she had never tried.

I gave her no mark at all because by that time I was prejudiced and couldn't trust my judgment.

Frank Broadyke was a wow. He had enthusiastically adopted Talbott's suggestion that if he, Broadyke, had undertaken to kill anyone it would have been Talbott and not Keyes, since it implied that Keyes' eminence in his profession had been on account of Talbott's salesmanship instead of Keyes' ability as a designer. Broadyke liked that very much and kept going back to it and plugging it. He admitted that the steady decrease in his own volume of business had been coincident with the rise of Keyes', and he further admitted, when the matter was mentioned by Dorothy, that only three days before the murder Keyes had started an action at law against him for damages to the tune of a hundred thousand dollars, complaining that Broadyke had stolen designs from Keyes' office which had got him contracts for a concrete mixer and an electric washing machine. But what the hell, he maintained, the man he would naturally have it in for was Vic Talbott, who had stampeded the market with his high-pressure sales methods—and his personality. Ask any reputable industrial designer; ask all of them. Keyes had been a mediocre gadget contriver, with no real understanding of the intricate and intimate relationship between function and design. I see from my notebook that he permitted himself to say that four times altogether.

He had been doing his best to recover lost ground. He partook, he said, of the nature of the lark; the sunrise stirred and inspired him; that was his time of day. All his brilliant early successes had been conceived before the dew was dry in shady places. In the afternoon and evening he was no better than a clod. But eventually he had got lazy and careless, stayed up late and got up late, and it was then his star had begun to dim. Recently, quite recently, he had determined to light the flame again, and only a month ago he had started getting to his office before seven o'clock, three hours before the staff was due to arrive. To his satisfaction and delight, it was beginning to work. The flashes of inspiration were coming back. That very Tuesday morning, the morning Keyes was killed, he had greeted his staff when they arrived by showing them a revolutionary and irresistible design for an electric egg beater.

Had anyone, Wolfe wanted to know, been with him in his office that morning during the parturition, say from half-past six to eight o'clock? No. No one.

For alibi, Broadyke, of those three, came closest to being naked.

Since I had cottoned to Audrey Rooney and would have married her any second if it wasn't that I wouldn't want my wife to be a public figure and there was her picture on the calendar on the wall of Sam's Diner, it was a setback to learn that her parents in Vermont had actually named her Annie, and she had changed it herself. Okay if she hadn't cared for Annie with Rooney, but good God, why Audrey? Audrey. It showed a lack in her.

It did not, of course, indict her for murder, but her tale helped out on that. She had worked in the Keyes office as Victor Talbott's secretary, and a month ago Keyes had fired her because he suspected her of swiping designs and selling them to Broadyke. When she had demanded proof and Keyes hadn't been able to produce it, she had proceeded to raise hell, which I could well believe. She had forced her way into his private room at the office so often that he had been compelled to hire a husky to keep her out. She had tried to get the rest of the staff, forty of them, to walk out on him until justice had been done her, and had darned near succeeded. She had tried to get at him at his home but failed. Eight days before his death, on a Monday morning, he had found her waiting for him when he arrived at the Stillwell Riding Academy to get his four legs. With the help of the stable hand, by name Wayne Safford, he had managed to mount and clatter off for the park.

But next morning Annie Audrey was there again, and the next one too. What was biting her hardest, as she explained to Wolfe at the outset, was that Keyes had refused to listen to her, had never heard her side, and was so mean and stubborn he didn't intend to. She thought he should. She didn't say in so many words that another reason she kept on showing up at the academy was that the stable hand didn't seem to mind, but that could be gathered. The fourth morning, Thursday, Vic Talbott had arrived too, to accompany Keyes on his ride. Keyes, pestered by Audrey, had poked her in the belly with his crop; Wayne Safford had pushed Keyes hard enough to make him stumble and fall; Talbott had intervened and taken a swing at Wayne; and Wayne had socked Talbott and knocked him into a stall that hadn't been cleaned.

Evidently, I thought, Wayne held back when he was boxing in a nicely furnished office on a Kerman rug; and I also thought that if I had been Keyes I would have tried designing an electric horse for my personal use. But the next day he was back for more, and did get more comments from Audrey, but that was as far as it went; and three days later, Monday, it was the same. Talbott wasn't there either of those two days.

Tuesday morning Audrey got there at a quarter to six, the advantage of the early arrival being that she could make the coffee while Wayne curried horses. They ate cinnamon rolls with the coffee. Wolfe frowned at that because he hates cinnamon rolls. A little after six a phone call came from the Hotel Churchill not to saddle Talbott's horse and to tell Keyes he wouldn't be there. At six-thirty Keyes arrived, on the dot as usual, responded only with grimly tightened lips to Audrey's needling, and rode off. Audrey stayed on at the academy, was there continuously for another hour, and was still there at twenty-five minutes to eight, when Keyes' horse came wandering in under an empty saddle.

Was Wayne Safford also there continuously? Yes, they were together all the time.

So Audrey and Wayne were fixed up swell. When it came Wayne's turn he didn't contradict her on a single point, which I thought was very civilized behavior for a stable hand. He too made the mistake of mentioning cinnamon rolls, but otherwise turned in a perfect score.

When they had gone, more than two hours after midnight, I stood, stretched and yawned good, and told Wolfe, "Five mighty fine clients. Huh?"

He grunted in disgust and put his hands on the rim of his desk to push his chair back.

"I could sleep on it more productively," I stated, "if you would point. Not at Talbott, I don't need that. I'm a better judge of love looks than you are, and I saw him looking at Dorothy, and he has it bad. But the clients? Pohl?"

"He needs money, perhaps desperately, and now he'll get it."

"Broadyke?"

"His vanity was mortally wounded, his business was going downhill, and he was being sued for a large sum."

"Dorothy?"

"A daughter. A woman. It could have gone back to her infancy, or it could have been a trinket denied her today."

"Safford?"

"A primitive romantic. Within three days after he met that girl the fool was eating cinnamon rolls with her at six o'clock in the morning. What about his love look?"

I nodded. "Giddy."

"And he saw Mr. Keyes strike the girl with his riding crop."

"Not strike her, poke her."

"Even worse, because more contemptuous. Also the girl had persuaded him that Mr. Keyes was persisting in a serious injustice to her."

"Okay, that'll do. How about her?"

"A woman either being wronged or caught wronging another. In either case, unhinged."

"Also he poked her with his crop."

"No," Wolfe disagreed. "Except in immediate and urgent retaliation, no woman ever retorts to physical violence from a man in kind. It would not be womanly. She devises subtleties." He got to his feet. "I'm sleepy." He started for the door.

Following, I told his back, "I know one thing, I would collect from every damn one of them in advance. I can't imagine why Cramer wanted to see them again, even Talbott, after a whole week with them. Why don't he throw in and draw five new cards? He's sore as a pup. Shall we phone him?"

"No." We were in the hall. Wolfe, heading for the elevator to ascend to his room on the second floor, turned. "What did he want?"

"He didn't say, but I can guess. He's at a dead stop in pitch-dark in the middle of a six corners, and he came to see if you've got a road map."

I made for the stairs, since the elevator is only four by six, and with all of Wolfe inside, it would already be cramped.

VII

"Forty trump," Orrie Cather said at 10:55 Wednesday morning.

I had told them the Keyes case had knocked on our door and we had five suspects for clients, and that was all. Wolfe had not seen fit to tell me what their errands would be, so I was entertaining at cards instead of summarizing the notebooks for them. At eleven sharp we ended the game, and Orrie and I shelled out to Saul, as usual, and a few minutes later the door from the hall opened and Wolfe entered. He greeted the two hired hands, got himself installed behind his desk, rang for beer, and asked me, "You've explained things to Saul and Orrie, of course?"

"Certainly not. For all I knew it's classified."

He grunted and told me to get Inspector Cramer. I dialed the number and had more trouble getting through than usual, finally had Cramer and signaled to Wolfe, and, since I got no sign to keep off, I stayed on. It wasn't much of a conversation.

"Mr. Cramer? Nero Wolfe."

"Yeah. What do you want?"

"I'm sorry I was busy last evening. It's always a pleasure to see you. I've been engaged in the matter of Mr. Keyes' death, and it will be to our mutual interest for you to let me have a little routine information."

"Like what?"

"To begin with, the name and number of the mounted policeman who saw Mr. Keyes in the park at ten minutes past seven that morning. I want to send Archie—"

"Go to hell." The connection went.

Wolfe hung up, reached for the beer tray which Fritz had brought in, and told me, "Get Mr. Skinner of the District Attorney's office."

I did so, and Wolfe got on again. In the past Skinner had had his share of moments of irritation with Wolfe, but at least he hadn't had the door slammed in his face the preceding evening and therefore was not boorish. When he learned that Wolfe was on the Keyes case he wanted to know plenty, but Wolfe stiff-armed him without being too rude and soon had what he was after. Upon Wolfe's assurance that he would keep Skinner posted on developments at his end, which they both knew was a barefaced lie, the Assistant D. A. even offered to ask headquarters to arrange for me to see the cop. And did so. In less than ten minutes after Wolfe and he were finished, a call came from Centre Street to tell me that Officer Hefferan would meet me at 11:45 at the corner of Sixty-sixth Street and Central Park West.

During the less than ten minutes, Wolfe had drunk beer, asked Saul about his family, and told me what I was expected to find out from the cop. That made me sore, but even more it made me curious. When we're on a case it sometimes happens that Wolfe gets the notion that I have got involved on some angle or with some member of the cast, and that therefore it is necessary to switch me temporarily onto a siding. I had about given up wasting nervous energy resenting it. But what was it this time? I had bought nobody's version and was absolutely fancy free, so why should he send me out to chew the rag with a cop and keep Saul and Orrie for more important errands? It was beyond me, and I was glaring at him and about to open up, when the phone rang again.

It was Ferdinand Pohl, asking for Wolfe. I was going to keep out of it, since the main attack was to be entrusted to others, but Wolfe motioned me to stay on.

"I'm at the Keyes office," Pohl said, "Forty-seventh and Madison. Can you come up here right away?"

"Certainly not," Wolfe said in a grieved tone. It always riled him that anybody in the world didn't know that he never left his house on business, and rarely for anything whatever. "I work only at home. What's the matter?"

"There's someone here I want you to talk to. Two members of the staff. With their testimony I can prove that Talbott took those designs and sold them to Broadyke. This clinches it that it was Talbott who killed Keyes. Of us five, the only ones that could possibly be suspected were Miss Rooney and that stable hand, with that mutual alibi they had, and this clears her—and him too, of course."

"Nonsense. It does nothing of the sort. It proves that she was unjustly accused of theft, and an unjust accusation rankles more than a just one. Now you can have Mr. Talbott charged with larceny, at least. I'm extremely busy. Thank you very much for calling. I shall need the cooperation of all of you."

Pohl wanted to prolong it, but Wolfe got rid of him, drank more beer, and turned to me. "You're expected there in twenty minutes, Archie, and considering your tendency to get arrested for speeding—"

I had had one ticket for speeding in eight years. I walked to the door but turned to remark bitterly, "If you think you're just sending me out to play, try again. Who was the last to see Keyes alive? The cop. He did it. And who will I deliver him to—you? No. Inspector Cramer!"

VIII

It was sunny and warm for October, and the drive uptown would have been pleasant if I hadn't been prejudiced by my feeling that I was being imposed on. Parking on Sixty-fifth Street, I walked around the corner and up a block, and crossed Central Park West to where a man in uniform was monkeying with his horse's bridle. I have met a pack of guardians of the peace on my rounds, but this rugged manly face with a pushed-in nose and bright big eyes was new to me. I introduced myself and showed credentials and said it was nice of him, busy as he was, to give me his time. Of course that was a blunder, but I've admitted I was prejudiced.

"Oh," he said, "one of our prominent kidders, huh?"

I made for cover. "About as prominent," I declared, "as a fish egg in a bowl of caviar."

"Oh, you eat caviar."

"Goddam it," I muttered, "let's start over again." I walked four paces to a lamp post, wheeled, returned to him, and announced, "My name's Goodwin and I work for Nero Wolfe. Headquarters said I could ask you a couple of questions and I'd appreciate it."

"Uh-huh. A friend of mine in the Fifteenth Squad has told me about you. You damn near got him sent to the marshes."

"Then you were already prejudiced. So was I, but not against you. Not even against your horse. Speaking of horses, that morning you saw Keyes on his horse, not long before he was killed, what time was it?"

"Ten minutes past seven."

"Within a minute or two?"

"Not within anything. Ten minutes past seven. I was on the early shift then, due to check out at eight. As you say, I'm so busy that I have no time, so I was hanging around expecting to see Keyes go by as per schedule. I liked to see his horse—a light chestnut with a fine spring to him."

"How did the horse look that morning—same as usual? Happy and healthy?" Seeing the look on his face, I added hastily, "I've sworn off kidding until tomorrow. I actually want to know, was it his horse?"

"Certainly it was! Maybe you don't know horses. I do."

"Okay. I used to too, when I was a boy on a farm in Ohio, but we haven't corresponded lately. What about Keyes that morning, did he look sick or well or mad or glad or what?"

"He looked as usual, nothing special."

"Did you speak to each other?"

"No."

"Had he shaved that morning?"

"Sure he had." Officer Hefferan was controlling himself. "He had used two razors, one on the right side and another one on the left, and he wanted to know which one did the best job, so he asked me to rub his cheeks and tell him what I thought."

"You said you didn't speak."

"Nuts."

"I agree. Let's keep this frankly hostile. I shouldn't have asked about shaving, I should have come right out and asked what I want to know, how close were you to him?"

"Two hundred and seventy feet."

"Oh, you've measured it?"

"I've paced it. The question came up."

"Would you mind showing me the spot? Where he was and where you were?"

"Yes, I'd mind, but I've got orders."

The courteous thing would have been for him to lead his horse and walk with me, so he didn't do that. He mounted his big bay and rode into the park, with me tagging along behind; and not only that, he must have given it a private signal that they mustn't be late. I never saw a horse walk so fast. He would have loved to lose me and blame it on me, or at least make me break into a trot, but I gave my legs the best stretch they had had in years, bending my elbows and pumping my lungs, and I wasn't more than thirty paces in the rear when he finally came to a stop at the crest of a little knoll. There were a lot of trees, big and little, off to the right down the slope, and clumps of bushes were on the left, but in between there was a good view of a long stretch of the bridle path. It was almost at a right angle to our line of vision, and at its nearest looked about a hundred yards away.

He did not dismount. There is no easier way in the world to feel superior to a man than to talk to him from on top of a horse.

Speaking, I handled things so as not to seem out of breath. "You were here?"

VIII

It was sunny and warm for October, and the drive uptown would have been pleasant if I hadn't been prejudiced by my feeling that I was being imposed on. Parking on Sixty-fifth Street, I walked around the corner and up a block, and crossed Central Park West to where a man in uniform was monkeying with his horse's bridle. I have met a pack of guardians of the peace on my rounds, but this rugged manly face with a pushed-in nose and bright big eyes was new to me. I introduced myself and showed credentials and said it was nice of him, busy as he was, to give me his time. Of course that was a blunder, but I've admitted I was prejudiced.

"Oh," he said, "one of our prominent kidders, huh?"

I made for cover. "About as prominent," I declared, "as a fish egg in a bowl of caviar."

"Oh, you eat caviar."

"Goddam it," I muttered, "let's start over again." I walked four paces to a lamp post, wheeled, returned to him, and announced, "My name's Goodwin and I work for Nero Wolfe. Headquarters said I could ask you a couple of questions and I'd appreciate it."

"Uh-huh. A friend of mine in the Fifteenth Squad has told me about you. You damn near got him sent to the marshes."

"Then you were already prejudiced. So was I, but not against you. Not even against your horse. Speaking of horses, that morning you saw Keyes on his horse, not long before he was killed, what time was it?"

"Ten minutes past seven."

"Within a minute or two?"

"Not within anything. Ten minutes past seven. I was on the early shift then, due to check out at eight. As you say, I'm so busy that I have no time, so I was hanging around expecting to see Keyes go by as per schedule. I liked to see his horse—a light chestnut with a fine spring to him."

"How did the horse look that morning—same as usual? Happy and healthy?" Seeing the look on his face, I added hastily, "I've sworn off kidding until tomorrow. I actually want to know, was it his horse?"

"Certainly it was! Maybe you don't know horses. I do."

"Okay. I used to too, when I was a boy on a farm in Ohio, but we haven't corresponded lately. What about Keyes that morning, did he look sick or well or mad or glad or what?"

"He looked as usual, nothing special."

"Did you speak to each other?"

"No."

"Had he shaved that morning?"

"Sure he had." Officer Hefferan was controlling himself. "He had used two razors, one on the right side and another one on the left, and he wanted to know which one did the best job, so he asked me to rub his cheeks and tell him what I thought."

"You said you didn't speak."

"Nuts."

"I agree. Let's keep this frankly hostile. I shouldn't have asked about shaving, I should have come right out and asked what I want to know, how close were you to him?"

"Two hundred and seventy feet."

"Oh, you've measured it?"

"I've paced it. The question came up."

"Would you mind showing me the spot? Where he was and where you were?"

"Yes, I'd mind, but I've got orders."

The courteous thing would have been for him to lead his horse and walk with me, so he didn't do that. He mounted his big bay and rode into the park, with me tagging along behind; and not only that, he must have given it a private signal that they mustn't be late. I never saw a horse walk so fast. He would have loved to lose me and blame it on me, or at least make me break into a trot, but I gave my legs the best stretch they had had in years, bending my elbows and pumping my lungs, and I wasn't more than thirty paces in the rear when he finally came to a stop at the crest of a little knoll. There were a lot of trees, big and little, off to the right down the slope, and clumps of bushes were on the left, but in between there was a good view of a long stretch of the bridle path. It was almost at a right angle to our line of vision, and at its nearest looked about a hundred yards away.

He did not dismount. There is no easier way in the world to feel superior to a man than to talk to him from on top of a horse.

Speaking, I handled things so as not to seem out of breath. "You were here?"

"Right here."

"And he was going north."

"Yep." He gestured. "That direction."

"You saw him. Did he see you?"

"Yes. He lifted his crop to me and I waved back. We often did that."

"But he didn't stop or gaze straight at you."

"He didn't gaze straight or crooked. He was out for a ride. Listen, brother." The mounted man's tone indicated that he had decided to humor me and get it over. "I've been through all this with the Homicide boys. If you're asking was it Keyes, it was. It was his horse. It was his bright yellow breeches, the only ones that color around, and his blue jacket and his black derby. It was the way he sat, with his shoulders hunched and his stirrups too long. It was Keyes."

"Good. May I pat your horse?"

"No."

"Then I won't. It would suit me fine if the occasion arose someday for me to pat you. When I'm dining with the inspector this evening I'll put in a word for you, not saying what kind."

I hoofed it out of the park and along Sixty-sixth Street to Broadway, found a drugstore and a phone booth, wriggled onto the stool, and dialed my favorite number. It was Orrie Cather's voice that answered. So, I remarked to myself, he's still there, probably sitting at my desk; Wolfe's instructions for him must be awful complicated. I asked for Wolfe and got him.

"Yes, Archie?"

"I am phoning as instructed. Officer Hefferan is a Goodwin-hater, but I swallowed my pride. On the stand he would swear up and down that he saw Keyes at the place and time as given, and I guess he did, but a good lawyer could shoot it full of ifs and buts."

"Why? Is Mr. Hefferan a shuttlecock?"

"By no means. He knows it all. But it wasn't a closeup."

"You'd better let me have it verbatim."

I did so. By years of practice I had reached the point where I could relay a two-hour conversation, without any notes but practically word for word, and the brief session I had just come from gave me no trouble at all. When I had finished Wolfe said, "Indeed."

Silence.

I waited a full two minutes and then said politely, "Please tell Orrie not to put his feet on my desk."

In another minute Wolfe's voice came. "Mr. Pohl has telephoned again, twice, from the Keyes office. He's a jackass. Go there and see him. The address—"

"I know the address. What part of him do I look at?"

"Tell him to stop telephoning me. I want it stopped."

"Right. I'll cut the wires. Then what do I do?"

"Phone in again and we'll see."

It clicked off. I wriggled off the stool and out of the booth and stood muttering to myself until I noticed that the line of girls on stools at the soda fountain, especially one of them with blue eyes and dimples, was rudely staring at me. I told her distinctly, "Meet me at Tiffany's ring counter at two o'clock," and strode out. Since I wouldn't be able to park within a mile of Forty-seventh and Madison, I decided to leave my car where it was and snare a taxi.

IX

ONE QUICK look around the Keyes establishment on the twelfth floor was enough to show where a good slice of the profits had gone, unless that was what Pohl's hundred grand had been used for. Panels of four kinds of blond wood made up both the walls and ceiling, and the furniture matched. The seats of the chairs for waiting callers were upholstered in blue and black super-burlap, and you had to watch yourself on the rugs not to twist an ankle. Everywhere, in glass cases against the walls, on pedestals scattered around, and on platforms and tables, were models of almost anything you could think of, from fountain pens to airplanes.

When a woman with pink earrings learned that I sought Mr. Pohl she gave me a wary and reproachful look, but she functioned. After a little delay I was waved through a door and found myself at the end of a long wide corridor. There was no one in sight and I had been given no directions, so it was a case of hide and seek. The best opening move seemed to be to walk down the corridor, so I started, glancing into open doors on either side as I passed. The same scale of interior architecture seemed to prevail throughout, with wide variations in style and color. At the fourth door on the right I saw him, and he called to me, simultaneously.

"Come in, Goodwin!"

I entered. It was a big room with three wide windows, and at a quick glance appeared to be the spot where they had really decided to spread themselves. The rugs were white and the walls were black, and the enormous desk that took all of one end was either ebony or call in an expert. The chair behind the desk, in which Pohl was seated, was likewise.

"Where's Wolfe?" Pohl demanded.

"Where he always is," I replied, negotiating rugs. "At home, sitting down."

He was scowling at me. "I thought he was with you. When I phoned him a few minutes ago he intimated that he might be. He's not coming?"

"No. Never. I'm glad you phoned him again because, as he told you this morning in my hearing, he'll need the cooperation of all of you."

"He'll get mine," Pohl stated grimly. "Since he's not coming for it himself, I suppose I ought to give this to you." He took papers from his breast pocket, looked through them, selected one, and held it out. I stepped to the desk to take it.

It was a single sheet, with "Memo from Sigmund Keyes" on it, printed fancy, and scrawled in ink was a list of towns:

> Dayton, Ohio Aug. 11 & 12
> Boston Aug. 21
> Los Angeles Aug. 27 to Sept. 5
> Meadville, Pa. Sept. 15
> Pittsburgh Sept. 16 & 17
> Chicago Sept. 24–26
> Philadelphia Oct. 1

"Much obliged," I thanked him, and stuck it in my pocket. "Covers a lot of country."

Pohl nodded. "Talbott gets around, and he's a good salesman, I admit that. Tell Wolfe I did just as he said, and I got it out of a record right here in Keyes' desk, so no one knows anything about it. Those are all the out-of-town trips Talbott has made since August first. I have no idea what Wolfe wants it for, but by God it shows he's on the job, and who ever does know what a detective is after? I don't give a damn how mysterious it is as long as I can help him get Talbott."

I had an eye cocked at him, trying to decide whether he was really as naïve as he sounded. It gave me one on Wolfe, knowing that he had tried to keep Pohl away from a phone by giving him work to do, and here Pohl had cleaned it up in no time at all and was ready to ask for more. But instead of asking Wolfe for more, he asked me. He shot it at me.

"Go out and get me some sandwiches and coffee. There's a place on Forty-sixth Street, Perrine's."

I sat down. "That's funny, I was about to ask you to get me some. I'm tired and hungry. Let's go together."

"How the hell can I?" he demanded.

"Why not?"

"Because I might not be able to get in again. This is Keyes' room, but Keyes is dead, and I own part of this business and I've got a right here! Dorothy has tried to chase me out—damn her, she used to sit on my lap! I want certain information, and she has ordered the staff not to give me any. She threatened to get the police to put me out, but she won't do that. She's had enough of the police this last week." Pohl was scowling at me. "I prefer corned beef, and the coffee black, no sugar."

I grinned at his scowl. "So you're squatting. Where's Dorothy?"

"Down the hall, in Talbott's room."

"Is Talbott there?"

"No, he hasn't been in today."

I glanced at my wrist and saw twenty minutes past one. I stood up. "Rye with mustard?"

"No. White bread and nothing on it—no butter."

"Okay. On one condition, that you promise not to phone Mr. Wolfe. If you did you'd be sure to tell him that you got what he's after, and I want to surprise him with it."

He said he wouldn't, and that he wanted two sandwiches and plenty of coffee, and I departed. Two men and a woman who were standing in the corridor, talking, inspected me head to foot as I passed but didn't try to trip me, and I went on out to the elevators, descended, and got directed to a phone booth in the lobby.

Orrie Cather answered again, and I began to suspect that he and Saul were continuing the pinochle game with Wolfe.

"I'm on my way," I told Wolfe when he was on, "to get corned-beef sandwiches for Pohl and me, but I've got a plan. He promised not to phone you while I'm gone, and if I don't go back he's stuck.

He has installed himself in Keyes' room, which you ought to see, against Dorothy's protests, and intends to stay. Been there all day. What shall I do, come home or go to a movie?"

"Has Mr. Pohl had lunch?"

"Certainly not. That's what the sandwiches are for."

"Then you'll have to take them to him."

I remained calm because I knew he meant it from his heart, or at least his stomach. He couldn't bear the idea of even his bitterest enemy missing a meal.

"All right," I conceded, "and I may get a tip. By the way, that trick you tried didn't work. Right away he found a record of Talbott's travels in Keyes' desk and copied it off on a sheet from Keyes' memo pad. I've got it in my pocket."

"Read it to me."

"Oh, you can't wait." I got the paper out and read the list of towns and dates to him. Twice he said I was going too fast, so apparently he was taking it down. When that farce was over I asked, "After I feed him, then what?"

"Call in again when you've had your lunch."

I banged the thing on the hook.

X

THEY were good sandwiches. The beef was tender and full of hot salty sap, with just the right amount of fat, and the bread had some character. I was a little short on milk, having got only a pint, but stretched it out. In between bites we discussed matters, and I made a mistake. I should of course have told Pohl nothing whatever, especially since the more I saw of him the less I liked him, but the sandwiches were so good that I got careless and let it out that as far as I knew no attack had been made on the phone girl and the waiter at the Hotel Churchill. Pohl was determined to phone Wolfe immediately to utter a howl, and in order to stop him I had to tell him that Wolfe had other men on the case and I didn't know who or what they were covering.

I was about to phone myself when the door opened and Dorothy Keyes and Victor Talbott walked in.

I stood up. Pohl didn't.

"Hello hello," I said cheerfully. "Nice place you have here."

Neither of them even nodded to me. Dorothy dropped into a chair against a wall, crossed her legs, and turned her gaze on Pohl with her chin in the air.

Talbott marched over to us at the ebony desk, stopped at my elbow, and told Pohl, "You know damn well you've got no right here, going through things and trying to order the staff around. You have no right here at all. I'll give you one minute to get out."

"*You*'ll give me?" Pohl sounded nasty and looked nasty. "You're a paid employee, and you won't be that long, and I'm part owner, and you say *you*'ll give me! Trying to order the staff around, am I? I'm giving the staff a chance to tell the truth, and they're doing it. Two of them have spent an hour in a lawyer's office, getting it on paper. A complaint has been sworn against Broadyke for receiving stolen goods, and he's been arrested by now."

Talbott said, "Get out," without raising his voice.

Pohl, not moving, said, "And I might also mention that a complaint has been sworn against you for stealing the goods. The designs you sold to Broadyke. Are you going to try to alibi that too?"

Talbott's jaw worked a couple of seconds before it let his lips open for speech. His teeth stayed together as he said, "You can leave now."

"Or I can stay. I'll stay." Pohl was sneering, and it made his network of face creases deeper. "You may have noticed I'm not alone."

I didn't care for that. "Just a minute," I put in. "I'll hold your coats, and that's all. Don't count on me, Mr. Pohl. I'm strictly a spectator, except for one thing, you haven't paid me for your sandwiches and coffee. Ninety-five cents before you go, if you're going."

"I'm not going. It's different here from what it was in the park that morning, Vic. There's a witness."

Talbott took two quick steps, used a foot to shove the big ebony chair back free of the desk, made a grab in the neighborhood of Pohl's throat, got his necktie, and jerked him out of the chair. Pohl came forward and tried to come up at the same time, but Talbott, moving fast, kept going with him, dragging him around the corner of the desk.

I had got upright and backed off, not to be in the way.

Suddenly Talbott went down, flat on his back, an upflung hand gripping a piece of the necktie. Pohl was not very springy, even for his age, but he did his best. He scrambled to his feet, started yelling, "Help! Police! Help!" at the top of his voice, and seized the chair I had been sitting on and raised it high. His idea was to drop it on the prostrate enemy, and my leg muscles tightened for quick action, but Talbott leaped up and yanked the chair away from him. Pohl ran. He scooted around behind the desk, and Talbott went after him. Pohl, yelling for help again, slid around the other end, galloped across the room to a table which held a collection of various objects, picked up an electric iron, and threw it. Missing Talbott, who dodged, it crashed onto the ebony desk and knocked the telephone to the floor. Apparently having an iron thrown at him made Talbott mad, for when he reached Pohl, instead of trying to get a hold on something more substantial than a necktie, he hauled off and landed on his jaw, in spite of the warning I had given him the day before.

"Off of that, you!" a voice boomed.

Glancing to the right, I saw two things: first, that Dorothy, still in her chair, hadn't even uncrossed her legs, and second, that the law who had entered was not a uniformed pavement man but a squad dick I knew by sight. Evidently he had been somewhere around the premises, but it was the first I had seen of him.

He crossed to the gladiators. "This is no way to act," he declared.

Dorothy, moving swiftly, was beside him. "This man," she said, indicating Pohl, "forced his way in here and was told to leave but wouldn't. I am in charge of this place and he has no right here. I want a charge against him for trespassing or disturbing the peace or whatever it is. He tried to kill Mr. Talbott with a chair and then with that iron he threw at him."

I, having put the phone back on the desk, had wandered near, and the law gave me a look.

"What were you doing, Goodwin, trimming your nails?"

"No, sir," I said respectfully, "it was just that I didn't want to get stepped on."

Talbott and Pohl were both speaking at once.

"I know, I know," the dick said, harassed. "Ordinarily, with people like you, I would feel that the thing to do was to sit down and discuss it, but with what happened to Keyes things are different from ordinary." He appealed to Dorothy. "You say you're making a charge, Miss Keyes?"

"I certainly am."

"So am I," Talbott stated.

"Then that's that. Come along with me, Mr. Pohl."

"I'm staying here." Pohl was still panting. "I have a right here and I'm staying here."

"No, you're not. You heard what the lady said."

"Yes, but you didn't hear what I said. I was assaulted. She makes a charge. So do I. I was sitting quietly in a chair, not moving, and Talbott tried to strangle me, and he struck me. Didn't you see him strike me?"

"It was in self-defense," Dorothy declared. "You threw an iron—"

"To save my life! He assaulted—"

"All I did—"

"Hold it," the law said curtly. "Under the circumstances you can't talk yourselves into anything with me. You men will come along with me, both of you. Where's your hats and coats?"

They went. First they used up more breath on words and gestures, but they went, Pohl in the lead, with only half a necktie, Talbott next, and the law in the rear.

Thinking I might as well tidy up a little, I went and righted the chair Pohl had tried to use, then retrieved the iron and put it back on the table, and then examined the beautiful surface of the desk to see how much damage had been done.

"I suppose you're a coward, aren't you?" Dorothy inquired.

She had sat down again, in the same chair, and crossed the same legs. They were all right; I had no kick coming there.

"It's controversial," I told her. "It was on the Town Meeting of the Air last week. With a midget, if he's unarmed, I'm as brave as a lion. Or with a woman. Try picking on me. But with—" A buzz sounded.

"The phone," Dorothy said.

I pulled it to me and got the receiver to my ear.

"Is Miss Keyes there?"

"Yes," I said, "she's busy sitting down. Any message?"

"Tell her Mr. Donaldson is here to see her."

I did so, and for the first time saw an expression that was unquestionably human on Dorothy's face. At sound of the name Donaldson all trace of the brow-lifter vanished. Muscles tightened all over and color went. She may or may not have been what she had just called me, I didn't know because I had never seen or heard of Donaldson, but she sure was scared stiff.

I got tired waiting and repeated it. "Mr. Donaldson is here to see you."

"I—" She wet her lips. In a moment she swallowed. In another moment she stood up, said in a voice not soft at all, "Tell her to send him to Mr. Talbott's room," and went.

I forwarded the command as instructed, asked for an outside line, and, when I heard the dial tone, fingered the number. My wrist watch said five past three, and it stopped my tongue for a second when once more I heard Orrie's voice.

"Archie," I said shortly. "Let me speak to Saul."

"Saul? He's not here. Been gone for hours."

"Oh, I thought it was a party. Then Wolfe."

Wolfe's voice came. "Yes, Archie?"

"I'm in Keyes' office, sitting at his desk. I'm alone. I brought Pohl his lunch, and he owes me ninety-five cents. It just occurred to me that I've seen you go to great lengths to keep your clients from being arrested. Remember the time you buried Clara Fox in a box of osmundine and turned the hose on her? Or the time—"

"What about it?"

"They're scooping up all the clients, that's all. Broadyke has been collared for receiving stolen goods—the designs he bought from Talbott. Pohl has been pulled in for disturbing the peace, and Talbott for assault and battery. Not to mention that Miss Keyes has just had the daylights scared out of her."

"What are you talking about? What happened?"

I told him and, since he had nothing to do but sit and let Orrie answer the phone for him, I left nothing out. When I was through I offered the suggestion that it might be a good plan for me to stick around and find out what it was about Mr. Donaldson that made young women tremble and turn pale at sound of his name.

"No, I think not," Wolfe said, "unless he's a tailor. Just find out if he's a tailor, but discreetly. No disclosure. If so, get his address. Then find Miss Rooney—wait, I'll give you her address—"

"I know her address."

"Find her. Get her confidence. Get alone with her. Loosen up her tongue."

"What am I after—no, I know what I'm after. What are you after?"

"I don't know. Anything you can get. Confound it, you know what a case like this amounts to, there's nothing for it but trial and error—"

Movement over by the door had caught my eye, and I focused on it. Someone had entered and was approaching me.

"Okay," I told Wolfe. "There's no telling where she is, but I'll find her if it takes all day and all night." I hung up and grinned at the newcomer and greeted her.

"Hello, Miss Rooney. Looking for me?"

XI

ANNIE AUDREY was all dressed up in a neat brown wool dress with red threads showing on it in little knots, but she didn't look pleased with herself or with anyone else. You wouldn't think a face with all that pink skin could look so sour. With no greeting, not even a nod, she demanded as she approached, "How do you get to see a man that's been arrested?"

"That depends," I told her. "Don't snap at me like that. I didn't arrest him. Who do you want to see, Broadyke?"

"No." She dropped onto a chair as if she needed support quick. "Wayne Safford."

"Arrested what for?"

"I don't know. I saw him at the stable this morning and then I went downtown to see about a job. A while ago I phoned Lucy, my best friend here, and she told me there was talk about Vic Talbott selling those designs to Broadyke, so I came to find out what was happening and when I learned that Talbott and Pohl had both been arrested I phoned Wayne to tell him about it, and the man there answered and said a policeman had come and taken Wayne with him."

"For why?"

"The man didn't know. How do I get to see him?"

"You probably don't."

"But I have to!"

I shook my head. "You believe you have to, and I believe you have to, but the cops won't. It depends on what his invitation said. If they just want to consult him about sweating horses he may be home in an hour. If they've got a hook in him, or think they have, God knows. You're not a lawyer or a relative."

She sat and looked at me, sourer than ever. In a minute she spoke, bitterly. "You said yesterday I may be nice."

"Meaning I should mount my bulldozer and move heaven and earth?" I shook my head again. "Even if you were so nice it made my head swim, the best I could do for you this second would be to hold your hand, and judging from your expression that's not what you have in mind. Would you mind telling me what you have got in your mind besides curiosity?"

She got up, circled two corners of the desk to reach the phone, put it to her ear, and in a moment told the transmitter, "This is Audrey, Helen. Would you get me— No. Forget it."

She hung up, perched on a corner of the desk, and started giving me the chilly eye again, this time slanting down instead of up.

"It's me," she declared.

"What is?"

"This trouble. Wherever I am there's trouble."

"Yeah, the world's full of it. Wherever anybody is there's trouble. You get shaky ideas. Yesterday you were scared because you thought they were getting set to hang a murder on you, and not one of them has even hinted at it. Maybe you're wrong again."

"No, I'm not." She sounded grim. "There was that business of accusing me of stealing those designs. They didn't have to pick me for that, but you notice they did. Now all of a sudden that's cleared up, I'm out of that, and what happens? Wayne gets arrested for murder. Next thing—"

"I thought you didn't know what they took him for."

"I don't. But you'll see. He was with me, wasn't he?" She slid off the desk and was erect. "I think—I'm pretty sure—I'm going to see Dorothy Keyes."

"She's busy with a caller."

"I know it, but he may be gone."

"A man named Donaldson, and I'm wondering about him. I have a hunch Miss Keyes is starting a little investigation on her own. Do you happen to know if this Donaldson is a detective?"

"I know he isn't. He's a lawyer and a friend of Mr. Keyes. I've seen him here several times. Do you—"

What interrupted her was a man coming in the door and heading for us.

It was a man I had known for years. "We're busy," I told him brusquely. "Come back tomorrow."

I should have had sense enough to give up kidding Sergeant Purley Stebbins of the Homicide Squad long ago, since it always glanced off and rolled away. When he got sore, as he often did, it wasn't at the kidding but at what he considered my interference with the performance of his duty.

"So you're here," he stated.

"Yep. Miss Rooney, this is Sergeant—"

"Oh, I've met him before." Her face was just as sour at him as it had been at me.

"Yeah, we've met," Purley acquiesced. His honest brown eyes were at her. "I've been looking for you, Miss Rooney."

"Oh, my Lord, more questions?"

"The same ones. Just checking up. You remember that statement you signed, where you said that Tuesday morning you were at the riding academy with Safford from a quarter to six until after half-past seven, and both of you were there all the time? You remember that?"

"Certainly I do."

"Do you want to change it now?"

Audrey frowned. "Change what?"

"Your statement."

"Of course not. Why should I?"

"Then how do you account for the fact that you were seen riding a horse into the park during that period, and Safford, on another horse, was with you, and Safford has admitted it?"

"Count ten," I snapped at her, "before you answer. Or even a hun—"

"Shut up," Purley snarled. "How do you account for it, Miss Rooney? You must have figured this might come and got something ready for it. What's the answer?"

Audrey had left her perch on the desk to get on her feet and face the pursuer. "Maybe," she suggested, "someone couldn't see straight. Who says he saw us?"

"Okay." Purley hauled a paper from his pocket and unfolded it. He looked at me. "We're careful about these little details when that fat boss of yours has got his nose in." He held the paper so Audrey could see it. "This is a warrant for your arrest as a material witness. Your friend Safford wanted to read his clear through. Do you?"

She ignored his generous offer. "What does it mean?" she demanded.

"It means you're going to ride downtown with me."

"It also means—" I began.

"Shut up." Purley moved a step. His hand started for her elbow, but didn't reach it, for she drew back and then turned and was on her way. He followed and was at her heels as she went out the door. Apparently she thought she had found a way to get to see her Wayne.

I sat a little while with my lips screwed up, gazing at the ashtray on the desk. I shook my head at nothing in particular, just the state of things, reached for the phone, got an outside line, and dialed again.

Wolfe's voice answered.

"Where's Orrie?" I demanded. "Taking a nap on my bed?"

"Where are you?" Wolfe inquired placidly.

"Still in Keyes' office. More of the same. Two more gone."

"Two more what? Where?"

"Clients. In the hoosegow. We're getting awful low—"

"Who and why?"

"Wayne Safford and Audrey Rooney." I told him what had happened, without bothering to explain that Audrey had walked in before our previous conversation had ended. At the end I added, "So four out of five have been snaffled, and Talbott too. We're in a fine fix. That leaves us with just one, Dorothy Keyes, and it wouldn't surprise me if she was also on her way, judging from the look on her face when she heard who was— Hold it a minute."

What stopped me was the sight of another visitor entering the room. It was Dorothy Keyes. I told the phone, "I'll call back," hung up, and left my chair.

Dorothy came to me. She was still human, more so if anything. The perky lift of her was completely gone, the color scheme of her visible skin was washed-out gray, and her eyes were pinched with trouble.

"Mr. Donaldson gone?" I asked her.

"Yes."

"It's a bad day all around. Now Miss Rooney and Wayne Safford have been pinched. The police seem to think they left out something about that Tuesday morning. I was just telling Mr. Wolfe when you came—"

"I want to see him," she said.

"Who? Mr. Wolfe?"

"Yes. Immediately."

"What about?"

I'll be damned if her brows didn't go up. The humanity I thought I had seen was only on the surface.

"I'll tell him that," she stated, me being mud. "I must see him at once."

"You can't, not at once," I told her. "You could rush there in a taxi, but you might as well wait till I go to Sixty-fifth Street and get my car, because it's after four o'clock and he's up with the orchids, and he wouldn't see you until six even though you are the only client he's got still out of jail."

"But this is urgent!"

"Not for him it isn't, not until six o'clock. Unless you want to tell me about it. I'm permitted upstairs. Do you?"

"No."

"Then shall I go get my car?"

"Yes."

I went.

XII

At three minutes past six Wolfe, down from the plant rooms, joined us in the office. By the time Dorothy and I had got there she had made it perfectly plain that as far as I was concerned she was all talked out, our conversation during the ride downtown having consisted of her saying at one point, "Look out for that truck," and me replying, "I'm driving," so during the hour's wait I hadn't even asked her if she wanted a drink. And when Wolfe had entered and greeted her, and got his bulk adjusted in his chair behind his desk, the first thing she said was, "I want to speak to you privately."

Wolfe shook his head. "Mr. Goodwin is my confidential assistant, and if he didn't hear it from you he soon would from me. What is it?"

"But this is very—personal."

"Most things said in this room by visitors are. What is it?"

"There is no one I can go to but you." Dorothy was in one of the yellow chairs, facing him, leaning forward to him. "I don't know where I stand, and I've got to find out. A man is going to tell the police that I forged my father's name to a check. Tomorrow morning."

Her face was human again, with her eyes pinched.

"Did you?" Wolfe asked.

"Forge the check? Yes."

I lifted my brows.

"Tell me about it," Wolfe said.

It came out, and was really quite simple. Her father hadn't given her enough money for the style to which she wanted to accustom herself. A year ago she had forged a check for three thousand dollars, and he had of course discovered it and had received her promise that she would never repeat. Recently she had forged another one, this time for five thousand dollars, and her father had been very difficult about it, but there had been no thought in his head of anything so drastic as having his daughter arrested.

Two days after his discovery of this second offense he had been killed. He had left everything to his daughter, but had made a lawyer named Donaldson executor of the estate, not knowing, according to Dorothy, that Donaldson hated her. And now Donaldson had found the forged check among Keyes' papers, with a memorandum attached to it in Keyes' handwriting, and had called on Dorothy that afternoon to tell her that it was his duty, both as a citizen and as a lawyer, considering the manner of Keyes' death, to give the facts to the police. It was an extremely painful duty, he had asserted, but he would just have to grin and bear it.

I will not say that I smirked as I got these sordid facts scratched into my notebook, but I admit that I had no difficulty in keeping back the tears.

Wolfe, having got answers to all the questions that had occurred to him, leaned back and heaved a sigh. "I can understand," he murmured, "that you felt impelled to get rid of this nettle by passing it on to someone. But even if I grasped it for you, what then? What do I do with it?"

"I don't know." It is supposed to make people feel better to tell their troubles, but apparently it made Dorothy feel worse. She sounded as forlorn as she looked.

"Moreover," Wolfe went on, "what are you afraid of? The property, including the bank balance, now belongs to you. It would be a waste of time and money for the District Attorney's office to try to get you indicted and brought to trial, and it wouldn't even be considered. Unless Mr. Donaldson is an idiot he knows that. Tell him so. Tell him I say he's a nincompoop." Wolfe wiggled a finger at her. "Unless he thinks you killed your father and wants to help get you electrocuted. Does he hate you that much?"

"He hates me," Dorothy said harshly, "all he can."

"Why?"

"Because once I let him think I might marry him, and he announced it, and then I changed my mind. He has strong feelings. It was strong when he loved me, and it is just as strong now when he hates me. Any way he can use that check to hurt me, he'll do it."

"Then you can't stop him, and neither can I. The forged check and your father's memorandum are legally in his possession, and nothing can keep him from showing them to the police. Does he ride horseback?"

"Oh, my God," Dorothy said hopelessly. She stood up. "I thought you were clever! I thought you would know what to do!" She made for the door, but at the sill she turned. "You're just a cheap shyster too! I'll handle the dirty little rat myself!"

I got up and went to the hall to let her out, to make sure that the door was properly closed behind her. When I was back in the office I sat down and tossed the notebook into a drawer and remarked, "Now she's got us all tagged. I'm a coward, you're a shyster, and the executor of her father's estate is a rat. That poor kid needs some fresh contacts."

Wolfe merely grunted, but it was a good-humored grunt, for the dinner hour was near, and he never permits himself to get irritated just before a meal.

"So," I said, "unless she does some fancy handling in a hurry she will be gathered in before noon tomorrow, and she was the last we had. All five of them, and also the suspect we were supposed to pin it on. I hope Saul and Orrie are doing better than we are. I have a date for dinner and a show with a friend, but I can break it if there's anything I can be doing—"

"Nothing, thank you."

I glared at him. "Oh, Saul and Orrie are doing it?"

"There's nothing for this evening, for you. I'll be here, attending to matters."

Yes, he would. He would be here, reading books, drinking beer, and having Fritz tell anyone who called that he was engaged. It wasn't the first time he had decided that a case wasn't worth the effort and to hell with it. On such occasions my mission was to keep after him until I had him jarred loose, but this time my position was that if Orrie Cather could spend the afternoon in my chair he could damn well do my work. So I let it lay and went up to my room to redecorate for the evening out.

It was a very nice evening on all counts. Dinner at Lily Rowan's, while not up to the standard Fritz had got my palate trained to, was always good. So was the show, and so was the dance band at the Flamingo Club, where we went afterward to get better acquainted, since I had only known her seven years. What with this and that I didn't get home until after three o'clock, and, following routine, looked in at the office to jiggle the handle of the safe and glance around. If there was a message for me Wolfe always left it on my desk under a paperweight, and there one was, on a sheet from his pad, in his small thin handwriting that was as easy to read as type.

I ran through it.

> AG: Your work on the Keyes case has been quite satisfactory. Now that it is solved, you may proceed as arranged and go to Mr. Hewitt's place on Long Island in the morning to get those plants. Theodore will have the cartons ready for you. Don't forget to watch the ventilation.
>
> NW

I read it through again and turned it over to look at the back, to see if there was another installment, but it was blank.

I sat at my desk and dialed a number. None of my closest friends or enemies was there, but I got a sergeant I knew named Rowley, and asked him, "On the Keyes case, do you need anything you haven't got?"

"Huh?" He always sounded hoarse. "We need everything. Send it C.O.D."

"A guy told me you had it on ice."

"Aw, go to bed."

He was gone. I sat a moment and then dialed again, the number of the *Gazette* office. Lon Cohen had gone home, but one of the journalists told me that as far as they knew the Keyes case was still back on a shelf, collecting dust.

I crumpled Wolfe's message and tossed it in the wastebasket, muttered, "The damn fat faker," and went up to bed.

XIII

IN THE Thursday morning papers there wasn't a single word in the coverage of the Keyes case to indicate that anyone had advanced even an inch in the hot pursuit of the murderer.

And I spent the whole day, from ten to six, driving to Lewis Hewitt's place on Long Island, helping to select and clean and pack ten dozen yearling plants, and driving back again. I did no visible fuming, but you can imagine my state of mind, and on my way home, when a cop stopped me as I was approaching Queensboro Bridge, and actually went so low as to ask me where the fire was, I had to get my tongue between my teeth to keep myself from going witty on him.

While I was lugging the last carton of plants up the stoop I had a surprise. A car I had often seen before, with PD on it, rolled up to the curb and stopped behind the sedan, and Inspector Cramer emerged from it.

"What has Wolfe got now?" he demanded, coming up the steps to me.

"A dozen zygopetalum," I told him coldly, "a dozen renanthera, a dozen odontoglossum—"

"Let me by," he said rudely.

I did so.

What I should have done, to drive it in that I was now a delivery boy and not a detective, was to go on helping Theodore get the orchids upstairs, and I set my teeth and started to do that, but it wasn't long before Wolfe's bellow came from the office. "Archie!"

I went on in. Cramer was in the red leather chair with an unlighted cigar tilted toward the ceiling by the grip of his teeth. Wolfe, his tightened lips showing that he was enjoying a quiet subdued rage, was frowning at him.

"I'm doing important work," I said curtly.

"It can wait. Get Mr. Skinner on the phone. If he has left his office, get him at home."

I would have gone to much greater lengths if Cramer hadn't been there. As it was, all I did was snort as I crossed to my desk and sat down and started to dial.

"Cut it!" Cramer barked savagely.

I went on dialing.

"I said stop it!"

"That will do, Archie," Wolfe told me. I turned from the phone and saw he was still frowning at the inspector but his lips had relaxed. He used them for speech. "I don't see, Mr. Cramer, what better you can ask than the choice I offer. As I told you on the phone, give me your word that you'll cooperate with me on my terms, and I shall at once tell you about it in full detail, including of course the justification for it. Or refuse to give me your word, that's the alternative, and I shall ask Mr. Skinner if the District Attorney's office would like to cooperate with me. I guarantee only that no harm will be done, but my expectation is that the case will be closed. Isn't that fair enough?"

Cramer growled like a tiger in a cage having a chair poked at him.

"I don't understand," Wolfe declared, "why the devil I bother with you. Mr. Skinner would jump at it."

Cramer's growl became words. "When would it be—tonight?"

"I said you'd get details after I get your promise, but you may have that much. It would be early tomorrow morning, contingent upon delivery of a package I'm expecting—by the way, Archie, you didn't put the car in the garage?"

"No, sir."

"Good. You'll have to go later, probably around midnight, to meet an airplane. It depends on the airplane, Mr. Cramer. If it arrives tomorrow instead of tonight, we'd have to postpone it until Saturday morning."

"Where? Here in your office?"

Wolfe shook his head. "That's one of the details you'll get. Confound it, do I mean what I say?"

"Search me. I never know. You say you'll take my word. Why not take my word that I'll either do it or forget I ever heard it?"

"No. Archie, get Mr. Skinner."

Cramer uttered a word that was for men only. "You and your goddam charades," he said bitterly. "Why do you bother with me? You know damn well I'm not going to let you slip it to the D. A.'s office, because you may really have it. You have before. Okay. On your terms."

Wolfe nodded. The gleam in his eye came and went so fast that it nearly escaped even me.

"Your notebook, Archie. This is rather elaborate, and I doubt if we can finish before dinner."

XIV

"I'LL EXPLAIN gladly," I told Officer Hefferan, "if you'll descend from that horse and get level with me. That's the democratic way to do it. Do you want me to get a stiff neck, slanting up at you?"

I yawned wide without covering it, since there was nothing there but nature and a mounted cop. Being up and dressed and breakfasted and outdoors working at seven in the morning was not an all-time record for me, but it was unusual, and I had been up late three nights in a row: Tuesday the congregation of clients, Wednesday the festivities with Lily Rowan, and Thursday the drive to La Guardia to meet the airplane, which had been on schedule.

Hefferan came off his high horse and was even with me. We were posted on top of the little knoll in Central Park to which he had led me the day I had made his acquaintance. It promised to be another warm October day. A little breeze was having fun with the leaves on the trees and bushes, and birds were darting and hopping around, discussing their plans for the morning.

"All I'm doing," Hefferan said to make it plain, "is obeying orders. I was told to meet you here and listen to you."

I nodded. "And you don't care for it. Neither do I, you stiff-back Cossack, but I've got orders too. The setup is like this. As you know, down there behind that forest"—I pointed—"is a tool shed. Outside the shed Keyes' chestnut horse, saddled and bridled, is being held by one of your colleagues. Inside the shed there are two women named Keyes and Rooney, and four men named Pohl, Talbott, Safford, and Broadyke. Also Inspector Cramer is there with a detachment from his squad. One of the six civilians, chosen by secret ballot, is at this moment changing his or her clothes, putting on bright yellow breeches and a blue jacket, just like the outfit Keyes wore. Between you and me and your horse, the choosing was a put-up job, handled by Inspector Cramer. Dressed like Keyes, the chosen one is going to mount Keyes' horse and ride along that stretch of the bridle path, with shoulders hunched and stirrups too long, catch sight of you, and lift his or her crop to you in greeting. Your part is to be an honest man. Pretend it's not me telling you this, but someone you dearly love like the Police Commissioner. You are asked to remember that what you were interested in seeing was the horse, not the rider, and to put the question to yourself, did you actually recognize Keyes that morning, or just the horse and the getup?"

I appealed to him earnestly. "And for God's sake don't say a word to me. You wouldn't admit anything whatever to me, so keep your trap shut and save it for later, for your superiors. A lot depends on you, which may be regrettable, but it can't be helped now.

"If it won't offend you for me to explain the theory of it, it's this: The murderer, dressed like Keyes but covered with a topcoat, was waiting in the park uptown behind that thicket at half-past six, when Keyes first rode into the park and got onto the bridle path. If he had shot Keyes out of the saddle from a distance, even a short one, the horse would have bolted, so he stepped out and stopped Keyes, and got hold of the bridle before he pulled the trigger. One bullet for one. Then he dragged the body behind the thicket so it couldn't be seen from the bridle path, since another early-morning rider might come along, took off his topcoat—or maybe a thin raincoat—and stuffed it under his jacket, mounted the horse, and went for a ride through the park. He took his time so as to keep to Keyes' customary schedule. Thirty minutes later, approaching that spot"—I pointed to where the bridle path emerged from behind the trees—"he either saw you up here or waited until he did see you up here, and then rode on along that stretch, giving you the usual salute by lifting his crop. But the second he got out of sight at the other end of the stretch he acted fast. He got off the horse and just left it there, knowing it would make its way back to its own exit from the park, and he beat it in a hurry, either to a Fifth Avenue bus or the subway, depending on where he was headed for. The idea was to turn the alibi on as soon as possible, since he couldn't be sure how soon the horse would be seen and the search for Keyes would be started. But at the worst he had established Keyes as still alive at ten minutes past seven, down here on that stretch, and the body would be found way uptown."

"I believe," Hefferan said stiffly, "I am on record as saying I saw Keyes."

"Scratch it," I urged him. "Blot it out. Make your mind a blank, which shouldn't—" I bit it off, deciding it would be undiplomatic, and glanced at my wrist. "It's nine minutes past seven. Where were you that morning, on your horse or off?"

"On."

"Then you'd better mount, to have it the same. Let's be particular—jump on! There he comes!"

I admit the Cossack knew how to get on top of a horse. He was erect in the saddle quicker than I would have had a foot in a stirrup, and had his gaze directed at the end of the stretch of the bridle path where it came out of the trees. I also admit the chestnut horse looked fine from up there. It was rangy but not gangly, with a proud curve to its neck, and, as Hefferan had said, it had a good set of springs. I strained my eyes to take in the details of the rider's face, but at that distance it couldn't be done. The blue of the jacket, yes, and the yellow of the breeches, and the hunched shoulders, but not the face.

No sound came from Hefferan. As the rider on the bridle path neared the end of the open stretch I strained my eyes again, hoping something would happen, knowing as I did what he would find confronting him when he rounded the sharp bend at the finish of the stretch—namely, four mounted cops abreast.

Something happened all right, fast, and not on my list of expectations. The chestnut was out of sight around the bend not more than half a second, and then here he came back, on the jump, the curve gone out of his neck. But he or his rider had had enough of the bridle path. Ten strides this side of the bend the horse swerved sharp and darted off to the left, off onto the grass in one beautiful leap, and then dead ahead, due east toward Fifth Avenue, showing us his tail. Simultaneously here came the quartet of mounted cops, like a cavalry charge. When they saw what the chestnut had done their horses' legs suddenly went stiff, slid ten feet in the loose dirt, and then sashayed for the bound onto the grass, to follow.

Yells were coming from a small mob that had run out of the forest which hid the tool shed. And Hefferan left me. His horse's ham jostled my shoulder as it sprang into action, and divots of turf flew through the air as it bounded down the slope to join the chase. The sound of gunshots came from the east, and that finished me. I would have given a year's pay, anything up to a kingdom, for a horse, but, having none, I lit out anyway.

Down the slope to the bridle path I broke records, but on the other side it was upgrade, and also I had to dodge trees and bushes and jump railings. I was making no detours to find crossings, but heading on a beeline for the noises coming from the east, including another round of shots. One funny thing, even busy as I was trying to cover ground, I was hoping they wouldn't hit that chestnut horse. Finally the border of the park was in sight, but I could see nothing moving, though the noises seemed to be louder and closer. Straight ahead was the stone wall enclosing the park, and, unsure which way to turn for the nearest entrance, I made for the wall, climbed it, stood panting, and surveyed.

I was at Sixty-fifth and Fifth Avenue. One block up, outside a park entrance, the avenue was so cluttered that it was blocked. Cars, mostly taxis, were collecting at both fringes of the intersection, and the pedestrians who hadn't already arrived were on their way, from all directions. A bus had stopped and passengers were piling out. The tallest things there were the horses. I got the impression that there were a hell of a lot of horses, but probably it wasn't more than six or seven. They were all bays but one, the chestnut, and I was glad to see that it looked healthy as I cantered up the pavement toward the throng. The chestnut's saddle was empty.

I was pushing my way through to the center when one in uniform grabbed my arm, and I'll be damned if Officer Hefferan didn't sing out, "Let him come, that's Nero Wolfe's man Goodwin!" I would have been glad to thank him cordially, but didn't have enough breath yet to speak. So I merely pushed on and, using only my eyes, got my curiosity satisfied.

Victor Talbott, in blue jacket and yellow breeches, apparently as unhurt as the chestnut, was standing there with a city employee hanging onto each arm. His face was dirty and he looked very tired.

XV

"You will be glad to know," I told Wolfe late that afternoon, "that none of these bills we are sending to our clients will have to be addressed care of the county jail. That would be embarrassing."

It was a little after six, and he was down from the plant rooms and had beer in front of him. I was at my typewriter, making out the bills.

"Broadyke," I went on, "claims that he merely bought designs that were offered him, not knowing where they came from, and he can probably make it stick. Dorothy has agreed on a settlement with Pohl and will press no charge. As for Dorothy, it's hers now anyway, as you said, so what the hell. And Safford and Audrey can't be prosecuted just for going to ride in the park, even if they omitted it in their statements just to avoid complications. By the way, if you wonder why they allocated fifteen per cent of our fee to a stable hand, he is not a stable hand. He owns that riding academy, by gum, so Audrey hasn't sold out cheap at all—anything but. They'll probably be married on horseback."

Wolfe grunted. "That won't improve their chances any."

"You're prejudiced about marriage," I reproached him. "I may try it myself someday. Look at Saul, staked down like a tent but absolutely happy. Speaking of Saul, why did you waste money having him and Orrie phoning and calling on New York tailors?"

"It wasn't wasted," Wolfe snapped. He can't stand being accused of wasting money. "There was a slim chance that Mr. Talbott had been ass enough to have his costume made right here. The better chance, of course, was one of the cities he had recently visited, and the best of all was the one farthest away. So I telephoned Los Angeles first, and the Southwest Agency put five men on it. Also Saul and Orrie did other things. Saul learned, for instance, that Mr. Talbott's room at the hotel was so situated that, by using stairs and a side entrance, he could easily have left and returned at that time of day without being recognized." Wolfe snorted. "I doubt if Mr. Cramer even considered that. Why should he? He had taken that policeman's word that he had seen Mr. Keyes on a horse, alive and well, at ten minutes past seven."

"Good here," I agreed. "But, assuming that it might have been the murderer, not Keyes, the cop had seen alive on a horse, why did you immediately pick Talbott for it?"

"I didn't. The facts did. The masquerade, if there was one, could have helped no one but Mr. Talbott, since an alibi for that moment at that spot would have been useless for any of the others. Also the greeting exchanged at a distance with the policeman was an essential of the plan, and only Mr. Talbott, who often rode with Mr. Keyes, could have known there would be an opportunity for it."

"Okay," I conceded. "And you phoned Pohl to find out where Talbott had been recently. My God, Pohl actually helped on it! By the way, the Southwest Agency put an airmail stamp on the envelope containing their bill, so I guess they want a check. Their part of the charge is reasonable enough, but that tailor wants three hundred bucks for making a blue jacket and a pair of yellow breeches."

"Which our clients will pay," Wolfe said placidly. "It isn't exorbitant. It was five o'clock in the afternoon there when they found him, and he had to be persuaded to spend the night at it, duplicating the previous order."

"Okay," I conceded again. "I admit it had to be a real duplicate, label and all, to panic that baby. He had nerve. He gets his six-o'clock call at his hotel, says to wake him again at seven-thirty, beats it to the street without being seen, puts on his act, and gets back to his room in time to take the seven-thirty call. And don't forget he was committed right from the beginning, at half-past six, when he shot Keyes. From there on he had to make his schedule. Some nerve."

I got up and handed the bills, including copies of the itemized expense account, across to Wolfe for his inspection.

"You know," I remarked, sitting down again, "that was close to the top for a shock to the nervous system, up there this morning. When he got picked to double for Keyes that must have unsettled him a little to begin with. Then he gets ushered into the other room to change, and is handed a box that has on it "Cleever of Hollywood." He opens it, and there is an outfit exactly like the one he had had made, and had got well rid of somehow along with the gun, and there again is a label in the jacket, "Cleever of Hollywood." I'm surprised he was able to get it on and buttoned up, and walk out to the horse and climb into the saddle. He did have nerve. I suppose he intended just to keep on going, but as he rounded the bend there were the four mounted cops and flup went his nerves, and I don't blame him. I admit I hadn't the faintest idea, when I was phoning you that list of towns Pohl had given me—hey! Good God!"

Wolfe looked up. "What's the matter?"

"Give me back that expense list! I left out the ninety-five cents for Pohl's sandwiches!"

DISGUISE FOR MURDER

I

WHAT I felt like doing was go out for a walk, but I wasn't quite desperate enough for that, so I merely beat it down to the office, shutting the door from the hall behind me, went and sat at my desk with my feet up, leaned back and closed my eyes, and took some deep breaths.

I had made two mistakes. When Bill McNab, garden editor of the *Gazette*, had suggested to Nero Wolfe that the members of the Manhattan Flower Club be invited to drop in some afternoon to look at the orchids, I should have fought it. And when the date had been set and the invitations sent, and Wolfe had arranged that Fritz and Saul should do the receiving at the front door and I should stay up in the plant rooms with him and Theodore, mingling with the guests, if I had had an ounce of brains I would have put my foot down. But I hadn't, and as a result I had been up there a good hour and a half, grinning around and acting pleased and happy. "No, sir, that's not a brasso, it's a laelio." "No, madam, I doubt if you could grow that miltonia in a living room—so sorry." "Quite all right, madam—your sleeve happened to hook it—it'll bloom again next year."

It wouldn't have been so bad if there had been something for the eyes. It was understood that the Manhattan Flower Club was choosy about who it took in, but obviously its standards were totally different from mine. The men were just men, okay as men go, but the women! It was a darned good thing they had picked on flowers to love, because flowers don't have to love back. I didn't object to their being alive and well, since after all I've got a mother too, and three aunts, and I fully appreciate them, but it would have been a relief to spot just one who could have made my grin start farther down than the front of my teeth.

There had in fact been one—just one. I had got a glimpse of her at the other end of the crowded aisle as I went through the door from the cool room into the moderate room, after showing a couple of guys what a bale of osmundine looked like in the potting room. From ten paces off she looked absolutely promising, and when I had maneuvered close enough to make her an offer to answer questions if she had any, there was simply no doubt about it, and the first quick slanting glance she gave me said plainly that she could tell the difference between a flower and a man, but she just smiled and shook her head and moved on by with her companions, an older female and two males. Later I had made another try and got another brushoff, and still later, too long later, feeling that the damn grin might freeze on me for good if I didn't take a recess, I had gone AWOL by worming my way through to the far end of the warm room and sidling on out.

All the way down the three flights of stairs new guests were coming up, though it was then four o'clock. Nero Wolfe's old brownstone house on West Thirty-fifth Street had seen no such throng as that within my memory, which is long and good. One flight down I stopped off at my bedroom for a pack of cigarettes, and another flight down I detoured to make sure the door of Wolfe's bedroom was locked. In the main hall downstairs I halted a moment to watch Fritz Brenner, busy at the door with both departures and arrivals, and to see Saul Panzer emerge from the front room, which was being used as a cloakroom, with someone's hat and topcoat. Then, as aforesaid, I entered the office, shutting the door from the hall behind me, went and sat at my desk with my feet up, leaned back and closed my eyes, and took some deep breaths.

I had been there maybe eight or ten minutes, and was getting relaxed and a little less bitter, when the door opened and she came in. Her companions were not along. By the time she had closed the door and turned to me I had got to my feet, with a friendly leer, and had begun, "I was just sitting here thinking—"

The look on her face stopped me. There was nothing wrong with it basically, but something had got it out of kilter. She headed for me, got halfway, jerked to a stop, sank into one of the yellow chairs, and squeaked, "Could I have a drink?"

Upstairs her voice had not squeaked at all. I had liked it.

"Scotch?" I asked her. "Rye, bourbon, gin—"

She just fluttered a hand. I went to the cupboard and got a hooker of Old Woody. Her hand was shaking as she took the glass, but she didn't spill any, and she got it down in two swallows, as if it had been milk, which wasn't very ladylike. She shuddered all over and shut her eyes. In a minute she opened them again and said hoarsely, the squeak gone, "Did I need that!"

"More?"

She shook her head. Her bright brown eyes were moist, from the whisky, as she gave me a full straight look with her head tilted up. "You're Archie Goodwin," she stated.

I nodded. "And you're the Queen of Egypt?"

"I'm a baboon," she declared. "I don't know how they ever taught me to talk." She looked around for something to put the glass on, and I moved a step and reached for it. "Look at my hand shake," she complained. "I'm all to pieces."

She kept her hand out, looking at it, so I took it in mine and gave it some friendly but gentle pressure. "You do seem a little upset," I conceded. "I doubt if your hand usually feels clammy. When I saw you upstairs—"

She jerked the hand away and blurted, "I want to see Nero Wolfe. I want to see him right away, before I change my mind." She was gazing up at me, with the moist brown eyes. "My God, I'm in a fix now all right! I'm one scared baboon! I've made up my mind, I'm going to get Nero Wolfe to get me out of this somehow—why shouldn't he? He did a job for Dazy Perrit, didn't he? Then I'm through. I'll get a job at Macy's or marry a truck driver! I want to see Nero Wolfe!"

I told her it couldn't be done until the party was over.

She looked around. "Are people coming in here?"

I told her no.

"May I have another drink, please?"

I told her she should give the first one time to settle, and instead of arguing she arose and got the glass from the corner of Wolfe's desk, went to the cupboard, and helped herself. I sat down and frowned at her. Her line sounded fairly screwy for a member of the Manhattan Flower Club, or even for a daughter of one. She came back to her chair, sat, and met my eyes. Looking at her straight like that could have been a nice way to pass the time if there had been any chance for a meeting of minds, but it was easy to see that what her mind was fighting with was connected with me only accidentally.

"I could tell you," she said, hoarse again.

"Many people have," I said modestly.

"I'm going to."

"Good. Shoot."

"I'm afraid I'll change my mind and I don't want to."

"Okay. Ready, go."

"I'm a crook."

"It doesn't show," I objected. "What do you do, cheat at canasta?"

"I didn't say I'm a cheat." She cleared her throat for the hoarseness. "I said I'm a crook. Remind me someday to tell you the story of my life, how my husband got killed in the war and I broke through the gate. Don't I sound interesting?"

"You sure do. What's your line, orchid-stealing?"

"No. I wouldn't be small and I wouldn't be dirty—that's what I thought, but once you start it's not so easy. You meet people and you get involved. You can't go it alone. Two years ago four of us took over a hundred grand from a certain rich woman with a rich husband. I can tell you about that one, even names, because she couldn't move anyhow."

I nodded. "Blackmailers' customers seldom can. What—"

"I'm not a blackmailer!" Her eyes were blazing.

"Excuse me. Mr. Wolfe often says I jump to conclusions."

"You did that time." She was still indignant. "A blackmailer's not a crook, he's a snake! Not that it really matters. What's wrong with being a crook is the other crooks—they make it dirty whether you like it or not. I've been up to my knees in it. It makes a coward of you too—that's the worst. I had a friend once—as close as a crook ever comes to having a friend—and a man killed her, strangled her, and if I had told what I knew about it they could have caught him, but I was afraid to go to the cops, so he's still loose. And she was my friend! That's getting down toward the bottom. Isn't it?"

"Fairly low," I agreed, eying her. "Of course I don't know you any too well. I don't know how you react to two stiff drinks. Maybe your hobby is stringing private detectives. If so, why don't you wait for Mr. Wolfe? It would be more fun with two of us."

She simply ignored it. "I realized long ago," she went on as if it were a one-way conversation, "that I had made a mistake. I wasn't what I had thought I was going to be—a romantic reckless outlaw.

You can't do it that way, or anyhow I couldn't. I was just a crook and I knew it, and about a year ago I decided to break loose. A good way to do it would have been to talk to someone the way I'm talking to you now, but I didn't have sense enough to see that. And so many people were involved. It was so involved! You know?"

I nodded. "Yeah, I know."

"So I kept putting it off. We got a good one in December and I went to Florida for a vacation, but down there I met a man with a lead and we followed it up here just a week ago. That's what I'm working on now. That's what brought me here today. This man—"

She stopped abruptly.

"Well?" I invited her.

She looked dead serious, not more serious, but a different kind. "I'm not putting anything on him," she declared. "I don't owe him anything and I don't like him, but this is strictly about me and no one else—only I had to explain why I'm here. I wish to God I'd never come!"

There was no question about that coming from her heart, unless she had done a lot of rehearsing in front of a mirror.

"It got you this talk with me," I reminded her.

She was looking straight through me and beyond. "If only I hadn't come! If only I hadn't seen him!" She leaned toward me for emphasis. "I'm either too smart or not smart enough, that's my trouble. I should have looked away from him, turned away quick, when I realized I knew who he was, before he turned and saw it in my eyes. But I was so shocked I couldn't help it! For a second I couldn't move. God, I was dumb! I stood there staring at him, thinking I wouldn't have recognized him if he hadn't had a hat on, and then he looked at me and saw what was happening. I knew then all right what an awful fool I was, and I turned away and moved off, but it was too late. I know how to manage my face with nearly anybody, anywhere, but that was too much for me. It showed so plain that Mrs. Orwin asked me what was the matter with me and I had to try to pull myself together—then seeing Nero Wolfe gave me the idea of telling him, only of course I couldn't right there with the crowd—and then I saw you going out and as soon as I could break away I came down to find you."

She tried smiling at me, but it didn't work so good. "Now I feel some better," she said hopefully.

I nodded. "That's good bourbon. Is it a secret who you recognized?"

"No. I'm going to tell Nero Wolfe."

"You decided to tell me." I flipped a hand. "Suit yourself. Whoever you tell, what good will that do?"

"Why—then he can't do anything to me."

"Why not?"

"Because he wouldn't dare. Nero Wolfe will tell him that I've told about him, so that if anything happened to me he would know it was him, and he'd know who he is—I mean Nero Wolfe would know—and so would you."

"We would if we had his name and address." I was studying her. "He must be quite a specimen, to scare you that bad. And speaking of names, what's yours?"

She made a little noise that could have been meant for a laugh. "Do you like Marjorie?"

"So-so."

"I used Evelyn Carter in Paris once. Do you like that?"

"Not bad. What are you using now?"

She hesitated, frowning.

"Good Lord," I protested, "you're not in a vacuum, and I'm a detective. They took the names down at the door."

"Cynthia Brown," she said.

"I like that fine. That's Mrs. Orwin you came with?"

"Yes."

"She's the current customer? The lead you picked up in Florida?"

"Yes. But that's—" She gestured. "That's finished. That's settled now, since I'm telling you and Nero Wolfe. I'm through."

"I know. A job at Macy's or marry a truck driver. There's one thing you haven't told me, though—who was it you recognized?"

She turned her head for a glance at the door and then turned it still farther to look behind her. When her face came back to me it was out of kilter again, with the teeth pinching the lower lip.

"Can anyone hear us?" she asked.

"Nope. That other door goes to the front room—today the cloakroom. Anyhow this room's soundproofed, including the doors."

She glanced at the hall door again, returned to me, and lowered her voice. "This has to be done the way I say."

"Sure, why not?"

"I wasn't being honest with you."

"I wouldn't expect it from a crook. Start over."

"I mean—" She used the teeth on the lip again. "I mean I'm not just scared about myself. I'm scared all right, but I don't just want Nero Wolfe for what I said. I want him to get him for murder, but he has to keep me out of it. I don't want to have anything to do with any cops—not now I don't especially. I'm through. If he won't do it that way—do you think he will?"

I was feeling a faint tingle at the base of my spine. I only get that on special occasions, but this was unquestionably something special, if Marjorie Evelyn Carter Cynthia Brown wasn't taking me for a ride to pay for the drinks.

I gave her a hard look and didn't let the tingle get into my voice. "He might, for you, if you pay him. What kind of evidence have you got? Any?"

"I saw him."

"You mean today?"

"I mean I saw him then." She had her hands clasped tight. "I told you—I had a friend. I stopped in at her apartment that afternoon. I was just leaving—Doris was inside, in the bathroom—and as I got near the entrance door I heard a key turning in the lock, from the outside. I stopped, and the door came open and a man came in. When he saw me he just stood and stared. I had never met Doris's bank account and I knew she didn't want me to, and since he had a key I supposed of course it was him, making an unexpected call, so I mumbled something about Doris being in the bathroom and went past him, through the door and on out."

She paused. Her clasped hands loosened and then tightened again.

"I'm burning my bridges," she said, "but I can deny all this if I have to. I went and kept a cocktail date, and then phoned Doris's number to ask if our dinner date was still on, considering the visit of the bank account. There was no answer, so I went back to her apartment and rang the bell, and there was no answer to that either. It was a self-service elevator place, no doorman or hallman, so there was no one to ask anything. Her maid found her body the next morning. The papers said she had been killed the day before. That man killed her. There wasn't a word about him—no one had seen him enter or leave. And I didn't open my mouth! I was a lousy coward!"

"And today all of a sudden there he is, looking at orchids?"

"Yes."

"It's a pretty good script," I acknowledged. "Are you sure—"

"It's no script! I wish to God it was!"

"Okay. Are you sure he knows you recognized him?"

"Yes. He looked straight at me, and his eyes—"

She was stopped by the house phone buzzing. Stepping to my desk, I picked it up and asked it, "Well?"

Nero Wolfe's voice, peevish, came. "Archie!"

"Yes, sir."

"What the devil are you doing? Come back up here!"

"Pretty soon. I'm talking with a prospective client—"

"This is no time for clients! Come at once!"

The connection went. He had slammed it down. I hung up and went back to the prospective client. "Mr. Wolfe wants me upstairs. He didn't stop to think in time that the Manhattan Flower Club has women in it as well as men. Do you want to wait here?"

"Yes."

"If Mrs. Orwin asks about you?"

"I didn't feel well and went home."

"Okay. I shouldn't be long—the invitations said two-thirty to five. If you want a drink, help yourself. What name does this murderer use when he goes to look at orchids?"

She looked blank. I got impatient.

"Damn it, what's his name? This bird you recognized."

"I don't know."

"You don't?"

"No."

"Describe him."

She thought it over a little, gazing at me, and then shook her head. "I don't think—" she said doubtfully. She shook her head again, more positive. "Not now. I want to see what Nero Wolfe says first." She must have seen something in my eyes, or thought she did, for suddenly she came up out of her chair and moved to me and put a hand on my arm. "That's all I mean," she said earnestly. "It's not you—I know you're all right." Her fingers tightened on my forearm. "I might as well tell you—you'd never want any part of me anyhow—this is the first time in years, I don't know how long, that I've talked to a man just straight

—you know, just human? You know, not figuring on something one way or another. I—" She stopped for a word, and a little color showed in her cheeks. She found the word. "I've enjoyed it very much."

"Good. Me too. Call me Archie. I've got to go, but describe him. Just sketch him."

But she hadn't enjoyed it that much. "Not until Nero Wolfe says he'll do it," she said firmly.

I had to leave it at that, knowing as I did that in three more minutes Wolfe might have a fit. Out in the hall I had the notion of passing the word to Saul and Fritz to give departing guests a good look, but rejected it because (a) they weren't there, both of them presumably being busy in the cloakroom, (b) he might have departed already, and (c) I had by no means swallowed a single word of Cynthia's story, let alone the whole works. So I headed for the stairs and breasted the descending tide of guests leaving.

Up in the plant rooms there were plenty left. When I came into Wolfe's range he darted me a glance of cold fury, and I turned on the grin. Anyway, it was a quarter to five, and if they took the hint on the invitation it wouldn't last much longer.

II

THEY didn't take the hint on the dot, but it didn't bother me because my mind was occupied. I was now really interested in them—or at least one of them, if he had actually been there and hadn't gone home.

First there was a chore to get done. I found the three Cynthia had been with, a female and two males, over by the odontoglossum bench in the cool room. Getting through to them, I asked politely, "Mrs. Orwin?"

She nodded at me and said, "Yes?" Not quite tall enough but plenty plump enough, with a round full face and narrow little eyes that might have been better if they had been wide open, she struck me as a lead worth following. Just the pearls around her neck and the mink stole over her arm would have made a good haul, though I doubted if that was the kind of loot Cynthia specialized in.

"I'm Archie Goodwin," I said. "I work here."

I would have gone on if I had known how, but I needed a lead myself, since I didn't know whether to say Miss Brown or Mrs. Brown. Luckily one of the males horned in.

"My sister?" he inquired anxiously.

So it was a brother-and-sister act. As far as looks went he wasn't a bad brother at all. Older than me maybe, but not much, he was tall and straight, with a strong mouth and jaw and keen gray eyes. "My sister?" he repeated.

"I guess so. You are—"

"Colonel Brown. Percy Brown."

"Yeah." I switched back to Mrs. Orwin. "Miss Brown asked me to tell you that she went home. I gave her a little drink and it seemed to help, but she decided to leave. She asked me to apologize for her."

"She's perfectly healthy," the colonel asserted. He sounded a little hurt. "There's nothing wrong with her."

"Is she all right?" Mrs. Orwin asked.

"For her," the other male put in, "you should have made it three drinks. Three big ones. Or just hand her the bottle."

His tone was mean and his face was mean, and anyhow that was no way to talk in front of the help in a strange house, meaning me. He was some younger than Colonel Brown, but he already looked enough like Mrs. Orwin, especially the eyes, to make it more than a guess that they were mother and son. That point was settled when she commanded him, "Be quiet, Gene!" She turned to the colonel. "Perhaps you should go and see about her?"

He shook his head, with a fond but manly smile at her. "It's not necessary, Mimi. Really."

"She's all right," I assured them and pushed off, thinking there were a lot of names in this world that could stand a reshuffle. Calling that overweight narrow-eyed pearl-and-mink proprietor Mimi was a paradox.

I moved around among the guests, being gracious. Fully aware that I was not equipped with a Geiger counter that would flash a signal if and when I established contact with a strangler, the fact remained that I had been known to have hunches, and it would be something for my scrapbook if I picked one as the killer of Doris Hatten and it turned out later to be sunfast.

Cynthia Brown hadn't given me the Hatten, only the Doris, but with the context that was enough. At the time it had happened, some five months ago, early in October, the papers had given it a big play of course. She had been strangled with her own scarf, of white silk with the Declaration of Independence printed on it, in her cozy fifth-floor apartment in the West Seventies, and the scarf had been left around her neck, knotted at the back. The cops had never got within a mile of charging anyone, and Sergeant Purley Stebbins of Homicide had told me that they had never even found out who was paying the rent, but there was no law against Purley being discreet.

I kept on the go through the plant rooms, leaving all switches open for a hunch. Some of them were plainly preposterous, but with everyone else I made an opportunity to exchange some words, fullface and close up. That took time, and it was no help to my current and chronic campaign for a raise in wages, since it was the women, not the men, that Wolfe wanted off his neck. I stuck at it anyhow. It was true that if Cynthia was on the level, and if she hadn't changed her mind by the time I got Wolfe in to her, we would soon have specifications, but I had had that tingle at the bottom of my spine and I was stubborn.

As I say, it took time, and meanwhile five o'clock came and went, and the crowd thinned out. Going on five-thirty the remaining groups seemed to get the idea all at once that time was up and made for the entrance to the stairs. I was in the moderate room when it happened, and the first thing I knew I was alone there, except for a guy at the north bench, studying a row of dowianas. He didn't interest me, as I had already canvassed him and crossed him off as the wrong type for a strangler, but as I glanced his way he suddenly bent forward to pick up a pot with a flowering plant, and as he did so I felt my back stiffening. The stiffening was a reflex, but I knew what had caused it: the way his fingers closed around the pot, especially the thumbs. No matter how careful you are of other people's property, you don't pick up a five-inch pot as if you were going to squeeze the life out of it.

I made my way around to him. When I got there he was holding the pot so that the flowers were only a few inches from his eyes.

"Nice flower," I said brightly.

He nodded. "What color do you call the sepals?"

"Nankeen yellow."

He leaned to put the pot back, still choking it. I swiveled my head. The only people in sight, beyond the glass partition between us and the cool room, were Nero Wolfe and a small group of guests, among whom were the Orwin trio and Bill McNab, the garden editor of the *Gazette*. As I turned my head back to my man he straightened up, pivoted on his heel, and marched off without a word. Whatever else he might or might not have been guilty of, he certainly had bad manners.

I followed him, on into the warm room and through, out to the landing, and down the three flights of stairs. Along the main hall I was courteous enough not to step on his heel, but a lengthened stride would have reached it. The hall was next to empty. A woman, ready for the street in a caracul coat, was standing there, and Saul Panzer was posted near the front door with nothing to do. I followed my man on into the front room, the cloakroom, where Fritz Brenner was helping a guest on with his coat. Of course the racks were practically bare, and with one glance my man saw his property and went to get it. His coat was a brown tweed that had been through a lot more than one winter. I stepped forward to help, but he ignored me without even bothering to shake his head. I was beginning to feel hurt. When he emerged to the hall I was beside him, and as he moved to the front door I spoke.

"Excuse me, but we're checking guests out as well as in. Your name, please?"

"Ridiculous," he said curtly, and reached for the knob, pulled the door open, and crossed the sill. Saul, knowing I must have had a reason for wanting to check him out, was at my elbow, and we stood watching his back as he descended the seven steps of the stoop.

"Tail?" Saul muttered at me.

I shook my head and was parting my lips to mutter something back, when a sound came from behind us that made us both whirl around —a screech from a woman, not loud but full of feeling. As we whirled, Fritz and the guest he had been serving came out of the front room, and all four of us saw the woman in the caracul coat come running out of the office into the hall. She kept coming, gasping something, and the guest, making a noise like an alarmed male, moved to meet her. I moved faster, needing about eight jumps to the office door and two inside. There I stopped.

Of course I knew the thing on the floor was Cynthia, but only because I had left her in there in those clothes. With the face blue and contorted, the tongue halfway out, and the eyes popping, it could have been almost anybody. I knelt and slipped my hand inside her dress front, kept it there ten seconds, and felt nothing.

Saul's voice came from behind. "I'm here."

I got up and went to the phone on my desk and started dialing, telling Saul, "No one leaves. We'll keep what we've got. Have the door open for Doc Vollmer." After only two whirs the nurse answered, and put Vollmer on, and I snapped it at him. "Doc, Archie Goodwin. Come on the run. Strangled woman. Yeah, strangled."

I pushed the phone back, reached for the house phone and buzzed the plant rooms, and after a wait had Wolfe's irritated bark in my ear. "Yes?"

"I'm in the office. You'd better come down. That prospective client I mentioned is here on the floor, strangled. I think she's gone, but I've sent for Vollmer."

"Is this flummery?" he roared.

"No, sir. Come down and look at her and then ask me."

The connection went. He had slammed it down. I got a sheet of thin tissue paper from a drawer, tore off a corner, and went and placed it carefully over Cynthia's mouth and nostrils. In ten seconds it hadn't stirred.

Voices had been sounding from the hall. Now one of them entered the office. Its owner was the guest who had been in the cloakroom with Fritz when the screech came. He was a chunky broad-shouldered guy with sharp domineering dark eyes and arms like a gorilla's. His voice was going strong as he started toward me from the door, but it stopped when he had come far enough to get a good look at the object on the floor.

"My God," he said huskily.

"Yes, sir," I agreed.

"How did it happen?"

"Don't know."

"Who is it?"

"Don't know."

He made his eyes come away from it and up until they met mine, and I gave him an A for control. It really was a sight.

"The man at the door won't let us leave," he stated.

"No, sir. You can see why."

"I certainly can." His eyes stayed with me, however. "But we know nothing about it. My name is Carlisle, Homer N. Carlisle. I am the executive vice-president of the North American Foods Company. My wife was merely acting under impulse; she wanted to see the office of Nero Wolfe, and she opened the door and entered. She's sorry she did, and so am I. We have an appointment, and there's no reason why we should be detained."

"I'm sorry too," I told him, "but one thing, if nothing else—your wife discovered the body. We're stuck worse than you are, with a corpse here in our office, and we haven't even got a wife who had an impulse. We got it for nothing. So I guess— Hello, Doc."

Vollmer, entering and nodding at me on the fly, was panting a little as he set his black case on the floor and knelt beside it. His house was down the street and he had had only two hundred yards to trot, but he was taking on weight. As he opened the case and got out the stethoscope, Homer Carlisle stood and watched with his lips pressed tight, and I did likewise until I heard the sound of Wolfe's elevator. Crossing to the door and into the hall, I surveyed the terrain. Toward the front Saul and Fritz were calming down the woman in the caracul coat, now Mrs. Carlisle to me. Nero Wolfe and Mrs. Mimi Orwin were emerging from the elevator. Four guests were coming down the stairs: Gene Orwin, Colonel Percy Brown, Bill McNab, and a middle-aged male with a mop of black hair.

I stayed by the office door to block the quartet on the stairs. As Wolfe headed for me, Mrs. Carlisle darted to him and grabbed his arm. "I only wanted to see your office! I want to go! I'm not—"

As she pulled at him and sputtered, I noted a detail. The caracul coat was unfastened, and the ends of a silk scarf, figured and gaily colored, were flying loose. Since at least half of the female guests had sported scarfs, I mention it only to be honest and admit that I had got touchy on that subject.

Wolfe, who had already been too close to too many women that day to suit him, tried to jerk away, but she hung on. She was the big-boned flat-chested athletic type, and it could have been quite a tussle, with him weighing twice as much as her and four times as big around, if Saul hadn't rescued him by coming in between and prying her loose. That didn't stop her tongue, but Wolfe ignored it and came on toward me.

"Has Dr. Vollmer come?"

"Yes, sir."

The executive vice-president emerged from the office, talking. "Mr. Wolfe, my name is Homer N. Carlisle and I insist—"

"Shut up," Wolfe growled. On the sill of the door to the office, he faced the audience. "Flower lovers," he said with bitter scorn. "You told me, Mr. McNab, a distinguished group of sincere and devoted gardeners. Pfui! Saul!"

"Yes, sir."

"Are you armed?"

"Yes, sir."

"Put them all in the dining room and keep them there. Let no one touch anything around this door, especially the knob. Archie, come with me."

He wheeled and entered the office. Following, I used my foot to swing the door nearly shut, leaving no crack but not latching it. When I turned Vollmer was standing, facing Wolfe's scowl.

"Well?" Wolfe demanded.

"Dead," Vollmer told him. "With asphyxiation from strangling sometimes you can do something, but it wasn't even worth trying."

"How long ago?"

"I don't know, but not more than an hour or two. Two hours at the outside, probably less."

Wolfe looked at the thing on the floor, with no change in his scowl, and back at Doc. "You say strangling. Finger marks?"

"No. A constricting band of something with pressure below the hyoid bone. Not a stiff or narrow band; something soft like a strip of cloth—say a scarf."

Wolfe switched to me. "You didn't notify the police."

"No, sir." I glanced at Vollmer and back. "I need a word."

"I suppose so." He spoke to Doc. "If you will leave us for a moment? The front room?"

Vollmer hesitated, uncomfortable. "As a doctor called to a violent death I'd catch hell. Of course I could say—"

"Then go to a corner and cover your ears."

He did so. He went to the farthest corner, the angle made by the partition of the bathroom, pressed his palms to his ears, and stood facing us.

I addressed Wolfe with a lowered voice. "I was here, and she came in. She was either scared good or putting on a very fine act. Apparently it wasn't an act, and I now think I should have alerted Saul and Fritz, but it doesn't matter what I now think. Last October a woman named Doris Hatten was killed—strangled—in her apartment. No one got elected. Remember?"

"Yes."

"She said she was a friend of Doris Hatten's and was at her apartment that day and saw the man that did the strangling, and that he was here this afternoon. She said he was aware that she had recognized him, that's why she was scared, and she wanted to get you to help by telling him that we were wise and he'd better lay off. No wonder I didn't gulp it down. I realize that you dislike complications and therefore might want to scratch this out, but at the end she touched a soft spot by saying that she had enjoyed my company, so I prefer to open up to the cops."

"Then do so. Confound it!"

I went to the phone and started dialing WAtkins 9-8241. Doc Vollmer came out of his corner and went to get his black case from the floor and put it on a chair. Wolfe was pathetic. He moved around behind his desk and lowered himself into his own oversized custom-made number, the only spot on earth where he was ever completely comfortable, but there smack in front of him was the object on the floor, so after a moment he made a face, got back onto his feet, grunted like an outraged boar, went across to the other side of the room to the shelves, and inspected the backbones of books.

But even that pitiful diversion got interrupted. As I finished with my phone call and hung up, sudden sounds of commotion came from the hall. Dashing across, getting fingernails on the edge of the door and pulling it open, and passing through, I saw trouble. A group was gathered in the open doorway of the dining room, which was across the hall. Saul Panzer went bounding past me toward the front. At the front door Colonel Percy Brown was stiff-arming Fritz Brenner with one hand and reaching for the doorknob with the other. Fritz, who is chef and housekeeper, is not supposed to double in acrobatics, but he did fine. Dropping to the floor, he grabbed the colonel's ankles and jerked his feet out from under him. Then I was there, and Saul with his gun out; and there with us was the guest with the mop of black hair.

"You damn fool," I told the colonel as he sat up. "If you'd got outdoors Saul would have winged you."

"Guilt," said the black-haired guest emphatically. "The compression got unbearable and he exploded. I was watching him. I'm a psychiatrist."

"Good for you." I took his elbow and turned him. "Go back in and watch all of 'em. With that wall mirror you can include yourself."

"This is illegal," stated Colonel Brown, who had scrambled to his feet and was short of breath.

Saul herded them to the rear. Fritz got hold of my sleeve. "Archie, I've got to ask Mr. Wolfe about dinner."

"Nuts," I said savagely. "By dinnertime this place will be more crowded than it was this afternoon. Company is coming, sent by the city. It's a good thing we have a cloakroom ready."

"But he has to eat; you know that. I should have the ducks in the oven now. If I have to stay here at the door and attack people as they try to leave, what will he eat?"

"Nuts," I said. I patted him on the shoulder. "Excuse my manners, Fritz, I'm upset. I've just strangled a young woman."

"Nuts," he said scornfully.

"I might as well have," I declared.

The doorbell rang. I reached for the switch and turned on the stoop light and looked through the panel of one-way glass. It was the first consignment of cops.

III

IN MY opinion Inspector Cramer made a mistake. Opinion, hell, of course he did. It is true that in a room where a murder has occurred the city scientists—measurers, sniffers, print-takers, specialists, photographers—may shoot the works, and they do. But except in rare circumstances the job shouldn't take all week, and in the case of our office a couple of hours should have been ample. In fact, it was. By eight o'clock the scientists were through. But Cramer, like a sap, gave the order to seal it up until further notice, in Wolfe's hearing. He knew damn well that Wolfe spent at least three hundred evenings a year in there, in the only chair and under the only light that he really liked, and that was why he did it. It was a mistake. If he hadn't made it, Wolfe might have called his attention to a certain fact as soon as

Wolfe saw it himself, and Cramer would have been saved a lot of trouble.

The two of them got the fact at the same time, from me. We were in the dining room—this was shortly after the scientists had got busy in the office, and the guests, under guard, had been shunted to the front room—and I was relating my conversation with Cynthia Brown. They wanted all of it, or Cramer did rather, and they got it. Whatever else my years as Wolfe's assistant may have done for me or to me, they have practically turned me into a tape recorder, and Wolfe and Cramer didn't get a rewrite of that conversation, they got the real thing, word for word. They also got the rest of my afternoon, complete. When I finished, Cramer had a slew of questions, but Wolfe not a one. Maybe he had already focused on the fact above referred to, but neither Cramer nor I had. The shorthand dick seated at one end of the dining table had the fact too, in his notebook along with the rest of it, but he wasn't supposed to focus.

Cramer called a recess on the questions to take steps. He called men in and gave orders. Colonel Brown was to be photographed and fingerprinted and headquarters records were to be checked for him and Cynthia. The file on the murder of Doris Hatten was to be brought to him at once. The lab reports were to be rushed. Saul Panzer and Fritz Brenner were to be brought in.

They came. Fritz stood like a soldier at attention, grim and grave. Saul, only five feet seven, with the sharpest eyes and one of the biggest noses I have ever seen, in his unpressed brown suit, and his necktie crooked—he stood like Saul, not slouching and not stiff. He would stand like that if he were being awarded the Medal of Honor or if he were in front of a firing squad.

Of course Cramer knew both of them. He picked on Saul. "You and Fritz were in the hall all afternoon?"

Saul nodded. "The hall and the front room, yes."

"Who did you see enter or leave the office?"

"I saw Archie go in about four o'clock—I was just coming out of the front room with someone's hat and coat. I saw Mrs. Carlisle come out just after she screamed. In between those two I saw no one either enter or leave. We were busy most of the time, either in the hall or the front room."

Cramer grunted. "How about you, Fritz?"

"I saw no one." Fritz spoke louder than usual. "I didn't even see Archie go in." He took a step forward, still like a soldier. "I would like to say something."

"Go ahead."

"I think a great deal of all this disturbance is unnecessary. My duties here are of the household and not professional, but I cannot help hearing what reaches my ears, and I am aware of the many times that Mr. Wolfe has found the answer to problems that were too much for you. This happened here in his own house, and I think it should be left entirely to him."

I yooped, "Fritz, I didn't know you had it in you!"

"All this disturbance," he insisted firmly.

"I'll be goddamned." Cramer was goggling at him. "Wolfe told you to say that, huh?"

"Bah." Wolfe was contemptuous. "It can't be helped, Fritz. Have we plenty of ham?"

"Yes, sir."

"Sturgeon?"

"Yes, sir."

"Later, probably. For the guests in the front room, but not the police. Are you through with them, Mr. Cramer?"

"No." Cramer went back to Saul. "You checked the guests in?"

"Yes."

"How?"

"I had a list of the members of the Manhattan Flower Club. They had to show their membership cards. I checked on the list those who came. If they brought a wife or husband, or any other guest, I took the names."

"Then you have a record of everybody?"

"Yes."

"How complete is it?"

"It's complete and it's accurate."

"About how many names?"

"Two hundred and nineteen."

"This place wouldn't hold that many."

Saul nodded. "They came and went. There wasn't more than a hundred or so at any one time."

"That's a help." Cramer was getting more and more disgusted, and I didn't blame him. "Goodwin says he was there at the door with you when that woman screamed and came running out of the office, but that you hadn't seen her enter the office. Why not?"

"We had our backs turned. We were watching a man who had just left go down the steps. Archie had asked him for his name and he had said that was ridiculous. If you want it, his name is Malcolm Vedder."

"The hell it is. How do you know?"

"I had checked him in along with the rest."

Cramer stared. "Are you telling me that you could fit that many names to that many faces after seeing them just once?"

Saul's shoulders went slightly up and down. "There's more to people than faces. I might go wrong on a few, but not many. I was at that door to do a job and I did it."

"You should know by this time," Wolfe rumbled, "that Mr. Panzer is an exceptional man."

Cramer spoke to a dick standing by the door. "You heard that name, Levy—Malcolm Vedder. Tell Stebbins to check it on that list and send a man to bring him in."

The dick went. Cramer returned to Saul. "Put it this way. Say I sit you here with that list, and a man or woman is brought in, and I point to a name on the list and ask you if that person came this afternoon under that name. Could you tell me positively?"

"I could tell you positively whether the person had been here or not, especially if he was wearing the same clothes and hadn't been disguised. On fitting him to his name I might go wrong in a few cases, but I doubt it."

"I don't believe you."

"Mr. Wolfe does," Saul said complacently. "Archie does. I have developed my faculties."

"You sure have. All right, that's all for now. Stick around."

Saul and Fritz went. Wolfe, in his own chair at the end of the dining table, where ordinarily, at this hour, he sat for a quite different purpose than the one at hand, heaved a deep sigh and closed his eyes. I, seated beside Cramer at the side of the table that put us facing the door to the hall, was beginning to appreciate the kind of problem we were up against. The look on Cramer's face indicated that he was appreciating it too. The look was crossing my bow, direct at Wolfe.

"Goodwin's story," Cramer growled. "I mean her story. What do you think?"

Wolfe's eyes came open a little. "What followed seems to support it. I doubt if she would have arranged for that"—he flipped a hand in the direction of the office across the hall—"just to corroborate a tale. I accept it. I credit it."

"Yeah. I don't need to remind you that I know you well and I know Goodwin well. So I wonder how much chance there is that in a day or so you'll suddenly remember that she had been here before today, or one or more of the others had, and you've got a client, and there was something leading up to this."

"Bosh," Wolfe said dryly. "Even if it were like that, and it isn't, you would be wasting time. Since you know us, you know we wouldn't remember until we got ready to."

Cramer glowered. Two scientists came in from across the hall to report. Stebbins came to announce the arrival of an assistant district attorney. A dick came to relay a phone call from a deputy commissioner. Another dick came in to say that Homer Carlisle was raising hell in the front room. Meanwhile Wolfe sat with his eyes shut, but I got an idea of his state of mind from the fact that intermittently his forefinger was making little circles on the polished top of the table.

Cramer looked at him. "What do you know," he asked abruptly, "about the killing of that Doris Hatten?"

"Newspaper accounts," Wolfe muttered. "And what Mr. Stebbins has told Mr. Goodwin, casually."

"Casual is right," Cramer got out a cigar, conveyed it to his mouth, and sank his teeth in it. He never lit one. "Those damn houses with self-service elevators are worse than walk-ups for a checking job. No one ever sees anyone coming or going. If you're not interested, I'm talking to hear myself."

"I am interested." Wolfe's eyes stayed shut.

"Good. I appreciate it. Even so, self-service elevator or not, the man who paid the rent for that apartment was lucky. He may have been clever and careful, but also he was lucky. Never to have anybody see him enough to give a description of him—that took luck."

"Possibly Miss Hatten paid the rent herself."

"Sure," Cramer conceded, "she paid it all right, but where did she get it from? No visible means of support—he sure wasn't visible, and three good men spent a month trying to start a trail, and one of them is still at it. There was no doubt about its being that kind of a setup; we did get that far. She had only been living there two months, and when we found out how well the man who paid for it had kept himself covered, as tight as a drum, we decided that maybe he had installed her there just for that purpose. That was why we gave it all we had. Another reason was that the papers started hinting that we knew who he was and that he was such a big shot we were sitting on the lid."

Cramer shifted his cigar one tooth over to the left. "That kind of thing used to get me sore, but what the hell, for newspapers that's just routine. Big shot or not, he didn't need us to do any covering for him—he had done too good a job himself. Now, if we're to take it the way this Cynthia Brown gave it to Goodwin, it might have been the man who paid the rent and it might not. That makes it pie. I would hate to tell you what I think of the fact that Goodwin sat there in your office and was told right here on these premises and all he did was go upstairs and watch to see if anybody squeezed a flowerpot!"

"You're irritated," I said charitably. "Not that he *was* on the premises, that he *had* been. Also I was taking it with salt. Also she was saving specifications for Mr. Wolfe. Also—"

"Also I know you. How many of those two hundred and nineteen people were men?"

"I would say a little over half."

"Then how do *you* like it?"

"I hate it."

Wolfe grunted. "Judging from your attitude, Mr. Cramer, something that has occurred to me has not occurred to you."

"Naturally. You're a genius. What is it?"

"Something that Mr. Goodwin told us. I want to consider it a little."

"We could consider it together."

"Later. Those people in the front room are my guests. Can't you dispose of them?"

"One of your guests," Cramer rasped, "was a beaut, all right." He spoke to the dick by the door. "Bring in that woman—what's her name? Carlisle."

IV

MRS. HOMER N. CARLISLE came in with all her belongings: her caracul coat, her gaily colored scarf, and her husband. Perhaps I should say that her husband brought her. As soon as he was through the door he strode across to the dining table and delivered a harangue. I don't suppose Cramer had heard that speech, with variations, more than a thousand times. This time it was pretty effective. Solid and broad-shouldered, Mr. Carlisle looked the part. His sharp dark eyes flashed, and his long gorilla-like arms were good for gestures. At the first opening Cramer, controlling himself, said he was sorry and asked them to sit down.

Mrs. Carlisle did. Mr. Carlisle didn't.

"We're nearly two hours late now," he stated. "I know you have your duty to perform, but citizens have a few rights left, thank God. Our presence here is purely adventitious." I would have been impressed by the adventitious if he hadn't had so much time to think it up. "I warn you that if my name is published in connection with this miserable affair, a murder in the house of a private detective, I'll make trouble. I'm in a position to. Why should it be? Why should we be detained? What if we had left five or ten minutes earlier, as others did?"

"That's not quite logical," Cramer objected.

"Why not?"

"No matter when you left it would have been the same if your wife had acted the same. She discovered the body."

"By accident!"

"May I say something, Homer?" the wife put in.

"It depends on what you say."

"Oh," Cramer said significantly.

"What do you mean, oh?" Carlisle demanded.

"I mean that I sent for your wife, not you, but you came with her, and that tells me why. You wanted to see to it that she wasn't indiscreet."

"What the hell has she got to be indiscreet about?"

"I don't know. Apparently you do. If she hasn't, why don't you sit down and relax while I ask her a few questions?"

"I would, sir," Wolfe advised him. "You came in here angry, and you blundered. An angry man is a jackass."

It was a struggle for the executive vice-president, but he made it. He clamped his jaws and sat. Cramer went to the wife.

"You wanted to say something, Mrs. Carlisle?"

"Only that I'm sorry." Her bony hands, the fingers twined, were on the table before her. "For the trouble I've caused."

"I wouldn't say you caused it exactly—except for yourself and your husband." Cramer was mild. "The woman was dead, whether you went in there or not. But, if only as a matter of form, it was essential for me to see you, since you discovered the body. That's all there is to it as far as I know. There's no question of your being involved more than that."

"How the hell could there be?" Carlisle blurted.

Cramer ignored him. "Goodwin here saw you standing in the hall not more than two minutes, probably less, prior to the moment you screamed and ran out of the office. How long had you then been downstairs?"

"We had just come down. I was waiting for my husband to get his things."

"Had you been downstairs before that?"

"No—only when we came in."

"What time did you arrive?"

"A little after three, I think—"

"Twenty past three," the husband put in.

"Were you and your husband together all the time? Continuously?"

"Of course. Well—you know how it is—he would want to look longer at something, and I would move on a little—"

"Certainly we were," Carlisle said irritably. "You can see why I made that remark about it depending on what she said. She has a habit of being vague. This is no time to be vague."

"I am not actually vague," she protested with no heat, not to her husband but to Cramer. "It's just that everything is relative. There would be no presence if there were no absence. There would be no innocence if there were no sin. Nothing can be cut off sharp from anything else. Who would have thought my wish to see Nero Wolfe's office would link me with a horrible crime?"

"My God!" Carlisle exploded. "Hear that? Link. *Link!*"

"Why did you want to see Wolfe's office?" Cramer inquired.

"Why, to see the globe."

I gawked at her. I had supposed that naturally she would say it was curiosity about the office of a great and famous detective. Apparently Cramer reacted the same as me. "The globe?" he demanded.

"Yes, I had read about it and I wanted to see how it looked. I thought a globe that size, three feet in diameter, would be fantastic in an ordinary room— Oh!"

"Oh what?"

"I didn't see it!"

Cramer nodded. "You saw something else instead. By the way, I forgot to ask, did you know her? Had you ever seen her before?"

"You mean—her?"

"Yes. Her name was Cynthia Brown."

"We had never known her or seen her or heard of her," the husband declared.

"Had you, Mrs. Carlisle?"

"No."

"Of course she came as the guest of a Mrs. Orwin; she wasn't a member of this flower club. Are you a member?"

"My husband is."

"We both are," Carlisle stated. "Vague again. It's a joint membership. In my greenhouse at my country home I have over four thousand plants, including several hundred orchids." He looked at his wrist watch. "Isn't this about enough?"

"Plenty," Cramer conceded. "Thank you, both of you. We won't bother you again unless we have to. Levy, pass them out."

Mrs. Carlisle got to her feet and moved off, but halfway to the door she turned. "I don't suppose—would it be possible for me to look at the globe now? Just a peek?"

"For God's sake!" Her husband took her by the arm. "Come on. Come on!"

When the door had closed behind them Cramer glared at me and then at Wolfe. "This is sure a sweet one," he said grimly. "Say it's within the range of possibility that Carlisle is it, and the way it stands right now, why not? So we look into him. We check back on him for six months, and try doing it without getting roars out of him—a man like that, in his position. However, it can be done—by three or four men in two or three weeks. Multiply that by what? How many men were here?"

"Around a hundred and twenty," I told him. "Ten dozen. But you'll find that at least half of them are disqualified one way or another. As I told you, I took a survey. Say sixty."

"All right, multiply it by sixty. Do you care for it?"

"No."

"Neither do I." Cramer took the cigar from his mouth, removed a nearly severed piece with his fingers and put it in an ashtray, and replaced the cigar with a fresh tooth-hold. "Of course," he said sarcastically, "when she sat in there telling you about him the situation was different. You wanted her to enjoy being with you. You couldn't reach for the phone and tell us you had a self-confessed crook who could put a quick finger on a murderer and let us come and take over—hell no! You had to save it for a fee for Wolfe! You had to sit and admire her legs!"

"Don't be vulgar," I said severely.

"You had to go upstairs and make a survey! You had to— Well?"

Lieutenant Rowcliff had opened the door and entered. There were some city employees I liked, some I admired, some I had no feeling about, some I could have done without easy—and one whose ears I was going to twist someday. That was Rowcliff. He was tall, strong, handsome, and a pain in the neck.

"We're all through in there, sir," he said importantly. "We've covered everything. Nothing is being taken away, and it is all in order. We were especially careful with the contents of the drawers of Wolfe's desk, and also we—"

"My desk!" Wolfe roared.

"Yes, your desk," Rowcliff said precisely, smirking.

The blood was rushing into Wolfe's face.

"She was killed there," Cramer said gruffly. "She was strangled with something, and murderers have been known to hide things. Did you get anything at all?"

"I don't think so," Rowcliff admitted. "Of course the prints have to be sorted, and there'll be lab reports. How do we leave it?"

"Seal it up and we'll see tomorrow. You stay here and keep a photographer. The others can go. Tell Stebbins to send that woman in—Mrs. Irwin."

"Orwin, sir."

"I'll see her."

"Yes, sir." Rowcliff turned to go.

"Wait a minute," I objected. "Seal what up? The office?"

"Certainly," Rowcliff sneered.

I said firmly, to Cramer, not to him, "You don't mean it. We work there. We live there. All our stuff is there."

"Go ahead, Lieutenant," Cramer told Rowcliff, and he wheeled and went.

I set my jaw. I was full of both feelings and words, but I knew they had to be held in. This was not for me. This was far and away the worst Cramer had ever pulled. It was up to Wolfe. I looked at him. The blood had gone back down again; he was white with fury, and his mouth was pressed to so tight a line that there were no lips.

"It's routine," Cramer said aggressively.

Wolfe said icily, "That's a lie. It is not routine."

"It's *my* routine—in a case like this. Your office is not just an office. It's the place where more fancy tricks have been played than any other spot in New York. When a woman is murdered there, soon after a talk with Goodwin for which we have no word but his, I say sealing it is routine."

Wolfe's head came forward an inch, his chin out. "No, Mr. Cramer. I'll tell you what it is. It is the malefic spite of a sullen little soul and a crabbed and envious mind. It is the childish rancor of a primacy too often challenged and offended. It is the feeble wriggle—"

The door came open to let Mrs. Orwin in.

V

WITH Mrs. Carlisle the husband had come along. With Mrs. Orwin it was the son. His expression and manner were so different I would hardly have known him. Upstairs his tone had been mean and his face had been mean. Now his narrow little eyes were doing their damnedest to look frank and cordial and one of the boys. He leaned across the table at Cramer, extending a hand.

"Inspector Cramer? I've been hearing about you for years! I'm Eugene Orwin." He glanced to his right. "I've already had the pleasure of meeting Mr. Wolfe and Mr. Goodwin—earlier today, before this terrible thing happened. It *is* terrible."

"Yes," Cramer agreed. "Sit down."

"I will in a moment. I do better with words standing up. I would like to make a statement on behalf of my mother and myself, and I hope you'll permit it. I'm a member of the bar. My mother is not feeling well. At the request of your men she went in with me to identify the body of Miss Brown, and it was a bad shock, and we've been detained now more than two hours."

His mother's appearance corroborated him. Sitting with her head propped on a hand and her eyes closed, obviously she didn't care as much about the impression they made on the inspector as her son did. It was doubtful whether she was paying any attention to what her son was saying.

"A statement would be welcome," Cramer told him, "if it's relevant."

"I thought so," Gene said approvingly. "So many people have an entirely wrong idea of police methods! Of course you know that Miss Brown came here today as my mother's guest, and therefore it might be supposed that my mother knows her well. But actually she doesn't. That's what I want to make clear."

"Go ahead."

Gene glanced at the shorthand dick. "If it's taken down I would like to go over it when convenient."

"You may."

"Then here are the facts. In January my mother was in Florida. You meet all kinds in Florida. My mother met a man who called himself Colonel Percy Brown—a British colonel in the Reserve, he said. Later on he introduced his sister Cynthia to her. My mother saw a great deal of them. My father is dead, and the estate, a rather large one, is in her control. She lent Brown some money—not much; that was just an opener. A week ago—"

Mrs. Orwin's head jerked up. "It was only five thousand dollars, and I didn't promise him anything," she said wearily, and propped her head on her hand again.

"All right, Mother." Gene patted her shoulder. "A week ago she returned to New York, and they came along. The first time I met them I thought they were impostors. He didn't sound like an Englishman, and certainly she didn't. They weren't very free with family details, but from them and Mother, chiefly Mother, I got enough to inquire about and sent a cable to London. I got a reply Saturday and another one this morning, and there was more than enough to confirm my suspicion, but not nearly enough to put it up to my mother. When she likes people she can be very stubborn about them—not a bad trait, not at all; I don't want to be misunderstood and I don't want her to be. I was thinking it over, what step to take next. Meanwhile, I thought it best not to let them be alone with her if I could help it—as you see, I'm being utterly frank. That's why I came here with them today—my mother is a member of that flower club; I'm no gardener myself."

His tone implied a low opinion of male gardeners, which was none too bright if his idea was to get solid with Wolfe as well as Cramer.

He turned a palm up. "That's what brought me here. My mother came to see the orchids, and she invited Brown and his sister to come simply because she is goodhearted. But actually she doesn't know them, she knows nothing about them, because what they have told her is one thing and what they really are is something else. Then this happened, and in the past hour, after she recovered a little from the shock of being taken in there to identify the corpse, I have explained to her what the situation is."

He put his hands on the table and leaned on them, forward at Cramer. "I'm going to be quite frank, Inspector. Under the circumstances, I can't see that it would serve any useful purpose to let it be published that that woman came here with my mother. What good would it do? How would it further the cause of justice? I want to make it perfectly clear that we have no desire to evade our responsibility as citizens. But how would it help to get my mother's name in the headlines?"

He straightened, backed up a step, and looked affectionately at Mother.

"Names in headlines aren't what I'm after," Cramer told him, "but I don't run the newspapers. If they've already got it I can't stop them. I'd like to say I appreciate your frankness. So you only met Miss Brown a week ago. How many times had you seen her altogether?"

Three times, Gene said. Cramer had plenty of questions for both mother and son. It was in the middle of them that Wolfe passed me a slip of paper on which he had scribbled:

> Tell Fritz to bring sandwiches and coffee for you and me.
> Also for those left in the front room. No one else. Of course
> Saul and Theodore.

I left the room, found Fritz in the kitchen, delivered the message, and returned.

Gene stayed cooperative to the end, and Mrs. Orwin tried, though it was an effort. They said they had been together all the time, which I happened to know wasn't so, having seen them separated at least twice during the afternoon—and Cramer did too, since I had told him. They said a lot of other things, among them that they hadn't left the plant rooms between their arrival and their departure with Wolfe; that they had stayed until most of the others were gone because Mrs. Orwin wanted to persuade Wolfe to sell her some plants; that Colonel Brown had wandered off by himself once or twice; that they had been only mildly concerned about Cynthia's absence because of assurances from Colonel Brown and me; and so on and so forth. Before they left, Gene made another try for a commitment to keep his mother's name out of it, and Cramer appreciated his frankness so much that he promised to do his best. I couldn't blame Cramer; people like them might be in a position to call almost anybody, even the commissioner or the mayor, by his first name.

Fritz had brought trays for Wolfe and me, and we were making headway with them. In the silence that followed the departure of the Orwins, Wolfe could plainly be heard chewing a mouthful of mixed salad.

Cramer sat frowning at us. He spoke not to Wolfe but to me. "Is that imported ham?"

I shook my head and swallowed before I answered. "No, Georgia. Pigs fed on peanuts and acorns. Cured to Mr. Wolfe's specifications. It smells good but it tastes even better. I'll copy the recipe for you— no, damn it, I can't, because the typewriter's in the office. Sorry." I put the sandwich down and picked up another. "I like to alternate— first a bite of ham, then sturgeon, then ham, then sturgeon . . ."

I could see him controlling himself. He turned his head. "Levy! Get that Colonel Brown in."

"Yes, sir. That man you wanted—Vedder—he's here."

"Then I'll take him first."

VI

Up in the plant rooms Malcolm Vedder had caught my eye by the way he picked up a flowerpot and held it. As he took a chair across the dining table from Cramer and me, I still thought he was worth another good look, but after his answer to Cramer's third question I relaxed and concentrated on my sandwiches. He was an actor and had had parts in three Broadway plays. Of course that explained it. No actor would pick up a flowerpot just normally, like you or me. He would have to dramatize it some way, and Vedder had happened to choose a way that looked to me like fingers closing around a throat.

Now he was dramatizing this by being wrought up and indignant about the cops dragging him into an investigation of a sensational murder. He kept running the long fingers of both his elegant hands through his hair in a way that looked familiar, and I remembered I had seen him the year before as the artist guy in *The Primitives.*

"Typical!" he told Cramer, his eyes flashing and his voice throaty with feeling. "Typical of police clumsiness! Pulling *me* into this! The newspapermen out front recognized me, of course, and the damned photographers! My God!"

"Yeah," Cramer said sympathetically. "It'll be tough for an actor, having your picture in the paper. We need help, us clumsy police, and you were among those present. You're a member of this flower club?"

No, Vedder said, he wasn't. He had come with a friend, a Mrs. Beauchamp, and when she had left to keep an appointment he had remained to look at more orchids. If only he had departed with her he would have avoided this dreadful publicity. They had arrived about three-thirty, and he had remained in the plant rooms continuously until leaving with me at his heels. He had seen no one that he had ever known or seen before, except Mrs. Beauchamp. He knew nothing of any Cynthia Brown or Colonel Percy Brown. Cramer went through all the regulation questions and got all the expected negatives, until he suddenly asked, "Did you know Doris Hatten?"

Vedder frowned. "Who?"

"Doris Hatten. She was also—"

"Ah!" Vedder cried. "She was also strangled! I remember!"

"Right."

Vedder made fists of his hands, rested them on the table, and leaned forward. His eyes had flashed again and then gone dead. "You know," he said tensely, "that's the worst of all, strangling—especially a woman." His fists opened, the fingers spread apart, and he gazed at them. "Imagine strangling a beautiful woman!"

"Did you know Doris Hatten?"

"Othello," Vedder said in a deep resonant tone. His eyes lifted to Cramer, and his voice lifted too. "No, I didn't know her; I only read about her." He shuddered all over and then, abruptly, he was out of his chair and on his feet. "Damn it all," he protested shrilly, "I only came here to look at orchids! God!"

He ran his fingers through his hair, turned, and made for the door. Levy looked at Cramer with his brows raised, and Cramer shook his head impatiently.

I muttered at Wolfe, "He hammed it, maybe?"

Wolfe wasn't interested.

The next one in was Bill McNab, garden editor of the *Gazette*. I knew him a little, but not well, most of my newspaper friends not being on garden desks. He looked unhappier than any of the others, even Mrs. Orwin, as he walked across to the table, to the end where Wolfe sat.

"I can't tell you how much I regret this, Mr. Wolfe," he said miserably.

"Don't try," Wolfe growled.

"I wish I could, I certainly do. What a really, really terrible thing! I wouldn't have dreamed such a thing could happen—the Manhattan Flower Club! Of course, she wasn't a member, but that only makes it worse in a way." McNab turned to Cramer. "I'm responsible for this."

"You are?"

"Yes. It was my idea. I persuaded Mr. Wolfe to arrange it. He let me word the invitations. And I was congratulating myself on the great success! The club has only a hundred and eighty-nine members, and there were over two hundred people here. Then this! What can I do?" He turned. "I want you to know this, Mr. Wolfe. I got a message from my paper; they wanted me to do a story on it for the news columns, and I refused point-blank. Even if I get fired—I don't think I will."

"Sit down a minute," Cramer invited him.

McNab varied the monotony on one detail, at least. He admitted that he had left the plant rooms three times during the afternoon, once to accompany a departing guest down to the ground floor, and twice to go down alone to check on who had come and who hadn't. Aside from that, he was more of the same. He had never heard of Cynthia Brown. By now it was beginning to seem not only futile but silly to spend time on seven or eight of them merely because they happened to be the last to go and so were at hand. Also it was something new to me from a technical standpoint. I had never seen one stack up like that. Any precinct dick knows that every question you ask of everybody is aimed at one of the three targets: motive, means, and opportunity. In this case there were no questions to ask because those were already answered. Motive: the guy had followed her downstairs, knowing she had recognized him, had seen her enter Wolfe's office and thought she was doing exactly what she was doing, getting set to tell Wolfe, and had decided to prevent that the quickest and best way he knew. Means: any piece of cloth; even his handkerchief would do. Opportunity: he was there—all of them on Saul's list were.

So if you wanted to learn who strangled Cynthia Brown, first you had to find out who had strangled Doris Hatten, and the cops had already been working on that for five months.

As soon as Bill McNab had been sent on his way, Colonel Percy Brown was brought in.

Brown was not exactly at ease, but he had himself well in hand. You would never have picked him for a con man, and neither would I. His mouth and jaw were strong and attractive, and as he sat down he leveled his keen gray eyes at Cramer and kept them there. He wasn't interested in Wolfe or me. He said his name was Colonel Percy Brown, and Cramer asked him which army he was a colonel in.

"I think," Brown said in a cool even tone, "it will save time if I state my position. I will answer fully and freely all questions that relate to what I saw or heard or did since I arrived here this afternoon. To that extent I'll help you all I can. Answers to any other questions will have to wait until I consult my attorney."

Cramer nodded. "I expected that. The trouble is I'm pretty sure I don't give a damn what you saw or heard this afternoon. We'll come back to that. I want to put something to you. As you see, I'm not even wanting to know why you tried to break away before we got here."

"I merely wanted to phone—"

"Forget it." Cramer put the remains of his second cigar, not more than a scraggly inch, in the ashtray. "On information received, I think it's like this. The woman who called herself Cynthia Brown, murdered here today, was not your sister. You met her in Florida six or eight weeks ago. She went in with you on an operation of which Mrs. Orwin was the subject, and you introduced her to Mrs. Orwin as your sister. You two came to New York with Mrs. Orwin a week ago, with the operation well under way. As far as I'm concerned, that is only background. Otherwise I'm not interested in it. My work is homicide, and that's what I'm working on now."

Brown was listening politely.

"For me," Cramer went on, "the point is that for quite a period you have been closely connected with this Miss Brown, associating with her in a confidential operation. You must have had many intimate conversations with her. You were having her with you as your sister, and she wasn't, and she's been murdered. We could give you merry hell on that score alone."

Brown had no use for his tongue. His face said no comment.

"It'll never be too late to give you hell," Cramer assured him, "but I wanted to give you a chance first. For two months you've been on intimate terms with Cynthia Brown. She certainly must have mentioned an experience she had last October. A friend of hers named Doris Hatten was murdered—strangled. Cynthia Brown had information about the murderer which she kept to herself; if she had come out with it she'd be alive now. She must have mentioned that to you; you can't tell me she didn't. She must have told you all about it. Now you can tell me. If you do we can nail him for what he did here today, and it might even make things a little smoother for you. Well?"

Brown had pursed his lips. They straightened out again, and his hand came up for a finger to scratch his cheek.

"I'm sorry," he said.

"For what?"

"I'm sorry I can't help."

"Do you expect me to believe that during all those weeks she never mentioned the murder of her friend Doris Hatten?"

"I'm sorry I can't help."

Cramer got out another cigar and rolled it between his palms, which was wasted energy since he didn't intend to draw smoke through it. Having seen him do it before, I knew what it meant. He still thought he might get something from this customer and was taking time out to control himself.

"I'm sorry too," he said, trying not to make it a growl. "But she must have told you something of her previous career, didn't she?"

"I'm sorry." Brown's tone was firm and final.

"Okay. We'll move on to this afternoon. On that you said you'd answer fully and freely. Do you remember a moment when something about Cynthia Brown's appearance—some movement she made or the expression on her face—caused Mrs. Orwin to ask her what was the matter with her?"

A crease was showing on Brown's forehead. "I don't believe I do," he stated.

"I'm asking you to try. Try hard."

Silence. Brown pursed his lips and the crease in his forehead deepened. Finally he said, "I may not have been right there at the moment. In those aisles—in a crowd like that—we weren't rubbing elbows continuously."

"You do remember when she excused herself because she wasn't feeling well?"

"Yes, of course."

"Well, this moment I'm asking about came shortly before that. She exchanged looks with some man nearby, and it was her reaction to that that made Mrs. Orwin ask her what was the matter. What I'm interested in is that exchange of looks. If you saw it and can remember it, and can describe the man she exchanged looks with, I wouldn't give a damn if you stripped Mrs. Orwin clean and ten more like her."

"I didn't see it."

"You didn't."

"No."

"You didn't say you're sorry."

"I am, of course, if it would help—"

"To hell with you!" Cramer banged his fist on the table so hard the trays danced. "Levy! Take him out and tell Stebbins to send him down and lock him up. Material witness. Put more men on him. He's got a record somewhere. Find it!"

"I wish to phone my attorney," Brown said quietly but emphatically.

"There's a phone down where you're going," Levy told him. "If it's not out of order. This way, Colonel."

As the door closed behind them Cramer glared at me as if daring me to say that I was sorry too. Letting my face show how bored I was, I remarked casually, "If I could get in the office I'd show you a swell book on disguises; I forget the name of it. The world record is sixteen years—a guy in Italy fooled a brother and two cousins who had known him well. So maybe you ought to—"

Cramer turned from me rudely and said, "Gather up, Murphy. We're leaving." He shoved his chair back, stood up, and shook his ankles to get his pants legs down. Levy came back in, and Cramer addressed him. "We're leaving. Everybody out. To my office. Tell Stebbins one man out front will be enough—no, I'll tell him—"

"There's one more, sir."

"One more what?"

"In the front room. A man."

"Who?"

"His name is Nicholson Morley. He's a psychiatrist."

"Let him go. This is a goddam joke."

"Yes, sir."

Levy went. The shorthand dick had collected notebooks and other papers and was putting them into a battered briefcase. Cramer looked at Wolfe. Wolfe looked back at him.

"A while ago," Cramer rasped, "you said something had occurred to you."

"Did I?" Wolfe inquired coldly.

Their eyes went on clashing until Cramer broke the connection by turning to go. I restrained an impulse to knock their heads together. They were both being childish. If Wolfe really had something, anything at all, he knew damn well Cramer would gladly trade the seals on the office doors for it sight unseen. And Cramer knew damn well he could make the deal himself with nothing to lose. But they were both too sore and stubborn to show any horse sense.

Cramer had circled the end of the table on his way out when Levy re-entered to report, "That man Morley insists on seeing you. He says it's vital."

Cramer halted, glowering. "What is he, a screwball?"

"I don't know, sir. He may be."

"Oh, bring him in." Cramer came back around the table to his chair.

VII

This was my first really good look at the middle-aged male with the mop of black hair. His quick-darting eyes were fully as black as his hair, and the appearance of his chin and jowls made it evident that his beard would have been likewise if he gave it half a chance. He sat down and was telling Cramer who and what he was.

Cramer nodded impatiently. "I know. You have something to say, Dr. Morley?"

"I have. Something vital."

"Let's hear it."

Morley got better settled in his chair. "First, I assume that no arrest has been made. Is that correct?"

"Yes—if you mean an arrest with a charge of murder."

"Have you a definite object of suspicion, with or without evidence in support?"

"If you mean am I ready to name the murderer, no. Are you?"

"I think I may be."

Cramer's chin went up. "Well? I'm in charge here."

Dr. Morley smiled. "Not quite so fast. The suggestion I have to offer is sound only with certain assumptions." He placed the tip of his right forefinger on the tip of his left little finger. "One: that you have no idea who committed this murder, and apparently you haven't." He moved over a finger. "Two: that this was not a commonplace crime with a commonplace discoverable motive." To the middle finger. "Three: that nothing is known to discredit the hypothesis that this girl—I understand from Mrs. Orwin that her name was Cynthia Brown—that she was strangled by the man who strangled Doris Hatten on October seventh last year. May I make those assumptions?"

"You can try. Why do you want to?"

Morley shook his head. "Not that I want to. That if I am permitted to, I have a suggestion. I wish to make it clear that I have great respect for the competence of the police, within proper limits. If the man who murdered Doris Hatten had been vulnerable to police techniques and resources, he would almost certainly have been caught. But he wasn't. You failed utterly. Why?"

"You're telling me."

"Because he was out of bounds for you. Because your exploration of motive is restricted by your preconceptions." Morley's black eyes gleamed. "You're a layman, so I won't use technical terms. The most powerful motives on earth are motives of the personality, which cannot be exposed by any purely objective investigation. If the personality is twisted, distorted, as it is with a psychotic, then the motives are twisted too. As a psychiatrist I was deeply interested in the published reports of the murder of Doris Hatten—especially the detail that she was strangled with her own scarf. When your efforts to find the culprit—thorough, no doubt, and even brilliant—ended in complete failure, I would have been glad to come forward with a suggestion, but I was as helpless as you."

"Get down to it," Cramer muttered.

"Yes." Morley put his elbows on the table and paired all his fingertips. "Now today. On the basis of the assumptions I began with, it is a tenable theory, worthy to be tested, that this was the same man. If so he has made a mistake. Apparently no one got in here today without having his name checked; the man at the door was most efficient. So it is no longer a question of finding him among thousands or millions; it's a mere hundred or so, and I am willing to contribute my services. I don't think there are more than three or four men in New York qualified for such a job, and I am one of them. You can verify that."

The black eyes flashed. "I admit that for a psychiatrist this is a rare opportunity. Nothing could be more dramatic than a psychosis exploding into murder. I don't pretend that my suggestion is entirely unselfish. All you have to do is to have them brought to my office—one at a time, of course. With some of them ten minutes will be enough, but with others it may take hours. When I have—"

"Wait a minute," Cramer put in. "Are you suggesting that we deliver everyone that was here today to your office for you to work on?"

"No, not everyone, only the men. When I have finished I may have nothing that can be used as evidence, but there's an excellent chance that I can tell you who the strangler is, and when you once know that—"

"Excuse me," Cramer said. He was on his feet. "Sorry to cut you off, Doctor, but I must get downtown." He was on his way. "I'm afraid your suggestion wouldn't work. I'll let you know—"

He went, and Levy and Murphy with him.

Dr. Morley pivoted his head to watch them go, kept it that way a moment, and then came back to us. He looked disappointed but not beaten. The black eyes, after resting on me briefly, darted to Wolfe.

"You," he said, "are intelligent and literate. I should have had you more in mind. May I count on you to explain to that policeman why my suggestion is the only hope for him?"

"No," Wolfe said curtly.

"He's had a hard day," I told Morley. "So have I. Would you mind closing the door after you?"

He looked as if he had a notion to start on me as a last resort, so I got up and circled around to the door, which had been left open, and remarked to him, "This way, please."

He arose and walked out without a word. I shut the door, had a good stretch and yawn, crossed to open a window and stick my head out for a breath of air, closed the window, and looked at my wrist watch.

"Twenty minutes to ten," I announced.

Wolfe muttered, "Go look at the office door."

"I just did, as I let Morley out. It's sealed. Malefic spite."

"See if they're gone and bolt the door. Send Saul home and tell him to come at nine in the morning. Tell Fritz I want beer."

I obeyed. The hall and front room were uninhabited. Saul, whom I found in the kitchen with Fritz, said he had made a complete tour upstairs and everything was in order. I stayed for a little chat with him while Fritz took a tray to the dining room. When I left him and went back Wolfe, removing the cap from a bottle of beer with the opener Fritz had brought on the tray, was making a face, which I understood. The opener he always used, a gold item that a satisfied client had given him years ago, was in the drawer of his desk in the office. I sat and watched him pour beer.

"This isn't a bad room to sit in," I said brightly.

"Pfui! I want to ask you something."

"Shoot."

"I want your opinion of this. Assume that we accept without reservation the story Miss Brown told you. By the way, do you?"

"In view of what happened, yes."

"Then assume it. Assume also that the man she had recognized, knowing she had recognized him, followed her downstairs and saw her enter the office; that he surmised that she intended to consult me; that he postponed joining her in the office either because he knew you were in there with her or for some other reason; that he saw you come out and go upstairs; that he took an opportunity to enter the office unobserved, got her off guard, killed her, got out unobserved, and returned upstairs. All of those assumptions seem to be required, unless we discard all that and dig elsewhere."

"I'll take it that way."

"Very well. Then we have significant indications of his character. Consider it. He has killed her and is back upstairs, knowing that she was in the office talking with you for some time. He would like to know what she said to you. Specifically, he would like to know whether she told you about him, and if so how much. Had she or had she not named or described him in his current guise? With that question unanswered, would a man of his character as indicated leave the house? Or would he prefer the challenge and risk of remaining until the body had been discovered, to see what you would do? And I too, of course, after you had talked with me, and the police?"

"Yeah." I chewed my lip. There was a long silence. "So that's how your mind's working. I could offer a guess."

"I prefer a calculation to a guess. For that a basis is needed, and we have it. We know the situation as we have assumed it, and we know something of his character."

"Okay," I conceded, "a calculation. I'll be damned. The answer I get, he would stick around until the body was found, and if he did, then he is one of the bunch Cramer has been talking with. So that's what occurred to you, huh?"

"No. By no means. That's a different matter. This is merely a tentative calculation for a starting point. If it is sound, I know who the murderer is."

I gave him a look. Sometimes I can tell how much he is putting on and sometimes I can't. I decided to buy it. With the office sealed up by the crabbed and envious mind of Inspector Cramer, he was certainly in no condition to entertain himself by trying to string me.

"That's interesting," I said admiringly. "If you want me to get him on the phone I'll have to use the one in the kitchen."

"I want to test the calculation."

"So do I."

"But there's a difficulty. The test I have in mind, the only one I can contrive to my satisfaction—only you can make it. And in doing so you would have to expose yourself to great personal risk."

"For God's sake." I gawked at him. "This is a brand-new one. The errands you've sent me on! Since when have you flinched or faltered in the face of danger to me?"

"This danger is extreme."

"So is the fix you're in. The office is sealed, and in it are the book you're reading and the television set. Let's hear the test. Describe it. All I ask is ninety-nine chances in a hundred."

"Very well." He turned a hand over. "The decision will be yours. The typewriter in the office is inaccessible. Is that old one in your room in working order?"

"Fair."

"Bring it down here, and some sheets of blank paper—any kind. I'll need a blank envelope."

"I have some."

"Bring one. Also the telephone book, Manhattan, from my room."

I went to the hall and up two flights of stairs. Having collected the first three items in my room, I descended a flight, found that the door of Wolfe's room was still locked, and had to put the typewriter on the floor to get out my keys. With a full cargo I returned to the dining room, unloaded, and was placing the typewriter in position on the table when Wolfe spoke.

"No, bring it here. I'll use it myself."

I lifted my brows at him. "A page will take you an hour."

"It won't be a page. Put a sheet of paper in it."

I did so, got the paper squared, lifted the machine, and put it in front of him. He sat and frowned at it for a long minute and then started pecking. I turned my back on him to make it easier to withhold remarks about his two-finger technique, and passed the time by trying to figure his rate. That was hopeless, because at one moment he would be going at about twelve words a minute and then would come a sudden burst of speed, stepping it up to twenty or more. All at once there was the sound of the ratchet turning as he pulled the paper out, and I supposed he had ruined it and was going to start over, but when I turned to look his hand was extended to me with the sheet in it.

"I think that will do," he said.

I took it and read what he had typed:

> She told me enough this afternoon so that I know who to send this to, and more. I have kept it to myself because I haven't decided what is the right thing to do. I would like to have a talk with you first, and if you will phone me tomorrow, Tuesday, between nine o'clock and noon, we can make an appointment; please don't put it off or I will have to decide myself.

I read it over three times. I looked at Wolfe. He had put an envelope in the typewriter and was consulting the phone book.

"It's all right," I said, "except that I don't care for the semicolon after 'appointment.' I would have put a period and started a new sentence."

He began pecking, addressing the envelope. I waited until he had finished and rolled the envelope out.

"Just like this?" I asked. "No name or initials signed?"

"No."

"I admit it's nifty," I admitted. "Hell, we could forget the calculation and send this to every guy on that list and wait to see who phoned. He has just about got to phone—and also make a date."

"I prefer to send it only to one person—the one indicated by your report of that conversation. That will test the calculation."

"And save postage." I glanced at the paper. "The extreme danger, I suppose, is that I'll get strangled. Or of course in an emergency like this he might try something else. He might even arrange for help. If you want me to mail this I'll need that envelope."

"I don't want to minimize the risk of this, Archie."

"Neither do I. I'll have to borrow a gun from Saul; ours are in the office. May I have that envelope? I'll have to go to Times Square to mail it."

"Yes. Before you do so, copy that note; we should have a copy. Keep Saul here in the morning. If and when the phone call comes you will have to use your wits to arrange the appointment as advantageously as possible. Discussion of plans will have to wait upon that."

"Right. The envelope, please?"

He handed it to me.

VIII

As FAR as Wolfe was concerned, the office being sealed made no difference in the morning up to eleven o'clock, since his schedule had him in the plant rooms from nine to eleven. With me it did. From breakfast on was the best time for my office chores, including the morning mail.

That Tuesday morning, however, it didn't matter much, since I was kept busy from eight o'clock on by the phone and the doorbell. After nine Saul was there to help, but not with the phone because the orders were that I was to answer all calls. They were mostly from newspapers, but there were a couple from Homicide—once Rowcliff and once Purley Stebbins—and a few scattered ones, including one with comic relief from the president of the Manhattan Flower Club. I took them on the extension in the kitchen. Every time I lifted the thing and told the transmitter, "Nero Wolfe's office, Archie Goodwin speaking," my pulse went up a notch and then had to level off again. I had one argument, with a bozo in the District Attorney's office who had the strange idea that he could order me to report for an interview at eleven-thirty sharp, which ended by my agreeing to call later to fix an hour.

A little before eleven I was in the kitchen with Saul, who at Wolfe's direction had been briefed to date, trying to come to terms on a bet. I was offering him even money that the call would come by noon and he was holding out for five to three, having originally asked for two to one. I was suggesting sarcastically that we change sides when the phone rang and I got it and said distinctly, "Nero Wolfe's office, Archie Goodwin speaking."

"Mr. Goodwin?"

"Right."

"You sent me a note."

My hand wanted to grip the phone the way Vedder had gripped the flowerpot, but I wouldn't let it.

"Did I? What about?"

"You suggested that we make an appointment. Are you in a position to discuss it?"

"Sure. I'm alone and no extensions are on. But I don't recognize your voice. Who is this?"

That was just putting a nickel's worth of breath on a long shot. Saul, at a signal from me, had raced up to the extension in Wolfe's room, and this bird might possibly be completely loony. But no.

"I have two voices. This is the other one. Have you made a decision yet?"

"No. I was waiting to hear from you."

"That's wise, I think. I'm willing to discuss the matter. Are you free for this evening?"

"I can wiggle free."

"With a car to drive?"

"Yeah, I have a car."

"Drive to a lunchroom at the northeast corner of Fifty-first Street and Eleventh Avenue. Get there at eight o'clock. Park your car on Fifty-first Street, but not at the corner. Got that?"

"Yes."

"You will be alone, of course. Go in the lunchroom and order something to eat. I won't be there, but you will get a message. You'll be there at eight o'clock?"

"Yes. I still don't recognize your voice. I don't think you're the person I sent the note to."

"I am. It's good, isn't it?"

The connection went.

I hung up, told Fritz he could answer calls now, and hotfooted it to the stairs and up a flight. Saul was there on the landing.

"Whose voice was that?" I demanded.

"Search me. You heard all I did." His eyes had a gleam in them, and I suppose mine did too.

"Whoever it was," I said, "I've got a date. Let's go up and tell the genius. I've got to admit he saved a lot of postage."

We mounted the other two flights and found Wolfe in the cool room, inspecting a bench of dendrobiums for damage from the invasion of the day before. When I told him about the call he merely nodded, not even taking the trouble to smirk, as if picking a murderer first crack out of ten dozen men was the sort of thing he did between yawns.

"That call," he said, "validates our assumptions and verifies our calculation, but that's all. If it had done more than that it wouldn't have been made. Has anyone come to take those seals off?"

I told him no. "I asked Stebbins about it and he said he'd ask Cramer."

"Don't ask again," he snapped. "We'll go down to my room."

If the strangler had been in Wolfe's house the rest of that day he would have felt honored—or anyway he should. Even during Wolfe's afternoon hours in the plant rooms, from four to six, his mind was on my appointment, as was proved by the crop of new slants and ideas that poured out of him when he came down to the kitchen. Except for a trip to Leonard Street to answer an hour's worth of questions by an assistant district attorney, my day was devoted to it too. My most useful errand, though at the time it struck me as a waste of time and money, was one made to Doc Vollmer for a prescription and then to a drugstore under instructions from Wolfe.

When I got back from the D. A.'s office Saul and I got in the sedan and went for a reconnaissance. We didn't stop at Fifty-first Street and Eleventh Avenue, but drove past it four times. The main idea was to find a place for Saul. He and Wolfe both insisted that he had to be there with his eyes and ears open, and I insisted that he had to be covered enough not to scare off my date, who could spot his big nose a mile off. We finally settled for a filling station across the street from the lunchroom. Saul was to have a taxi drive in there at eight o'clock, and stay in the passenger's seat while the driver tried to get his carburetor adjusted. There were so many contingencies to be agreed on that if it had been anyone but Saul I wouldn't have expected him to remember more than half. For instance, in case I left the lunchroom and got in my car and drove off Saul was not to follow unless I cranked my window down.

Trying to provide for contingencies was okay in a way, but at seven o'clock, as the three of us sat in the dining room, finishing the roast duck, I had the feeling that we might as well have spent the day playing pool. Actually it was strictly up to me, since I had to let the other guy make the rules until and unless it got to where I felt I could take over and win. And with the other guy making the rules no one gets very far, not even Nero Wolfe, arranging for contingencies ahead of time; you meet them as they come, and if you meet one wrong it's too bad.

Saul left before I did, to find a taxi driver that he liked the looks of. When I went to the hall for my hat and raincoat, Wolfe came along, and I was really touched, since he wasn't through yet with his after-dinner coffee.

"I still don't like the idea," he insisted, "of your having that thing in your pocket. I think you should slip it inside your sock."

"I don't." I was putting the raincoat on. "If I get frisked, a sock is as easy to feel as a pocket."

"You're sure that gun is loaded?"

"For God's sake. I never saw you so anxious. Next you'll be telling me to put on my rubbers."

He even opened the door for me.

It wasn't actually raining, merely trying to make up its mind whether to or not, but after a couple of blocks I reached to switch on the windshield wiper. As I turned uptown on Tenth Avenue the dash clock said 7:47; as I turned left on Fifty-first Street it had only got to 7:51. At that time of day in that district there was plenty of space, and I rolled to the curb and stopped about twenty yards short of the corner, stopped the engine and turned off the lights, and cranked my window down for a good view of the filling station across the street. There was no taxi there. I glanced at my wrist watch and relaxed. At 7:59 a taxi pulled in and stopped by the pumps, and the driver got out and lifted the hood and started peering. I put my window up, locked three doors, pulled the key out, got myself out, locked the door, walked to the lunchroom, and entered.

There was one hash slinger behind the counter and five customers scattered along on the stools. I picked a stool that left me elbow room, sat, and ordered ice cream and coffee. That made me slightly conspicuous in those surroundings, but I refused to insult Fritz's roast duck, which I could still taste. The counterman served me and I took my time. At 8:12 the ice cream was gone and my cup empty, and I ordered a refill. I had about got to the end of that too when a male entered, looked along the line, came straight to me, and asked me what my name was. I told him, and he handed me a folded piece of paper and turned to go.

He was barely old enough for high school, and I made no effort to hold him, thinking that the bird I had a date with was not likely to be an absolute sap. Unfolding the paper, I saw neatly printed in pencil:

> Go to your car and get a note under the windshield wiper. Sit in the car to read it.

I paid what I owed, walked to my car and got the note as I was told, unlocked the car and got in, turned on the light, and read in the same print:

> Make no signal of any kind. Follow instructions precisely. Turn right on 11th Ave. and go slowly to 56th St. Turn right on 56th and go to 9th Ave. Turn right on 9th Ave. Right again on 45th. Left on 11th Ave. Left on 38th. Right on 7th Ave. Right on 27th St. Park on 27th between 9th and 10th Aves. Go to No. 814 and tap five times on the door. Give the man who opens the door this note and the other one. He will tell you where to go.

I didn't like it much, but I had to admit it was a handy arrangement for seeing to it that I went to the conference unattached or there wouldn't be any conference. It had now decided to rain. Starting the engine, I could see dimly through the misty window that Saul's taxi driver was still monkeying with his carburetor, but of course I had to resist the impulse to crank the window down to wave so long. Keeping the instructions in my left hand, I rolled to the corner, waited for the light to change, and turned right on Eleventh Avenue. Since I had not been forbidden to keep my eyes open I did so, and as I stopped at Fifty-second for the red light I saw a black or dark blue sedan pull away from the curb behind me and creep in my direction. I took it for granted that that was my chaperon, but even so I followed directions and kept to a crawl until I reached Fifty-sixth and turned right.

In spite of all the twistings and turnings and the lights we had to stop at, I didn't get the license number of the black sedan for certain until the halt at Thirty-eighth Street and Seventh Avenue. Not that that raised my pulse any, license plates not being welded on, but what the hell, I was a detective, wasn't I? It was at that same corner, seeing a flatfoot on the sidewalk, that I had half a notion to jump out, summon him, and tackle the driver of the sedan. If it was the strangler, I had the two printed notes in my possession, and I could at least have made it stick enough for an escorted trip to the Fourteenth Precinct Station for a chat. I voted it down, and was soon glad of it.

The guy in the sedan was not the strangler, as I soon learned. On Twenty-seventh Street there was space smack in front of Number 814 and I saw no reason why I shouldn't use it. The sedan went to the curb right behind me. After locking my car I stood on the sidewalk a moment, but my chaperon just sat tight, so I kept to the instructions, mounted the steps to the stoop of the run-down old brownstone, entered the vestibule, and knocked five times on the door. Through the glass panel the dimly lit hall looked empty. As I peered in, thinking I would either have to knock a lot louder or ignore instructions and ring the bell, I heard footsteps behind and turned. It was my chaperon.

"Well, we got here," I said cheerfully.

"You damn near lost me at one light," he said accusingly. "Give me them notes."

I handed them to him—all the evidence I had. As he unfolded them for a look I took him in. He was around my age and height, skinny but with muscles, with outstanding ears and a purple mole on his right jaw. If it was him I had a date with I sure had been diddled. "They look like it," he said, and stuffed the notes in a pocket. From another pocket he produced a key, unlocked the door, and pushed it open. "Follow me."

I did so, to the stairs and up. As we ascended two flights, with him in front, it would have been a cinch for me to reach and take a gun off his hip if there had been one there, but there wasn't. He may have preferred a shoulder holster like me. The stair steps were bare worn wood, the walls had needed plaster since at least Pearl Harbor, and the smell was a mixture I wouldn't want to analyze. On the second landing he went down the hall to a door at the rear, opened it, and signaled me through with a jerk of his head.

There was another man there, but still it wasn't my date—anyway I hoped not. It would be an overstatement to say the room was furnished, but I admit there was a table, a bed, and three chairs, one of them upholstered. The man, who was lying on the bed, pushed himself up as we entered, and as he swung around to sit, his feet barely reached the floor. He had shoulders and a torso like a heavyweight wrestler, and legs like an underweight jockey. His puffed eyes blinked in the light from the unshaded bulb as if he had been asleep.

"That him?" he demanded and yawned.

Skinny said it was. The wrestler-jockey, W-J for short, got up and went to the table, picked up a ball of thick cord, approached me and spoke. "Take off your hat and coat and sit there." He pointed to one of the straight chairs.

"Hold it," Skinny commanded him. "I haven't explained yet." He faced me. "The idea is simple. This man that's coming to see you don't want any trouble. He just wants to talk. So we tie you in that chair and leave you, and he comes and you have a talk, and after he leaves we come back and cut you loose and out you go. Is that plain enough?"

I grinned at him. "It sure is, brother. It's too damn plain. What if I won't sit down? What if I wiggle when you start to tie me?"

"Then he don't come and you don't have a talk."

"What if I walk out now?"

"Go ahead. We get paid anyhow. If you want to see this guy, there's only one way: we tie you in the chair."

"We get more if we tie him," W-J objected. "Let me persuade him."

"Lay off," Skinny commanded him.

"I don't want any trouble either," I stated. "How about this? I sit in the chair and you fix the cord to look right but so I'm free to move in case of fire. There's a hundred bucks in the wallet in my breast pocket. Before you leave you help yourselves."

"A lousy C?" W-J sneered. "For Chrissake shut up and sit down."

"He has his choice," Skinny said reprovingly.

I did indeed. It was a swell illustration of how much good it does to try to consider contingencies in advance. In all our discussions that day none of us had put the question, what to do if a pair of smooks offered me my pick of being tied in a chair or going home to bed. As far as I could see, standing there looking them over, that was all there was to it, and it was too early to go home to bed.

Thinking it would help to know whether they really were smooks or merely a couple of rummies on the payroll of some fly-specked agency, I decided to try something. Not letting my eyes know what my hand was about to do, I suddenly reached inside my coat to the holster, and then they had something more interesting than my face to look at: Saul's clean shiny automatic.

The wrestler-jockey put his hands up high and froze. Skinny looked irritated.

"For why?" he demanded.

"I thought we might all go for a walk down to my car. Then to the Fourteenth Precinct, which is the closest."

"What do we do then?"

There he had me.

"You either want to see this guy or you don't," Skinny explained patiently. "Seeing how you got that gun out, I guess he must know you. I don't blame him wanting your hands arranged for." He turned his palms up. "Make up your mind."

I put the gun back in the holster, took off my hat and raincoat and hung them on a hook on the wall, moved one of the straight chairs so the light wouldn't glare in my eyes, and sat.

"Okay," I told them, "but by God, don't overdo it. I know my way around and I can find you if I care enough, don't think I can't."

They unrolled the cord, cutting pieces off, and went to work. W-J tied my left wrist to the rear left leg of the chair while Skinny did the right. They were both thorough, but to my surprise Skinny was rougher. I insisted it was too tight, and he gave a stingy thirty-second of an inch. They wanted to do my ankles the same way, to the bottoms of the front legs of the chair, but I claimed I would get cramps sitting like that, and I was already fastened to the chair, and it would be just as good to tie my ankles together. They discussed it, and I had my way. Skinny made a final inspection of the knots and then went over me. He took the gun from my shoulder holster and tossed it on the bed, made sure I didn't have another one, and left the room.

W-J picked up the gun and scowled at it. "These goddam things," he muttered. "They make more trouble." He went to the table and put the gun down on it, tenderly, as if it were something that might break. Then he crossed to the bed and stretched out on it.

"How long do we have to wait?" I asked.

"Not long. I wasn't to bed last night." He closed his eyes.

He got no nap. His barrel chest couldn't have gone up and down more than a dozen times before the door opened and Skinny came in. With him was a man in a gray pin-stripe suit and a dark gray Homburg, with a gray topcoat over his arm. He had gloves on. W-J got off the bed and onto his toothpick legs. Skinny stood by the open door. The man put his hat and coat on the bed, came and took a look at my fastenings, and told Skinny, "All right, I'll come for you." The two rummies departed, shutting the door. The man stood facing me, looking down at me, and I looked back.

He smiled. "Would you have known me?"

"Not from Adam," I said, both to humor him and because it was true.

IX

I wouldn't want to exaggerate how brave I am. It wasn't that I was too damn fearless to be impressed by the fact that I was thoroughly tied up and the strangler was standing there smiling at me; I was simply astounded. It was an amazing disguise. The two main changes were the eyebrows and eyelashes; these eyes had bushy brows and long thick lashes, whereas yesterday's guest hadn't had much of either one. The real change was from the inside. I had seen no smile on the face of yesterday's guest, but if I had it wouldn't have been like this one. The hair made a difference too, of course, parted on the side and slicked down.

He pulled the other straight chair around and sat. I admired the way he moved. That in itself could have been a dead giveaway, but the movements fitted the getup to a T. Finding the light straight in his eyes, he shifted the chair a little.

"So she told you about me?" he said, making it a question.

It was the voice he had used on the phone. It was actually different, pitched lower for one thing, but with it, as with the face and movements, the big change was from the inside. The voice was stretched tight, and the palms of his gloved hands were pressed against his kneecaps with the fingers straight out.

I said, "Yes," and added conversationally, "When you saw her go in the office why didn't you follow her in? Why did you wait?"

"That isn't—" he said, and stopped.

I waited politely.

He spoke. "I had seen you leave, upstairs, and I suspected you were in there."

"Why didn't she scream or fight?"

"I talked to her. I talked a little first." His head gave a quick jerk, as if a fly were bothering him and his hands were too occupied to attend to it. "What did she tell you?"

"About that day at Doris Hatten's apartment—you coming in and her going out. And of course her recognizing you there yesterday."

"She is dead. There is no evidence. You can't prove anything."

I grinned. "Then you're wasting a lot of time and energy and the best disguise I ever saw. Why didn't you just toss my note in the wastebasket? Let me answer. You didn't dare. In getting evidence, knowing exactly what and who to look for makes all the difference. And you knew I knew."

"And you haven't told the police?"

"No."

"Nor Nero Wolfe?"

"No."

"Why not?"

I shrugged—not much of a shrug, on account of my status quo. "I may not put it very well," I said, "because this is the first time I have ever talked with my hands and feet tied and I find it cramps my style. But it strikes me as the kind of coincidence that doesn't happen very often. I'm fed up with the detective business and I'd like to quit. I have something that's worth a good deal to you—say fifty thousand dollars. It can be arranged so that you get what you pay for. I'll go the limit on that, but it has to be closed damn quick. If you don't buy I'm going to have a tough time explaining why I didn't remember sooner what she told me. Twenty-four hours from now is the absolute limit."

"It couldn't be arranged so I would get what I paid for."

"Sure it could. If you don't want me on your neck the rest of your life, believe me, I don't want you on mine either."

"I suppose you don't." He smiled, or at least he apparently thought he was smiling. "I suppose I'll have to pay."

There was a sudden noise in his throat as if he had started to choke. He stood up. "You're working your hand loose," he said huskily and moved toward me.

It might have been guessed from his voice, thick and husky from the blood rushing to his head, but it was plain as day in his eyes, suddenly fixed and glassy like a blind man's eyes. Evidently he had come there fully intending to kill me and had now worked himself up to it. I felt a crazy impulse to laugh. Kill me with what?

"Hold it!" I snapped at him.

He halted, muttered, "You're getting your hand loose," and moved again, passing me to get behind.

With what purchase I could get on the floor with my bound feet, I jerked my body and the chair violently aside and around and had him in front of me again.

"No good," I told him. "They only went down one flight. I heard 'em. It's no good anyway. I've got another note for you—from Nero Wolfe—here in my breast pocket. Help yourself, but stay in front of me."

His eyes stayed glassy on me.

"Don't you want to know what it says?" I demanded. "Get it!"

He was only two steps from me, but it took him four small slow ones. His gloved hand went inside my coat to the breast pocket, and came out with a folded slip of yellow paper—a sheet from one of Wolfe's memo pads. From the way his eyes looked, I doubted if he would be able to read, but apparently he was. I watched his face as he took it in, in Wolfe's straight precise handwriting:

> If Mr. Goodwin is not home by midnight the information given him by Cynthia Brown will be communicated to the police and I shall see that they act immediately.
>
> Nero Wolfe

He looked at me, and slowly his eyes changed. No longer glassy, they began to let light in. Before he had just been going to kill me. Now he hated me.

I got voluble. "So it's no good, see? He did it this way because if you had known I had told him you would have sat tight. He figured that you would think you could handle me, and I admit you tried your best. He wants fifty thousand dollars by tomorrow at six o'clock, no later. You say it can't be arranged so you'll get what you pay for, but we say it can and it's up to you. You say we have no evidence, but we can get it—don't think we can't. As for me, I wouldn't advise you even to pull my hair. It would make him sore at you, and he's not sore now, he just wants fifty thousand bucks."

He had started to tremble and knew it, and was trying to stop.

"Maybe," I conceded, "you can't get that much that quick. In that case he'll take your IOU. You can write it on the back of that note he sent you. My pen's here in my vest pocket. He'll be reasonable about it."

"I'm not such a fool," he said harshly. He had stopped trembling.

"Who said you were?" I was sharp and urgent and thought I had loosened him. "Use your head, that's all. We've either got you cornered or we haven't. If we haven't, what are you doing here? If we have, a little thing like your name signed to an IOU won't make it any worse. He won't press you too hard. Here, get my pen, right here."

I still think I had loosened him. It was in his eyes and the way he stood, sagging a little. If my hands had been free, so I could have got the pen myself and uncapped it and put it between his fingers, I would have had him. I had him to the point of writing and signing, but not to the point of taking my pen out of my pocket. But of course if my hands had been free I wouldn't have been bothering about an IOU and a pen.

So he slipped from under. He shook his head, and his shoulders stiffened. The hate that filled his eyes was in his voice too. "You said twenty-four hours. That gives me tomorrow. I'll have to decide. Tell Nero Wolfe I'll decide."

He crossed to the door and pulled it open. He went out, closing the door, and I heard his steps descending the stairs; but he hadn't taken his hat and coat, and I nearly cracked my temples trying to use my brain. I hadn't got far when there were steps on the stairs again, coming up, and in they came, all three of them. W-J was blinking again; apparently there was a bed where they had been waiting. My host ignored him and spoke to Skinny.

"What time does your watch say?"

Skinny glanced at his wrist. "Nine-thirty-two."

"At half-past ten, not before that, untie his left hand. If he has a knife where he can get at it with his left hand, take it and—no, keep it. Leave him like that and go. It will take him five minutes or more to get his other hand and his feet free. Have you any objection to that?"

"Hell no. He's got nothing on us."

"Will you do it that way?"

"Right. Ten-thirty on the nose."

The strangler took a roll of bills from his pocket, having a little difficulty on account of his gloves, peeled off two twenties, went to the table with them, and gave them a good rub on both sides with his handkerchief.

He held the bills out to Skinny. "I've paid the agreed amount, as you know. This extra is so you won't get impatient and leave before half-past ten."

"Don't take it!" I called sharply.

Skinny, the bills in his hand, turned. "What's the matter, they got germs?"

"No, but they're peanuts, you sap! He's worth ten grand to you! As is! Ten grand!"

"Nonsense," the strangler said scornfully and started for the bed to get his hat and coat.

"Gimme my twenty," W-J demanded.

Skinny stood with his head cocked, regarding me. He looked faintly interested but skeptical, and I saw it would take more than words. As the strangler picked up his hat and coat and turned, I jerked my body violently to the left and over I went, chair and all. I have no idea how I got across the floor to the door. I couldn't simply roll on account of the chair, I couldn't crawl without hands, and I didn't even try to jump. But I made it, and not slow, and was there, down on my right side, the chair against the door and me against the chair, before any of them snapped out of it enough to reach me.

"You think," I yapped at Skinny, "it's just a job? Let him go and you'll find out! Do you want his name? Mrs. Carlisle—Mrs. Homer N. Carlisle. Do you want her address?"

The strangler, on his way to me, stopped and froze. He—or I should say she—stood stiff as a bar of steel, the long-lashed eyes aimed at me.

"Missus?" Skinny demanded incredulously. "Did you say Missus?"

"Yes. She's a woman. I'm tied up, but you've got her. I'm helpless, so you can have her. You might give me a cut of the ten grand." The strangler made a movement. "Watch her!"

W-J, who had started for me and stopped, turned to face her. I had banged my head and it hurt. Skinny stepped to her, jerked both sides of her double-breasted coat open, released them, and backed up a step. "It could be a woman," he said judiciously.

"Hell, we can find that out easy enough." W-J moved. "Dumb as I am, I can tell *that*."

"Go ahead," I urged. "That will check her and me both. Go ahead!"

She made a noise in her throat. W-J got to her and put out a hand. She shrank away and screamed, "Don't touch me!"

"I'll be goddamned," W-J said wonderingly.

"What's this gag," Skinny demanded, "about ten grand?"

"It's a long story," I told him, "but it's there if you want it. If you'll cut me in for a third it's a cinch. If she gets out of here and gets safe home we can't touch her. All we have to do is connect her as she is—here now, disguised—with Mrs. Homer N. Carlisle, which is what she'll be when she gets home. If we do that we've got her shirt. As she is here now, she's red hot. As she is at home, you couldn't even get in."

I had to play it that way. I just didn't dare say call a cop, because if he felt about cops the way some rummies do he might have dragged me away from the door and let her go.

"So what?" Skinny asked. "I didn't bring my camera."

"I've got something better. Get me loose and I'll show you."

Skinny didn't like that. He eyed me a moment and turned for a look at the others. Mrs. Carlisle was backed against the bed, and W-J stood studying her with his fists on his hips. Skinny returned to me. "I'll do it. Maybe. What is it?"

"Damn it," I snapped, "at least put me right side up. These cords are eating my wrists."

He came and got the back of the chair with one hand and my arm with the other, and I clamped my feet to the floor to give us leverage. He was stronger than he looked. Upright on the chair again, I was still blocking the door.

"Get a bottle," I told him, "out of my right-hand coat pocket—no, here, the coat I've got on. I hope to God it didn't break."

He fished it out. It was intact. He held it to the light to read the label.

"What is it?"

"Silver nitrate. It makes a black indelible mark on most things, including skin. Pull up her pants leg and mark her with it."

"Then what?"

"Let her go. We'll have her. With the three of us able to explain how and when she got marked, she's sunk."

"How come you've got this stuff?"

"I was hoping for a chance to mark her myself."

"How much will it hurt her?"

"None at all. Put some on me—anywhere you like, as long as it don't show."

"You'd better give me the story—why she'll be sunk. I don't care how long it is."

"Not till she's marked." I was firm. "I will as soon as you mark her."

He studied the label again. I watched his face, hoping he wouldn't ask if the mark would be permanent because I didn't know what answer would suit him, and I had to sell him.

"A woman," he muttered. "By God, a woman!"

"Yeah," I said sympathetically. "She sure made a monkey of you." He swiveled his head and called, "Hey!"

W-J turned. Skinny commanded him, "Pin her up! Don't hurt her."

W-J reached for her. But, as he did so, all of a sudden she was neither man nor woman, but a cyclone. Her first leap, away from his reaching hand, was sidewise, and by the time he had realized he didn't have her she had got to the table and grabbed the gun. He made for her and she pulled the trigger and down he went, tumbling right at her feet. By that time Skinny was almost to her and she whirled and blazed away again. He kept going, and from the force of the blow on my left shoulder I might have calculated, if I had been in a mood for calculating, that the bullet had not gone through Skinny before it hit me. She pulled the trigger a third time, but by then Skinny had her wrist and was breaking her arm.

"She got me!" W-J was yelling indignantly. "She got me in the leg!"

Skinny had her down on her knees.

"Come and cut me loose," I called to him, "and give me that gun, and go find a phone."

Except for my wrists and ankles and shoulder and head, I felt fine all over.

X

"I HOPE you're satisfied," Inspector Cramer said sourly. "You and Goodwin have got your pictures in the paper again. You got no fee, but a lot of free publicity. I got my nose wiped."

Wolfe grunted comfortably.

It was seven o'clock the next evening, and the three of us were in the office, me at my desk with my arm in a sling, Cramer in the red leather chair, and Wolfe on his throne back of his desk, with a glass of beer in his hand and a second unopened bottle on the tray in front of him. The seals had been removed by Sergeant Stebbins a little before noon, in between other chores. The whole squad had been busy with chores: visiting W-J at the hospital, conversing with Mr. and Mrs. Carlisle at the D. A.'s office, starting to round up circumstantial evidence to show that Mr. Carlisle had furnished the necessary for Doris Hatten's rent and Mrs. Carlisle knew it, pestering Skinny, and other items. I had been glad to testify that Skinny, whose name was Herbert Marvel and who ran a little agency in a mid-town one-room office, was one hundred proof and that, as soon as I had convinced him that his well-dressed male client was a female public enemy, he had been simply splendid. Of course, when Skinny had returned to the room after going to phone, he and I had had a full three minutes for a meeting of minds before the cops came. I had used twenty seconds of the three minutes satisfying my curiosity. In Mrs. Carlisle's right-hand coat pocket was a slip noose made of strong cord. So that was her idea when she had moved to get behind me. Someday, when the trial is over and Cramer has cooled off, I'll try getting it for a souvenir.

Cramer had refused the beer Wolfe had courteously offered. "What I chiefly came for," he went on, "was to let you know that I realize there's nothing I can do. I know damn well Cynthia Brown described her to Goodwin, and probably gave him her name too, and Goodwin told you. And you wanted to hog it. I suppose you thought you could pry a fee out of somebody. Both of you suppressed evidence."

He gestured. "Okay, I can't prove it. But I know it, and I want you to know I know it. And I'm not going to forget it."

Wolfe drank, wiped his lips, and put the glass down. "The trouble is," he murmured, "that if you can't prove you're right, and of course you can't, neither can I prove you're wrong."

"Oh, yes, you can. But you haven't and you won't!"

"I would gladly try. How?"

Cramer leaned forward. "Like this. If she hadn't been described to Goodwin, how did you pick her for him to send that blackmail note to?"

Wolfe shrugged. "It was a calculation, as I told you. I concluded that the murderer was among those who remained until the body had been discovered. It was worth testing. If there had been no phone call in response to Mr. Goodwin's note the calculation would have been discredited, and I would—"

"Yeah, but why her?"

"There were only two women who remained. Obviously it couldn't have been Mrs. Orwin; with her physique she would be hard put to pass as a man. Besides, she is a widow, and it was a sound presumption that Doris Hatten had been killed by a jealous wife, who—"

"But why a woman? Why not a man?"

"Oh, that." Wolfe picked up the glass and drained it with more deliberation than usual, wiped his lips with extra care, and put the glass down. He was having a swell time. "I told you in my dining room" —he pointed a finger—"that something had occurred to me and I wanted to consider it. Later I would have been glad to tell you about it if you had not acted so irresponsibly and spitefully in sealing up this office. That made me doubt if you were capable of proceeding properly on any suggestion from me, so I decided to proceed myself. What had occurred to me was simply this: that Miss Brown had told Mr. Goodwin that she wouldn't have recognized 'him' if he hadn't had a hat on. She used the masculine pronoun, naturally, throughout that conversation, because it had been a man who had called at Doris Hatten's apartment that October day, and he was fixed in her mind as a man. But it was in my plant rooms that she had seen him that afternoon, and no man wore his hat up there. The men left their hats downstairs. Besides, I was there and saw them. But nearly all the women had hats on." Wolfe upturned a palm. "So it was a woman."

Cramer eyed him. "I don't believe it," he said flatly.

"You have a record of Mr. Goodwin's report of that conversation. Consult it."

"I still wouldn't believe it."

"There were other little items." Wolfe wiggled a finger. "For example: the strangler of Doris Hatten had a key to the door. But surely the provider, who had so carefully avoided revealment, would not have marched in at an unexpected hour to risk encountering strangers. And who so likely to have found an opportunity, or contrived one, to secure a duplicate key as the provider's jealous wife?"

"Talk all day. I still don't believe it."

Well, I thought to myself, observing Wolfe's smirk and for once completely approving of it, Cramer the office-sealer has his choice of believing it or not and what the hell.

As for me, I had no choice.